NECROPOLIS

ANTHONY HOROWITZ

NECROPOLIS

BOOK FOUR OF
THE GATEKEEPERS

SCHOLASTIC PRESS • NEW YORK

Library of Congress Cataloging-in-Publication Data

Horowitz, Anthony, 1955–
     Necropolis / Anthony Horowitz. — 1st ed.
          p.   cm. — (Gatekeepers ; bk. 4)
     Summary: To stop the evil corporation Nightrise from unleashing its devastating power around the globe, fifteen-year-old Matt and three other Gatekeepers travel to Hong Kong to find Scarlet, the final Gatekeeper, whose fate is inextricably joined to their own.
     ISBN-13: 978-0-439-68003-5 (hardcover : alk. paper)
     ISBN-10: 0-439-68003-4 (hardcover : alk. paper)
[1. Supernatural—Fiction.   2. Hong Kong (China)—Fiction.)   I. Title.
     PZ7.H7875Ne 2009
     [Fic]—dc22

                                        2008044892

10 9 8 7 6 5 4 3 2 1   09 10 11 12 13 14

            Printed in the U.S.A.   23
            First edition, April 2009

        Text was set in New Baskerville.
        Book design by Steve Scott

For Nicholas

Prologue

NIGHTRISE CORPORATION
STRICTLY CONFIDENTIAL
Memorandum from the Chairman's Office: October 15

We are about to take power.

Four months ago, on June 25, the gate built into the Nazca Desert opened and the Old Ones finally returned to the world that once they ruled. They are with us now, waiting for the command to reveal themselves and to begin a war that, this time, they cannot lose.

Why has that command not been given?

The triumph of Nazca was tainted by the presence of two children, teenaged boys. One has already become familiar to us . . . indeed, we have been watching him for much of his life. His name, or the name by which he is now known, is Matthew Freeman. He is fifteen and English. The other was a Peruvian street urchin who calls himself Pedro and grew up in the slums of Lima. Between them, they were responsible for the death of our friend and colleague Diego Salamanda. Incredibly, too, they wounded the King of the Old Ones even at the moment of his victory.

These are not ordinary children. They are two of the so-called Gatekeepers who were part of the great battle, more than ten thousand years ago, when the Old Ones were defeated and banished. It is absolutely crucial this time, if our plans are to succeed and a new world is to be created, that we understand the nature of the Five.

1. Ten thousand years ago, five children led the last survivors of humanity against the Old Ones. The battle took place in Great Britain, but at a time when the country was not yet an island, before the ice sheets had melted in the north.

2. By cunning, by a trick, the children won, and the Old Ones were banished. Two gates were constructed to keep them out: one in Yorkshire, in the north of England, the other in Peru. One gate held. The other we managed to smash.

3. The Five existed then. The Five are here now. It is as if they have been reborn on the other side of time . . . but it is not quite as simple as that. They are the same children, somehow living in two different ages.

4. Kill one of the children now and he or she will be "replaced" by one of the children from the past. This is the single, crucial fact that makes them so dangerous an enemy. Killing them is almost no use at all. If we want to control them, they have to be taken alive.

5. Alone, these children are weak and can be beaten. Their powers are unpredictable and not fully in their control. But when they come together, they become stronger. This is the great danger for us. If all five of them join forces at any time, anywhere in the world, they may be able to create a third gate, and everything we have worked for will be lost.

The fifth of the Five

So far only four of the children have been identified. The English boy and the Peruvian boy have now been joined by twin American brothers, Scott and Jamie Tyler, who were revealed to us by our Psi project. At the time, they were working in a theatre in Nevada.

Note that Scott Tyler was thoroughly programmed whilst held captive by our agents in Nevada. Although he was subsequently reunited with his twin brother, it is still possible that he can be turned against his friends. A psychological report (appendix 1) is attached.

• • •

We know very little about the fifth of the Five. She is a girl. Like the others, she will be fifteen years old. We expect her to be of Chinese heritage, quite probably still living in the East. In the old world, her name was Scar. It is certain that the other four will be searching for her, and we have to face the fact that they may succeed.

We must therefore find her first.

We have agents in every country searching for her. Many politicians and police forces are now working actively for us. The Psi project continues throughout Europe and Asia, and we are still investigating teenagers with possible psychic/paranormal abilities. There is every chance that the girl will reveal herself to us. It is likely that she still has no idea who and what she really is.

Once we have the girl in our hands, we can use her to draw the rest of the Gatekeepers into a trap. One at a time, we will bring them to the Necropolis. And once we have all five of them, we can hold them separately, imprison them, torture them, and keep them alive until the end of time.

Everything is now set. The Gatekeepers have no idea how strong we are, how far we have advanced. Our eyes are everywhere, all around the world, and very soon the battle will begin.

We just have to find the girl.

Ia sakkath. Iak sakkakh. Ia sha xul.

ONE

Road Sense

The girl didn't look before crossing the road.

That was what the driver said later. She didn't look left or right. She'd seen a friend on the opposite sidewalk, and she simply walked across to join him, not noticing that the lights had turned green, forgetting that this was always a busy intersection and that this was four o'clock in the afternoon when people were trying to get their work finished, hurrying on their way home. The girl just set off without thinking. She didn't so much as glimpse the white van heading toward her at fifty miles an hour.

But that was typical of Scarlett Adams. She always was a bit of a dreamer, the sort of person who'd act first and then think about what she'd done only when it was far too late. The field hockey ball that she had tried to thwack over the school roof, but which had instead gone straight through the headmistress's window. The groundsman she had pushed, fully clothed, into the swimming pool. It might have been a good idea to check first that he could swim. The sixty-foot-tall tree she'd climbed up, only to realize that there was no possible way back down.

Fortunately, her school made allowances. It helped that Scarlett was generally popular, was liked by most of the teachers, and, even if she was never top of the class, managed to be never too near the bottom. Where she really excelled was at sports. She was captain of the field hockey team (despite the occasional misfires), a strong tennis player, and an all-round winner when it came to track and field. No school will give too much trouble to someone who brings home the trophies, and Scarlett was responsible for a whole clutch of them.

The school was called St. Genevieve's, and from the outside it could have been a stately home or perhaps a private hospital for the very rich. It stood on its own grounds, set back from the road, with ivy growing up the walls, sash windows, and a bell tower perched on top of the roof. The uniform, it was generally agreed, was the most hideous in England: a mauve dress, a yellow jersey, and, in summer months, a straw hat. Everyone hated the straw hats. In fact it was a tradition for every girl to set the wretched things on fire on their last day.

St. Genevieve's was a private school, one of many that were clustered together in the center of Dulwich, in South London. It was a strange part of the world, and everyone who lived there knew it. To the west there was Streatham and to the east Sydenham, both areas with high-rise apartment buildings, drugs, and knife crimes. But in Dulwich, everything was green. There were old-fashioned tea shops, the sort that spelled themselves *shoppes*, and flower baskets hanging off the lampposts. Most of the cars seemed to be SUVs, and the mothers who drove them were all on first-name terms. Dulwich College, Dulwich Preparatory School, Alleyn's, St. Genevieve's . . . they were only a stone's throw away from each other, but of course nobody threw stones at each other. Not in this part of town.

It was obvious from her appearance that Scarlett hadn't been born in England. Her parents might be Mr. and Mrs. Typical Dulwich — her mother tall, blond, and elegant, her father looking like the lawyer he always had been, with graying hair, a round face, and glasses — but she looked nothing like them. Scarlett had long black hair, strange hazel-green eyes, and the soft brown skin of a girl born in China, Hong Kong, or some other part of Central Asia. She was slim and small, with a dazzling smile that had gotten her out of trouble on many occasions. She wasn't their biological daughter. Everyone knew that. She had known it herself from the earliest age.

She had been adopted. Paul and Vanessa Adams were unable to have children of their own, and they had found her in an orphanage in Jakarta. Nobody knew how she had gotten there. The identity of her birth mother was a mystery. Scarlett tried not to think about her past, where she had come from, but she often wondered what would have happened if the couple who had come all the way from London had chosen the baby in cot seven or nine rather than the one in cot eight. Might she have ended up planting rice somewhere in Indonesia or sewing Nike sneakers in some city sweatshop? It was enough to make her shudder . . . the thought alone.

Instead of which, she found herself living with her parents on a quiet street, just round the corner from North Dulwich Station, which was in turn about a fifteen-minute walk from her school. Her father, Paul Adams, specialized in international business law. Her mother, Vanessa, ran a travel company that put together packages in China and the Far East. The two of them were so busy that they seldom had time for Scarlett — or, indeed, for each other. From the time Scarlett had been five, they had employed a full-time housekeeper to look after all of them. Christina Murdoch was short, dark-haired, and seemed to have no sense of humor at all. She had come to London from Glasgow, and her father was a vicar. Apart from that, Scarlett knew little about her. The two of them got on well enough, but they had both agreed without actually saying it that they were never going to be friends.

One of the good things about living in Dulwich was that Scarlett did have plenty of friends and they all lived very nearby. There were two girls from her class on the same street and there was also a boy — Aidan Ravitch — just five minutes away. It was Aidan who had prompted her to cross the road.

Aidan was in his second year at The Hall, yet another local private school, and had come to London from Los Angeles. He was tall for his age and good-looking in a relaxed, awkward sort of way, with shaggy hair and slightly crumpled features. There was no uniform at his school, and he wore the same hoodie, jeans, and sneakers day in, day out. Aidan didn't understand the English. He claimed to be completely mystified by such things as rugby, tea, and *Doctor Who*. English policemen in particular baffled him. "Why do they have to wear those stupid hats?" he would ask. He was Scarlett's closest friend, although both of them knew that Aidan's father worked for an American bank and could be transferred back home any day. Meanwhile, they spent as much time together as they could.

The accident happened on a warm, summer afternoon. Scarlett was thirteen at the time.

It was a little after four, and Scarlett was on her way home from school. The very fact that she was allowed to walk home on her own meant a lot to her. It was only on her last birthday that her parents had finally relented . . . until then, they had insisted that Mrs. Murdoch should meet her at the school gates every day, even though there were far younger girls who were allowed to face the perils of Dulwich High Street without an armed escort. She had never been quite sure what they were so worried about. There was no chance of her getting lost. Her route took her past a flower shop, an organic grocer's, and a pub — The Crown and Grayhound — where she might spot a few old men, sitting in the sun with their lemonade shandies. There were no drug dealers, no child snatchers or crazed killers in the immediate area. And she was hardly on her own anyway. From half past three onward, the streets were crowded with boys and girls streaming in every direction, on their way home.

She had reached the traffic lights on the other side of the village — where five roads met with shops on one side, a primary school on the other — when she noticed him. Aidan was on his own, listening to music. She could see the familiar white wires trailing down from his ears. He saw her, smiled, and called out her name. Without thinking, she began to walk toward him.

The van was being driven by a twenty-five-year-old delivery man called Michael Logue. He would have to give all his details to the police later on. He was delivering spare parts to a sewing machine factory in Bickley and, thanks to the London traffic, he was late. He was almost certainly speeding as he approached the intersection. But on the other hand, the lights were definitely green.

Scarlett was about halfway across when she saw him, and by that time it was far too late. She saw Aidan's eyes widen in shock, and that made her turn her head, wanting to know what it was that he had seen. She froze. The van was almost on top of her. She could see the driver, staring at her from behind the wheel, his face filled with horror, knowing what was about to happen, unable to do anything about it. The van seemed to be getting bigger and bigger as it drew closer. Even as she watched, it completely filled her vision.

And then everything happened at once.

Aidan shouted out. The driver frantically spun the wheel. The van tilted. And Scarlett found herself being thrown forward, out of the way, as something — or someone — smashed into her back with incredible force. She wanted to cry out, but her breath caught in her throat and her knees buckled underneath her. Somewhere in her mind, she was aware that a passerby had leaped off the sidewalk and that he was trying to save her. His arm was around her waist, his shoulder and head pressed into the small of her back. But how had he managed to get to her so fast? Even if he had seen the van coming and sprinted toward her immediately, he surely wouldn't have reached her in time. He seemed to know what was going to happen almost before it did.

The van shot past, missing her by inches. She actually felt the warm breeze slap her face and smelled the petrol fumes. There had been two books in her hand: a French dictionary and a math notebook . . . an hour and a half's homework for the evening ahead. As she was carried forward, her hand and arm jerked, out of control, and the books were hurled into the air, landing on the road and sliding across the tarmac as if she had deliberately thrown them away. Scarlett followed them. With the man still grabbing hold of her, she came crashing down. There was a moment of sharp pain as she hit the ground and all the skin was taken off one knee. Behind her, there was the screech of tires, a blast of a horn, and then the ominous sound of metal hitting metal. A car alarm went off. Scarlett lay still.

For what felt like a whole minute, nobody did anything. It was as if someone had taken a photograph and framed it with a sign reading ACCIDENT IN DULWICH. Then Scarlett sat up and twisted round. The man who had saved her was lying stretched out in the road, and she was only aware that he was Chinese, in his twenties, with black hair, and that he was wearing jeans and a loose-fitting jacket. She looked past him. The white van had swerved round a traffic island, mounted the sidewalk, and smashed into a car parked in front of the primary school. It was this car's alarm that had gone off. The driver of the van was slumped over the wheel, his head covered in broken glass.

Scarlett turned back. A crowd had already formed — perhaps it had been there from the start — and people were hurrying toward her, rushing past Aidan, who seemed to be rooted to the spot. He was shaking his head as if denying that he had been to blame. There were twenty or thirty schoolkids, some of them already taking photographs with their mobile phones. A policeman had appeared so quickly that he could have popped out of a trapdoor in the pavement. He was the first to reach her.

"Are you all right? Don't try to move. . . ."

Scarlett ignored him. She put out a hand for support and eased herself back onto her feet. Her knee was on fire and her shoulder felt as if it had been beaten with an iron club, but she was already fairly sure that she hadn't been seriously hurt.

She looked at Aidan, then at the white van. A few people were already helping the driver out, laying him on the sidewalk. Steam was rising out of the crumpled hood. Next to her, the policeman was speaking urgently into his shoulder mike, doing all the stuff with Delta Bravo Oscar Charlie, summoning help.

Finally, Aidan made it over to her. "Scarl . . . ?" That was his name for her. "Are you okay?"

She nodded, suddenly tearful without knowing why. Maybe it was just the shock, the knowledge of what could have been. She wiped her face with the back of her hand, noticing that her nails were grimy and all her knuckles were grazed. Her dress was torn. She realized she must look like a total wreck.

"You were nearly killed . . . !" Why was Aidan telling her that? She had more or less worked it out for herself.

Even so, his words reminded her of the man who had saved her. She looked down and was surprised to see that he was no longer there. For a moment she thought that it was a conjuring trick, that he had simply vanished into thin air. Then she saw him, already on the far side of the road — the side that she had been heading toward — hurrying past the shops. He reached a hair salon on the corner, where a woman with hair that was too blond to be true had just come out. He pushed past her and then he was gone.

Why? He hadn't even stayed long enough to be thanked.

After that, things unraveled more slowly. An ambulance arrived, and although Scarlett didn't need it, the van driver had to be put on a stretcher and carried away. Scarlett herself was examined but nothing was broken, and in the end she was allowed to go home. Aidan went with her. An officer accompanied them both. Scarlett wondered how that would go down with Mrs. Murdoch. Somehow she knew it wasn't going to mean laughter and backslapping at bedtime.

In fact, the accident had several consequences.

Paul and Vanessa Adams were told what had happened when they got home that night, and as soon as they had got over the shock, the knowledge of how close they had come to losing their only child, they began to argue about whose fault it was: their own for allowing Scarlett too much freedom, Aidan's for distracting her, or Scarlett's for showing so little road sense, even at the age of thirteen. In the end, they decided that in the future, Mrs. Murdoch would take up her old position at the school gates. It would be another nine months before Scarlett was allowed to walk home on her own again.

The identity of the man who had saved her remained a mystery. Where had he come from? How had he seen what was about to happen? Why had he been in such a hurry to get away? Mrs. Murdoch decided that he must be an illegal immigrant, that he had taken off at the sight of the approaching policeman. For her part, Scarlett was just sorry that she hadn't been able to thank him. And if he was in some sort of trouble, she would have liked to have helped him.

That was the night she had her first dream.

Scarlett had never been one for vivid dreams. Normally she got home, ate, did her homework, spent forty minutes on her PlayStation, and then plunged into a deep, empty sleep that would be ended all too quickly by Mrs. Murdoch shaking her awake for the start of another school day. But this dream was more than vivid. It was so realistic, so detailed, that it was almost like being inside a film. And there was something else that was strange about it. As far as she could see, it had no connection to her life or to anything that had happened during the day.

She dreamed that she was in a gray-lit world that might be another planet . . . the moon perhaps. In the distance, she could see a vast ocean stretching out to the horizon and beyond — but there were no waves. The surface of the water could have been a single sheet of metal. Everything was dead. She was surrounded by sand dunes — at least, that was what she thought they were, but they were actually made of dust. They had somehow blown there and — like the dust on the moon — it would stay the same forever. She walked forward. But she left no footprints.

There were four boys standing together, a short distance away.

The boys were searching for her. If she listened carefully, she could actually hear them calling her name. She tried to call back, but although there was no wind, not even a breeze, something snatched the words away.

The boys weren't real. They couldn't be. . . . Scarlett had never seen them before. And yet, somehow, she was sure that she knew their names.

Scott. Jamie. Pedro. And Matt.

She knew them from somewhere. They had met before.

That was the first time, but over the next two years, she had the same dream again and again. And gradually, it began to change. It seemed to her that every time she saw the boys, they were a little farther away, until finally she had to get used to the fact that she was completely on her own. Every time she went to sleep, she found herself hoping she would see them. More than that. She needed to meet them.

She never spoke about her dreams, not even to Aidan. But somewhere in the back of her mind, she knew that finding the four boys had become the single most important thing in her life.

TWO
The Door

Two years later, Scarlett had turned fifteen — and she had become an orphan for a second time.

Paul and Vanessa Adams hadn't died, but their marriage had, one inch at a time. In a way, it was amazing they had stayed together so long. Scarlett's father had just started a new job, working for a multinational corporation based in Hong Kong. Meanwhile, her mother was spending more and more time with her own business, looking after customers who seemed to demand her attention twenty-four hours a day. They were seeing less and less of each other and suddenly realized that they preferred it that way. They didn't argue or shout at each other. They just decided they would be happier apart.

They told Scarlett the news at the end of the summer holidays and, for her part, she wasn't quite sure what to feel. But the truth was that in the short term it would make little difference to her life. Most of the time she was on her own with Mrs. Murdoch anyway, and although she'd always been glad to see her parents, she'd gotten used to the fact that they were seldom, if ever, around. The three of them had one last meeting in the kitchen, the two adults sitting with grim faces and large glasses of wine.

"Your mother is going to set up a company in Melbourne, in Australia," Paul said. "She has to go where the market is, and Melbourne is a wonderful opportunity." He glanced at Vanessa, and in that moment, Scarlett knew that he wasn't telling the whole truth. Maybe the Australians were desperate for exotic holidays. But the fact was that she had chosen somewhere as far away as possible. Maybe she had met someone else. Whatever the reason, she wanted to carve herself a whole new life. "As for me, Nightrise has asked me to move to the Hong Kong office. . . ."

The Nightrise Corporation. That was the company that employed her dad.

"I know this is very difficult for you, Scarly," he went on. "Two such huge changes. But we both want to look after you. You can come with either of us."

In fact, it wasn't difficult for Scarlett. She had already thought about it and made up her mind. "Why can't I stay here?" she asked.

"On your own?"

"Mrs. Murdoch will look after me. You're not going to sell the house, are you? This is my home! Anyway, I don't want to leave St. Genevieve's. And all my friends are here. . . ."

Of course, both her parents protested. They wanted Scarlett to come with them. How could she possibly manage without them? But all of them knew that it was actually the best, the easiest solution. Mrs. Murdoch had been with the family for ten years and probably knew Scarlett as well as anyone. In a way, they couldn't have been happier if they had suggested it themselves. It might not be conventional, but it was clearly for the best.

And so it was agreed. A few weeks later, Vanessa left, hugging Scarlett and promising that the two of them would see each other again very soon. And yet, somehow, Scarlett wondered just how likely that would be. She had always tried to be close to Vanessa, recognizing at the same time that they had almost nothing in common. They weren't a real mother and daughter and so — as far as Scarlett was concerned — this wasn't a real divorce.

Paul Adams left for Hong Kong shortly afterward, and suddenly Scarlett found herself in a new phase of life, virtually on her own. But, as she had expected, it wasn't so very different from what she had always been used to. Mrs. Murdoch was still there, cooking, cleaning, and making sure she was ready for school. Her father telephoned her regularly to check up on her. Vanessa sent long e-mails. Her teachers — who had been warned what had happened — kept a close eye on her. She was surprised how quickly she got used to things.

She was happy. She had plenty of friends, and Aidan was still around. The two of them saw more of each other than ever, going shopping together, listening to music, taking Aidan's dog — a black retriever — out on Dulwich Common. She was allowed to walk home from school on her own again. In fact, as if to recognize her new status, she found herself being given a whole lot more freedom. On weekends, she went into town to the cinema. She stayed overnight with other girls from her class. She had been given a big part in the Christmas play, which meant late afternoon rehearsals and hours in the evening learning her lines. It all helped to fill the time and to make her think that her life wasn't so very unusual after all.

Everything changed one day in November. That was when Miss Chaplin announced her great Blitz project — a visit to London's East End.

Joan Chaplin was the art teacher at St. Genevieve's, and she was famous for being younger, friendlier, and more easygoing than any of the dinosaurs in the staff room. She was always finding new ways to interest the girls, organizing field trips to exhibitions and events all over London. One class had gone to see the giant crack built into the floor of the Tate Modern. For another it had been a shark suspended in a tank, an installation by the artist Damien Hirst. Weeks later, they had still been arguing whether it was serious art or just a dead fish.

As part of their history coursework, a lot of the girls were studying the Blitz, the bombing of London by the Germans during the Second World War. Miss Chaplin had decided that they should take an artistic as well as a historical interest in what had happened.

"I want you to capture the spirit of the Blitz," she explained. "What's the point of studying it if you don't feel it too?" She paused as if waiting for someone to argue, then went on. "You can use photography, painting, collage, or even clay modeling if you like. But I want you to give me an idea of what it might have been like to live in London during the winter of 1940."

There was a mutter of agreement around the class. Walking around London had to be more fun than reading about it in books. Scarlett was particularly pleased. History and art had become two of her favorite subjects, and she saw that here was an opportunity to do them both at the same time.

"Next Monday, we're going to Shoreditch," Miss Chaplin went on. "It was an area of London that was very heavily bombed. We'll visit many of the streets, trying to imagine what it was like, and we'll look at some of the buildings that survived."

She glanced outside. The art room was on the ground floor, at the back of the school, with a view over the garden, sloping down with flower beds at the bottom and three tennis courts beyond. It was Friday and it was raining. The rain was sheeting down and the grass was sodden. It had been like that for three days.

"Of course," she went on, "the trip won't be possible if the weather doesn't cheer up — and I have to warn you that the forecast hasn't been too promising. But maybe we'll be lucky. Either way, remember to bring a permission slip from your parents." Then she had a sudden thought and smiled. "What do you think, Scarlett?"

It had become a sort of joke at St. Genevieve's.

Scarlett Adams always seemed to know what the weather was going to do. Nobody could remember when it had first started but everyone agreed — you could tell how the day was going to be simply by the way Scarlett dressed. If she forgot her scarf, it would be warm. If she brought in an umbrella, it would rain. After a bit, people began to ask her opinion. If there was an important tennis match or a picnic planned by the river, have a word with Scarlett. If there was any chance of a cross-country run being called off, she would know.

Of course, she wasn't always right. But it seemed she could be relied upon about ninety percent of the time.

Now she looked out of the window. It was horrible outside. The clouds, gray and unbroken, were smothering the sky. She could see raindrops chasing each other across the glass. "It'll be fine," she said. "It'll clear up after the weekend."

Miss Chaplin nodded. "I do hope you're right."

She was. It rained all day Sunday and was still drizzling on Sunday night. But Monday morning, when Scarlett woke up, the sky was blue. Even Mrs. Murdoch was whistling as she put together the packed lunch requested by the school. It was as if a last burst of summer had decided to put in a surprise appearance.

The bus came to the school at midday. The lesson — combining art and history — was actually going to take place over two periods plus lunch and, allowing for the traffic, the girls wouldn't be back until the end of school. As they pulled out of St. Genevieve's, Miss Chaplin talked over the intercom, explaining what they were going to do.

"We'll be stopping for lunch at St. Paul's Cathedral," she said. "It was very much part of the spirit of the Blitz because, despite all the bombing, it was not destroyed. The coach will then take us to Shoreditch, and we're going to walk around the area. It's still a bit wet underfoot, so I want us to go indoors. The place I've chosen is St. Meredith's, on Moore Street. It's one of the oldest churches in London. In fact, there was a chapel there as long ago as the thirteenth century."

"Why are we visiting another church?" one of the girls asked.

"Because it also played an important part in the war. A lot of local people used to hide there during the bombing. They actually believed it had the power to protect them . . . that they'd be safe there."

She paused. The coach had reached the River Thames, crossing over Blackfriars Bridge. Scarlett looked out of the window. The water was flowing very quickly after all the rain. In the distance, she could just make out part of the London Eye, the silver framework glinting in the sunlight. The sight of it made her sad. She had ridden on it with her parents, at the end of the summer. It had been one of the last things the three of them had done while they were still a family.

". . . actually took a direct hit on October 2, 1940." Miss Chaplin was still talking about St. Meredith's. Scarlett had allowed her thoughts to wander, and she'd missed half of what the teacher had said. "It wasn't destroyed, but it was badly damaged. Bring your sketchbooks with you and we can work in there. We have permission and you can go anywhere you like. See if you can feel the atmosphere. Imagine what it was like, being there with the bombs going off all around."

Miss Chaplin flicked off the microphone and sat down again, next to the driver.

Scarlett was a few rows behind her, sitting next to a girl named Amanda, who was one of her closest friends and lived on the same road as her. She noticed that Amanda was frowning.

"What is it?" she asked.

"St. Meredith's," Amanda said.

"What about it?"

It took Amanda a few moments to remember. "There was a murder there. About six months ago."

"You're not being serious."

"I am."

If it had been anyone else, Scarlett might not have believed her. But she knew that Amanda had a special interest in murder. She loved reading Agatha Christie and she was always watching whodunnits on TV. "So who got murdered?" she asked.

"I can't remember," Amanda said. "It was some guy. A librarian, I think. He was stabbed."

Scarlett wasn't sure it sounded very likely, and when the coach stopped off at St. Paul's, she went over to Miss Chaplin. To her surprise, the teacher didn't even hesitate. "Oh yes," she said cheerfully. "There was an incident there this summer. A man was attacked by a homeless person. I'm not sure the police ever caught anyone, but it all happened a long time ago. It doesn't bother you, does it, Scarlett?"

"No," Scarlett said. "Of course not."

But that wasn't quite true. It did secretly worry her, even if she wasn't sure why. She had a sense of foreboding that only grew worse as they got closer to the church.

The art teacher had chosen this part of London for a reason. It was a patchwork of old and new, with great gaps where whole buildings and perhaps even streets had been taken out by the Germans. Most of the shops were shabby and depressing, with plastic signs and dirty windows full of products that people might need but which they couldn't possibly want: vacuum cleaners, dog food, one hundred items at less than a pound. There was an ugly parking garage towering high over the buildings, but it was hard to imagine anyone stopping here. The traffic rumbled past in four lanes, anxious to be on its way.

But even so, there were a few clues as to what the area might once have been like. A cobbled alleyway, a gas lamp, a red telephone box, a house with pillars and iron railings. The London of seventy years ago. That was what Miss Chaplin had brought them all to find.

They turned onto Moore Street. It was a dead end, narrow and full of puddles and potholes. A pub stood on one side, opposite a launderette that had shut down. St. Meredith's was at the bottom, a solid, redbrick church that looked far too big to have been built in this part of town. The war damage was obvious at once. The steeple had been added quite recently. It wasn't even the same color as the rest of the building and didn't quite match the huge oak doors or the windows with their heavy stone frames.

Scarlett felt even more uneasy once they were inside. She jumped as the door boomed shut behind her, cutting out the London traffic, much of the light — indeed, any sense that they were in a modern city at all. The interior of the church stretched into the distance to the silver cross high up on the altar, caught in a single shaft of dusty light. Otherwise, the stained-glass windows held the sun back, the different colors blurring together. Hundreds of candles flickered uselessly in iron holders. She could make out little side-chapels, built into the walls. Even without her remembering the murder that had happened there,

St. Meredith's didn't strike her as a particularly holy place. It was simply creepy.

But nobody else seemed to share her feelings. The other girls had taken out their sketchbooks and were sitting in the pews, chatting to each other and drawing what they had seen outside. Miss Chaplin was examining the pulpit — a carving of an eagle. Presumably, most Londoners chose not to pray at two o'clock in the afternoon. They had the place to themselves.

Scarlett looked for Amanda, but her friend was talking to another girl on the other side of the transept, so she sat down on her own and opened her pad. She needed to put the murder out of her mind. Instead, she thought about the men and women who had sheltered here during the Blitz. Had they really believed that St. Meredith's had some sort of magical power to avoid being hit, that they would be safer here than in a cellar or a Tube station? She thought about them sitting there with their fingers crossed while the Luftwaffe roared overhead. Maybe that was what she would draw.

She shivered. She was wearing a coat, but it was very cold inside the church. In fact, it felt colder inside than out. A movement caught her eye. A line of candles had flickered, all the flames bending together, caught in a sudden breeze. Had someone just come in? No. The door was still shut. Nobody could have opened or closed it without being heard.

A boy walked past. At first, Scarlett barely registered him. He was in the shadows at the side of the church, between the columns and the side-chapels, moving toward the altar. He made absolutely no sound. Even his feet against the marble floor were silent. He could have been floating. She turned to follow him as he went, and just for a second, his face was illuminated by a naked bulb hanging on a wire.

She knew him.

For a moment, she was confused as she tried to think where she had seen him before. And then suddenly she remembered. It was crazy. It couldn't be possible. But at the same time, there could be no doubt.

It was one of the boys from her dreams, one of the four she had seen walking together in that gray desert. She even knew his name.

It was Matt.

In a normal dream, Scarlett wouldn't see people's faces — or if she did, she would forget them when she woke up. But she had experienced this dream again and again over a period of two years. She'd learned to recognize Matt and the others almost as soon as she was asleep and that was why she knew him now. Short, dark hair. Broad shoulders. Pale skin and eyes that were an intense blue. He was about her age although there was something about him that seemed older. Maybe it was just the way he walked, the sense of purpose. He walked like someone in trouble.

What was he doing here? How had he even got in? Scarlett turned to a girl who was sitting close to her, drawing a major explosion from the look of the scribble on her pad.

"Did you see him?" she asked.

"Who?"

"That boy who just went past."

The other girl looked around her. "What boy?"

Scarlett turned back. The boy had disappeared from sight. For a moment, she was thrown. Had she imagined him? But then she saw him again, some distance away. He had stopped in front of a door. He seemed to hesitate, then turned the handle and went through. The door closed behind him.

She followed him. She had made the decision without even thinking about it. She just put down her sketchbook, got up, and went after him. It was only when she reached the door that she asked herself what she was doing, chasing after someone she had never met, someone who might not even exist. Suppose she ran into him? What was she going to say? "Hi, I'm Scarlett and I've been dreaming about you. Fancy a Big Mac?" He'd think she was mad.

The door he had passed through was in the outer wall, underneath a stained-glass window that was so dark and grimy that the picture was lost. Scarlett guessed it must lead out into the street, perhaps into the cemetery, if the church had one. There was something strange about it. The door was very small, out of proportion with the rest of St. Meredith's. There was a symbol carved into the wooden surface — a five-pointed star.

She hesitated. The girls weren't supposed to leave the church. On the other hand, she wouldn't exactly be going far. If there was no sign of the boy on the other side, she could simply come back in again. The door had an iron ring for a handle. She turned it and went through.

To her surprise, she didn't find herself outside in the

street. Instead, she was standing in a wide, brightly lit corridor. There were flaming torches slanting out of iron brackets set in the walls, the fire leaping up toward the ceiling, which was high and vaulted. The corridor had no decoration of any kind, and it seemed both old and new at the same time, the plasterwork crumbling to reveal the brickwork underneath. It had to be some sort of cloister — somewhere the priests went to be on their own. But the corridor was nothing like the rest of St. Meredith's. It was a different color. It was the wrong size and shape.

It was also very cold. The temperature seemed to have fallen dramatically. As she breathed out, Scarlett saw white mist in front of her face. It was as if she were standing inside a fridge. She had to remind herself that this was the first week of November. It felt like the middle of winter. She rubbed her arms, fighting off the biting cold.

There was a man sitting in a wooden chair opposite her, facing the door. She hadn't noticed him at first because he was in shadow, between two of the torches. He was dressed like a monk with a long, dirty brown habit that went all the way down to his bare feet. He was wearing sandals, and a hood over his head. He was slumped forward with his face toward the floor. Scarlett had already decided to turn round and go back the way she had come, but before she could move, he suddenly looked up. The hood fell back. She gasped.

He was one of the ugliest men she had ever seen. He was completely bald, the skin stretched over a skull that was utterly white and dead. His head was the wrong shape — narrow, with part of it caved in on one side, like an egg that had been hit with a spoon. His eyes were black and sunken, and he had horrible teeth that revealed themselves as he smiled at her, his thin lips sliding back like a knife wound. What had he been doing, sitting there? She looked left and right, but they were on their own. The boy named Matt — if it had even been him — was gone.

The man spoke. The words cracked in his throat, and Scarlett didn't understand any of them. He could have been speaking Russian or Polish . . . whatever it was, it wasn't English. She backed away toward the door.

"I'm very sorry," she said. "I think I've come the wrong way."

She turned round and scrambled for the handle. But she never made it. The monk had moved very quickly. She felt his hands grab hold of her shoulders and drag her backward, away from the door. He was very strong. His fingers dug into her like steel pincers.

"Let go!" she shouted.

His arm sneaked over her shoulder and around her throat. He was holding her with incredible force. She could feel the bone cutting into her windpipe, blocking the air supply. And he was screaming out more words that she couldn't understand, his voice high-pitched and animal. Another monk appeared at the end of the corridor. Scarlett didn't really see him. She was just aware of him rushing toward them, the long robes flapping.

Still she fought back. She reached with both hands, clawing for the monk's eyes. She kicked back with one foot, then tried to elbow him in his stomach. But she couldn't reach him. And then the second monk threw himself onto her.

The next thing she knew, she was on her back, her arms stretched out above her head. Her legs had been knocked out from underneath her. The two men had grabbed hold of her, and there was nothing she could do. She twisted and writhed, her hair falling over her face. The monks just laughed.

Scarlett felt her heels bumping over the stone-cold floor as the two men dragged her away.

THREE
Father Gregory

The cell was tiny — less than 33 feet square — and there was nothing in it at all, not even a chair or a bench. The walls were brick with a few traces of flaking paint, suggesting they might have been decorated at some time. The door had been fashioned out of three slabs of wood, fastened together with metal bands. There was a single window, barred and set high up so that even for someone taller than Scarlett, there wouldn't be any chance of a view. From where she was sitting, slumped miserably on the stone floor, she could just make out a narrow strip of sky. But even that was enough to send a shiver down her spine.

It was dark. Not quite night, but very nearly. She realized that it would be pitch-black in the cell in just a couple of hours as they hadn't left her a candle or an electric light. But how was that possible? It had been around two o'clock when she had entered St. Meredith's, and the sun had been shining. Suddenly, it was early evening. So what had happened to the time in between?

Scarlett was shivering — and not just because of the shock of what she had been through. It was freezing in the cell. There was no glass in the window and no heating. The bare brickwork only made it worse. Fortunately, she had been wearing her winter coat when she set off on the school trip. Now she drew it around her, trying to bury herself in its folds. She had never been so cold. She could actually feel the bones in her arms and legs. They were so hard and brittle that she thought they might shatter at any time.

Desperately, she tried to work out what had happened. For no reason that she could even begin to imagine, two men she had never met had grabbed her and thrown her into a cell. Could she have strayed into a secret wing of St. Meredith's, somewhere that no one was meant to go? The single strip of sky told her otherwise. That and the freezing weather. She remembered that the monk had spoken in a foreign language.

She was no longer in London.

It seemed crazy, but she had to accept it. Maybe she had blacked out at the moment she had been seized. Maybe they had drugged her and she had been unconscious without even knowing it. Everything told her that this wasn't England. Somehow she had been spirited away.

With a spurt of anger, she scrambled to her feet and went over to the door. She wasn't just going to sit here and wait for them to come back. Suppose they never did come back? She might die in this place. But she quickly saw that there was no way through the door — not unless it was unlocked from the other side. It was massive and solid, with a single keyhole built for an antique key. She tried to squint through it, but there was nothing to see. She straightened up, then hammered her fists against the wood.

"Hey! Come back! Let me out of here!"

But nobody came. She wasn't even sure if her voice could be heard outside the cell.

That left the window. Could she possibly climb up, using the rough edges of the brickwork to support herself? Scarlett tried, but her fingertips couldn't get enough grip, and anyway the bars at the top were too close to squeeze through, even assuming she could drop down on the other side. No. She was in a solid box with no trapdoors, no secret passages, no magic way out. She would just have to stay here until somebody came.

She sank back into a corner, trying to preserve what little body warmth she had left by curling herself into a ball. The strange thing was, she should have been terrified. She was completely helpless, a prisoner. This was an evil place. But she still couldn't accept the reality of what had happened to her and because of that, it was difficult to keep feeling scared. This was all like some bad dream. Once she had worked out how she had got here, then maybe she could start worrying about what was going to happen next.

An hour passed, or maybe two. Finally there was a rattle of a key in the lock, the door swung open again, and two monks came into the cell. Scarlett couldn't say if they were the ones who had grabbed her in the corridor, as all these people were dressed the same way. Their hoods were up and they were skeleton-thin. Even if you stood them up against a wall, it would have been difficult to tell them apart.

One of them barked out a command in the strange, harsh language she had heard before, and when he saw that she didn't understand, he made a rough gesture, telling her to stand up. Scarlett did as she was instructed. Her face gave nothing away, but she was already thinking. If they took her out of here, maybe she would be able to break away. She would run back down the corridor and find the nearest exit. Whatever country she was in, there would have to be a police officer or someone else around. She would make herself understood, somehow find her way home.

But right now, the two monks were watching her too closely. They led her out with one standing next to her and the other directly behind, so close that she could actually smell them. Neither man had washed, not for a long time. As they reached the corridor, Scarlett hesitated and felt a hand pushing her roughly forward. She turned left. The three of them set off together.

Where was she? The place had the feel of an old palace or a monastery that had been abandoned long ago. Everything about it was broken down and neglected, from the peeling walls to the paved floor, which was slanting and uneven with some sort of mold growing through the cracks. Naked lightbulbs hung on single wires (so at least there was electricity), but they were dull and flickering, barely able to light the way. The air was damp and there was a faint smell of sewage.

Scarlett noticed an oil painting in a gilt frame. It showed a crucifixion scene, but the colors were faded, the canvas torn. An antique cabinet with two iron candlesticks stood beneath it, one door open and papers scattered on the floor. Scarlett and the monks turned a corner, and for the first time she was able to see outside. A series of arches led onto a terrace with a garden beyond. Scarlett stopped dead. Her worst fears had been realized. She knew now that she definitely wasn't in England.

The garden was covered in snow. There were trees with no leaves, their branches heavy with the stuff. The ground was also buried and, in the distance, barely visible in the darkness, she could see white-topped mountains. There were no other buildings, no lights showing anywhere. The monastery was in some sort of wilderness — but how had she gotten here? Had she been knocked out and put on a plane? Scarlett searched back in her memory, but there was nothing there . . . nothing to indicate a journey, leaving England or arriving anywhere else. Then one of the monks jabbed her in the back, and she was forced to start moving again.

They came to a hallway lit by a huge chandelier, not electric but jammed with rows of candles, at least a hundred of them, the wax dripping slowly down and congealing into a series of growths that reminded Scarlett of the sort of shapes she had once seen in a cave. Some of the wax had splattered onto a round table beneath. An empty bottle lay on its side along with dirty plates and glasses, moldering pieces of bread. There had been a dinner here — days, maybe weeks before. There were no rats or cockroaches. It was too cold.

Several doors led out of the hallway. As one monk led her to the nearest of them, the other pushed her inside. This hurt her, and Scarlett spun round and swore at him. The monk just smiled and backed away. The other man went with him. The door closed.

Scarlett turned back and examined her new surroundings. This was the only halfway comfortable room she had seen so far. It was furnished with a rug on the floor, two armchairs, bookshelves, and a desk. It was warmer too. A coal fire was burning in a grate, and although the flames were low, she could feel the heat it was giving out and smell it in the air. More paintings hung on the walls, all with religious subjects. There was a window, but it had become too dark to see outside.

A man was sitting behind the desk. He also wore a habit, but his was black. So far he had said nothing, but his eyes were fixed on Scarlett. With an uneasy feeling, she walked over to him. He was old — at least twenty years older than the others, with the same bald head and sunken eyes. There were tufts of white hair around his ears and he had thick white eyebrows that could have been glued in place. His nose was long and too thin for his face. His fingers, spread out across the surface of the desk, were the same. He was watching Scarlett intensely, and as she drew closer, she saw that there was a growth — a sty — sitting on one of his eyes. The whole socket was red and dripping. It was as if, like the rest of the building, he was rotting away. Scarlett shuddered and felt ill.

The man still hadn't spoken. Scarlett drew level with him so that the desk was between them. Despite everything, she had decided that she wasn't going to let him intimidate her. "Who are you?" she demanded. "Where am I? Why have you brought me here?"

His eyes widened in surprise. At least, one of them did. The diseased eye had long since lost any movement. "You are English?" he said.

Scarlett was taken by surprise. She hadn't expected him to speak her language. "Yes," she said.

"Please. Sit down." He gestured at one of the chairs. "Would you like a hot drink? Some tea should be arriving soon."

Scarlett shook her head. "I don't want any tea," she snapped. "I want to go back where I came from. Why are you keeping me here?"

"I asked you to sit down," the monk said. "I would suggest that you do as you are told."

He hadn't raised his voice. He didn't even sound threatening. But somehow Scarlett knew it would be a mistake to disobey him. She could see it in his eyes. The pupils were black and dead and slightly unfocused. They were the sort of eyes that might belong to someone who was mad.

She sat down.

"That's better," he said. "Now, let's introduce ourselves. What is your name?"

"I'm Scarlett Adams."

"Scarlett Adams." He repeated it with a sort of satisfaction, as if that was what he had expected to hear. "Where are you from?"

"I live in Dulwich. In London. Please, will you tell me where I am?"

He lifted a single finger. The nail was yellow and bent out of shape. "I will tell you everything you wish to know," he said. His English was perfect although it was obvious that it wasn't his first language. He had an accent that Scarlett couldn't place, and he strung his words together very carefully, like a craftsman making a necklace. "But first tell me this," he went on. "You really have no idea how you came here?"

"No." Scarlett shook her head. "I was in a church."

"In London?"

"Yes. I went through a door. One of the people here grabbed hold of me. That's all I can remember."

He nodded slowly. His eyes had never left her, and Scarlett felt a terrible urge to look away, as if somehow he was going to swallow her up.

"You are in Ukraine," the man said suddenly.

"Ukraine?" Everything seemed to spin for a minute. "But that's . . .".

It was somewhere in Russia. It was on the other side of the world.

"This is the Monastery of the Cry for Mercy. I am Father Gregory." He looked at his guest a little sadly, as if he was disappointed that she didn't understand. "Your coming here is a great miracle," he said. "We have been waiting for you for almost twenty years."

"That's not possible. What do you mean? I haven't been alive for twenty years." Scarlett was getting tired of this. She was feeling sick with exhaustion, with confusion. "How come you speak English?" she asked. She knew it was a stupid question, but she needed a simple answer. She wanted to hear something that actually made sense.

"I have traveled all over the world," Father Gregory replied. "I spent six years in your country, in a seminary near the city of Bath."

"Why did you say you've been waiting for me? What do you mean?"

The door suddenly opened and one of the monks came in, carrying a bronze tray with two cups of tea. Scarlett guessed that Father Gregory must have ordered it before she was brought in because there was no obvious method of communication in the office, no telephone or computer, nothing modern apart from a desk lamp throwing out a pool of yellow light. The monk set down the tray and left.

"Help yourself," Father Gregory said.

Scarlett did as she was told. The liquid was boiling hot and burned her fingers as she lifted the cup. She took a sip. The tea tasted herbal and heavily sugared, so sweet that it stuck to her lips. She set it down again.

"I will tell you my story because it pleases me to do so," Father Gregory said. "Because I sometimes wondered if this day would ever come. That you are sitting here now, in this place, is more than a miracle. My whole life has been leading to this moment. It is perhaps the very reason why I was meant to live."

Scarlett didn't interrupt him. The more he talked, the more passionate he became. She could see the coal fire reflected in his eyes, but even if the fire hadn't been there, there might still have been the same glow.

"I was born sixty-two years ago in Moscow, which was then the capital of the Soviet Union. My father was a politician, but from my earliest age, I knew that I wanted to enter the Church. Why? I did not like the world into which I had been born. Even when I was at school, I found the other children spiteful and stupid. I was small for my age and often bullied. I never found it easy to make friends. I did not much like my parents either. They didn't understand me. They didn't even try.

"I was nineteen when I told my father that I wanted to take holy orders. He was horrified. I was his only son, and he had always assumed that I would go into politics, like him. He tried to talk me out of it. He arranged for me to travel around the world, hoping that if I saw all the riches that the West had to offer, it would change my mind.

"In fact, it did the exact opposite. Everything I saw in Europe and America disgusted me. Wealthy families with huge homes and expensive cars, living just a mile away from children who were dying because they could not afford medicine. Countries at war, the people killing and maiming each other because of politicians too stupid to find another way. The noise of modern life: the planes and the cars, the concrete smothering the land. The pollution and the garbage. The people, in their millions, scurrying on their way to jobs they hated. . . ."

Scarlett shrugged. "So you weren't happy," she said. "What's that got to do with me?"

"It has everything to do with you, and if you interrupt me again, I will have you whipped until the skin peels off your back."

Father Gregory paused. Scarlett was completely shocked but didn't want to show it. She said nothing.

"I entered a seminary in England," he continued, "and trained to become a monk. I spent six years there, then another three in Tuscany before finally I came here. That was thirty years ago. This was a very beautiful and very restful place when I first arrived, a refuge from the rest of the world. The weather was harsh and, in the winter, the days

36

were short. But the way of life suited me. Prayer six times a day, simple meals and silence while we ate. We cultivated all our food ourselves. I have spent many hundreds of hours hacking at the barren soil that surrounds us. When I wasn't in the fields, I was helping in the local villages, tending to the poor and the sick.

"A holy life, Scarlett. And so it might have remained. But then everything changed. And all because of a door in a wall."

Father Gregory hadn't touched his tea, but suddenly he picked up his glass between his finger and thumb and tipped the scalding liquid back. Scarlett saw his throat bulge. It was like watching a sick man take his medicine.

"It puzzled me from the start. A door that seemed to belong to a different building with a strange device — a five-pointed star — that had nothing to do with this place. A door that went nowhere." He lifted a hand to stop her from interrupting. "It went nowhere, child. Believe me. There was a brief corridor on the other side and then a blank wall.

"The monastery was then run by an abbot who was much older than me. His name was Father Janek. And one day, walking in the cloisters, I asked him about it.

"He wouldn't tell me. A simple lie might have ended my curiosity, but Father Janek was too good a man to lie. Instead, he told me not to ask any more questions. He quickened his pace and as he walked away, I saw that he was afraid.

"From that day on, I was fascinated by the door. We had an extensive library here, Scarlett, with more than ten thousand books — although most of them have now moldered away. Some of them were centuries old. I searched through them. It took me many years. But slowly — a sentence here, a fragment there — a story began to emerge. But in the end, it was one book, a secret copy of a diary written by a Spanish monk in 1532 that told me everything I wanted to know."

He stopped and ran his eyes over the girl as if she were the most precious thing he had ever seen. Scarlett was revolted and didn't try to hide it. She could see saliva on the old man's lips.

"The Old Ones," he whispered, and although Scarlett had never heard those words before, they meant something to her, some memory from the far distant past. "The diary told me about the great battle that had taken place ten thousand years ago when the Old Ones ruled the world and mankind were their slaves. Pure evil. The Bible talks of devils . . . of Lucifer and Satan. But that's just storytelling. The Old Ones were real. They were here. And the one who ruled over them, Chaos, was more powerful than anything in the universe."

"So what happened to them?" Scarlett asked. Her voice had almost dropped to a whisper. Apart from the flames, twisting in the hearth, everything in the room was still.

"They were defeated and cast out. There were five children. . . ." he spoke the word with contempt. "They came to be known as the Gatekeepers. Four boys and a girl." He leveled his eyes on Scarlett, and she knew what he was going to say next. "You are the girl."

Scarlett shook her head. "You're wrong. That's insane. I'm not anything. I'm just a schoolgirl. I go to school in London. . . ."

38

"How do you think you got here?" The monk pointed in the direction of the corridor with a single trembling finger. Some sort of liquid was leaking out of his damaged eye, a single tear. "You have seen the monastery and the snow. You know you are not in London now."

"You drugged me."

"You came through the door! It was all there in the diary. There were twenty-five doorways built all around the world. They were there for the Gatekeepers so that when the time came, they would be able to travel great distances in seconds. Only the Gatekeepers can use them. Nobody else. When I pass through the door, I find myself in a corridor, a dead end. But it's not the same for you. It brought you here."

Scarlett shook her head. Nothing she had heard made any sense at all. She didn't even know where to begin. "I'm not ten thousand years old," she said. "Look at me! You can see for yourself. I'm fifteen!"

"You have lived twice, at two different times." Father Gregory laughed delightedly. "It's beyond belief," he said. "Finally to meet one of the Gatekeepers after all these years and to find that she has no idea who or what she is."

"You mentioned there was an abbot here," Scarlett said. "I want to talk to him."

"Father Janek is dead." He sighed. "I haven't told you the rest of my story. Maybe then you will understand." He nodded at her glass. "You haven't drunk your tea."

"I don't want it."

"I would take what you are given while you still can, child. There is much pain for you ahead."

Scarlett's tea was right in front of her. Briefly, she thought about picking it up and flinging it in his face. But it wouldn't do much good. It was probably lukewarm by now.

"The discovery of the diary, along with all the other fragments, changed my life," Father Gregory continued. "I began to think about the reasons why I had come to the monastery in the first place. Did I really think that religion — prayer and fasting — would help me change the world? Or was I just using religion to hide from it? Suddenly I knew what had brought me here. Hatred. I hated the world. I hated mankind. And praying to God to save us was ridiculous. God isn't interested! If He was, don't you think He'd have done something centuries ago?

"My whole life had been devoted to an illusion. All those prayers, the same words repeated again and again. Did they really make any sense? Of course not! The cries for mercy that would never come. Kneeling and making signs, singing hymns while, outside in the street, people were killing each other and trying to make as much money as they could to spend on themselves and to hell with everyone else. Do you never read the papers? What do you see in them except for murder and lust and greed, all day, every day? Do you not see the nature of the world in which you live?

"There is no God, Scarlett. I know that now. But there are the Old Ones. They are our natural masters. They deserve to rule the world because the world is evil and so are they."

He paused for breath. Scarlett looked at him with a mixture of pity and disgust. She had already decided that this wasn't about God or about religion. It was about a man who had nothing inside him. The years had hollowed out Father Gregory until there was nothing left.

"I will finish my story, and then you must be taken back to your cell," he said. "You will not be staying with us very long, Scarlett. You have a long journey to make. You will not return."

Scarlett said nothing. She knew that he was trying to frighten her. She also knew that he was succeeding. A long journey . . . where? And how would they take her there? Would they force her through another door?

Father Gregory closed his eyes for a few seconds, then continued.

"When I came here, there were twenty-four brothers at the Monastery of the Cry for Mercy," he explained. "Some of them, I knew, felt the same as me. They were disillusioned. Their life was hard. There were no rewards. The local people, the ones we were helping, weren't even grateful. Gradually, I began to sound the brothers out. I shared with them the knowledge I had discovered. How many of them would abandon their religion and turn instead to the Old Ones? In the end, there were seven of us. Seven out of twenty-four. Ready to begin a new adventure.

"We could, of course, have left. But I already knew that was out of the question. We were here for a reason, and that reason was the door. It had been here long before the monastery existed. Indeed, why was the monastery built in this place at all? It was because the architects knew that the door was in some way magical even if they had forgotten what its true purpose was. Do you see, child? The monastery was built around the door just as you will find holy places connected to the other doors all over the world: churches, temples, burial sites, caves.

"The seven of us agreed that we would stay here and serve the Old Ones. We would guard the door and should a child ever pass through it, we would know that we had found one of the Gatekeepers, and we would seize hold of them just as we have taken hold of you. . . ."

"What happened to Father Janek and the other monks?" Scarlett asked, although she wasn't sure she wanted to know.

"I killed Father Janek. I crept into his room while he slept and cut his throat. Then we continued around the monastery and did the same to all the others. Seventeen men died that night, and in the morning, the corridors were awash with blood. But don't mourn for them. They would have died happily. They would think they were going to heaven, into the embrace of their God.

"We have been here ever since. Of course, with so few of us, the monastery has fallen into disrepair. Once, the villagers brought us food because they revered us. Now they give it to us because they are afraid. We have survived a very long time, always waiting, always watching the door. Because we knew that you would come. And recently we realized that our time had come. We were expecting you."

"How?"

"Because the Old Ones have returned to the world. Even now, they are gathering strength, waiting to take back what was always theirs. Their agents have contacted us. Very soon, we will hand you over to them. And then we will have our reward."

"What will happen to me?"

"The Old Ones will not kill you. You don't need to be afraid. But they will need to keep you close to them, and you still must pay for what you did to them so many years ago."

"I didn't do anything! I don't know what you're talking about. . . ."

Father Gregory nodded his head sadly. "A great pity," he murmured. "I had expected more of you. A warrior or a great magician. But you really are nothing. A little girl, as you said, from school. Maybe the Old Ones will let me torture you for a while before you go. I would like that very much. To pay you back for the disappointment. We will see. . . ."

He stood up and went over to the door. He walked with a limp, and it occurred to Scarlett that as well as the diseased eye, he might have a withered leg. It took him a while even to cross the room, and she briefly wondered if she might be able to overpower him. But it wouldn't have done any good. When he opened the door, the two monks who had brought her there were waiting on the other side.

"They will take you back to your cell," he said. "They will also bring you food and water. I imagine you will be with us a few days."

Scarlett stood up and walked past him. There was nothing else she could do. For a brief moment, the two of them stood shoulder to shoulder in the doorway. Father Gregory reached out and stroked her hair. Scarlett shuddered. She didn't even try to hide her revulsion.

"Good-bye, Scarlett," he said. "You have no idea how glad I am that we have met."

Scarlett let the two monks walk her away. She didn't look back.

FOUR
Dragon's Breath

They took Scarlett back to the same cell she had occupied — but they had been busy while she was away. Someone had carried in a bed — although the moment she saw it, she knew she wasn't going to be allowed the privilege of a comfortable sleep. It was little more than a cot with sagging springs and a metal frame; she wouldn't even be able to stretch out without her feet going over the end. There were just two coarse blankets to protect her from the chill of the night and no pillow.

They had also supplied her with a table, a chair, and a bucket that she guessed she was expected to use as a toilet, although she didn't even want to think about that. A candle in a glass lantern now lit the room, and they had provided her with a meager dinner. A bowl of thin vegetable soup, a hunk of bread, and a mug were waiting on the table. There was a spoon to eat with — and if Scarlett had any thought of using it as a weapon, her hopes were soon dashed. It was flimsy, made of tin. They hadn't bothered with a knife or a fork.

She didn't feel like eating yet. If anything, the sight of the starvation rations brought home the full horror of her situation. These people were utterly merciless. They wanted her to live, but they didn't care how miserable or painful her life became — they had made that much clear. Scarlett sat down on the bed and sank her head into her hands. She thought she was going to cry, but the tears didn't come. The Old Ones. The Gatekeepers. The twenty-five doors around the world. Everything that Father Gregory had said seemed to spin round and round her, sucking her ever farther into a tunnel of misery and despair. How could this have happened to her? Could any of it really be true?

Somehow, she forced herself to go over it, to unpick the words. Much of what Father Gregory had said sounded completely insane. But at the same time, she had to admit that a lot of it was strangely familiar. There were echoes. There had been strange incidents in her life and they had taken place long before she walked through the church door.

The dreams, for one. Father Gregory had mentioned five children — four boys and a girl. Scarlett had been dreaming exactly the same thing for almost two years. And how had this all started? She had actually seen Matt, in St. Meredith's. He had been the one who had led her through the door, although now she wondered if he had really been there at all. He had been silent, ghostlike. It wasn't that she had imagined him. But perhaps what she had experienced was some sort of vision. If he had really gone through the door, wouldn't he be here now?

And then there was the door itself. Scarlett had tried to persuade herself that she had been drugged and kidnapped, but the more she thought about it, the more she accepted that it hadn't happened that way. Father Gregory had told her the truth. She had gone through a door in London and ended up in Ukraine. There had been no flight, no drugs. And if she accepted that, what choice did she have but to accept the rest?

She went over to the table and examined the food. It looked far from appetizing, but she made herself swallow it, the soup cold and greasy, the bread several days old. Still, it was all she was going to get, and she needed her strength. The candle in the lamp was only an inch tall, and she wondered how long it would last. When it went out, she would be left in total blackness. The thought made her shudder. There was already so much to be afraid of, but being on her own, locked up in the dark, was somehow worse than any of it.

It would be better if she could sleep. She didn't undress. It was far too cold to even think of taking off her coat. She climbed onto the bed and pulled the two blankets over her, burrowing into them like an animal in a cave. She lay like that for a long time, and when sleep did finally come, she didn't even notice it. She only knew that she was no longer awake when she realized that she had begun to dream.

She was back in the strange, airless world that she had visited so many times before. She recognized it and was glad to be there. She was desperate to see Matt and the other three boys. If anyone could help her, they could. At least they might show her a way to break out.

But there was no sign of them. While part of her slept, alone in her cell, the other part was stranded here, alone on the edge of a grim and lifeless sea.

Something in the dreamworld had changed. Scarlett

became aware of it very slowly, not seeing anything but sensing it, a sort of throbbing in the air that was coming from very far away, from the other side of the horizon. She heard a faint rumble of thunder and saw a tiny streak of lightning, like a hairline crack in the fabric of the world. Her head was pounding. She noticed the water, the surface of the ocean, begin to shiver. A gust of wind tugged at her hair. The sand, or the gray dust, or whatever it was, spun in eddies around her feet, then leaped up, half blinding her and stinging her cheeks. She backed away, knowing that she needed to hide. She still didn't know what she was hiding from.

And then, in a single moment, the ocean split open. It was as if it had been sliced in half by some vast, invisible knife — and the black water rushed in, millions of gallons pouring from left and right into the chasm — a mile long — that had been formed. At the same time, something rose up, twisting toward the surface. At first, she thought it was a snake, some sort of monstrous sea serpent that had been resting for centuries on the ocean bed and had only now woken up. She smelled its breath — how was that possible . . . how could you smell anything in a dream? — and cried out as it rushed toward her, its eyes blazing, flames exploding around its mouth. It was a dragon! Straight out of ancient folklore. And yet it was horribly real, howling so loudly that she thought her head would burst.

SIGNAL ONE

The two words had appeared in front of her. They were written in neon: huge red letters hanging from some

48

sort of frame, the light so intense that they burned her eyes. Where had they come from? They must have risen out of the ground because only a moment before, the landscape had been empty. The neon buzzed and flickered as some sort of electric power coursed through it. Scarlett looked down at her hands and saw that they were blood red, reflecting the light. It was as if she were on fire.

SIGNAL ONE . . . SIGNAL ONE . . .

It flashed on and off. The dragon was there one minute, then gone the next, lost in the darkness, reappearing in the light. Each time she saw it, it was a little closer. The wind was blasting her. If it got any stronger, it would throw her off her feet. She tried to run, but she couldn't move. The dragon opened its mouth, showing teeth like kitchen knives.

And that was when she woke up and found herself still lying on top of the bed and covered by the two blankets, with the first, dreary light of the morning creeping in through the window. It was ice-cold all around.

Scarlett sat up. She was already beginning to shiver. What had that all been about? *Signal One?* She had never seen the two words written down before. She had no idea what they meant, even if she was certain that they must be important. They had been shown to her for a reason.

She looked up at the window and guessed that it must be about five or six o'clock in the morning. It was difficult to say without her watch. Presumably the monks would bring her some sort of breakfast. They had made it clear that they needed to keep her alive. Could she somehow overpower them when they came in, fight her way through the door and make a run for it? She doubted it. The monks were thin and malnourished, but they were still a lot stronger than her. If only she had a weapon — that would make all the difference.

Sitting on the edge of the bed, she searched through her pockets. All she had was a blunt pencil, left over from art class, a comb, and a transit card. The sight of it made her sad. It was so ordinary, a reminder of everything she had left behind. How many thousands of miles was she now from London buses and Tube trains?

There was nothing she could use. She considered taking off her coat, throwing it in the face of whoever carried in her food. But it was a stupid plan. She still didn't know there was going to be any food, and anyway, it wouldn't work. They would just laugh at her before they took her away and whipped her or whatever else they planned to do.

There had to be a way out of the cell. Scarlett got up and examined the door a second time, running her hands over the hasps, pressing against it with all her weight. It was so solid it might as well have been cemented into the wall. That just left the window. There were three bars and no glass. The cell had been built to house a man, not a child — and certainly not a girl. Might it be possible to squeeze through, after all?

She hadn't been able to reach the window before, but maybe these monks, as clever as they might be, had made a mistake. They had supplied her with a table and a chair. Quickly, she dragged the table over to the window, put the chair on top, and climbed up.

For the first time, she was able to look outside. There was a view down a hill, the ground steep and rugged, thick patches of snow piled up against black rocks. A few buildings stood in the near distance, scattered around. They looked like barns and abandoned farmhouses that might belong to the monastery but that were more likely part of a village, just out of sight. A series of icicles hung above her, suspended from a gutter that ran the full length of the building. She had forgotten how cold it was, but she was quickly reminded by a sudden snow flurry blowing in off the roof. Her lips and cheeks were already numb. It had to be less than zero out there.

There was no way down. The bars were too close together, and even if she had managed to slip through, she'd be at least sixty feet above the ground. Try to jump from this height and she would break both her legs.

She was still in the cell two hours later when the door opened and they finally brought her something to eat.

Breakfast was a bowl of cold porridge and a tin mug of water, carried in by a monk she hadn't yet met — for his face certainly wasn't one that she would have forgotten. It was horribly burned. One whole side of it was dead and disfigured as if he had fallen asleep with his head resting on an oven. Scarlett turned her eyes away from him. Was there anyone at Cry for Mercy who hadn't rotted over the past twenty years? A second monk stood with him, guarding the door.

"You . . . eat . . . little . . . girl." Burnt Face was proud of his English, but his accent was so thick, she could barely make out the words.

He set the tray down, and Scarlett moved toward him.

Her hands were clasped behind her back, and she was clearly on the edge of tears. "Please," she said. "Please let me out. . . ." Her voice was trembling.

The sight of the girl, pale and bleary-eyed after the long night, seemed to amuse him. "Out?" He sneered at her. "No out . . ."

"But you don't understand. . . ." She was closer to him now, and as he straightened up, she brought her hands round and lashed out.

She was holding an icicle.

She had broken it off the gutter and was holding it like a knife. The point was needle sharp. Using all her strength, she drove it into the flesh between his shoulder and his neck. The monk screamed. Blood gushed out. He fell to his knees, as if in prayer.

Scarlett was already moving. She knew that she had to take advantage of the surprise, that speed was all she had on her side. The second monk had frozen, completely shocked by what had just happened. Before he could react, she threw herself at him, head and shoulders down, like a bull. She hit him hard in the stomach and heard the breath explode out of him. His hands grabbed for her, but then he was down, writhing on the floor. She pulled away and began to run.

According to Father Gregory, there were just seven monks in the Monastery of the Cry for Mercy, and she had just taken out two of them. How long would it be before the ones that remained set off after her? Scarlett had to find the door that had brought her here. She knew where it was — a short way down the corridor, only a minute from the cell. With a bit of luck, she would be gone before they knew what had happened.

It was only when she had taken twenty paces that she knew she had gone wrong. Somehow she had managed to get lost. She was in another long corridor — one that she didn't recognize. There was a picture of some holy person hanging crookedly on the wall. An ornate wooden chest. Another passageway with a flight of stone steps leading down. For a moment they looked tempting. They might lead her out of the monastery. But at the same time, she knew they would take her farther away from the door. The door was the fast way back to St. Meredith's. She had to find it.

In the distance, a bell began to ring. Not a call to prayers. An alarm. She heard shouting. The second of the two monks — the one she had hit — must have recovered. Forcing herself not to panic, she continued forward even though she knew she was heading in the wrong direction, and that the farther she went, the more lost she would become. She heard flapping ahead of her, the sound of sandals hitting the stone floor, and a moment later another monk appeared. He saw her and cried out. There was an opening to one side. She took it, passing between the wood-paneled walls and a great tapestry, hanging in shreds, the fabric moldering away.

The passage emerged in a second corridor, and with a surge of relief she realized that she knew where she was. Somehow she had found her way back. There was the table with the candlesticks, the painting of the crucifixion. The door was just beyond. There was nobody in the way.

The noise of the sandals. If the monk had been barefoot, Scarlett might not have heard him. But even without looking round, she knew that someone had caught up with her, that he was running toward her even now. In a single movement she reached out, grabbed a heavy iron candlestick, and swung it round. She'd timed it exactly right. The end of the candlestick smashed into the side of the monk's bald head, knocking him out. Scarlett hit him a second time, just to be sure, then dropped the candlestick and made for the door.

Someone appeared at the far end of the corridor.

It was Father Gregory. He saw Scarlett and screamed something — maybe in English, maybe in his own language. The words were trapped in his throat. The door was now between the two of them, exactly halfway. Scarlett wondered if she could reach it. Father Gregory was dancing on his feet as if he had just been electrocuted. His good eye was wide and staring, making the other one look all the more diseased. Scarlett was about a hundred feet away, panting, gathering all her strength for one last effort.

The two of them set off at the same moment.

In a way, it was weird. Scarlett wasn't running away. She was actually hurtling toward the one man she most wanted to avoid. But she had to reach the door before he did. She had made her decision. It was the only way home.

Father Gregory was surprisingly fast. His limp had disappeared and he moved with incredible speed, his fury propelling him forward. Scarlett didn't dare look at him.

She was aware of him getting closer and closer, but her eyes were fixed on the door. There it was in front of her. She lunged forward and grabbed hold of the handle, but at the same moment his hands fell on her, seizing hold of the top of her coat, his fingers against her neck. She heard him cry out in triumph. His breath was against her skin.

She didn't let go of the door. She wasn't going to let him drag her back. Instead, she dropped down, twisting her shoulders so that the coat was pulled over her head. She had already undone the buttons and she felt it come loose, falling away. Father Gregory lost his balance and, still holding the coat, fell back. Scarlett was free. She jerked the door open and threw herself forward. For a few seconds her vision was blurred. The doorway seemed to rush past. She heard Gregory screaming at her, suddenly a long way away.

The door slammed shut behind her.

She was lying, sobbing and shaking on the floor of St. Meredith's. And there was a man standing in front of her, a young policeman dressed in blue, staring at her with a look of complete bewilderment.

"Who are you?" he demanded.

"I'm . . . Scarlett Adams." She could barely get the words out.

"Where have you been? What have you been doing?" The policeman shook his head in disbelief. "You'd better come with me!"

FIVE
Front Page News

Scarlett had only been missing for eighteen hours, but she was a fifteen-year-old student on a school trip in the middle of London, and her disappearance had been enough to trigger a major panic, with newspaper headlines, TV bulletins, and a nationwide search. Both her parents had been informed at once, and Paul Adams was already on a plane, on his way back from Hong Kong. He was actually in midair when Scarlett was found.

Scarlett had begun to realize that she was in trouble almost from the moment she found herself back in St. Meredith's, sitting opposite the policeman, who had immediately launched into a series of questions.

"Where have you been?" he asked again.

Scarlett was still in shock, thinking about her narrow escape from Father Gregory. She pointed at the door with a trembling finger. "There . . ."

"What do you mean?" The policeman was young and out of his depth. He had already radioed for backup, and an ambulance was on the way. Even so, he was the first on the scene. There might even be a promotion in this. He took out a notebook and prepared to write down anything Scarlett said.

"The monastery," Scarlett muttered. "I was in the monastery."

"And what monastery was that?"

"On the other side of the door."

The policeman walked over to the door and opened it before Scarlett realized what he was going to do. At the last minute, she screamed at him, a single word.

"Don't!"

She had visions of Father Gregory flying in, dragging her back to her cell. She was sure the nightmare was about to begin all over again. But the policeman was just standing there, scratching his head. There was no monastery on the other side of the door, no monks — just an alleyway, a brick wall, a line of trash cans. It was drizzling — gray, London weather. Scarlett looked past him. She couldn't quite believe what she was seeing.

And that was when she knew that she was going to have to start lying. How could she explain where she had been and what had really happened to her? Magic doors? Psycho monks in Ukraine? People would think she was mad. Worse than that, they might decide that the whole thing had been a schoolgirl prank. She would be expelled from St. Genevieve's. Her father would kill her. She had to come up with an answer that made sense.

The next forty-eight hours were a nightmare almost as bad as the one she had left behind. More policemen and paramedics arrived, and suddenly the church was crowded with people all asking questions and arguing amongst themselves. Scarlett didn't seem to be hurt, but even so, she was wrapped in a blanket and whisked off to the hospital. Somehow, the press had already found out that she was back. The street was jammed with photographers and journalists threatening to mob her as she was bundled into the ambulance, and there were more of them waiting when she was helped out on the other side. All Scarlett could do was keep her head down, ignore the flashes of the cameras, and wish that the whole thing would be over soon.

Mrs. Murdoch was called to the hospital and stayed with Scarlett as she was examined by a doctor and a nurse. The housekeeper looked shell-shocked. It was obvious that nothing like this had ever happened to her before. The doctor took Scarlett's pulse and heart rate and then asked her to strip down to her underwear.

"Where did you get these?" He had noted a series of scratches running down her back.

"I don't know. . . ." Scarlett guessed that she had been hurt in her final confrontation with Father Gregory, but she wasn't going to talk about that now. She was pretending that she was too dazed to explain anything.

"How about this, Scarlett?" The nurse had found blood on her school jersey. "Is this your blood?"

"I don't think so."

The jersey was placed in a bag to be handed over to the police for forensic examination. It occurred to Scarlett that they would be unable to find a match for it . . . not unless their database extended all the way to Ukraine.

Finally, Scarlett was allowed to take a shower and was given new clothes to wear. Two policewomen had arrived to interview her. Mrs. Murdoch stayed with her, and just for once Scarlett was glad to have her around. She wouldn't have wanted to go through all this on her own.

"Do you remember what happened to you from the time of your disappearance? Perhaps you'd like to start when you arrived at the church. . . ."

The policewomen were both in their thirties, kind but severe. The rumor was already circulating that Scarlett had never been in any danger at all and that this whole thing was a colossal waste of police time. By now, Scarlett had worked out what she was going to say. She knew that it would sound pretty lame. But it would just have to do.

"I don't remember anything," she said. "I wasn't feeling well in the church. I was dizzy. So I went outside to get some fresh air — and after that, everything is blank. I think I fell over. I don't know. . . ."

"You fainted?"

"I think so. I want to help you. But I just don't know. . . ."

The two policewomen looked doubtful. They had been on the force long enough to know when someone was lying, and it was obvious to them that Scarlett was hiding something. But there wasn't much they could do. They asked her the same questions over and over again and received exactly the same answers. She had fallen ill. She had fainted. She couldn't remember anything else. And what other explanation could there be?

The interview ended when Paul Adams appeared. A taxi had brought him straight from Heathrow Airport, and he burst into the room, his suit crumpled, his face a mixture of anxiety, relief, and irritation, all three of them compounded by a generous dose of jet lag.

"Scarly!" He went over and hugged his daughter.

"Hello, Dad."

"I can't believe they've found you. Are you hurt? Where have you been?" The two policewomen exchanged a glance. Paul Adams turned to them. "If you don't mind, I'd like to take my daughter home. Mrs. Murdoch . . ."

They left the hospital by a back exit, avoiding the press pack who were still camped out at the front. By now, Scarlett was exhausted. She had been found midmorning, but it was early evening before she was released. She was desperate to go to bed, and once she got there, she slept through the entire night. Maybe that was just as well. She would need all her strength for the headlines that were waiting for her the next day.

MISSING SCHOOLGIRL FOUND AFTER JUST ONE DAY

POLICE ASK — WAS THIS A PRANK?

Mystery still surrounds the return of fifteen-year-old schoolgirl Scarlett Adams, who was discovered by police just one day after she went missing on a school trip. Scarlett was feared abducted after she vanished during a visit to St. Meredith's church in East London, prompting a national search. She was later found unhurt inside the church itself.

Although she received hospital treatment for minor scratches, there was no indication that she had been assaulted or kept against her will. So far, the girl — described as "bright and sensible" by the teachers at the £15,000-a-year private school that she attends in Dulwich — has been unable to offer any explanation, claiming that she is suffering from memory loss. Her father, Paul Adams, a corporate lawyer, angrily dismissed claims that the whole incident might have been a schoolgirl prank. "Scarlett has obviously suffered a traumatic experience, and I'm just glad to have her back," he said.

Meanwhile, the police seem anxious to close the file. "What matters is that Scarlett is safe," Detective Chris Kloet said, speaking from New Scotland Yard. "We may never know what happened to her in the eighteen hours she was gone, but we are satisfied that no crime seems to have been committed."

The report had been sent ten thousand miles by fax. It was being examined by a boy in a room in Nazca, Peru. After he was done reading it, he got up and went over to a desk. He held the sheet of paper under a light. There was a picture of Scarlett next to the text. She had been photographed holding a hockey stick with two more girls, one on each side. A team photo. The boy examined her carefully. She was quite good-looking, he thought. Asian, he would have said. Almost certainly the same age as him.

"When did this arrive?" he asked.

"Half an hour ago," came the reply.

The boy's name was Matthew Freeman. He was the first of the Gatekeepers and, without quite knowing how, he had become their unelected leader. Four months ago, he had faced the Old Ones in the Nazca Desert and had tried to close the barrier, the huge gate, that for centuries had kept them at bay. He had failed. The King of the Old Ones had cut him down where he stood, leaving him for dead. The last thing he had seen was the armies of the Old Ones, spreading out and disappearing into the night.

It had taken him six weeks to recover from his injuries, and since then he had been resting, trying to work out what to do next. He was staying in a Peruvian farmhouse, a hacienda just outside the town of Nazca itself. Richard Cole, the journalist who had traveled with him from England, was still with him. Richard was his closest friend. It was he who had just come into the room.

"It's got to be her," Matt said.

Richard nodded. "She was in St. Meredith's. She must have gone through the same door that you went through. God knows what happened to her. She was missing for eighteen hours."

"Her name is Scarlett."

"Scar." Richard nodded again.

Matt thought for a moment, still clutching the article. He had spent the past four months searching for Scarlett in the only way that he could — through his dreams. Night after night he had visited the strange dreamworld that had become so familiar to him. It had helped him in the past. He was certain that she had to be there somewhere. Perhaps it would lead him to her, helping him again.

And now, quite unexpectedly, she had turned up in the real world. There could be no doubt that this was her, the fifth of the Five. And she was in England, in London! A student at an expensive private school.

"We have to go to her," Matt said. "We must leave at once."

"I'm checking out tickets now."

Matt turned the photograph round in the light, tilting it toward himself. "Scar," he muttered. "Now we know where she is."

"That's right," Richard said. He looked grave. "But the Old Ones will know it too."

SIX
Matt's Diary [1]

I never asked for any of this. I never wanted to be part of it. And even now, I don't understand exactly what is happening or why it had to be me.

I hoped that writing this diary might help. It was Richard's idea, to put it all down on paper. But it hasn't worked out the way I hoped. The more I think about my life, the more I write about it, the more confused it all becomes.

Sometimes I try to go back to where it all began, but I'm not sure anymore where that was. Was it the day my parents died? Or did it start in Ipswich, the evening I decided to break into a warehouse with my best friend . . . who was actually anything but? Maybe the decision had already been made the day I was born. Matthew Freeman, you will not go to school like other kids. You won't play football and take your A-levels and have a career. You are here for another reason. You can argue if you like, but that's just the way it's got to be.

I think a lot about my parents even though sometimes it's hard to see their faces, and their voices have long since faded out. My dad was a doctor, a GP with a practice round the corner from the house. I can just about remember a man with a beard and gold-rimmed glasses. He was very political. We were recycling stuff long before it was fashionable, and he used to get annoyed about the National Health Service — too many managers, too much red tape. At the same time, he used to laugh a lot. He read to me at night . . . Roald Dahl . . . *The Twits* was one of his favorites. And there was a comedy show on TV that he never missed. It was on Sunday night, but I've forgotten its name.

My mum was a lot smaller than him. She was always on a diet, although I don't think she really needed to lose weight. I suppose it didn't help that she was a great cook. She used to make her own bread and cakes, and around September she'd set up a production line for Christmas puddings, which she'd sell off for charity. Sometimes she talked about going back to work, but she liked to be there when I got back from school. That was one of her rules. She wouldn't let me come home to an empty house.

I was only eight years old when they died, and there's so much about them I never knew. I guess they were happy together. Whenever I think back, the sun always seems to be shining, which must mean something. I can still see our house and our garden with a big rosebush sprawling over the lawn. Sometimes I can even smell the flowers.

Mark and Kate Freeman. Those were their names. They died in a car accident on their way to a wedding, and the thing is, I knew it was going to happen. I dreamed that their car was going to drive off a bridge and into a river, and I woke up knowing that they were both going to die. But I didn't tell them. I knew my dad would never have believed me. So I pretended I was sick. I cried and kicked my heels. I let them go, but I made them leave me behind.

I could have saved them. I tell myself that over and over again. Maybe my dad wouldn't have believed me. Maybe he would have insisted on going, no matter what I said. But I could have poured paint over the car or something. I could even have set fire to it. There were all sorts of ways that I could have made it impossible for them to leave the house.

But I was too scared. I had a power and I knew that it made me different from everyone else and that was the last thing I wanted to be. Freakshow Matt . . . not me, thanks. So I said nothing. I stayed back and watched them go, and since then I've seen the car pull away a thousand times and I've yelled at my eight-year-old self to do something and I've hated myself for being so stupid. If I could go back in time, that's where I would start, because that's where it all went wrong.

After that, things happened very quickly. I was fostered by a woman called Gwenda Davis, who was related in some way to my mother — her half sister or something. For the next six years, I lived with her and her partner, Brian, in a terraced house in Ipswich. I hated both of them. Gwenda was shallow and self-centered, but Brian was worse. They had what I think is called an abusive relationship, which means that he used to beat her around. He hit me too. I was scared of him — I admit it. Sometimes I would see him looking at me in the same way, and I would make sure my bedroom door was locked at night.

And yet, here's something strange. I might as well admit it. In a way, I was almost happy in Ipswich. Sometimes

I thought of it as a punishment for what I'd done — or hadn't done — and part of me figured that I deserved it. I was resigned to my life there. I knew it was never going to get any better and at least I was able to create an identity for myself. I could be anyone I wanted to be.

I bunked off school. I was never going to pass any exams, so what did I care? I stole stuff from local shops. I started smoking when I was twelve. My friend Kelvin bought me my first packet of Marlboro Lights — although, of course, he made me pay him back twice what they'd cost. I never took drugs. But if I'd stayed with him much longer, I probably would have. I'd have ended up like one of those kids you read about in the newspapers, dead from an overdose, a body next to a railway line. Nobody would have cared, not even me. That was just the way it would have been.

But then along came Jayne Deverill, and suddenly everything changed, because it turned out she was a witch. I know how crazy that sounds. I can't believe I just wrote it. But she wasn't a witch like in a movie. I mean, she didn't have a long nose and a pointy hat or anything like that. She was the real thing: evil, cruel, and just a little bit mad. She and her friends had been watching me, waiting for me to fall into their hands because they needed me to help them unlock a mysterious gate hidden in a wood in Yorkshire. And it seemed that, after all, I wasn't just some loser with a criminal record who'd gotten his parents killed. I was one of the Five. A Gatekeeper. The hero of a story that had begun ten thousand years before I was born.

How did I feel about that? How do I feel about it now?

I have no choice. I am trapped in this and will have to stick with it until the bitter end. And I do think the end will be a hard one. The forces we're up against — the Old Ones and their allies around the world — are too huge. They are like a nightmare plague, spreading everywhere, killing everything they touch. I have powers. I've accepted that now, and recently I've learned how to use them. But I am still only fifteen years old — I had my birthday out here in Nazca — and when I think about the things that are being asked of me, I am scared.

I can't run away. There's nowhere for me to hide. If I don't fight back, the Old Ones will find me. They will destroy me more surely and more painfully than even those cigarettes would have managed. After I was arrested, I never smoked again, by the way. That was one of the ways that I changed. I think I have accepted my place in all this. First of all, I have to survive. But that's not enough. I also have to win.

At least I'm no longer alone.

When this all began, I knew that I was one of five children, all the same age as me, and that one day we would meet. I knew this because I had seen them in my dreams.

Pedro was the first one I came across in real life. He has no last name. He lost it — along with his home, his possessions, and his entire family when the village in Peru where he lived was hit by a flood. He was six years old. After that, he moved to the slums of Lima and managed to scratch out a living there. The first time I saw him, he was begging on the street. We met when I was unconscious and he was trying to rob me. But that was the way he was brought up. For him, there was never any right or wrong — it was just a question of finding the next meal. He couldn't read. He knew nothing about the world outside the crumbling shanty town where he lived. And of course he could hardly speak a word of English.

I don't think I'd ever met anyone quite so alien to me . . . and by that I mean he could have come from another planet. For a start (and there's no pleasant way to put this) he stank. He hadn't washed or had a bath in years, and the clothes he wore had been worn by at least ten people before him. Even after everything I'd been through, I was rich compared to him. At least I'd grown up with fresh tap water. I'd never starved.

Almost from the very start, we became friends. It probably helped that Pedro decided to save my life when the police chief, a man called Rodriguez, was cheerfully beating me up. But it was more than that. Think about the odds of our ever finding each other, me living in a provincial town in England and him, a street urchin surviving in a city ten thousand miles away. We were drawn together because that was how it was meant to be. We were two of the Five.

Pedro is pure Inca: a descendant of the people who first lived in Peru. More than that, he's somehow connected with Manco Capac, one of the sun gods. The Incas showed me a picture of Manco — it was actually on a disc made of solid gold — and the two of them looked exactly the same. I'm not sure I completely understand what's going on here. Is Pedro some sort of ancient god? If so, what does that make me?

Like me, Pedro has a special power. His is the ability to heal. The only reason I'm able to walk today is because of him. We were both injured in the Nazca Desert. He broke his leg, but I was cut down and left for dead . . . and I would have died if he hadn't come back and stayed with me for a couple of weeks. It's called radiesthesia, which is probably the longest word I know. I've only managed to spell it right because I've looked it up in the dictionary. It's something to do with the transfer of energy. Basically, it means that I got better thanks to him. And as a result, Pedro is more than a friend. He's almost like a long-lost brother — and if that sounds corny, too bad. That's how I feel.

And then came Scott and Jamie Tyler.

They really were brothers . . . twins, in fact. Formerly the telepathic twins, performing with *The Circus of the Mind* at the Reno Playhouse in Nevada. While Pedro and I had been fighting (and losing) in the Nazca Desert, they'd been having adventures of their own, chased across America by an organization called the Nightrise Corporation. They'd also managed to get tangled up in the American election and were there when one of the candidates was almost assassinated.

Scott and Jamie are more or less identical. They're thin to the point of being skinny, and you can tell straight away that they have Native American blood — they were descended from the Washoe tribe. They have long, dark hair, dark eyes, and a sort of watchful quality. Physically, I would have said that Jamie was the younger of the two, but when they finally reached us — they traveled through a doorway that took them from Lake Tahoe in Nevada to a temple in Cuzco, Peru — he was very much in charge. His brother had been taken prisoner and tortured. We're still not sure what they did to him, and Pedro has spent long hours alone with him, trying to repair the damage. But Scott is still suffering. He's withdrawn. He doesn't talk very much. I sometimes wonder if we'll be able to rely on him when the time comes.

It's been more than four months since I faced the Old Ones in the Nazca Desert, and I still haven't recovered from my own injuries. I'm in pain a lot of the time. There are no scars, but I can feel something wrong inside me. Sometimes I wake up at night and it's as if I've just been stabbed. Even Pedro still has a limp. So between the four of us, I certainly wouldn't bet any money on our taking on unimaginable forces of darkness and saving the world. I'm sorry, but that's how it is.

Jamie is very bright. He seems to see things more clearly than any of us, mainly because he was there at the very start. It's too complicated to explain right now, but somehow he traveled back in time and met us . . . before we were us. Yes. There was a Matt ten thousand years ago who looked like me and sounded like me and who may even have been me. Jamie says that we've all lived twice. I just hope it was more fun the first time.

Four months!

We've all been hanging out in this house near the coast, to the south of Lima. It belongs to a professor named Joanna Chambers who's an expert on pretty much any-thing to do with Peru. The house is wooden and painted white, constructed a bit like a hacienda, which is a Spanish farmhouse. There's a large central room that opens onto a veranda during the day and a wide staircase that connects the two floors. Everything is very old-fashioned. There are scatter rugs and a big open fireplace and fans that turn slowly beneath the ceiling, circulating the air.

We've passed the time reading, watching TV (the house has satellite and we've also shipped in a supply of DVDs), and surfing the Net, looking out for any news of the Old Ones. The professor insists that we do three or four hours of lessons, although it's been ages since any of us went to school and Pedro never stepped into one in his life. We've played football in the garden, passing the ball around the llamas that wander onto the grass, and we've gone for hikes in the desert. And, I suppose, we've been gathering strength, slowly recovering from everything we've been through.

But even so, there have been times when it all seems unreal, sitting here, doing nothing in the full knowledge that somewhere in the world the Old Ones must be spreading their power base, preparing to strike at humanity. They'll be making friends in all the right places. . . . As far as we know, they could be all over Europe. Their aim is to start a total war, to kill as many people as possible, and then to toy with the rest, maiming and torturing until there's nobody left. Why do they want to do this? There is no why. The Old Ones feed on pain in the same way that cancer will attack a healthy organism. It's their nature.

Sometimes, in the evening, the six of us will play per-udo, which is a Peruvian game, a bit like liar dice. Me, Richard, Pedro, Scott, Jamie, and the professor. We'll sit there, throwing dice and behaving as if nothing is happening, as if we're just a bunch of friends on an extended holiday. And secretly I want to get up and punch the wall. We're safe and comfortable in Nazca. But every moment we're here, we're losing. Our enemy is gaining the upper hand.

What else can we do? The Old Ones have disappeared. And even if we knew what they were doing, we're not yet strong enough to take them on. Only four of the Gatekeepers have come together. There have to be five.

And now there are. At last we've found Scar.

It's hard to believe that today I actually held a picture of her in my hands. Now she has a name — Scarlett Adams. We know where she lives. We can actually reach out to her and tell her the truth about who she is — or was.

Ten thousand years ago, she was in charge of her own private army. Jamie actually met her and fought with her at the final battle when the King of the Old Ones was banished and the first great gate was constructed. She must have a power — we all do. But he never found out what it was. When he met her, he said she was brave and resourceful. She could ride a horse, fight with a sword, lead an army of men who were at least twice her age. But she never did anything that looked like magic . . . at least, not anything that he noticed.

Very soon, we will leave Nazca. I really want to see England again.

And now I'm going to bed.

Richard is worried that Scar turning up is the start of a new phase. The Old Ones have left us alone, but now they'll have been alerted. If they were planning a move against us, this is the time when they'll make it.

But I don't care. There are five of us, and that means that soon this whole thing will be over. We'll get together and do whatever it takes to bring it all to an end. After that, I'll go back to school. I'll take my exams. I'll have an ordinary life.

That's all I want. I can hardly wait.

SEVEN

Last Night in Nazca

Twenty-four hours after the fax had arrived, Professor Chambers organized a dinner. It was her way of saying good-bye. The following day, Matt, Richard, Pedro, Jamie, and Scott would be leaving for England — the professor had arranged passports for all of them — and at last she would have the house to herself.

Joanna Chambers had spent most of her life in Peru, studying the Incas, the ancient Moche and Chimu tribes and, of course, the Nazca Lines. She was an expert on a dozen different subjects, a qualified pilot, a good shot with a rifle or a handgun, and a terrible cook. Fortunately, the meal had been prepared by the local help: creole soup, followed by lomo saltado — a dish made with grilled beef, onions, and rice. There were two jugs of pisco sour, a frothing, white drink made from grape brandy, lemon, and egg white — it tasted much better than it looked.

Richard Cole was sitting at the head of the table. He had changed in the past few months. His hair had been bleached by the sun and he had grown it so that it fell in long strands over his collar. He had a permanent desert tan, and although he didn't quite have a beard, he looked rough and unshaven. Tonight, he had changed into jeans and a white linen shirt. Normally he slouched around in shorts and sandals, and if the house had been nearer the sea, he might easily have been mistaken for a surfer. He started every morning with a five-mile run. He was keeping himself in shape.

Scott and Jamie Tyler were sitting on one side of the table, together as usual. Matt and Pedro were on the other. There was one empty seat, and someone had placed the article with the picture of Scarlett Adams on the table in front of it, as if she were there in spirit.

All six of them were in a good mood. The food had been excellent, and the drink had helped. Upstairs, their suitcases were packed and ready in the various rooms. Professor Chambers waited until the food had been cleared away, then tapped a fork against her glass and rose to her feet. Matt had never seen her wearing a dress, and tonight was no exception. She had put on a crumpled safari suit and there was a small bunch of flowers in her buttonhole.

"We ought to go to bed," she began. "You have a long journey to make tomorrow — but I just want to wish you bon voyage. I can't say I'm too sorry that you're finally on your way. . . ." There were protests around the table, and she held up a hand for silence. "It's been impossible to get any work done with all your infernal noise, football games out on the front lawn, four boys clumping up and down the stairs, and all the rest of it.

"But I will miss you. I've enjoyed having you here. That's the truth of it. And although it's wonderful that Scar has finally turned up, I can't help wondering what lies ahead of you." She stopped for a moment. "I feel a bit like a mother sending my sons off to war. I can only hope that one day I'll see you again. I can only hope that you'll come back safe."

She lifted her glass.

"Anyway, here's a toast to all five of you. The Five, I should say. Look after yourselves. Beat the Old Ones. Do what you have to do. And now let's get some hot chocolate and have a final game of perudo. You have an early start."

Later that night, Richard and Matt found themselves standing on the veranda outside the main room. It was a beautiful night with a full moon, an inky sky, and stars everywhere. Matt could hear classical music coming from inside the house. Professor Chambers had an old-fashioned radio that she liked to listen to while she worked. Scott and Jamie were sharing a room on the first floor. Pedro was probably watching TV.

"I can't believe we're going home," Matt said.

"England." Richard gazed into the darkness as if he could see it on the horizon. "Do you have any idea what happens when we get there?"

Matt shook his head. "I don't know. I've thought about it. I've tried to work out some sort of plan. Maybe it would be easier if we knew what the Old Ones have been doing all this time." He thought for a moment. "Maybe we'll know when the five of us get together. Maybe it will all make sense."

Matt stared into the darkness. The nights in Nazca were always huge. Even without seeing it, he could feel the desert stretching out to the mountains. There seemed to be five times more stars in the southern hemisphere than he'd ever seen in Europe. The sky was bursting with them.

"What you said yesterday . . ." He turned to Richard. "About the Old Ones . . ."

"They were looking for kids with special powers," Richard said. "That's how they found Scott and Jamie. If Scarlett went through the door at St. Meredith's, they'll know about it. They'll have read the article too."

"You think they'll be waiting for us?"

"Scarlett's being watched by the Nexus. Her father's with her. She took a couple of days off school. So far everything seems okay. She doesn't seem to be in any danger."

Richard had been in constant touch with the Nexus, the strange collection of millionaires, politicians, psychics, and churchmen who knew about the Old Ones and had come together in a sort of secret society to fight them. It had to be secret because they were afraid of being ridiculed. How could they admit that they believed in devils and demons? The Nexus had made it their job to look after Matt and the other Gatekeepers. At one stage, they had paid for him to go to a private school. They were still paying for everything while the four of them were out here.

And they were also protecting Scarlett Adams. They had moved in the moment she had been identified in the national press, hiring a team of private detectives to watch over her night and day. They were lucky that she lived in England. That made things easier. One of the Nexus members was a senior police officer named Tarrant, and he had arranged for all her calls to be monitored. Meanwhile, Scarlett had gone back to school. Her father was still with her in London, and there was a Scottish helper living in the house. By now, Richard knew a great deal about her. She was in the school play. She had a boyfriend named Aidan, and she regularly beat him at tennis. She seemed to have a happy life.

Richard and Matt were about to rip all that up. Somewhere inside him, Matt felt guilty about that — but he knew he couldn't avoid it. She had been born for a purpose. His job was to tell her what that purpose was.

Somewhere, an owl hooted in the darkness. The house was on the outskirts of Nazca, but Richard and Matt could make out the lights of the town, twinkling in the distance. Everything was very peaceful, but they knew that it was an illusion. Soon the whole world would change.

"I'm not sure you should go," Richard said suddenly.

"What do you mean?" Matt was surprised. Everything was ready. The tickets had been bought.

"I've been thinking about it . . . this trip to England. You and Pedro and Scott and Jamie . . . all on the same plane. Suppose the Old Ones have control of American airspace. They could smash you into the side of a mountain. Or a building."

"They don't want to kill us," Matt said. He was fairly sure about that. "If they kill us, we'll all be replaced by our past selves. That's how it works. And what good will that do them? They'll only have to start searching for us all over again. It's easier for them to keep us alive."

Richard shook his head. "They could still force the plane down somewhere and capture you."

Matt considered the possibility. The trouble was that the Old Ones had been silent for months. They seemed to have slipped into the shadows, as if they had never existed at all. Richard had been scouring the Internet, waiting to hear of a news event, some horror happening somewhere in the world that might suggest the Old Ones were involved. There were plenty of stories. The war in Afghanistan. Ethnic cleansing in Darfur. Misery and starvation in Zimbabwe. But that was just everyday news. That would happen even without the Old Ones. He had been looking for something else.

"What do you think they're doing?" Matt asked. "Why do you think they haven't shown themselves?"

Richard shrugged. "I guess they've been waiting," he said.

"Waiting for what?"

"Waiting for Scar."

There was a movement on the veranda, and Matt tensed for a moment, then relaxed. He could tell it was Professor Chambers, even without turning round. The smell of her cigar had given her away and, sure enough, there it was. She was clutching it in one hand with a glass of Peruvian brandy in the other.

"Are you two going in?" she asked. "I'm putting on the alarms."

The house was completely surrounded by a security system that had been installed shortly after Richard, Pedro, and Matt had arrived. There were no fences or uniformed guards — the professor had said she couldn't live like that. The system was invisible. But there was a series of infrared beams at the perimeter, and the garden itself had pressure pads concealed in different places under the lawn. Most sophisticated of all was the radar dish mounted on the roof, sweeping the entire area. It could pick up any movement a hundred yards away. That was how they had been living. It might look as if they were free, but they had all been aware that they were actually in a state of siege.

·"We were just talking about tomorrow," Richard said.

"It'll be here soon." Chambers blew smoke. "It's after ten. Shouldn't you be in bed?"

Richard tapped Matt on the shoulder. "After you."

The three of them went inside. Matt said good night to Richard and climbed the stairs to the small room he had chosen at the back of the house. He liked it there. When he was lying in bed, his head was directly underneath a slanting roof with a skylight so, lying on his back, he could look up at the stars. His small canvas bag was already packed and sitting on the floor. He wasn't taking much with him. If he needed anything in London, he could always buy it there.

Matt undressed quickly, washed, and slipped between the sheets. For the last few months, he had been searching for Scar in the only way that he could — in his dreams. Time and again he had visited the dreamworld. He had been there so often that he knew the landscape well: the shoreline stretching along a great sea with everything dead and gray, the island where he had once found himself trapped.

The dreamworld baffled him. Was it a dream or was it

a real world? That was the first question. And was it there to help him or to throw him off balance? On the one hand, it was a frightening place, conjuring up strange, violent images that he couldn't understand: giant swans, walking statues, guns, and knives. But at the same time, Matt didn't think he was in any danger there. The more he visited it, the more he felt it was on his side. He wondered if anyone actually lived there — or was it simply there for the Gatekeepers, its only inhabitants?

At any event, he had gone back there almost every night, floating out of the bed, out of the room, out of himself. Then he had begun to travel, searching for Scar. Sometimes he would see a flicker of lightning, an approaching storm. Once, he found footprints. Another time he came upon a grove of trees, which at least proved that the place wasn't entirely dead, that things could grow there.

But there had never been any sign of Scar.

There was no point in searching for her tonight. In just twenty-four hours he would be meeting her anyway. But even so — maybe it was just habit — he found himself back in the dreamworld almost at once. As usual, he was on his own. He was climbing a steep hill, but it took no more effort than if he had been walking on level ground. Far behind him, the wilderness stretched out, wide and empty.

And then he noticed something strange. The ground underneath his feet had changed. He knelt down and examined it, brushing aside the dust that covered everything. It was true. He was standing on a path fashioned out of paving stones that had been brought here and laid in place. He could see the joins, the cement gluing everything together. Even though he was asleep, Matt felt a surge of excitement. A man-made path! This was completely new and confirmed what he had always thought: The dreamworld was inhabited. There might be buildings, even whole cities there.

He looked up. The path had to lead somewhere. There could be something on the other side of the hill.

But he wasn't going to find out — not then. Suddenly he was awake. Someone was shaking him, calling his name. The lights were on in his room. He opened his eyes. It was Richard.

"Wake up, Matt," he was saying. "There's someone here."

EIGHT
The Man from Lima

Matt heaved himself out of bed, threw on some shorts and a T-shirt, and ran downstairs barefoot. The whole house was awake. There were lights on everywhere and the alarm system was buzzing, warning them that somebody was approaching.

It had already occurred to him that this sudden interruption must be connected to the fact that Scarlett had been found. If all five of the Gatekeepers were now out there and known to each other, that made them a greater danger to the Old Ones, and it was no surprise that they'd want to take action. It was exactly what he and Richard had been worrying about. On the other hand, it could be a false alarm. Over the past four months, there had been plenty enough of those. Sometimes the children came out from the town, looking for food or something to steal. Professor Chambers kept llamas for their wool, and one of them might have broken loose. The system was sensitive. Even a bat or a large moth might have been enough to set it off.

Matt hurried into the main room. There was a computer standing on a table in the corner and it had already activated itself, automatically connecting to the radar on

the roof. It showed a single blip moving slowly and pur-
posefully toward the front door. It was half past one. A bit
late for a visitor.

Jamie and Scott had come downstairs, fully dressed.
Pedro followed them — barefoot like Matt, but then he
often preferred to walk without shoes. He was yawning
and pulling on a sweater. Joanna Chambers had arrived
ahead of everyone. She was wearing an old dressing gown.
Matt watched her open the gun cabinet and take out a
rifle. So far, nobody had spoken.

"What's happening?" Jamie asked.

"A single figure moving through the garden." She
nodded at the computer. "It looks like there's only one of
them, but we can't be sure."

Richard went over and examined the screen. "I'd say
he's trying not to be seen," he muttered. "Why don't we
take a look at him?"

He leaned over and pressed a switch. This was another
part of the security system. The entire garden was instantly
lit up by a series of arc lamps so bright that it was as if he
had set off a magnesium flare. Matt blinked. It was quite
shocking to see the brilliant colors, the wide green lawn,
so late at night.

There was a single figure, a man, trapped in the
middle of the lawn. He was dressed in a linen jacket, jeans,
and a polo shirt buttoned up to the neck. There was a
canvas bag across his shoulder. As the lights had come
on, he had frozen and stood there with his hands half
covering his eyes, momentarily blinded. He seemed to
be on his own. He certainly wasn't carrying any visible

weapons. Richard opened the French windows. Professor Chambers stepped outside.

"Stay where you are!" she shouted. "I have a gun pointing at you."

"There is no need for that!" the man shouted back in heavily accented English. "I am a friend."

"What do you want?"

"I want to speak to the boy. Matthew Freeman. Is he here?"

Richard glanced at Matt, who moved forward, stepping through the French windows. He was careful not to go too far. Professor Chambers lifted the gun, covering him. "What's your name?" he called out.

"Ramon." The man cupped his hand over his eyes, shielding them, trying to make him out.

"Where have you come from?"

"From Lima." The man hesitated, unsure what to do, whether to move forward or not. He seemed to be pinned there by the light. "Please . . . are you Matthew? I am here because I want to help you."

Pedro had come over to the window. He was standing next to Matt. "Why does he come, like a thief, in the middle of the night?" he muttered. Matt nodded. He knew that Pedro was the most suspicious of them all. Maybe it was something to do with the life he'd once led.

Richard agreed. "We can ask him to come back in the morning," he muttered.

But Matt wasn't so sure. "What do you want?" he shouted.

The man hadn't moved. "I will show you when I am

inside," he said. He looked around him. "Please . . . it is not safe for me out here."

Matt knew he had to make a decision. It was something he was finding more and more. Although he was in the professor's house and she and Richard were far older than him, he always seemed to be the one in charge.

Quickly, he turned over the options. They were all supposed to be leaving the house at ten o'clock the next morning, driving up to Lima to catch the flight that would take them to London. This was no time to be meeting with complete strangers. On the other hand, there were six of them and one of him. Professor Chambers had a weapon. And the man seemed genuine enough.

"All right!" Matt called out. "Come in. . . ."

The man began to walk toward the house. At the same time, Richard went over to the cabinet and reached inside. There was another gun there. He wasn't taking any chances.

The man came into the main room, Professor Chambers following him with the rifle. Now that he was inside, Matt could see that he was a few years older than Richard, with the dark hair and olive skin of a native Peruvian. He had obviously been on the road for a while. He was dusty and unshaven, and his clothes were crumpled, with sweat patches under the arms. There was a haunted look in his eyes. From the look of him, he didn't seem to be a threat.

The first thing he did was to take a pair of spectacles out of his top pocket and put them on. Now he looked like a schoolteacher or perhaps an accountant working in a small, local office. He had a cheap watch on his wrist, and his shoes were scuffed and down-at-heel. He looked straight at Matt. "Are you Matthew Freeman?" He blinked. "I did not think I would find you here."

"Sit down," Richard said.

The man sat on the sofa with his back to the French windows. Richard pressed the button that turned off the garden lights, and everything outside the room disappeared into blackness again. It had clouded over during the night. The moon and the stars had disappeared. Richard came back over to the sofa and sat down on one of the arms. He hadn't reset the security system. But then the visitor wouldn't be staying very long. Scott and Jamie perched on the edge of the coffee table. Professor Chambers sat in a chair with the rifle between her knees.

"So what do you want?" she demanded.

"I will tell you everything you want to know," Ramon said. "But can I first ask you for a drink? I have been traveling all day and I had to wait until night before coming here. Believe me — if I had been seen, I would have been killed."

"I'll get it," Pedro said. He went into the kitchen, returning a moment later with a glass of water. The man took it in both hands and gulped greedily.

"How do you know about me?" Matt asked.

"I know a great deal about you, Matthew. May I call you that? I know how you came to Peru and I think I know what you have been doing since you arrived here. I was present, also, the night you came to the hacienda at Ica, although perhaps you did not see me. I was there because I was hired to work for Diego Salamanda."

Ramon must have known the effect the name would have on everyone in the room. Salamanda had been the chairman and owner of a huge news corporation in South America. Deliberately deformed as a child — his head had been grotesquely stretched — he had used his power and wealth to bring back the Old Ones. Matt and Pedro had gone to his hacienda searching for Richard, and later on Matt and Salamanda had confronted each other in the Nazca Desert. Matt had killed him, turning back the bullets fired from his own gun.

"Please — do not think of me as your enemy," Ramon continued, hastily. "I swear to you that I was not part of his plans." He paused. Beads of sweat stood out on his forehead. "I am not even in business. I am a lecturer at Lima University and Señor Salamanda paid me to help him with a special project. I should explain that my specialty is ancient history." He bowed in the direction of Professor Chambers. "I have heard you speak many times, Señora. I was there, for example, last April when you gave the presentation at the Museo Nacional de Antropología. I thought it was a brilliant talk."

Professor Chambers thought for a moment. "It's true that I was there," she said. "But anyone could know that."

"Señor Salamanda told me that he was in possession of a diary that he wanted me to interpret on his behalf," Ramon went on. "The diary had been written in the sixteenth century by a man called Joseph of Cordoba. This man traveled here to Peru with the Spanish conquistadors.

89

Salamanda told me that he bought the diary from a book-seller in London, a man called William Morton."

"He didn't buy it," Matt said. "He stole it. He killed William Morton to get it." Matt knew because he had been there at the time. Morton had been demanding two million pounds, but all he had got was a knife in the back.

"I did not know these things," Ramon exclaimed. "I was innocent. My job was to work only on the text, to unlock its secrets, and I spent many, many hours in his office and also at his home in Ica. The diary was never allowed to leave his side. He made it clear to me from the start that it was the most precious thing to him in the world. And as I read it, as I began to study it, I realized why. It told this extraordinary history . . . the Old Ones, a battle many thousands of years ago, and a gate that could be unlocked by the stars."

He lowered his head.

"I know that I am responsible for what happened last June. I did the work that I was paid to do and I helped Salamanda to open the gate. I have allowed a terrible thing to happen and it has been on my conscience ever since." He twisted on the sofa, urging them to believe him. "I am not a bad man. I am a Catholic. I go to church. I believe in heaven and hell. And I have been thinking . . . what can I do to make amends for what I have done? What can I do to undo the damage that I have caused? And I knew, finally, that I must find you. So I came."

"How did you know where we were?" Jamie asked.

"Señor Salamanda often mentioned the name of Professor Chambers. I guessed that you would be with her, and I have brought you something. You will not shoot me if I reach into my bag?"

He glanced at the professor, then reached beside him. He took out an old, leather-bound book and laid it on the table. Nobody in the room said anything. But they all knew what it was. It was hard to believe that it was actually there, in front of them. The cover was dark brown with a few faint tracings of gold, tied with a cord. The edges of the pages were rough and uneven. Matt recognized it at once. It contained everything they needed to know about the Old Ones. It might even describe how they could be defeated.

"It is the diary of the mad monk," Ramon said.

And it was. The small, square book sitting there in the middle of the table was, supposedly, the only copy in the world. There was no limit to how many secrets it might contain, how valuable it might be.

"How did you get it?" Richard demanded.

"I stole it!" Ramon took out a handkerchief and wiped it across his forehead. "I thought it would be impossible, but in fact it was easy. You see, I still had my electronic passkey to the office of Salamanda News International in Lima. And I had this crazy idea. Maybe the key had not been canceled. Señor Salamanda was dead, but surely they had forgotten about me. Two days ago, I returned to the office. Nobody saw me, although by now they will know that it is gone. I took it from his desk and hurried away into the night. It is possible that the cameras will have identified me and that they will be searching for me even now."

Richard was still suspicious. "What do you want from us?" he asked. "Do you want us to pay you?"

Ramon shook his head. "Can you not understand me?" he exclaimed. He clasped his hands in front of him. "I am twenty-eight years old. Next year I hope to be married. When I was given this work by Señor Salamanda, I knew nothing. It was just, for me, a job."

He pushed the diary away.

"Here! You can have it without payment. It is yours. I brought it to you only because I thought you might make use of it in this great . . ." He searched for the word in English. ". . . *lucha*. Struggle. I want nothing from you. I am sorry that I came."

There was a pause. Matt knew that he had just been given a fantastic prize. The diary might explain the dream-world. It might tell them the history of the twenty-five doorways that stood in so many different countries. Who had built them, and when? It might even help them work out what they were supposed to do when the five of them finally met in London. Ramon was right: Salamanda had been prepared to kill to get his hands on the diary, and now it had just been handed to them, out of the blue.

Jamie leaned forward and picked it up. He unwound the cord, and the diary opened in his hands. He examined the page in front of him. It was covered in handwriting that would have been almost unreadable even if it hadn't been in Spanish. There were tiny diagrams in the margins. Suddenly his eyes lit up. He pointed to a single word.

"Sapling," he said. "That was my name when I went back in time. Sapling was killed and I took his place."

The diary was real. Matt had no doubt of it. But what about the man who had brought it to them? He looked genuine, but Richard had been expecting some sort of trap, and this could well be it. Suddenly Matt had an idea. There was an easy way to find out. "Jamie," he said. "Ask him if he's telling the truth."

Jamie understood at once. But before he could act, Scott stood up. "I'll do it," he said.

Scott walked forward and stopped in front of the visitor. He looked Ramon straight in the eyes. "Are you telling the truth?" he demanded.

"On my mother's grave," Ramon replied, crossing himself and then kissing his thumb. "I'm only here because it is the right thing to do. Because I want to help."

Scott concentrated. This was his power, the ability that had kept audiences entertained for the many months when he was performing in Reno. They had thought it was a trick, but in fact it was real. He could read minds.

Unfortunately, it wasn't quite as easy as that sounded. It wasn't like throwing a switch. Scott and Jamie had a connection with each other. When they were in the same room or even a short distance away, they could communicate with each other just by thinking. But when it came to other people, strangers like Ramon, what they saw was confused, chaotic. Nothing was ever black-and-white.

Perhaps a minute passed. Then Scott nodded. "He's telling the truth," he said.

"I promise you . . ." Ramon knew that he had been tested in some way. The words came pouring out. "I don't care if you don't trust me. I'll leave you with the diary. I'll go. I have no other reason to be here."

"You said it wasn't safe for you outside," Richard said. "Were you followed?"

Ramon shook his head and swallowed nervously. "I don't think so. After I took the diary, I hid in Lima. I wanted to see if the police would come. Then, when nothing happened, I took a tourist bus to Paracas. I thought it was less likely that I would be noticed that way. By now they will know that the diary is missing. They will know that I have taken it. And although Salamanda is gone, there are people in his organization who will still wish to continue what he began."

"So where will you go now?" Professor Chambers asked. "Do you have somewhere to hide?"

"I was hoping . . ." Ramon began. There was a strange sound, a whistling that came through the air, then the tearing of fabric. He looked down. There was something sticking out of his shirt. Puzzled, he reached down and touched it, then tried to pull it free. It wouldn't move, and when he released it, his hand was wet with blood.

They had all heard it but hadn't realized what it was. A fence post. It had been thrown with impossible force from out of the darkness. It must have traveled more than fifty yards before the pointed end smashed into the back of the sofa, penetrating through the leather and padding before impaling the man who was sitting there. Ramon's eyes widened. He tried to speak. Then he slumped forward, pinned into place, unable even to fall.

The alarms hadn't gone off. The radar screen was empty. Professor Chambers sprang to her feet and pressed the button to turn on the outside lights. Nothing happened.

Something was moving in the garden. There were figures, edging forward, dressed in filthy, tattered clothes that hung off them as if they were rotting away. Matt could just make them out in the light spilling from the room. It was suddenly very cold, and he knew at once that dark forces were at work and whatever the figures were, coming toward him, they weren't human.

They had come for the diary.

NINE
Night Attack

Slowly, determinedly, they closed in on the house.

There were more than a dozen of them: nightmare figures, shuffling across the lawn. Where had they come from? Matt could imagine them climbing out of the local cemetery. There was something corpse-like about them. A gleam of light from the living room caught one of their faces, and he saw glistening bone, one empty eye socket, dried blood streaking down the side of the cheek and neck. At that moment he was sure of it: These creatures couldn't be killed. They were already dead.

As if to prove him wrong, Professor Chambers stepped forward and fired a shot at the nearest of them. Matt saw a great gout of blood explode out of the back of its head. It fell facedown and lay shuddering in the grass. So at least they could be stopped! She fired again, hitting another of them in the shoulder. The creature twitched as if shrugging the bullet off. Blood spread across what was left of its shirt — but it kept on coming. It didn't seem to feel pain.

Richard was already on his feet, loading the revolver that he had taken from the gun cabinet. A few weeks before, Matt had smiled when he had stumbled across him, shooting tin cans in the desert. Now he was glad that Richard had decided to practice.

When the attack had begun, Scott and Jamie had snatched up a couple of makeshift weapons — anything they could get their hands on. Jamie had a baseball bat. Scott had found a kitchen knife, which he was holding in front of him, the blade slanting up. Pedro had backed away to the other side of the room. He was standing with his back to a full-length window, his eyes darting left and right, waiting for the first attack.

He wasn't looking behind him.

"Pedro . . . ! Watch out!" Richard shouted in warning.

One of the creatures was looming out of the shadows on the other side of the glass. Pedro spun round just in time to see a dead white face, staring eyes, gray lips, hands stretching toward him. The creature didn't stop. It walked straight through the window, smashing the glass and entering the room with blood streaming down its face. Shards of broken glass were sticking out of its flesh, but it didn't seem to notice. Richard lifted his revolver and shot it twice in the head. It crumpled and fell at Pedro's feet. At the same time, Richard twisted round and fired again. Another of the creatures had reached the open French windows and was about to step inside. It threw up its hands and fell back with a bullet between its eyes.

But there were still many more of them moving slowly across the lawn, unafraid of dying, determined only to reach the house. Perhaps Ramon had been a diversion after all. While he had been talking, the night attackers had completely surrounded the house. Matt heard the sound of wood splintering upstairs and knew that some of them must have climbed up to the balcony and broken in that way. Jamie stepped forward, grabbed the diary, and threw it to Scott in a single movement. Scott caught it without even looking and slipped it into his jacket. Neither of them had spoken, and Matt knew that the two of them must have communicated telepathically. He had seen them do it often enough. Each one of them knew instantly what the other was going to do. They were almost like reflections of each other.

As Richard reloaded, Joanna Chambers fired again. She pulled some more bullets out of her dressing gown pocket, and as she fumbled with the loading mechanism, one of the creatures launched itself at her, grabbing hold of her with one hand, lifting an ancient-looking knife with the other. The blade was black with a broken, serrated edge. It stabbed down.

Matt stopped him.

Six months ago, he wouldn't have been able to do it. But then he had been alone. Now four of the Gatekeepers had come together and Scott, Jamie, and Pedro had added their power to his. All he had to do was think about it and the blade snapped in half. The creature screamed in pain and a wisp of smoke rose from the palm of its hand as the hilt of the knife burned into it. By now, Chambers had loaded her rifle. She fired a single shot at point-blank range, putting the attacker out of its misery.

"We can't control them!" Jamie shouted.

If these creatures had been fully human, he might have been able to make them turn round and leave the house. He and Scott didn't just read minds — they were also able to control them. All their lives, the two brothers had recognized that they were living under a curse. Always, they had to be careful what they said. One unguarded thought, one word spoken in anger, could turn them into murderers. Once, Scott had almost killed a boy at school. And later, when their foster father committed suicide, Scott had known that he was secretly to blame.

But this time it wasn't going to work. Their attackers didn't seem to have minds that could be controlled. It was as if they had already been programmed to kill with no thoughts of their own. And there were too many of them. Matt glanced into the garden. It was still very dark outside, but he could make out a whole crowd of them, moving relentlessly across the lawn. There were more at the back of the house and yet more of them upstairs.

Matt heard a horrible gargling sound and turned just as a man — or the remains of one — stumbled over the sofa and launched himself at him. The man was naked to the waist, sweat and slime dripping off his chest. Matt nodded and the man was flung backward, crashing into the wall. He slid to the floor and lay still.

"They're on the stairs."

It was Scott who had seen them. The creatures from the balcony were making their way down, their movements slow, almost robotic. Jamie ran forward with the baseball bat and swung it into the face of the first man that he reached. There was a crunch of breaking bone. The man crumpled.

Matt looked all around him, wondering where the next attack was going to come from. At the same time, he smelled something. His eyes had begun to water and he was aware that it was getting more difficult to breathe. The temperature had risen too. Richard fired again, hitting one creature, then used the revolver as a club, smashing it into a second. "The house is on fire!" he yelled.

Matt didn't need to be told. Smoke was pouring down the staircase, sucked into the ground floor by the turning fans. He could already hear the crackle of burning wood. Stretched out in the hot Nazca sun — it almost never rained in this part of Peru — the professor's house would be bone dry. There were fire extinguishers in all the rooms, but they weren't going to be given a chance to use them. Left to itself, the fire would consume the whole building in minutes.

Richard fired two more shots before the gun clicked uselessly in his hand. He rummaged in his pocket, searching for more ammunition. Professor Chambers blasted off another round, but she too had only a few bullets left. And the creatures kept on coming. Kill one and another two or three would take its place. There seemed to be no end to them. Matt saw another one appear on the stairs, holding an iron post similar to the one that had killed Ramon. It had been torn free from the garden fence. He watched as the creature lifted it up to its shoulder, and realized too late what it was about to do.

The creature flung the rod like a spear, aiming straight at Pedro. Matt shouted a warning. Pedro twisted round.

The missile turned once in the air and then struck him a glancing blow on the side of the head. He cried out and fell to the floor, dazed and bleeding. Another creature — dressed bizarrely in the rags of a dinner suit — closed in on him. Matt couldn't reach him. He was too far away. But Scott was there. He still had the kitchen knife. He was standing between Pedro and his attacker. Matt waited for him to move.

Scott did nothing. He stood where he was, frozen to the spot. He wasn't even blinking. Matt could see his chest heaving and his hands seemed to be locked in place, the fingers bent. His whole body was rigid.

Matt knew what was happening. He had seen it before. Scott wasn't afraid. He wasn't a coward. But he had spent weeks with Nightrise, with the woman called Susan Mortlake, and in that time they had gotten into his mind. It was hard to imagine how much pain they had put him through, trying to turn him against his friends. This was the result. In moments of stress, he simply shut down. Even Pedro had so far been unable to help him. The wounds were too deep.

Pedro was lying still. There was a gash on the side of his head. Jamie was lashing out with the baseball bat, using it like a club or a sword. Matt looked for a weapon but couldn't see one. The man in the dinner jacket had reached Pedro and was standing over him. He had produced a second weapon, an axe which had been hanging for decoration on the wall. Desperately, Matt searched across the room, saw a jagged piece of broken glass on the floor and — using his power — swept it through the air and into the creature's throat. The creature screamed horribly and fell back in a fountain of its own blood.

"We have to get out of here!" Richard shouted.

The air was full of smoke. It was getting harder to breathe inside, but running out into the fresh air would be suicide. Nobody would be able to see anything in the darkness — and if these creatures had night vision, they would be in total command. Matt stood there, cursing himself. He knew that this was happening because of Scarlett. He had been expecting it. So why hadn't he been better prepared?

At any event, he knew that Richard was right. They had to get out of the house before they suffocated. The smoke didn't seem to have any effect on the attackers. It was as if their lungs had rotted away and they didn't need to breathe. Jamie threw the baseball bat at one of the creatures on the stairs, then ran over to his brother. Matt reached Pedro and helped him to his feet. At least he didn't seem to be too badly hurt. Professor Chambers blasted away with the rifle, clearing a way to the French windows.

"Look out!"

It was Richard who shouted the warning. Matt looked up just in time to see part of the ceiling come crashing down in a chaos of orange fire and black smoke. The flames were leaping up at the night. It seemed that most of the roof and part of the second floor had gone. Taking Pedro with him, he threw himself to one side and the falling debris missed them by inches, crashing down onto the sofa where Ramon, the man who had started all this, was sitting. The iron rod that had killed him was slanting out of his chest. He was watching it all like a disinterested spectator.

The six of them staggered out into the garden, leaving the burning house and the remaining creatures — nine or ten of them — behind. Professor Chambers fired one last shot. "No more ammo!" she called out to Richard, but there was a strain in her voice and Matt wondered if she had been hurt. He looked at her in alarm. There was a patch of red spreading across the front of her dressing gown. A dark gash showed in the material. But she wasn't going to let the pain slow her down. "How about you?" she demanded.

"Two more bullets," Richard replied.

Two more bullets, and the attackers were everywhere. Matt could see them clearly in the light of the flames, their eyes glowing red, their hands clutching knives, axes, chains, and lengths of barbed wire, which they flailed like whips. Pedro was leaning against him, blood running down the side of his face. Scott and Jamie were standing together, catching their breath. They had made it outside, but they had nowhere to run. Another creature lumbered toward Professor Chambers, who stood where she was, clutching her wound. Richard shot it twice.

Matt was almost ready to give up. He couldn't believe that it was going to end this way, surprised and surrounded in a garden in Nazca. Was this what the fight had all been about? He was a Gatekeeper. He had returned to the world after ten thousand years. Was he really going to allow himself to be beaten so easily?

And then the night exploded a second time, with lights bursting out all around them, slanting in from every direction. Matt and Pedro stood where they were, swaying on their feet. Jamie moved toward his brother. Richard and Professor Chambers swung round with their now useless guns. They were trapped, huddled together in a group with the blazing house behind them, the lights in front, surrounded on all sides. Matt tried to see who it was that had arrived at this late stage. Did he have the power to send them back? He bowed his head, drawing on the last of his strength.

Then, as if from nowhere, a volley of arrows was fired in his direction. But not at him. They had been aimed deliberately over his head. Some of the creatures on the edge of the house cried out and fell back as they were hit. Another volley followed, taking out more of them. The lights were coming from the headlights of four or five cars that had driven to the edge of the garden and parked in a semicircle. There were men running across the lawn. There were several gunshots. One of the men stopped and reached out for Professor Chambers, who more or less collapsed in his arms. The others continued into the house, blasting away with handguns, searching for any remaining attackers, and setting to work fighting the fire.

And suddenly Matt knew who they were.

They had helped Pedro and him when they had first come to Peru, spiriting them out of Cuzco through a network of underground tunnels. The two boys had stayed with them in their hidden city, Vilcabamba, high up in the mountains. They were Incas, the tribe that had once ruled

Peru, but which had been reduced to little more than a handful of survivors, living in secret. They had promised to look after Matt and the other Gatekeepers while they were in Peru. And they had come, true to their word.

They were armed with guns as well as their own traditional weapons, and they made short work of the attackers. Machetes swung through the darkness, slicing into rags and flesh. Bullets hammered through the night. It was over very quickly. Matt, Pedro, Scott, and Jamie waited on the lawn while the last of the creatures was finished off. Richard was now helping to support Joanna Chambers. All the color had left her face. She was barely able to stand.

One of the Incas came over to them. He was short with broad shoulders and a dark, serious face. "Are you okay?" he asked.

"We're all right," Richard said. "But Professor Chambers has been hurt."

"I am Tiso. We came when we heard the first alarm. I am sorry. We arrived too late."

"We're just glad you're here," Richard said. "Can we go back into the house? We need to get her inside. . . ."

But it was another half hour before the Incas had put out the flames and they could get back in. The roof and part of the first floor had gone, but there were still two bedrooms that were habitable and, once the debris and the dead bodies had been cleared, the six of them would be able to camp out on the ground floor.

The house would never be the same again. Matt looked at the charred wood and the soiled carpets, the broken windows and debris, and felt a mounting sadness. It had been such a beautiful place. Professor Chambers had lived there for much of her life, but then he and the others had come along and ruined it for her. In a few hours, they were supposed to be departing — on their way to London. And this was the mess that they were leaving behind.

Tiso and some of the other Incas helped carry Professor Chambers into her study, which had also survived. Richard went with her, and Pedro followed. His healing powers were going to be needed more than ever, although it looked as if the professor might be too badly injured even for him. She needed medical help — and sure enough, a doctor arrived a few minutes later, urgently summoned from the nearby town. Matt, Scott, and Jamie stayed outside while she was examined. None of them said anything. They were exhausted. Just a few hours before, they had been laughing together, having dinner, and playing dice games. And now this!

Matt glanced at Scott. "Where's the diary?" he asked. At that moment he almost wished they didn't have it. It didn't matter how valuable it was. It had so far brought them nothing but trouble.

Scott took it out of his jacket pocket and handed it over. "I'm sorry," he said. His voice was low. "I didn't help you, back there. I didn't help Pedro. I wanted to. But . . ." His voice trailed off.

"It doesn't matter," Matt said. "Everything happened so quickly. Anyway, Pedro's going to be okay."

"What are they doing in there?" Jamie stared at the closed study door. His voice was angry. He kicked out at the sofa where Ramon had been sitting. The dead man had been carried outside, but there was still a great gash in the leather to remind them of what had happened. He turned to his brother. "You got it wrong," he said. "You said he was telling the truth."

Scott blushed — with embarrassment or perhaps with anger. "I thought he was telling the truth," he said.

"You may have been right," Matt interrupted. The two brothers seldom argued, and he was surprised to see them starting now. "We can't be sure that Ramon was responsible for what happened tonight. He told us he was in danger, and he was certainly right about that. They killed him. So maybe the rest of his story was true."

"Can we use it?" Scott asked.

Matt opened the diary. There was a page covered with diagrams. One of them looked a bit like a motorcar, though as if drawn by a child, and he remembered that Joseph of Cordoba — the mad monk — was supposed to have been able to predict the future. He flicked through it. Some of the pages had been marked with a modern pen. Someone had scribbled down words and figures, underlining certain areas of the text. Diego Salamanda? The diary had belonged to him, and he could have spent weeks deciphering it. It seemed that he had left some of his handiwork behind.

Matt tried to make sense of some of the words, but the monk had written in ancient Spanish and his handwriting was almost illegible. "I can't read this language," he said. "And although Pedro can speak it, he can't read. . . ."

"Maybe the professor will be able to work it out," Jamie suggested.

Professor Chambers. Matt remembered how Richard

had looked when he had helped carry her in. The two of them had been inside for a long time.

And then the door of the study opened. Pedro came out. He shook his head briefly and sat down, looking miserable. The doctor followed him. He muttered a few words to Richard, then left the house, doing his best to avoid eye contact. That was when Matt knew that it wasn't going to be good news.

"Matt . . ." Richard called him over to the door. "She wants to see you," he said. His voice was hoarse. "She wants to say good-bye."

"Is she . . . ?" Matt realized what he'd just been told. "She can't be dying," he said. "What about Pedro? Can't he help her?"

"It's too late for Pedro. There's nothing he can do." Richard sighed. "We've called an ambulance for her, and it's on its way now. But she's not going to make it. I'm sorry, Matt. I don't know how it happened, but she was stabbed. There's been a lot of internal bleeding and . . ." He stopped and took a deep breath. "She's not in any pain. The doctor's seen to that. But there's nothing more we can do for her. Do you want me to come in with you?"

"No . . ." Matt went into the study.

Joanna Chambers was lying on the daybed that she liked to use as a place to think when she was working. As usual, her desk was completely covered in papers along with a bottle of brandy and a box of her favorite cigars. The old-fashioned radio that she liked to listen to was next to her computer, but it was turned off. Somehow that made Matt sadder than anything else, the thought that she would never listen to it again.

She was still in her dressing gown, but someone had drawn a blanket over her legs and chest. There was only one light on, and it was burning low, casting a soft glow across the room.

He thought she was asleep, but as he closed the door, she looked up. "Matt . . . ?"

He went over to her. "The ambulance is on its way," he muttered. "The doctor says —"

"Don't tell me any stuff and nonsense," she cut in, and just for a moment she sounded exactly like her old self. "There's nothing they can do for me, and anyway I'm not going into any local hospital. Dreadful place." She tried to shift her position, but she didn't have the strength. "Come and sit next to me."

Matt did as he was told. His eyes were stinging and there was an ache in his throat. Why did it have to happen like this? Why couldn't she be all right? He remembered Professor Chambers as he had first seen her, piloting her own plane. She had worked out the secret of the Nazca Lines, and she had been with him, in the middle of the desert, when they were attacked by the condors. He knew that without her, he would never have located the second gate. And since then, she had looked after them, never once complaining as her house was invaded and her work interrupted.

Matt had used his power to protect himself. Why hadn't he been able to do the same for her?

"Now you listen to me," she said. She found his hand

and clasped it. "You mustn't be upset about me. You have a very great responsibility, Matt. I don't think you have any idea yet what is going to be asked of you. And how old are you? Fifteen! It's not fair. . . ."

She closed her eyes for a few seconds, fighting for breath.

"The Old Ones will be beaten," she said. "Ever since the world began, there's always been good and evil, and somehow good's managed to muddle through. You'll see. It may not be easy. What happened today . . . silly, really. We should have known they would come."

She let go of his hand. She couldn't manage very much more.

"That's what I wanted to tell you," she said. Her voice was fading away. "I'm so glad I met you, really. I'm glad we had our time here. I've always loved this place, always been happy here. . . ."

She pointed at the door with one finger, telling him to leave her. Matt did as she said. Richard was waiting for him outside.

The ambulance arrived ten minutes later. But it was too late. Professor Chambers was already dead.

TEN
Council of War

Matt woke up with the smell of burnt wood in his nostrils and the taste of it in his mouth. He had slept for about two hours, but he might as well not have bothered. Even before he got out of bed, he knew that he was as tired as he had been when he got into it.

He'd had to share with Pedro. His own room had been destroyed by the fire, along with everything inside it — and it was only as he opened his eyes the following morning that he realized exactly what that meant. He no longer had a passport. He wasn't going to be traveling anywhere today, certainly not on a commercial flight — and that must have been just what the attack had set out to achieve. The Old Ones didn't want him arriving in London. They didn't want him anywhere near Scarlett Adams. And although there were policemen and private detectives looking out for her, she was completely isolated. One in England. Four in Peru. It certainly didn't add up to the Five.

Pedro was sitting cross-legged on his bed, wearing only a pair of shorts. There was a bandage on the side of his head. Matt guessed that he had been awake for a while. Pedro was always the first to get up, but then, of course, in his old life he would have been begging on the streets of Lima, waiting for the commuter traffic long before dawn. The two boys had been lying next to each other in twin beds.

"So what do we do now?" Pedro asked.

"I don't know, Pedro." Matt got out of bed and pulled on a fresh T-shirt. "We'll have to meet and decide."

"Will we still go to England?"

"Yes."

Pedro hadn't spoken very much about the journey, and Matt suspected that he was finding it difficult to get his head around it. He had never been out of Peru in his life. Even the notion of getting on a plane was completely alien to him. He had only flown once and that had been in a helicopter that had crashed. The thought of spending fifteen hours in the air and landing in a completely different world must have unnerved him.

"I am sad that the professor is dead," he said. "She was very kind."

"I know." Matt still wondered if he could have saved her. Was her death his fault? It seemed to him now that she had been doomed from the moment they had arrived, although he knew she would never have seen it that way. Even so . . . It had been two days since they had received the fax with the news about Scar. He wished now that they had all left at once.

There were now just five of them remaining: Matt, Pedro, Scott, Jamie, and Richard. They met outside, sitting at a wooden table in the shade of a silk-cotton tree — a kapok, as it was also known. Professor Chambers had liked taking the boys around her garden, showing them all the different plants and talking about them. This one had somehow found its way out of the rain forest, she had said, and she couldn't understand how it was growing here at all. The table had been set up in the shade, the umbrella-shaped canopy and creamy-white flowers of the kapok shielding them from the sun.

They might have been safer in the house, but they could hardly bear to look at it, the ruin that it had become. Somehow, it didn't seem likely that the Old Ones would return . . . not in the daylight. And anyway, the Incas were somewhere close, guarding them. Richard had brought out a tray of iced lemonade and a plate of empanadas, the little cheese pastries that they had often devoured. But nobody was hungry. They were exhausted and unhappy. Nobody knew what they were supposed to do.

One thing was sure: They couldn't stay here much longer. The house still had water and electricity, and they might even be able to repair the roof. But there was no alarm system. The Incas couldn't protect them indefinitely. And, more to the point, none of them wanted to be here. The moment Professor Chambers had been taken from the hacienda, all of its life seemed to have gone with her.

"Okay . . ." It was Richard who was the first to speak, and Matt was grateful to him for breaking the silence, for taking control. He was wearing a clean polo shirt and jeans, but he looked completely worn out, as if he hadn't slept at all.

"This is a council of war," he said. "Because it looks as

if the war has finally arrived. We have to talk about last night. We have to deal with it and put it behind us. And I might as well start by saying that it was mainly my fault." He held up a hand before anyone could interrupt him. "When Ramon came to the house, I turned off the security system. But I never put it back on again. Not the radar, anyway. Maybe that was the idea. Maybe that was why he was sent to us. A diversion . . ."

"It was my fault too," Scott cut in. "Matt wanted me to look into his mind and I did. But somehow he managed to fool me. I thought he was telling the truth."

"Maybe he was telling the truth," Matt said. "He brought us the diary . . . and do you really think he would have just sat there and allowed himself to be killed? Maybe they followed him from Lima. The whole point of last night could have been simply that they wanted the diary back."

"The question we've got to ask ourselves is — what are we going to do next?" Richard said. "It's been more than forty-eight hours since Scarlett Adams appeared in the newspapers. The Nexus are still watching her, but we can't leave her on her own much longer. On the other hand . . ." He nodded at Matt. "Matt has lost his passport, so he's not flying anywhere."

"We can use the door," Jamie said. "The same one that Scott and I came through. All we have to do is get to the Temple of Coricancha in Cuzco. We walk in . . . we walk out in London. We don't need a plane."

It seemed obvious. It was exactly the reason why the doors had been built in the first place. But Richard shook his head. "We can't use the doors," he said. "Think about it, Jamie. Salamanda had the diary and he obviously studied it carefully. If the Old Ones are looking for us — and it seems pretty likely that they are — that's exactly how they'll expect us to travel."

"Maybe they never saw the diary," Pedro said. "It was in the office of Señor Salamanda. He could never have shown it to them."

Richard was still unhappy. "It's too much of a risk. Anyway, they know about the door in St. Meredith's. Scarlett went through it. That's probably what started all this. They could be waiting for us there. I know it's boring, but I reckon we're much safer taking planes."

"But Matt doesn't have a passport," Scott said.

"The Nexus can get us into America," Richard replied. "I spoke to Nathalie Johnson this morning, and she's sending a private plane. It's already on its way. And she's been in touch with John Trelawney. The two of them have enough clout to get us through immigration. They can also get Matt a new passport. After all, they didn't have any difficulty getting one for Pedro. It'll take a couple of days, but we could be in England by Tuesday."

Scott and Jamie had met Nathalie Johnson before they came to Peru. She was an American businesswoman who had made a fortune out of computers before she had been drawn into the Nexus. John Trelawney was the senator who had been fighting in the presidential election. The result was going to be announced in just one day, and he was still the favorite to win. The two of them were powerful friends.

Jamie considered what Richard had said. "All right, then." He shrugged. "Let's go."

"Not all of us," Matt said.

There was a sudden silence around the table. All eyes were turned on him.

"I think we should separate," he said.

"Are you crazy . . . ?" Scott said.

"Why?" Pedro chimed in.

"What do you mean, Matt?" Jamie asked.

Everyone was talking at once. Matt wasn't surprised. Even as he had decided what he was going to do, he had known that the rest of them would be against it. They were supposed to stick together. Finding each other, coming together . . . it was what their lives were all about. Five Gatekeepers. So far, against all the odds, four of them had managed to do exactly that. They were one step away from finding the fifth. It seemed completely mad to split up now.

"We've just got to be careful," Matt explained. "Richard and I were talking about it last night, before we were attacked. If all four of us get onto one plane and the Old Ones somehow manage to get control of it, they'll have us at their mercy. They'll be able to do anything with us. All four of us at once."

"So what are you saying?" Jamie asked.

"We can't stay here," Pedro added.

"I'm going to London with Richard," Matt said. "We'll meet the Nexus as soon as we can and we'll meet Scarlett as soon as we know it's safe." He turned to Jamie. "I'd like you to come with us."

Jamie opened his mouth but said nothing. He understood the implications of what Matt had just suggested.

"You're leaving me behind," Scott muttered. His voice was low and sullen.

"It's just for a few days. A week, no longer."

"Is this because I messed up last night?"

"You didn't mess up." Matt had to choose his words carefully. In a way, Scott was right. He might not be to blame, but he still couldn't be completely trusted either. Matt looked at him, sitting slumped back from the table with his hands in his pockets, and saw the cold anger in his face. And there was something else. A sort of cruelty. When Scott had lived ten thousand years ago, his name had been Flint and it suited him. Sitting in the garden, his eyes were as hard as stone.

"Scott and I don't like being apart," Jamie said.

"I know that and I'm sorry," Matt said. "It's true that we're stronger together. That's why I want to stay in pairs. Two and two. If anything goes wrong in London, I'll need someone to back us up."

"So why not take Pedro?"

"Because Pedro doesn't know London. He's never been to England."

"Neither have I."

Matt sighed. "Jamie . . . if you really don't like the idea, I'll go on my own. I don't mind doing that. I just don't think we should all go. That's all. I'm trying to do what's best for everyone."

"And since when did you get to tell everyone what they should do?" Scott demanded. "I thought we were meant to be equal. Who put you in charge?"

There was another long pause. Richard opened his mouth to say something, then changed his mind. The day was getting warmer as the sun climbed over the mountains, but the atmosphere right then was anything but.

Matt looked across the lawn to the track that led back to the town of Nazca. He had been there a couple of days ago, kicking a ball, waiting for Professor Chambers to get back from the shops. Now she was dead, her house was in ruins, and the four of them were at each other's throats. How could things have gone wrong so quickly?

"Scott, I don't think . . . ," Jamie began.

"Are you on his side?" Scott directed his anger at his brother.

"We're all on the same side," Matt cut in. "And if we turn against each other, we might as well give up."

"You've never been on my side, Matt. You've never trusted me, not from the day I arrived here. Well, you go without me. You can all go without me. I don't care."

Scott got up angrily, knocking his chair over behind him. He didn't even notice. He walked away in the direction of the house and disappeared through the front door. Nobody spoke. Then Jamie stood up. "I'm sorry, Matt," he said. "I'll go and talk to him. He'll be all right."

Jamie followed his brother. That left Richard, Pedro, and Matt. Richard poured a glass of the lemonade. He offered it to Matt, who shook his head. Richard drank it himself.

"Where do you want me to go?" Pedro asked. "I don't think it is good for us to stay here."

Matt sighed. "I thought you'd go back to Vilcabamba with Tiso and the other Incas," he said. "I was hoping you could spend a bit more time with Scott. . . ." Pedro understood. Scott still needed help after his experiences as a prisoner of Nightrise.

"I'll do what I can," he said. "But Scott has a lot of pain. There are things happening here . . ." He tapped the side of his head. "I do not understand."

"You were nearly killed last night. He didn't help you."

"Yes. But he and Jamie are very close. Twins. Maybe it is not such a great idea to split them up."

There didn't seem to be anything more to say. Pedro collected the jug and the glasses and carried them in. Richard and Matt were left on their own.

"That went well," Matt said gloomily.

Richard finished his lemonade and set the glass down. "Don't be too hard on yourself," he said. "We're all feeling bad about last night, and Joanna's death. Jamie will talk to Scott. He knows you're doing the best you can. They'll work it out."

"I hope so."

"In just a week, you'll be in Vilcabamba. All of you. You've got the diary now. And despite what happened last night, you all came out of it okay. None of you was badly hurt. I'm sure you've made the right decision, Matt. It's all going to work out."

But Matt wasn't so sure. He twisted round and looked at the house, at the scorched wood, what was left of the roof, and suddenly he was aware that something was wrong, that it didn't quite add up.

If Ramon had been able to find them so easily, why had it taken the Old Ones so long? And if they had wanted the diary back so badly, why hadn't they sent a larger force? Matt had seen the sort of creatures the Old Ones had at their disposal. They had crawled out of the floor of the Nazca Desert . . . the armed soldiers, the giant animals, the hoards of shape-changers. But they hadn't been there last night.

Was he making the right decision, splitting them up? Or was this what he was meant to do? Was he reacting to decisions that had already been made?

Later that afternoon, two cars came to the house. One would take Pedro and Scott to Arequipa, the famous "White City" in the south of Peru. They would have to stay there overnight before flying to Cuzco. Because of the thin air high up in the Andes, planes were only able to take off and land in the morning. Two of the Incas would go with them and escort them up through the cloud forest to Vilcabamba.

Jamie, Richard, and Matt had a shorter drive to Nazca Airport where a private plane was already waiting to fly them up to Miami. They would wait in Miami until Matt's new passport arrived and then they would cross the Atlantic to England. If things went well, they would only be apart for a few days.

Matt took one last look at the professor's house. The town children would probably raid it in the next few days, stripping it of anything of value. He had been there for a long time. He had almost begun to think of it as his home, but now it was nothing. Burned out. Broken. Empty.

Richard loaded their bags into the trunk.

"Vilcabamba," Matt said.

"Vilcabamba," Pedro agreed.

The two of them shook hands. Scott and Jamie said nothing — but Matt knew that they were communicating even so.

It was all over very quickly. The four boys climbed into their different cars and went their separate ways.

ELEVEN
The Happy Garden

In London, Scarlett Adams was trying to get back to her old life.

The doctors had decided there was nothing wrong with her. The police had asked more questions but had finally given up. Maybe she had suffered from amnesia. Maybe the whole thing about her disappearance had been a prank — but either way, they had better things to do. Even the press had decided to leave her alone. A new president, a man named Charles Baker, had just been elected in the U.S.A., and according to all the reports, there had been something strange about the way the votes had been counted. It was turning into a huge scandal that left no room in the papers for a girl who had been missing for less than a day.

Just forty-eight hours after he had flown all the way to England, Paul Adams went back to Hong Kong.

Scarlett understood why he couldn't stay with her. He had only recently started his new job, working in the legal department of a huge company involved, amongst other things, in the manufacture of computer equipment and software. It hadn't made a good impression, shooting off to London at such short notice. He had to get back again.

Back to Nightrise.

Paul Adams took Scarlett out to dinner on his last night at home. The two of them went to a little Italian restaurant that he liked in Dulwich. He ordered half a bottle of wine for himself and a lemonade for her, and the two of them sat facing each other trying to think of things to say. Paul was wearing expensive jeans and a shirt that didn't really suit him. The truth was that he was only really comfortable in a jacket and tie. They were like a second skin to him. Maybe it was his age. He was forty-nine years old, and he had been a lawyer for more than half that time, devoting his life to contracts, complicated reports, and charts. It was hard to imagine what he had been like as a teenager.

"Are you going to be all right, Scarly?" he asked.

"Yes." Scarlett nodded.

Neither of them had spoken very much about St. Meredith's. Paul Adams seemed to have accepted her story. She had fallen ill. She had forgotten whatever had happened. Scarlett wondered why she hadn't confided in him. He had always been kind to her. Why was she lying to him now?

"I'm sorry, Dad," she said.

"There's nothing to be sorry about." Paul Adams paused and sipped his wine. "Do you really have no idea what happened to you?"

"I wish I did."

"You could tell me, you know. I wouldn't be cross with you. I mean, if there's some sort of secret or something you're afraid of. . . ."

Scarlett shook her head. "I told the police everything."

Paul Adams nodded. Then the waiter arrived with

spaghetti carbonara for him and a pizza for Scarlett. There was the usual business with the oversize pepper grinder, the sprinkle of parmesan cheese. At last they were on their own again.

"How's the job going?" Scarlett asked, deliberately changing the subject.

"Oh. It's not too bad." Paul Adams twirled his fork in the spaghetti. "Do you want to come to Hong Kong for the Christmas holidays? I've spoken to your mother, and she's happy for me to have you this year. I'll get a few days off and we can travel together."

"I'd like that," Scarlett said, although she wondered what it would be like, traveling, just the two of them. They seemed to have grown apart so quickly.

They ate in silence. Paul Adams didn't seem to be enjoying his food. He left half of it, then took off his glasses and began to rub them with his napkin. Looking at him just then, Scarlett thought how old he had become. It wasn't just his hair that was going gray. It was all of him.

"I'm sorry, Scarly," he said. "I'm afraid I've rather let you down, haven't I? If I'd known that Vanessa and I weren't going to stay together . . . maybe we should have thought twice about adopting a child, although, of course, I'm glad we did. I think the world of you. But it hasn't been fair. Leaving you on your own with Mrs. Murdoch."

"It was my decision," Scarlett reminded him.

"Well, yes. I suppose it was."

"Why do you have to work in Hong Kong?" Scarlett asked.

"It's a wonderful opportunity. Not just the money. Nightrise has offices all over the world, and if I can work

124

my way up the ladder . . ." His voice trailed off. "I'll only be there a couple of years. I've told them already. Then I want them to transfer me to the London office and we'll be together again."

"Don't worry about me, Dad. I'll be all right."

"Will you, Scarly? I hope so."

He left on the early flight the next day.

Scarlett had already gone back to school — and that hadn't been easy either. The headmistress, a gray-haired woman who looked more severe than she actually was, had made a speech in assembly, telling everyone to leave her alone, but of course they had been all over her, bombarding her with questions, desperate to know where she had really been. Scarlett had been on TV. She was a minor celebrity. Some of the younger girls even asked her for an autograph. On the other hand, some of the teachers had been less than happy to see her — Joan Chaplin in particular. The art teacher had taken some of the responsibility for Scarlett's disappearance, and she in turn blamed Scarlett for that.

The next couple of days passed with the usual routine of lessons and games. There were piles of homework and rehearsals for the Christmas play. Everything had returned to normal — at least, that was what Scarlett told herself. But in her heart, she knew that nothing was really normal at all. Maybe it never would be again.

She had already decided that there was only one person she could talk to and tell the truth about her disappearance. Not her father. Not Mrs. Murdoch. It had to be Aidan. He was her closest friend. He wouldn't laugh at her. She had already texted him, and the two of them met after school and walked home together, taking their time, allowing the other schoolkids to stream ahead.

She told him everything: the door, the monastery, Father Gregory, the escape. She was still talking as they turned into Dulwich Park, opposite the art gallery, taking the long way round, past the playground and across the grass.

"Do you think I'm mad?" she asked when she had finished. There had been times when she had begun to wonder herself. Could it be that the official version of events was actually true? Had she somehow hit her head against a wall and dreamed the whole thing?

"I always thought you were pretty strange," Aidan said.

"But to dream something like that . . ."

"You don't make it sound like a dream." His eyes brightened. "Hey — maybe we could go back to the church. We could go through the door a second time and see what happened."

Scarlett shuddered. "I couldn't do that."

"Why not? If you went with me, at least it would prove it was true."

"I couldn't go back. They might be waiting for me. They'd grab me, and the whole thing would just start again."

"I'd protect you!"

"They'd kill you. They'd kill both of us."

They had reached the other side of the park and were coming out of the Court Lane Gate on the north side. From here the road cut down to the lights where, two years before, Scarlett had almost been killed.

Scarlett had just turned the corner when she saw the car.

It was a silver Mercedes with tinted windows so that even though she could make out two people inside it, she couldn't see their faces. It was parked on the opposite side of the road, and she might not even have noticed it . . . except that it was the fourth time she had seen it. It had been in the street that morning, parked outside The Crown and Grayhound when she was on her way to school. Once again, there had been two people sitting inside. It had overtaken her when she was walking to the Italian restaurant with her father. And she had seen it from her bedroom, cruising down the street where she lived. She had made a note of the license plate number. It contained the letters GEN, which just happened to be the first three letters of St. Genevieve's. That was why she remembered it now.

She stopped.

"What is it?" Aidan asked.

"Those two men." She pointed at the car. "They're watching me."

"Scarl . . ."

"I mean it. I've seen them before."

Aidan looked in their direction. "Maybe they're journalists," he said. "You're still a mystery. They could be after an interview."

"They've been following me."

"I'll ask them, if you like."

They must have seen him coming or guessed what he had in mind. As Aidan stepped off the sidewalk, the driver started the engine up and tore away, disappearing round the corner with a screech of tires.

Scarlett didn't see the Mercedes again, but that wasn't the end of it. Quite the opposite. It told her something that she had been feeling all along.

She was being watched. She was sure of it. It had crept up on her over the past few days, before Paul Adams had left, a sense that she was trapped, like a specimen in a laboratory glass slide. She had found herself gazing at complete strangers in the street, convinced that they were spying on her. When she walked past a security camera outside a shop or an office, it almost seemed to swivel round, its single, glass eye focusing on her — and she could imagine someone in a secret room far away, staring at her on a television monitor, picking her out from the crowd.

Even when she was on her own in her room, she had got the sense of someone eavesdropping, and after a while, just the flapping of a curtain would be enough to unnerve her. When she made phone calls — it didn't matter if it was her mobile or a landline — she was sure she could hear something in the background. Breathing. A faint echo. Someone listening.

She wasn't imagining it. It was there.

Scarlett had tried to tell herself that none of this was possible. She knew that there was a word for what she was experiencing: paranoia. Why would anyone bother to watch her? Nobody was watching her. She was just freaked out by what had happened before.

"There were five children. They came to be known as the Gatekeepers. Four boys and a girl. You are the girl."

It was when she saw the Mercedes with Aidan that Scarlett understood that what had begun at St. Meredith's wasn't over yet. It had only really begun.

The next day — Friday — was miserable. Scarlett hadn't slept well. She was snappy with Mrs. Murdoch and managed to make a spectacular mess of a math test at school. She didn't want to be in class. She just wanted to go back to her room and close the door — to shut "them" out, even though she didn't have any idea who "they" might be.

That evening, she got a phone call. It was Aidan.

"Hi, Scarlett," he said. "I was wondering . . . do you want to come to a movie tomorrow?"

Just that one sentence and she knew that something was wrong. Scarlett didn't reply immediately. She cradled her mobile in the palm of her hand, playing back what she had just heard. First of all, Aidan never called her Scarlett. He called her Scarl. And there had been something weird about his tone of voice. He hadn't asked her out as if he really meant it. He sounded fake, as if he was reading from a script.

As if he knew he was being overheard.

She lifted the mobile again. "What do you want to see?"

"I don't know. The new Batman or something. We can go into the West End. . . ."

And that was odd too. Why travel all the way into town? Dulwich had a perfectly good cinema.

"Okay," she said. "What time do you want to meet?"

"Twelve?"

"I'll see you here. . . ."

129

Aidan arrived at exactly midday, dressed in his trademark hoodie and jeans. As they walked over to the Tube station together, Scarlett wondered if she hadn't read too much into the conversation the night before. He seemed completely relaxed and cheerful. The two of them chatted about school, fast food, and the American election, which was still in the news. Aidan was interested in politics even if it left Scarlett completely cold.

"Charles Baker is a creep," he said. "I can't believe anyone voted for him as president. The other guy, Trelawney, should have walked away with it."

"So why didn't he?"

"I don't know. Some people are saying they botched the voting slips. But I'm telling you, Scarl, the wrong guy won."

They reached the cinema, the Empire in Leicester Square, but as they approached the box office, Aidan suddenly grabbed Scarlett and dragged her to one side. In an instant, his whole mood changed. He made sure there was no one else around, then hurriedly began to speak.

"Scarl, I've got to tell you. Something really weird has happened."

"What is it?" Scarlett was completely thrown.

"I didn't know whether to tell you or not. But yesterday, when I called you, I was told to do it! This guy came up to me when I was coming out of school."

"What guy?"

"I'd never seen him before. At first I thought he was trying to sell me something. He was Chinese. A young guy. He asked me to get a message to you."

130

"Why didn't he tell me himself?"

"I'm only telling you what he told me." Aidan ran a hand through his long, shaggy hair. There was still no one in this part of the foyer. A short distance away, a family of four was just going in to the film. "He just came up to me and asked if he could talk to me. He knew my name. And he knew I was your friend."

"What did he want?"

"Listen — I don't want to freak you out, but he told me that he couldn't approach you himself because your phone was bugged and you were being watched. He said you were in danger." Aidan paused. "Has this got something to do with what happened in the church?"

"I don't know, Aidan," Scarlett said. All her fears had just been confirmed. She didn't know if that made her feel better or worse. She looked around her. "So where is this mysterious Chinese man? Are we meeting him here?"

"No. He's round the corner . . . in a restaurant. The Happy Garden. It's on Wardour Street, about five minutes away."

"So why are we here?"

"That was my idea. I had to tell you what was going on, but I couldn't do it on the Tube in case someone was listening. I'm sorry, Scarl. I didn't want to lie to you, but this guy sounded really serious. And it was only yesterday we saw that car at the park." Aidan drew a breath. "You don't have to go," he said. "Maybe you shouldn't go."

"Why not?"

"Maybe you should go to the police."

Scarlett had to admit that he had a point. Everyone

knew that when a strange adult approached a kid outside school, it was time to call the cops. But she had already made up her mind. If she didn't go to this restaurant, she might never find out who the man was or what he wanted.

"The Happy Garden," she muttered. "What sort of name is that?"

"It's a Chinese restaurant," Aidan said.

"Oh yes," she nodded. "I suppose it would be." She thought for a moment. "Did the man say anything else?"

"Yes. He said that the two of you had met before. On Dulwich Grove, two years ago. He must have been talking about the accident. . . ."

If Scarlett had had any doubts, that decided it. The man who had saved her, who hadn't waited to be thanked, had been Chinese. It had to be the same person. But what was he doing back in her life?

"What time am I supposed to be there?" she asked.

"Half past one."

She looked at her watch. It was just after one o'clock. "We're going to be early."

"So you're going?"

"I've got to, Aidan. I don't think anything too bad can happen in the middle of a Chinese restaurant. And anyway, you'll be with me." She paused. "Won't you?"

"Sure." Aidan nodded. "I wouldn't leave you on your own. Anyway, I can't wait to find out what this is all about."

They left the cinema the way they'd come, slipping quietly into the crowds in Leicester Square. It was unlikely that anyone had followed them all the way from Dulwich, but Scarlett wasn't taking any chances. They turned up an alleyway that led into Chinatown, an area that was packed with Chinese restaurants and supermarkets. From here, they crossed over Shaftesbury Avenue, heading for the address that Aidan had been given.

The afternoon was surprisingly warm. It was lunchtime, there were lots of people around. The smell of fried noodles hung in the air.

The explosion happened just as they were about to turn the corner onto Wardour Street. They didn't just hear it. They felt it too. The pavement actually shuddered under their feet and a gust of warm air punched into them, carrying with it a cloud of dust and soot. If they had been just ten seconds earlier, they might have been hit by the full impact. A bomb had gone off. A large one. It had happened somewhere near.

"Stop!" Aidan shouted.

He was too late. Scarlett had already run forward and turned the corner.

A scene of devastation greeted her on the other side. A building about halfway up the road had been blown to pieces. It was as if someone had punched a giant fist into it. There was glass and debris all over the pavement, and tongues of flame were licking out of the shattered brickwork. A taxi must have been passing at the moment the bomb went off. All its windows were broken and the driver had tumbled out, blind, blood pouring down his face. A woman was standing nearby, screaming and screaming, her clothes in tatters, covered in blood and broken glass.

There was smoke everywhere, but Scarlett could make out several people injured. She had seen images like this on TV, in Baghdad and Jerusalem. But this was Soho, the center of London. And she knew that she'd almost been part of it. It might have been Aidan and her, lying in the rubble.

Aidan caught up with her. "We should go," he said.

"But the restaurant . . ."

"That *is* the restaurant."

Scarlett couldn't move. She stared at the gaping hole, the smoke billowing out, the smashed furniture and the bodies. He was right.

"Come on!" Aidan pleaded.

Scarlett could already hear the sirens of the police cars and ambulances moving in from some other part of the city. It was amazing how quickly they had been alerted. She allowed Aidan to lead her away. She didn't want to be found there. Part of her even wondered if she might somehow have been to blame.

It was the first story on the news that night. A restaurant called the Happy Garden had been the target of a lethal attack. Three people had been killed and a dozen more had been injured by a bomb that had been concealed under one of the tables. According to the police, this wasn't a terrorist incident. They put the blame on Chinese gangs that had been operating in the West End.

"Police today are speculating that the attack is the result of rising tension within the Chinese community," the newscaster said.

Scarlett watched the broadcast with Mrs. Murdoch. The housekeeper was knitting. "Weren't you in Soho today, Scarlett?" she asked.

"No," Scarlett lied. "I was on the other side of the town. I was nowhere near."

"This is the most serious attack so far," the report went on. "It follows other incidents involving gangs in Peckham and Mile End. Any witnesses are urged to come forward. Scotland Yard has set up a special phone line for anyone with any information that might help."

Scarlett texted Aidan that night before she went to bed, and he texted back. They both agreed that it was just a coincidence. Despite what they had thought earlier, it would be absurd to suggest that a restaurant in the middle of London had been blown up just to stop them from meeting someone there.

But as she turned out the lights and tried to get to sleep, Scarlett knew that it wasn't. The newscaster had been lying. The police were lying. There were no gangs . . . just an enemy who was still playing with her and who wouldn't stop until she was completely in their control.

TWELVE
Matt's Diary [2]

Sunday

A bomb has gone off in London. I've just been watching it on the television news, and I wonder if it might have something to do with Scarlett. Richard thinks it's unlikely. According to the reports, the bomb had been hidden in a restaurant in Chinatown. It was something to do with Chinese gang warfare. Three people have been killed.

I saw the images on the big plasma screen TV in my hotel room. Dead people, ambulances, screaming relatives, smoke, and broken glass . . . it was hard to believe that it was all happening in the middle of Soho. You just don't expect it there. It made me feel even farther away than I actually was.

Miami. I've never been here before and I certainly never dreamed that I'd wind up in a five-star hotel overlooking the beach, surrounded by Cadillacs, Cuban music, and palm trees. The Nexus has certainly put us up in style while we wait for my new passport to arrive. The only trouble is, it's taking longer than we had hoped. We're now booked onto a flight leaving on Monday evening and we'll have to cool our heels until then. Scarlett will just have to manage without us for a couple more days. We'll be with her soon enough.

It feels strange, being back in a big city after spending so much time in a backwater like Nazca. Miami is full of rich people and expensive houses. It's too cold to swim at this time of the year, but a lot of life still seems to be happening in the street. We didn't do much today. I bought myself some new clothes, replacing the stuff that got lost in the fire. We walked. And tonight we ate on Ocean Drive, a long strip of fancy cafés and bars with bright pink neon lights, cocktails, and live bands. It was good to be able to enjoy ourselves, sitting there, watching the crowds go past.

Nobody noticed us. For a few hours we could pretend we were normal.

• • •

Monday afternoon
This morning, the passport finally arrived, delivered in a brown, sealed envelope by a motorbike rider who didn't say a word. Terrible photograph. The Nexus have sent Jamie a new passport too, and they've decided that we should both travel under false names, for extra security. So now I'm Martin Hopkins. He is Nicholas Helsey. Richard is going to stay as himself, but then, as far as we know, nobody is trying to kill him.

We have economy tickets. The Nexus could have flown us first class, but they didn't want us to stand out.

We had our final meal on Ocean Drive. A huge plate of nachos and two Cokes. Richard had a beer. I wondered what the waiter must have made of us: Richard in a gaudy, Hawaiian shirt, sitting between two teenagers, the two of us wearing sunglasses even though there wasn't a lot of sun. We'd bought them the day before and hadn't gotten round to taking them off. We liked them because they kept us anonymous. If anyone had asked, we were going to say that he was a teacher and that we were on a school exchange. It was a pretty unlikely story — but nothing compared to the truth.

I've spoken to Pedro via satellite phone a couple of times while we've been here. He and Scott reached Vilcabamba without any problem. We've agreed to contact each other every day while we are apart. If there's silence, we'll know something is wrong. Pedro told me that Scott was okay. But Scott didn't come on the line.

Jamie asked me something today. It took me by surprise. "Why did you really leave Scott behind? You didn't think you could rely on him, did you?"

"I never said that."

"But you thought it." He lowered his voice. "You have no idea what he went through with Mrs. Mortlake. It was worse than anything you can imagine."

"Has he talked to you about it?"

Jamie shook his head. "He's put up barriers. He won't go there. He's not the same anymore. I know that. But you have no idea how he looked after me all those years. When Uncle Don was beating me around or when I was in trouble at school, Scott was always there for me. The only reason he got caught was that he was helping me get away." He suddenly took off his sunglasses and laid them on the table. "Don't underestimate him, Matt. I know he's not himself right now, but he'll never let you down."

I hope Jamie is right. But I'm not sure.

I looked across the road. There were some little kids throwing a ball on a lawn beside the beach. A couple of rollerbladers swung by. A pale green convertible drove past with music blaring. And just a few feet away, we were talking about torture and thinking about a war that we might not be able to win. Two different worlds. I know which one I'd have preferred to be in.

We finished eating and went back to the hotel. Our car was already there. The concierge carried out our cases, and then it was a twenty-minute drive across the causeway. The water, stretching out on both sides, looked blue and inviting. We reached Miami International Airport and went in, joining the crowds at the check-in desks. Thousands of people traveling all over the world. And this is what I was thinking . . .

Suppose the Old Ones are already here. Suppose they control this airport. We are allowing ourselves to be swallowed up by a system . . . tickets, passports, security. How do we know we can trust it, that it will take us where we want to go, or even let us out again?

We got to the baggage check. Richard took one look at the X-ray machines and stopped. "I'm an idiot," he said.

"What is it?"

He was carrying a backpack on his shoulder, cradling it under one arm. He'd had it with him at the restaurant too and I knew that, among other things, the monk's diary was inside. But now he was watching as people took out their computers and removed their belts, and I could see that he was furious with himself. "The tumi," he said. "I meant to transfer it to my main luggage. They'll never let it through."

The tumi is a sacrificial knife. It was given to him by the prince of the Inca tribe just before we left Vilcabamba. I could understand Richard wanting to keep it close to him. It was made of solid gold, with semiprecious stones in the hilt, and it must have been worth a small fortune. But this was a mistake. He might try to argue that the tumi was an antique, an ornament, or just a souvenir, but given that the airlines wouldn't even allow you to carry a teaspoon unless it was made of plastic, there was no way it was going to be allowed on the plane.

It was too late to do anything now. There was a long line of people behind us, and we wouldn't have been allowed to turn back. Richard dumped the bag on the moving belt and grimaced as it disappeared inside the X-ray machine. I suppose he was hoping that the security people might glance away at the right moment and miss it. But that wasn't going to happen. The bag came out again. It was grabbed by an unsmiling woman with her name — Monica Smith — on a badge on her blue, short-sleeved shirt.

"Is this yours?" she asked.

"Yes." Richard prepared for the worst.

"Can you unzip this, please?"

"I can explain . . . ," Richard began.

"Just open it, please."

The tumi was right on the top. I could see the golden figure of the Inca god that squatted above the blade. I watched as the woman, wearing latex gloves, began to rifle through Richard's clothes. Briefly, she picked up the diary, then put it back again. She examined a magnifying glass that Richard had bought in Miami, trying to decipher the monk's handwriting. But she didn't even seem to notice that the tumi was there. She closed the bag again.

"Thank you," she said.

Richard looked at me. Neither of us said anything. We snatched up our belongings and hurried forward. It was only afterward that we understood what had happened.

The tumi has another name. It's also known as the invisible blade. When the prince of the Incas gave it to Richard, he said that no one would ever find it, that he would be able to carry it with him at any time. He also warned Richard that one day he would regret having it — something neither of us really like to think about.

But now we both realized what we had just seen. It was a bit of ancient magic. And it was all the more amazing because it happened in the setting of a modern, international airport.

•   •   •

Monday night

We took off exactly on time, and once the seat belt signs had been turned off, I sat back in my seat and began to write this. In the seat next to me, Jamie had plugged himself straight into the TV console, watching a film. Richard was across the aisle, working with a Spanish dictionary, trying to unravel the diary.

A bit later, I fell asleep.

And that was when I went back. I had wanted to visit the dreamworld again, ever since I had discovered the path set into the side of the hill. Was it really possible that a civilization of some sort had once lived there? Might they be living there still? The dreamworld was a sort of in-between place, connecting where we were now with the world that Jamie had visited and where he had fought his battle, ten thousand years ago. It was there to help us. The more we knew about it, the better prepared we would be.

• • •

I was right where I wanted to be, back on the hillside, halfway up the path. But that was how the dreamworld worked. Every time I fell asleep, I picked up exactly where I had left off. So if I woke up throwing a stone into the air, when I went back to sleep, I would immediately catch it again. And I was wearing the same clothes that I had on the plane. That was how it worked too.

The hill became steeper and the path turned into a series of steps. They had definitely been made by human hands. As I continued climbing up, they became ever more defined, and when I finally reached the summit, I found myself on a square platform with some sort of design — it looked like a series of Arabic letters — cut into it. The letters made no sense to me, but then I lifted my head and what I saw was so amazing that I'm surprised I didn't wake up at once and find myself back on the plane.

I was looking at a city, sprawling out in all directions, as far as the eye could see. More than that. From where I was standing, high up on the hill, I could see thousands of rooftops stretching all the way to the horizon, perhaps ten miles away, but I got the impression that if I managed to walk all the way to the other side, it would continue to the next horizon and maybe to the one after that.

It was impossible to say if the city was ancient or modern. It somehow managed to be both at the same time. Some of the buildings were huge, cathedral-like with arched windows and domes covered in tiles that could have been silver or zinc. Others were steel and glass structures that reminded me of an airport terminal, and then I realized that there were actually dozens of them and they were all identical, radiating out of central courtyards like the spokes of a wheel. Towers rose up at intervals, again with silver turrets. Everything was connected, either by spiral staircases or covered walkways.

There were no parks and no trees. There weren't any cars or people. In fact, I wasn't looking at a city at all. This vast construction was one single building: a massive cathedral, a massive museum, a massive . . . something. It was a mishmash of styles; some parts must have been added hundreds or even thousands of years after others — but it was all locked together. It was one. I couldn't work out where the center was. I couldn't see where it had originally begun. Nor could I imagine how it had come into being. It was as if someone had taken a single seed — one brick — and dropped it into a bubbling swamp. And this, after thousands of years of growth, was the result.

Leaving the platform behind me, I walked down the other side of the hill and made my way toward the outer wall. I was now following a road with a marble-like surface, and it was taking me directly toward a great big arch and, on the other side of it, an open door. The air was very still. I could actually hear my heart beating as I approached. I didn't think I was in danger, but there was something so weird about this place, so far removed from my experience, that I admit I was afraid. I didn't hesitate, though. I passed through the arch and suddenly I was inside, in a long corridor with a tiled, very polished floor and a high, vaulted ceiling held up by stone pillars: not quite a church, not quite a museum, but something similar to both.

"Can I help you?"

Another shock. I wasn't on my own. And the question was so normal, so polite that it just didn't seem to belong to this extraordinary place.

There was a man standing behind a lectern, the sort of things lecturers have in front of them when they talk. He was quite small, a couple of inches shorter than me, and he had one of those faces . . . I won't say it was carved out of stone (it was too warm and human for that) but it somehow seemed ages old, gnarled by time and experience.

From the look of him, I would have said he was an Arab, a desert tribesman, but without any of the trappings such as a headdress, white robes, or a dagger. Instead, he was dressed in a long, silk jacket — faded mauve and silver — with a large pocket on each side and baggy, white trousers. A beard would have suited him, but he didn't have one. His hair was steel gray. His eyes were the same color. They were regarding me with polite amusement.

"What is this place?" I asked.

"This place?" The man seemed surprised that I had asked. "This is the great library. And it's very good to see you again."

A library. I remembered something Jamie had told me. When he met Scarlett at Scathack Hill, she had mentioned visiting a library to him.

"We've never met."

"I think we have." The man smiled at me. I wasn't sure what language he was speaking. In the dreamworld, all languages are one and the same, and people can understand each other no matter where they've come from. "You're Matthew Freeman. At least, that's the name you call yourself. You're one of the Gatekeepers. The first of them, in fact."

"Do you have a name?"

"No. I'm just the Librarian."

"I'm looking for Scarlett," I said. "Scarlett Adams. Has she been here?"

"Scarlett Adams? Scarlett Adams? You mean . . . Scar! Yes, she most certainly has been here. But not for a long time. And she's not here now."

"Do you know where I can find her?"

"I'm afraid not."

We were walking down the corridor together, which was strange because I couldn't remember starting. And we had passed into a second room, part of the library . . . it was obvious now. I had never seen so many books. There were books on both sides of me, standing like soldiers, shoulder to shoulder, packed into wooden shelves that stretched on and on into the distance, finally — a trick of perspective — seeming to come together at a point. The shelves began at floor level and rose all the way to the ceiling, maybe a hundred rows in each block. The air was dry and smelled of paper. There must have been a million books in this room alone, and each one of them was as thick as an encyclopedia.

"You must like reading," I said.

"I never have time to read the books. I'm too busy looking after them."

"How many of you are there?"

"Just me."

"Who built the library?"

"I couldn't tell you, Matt. It was already here before I arrived."

"So what are these books? Do you have a crime section? And romance?"

"No, Matt." The Librarian smiled at the thought. "Although you will find plenty of crime, and plenty of romance for that matter, among their pages. But all the books in the library are biographies."

"Who of?"

"Of all the people who have ever lived and quite a few who are still to be born. We keep their entire lives here. Their beginnings, their marriages, their good days and their bad days, their deaths — of course. Everything they ever did."

We stopped in front of a door. There was a sign on it, delicately carved into the wood. A five-pointed star.

"I know this," I said.

"Of course you do."

"Where does this door go?"

"It goes anywhere you want it to."

"It's like the door at St. Meredith's!" I said.

"It works the same way . . . but there you have only twenty-four possible destinations. In your world, there are twenty-five doors, all connecting with each other — although none of them will bring you back here. This library, on the other hand, has a door in every room, and I have absolutely no idea how many rooms there are and wouldn't even know how to count them." The Librarian gestured with one hand. "After you."

"Where are we going?"

"Well, since you're here, why don't we have a look at your life? Aren't you curious?"

"Not really."

"Let's see. . . ."

• • •

We went through the door, and for all I knew at that moment, we crossed twenty miles to the other side of the city. We found ourselves in a chamber that was certainly very different from the one we had left, with plate-glass windows all around us, held in place by a latticework of steel supports. Maybe this was one of the airport terminals I had seen. The books here were on metal shelves, each one with a narrow walkway and a circular platform that moved up and down like an elevator but with no cables, no pistons, no obvious means of support.

We went up six levels and shuffled along the ledge with a railing on one side, the books on the other.

"Matt Freeman . . . Matt Freeman . . ." The Librarian muttered my name as we went.

"Are they in alphabetical order?" I asked. All the volumes looked the same except that some were thicker than others. I couldn't see any names or titles.

"No. It's more complicated than that."

I looked back at the door that we'd come through. It was now below and behind us. "How do the doors work?" I asked.

"How do you mean?"

"How do you know where they'll take you?"

He stopped and turned to look at me. "If you just wander through them, they'll take you anywhere," he said. "But if you know exactly where you want to go, that's where they'll take you."

"Can anyone use them?"

"The doors in your world were built just for the five of you."

"What about Richard?"

"You can each take a companion with you, if you're so minded. Just remember to decide where you're going before you step through or you could end up scattered all over the planet."

We continued on our way, but after another couple of minutes, the Librarian suddenly stopped, reached up, and took out a book. "Here you are," he said. "This is you."

I looked at the book suspiciously. Like all the others, it was oversize, bound in some gray fabric, old but perhaps never read. It looked more like a school book than a novel or a biography. I noticed that it had fewer pages than many of the others.

"Is that it?" I asked.

"Absolutely." The Librarian seemed disappointed that I wasn't more impressed.

"That's my whole life?"

"Yes."

"My whole life up to now . . ."

"Up to now and all the way to the end."

The thought of that made my head swim. "Does it say when I die?"

"The book is all about you, Matt," the Librarian explained patiently. "Inside its pages you will find everything you have ever done and everything you will do. Do you want to know when you next meet the Old Ones? You can read it here. And yes, it will tell you exactly when you will die and in what manner."

"Are you telling me that someone has written down everything that happens to me before it happens?" I know that was exactly what he had just said, but I had to get my head around it.

"Yes." He nodded.

"Then that means that I've got no choice. Everything I do has already been decided."

"Yes, Matt. But you have to remember, it was decided by you."

"But my decisions don't mean anything!" I pointed at the book, and suddenly I was beginning to hate the sight of it. "Whatever I do in my life, the end is still going to be the same. It's already been written."

"Do you want to read it?" the Librarian asked.

149

"No!" I shook my head. "Put it away. I don't want to see it."

"That's your choice," the Librarian said with a sly smile. He slid the book back into the space it had come from. But I had one last question.

"Who wrote the book?" I asked.

"There is no author listed. All the books in the library are anonymous. That's one of the reasons why it makes them so hard to catalog."

I was beginning to feel miserable. The dreamworld seemed to exist to help us, but every time we came here, it was simply confusing. Jamie and Pedro had both found this too. "You call yourself a librarian," I snapped at the man. "So why can't you be more helpful? Why don't you have any answers?"

He tapped the spine of the book. "All the answers are here," he said. "But you just refused to look at them."

"Then answer me this one question. Am I going to win or lose?"

"Win or lose?"

"Against the Old Ones." I swallowed. "Am I going to get killed?"

"We are experiencing some turbulence. . . ."

The Librarian was still looking at me, but he hadn't spoken those words. With a sense of frustration, I felt myself being sucked away. There was someone leaning over me. A member of the cabin crew.

"I'm sorry I've had to wake you up," she said. "The captain has put on the seat belt sign."

I looked at my watch. We still had four more hours in

the air. Richard and Jamie were asleep, but I knew I wouldn't be able to join them. I took out my notepad and started writing again.

Four hours until London.

Soon we will be home.

THIRTEEN
Crossing Paths

Scarlett thought she'd be safe, back at school. She'd slip back into the crowd, and nobody would notice her. After all, nothing exciting ever happened at school. Wasn't that the whole point? So, for the first time in her life, she found herself looking forward to the next Monday morning. There would be no bombs, no strange men in cars, no cryptic messages. She would be swallowed up by math and history and physics, and everything would be all right.

But it didn't happen that way.

Shortly before lunch, she was called into the headmistress's office. There was no explanation, just a brief: "Mrs. Ridgewell would like to see you at twelve fifteen." Scarlett was nervous as she climbed the stairs. In a way, she'd been expecting trouble ever since the trip to St. Meredith's. She had been the center of attention for far too long and for all the wrong reasons. Her work had gone rapidly downhill. She'd been told off twice for daydreaming in class. And then there had been that terrible math test. The teachers had already decided that all the publicity had gone to her head, and Scarlett fully expected Mrs. Ridgewell to read her the riot act. Get your head down. Pull your socks up. That sort of thing.

But what the headmistress said came right out of the blue.

"Scarlett, I'm afraid you're going to be leaving us for a few weeks. I've just had a phone call from your father. It seems that some sort of crisis has arisen. . . ."

"What crisis?" Scarlett asked.

"He didn't say. He was very mysterious, if you want to know the truth. But he wants you to join him immediately in Hong Kong. In fact, he's already arranged the flight."

There was a moment's silence while Scarlett took this in. There were all sorts of questions that she wanted to ask, but she began with the most obvious. "Has this got something to do with what happened to me?"

"I don't think so."

"Then what?"

"He didn't say." Mrs. Ridgewell sighed. She had been at St. Genevieve's for more than twenty years and it showed. Her office was cluttered and a little shabby, with antique furniture and books everywhere. A Siamese cat — it was named Chaucer — lay asleep in a basket in a corner. "You haven't had a very good term, have you, Scarlett?"

"No." Scarlett shook her head miserably. "I'm sorry, Mrs. Ridgewell. I don't know what's going on, really. Everything seems to have gone wrong."

"Well, maybe we should look on the bright side. A complete break for a few weeks might do you good. I'll ask your teachers to prepare some work for while you're out there — and, of course, we're going to have to recast the Christmas play. I have to say that it is all very inconvenient."

"Didn't he say anything?"

"I've told you everything I know, I'm afraid. I thought he would have discussed it with you."

"No. I haven't heard from him."

"Well, I'm sure there's nothing to worry about. He told me he'd call you tonight. So you've just got time to say good-bye to your friends."

"When am I leaving?"

"Your flight is tomorrow."

Tomorrow! Scarlett couldn't believe what she was hearing. Tomorrow was only a few hours away. How could her dad have done this to her? He hadn't mentioned anything when they were in the Italian restaurant. What crisis could possibly have arisen so quickly?

Scarlett spent the rest of the day in a complete daze. Her friends were equally surprised, although the truth was that she was beginning to get a bit of a reputation. She was weird. First the church and now this. She didn't even get to see Aidan. She looked for him on the way home and tried texting him, but he didn't reply. Mrs. Murdoch had already heard the news. She had started packing by the time Scarlett got home. And she didn't seem pleased.

"Not a word of warning," she muttered. "And no explanation. What do you suppose I'm meant to do, sitting here on my own?"

Paul Adams called that night as he had promised, but he didn't tell Scarlett anything she wanted to know.

"I'm really sorry, Scarly." His voice on the line was thin and very distant. "I didn't want to do this to you. But things have happened. . . . I don't want to explain until I see you."

"But you've got to tell me!" Scarlett protested. "Is Mom all right? Are you?"

"We're both fine. There's nothing for you to worry about. It's just that there are times when a family has to be together, and this is one of them."

"How long am I staying with you?"

"A couple of weeks. Maybe longer."

"Why?" There was silence at the other end of the line. "Can't you tell me anything?" Scarlett went on. "It's not fair. It's the middle of term and I'm going to miss the school play and all the parties and everything!"

"Look — I'm just going to have to ask you to trust me. You'll be here in twenty-four hours, and I want to explain everything to you face-to-face, not over the phone. Can you do that for me, Scarly? Just wait until you get out here . . . and try not to think too badly of me until you arrive."

"All right." What else could she say?

"I've booked you into business class, so at least you'll be comfortable. Make sure you bring lots of books. It's a long flight."

After they said good-bye, Scarlett stood there, holding the receiver. She was feeling resentful and she couldn't stop herself. This wasn't fair. She was being bundled onto a plane and flown to Hong Kong as if she were a parcel being sent by FedEx. She was fifteen years old. Surely she should have some control over her own life?

The taxi came at noon. Scarlett's flight was leaving Heathrow at half past three. Mrs. Murdoch helped carry the suitcases out and load them into the back. The housekeeper was coming with her as far as the airport and would then return to the house alone. It was a gray, overcast day, and the weather reflected Scarlett's mood. She twisted round as they pulled away and watched the house disappear behind her. She knew she was going to be abroad for only a couple of weeks, but even so she couldn't escape a strange feeling. She wondered if she would ever see her home again.

They reached the bottom of the street and were turning left onto Half Moon Lane. And that was when it happened. A car crash. Scarlett only saw part of it, and it was only later that she was able to piece together what had happened. A car had been driving toward them — it had just come from the main road — and a second car, a BMW, suddenly pulled out in front of it. Scarlett heard the screech of tires and the smash of impact and looked up in time to see the two cars ricocheting off each other, out of control. One of them had been forced off the road and was sliding down a private driveway. She could make out at least three people inside.

"London traffic!" The taxi driver sniffed. He completed the turn, and they picked up speed.

Scarlett twisted round and looked out the back — at the crumpled hood of one of the cars, steam rising into the air, glass scattered on the road. A bus had been forced to stop, and the driver was climbing down, perhaps to see if he could help. The accident was already disappearing into the distance behind them, and she supposed it was just a coincidence. It couldn't mean anything.

But even so, it made her uneasy. It reminded her of the moment — two years ago, and just a short distance away — when she had almost been killed. And that made her think of the man who had contacted Aidan, wanting to meet her at the restaurant that had been blown to pieces before she could arrive. Scarlett sank back into her seat, feeling anxious, unable to control what was happening to her. Mrs. Murdoch gazed out of the window with no expression on her face.

They parted company at the airport. Scarlett was flying as an unaccompanied minor — what the airline called a Skyflyer Solo. She had to suffer the indignity of a plastic label around her neck before she was led away. She said good-bye to Mrs. Murdoch, hugging her awkwardly. Then she picked up her hand luggage and headed for the departure gate.

∙ ∙ ∙

It had been so close. None of them would ever believe just how close it had actually been.

Matt Freeman had landed at the same airport earlier that morning. There had been a uniformed chauffeur waiting for him and the others, and soon they were sitting in the air-conditioned comfort of a new Jaguar, being driven to their hotel. Richard was dozing in the front seat. He had spent much of the flight working on the diary and had barely slept at all. Jamie was looking out for his first sight of the city. Matt could see that so far he was disappointed. They were driving through a wasteland of blank, modern warehouses and unwelcoming hotels — the sort of places that always surround airports — and Matt wanted to tell him that this wasn't London at all.

Then, twenty minutes later, they turned off the motor-way, and suddenly they were in the city itself, passing the Natural History Museum in Kensington — it was still closed for repairs following Matt's last visit there — then the Victoria and Albert Museum, Harrods, and Hyde Park Corner. Jamie stared, openmouthed. He had spent much of his life in the desert landscape of Nevada, and he wasn't used to seeing anything that was actually old. For him, London, with its monuments and palaces, was another world. He saw red buses, pigeons, policemen in blue uni-forms, taxis — it was like falling into a pile of picture postcards. His one disappointment was that Scott wasn't with him. The two brothers had never been so far apart.

The driver took them to a hotel in Farringdon, a quiet part of London with narrow streets and a meat market that had been around when the animals were driven there in herds rather than delivered from Europe, pre-packed in boxes. The Tannery, as it was called, was small and anonymous — Richard and Matt had stayed there before. It was just a few minutes away from the private house where the Nexus met. By the time they arrived, it was eleven o'clock. A meeting had been arranged for half past seven that evening, giving them the rest of the day to relax and unwind from the long flight.

They made their way into a reception area that was like the front room of someone's house, with thick car-pets, flowers, and the comforting tick of a grandfather clock. The receptionist was a tight-lipped woman who took care not to give too much away. She glanced disap-provingly at Richard — still in his Hawaiian shirt, looking more like a beach bum than ever — and the two boys who were with him, then asked for their passports and slid forward some forms for them to sign.

"How many nights?" she asked.

"We're not sure," Richard said.

"Two rooms. I see they've been prepaid. . . ."

The telephone rang. The receptionist plucked the receiver as if it were an overripe fruit and held it to her ear. "The Tannery Hotel," she said. A moment's silence. Her eyes fluttered and she handed the phone to Richard. "It's for you, Mr. Cole."

Richard took the phone. Whatever he was hearing, it wasn't good news. He muttered a few words, then put the phone down.

"What is it?" Matt asked.

"Scarlett Adams. . . . She's leaving London."

"What?" Matt couldn't believe what he had just said. "Where's she going?"

"We can still catch her." Richard looked at his watch. "She's going to Hong Kong. She's booked on the three-thirty flight. . . ."

"Not back to Heathrow!" Jamie groaned.

"No." Richard weighed up the options. He was finding it hard to concentrate. He needed a shave more than ever, and his eyes were red with jet lag. "We can't intercept her at Heathrow," he said. "It's too public. She's never met us. She might not even want to talk to us. But her taxi isn't collecting her until midday. We can reach her before she leaves."

The decision had been made. The three of them

dumped their luggage with the receptionist, turned round, and walked out again. Fortunately, the driver was still waiting. Richard went up to him and told him where they wanted to go. The driver didn't argue. Matt and Jamie got back in again.

They hadn't even seen their rooms. The next moment they were off again, threading their way through Farringdon and down to Blackfriars Bridge. It was now approaching the lunch hour, and London had changed. Although they had made good progress from the airport, the traffic had snarled up. Every traffic light was red. It felt as if the entire city had turned against them.

"Who was it on the phone?" Matt asked.

"Susan Ashwood. She's already in London."

Miss Ashwood was a medium who also happened to be blind. Matt had first met her in Yorkshire, and it had been she who had introduced him to the Nexus.

"How did she know?" Matt asked.

"The Nexus are still bugging Scarlett's phone. They had two people following her too. . . ."

It didn't look as if they were going to make it. The whole of South London had become one long traffic jam. The car crossed Tower Bridge — giving Jamie a quick glimpse of the River Thames and St. Paul's — but after that, the city just felt drab and overcrowded with an endless stretch of cheap shops and restaurants punctuated by new office developments that would have looked out-of-date the moment they were built. Bermondsey, Walworth, Camberwell . . . they crawled from one district to the next without ever noticing where one ended and the next began, and all the time they were aware of time ticking away. Half past eleven, twenty to twelve . . . they didn't seem to be getting any nearer.

"This is hopeless," Richard said. "Maybe we'd better go to Heathrow after all."

The driver shook his head. "We're nearly there," he said.

They dropped down a steep hill — Dog Kennel Hill, it was called — and, looking out of the window, Matt began to feel something very strange. He had never visited this part of London — he was sure of it. And yet, at the same time, he knew where he was. He glimpsed a radio mast in the distance, a road sign pointing to King's College Hospital. They meant something to him. He *had* been here before.

And then it hit him. Of course he knew this part of the city. He had lived here — from the time when he was a baby to when he had been about eight years old.

He should have remembered it. It hadn't been that long ago. But perhaps he had blocked it out. It wouldn't have been surprising after everything he had been through. Now it all came flooding back. The mast belonged to Crystal Palace. He had often played football there. He had gone into the hospital on his seventh birthday with suspected food poisoning. He remembered sitting miserably in the waiting room with a plastic bowl balanced on his knees. They drove past a very ordinary house, but Matt knew at once who lived there. It was a boy named Graham Fleming who had been his best friend at school. The two of them had always thought they would be inseparable.

Matt wondered if he was still living there. What would he say if the two of them met now?

And there was something else he remembered. If he went past Graham's house, turned the corner, and walked past the old scout hut, he would come to a small, terraced house in a leafy street where all the houses were small and terraced. Number 32. It would have a green door and — unless they'd finally mended it — a cracked front step. That was where he had once lived.

"How much farther?" Richard asked.

The driver glanced at the GPS. "We're a minute away," he said.

They went through a traffic light at a busy junction, then drove up toward North Dulwich station, turning onto Half Moon Lane, which was just opposite. Matt felt dazed. It was extraordinary to think that for half their lives, he and Scarlett had almost been neighbors. They might have passed each other a dozen times without even knowing it. She lived on Ardbeg Road, which was the next on the left, and just for a moment, the way ahead was clear. The driver accelerated, glad to be able to use the Jaguar's power.

"Look out!" Richard shouted.

A car shot out from a private driveway and smashed right into them.

Matt saw everything. He heard the roar of an engine, and that made him turn his head. The car was coming straight at them. The driver was staring at them, his hands clenched on the wheel, not even trying to avoid them. He was middle-aged, clean-shaven — and there was no emotion in his face. He should have been scared.

He should have been showing some sort of reaction, knowing what was about to happen. But there was nothing at all.

Half a second later, there was a huge crash of metal against metal as he smashed into them.

The other car was an SUV, and it was like being hit by a tank. The Jaguar was swept off the road, the world tilting away as it was hurled toward a wide, modern house with a short driveway sloping steeply down to the front door. There was a second collision as it hit the door, more crumpling metal. The house alarm went off. Jamie cried out as he was thrown sideways, his head hitting Matt's shoulder. Matt tasted blood and realized that he had bitten his tongue. The Jaguar was lying at an angle, almost underneath the front wheels of the BMW, which was still on the road above them. Both the windows on the driver's side had shattered. The engine had cut out.

For a moment, nobody moved. Then Richard swore — which at least meant he was alive. He twisted round in the front seat. "Are you two all right?" he asked.

"What happened?" Jamie groaned.

"An accident," Richard said. "Idiot . . . wasn't looking where he was going."

He was wrong — Matt knew that already. He had seen what had happened. The BMW driver had been waiting for them, knowing they would come this way. Why else would he have shot out like that, slamming straight into them? Matt had seen him, gripping the wheel. He had known exactly what he was doing.

Richard was already out of the car.

"Wait . . . ," Matt said.

But Richard hadn't heard. He staggered up onto the road, only now becoming aware that he was in pain. There were no cuts or bruises, but, like all of them, he had suffered from whiplash. "What the hell do you think you were doing?" he demanded when he got to the SUV.

The driver had gotten out and was standing in the road. He was a middle-aged man, well built, wearing a long black coat and leather gloves. His mouth was soft and flabby, with small teeth, like a child's. His skin was very pink. His head was almost perfectly round, like a soccer ball. He had curly hair.

"I'm so terribly sorry," he said. "I didn't see you. I was in a hurry. I hope none of you are hurt."

Richard was still angry, but he suddenly knew something was wrong. "You did it on purpose," he said. His voice had faltered. "You tried to kill us."

"Not at all. I just pulled out without looking. I can't tell you how sorry I am. Thank goodness you don't seem to be seriously hurt."

By now, Matt and Jamie had joined Richard. They had left their driver where he was, recovering from the shock of the accident. Jamie stared at the SUV driver, and the color drained out of his face. He knew at once what he was looking at. It was the last thing he had expected to find here.

"Matt . . . ," Jamie whispered. "He's a shape-changer."

Matt didn't doubt him. Jamie had met shape-changers when he had gone back in time. Shape-changers were able to take on human form, but it didn't quite fit. One of them, an old man who had suddenly become a giant scorpion, had almost killed Jamie at the fortress at Scathack Hill. He knew what he was talking about. And Matt could see it for himself. Everything about the BMW driver was fake, even the way he stood there, stiff and unnatural, like a dummy in a shop window. The words he was saying could have been written out for him, on a script.

"I'm insured," he continued. "There's absolutely nothing to worry about. It was my fault. No doubt about it."

Richard stared. None of them knew what to do. Barely a minute had passed since the collision, but already other people were arriving on the scene. A bus on its way to Brixton had pulled up, and the driver was climbing out of his cabin, coming over to help. Two more cars had stopped farther up the road. Matt had seen a taxi pull out of Ardbeg Road and thought it might be coming their way, but it had already turned and driven away.

They couldn't risk a fight. They were in the middle of a suburban, South London street. If they challenged the shape-changer, if he decided to drop his human form, chaos would break loose. And already the police had arrived. A squad car turned the corner and pulled over. Two officers got out.

"Good afternoon, officers." The BMW driver was pretending that he was pleased to see them. "Glad you're here. We're in a bit of a pickle."

His language was as fake as the rest of him, and for just a few seconds, Matt was tempted to take him on, to show the entire crowd what was really happening here. He could use his own power. Without so much as moving, he could tear a strip of metal off the shattered car and send it flying into the man. There were a dozen witnesses on the scene. How would they react when the blushing, curly-haired BMW driver turned into a half-snake or a half-crocodile and bled green blood? Maybe it was time to show the world the war that was about to engulf it.

It was Richard who stopped him.

"No, Matt."

He must have seen what Matt was thinking, because he muttered the two words under his breath, never taking his eyes off the man who was standing in front of them. Matt understood. For some reason, the shape-changer was playing with them. It was pretending that this was just an ordinary accident. If Matt took it on, if he began a fight here in the street, innocent people might get hurt. And he was in England with a fake passport and a false name. This was the wrong time to be answering questions. Right now he had everything to lose.

"I'm so very sorry," the shape-changer said.

"I saw what happened!" the bus driver exclaimed. He nodded at the BMW driver, his face filled with outrage. "He pulled out at fifty miles an hour. He didn't look. He didn't signal. It was all his fault."

"Is anyone hurt?" one of the officers asked.

"Our driver is in shock," Richard said.

The right-hand side of the Jaguar had taken the full force of the impact, and it looked as if the driver might have also broken his arm. He was only semiconscious and in pain. One of the officers helped him out and laid him on the pavement, and they waited about fifteen minutes for an ambulance to arrive. Meanwhile the other officer began questioning the BMW driver — "Mr. Smith." He had no ID.

"I was on my way to Chislehurst. I'm a piano teacher. I pulled out without looking. I can't tell you how dreadful I feel. . . ."

Matt watched as they Breathalyzed him, and it almost made him smile, seeing the man blow into the machine. His breath wasn't human, and if he'd drunk a crate of whiskey, it was unlikely that it would register. Meanwhile their driver was loaded into an ambulance and driven off to the hospital. Thirty minutes or more had gone by, and Richard was desperate to be on his way, but the police weren't having any of it. They would have to take a statement down at the station.

It was almost four o'clock by the time the police finished with them. Even if they had wanted to go to Heathrow, it would have been too late. Scarlett would already be in the air, on her way to Hong Kong. Richard had called the Nexus to let them know; he hoped they would be able to catch her in time.

They left the police station and dropped into a local café, but Matt refused the offer of a drink. He was angry and depressed. The Old Ones were outmaneuvering him at every turn. They seemed to know exactly what he was going to do, and the trap they had set had been childishly simple. He didn't mention the taxi that he had seen pulling out of Ardbeg Road, but it had already occurred to him that Scarlett might well have been inside it. Their paths had finally crossed . . . but seconds too late.

"Let's go to her house," Matt suggested.

"Why?" Richard didn't even look up from his tea.

"I don't know. She could still be there. But even if she isn't, now that we've come this far . . ."

Neither Richard nor Jamie spoke.

"I'd just like to see where she lives," Matt said.

The three of them walked back to Ardbeg Road. It reminded Matt a little of the street where he had once lived. All the houses were terraced with bay windows, neat front gardens, and shrubs to hide the trash cans. Scarlett's was about halfway down.

They rang the bell, not expecting it to be answered, but after about half a minute, the door opened and they found themselves being examined by a short, stern-looking woman with tied-back black hair and eyes that seemed to be expecting trouble.

"Yes?" she said. She had a Scottish accent.

"We're looking for Scarlett Adams," Matt said.

"I'm afraid you've missed her. She left this morning."

Richard moved forward. "Do you live here?" he asked.

"Yes. I'm the housekeeper. Are you friends of Scarlett's?"

"Not exactly," Matt said. "We've just arrived from America. We were hoping to see her."

"That's not going to be possible. She's going to be out of the country for a while."

"Do you know when she'll be back?"

"It could be a week or two. I'm very sorry, if you'd been here just a few hours ago, you'd have caught her. Do you want to leave a message?"

"No, thank you."

"Right."

The woman closed the door.

And that was it. There was nothing more to be done.

For a moment, nobody spoke. Then Richard sighed.

"Anyone fancy a trip to Hong Kong?" he said.

FOURTEEN
Puerto Fragrante

Originally, there had been twelve members of the Nexus — the organization that existed only to fight the Old Ones. Professor Sanjay Dravid had been the first to be killed, stabbed at the Natural History Museum the same night that he had met Matt. Later on, a man named Fabian had also died. That just left ten — powerful people who lived all over the world.

They had all flown in to meet Matt and Jamie and at half past seven that evening, they came together in the secluded, wood-paneled room that was their London base.

The building, which the Nexus owned, stood between two shops, and there was nothing, no name or other marking, to suggest that it was anything but a private house. The room itself, up on the first floor, was equally plain. It could have been the meeting place of some small business, perhaps a firm of expensive lawyers. There didn't seem to be much there — just a long table with thirteen antique chairs, a handful of telephones and a computer, and a lot of clocks showing the time all over the world. But the glass door that slid open automatically and then hissed shut, sealing itself as the ten men and women came in, suggested that there might be more to the place than met the eye. A sophisticated camera blinked quietly in the corridor. The Nexus arrived one at a time, each one entering a different six-digit code before they were allowed in.

Matt wasn't looking forward to seeing them again. He knew that they were supposed to be on his side, but even so, he felt a certain dread entering the room. It was like facing ten head teachers at the same time, knowing he was about to be expelled. There were only two people there who he felt he knew. He had met Susan Ashwood, the medium, at her home near Manchester, and although he had thought she was completely mad, at least he was fairly sure that her heart was in the right place. And he had gotten to know Nathalie Johnson in the past few months. She was the American computer billionaire who had helped Scott and Jamie, and she had traveled down to Nazca a couple of times to make sure they were all right.

But that still left eight strangers. There was an Australian, broad and bullish with a round face and close-cropped hair. His name was Harry Foster and he owned a newspaper empire. Next to him, there was a bishop who dressed like a bishop and talked like a bishop but who hadn't actually told Matt his name. He was about sixty years old. Tarrant, the senior policeman who had helped put taps on Scarlett's phone, was at the head of the table, dressed in a smart blue-and-silver uniform.

Among the others, Matt had noted a Frenchman in an expensive suit, a small Chinese man who was continually rubbing his hands, a German who was something big in politics, and two others who had made no impression on him at all. They might all be world leaders. But tonight they just looked tired and scared.

Richard, Jamie, and Matt had taken their places at the table, bunched together at one end. The three of them were in a gloomy mood. Every word that they spoke, every second that passed, only carried Scarlett Adams farther away from them.

"We made a mistake." Nathalie Johnson came straight to the point. "We knew who she was. We knew where she lived. We should have approached her ourselves."

"It was my fault," Susan Ashwood said. "I didn't want to frighten her. I thought it would be easier for her if she heard it all from you." She turned to Matt. "I hoped you'd be here sooner. I didn't realize we'd have to wait for the new passports."

"I thought you had people watching her," Matt cut in. "Weren't there two private detectives or something?"

"They were ex-policemen," Tarrant said. "Duncan and McKnight. Good men, both of them. I've worked with them before." He paused. "Scarlett may have caught sight of them. They were parked in a car outside a park in Dulwich and they had to be more careful after that. They kept their distance. But they were still on top of the case. Until last night . . ."

"What happened?" Richard asked.

"They've both disappeared. Vanished without a trace. I've tried to contact them, but I haven't had any luck. I have a feeling they may have been killed."

There was a brief silence while the rest of the room took this in. It was obvious to all of them that they had underestimated the Old Ones. From the moment Scarlett had been identified, they had been running rings around the Nexus.

"So why has she gone to Hong Kong?" Matt asked.

"Her father is there," Tarrant replied. "He's a lawyer. He works for the Nightrise Corporation."

"Nightrise?" Jamie spoke for the first time. Jet lag had hit him badly, and he was exhausted. He'd only managed to keep himself awake with a black coffee and a can of Red Bull. "They're the people who came after Scott and me. Are you saying her dad is one of them?"

"Nightrise is a legitimate business," Nathalie Johnson reminded him. "They have offices all over the world. They employ thousands of people. The vast majority of them probably have no idea who — or what — they're working for."

"Still —"

"We don't know, Jamie. His name is Paul Adams. He's divorced. He and his wife adopted Scarlett fifteen years ago, and as far as we can tell, he doesn't know anything about the Old Ones."

"So what do we do now?" Richard asked. "Scott and Pedro are still in Peru. Matt and Jamie are here. And Scarlett will soon be in Hong Kong. The one thing we know is that we have to get the five Gatekeepers together. How are we going to do that?"

"You may have to follow her there."

It was the bishop who had spoken, and the other members of the Nexus nodded. But for his part, Matt wasn't so sure. He knew nothing about the city except that some of the toys he'd played with when he was younger had been manufactured there. MADE IN HONG KONG. It had always been a sign that they would probably break five minutes after they came out of the packaging. Certainly, he had no desire to go there. He had flown enough for one week.

"If I may . . ." The Chinese man had a soft, very cultivated voice. He hadn't spoken until now. He was small, with heavy, plastic glasses and an off-the-rack suit. Perhaps he adopted this sort of appearance on purpose. It was as if he didn't want to be noticed. "My name is Mr. Lee," he said, bowing his head toward Matt. "If you are thinking of making the journey to Hong Kong, I may be able to help you. I have connections throughout Asia, especially in that area. However, I would like to make one observation if I may."

He waited for someone to speak against him, as if he was nervous that there might be someone at the table who didn't want to hear what he had to say. When nobody protested, he went on.

"There is something very strange happening in Hong Kong," he began. "I know the place well. In fact, I was there — passing through — just a week ago. On the face of it, there is nothing I can put my finger on. Life continues as normal. Business is done. Tourists arrive and leave. But there is something in the city that makes no sense. How can I put it? There is an atmosphere there that is not pleasant. Friends of mine who live there, people I have known for many years, seem to be in a hurry to leave, and when I ask them why, they are afraid to say. Those who remain are nervous."

"The Old Ones are there," Susan Ashwood said, as if she had known all along. She worked as a medium, talking to ghosts. Matt wondered if they had told her.

"That is what I believe, Miss Ashwood," Mr. Lee agreed. "It is hardly a coincidence. Nightrise is based in Hong Kong. It is quite possible that much of the city is now in the control of the Old Ones. And if that is the case, then the moment this girl, Scarlett Adams, arrives there, it will be as if she is in prison, and none of us will be able to reach her."

"We have to reach her," Richard said. "If we don't, we might as well all pack up. There have to be five Gatekeepers."

Mr. Lee nodded. "Then we have to get her out of there — and that means following her. We have failed here in London. Maybe Matthew and Jamie will have more success over there."

"You want to send the two of them to Hong Kong?"

"They have certain powers, Mr. Cole, which may be of use to them," Mr. Lee said. "In my opinion, they must find a way to enter the city, but without the Old Ones knowing they are on their way."

"The two of them traveled here with false names and false ID," Tarrant said. He sounded disapproving. "They can use them again."

"Absolutely." The Australian, Harry Foster, banged a fist on the table. "They could be on the next flight out of here. There must be fifty thousand people a day flying in and out of Hong Kong. Who's going to notice a couple of kids in a crowd like that?"

"I don't agree." Susan Ashwood shook her head. "If

Mr. Lee is correct and the Old Ones are there, it would be complete madness to attempt to go in by air. Matt and Jamie would be seized the moment they stepped off the plane — I don't care how many people there are at the airport."

"I have an office in Hong Kong," Harry Foster said. "I could look in there on my way back to Australia. Why don't you let me try to find her? I can explain what's going on and she — and her father, for that matter — can leave with me. I'll take them down to Sydney, and you can pick them up there."

"I think it's too dangerous," Mr. Lee said.

"Well, at least I can get a message to her. Let her know the score." The Australian took out a pad and scribbled a note to himself. "A letter to warn her that she's in danger. I can get someone in my Hong Kong office to deliver it by hand."

"I think we have to be very careful," Susan Ashwood said. "We all know what happened today. The Old Ones were waiting outside her house in Dulwich. They knew Matt was on his way and they were determined to stop him." She glanced at Tarrant. "You had two men watching Scarlett, and now you say they may have been killed. How many more mistakes do we have to make before we realize what we're up against?"

"Then maybe it's time to use one of the doors," Richard said.

He had the diary and he slid it onto the table in front of him. All ten members of the Nexus stared at it. Only a few months before, they had been prepared to spend two million pounds to get their hands on it, and here it was, right in front of them. They wanted to reach out and touch it. And yet at the same time, they were afraid of it, as if it was a snake that might bite.

"I've been trying to work this out ever since Ramon brought it to us," Richard went on. "I've read bits of it, though I won't pretend I've understood very much . . . even with a Spanish dictionary and a magnifying glass. But there is one thing we do know: Twenty-five doors were built around the world for the Gatekeepers to use. They all connect with each other and they can all be found in sacred places. One of them is in St. Meredith's. When Matt went through it, it took him directly to the Abbey of San Galgano in Tuscany."

"Scott and I found one of the doors in a cave at Lake Tahoe," Jamie added. "It took us to the Temple of Coricancha in Cuzco, Peru."

"That's four of them," Richard said. "But there are twenty-one more, and our friend, the mad monk, may have helped us. He's made a list. . . ."

He unfastened the diary and opened it, laying it flat so that everyone could see. Everyone leaned forward. There was a very detailed map covering two pages, drawn in different colors of ink. It was just about recognizable as the world, although a world seen by a child with only a basic knowledge of geography. America was the wrong shape, and it was too close to Europe. Australia was upside down.

Joseph of Cordoba had used more care decorating his work. He had sketched in little ships, crossing the various oceans with their sails unfurled. Insect-size animals

poked out of the different landmasses, helping to identify them. There was a tiger in India, a dragon in China
and, at the North Pole, what could have been a
polar bear.

"I don't know how much you know about old maps,"
Richard said, "but for what it's worth, I studied them a bit
at university. I did politics and geography. This one is
fairly typical of the sixteenth century. That was a time
when maps were becoming more important. Henry VIII
was one of the first monarchs to realize how much they
could give away about a country's defenses. And everyone
was using them to steal everyone else's trade routes. You
see these little bags here?" He took out a pencil and
pointed. "They're probably bags of spice. Joseph may have
drawn them to represent the Spice Islands because that
was what everyone wanted."

"There are stars," Jamie said.

They were scattered all over the pages — the five-
pointed stars that he and Matt knew so well.

"That's right. There are twenty-five of them — one for
each door. The only trouble is, like a lot of the maps being
drawn at the time, this one isn't very accurate. As far as I
can make out, there seem to be doors in London, Cairo,
Istanbul, Delhi, Mecca, Buenos Aires, and somewhere in
the outback of Southern Australia. There's one here, close
to the South Pole. But the world's changed quite a lot in
five hundred years, and trying to identify the exact loca-
tions isn't going to be easy."

"You mentioned a list," Tarrant said.

"Yes. . . ." Richard turned a page, and sure enough,
there was a long row of names, all of them in tiny

handwriting. "The problem we've got here is that the names don't quite match up with the modern places, and half of them are in Spanish. Here's one, for example: Muerto de Maria. It took me half the night to work that one out."

"The death of Mary," the bishop translated.

"Or Mary's death," Richard said. "Do you get it? Marydeath. Or the church of St. Meredith in London. It's like a crossword clue, although I don't suppose Joseph was doing it on purpose to confuse us. Coricancha isn't named at all. It's just represented by a flaming sun — but then, of course, the sun was sacred to the Incas."

"Is there a door in Hong Kong?" Matt asked.

"There's certainly a door somewhere nearby," Richard said. He turned the page back to the map. "You can see it here — and if you look at the list, there's a reference to a place called Puerto Fragrante and a little dragon symbol. But that could be anywhere."

"May I see?" Mr. Lee reached out and took the diary in both hands, holding it as if he was afraid it was about to crumble away. He looked at the map, then the list, then turned another page. "Someone has written in pencil," he said. "The words 'Tai Shan.'" He glanced at Richard. "Was that you?"

Richard shook his head. "That must have been Ramon," he said. "He made notes all over it when he was trying to decipher it for Salamanda, but as far as I can see, he didn't have time to work out too much. Anyway, he was mainly focusing on the Nazca Lines."

"There is a door in Hong Kong!" Mr. Lee exclaimed. "I can tell you that for certain. And I can even tell you exactly where it is." He laid the diary down. "Puerto Fragrante — the Spanish for Fragrant Harbor, I think — is another clue," he said. "In Cantonese, Fragrant Harbor translates as Heung Gong. Or in other words, Hong Kong. The city was originally given that name because of the smell of sandalwood that drifted across the sea. Whoever studied the diary has been good enough to confirm it for us. Tai Shan means 'the mountain of the East.' It is where the sun begins its daily journey. It is also the place where human souls go when they die. There is a very old and very sacred temple with that name in Hong Kong, in a part of the city called Wan Chai. . . ."

There was a sense of relief in the room. It was as if they had all made their minds up. Even Susan Ashwood nodded her head in agreement and seemed to relax. Only Matt didn't look so sure.

"You could leave tonight," Harry Foster said. "If things went your way, you could actually be there to meet her at the airport. You could pull her out before the Old Ones even knew you'd arrived."

"Wait a minute," Matt said. "We flew here from Miami because we didn't think the doors were safe. Why has anything changed?" Nobody answered, so he went on. "Salamanda had the diary. He'll have found out about the temple. . . ."

"Not necessarily," Foster insisted. "This guy, Ramon, was working on it. But he may not have passed on everything he knew. Anyway, Salamanda's dead."

"Maybe there is an element of risk. . . ." Susan Ashwood began.

"It's more than a risk. It's a trap."

Matt hadn't sat down and worked it out. It was just that all the doubts that had been in his mind had somehow come together, and he could suddenly see everything very clearly.

"The whole thing is a trap," he said. "And it always has been, right from the start. Why were we attacked in Nazca? Why was Professor Chambers killed? It's because the Old Ones wanted to get us on the move. They wanted us to do exactly what we've done.

"Think about it. Scarlett Adams goes through the door at St. Meredith's, and instantly the whole world knows about her. She's in all the newspapers, and the Old Ones find out who she is. And then, the very next day, Ramon turns up in Nazca. Somehow he's managed to track us down. He tells us that he's managed to steal the one thing we most want, and he hands it across without even asking for money. Why? Because he goes to church! Because he's planning to get married! His whole story was ridiculous. And it wasn't true. The Old Ones wanted us to have the diary."

"They killed him to get it back," Nathalie said.

"Did they? I think Ramon was as surprised to get that fence post through his chest as we were to see it happen. He must have been programmed — either drugged or hypnotized — to stop Scott and Jamie seeing into his mind. And then they killed him to make us believe that he had been telling the truth. Otherwise, it would have all seemed too easy."

Matt took a breath. Normally, he didn't like being

the center of attention, but this time he knew he was right.

"All along, there was something that bothered me about that night in Nazca," he went on. "If they really wanted the diary back so badly, why did they send such a small force? What happened to the giant spider, the fly soldiers, the shape-changers, the death-riders?" He turned to Jamie. "You've seen them. You've fought them. Nazca was peanuts compared to what you went through."

Jamie nodded but said nothing.

"They want me to come to Hong Kong. That's what this has all been about." Matt was getting tired. He had no idea what time it was according to his body clock. He just wanted to crawl into bed and forget everything for ten hours. "First of all, they got us out of Nazca. They managed to split us up. And now they've given us a nice invitation to walk straight into their hands. The moment I go through that door, I'll be finished. They're using Scarlett to get at me. I hurt them. I wounded their leader, Chaos — the King of the Old Ones, or whatever he calls himself. They want to make me pay."

There was a long silence.

"What do you want to do, Matt?" Susan Ashwood asked. And that made a change. Normally the Nexus told him what they wanted him to do.

"I still have to go to Hong Kong," Matt said.

"Matt —" Richard began.

Matt stopped him. "What Miss Ashwood said was right. They're not going to let any of you get anywhere near Scarlett. It has to be the two of us, Jamie and me. And you too, Richard, if you want to come. But maybe we can use this situation to our advantage. The Old Ones expect us to turn up in the Temple of Tai Shan. That's how they've arranged the trap. But suppose we arrive another way? We could still take them by surprise."

"You could go in by sea," Foster said. "There are cruise ships going in and out of Hong Kong all the time."

"May I suggest something?" Mr. Lee interrupted, asking permission again. "The best way to enter Hong Kong might be through Macao. It is part of China, a small stub of land on the South China Sea — and like Hong Kong, it is a Special Administrative Region, which is to say, it is — at least in part — independent. You can fly from one to the other in a very short time. Helicopters make the journey several times a day."

"And how do we get to Macao?" Richard asked.

"You cannot fly there direct. I believe you will have to go via Singapore. But it is, if you like, a back door into Hong Kong — and one that the Old Ones may have overlooked." He took out a handkerchief and polished the lenses of his glasses. "More than that, I have a connection in Macao who may agree to help you. He has many resources. In fact, if anyone knows the truth about what is going on in that part of the world, it will be him."

"Wait a minute. . . ." Richard was worried and he didn't try to hide it. He was wishing he'd never mentioned the diary in the first place. "Matt, are you really sure you have to go there?" he asked. "You've already said that it's you that they want. You say it's a trap. Now you're walking straight into it."

"We need Scarlett," Matt replied simply. "They have her. We can't win without her." He looked round. "Jamie, will you come with me?"

Jamie shrugged. "I've always wanted to see Hong Kong."

"Then it's agreed." Matt turned back to Mr. Lee. "How quickly can you get in touch with your friend?"

"His name is Han Shan-tung," Lee replied. "He is a man with great influence. He has many friends inside Hong Kong. But it may not be easy to find him. He travels a great deal. You may have to wait."

"We can't wait."

"It will just be a few days. But trust me. It would be foolish to enter the city without his support."

A few days. More waiting. Matt thought about Scarlett. In a few hours' time, she would be landing in Hong Kong. What would she find when she got there? How would she manage on her own?

But there was no other way. Somehow she would have to survive until he got there. He just hoped it wouldn't be too long.

FIFTEEN
Wisdom Court

The nightmare started almost from the moment Scarlett arrived at Hong Kong Airport.

She was still a Skyflyer Solo, and the airline had arranged for an escort to meet her at the plane and take her through immigration and customs. His name was Justin, and he was dark-haired, in his early twenties, dressed like a member of the cabin crew.

"Did you have a good flight?" He spoke with an Australian accent and seemed friendly enough.

"It was okay."

"You must be tired. Never mind — I'll see you through to the other side. Is this your first time in Hong Kong?"

"Yes."

"You're going to love it here!"

He prattled on as Scarlett followed him to passport control. It would have been easy to find her own way — there were signs written in English as well as Chinese — but she was glad to have company after eleven hours of sitting on her own in what had felt like outer space. The worst thing about the flight hadn't been the length or the boredom — it had been the sense of disconnection. She was going somewhere she didn't want to go, not even knowing why she was going there. What could be so urgent that her father had made her travel all this way? And why hadn't he been able to tell her on the phone?

The airport was surprisingly quiet, but then, it was only six o'clock in the morning and perhaps there hadn't been that many international flights. Even so, Scarlett felt uneasy. She examined the people around her as they stood on the travelator, being carried down the wide, silver-and-gray corridors. The other passengers looked more dead than alive, bleary-eyed and pale. Nobody was talking. Nobody seemed happy to be there.

And there was something else that struck her. Everyone was heading the same way. They were all pouring into the main building. People might be arriving in Hong Kong but, this morning, at any rate, no one seemed to be leaving.

They arrived at immigration, joining a queue that snaked back and forth up to a line of low, glass booths with officials in black-and-silver uniforms, seated on low stools. They all looked very much the same to Scarlett — small, with brown eyes and black, spiky hair.

And then it was her turn. The official who took her passport and arrivals card was young, polite. He opened the passport and examined her details, and as he did so, she noticed a surveillance camera just above him swivel round to examine her too. It was quite unnerving, the way it moved without making any sound, somehow picking her out from the rest of the crowd.

"Scarlett Adams." The official spoke her name and smiled. He wasn't asking her to confirm it. He was just reading it off the page as if he didn't quite understand what it meant. Then he reached out for his stamp, inked it, and brought it down on the passport with a bang.

And at that exact moment, he changed. Did it really happen or was her mind playing tricks with her after the long flight? It was his eyes. As the stamp hit the page, they seemed to flicker as if someone had blown smoke over them. Suddenly they were yellow. The pupils, which had been brown a second ago, were now black and diamond-shaped. The passport official glanced up at her and smiled, and right then she was afraid that he was going to leap out of his booth and tear into her. His eyes were no longer human. They were more like a crocodile's eyes.

Scarlett gasped out loud. She couldn't help herself. She was paralyzed, staring at the thing in front of her. The escort, standing next to her, hadn't noticed anything wrong. Nobody else had reacted. There was a stamp as another visa was issued in the booth next door, and Scarlett glanced in that direction as a student with a back-pack was allowed through. When she looked back, it was over. The official was normal again. He was holding out her passport, waiting for her to take it. She hesitated, then snatched it from him, not wanting to come into contact even with the tips of his fingers, as if she was half expecting them to turn into claws.

"We need to pick up your bags," Justin said.

"Right . . ."

He looked at her curiously. "Is something the matter, Scarlett?"

"No." She shook her head. "Everything's fine."

The suitcases took about ten minutes to arrive. Scarlett's was one of the first off the plane. Justin picked it up for her, and the two of them went through the customs area, which was empty. Presumably nobody bothered smuggling anything into Hong Kong. The arrivals gate was directly ahead of them and Scarlett hurried forward. Despite everything, she was looking forward to seeing her father again.

He wasn't there.

There were about a hundred people waiting on the other side of the barriers, quite a few of them dressed in chauffeur uniforms, some of them holding names on placards. She saw her own name almost at once. It was being held by a black man in a suit. He was tall and bald with a face that could have been carved — it showed no emotion. Somehow, he didn't seem to belong in Hong Kong. It wasn't just his color. It was his size. He towered over everyone else, staring over the crowd with empty eyes as if he didn't want to be there.

There was a woman standing next to him, and Scarlett took a dislike to her at first sight. Was she even a woman? She was certainly dressed in women's clothes, with a gray dress, an anorak, and fur-lined boots that came up to her knees. But she had the face and the physique of a man. Her shoulders were broad and square. Her neck was thick-set. She wore no makeup although she was badly in need of it. She had skin like very old leather. She was Chinese and half the height of the chauffeur, with black hair hanging lifelessly down and thick, plastic glasses that wouldn't have flattered her face even if there had been something to flatter. She reminded Scarlett of a prison warden. It was impossible to guess her age. Forty? Fifty? She didn't look as if she had ever been young.

Scarlett went over to her.

"Good morning, Scarlett," the woman said. "Welcome to Hong Kong. I hope you had a good flight."

"Who are you?" Scarlett asked. She wasn't in any mood to be polite.

The woman didn't take offense. "My name is Mrs. Cheng," she said. "But you can call me Audrey. This is Karl." The man in the suit lowered his head briefly. "Shall we go to the car?"

"Where's my dad?"

"I'm afraid he couldn't come."

"Where is he?"

"I will explain in the car."

The escort — Justin — had listened to all this with growing concern. It was his job to hand Scarlett over to the right person and that clearly didn't seem to be the case here. "Excuse me a minute," he interrupted. He turned to Scarlett. "Do you know these people?"

"No," Scarlett said.

"Well, I'm not sure you should go with them." He turned back to the woman. "Forgive me, Mrs. Cheng. I was told I was delivering this girl to her father. And I'm not sure . . ."

"You're being ridiculous," Mrs. Cheng interrupted. "You can see quite clearly that we were waiting for her. We are both employed by the Nightrise Corporation and were sent here by her father."

189

"I'm sorry. She doesn't know you, and right now I'm responsible for her. I think you'd better come over to the desk and talk to my supervisor."

Scarlett was beginning to feel embarrassed to have two adults quarreling over her, especially in the middle of such a public place. But Justin and Mrs. Cheng had reached an impasse. The Chinese woman was breathing heavily, and two dark spots had appeared in her cheeks. She was struggling to keep her temper. Suddenly she snapped out a command, her voice so low that it could barely be heard. The chauffeur, Karl, lumbered forward.

"Now hold on a minute . . . ," Justin began.

It looked as if Karl was going to punch him. But instead he simply reached out and laid a hand on Justin's shoulder, his long, black fingers curving around the escort's neck. There was no violence at all. Then he leaned down so that his eyes were level with the other man's.

And Justin caved in.

"You're making a fuss about nothing," Mrs. Cheng said.

"Yes . . ." He could barely get the word out.

"Why don't you phone the Nightrise offices when they open? They'll tell you everything you want to know."

"There's no need. Of course, the girl can go with you."

"Let him go, Karl."

Karl released him. Justin swayed on his feet, then abruptly walked away. It was as if he had forgotten about Scarlett. He wanted to have nothing more to do with her.

"Let's be on our way, Scarlett. We've wasted enough time here."

Scarlett picked up her suitcase and followed Karl and Mrs. Cheng down an escalator. A sliding door led to a private road with a number of smart executive saloons and limousines waiting for their pickups. Karl took the case and hoisted it into the trunk. Meanwhile, Mrs. Cheng had opened the door, ushering Scarlett into the back.

"Where are we going?" Scarlett asked.

"We will take you to your father's apartment."

"Is he there?"

"No." Audrey Cheng spoke English like many Chinese people, cutting the words short as if she were attacking them with a pair of scissors. "Your father had to go away on business."

"But that's not possible. He just got me out of school. He made me come all this way."

"He has written a note for you. It will explain."

They had left the airport. Karl drove them across a bridge that looked brand-new with steel cables sweeping down like tendrils in a web. The airport had been built on an island, one of several that surrounded Hong Kong. Everything here was cut into by the sea.

They reached the outskirts of the city, and Scarlett saw the first tower blocks, five of them in a row. They warned her just how different this world was going to be, how alien to everything she knew. All five tower blocks were exactly the same. They had almost no character. And they were huge. Each one of them must have had a thousand windows, stacked up forty or fifty floors in straight lines, one on top of another. From the road, the windows looked the size of postage stamps, and anyone looking out of them would have been no bigger than the Queen's head in the corner. It was impossible to say how many people lived there or what it would be like, coming home at night to your identical flat in your identical tower, identified only by a number on the door. This was a city that was far bigger than the people who lived in it. Hong Kong would treat its inhabitants in the same way that an anthill looks after its ants.

The motorway had turned into an ugly, concrete overpass that twisted through more office and apartment blocks. It was only seven o'clock in the morning, but already the traffic was building up. Soon it would start to jam. Looking down, Scarlett saw what looked suspiciously like a London bus, trundling along with far too many passengers crammed on board. But it was painted the wrong colors, with Chinese symbols covering one side. Hong Kong had once belonged to the British, of course. It had been handed back at the end of the nineties, and although it was now owned by China, it more or less looked after itself.

They passed a market where the stalls were still being set up and made their way down a narrow street with dozens of advertisements, all in Chinese, hanging overhead. Finally, they turned into a driveway that curved up to a set of glass doors in a smaller tower block. Scarlett saw a sign: WISDOM COURT. The car stopped. They had arrived.

Wisdom Court stood to the east of the city in what had to be an expensive area, since it had the one thing that mattered in a place like this: open space. The building was old-fashioned, with brickwork rather than steel or glass. It was only fifteen stories high and stood in its own grounds. There was a forecourt with half a dozen neat flower beds and a white marble fountain, water trickling out of a lion's head. There were two more lions with gaping mouths, one on each side of the door. Inside, the reception area could have belonged to a luxury hotel. There were palm trees in pots and a man in a uniform sitting behind a marble counter. Two elevators stood side by side at the end of the corridor.

They went up to the twelfth floor, Karl carrying the luggage. Audrey Cheng had barely looked at Scarlett since they had left the airport, but now she fished in her handbag and took out a key that she dangled in front of her, as if to demonstrate that she really did have a right to be here. They reached a door marked 1213. Mrs. Cheng turned the key in the lock, and they went in.

Was this really where her father lived? The apartment was clean and modern, with a long living room, floor-to-ceiling windows, and three steps down to a sunken kitchen and dining room. There were two bedrooms, each with its own bathroom. But at first sight there was nothing that connected it with him. The paintings on the walls were abstract blobs of color that could have hung in any hotel. The furniture looked new — a glass table, leather chairs, pale wooden cupboards. Had Paul Adams really gone out and chosen it all, or had it been there when he arrived? Everything was very tidy, not a bit like the warm and cozy clutter of their home in Dulwich.

Looking around, Scarlett did find a few clues that told her he had been there. There were some books about the

Second World War on the shelves. He always had been interested in history. The fridge had some of his favorite foods — a packet of smoked salmon, Greek yogurt, his usual brand of butter — and there was a bottle of malt whiskey, the one he always drank, on the counter. Some of his clothes were hanging in the wardrobe in the main bedroom, and there was a bottle of his aftershave beside the bath.

And there was the note.

It was printed out, not written, in an envelope addressed to Scarlett. There wasn't even a signature. Scarlett wondered if he had asked his secretary to type it. He only used two fingers and usually made lots of mistakes. The note was very short.

> *Dear Scarly,*
> *Really sorry to do this to you, but something came up and I've got to be out of Hong Kong for a few days. I'll try to call but if not, enjoy yourself, and I'll see you soon. No need to worry about anything. I'll explain all when we meet.*
> *Dad*

Scarlett lowered the note. "It doesn't say when he'll be back," she said.

"Maybe your father doesn't know."

"But he's the only reason I'm here!"

Mrs. Cheng spread her hands as if to apologize, but there was no sign of any regret in her face. "This afternoon I will take you into the place where your father

194

works," she promised. "We will go to Nightrise, and you will see the chairman. He will tell you more."

Karl had carried Scarlett's suitcase into the spare bedroom. So far he hadn't said a word. He was waiting at the front door.

"I'm sure you're tired," Mrs. Cheng said. "Why don't you have a rest, and we can explore the city later. Maybe you would like to do some shopping? We have many shops."

Scarlett didn't want to go shopping with Audrey Cheng. It seemed that the two of them were going to be together until Paul Adams returned. It wasn't fair. Had she really swapped Mrs. Murdoch for this woman?

"I would like a rest," she said.

"That's a good idea. I will be here. Call if there is anything you need."

Scarlett went into her room. She undressed and had a shower, then lay on the bed. She fell asleep instantly, darkness coming down like a falling shutter.

Once again she returned to the dreamworld, to the desert and the sea. She could sense the water behind her, but she was careful not to turn round. She remembered the creature that had begun to emerge — the dragon or whatever it was — and she didn't want to see it again.

Everything was very still. Her head was throbbing. There was something strange in the air. She looked for the four boys who she had once known so well and was disappointed to find that they were nowhere near.

Something glowed red.

She looked up and saw the sign, the neon letters hanging in their steel frame. They were flashing on and off, casting a glow across the sand around them. But the words were different. The last time she had seen them, they had read: SIGNAL ONE. She was sure of it.

Now they had changed. SIGNAL THREE. That was what they read. And the symbol beside them, the letter T, had swung upside down.

SIGNAL THREE

SIGNAL THREE

What did it mean? Scarlett didn't know. But behind her, far away in the sea, the dragon saw it and understood. She heard it howling and knew that once again it was rushing toward her, getting closer and closer, but still she refused to turn round.

And then it fell on her. It was huge, as big as the entire world. Scarlett screamed, and after that she remembered nothing more.

SIXTEEN
The Chairman

The view was amazing. Scarlett had to admit it despite herself. She had never seen anything quite like it.

It was the middle of the afternoon, her first day in Hong Kong, and she was standing in front of a huge, plate-glass window, sixty-six floors up in the headquarters of the Nightrise Corporation. The building was called The Nail and looked like one too — a silver shaft that could have been hammered into its position on Queen Street. She was in the chairman's office, a room so big that she could have played hockey in it, although the ball would probably have gotten lost in the thick-pile carpet. Paintings by Picasso and Van Gogh hung on the wall. They were almost certainly original.

From her vantage point, Scarlett could see that the city was divided in two. She was staying on Hong Kong Island, surrounded by the most expensive shops and hotels. But she was looking across the harbor to Kowloon, the grubbier, more down-at-heel neighbor. The two parts were separated by what had to be one of the busiest stretches of water in the world, with ships of every shape and size somehow crisscrossing around each other without colliding. There were cruise ships, big enough to hold a small army, tied up at the jetty with little sampans, Chinese rowing boats, darting around them. Tugs, cargo boats, and container ships moved slowly left and right while nimbler passenger ferries cut in front of them, carrying passengers over to the other side and back. There were even a couple of junks, old Chinese sailing ships that seemed to have floated in from another age.

The Hong Kong skyscrapers were in a world of their own, each one competing to be the tallest, the sleekest, the most spectacular, the most bizarre. And there was something extraordinary about the way they were packed together, so many billions of tons of steel and glass, so many people living and working on top of one another — it had already reminded Scarlett of an ant nest, but now she saw it was for the richest ants in the world. There weren't many sidewalks in Hong Kong. An intricate maze of covered walkways connected the different buildings, going from shopping center to shopping center, through whole cities of Armani and Gucci and Prada and Cartier and every other million-dollar designer name.

There was very little color anywhere. If there were any trees or parks, they had been swallowed up in the spread of the city. Even the water was like slate. Although it was late in the day, the light hadn't changed much since the morning. Everything was wrapped in a strange, silver mist that made the offices in Kowloon look distant and out of focus.

While she was being driven there, Scarlett had noticed quite a few people in the street had covered their mouths and noses with a square of white material, like surgeons, so that only their eyes showed. Was the air really that bad? She sniffed a couple of times but couldn't detect anything wrong. On the other hand, the air in the car was almost certainly being filtered. The same was true of the office. The windows here were over an inch thick, cutting out all the noise and the smells of outside.

"It's quite a sight, isn't it?"

Scarlett turned round. A man had crept up on her without making any sound. He was a European, about sixty, with white hair and thin, silver glasses and, although he was smiling, trying to be friendly, she found herself recoiling from him . . . as if he were a spider or a poisonous snake. There was something very unnatural about the man. He had clearly had a lot of work done to his face — Botox or plastic surgery — but there was a dead quality to his flesh. His eyes were a very pale blue, so pale that they had almost no color at all.

This was the chairman of the Nightrise Corporation. It had to be. He was wearing an expensive suit, white shirt, and red tie. Very successful people have a way of walking, pushing forward as if they expect the world to get out of the way, and that was how he was walking now. He had a deep, throaty voice — he could have been a heavy smoker — and spoke with a faint American accent. There was a silver band on the middle finger of his left hand. Not the wedding finger. Scarlett somehow doubted that he would be married. Who in their right mind would choose to live with such a man?

"It's all right," Scarlett said.

The chairman seemed disappointed by her reaction.

"There is no greater city on the planet," he muttered. He pointed out of the window. "That's Kowloon. Some people say that the best reason to go there is to admire the views back again, but there are many museums and temples to enjoy too. You can take the Star Ferry over the water. The crossing is quite an experience, although it is one I have never enjoyed."

"Do you get seasick?"

"No." He shook his head. "When I was twelve years old, a fortune-teller predicted that I would be killed in an incident involving a boat. I'm sure you will think me foolish, but I am very superstitious. It is something I have in common with the Chinese. They believe in luck as a force, almost like a spirit. This building, for example, had to be built in a certain way, with the main door slanting at an angle and mirrors placed at crucial points, according to the principals of feng shui. Otherwise, it would be considered unlucky. And you see over there?" He pointed to a factory complex on the other side of the water, in Kowloon. "How many chimneys does it have?"

Scarlett counted. "Five."

"It has four real chimneys. The extra one is fake. It is there because 'four' is the Chinese word for death — but on the other hand, they believe that five brings good luck. Do you see? They take these things very seriously, and so do I. As a result, I have never been close to the water and I have certainly never stepped on a boat."

He gestured at a low, leather sofa opposite his desk. "Please. Come and sit down."

Scarlett did as she was told. He came over and joined her.

"It's a great pleasure to meet you, Scarlett," he said. "Your father told me a lot about you."

"Where is my father?"

"I'm afraid I owe you an apology. I'm sure you were disappointed that he wasn't here to meet you. The fact is that we had a sudden crisis in Nanjing."

"Is that in China?"

"Yes. There was a legal problem that needed our immediate attention. Obviously, we didn't want to send him. But your father is very good at his job, and there was no one else."

"When will he be back?"

"It shouldn't be more than a week."

"A week?" Scarlett was shocked. "Can I talk to him?" she asked.

The chairman sighed. "That may not be very easy. There are some parts of China that have very bad communications. The landlines are down because of recent flooding, and there are whole areas where there's no reception for mobile phones. I'm sure he will try to call you. But it may take some time."

"So what am I supposed to do?" Scarlett asked. She didn't even try to keep the annoyance out of her voice.

"I want you to enjoy yourself," the chairman said. "Mrs. Cheng will be staying with you until your father returns, and Karl will drive you wherever you want to go. There are plenty of things to do in Hong Kong. Shopping, of course. Mrs. Cheng has the necessary funds. There's a Disneyland out on Lantau. We have all sorts of fascinating markets for you to explore. And you must go up to The Peak. Also, I have something for you."

He went over to the desk and opened a drawer. When he came back, he was holding a white cardboard box. "It's a small gift," he explained. "By way of an apology."

He handed the box over and she opened it. Inside, on a bed of cotton wool, lay a pendant made out of some green stone, shaped like a disc and threaded with a leather cord. Looking more closely, Scarlett saw that there was a small animal carved into the center — a locust or a lizard or a cross between the two, lying on its side with its legs drawn up, as if in the womb. It was very intricate. If the work hadn't been so finely done, it might have been ugly.

"It's jade," he explained. "And it's quite old. Yuan Dynasty. That's thirteenth century. Can I put it on you?"

He reached forward and lifted it out of the box. Compared to the delicacy of the piece, his fingers looked thick and clumsy. Scarlett allowed him to lower it over her head, even though she didn't like having his hands so close to her throat.

"It looks beautiful on you, Scarlett," he said. "I hope you'll look after it. It's very valuable, so you don't want to leave it lying around." He got to his feet. "But now I'm afraid I will have to abandon you. I have a board meeting. I'd much rather not go. But even though I'm the chairman, they still won't accept my cry for mercy. So I'll have to say good-bye, Scarlett. It was a pleasure to meet you."

My cry for mercy . . .

Why had he said that? Cry for Mercy was the name of the monastery where Scarlett had been kept prisoner, on the other side of the door. Of course, he couldn't possibly have known that, but nonetheless, he had chosen the words quite deliberately. Was he taunting her? The chairman was already moving back to the desk, but even as he had turned, Scarlett thought she had detected something in his eyes, behind his silver-framed glasses. Was she imagining it? He had just given her an expensive gift. And yet, for all his seeming kindness and concern, she could have sworn she had seen something else. A brief flash of cruelty.

Scarlett spent the rest of the afternoon shopping — or window-shopping, anyway. She didn't actually buy anything, which was unlike her. Back in England, Aidan had often teased her that she'd lash out money on a diving suit if it had the right designer label. But she wasn't in the mood. She wondered if she'd caught a cold. It was still very damp, with a thin drizzle that hung suspended in the air without ever hitting the ground. She was also more aware of the silver-gray mist that stretched across the entire city, even following her into the arcades. The skyscrapers disappeared into it, the top floors fading out like a badly developed photograph. There was no sense of distance in Hong Kong. The mist enclosed everything so that roads went nowhere and people and cars seemed to appear as if out of nothing.

She asked Audrey Cheng about it.

"It's pollution," she replied, in a matter-of-fact voice. "It's not ours. It blows in from mainland China. There's nothing we can do." She looked at her watch. "It's time for supper, Scarlett. Would you like to go home?"

Scarlett nodded.

And then a man appeared, a little way ahead of them. Scarlett noticed him because he had stopped, forcing the crowd to separate and pass by him on both sides. They were on Queen Street, one of the busiest stretches in Hong Kong, surrounded by glimmering shop windows filled with furs, gold watches, fancy cameras, and diamond rings. The man was young, Chinese, dressed in a suit with a white shirt and a striped tie. He was holding an envelope.

"Scarlett —" he began.

He disappeared. The moment he spoke her name, the crowd closed in on him. It was one of the most extraordinary things Scarlett had ever seen. One moment, the people had been moving along the sidewalk — hundreds of them, complete strangers. But it was as if someone, somewhere, had thrown a switch and suddenly they were acting as one. Scarlett tried to look past the seething mass, but it was impossible. She thought she heard a scream. Then the crowd parted. The man was gone.

Only the envelope remained. It was crumpled, lying on the sidewalk. Scarlett moved forward to pick it up, but someone got there ahead of her . . . a pedestrian walking past. It was just a man going home. She didn't even get a chance to look at his face. He snatched up the envelope and took it with him, continuing on his way.

"What was that?" Scarlett demanded.

"What?" Audrey Cheng looked at her with empty eyes.

"That man . . ."

"What man?"

"He called out my name. Then everyone closed in on

him." She still couldn't take in what she had just seen. "He had a letter. He wanted to give it to me."

"I didn't see him," Mrs. Cheng said.

"But I did. He was right there."

"You still have jet lag." Audrey Cheng signaled, and Karl drew up in the car. "It's easy to imagine things when you're tired."

Scarlett was glad to get back to Wisdom Court even though she wished her father had been there to greet her. She was going to sleep in his room. Audrey Cheng had taken the guest bedroom. Karl, it seemed, would spend the night elsewhere. She had been completely shaken by what she had seen. How could a whole crowd behave like that? She remembered the way they had suddenly turned. They could have been controlled by some inner voice that she alone had been unable to hear.

She ate dinner, said good night to Mrs. Cheng, and went to her room. She hadn't finished unpacking, and it was as she took out the last of her clothes that she made a discovery. Someone had placed a guidebook for Hong Kong at the bottom of her suitcase. She assumed it must have been Mrs. Murdoch, and if so, it was a kind gesture — although it was odd that she hadn't mentioned it. She flicked through it. The *World Traveler's Guide to Hong Kong and Macao.* Fully illustrated with thirty color plates and comprehensive maps. It was new.

But that wasn't the only thing she found that night.

Scarlett had brought a little jewelry with her — a couple of necklaces and a bracelet Aidan had given her on her last birthday. She decided to keep them safe by putting them into one of the drawers in the dressing table. As she pulled, the drawer stuck. That was probably why nobody had noticed that it wasn't completely empty. She pulled harder and it came free.

There was a small, red document at the very back. It took Scarlett a few seconds to recognize what it was, but then she took it out and opened it.

It was her father's passport.

Paul Edward Adams. There was his photograph. Blank face, glasses, neat hair. It was full of stamps from all over the world and it hadn't yet expired.

The chairman had lied to her.

If her father had left his passport in the apartment, he couldn't possibly have traveled to China. And now that she thought about it, there had been something strange about the note he had left her. Why had he typed it? It hadn't even been signed. It could have been written by anyone.

It was eleven o'clock in Hong Kong. Four in the afternoon in England. Scarlett got into bed, but she couldn't sleep. She lay there for a long time, thinking of the passport, the passport official with the crocodile eyes, the chairman joking about the cry for mercy, the man who had tried to give her a letter.

She had only been in Hong Kong for one day. Already she was wishing she hadn't come.

SEVENTEEN
Contact

Over the next few days, Scarlett tried to forget what had happened and put all her energies into being a tourist. There had to be another explanation for her father's passport. He might have a second copy. Or maybe his company had been able to arrange other travel documents for his visit to China. It was, after all, just the other side of the border. She made a conscious decision not to think about it. He would be back soon — and until then she would treat this as an extended holiday. Surely it had to be better than being at school.

So she took the Star Ferry to Kowloon and back again and had tea at the old-fashioned Peninsula Hotel — tiny sandwiches and palm trees and a string quartet in black tie playing classical music. She went to Disneyland, which was small and didn't have enough fast rides but was otherwise all right if you didn't mind hearing Mickey Mouse talking in Cantonese. She went up to The Peak, a mountain standing behind the city that offered panoramic views as if from a low-flying plane. There had been a time when you could see all the way to China from there, but pollution had put an end to that.

She visited temples and markets and went shopping and did everything she could to persuade herself that she was having a good time. But it didn't work. She was miserable. She wanted to go home.

For a start, she was missing her friends at school, particularly Aidan. She had tried texting him, but the atmosphere seemed to be interfering with the signal and she got nothing back. She tried to call her mother in Australia, but Vanessa Adams was away on a trip. Her secretary said that she would call Scarlett back, but she never did.

And it was worse than that. Scarlett didn't like to admit it. It was so unlike her. But she was scared.

It was hard to put her finger on what exactly was wrong, but her sense of unease, the fear that something was going to jump out at her from around the next corner, grew and grew. It was like walking through a haunted house. You don't see anything. Nothing actually happens. But you're nervous anyway because you know the house is haunted. That was how it was for Scarlett. Only in her case it wasn't a house — it was a whole city.

First of all, there were the crowds, the people in the street. Scarlett knew that everyone was in a hurry — to get to work, to get to meetings, to get home again. In that respect, all cities were the same. But the people in Hong Kong looked completely dead. Nobody showed any expression. They walked like robots, all of them moving at the same pace, avoiding each other's eyes. She realized now that what she had seen on Queen Street hadn't been an isolated incident. It was as if the city somehow controlled them. How long would it be, Scarlett wondered, before it began to control her too?

The strange, gray mist was still everywhere. Worse than

that, it seemed to be getting thicker, darker, changing color. Mrs. Cheng had said it was pollution, but it seemed to have a life of its own, lingering around the corners, hanging over everything. It drained the color from the streets and even transformed the skyscrapers. The higher floors looked dark and threatening, and it was easy to imagine that they were citadels from a thousand years ago. They didn't seem to belong to the modern world.

And then there was Wisdom Court. From the moment she had arrived there, Scarlett had been aware that something was wrong. It was just too quiet. But after two days there, going up and down in the elevator, in and out of the front door, she suddenly realized she hadn't seen anybody else. There were no sounds coming from the other flats, no doors slamming or babies crying. No cars ever pulled up. No smells of cooking or cleaning ever wafted up from the other floors. Apart from Mrs. Cheng, she seemed to be living there entirely on her own.

Of course, there was the receptionist. She had barely registered him to begin with. He was always sitting in the same place, in front of a telephone that never rang, staring at a front door that hardly ever opened. He wore a black jacket and a white shirt. His face was pale. He never changed. Nobody ever replaced him.

How was that possible? Scarlett found herself examining him more closely. The same man in the same place, morning, noon, and night. Didn't he ever eat? Didn't he need toilet breaks? It could have been a corpse sitting there, and once that thought had entered her head, she found herself hurrying through the reception area, doing her best to avoid him. Not that it would have made any difference. He never spoke to her.

On the third evening, after their visit to Disneyland, she challenged Mrs. Cheng. The Chinese woman was making dinner, tossing prawns and bean shoots in a wok.

"Where is everybody?"

"What do you mean, Scarlett?"

"We're on our own, aren't we? There's nobody else in this building."

"Of course there are other people here." Mrs. Cheng turned up the flame. "They're just busy. People in Hong Kong have very busy lives."

"But I haven't seen anybody. There's nobody else on this floor."

"Some of the apartments are being redecorated."

Scarlett gave up. She knew when she was being lied to. It was just another mystery to add to all the others.

The next day, Mrs. Cheng took her to a market in an area known as Wan Chai. As usual, Karl drove them. By now, Scarlett had gotten used to the fact that he accompanied them everywhere and never spoke. She even wondered if he was able to. His role seemed to be to act as a bodyguard. He was always just a few paces behind.

Scarlett had always liked markets, and in Hong Kong there was a vibrant street life, sitting side by side with the expensive Western shops and soaring offices. She had been keen to explore the Chinese streets, the stalls piled high with strange herbs and vegetables, soup noodles bubbling away in the open air, and the signs and advertisements, all in Chinese, filling the sky like the flags and banners of an invading army.

And yet these markets were full of horrible things. She saw dozens of live chickens trapped in tiny cages and — next to them — dead ones, beaten utterly flat and piled up like deformed pancakes. On the stand next door, there was an eel cut into two pieces, surrounded by a puddle of blood. A goat's head hung on a hook, its eyes staring lifelessly, severed arteries spilling out of its neck. It was surrounded by the other pieces of what had once been its body. And finally, there was a whole fish, split lengthways, the two bloody halves lying side by side. That was in many ways the most disgusting sight of all. The wretched creature was still alive. She could see its internal organs beating.

Mrs. Cheng took one look at it and smiled. "Fresh!" she said.

Scarlett wondered how long she could stay in Hong Kong without becoming a vegetarian.

They continued on their way, walking past a row of meat shops. Mrs. Cheng was going to cook again that night and she was looking for ingredients. As they paused for a moment, Scarlett noticed one of the butchers staring at her. He was completely bald with a large, round head and a strange, childlike face. He seemed fascinated by her, as if she were a film star or visiting royalty. And he wasn't concentrating on what he was doing.

He was chopping up a joint of meat with a small axe. Scarlett watched the blade come down once, twice . . .

On the third blow, the butcher missed the meat and hit his own left hand. She actually saw the metal cut diagonally into the flesh at the wrist, almost completely severing his thumb as well. Blood spouted. But that wasn't the real horror.

The butcher didn't notice.

He raised the axe again, unaware that his hand was lying flat on the chopping board, the thumb twitching, the pool of blood widening. He was so interested in Scarlett that he hadn't noticed what he'd done. Scarlett stared at him in total shock, and that must have warned him, because at that point he looked down and backed away immediately, cradling the injured hand, then disappearing into the dark interior of the shop.

What sort of man could just about cut off his own hand without any sort of reaction? On the chopping board, human blood mingled with animal blood. It was no longer possible to tell which was which.

Scarlett didn't eat meat that night. And as soon as she had finished dinner, she went back to her room. The apartment had cable TV and she watched a rerun of an old British comedy. It didn't make her laugh, but at least it reminded her of home. She was thinking more and more about leaving. If her father didn't arrive soon, she would insist on it. How could this have happened to her? How had she found herself on the wrong side of the world, on her own?

She went over to the window and looked out.

Hong Kong by night was even more stunning than it was by day. The windows were ablaze — thousands of them — and all the skyscrapers used light in different ways. Some seemed to be cut into strange shapes by great slices of white neon. Others changed color, going from green to blue to mauve as if by some sort of electronic magic. And quite a few of them carried television screens so huge that they could be read all the way across the harbor, advertisements and weather information glowing in the night, reflecting in the dark water below.

One such building was directly opposite her. As she gazed out, thinking about the butcher, thinking about the still-living fish that had been cut in half, she found herself being drawn almost hypnotically toward the building. It must have belonged to some sort of bank or financial center — the screen was displaying the performance of stocks and shares. But even as Scarlett watched, the long lists of numbers were wiped from left to right and replaced by four letters in burning gold.

SCAR

It was her own name, or at least half of it. She smiled, wondering what the letters actually stood for. South China Associated Railways? Steamed Chicken And Rice? But then four more letters appeared, tracking from the other side.

LETT

And that was no abbreviation. It *was* her. Scarlett. The two blocks had formed her name, and now they were flashing at her as if trying to attract her attention. She stood at the window, not quite believing what she was seeing. Was someone really trying to send her a message, using an electric sign on the side of a building to get it across?

A few seconds later, the screen changed. Now it had turned white, and the message it was displaying read:

PG 70

Scarlett was taken aback. Maybe she was mistaken after all. What did it mean? PG Tips was a type of tea, wasn't it? PG was also a type of movie rating. But what about the 70?

Scarlett waited, hoping that the sign would change a third time and tell her something more — but nothing happened. It seemed to have frozen. Then, abruptly, it went black, as if someone had deliberately turned it off. At the same moment, she heard police sirens, a lot of them, racing through the streets on the other side of the harbor in Kowloon.

There was a knock at the door.

Scarlett went over to the bed and sat down, then quickly picked up a magazine and opened it. Although she wasn't quite sure why, she had decided that she didn't want to be found at the window. "Come in," she called.

The door opened, and Audrey Cheng came in. She was wearing a tight jersey that showed off the shape of her body — round and lumpy. Her black hair was tied back in a bun. Her eyes, magnified by the cheap spectacles, were full of suspicion. "I just wanted to check you were all right, Scarlett," she said.

"I'm fine, thank you very much," Scarlett replied.

"Are you going to bed?"

"In a few minutes."

"Sleep well." She seemed pleasant enough, but Scarlett saw her eyes slide over to the window and knew exactly why she had come in. It was the message. She wanted to know if Scarlett had seen it.

And it *was* a message — Scarlett was sure of it now. Someone was trying to reach her and had decided that this was the only way. There was some sort of sense in that. A man had tried to hand her an envelope and had been dragged off the sidewalk. Mrs. Cheng and Karl were watching her all the time. Perhaps this was the only way.

But what did it mean? Scarlett had never been any good at puzzles. Aidan had always laughed at her attempts to do a crossword. PG 70. It obviously had nothing to do with tea or movies. Could it be an address, a map reference, the license plate of a car? She went back over to the window and looked out again, but the screen was still dark. Somehow, she doubted it would come back on again.

Eventually, she stopped thinking about it and tried to go to sleep — and that was when the answer suddenly arrived. Maybe not thinking about it had helped. PG. Wasn't that an abbreviation for page? Could it be that someone was trying to make her look at page seventy? But in what? There were about forty or fifty books in the bedroom, most of them old history books that could have nothing to do with Hong Kong.

She got out of bed and picked one off the shelf at random. Sure enough, page seventy took her to a fascinating description of the way Paris had been laid out in the nineteenth century. She tried a dictionary that had been lying on the table. Page seventy began with "Bandicoot . . . a type of rat" and continued with a whole lot of words beginning with *B*. How about a page in the telephone book? That would make sense if someone was trying to get in touch.

And then she remembered. There had been one book that she hadn't packed but that had turned up mysteriously in her luggage. The guide to Hong Kong and Macao.

She went back to her suitcase. She hadn't even taken it out — but then she hadn't needed a guide, not with Karl and Mrs. Cheng ferrying her every step of the way. She carried it over to the light, flicking through to page seventy, and found herself reading a description of a place called Yau Ma Tei — "a very interesting area in Kowloon," the text said. "Yau Ma Tei means 'hemp oil ground' in Cantonese, although you are unlikely to see any around now." There was a photograph opposite a market selling jade, which reminded her of the amulet that the chairman had given her. She was wearing it now and wondered if he had bought it there.

She was about to throw the book down — another false lead — when she noticed something. There was a pencil line against the text. It was so faint that she had almost missed it — but perhaps that was deliberate. The line drew her attention to a single paragraph.

Tin Hau Temple. You shouldn't miss this fascinating temple in a quiet square just north of the jade market. Tin Hau is the goddess of the sea, but the temple is also dedicated to Shing Wong, the city god, and Tou Tei, the earth god. Admission is free. And watch out for the fortune-tellers who practice their trade in the streets outside. If you're superstitious, you can have your palm read or your future foretold by a "bird of fortune."

And at the very end of the paragraph, also in pencil, was a message: *5:00* P.M.

Scarlett didn't get very much sleep that night. Someone was trying to reach her — and the risk was so great that they'd had to take huge precautions. First, they'd slipped a book into her suitcase. Maybe they'd bribed someone at the airport. Then they'd somehow taken over a whole office block to draw her attention to it. The message had been clever too. PG 70. Anyone whose first language was Chinese would have had difficulty working out what it meant. It had taken her long enough herself.

She had to visit the temple and she had to be there at five o'clock. Maybe someone who knew her father would be there. Maybe they'd be able to tell her where he really was.

There was a fire in Hong Kong that night. The office building with the giant screen burned to the ground, and when Scarlett woke up, the air was even darker and hazier than ever, the smoke mixing in with the pollution. She looked out of the window, but she couldn't see the other side of Victoria Harbor. The whole of Kowloon was covered in fog.

Mrs. Cheng was more chatty than usual at breakfast. She mentioned that nine people had been killed and insisted on turning on the television to see what had happened. Sure enough, there it was on a local news channel. The image was a little grainy and the announcer was speaking in Chinese, but Scarlett recognized the building, directly opposite Wisdom Court, right on the harbor front. The images had been taken the night before, and there were flames exploding all around it, the reflections dancing in the black water. Half a dozen fire engines had been called to the scene.

But the firemen weren't doing anything. The camera panned over them. None of them moved. None of them even unwound their hoses.

They just stood there and let the building burn.

EIGHTEEN
Birds of Fortune

The Tin Hau Temple was a low, narrow building, crouching behind a wall and surrounded by trees, almost as if it didn't want to be found. There were tower blocks on every side, the dirty brick walls crowding out the sky. But in the middle of it all, there was a space, a wide square with trees that seemed to sprout out of the very concrete itself. Some benches and tables had been set out, and there were groups of old men playing a Chinese version of chess. A few tourists were milling around, taking photographs of each other against the green, sloping roofs of the temple. The air smelled faintly of incense.

It hadn't been easy getting Mrs. Cheng to bring her here.

From the very start, Scarlett knew she had to be careful. Mrs. Cheng had shown her the news report for a reason. She hadn't been fooled by Scarlett's act of the night before, and she was letting her know it. If Scarlett asked straight out to go to the Tin Hau Temple at five o'clock, she would be more suspicious than ever.

"Is there any news from my dad?" As they cleared the breakfast plates away, Scarlett asked the same question she asked every morning.

"I'm sure he'll call you soon, Scarlett. He's very busy."

"Why can't I call him?"

"It's not possible. China is very difficult." She flicked on the dishwasher. "So where would you like to go today?"

This was the moment Scarlett had been waiting for. She shrugged her shoulders. "I don't know," she said.

"We could go out to Stanley Village. It is on the beach and there are some nice stalls."

Scarlett pretended to consider. "Actually," she said, "I wanted to buy some jade for my friend Amanda."

Mrs. Cheng nodded. "You can find jade in the Hollywood Road. But it's expensive."

"Can't we go to a market?"

"There's a jade market in Kowloon. . . ."

It was exactly what Scarlett wanted her to say. She had read the entire chapter in the guidebook and knew that the most famous jade market in Hong Kong was just round the corner from the temple. If they visited one, they'd be sure to walk over to the other. And that way she would arrive at Tin Hau without even having mentioned it.

She still had to make sure that they got there at the right time, so after they finished clearing up, she announced that she had some schoolwork to do. They didn't leave Wisdom Court until two o'clock. Scarlett would have preferred to have taken the subway that went all the way there, but as usual, Mrs. Cheng insisted that Karl should drive them. That meant he would be with them all afternoon. They were certainly keeping her close.

The jade market was in a run-down corner of Kowloon, just off the Nathan Road, which was a long, wide tourist strip known as "the Golden Mile." Not that there was much gold amongst the rather tacky shops that specialized in cheap electronics, fake designer watches, and cut-price suits. The market was located in a low-ceilinged warehouse, sheltered under one of the huge overpasses that seemed to be knotted into the city.

The pollution was even worse today. The weather was cold and damp, and the mist was thicker than ever. Scarlett could actually feel it clinging to her skin and wondered how the people of Hong Kong put up with it. She noticed that increasing numbers of them had resorted to the white masks on their faces. How long would it be before she joined them?

There were about fifty stalls in the jade market, selling necklaces, bracelets, and little figurines. Keeping one eye on her watch, Scarlett made a big deal out of choosing something, haggling with the stallholders, asking Mrs. Cheng for advice, before finally settling on a bracelet that cost her all of three pounds. As she handed over the money, it occurred to her that Amanda would actually like it — she just hoped that she would be able to give it to her sometime soon.

"Do you want to go back down to the peninsula?" Mrs. Cheng suggested as they came back out into the street. Karl was waiting for them, leaning against the car. He never seemed to have any trouble parking in Hong Kong. For some reason, the traffic cops — if there were any — never came close.

"Not really . . ." Scarlett looked around her. And she was in luck. There was a signpost pointing to the Tin Hau Temple. They were standing right in front of it. "Can we go there?" she said, trying to make the suggestion sound casual.

"We've already visited a lot of temples."

"Yes. But I'd quite like to see another."

It was true. They'd already been to the Man Mo in Central Hong Kong and to the Kuan Yin only the day before. They were strange places. Chinese temples seemed to mix religion and superstition — with fortune sticks and palm readers sitting comfortably among the altars and the incense. The people who went there didn't pray like an English congregation. They bowed repeatedly, muttering to themselves. They left offerings of food and silk on the tables. They burned sacks of paper in furnaces that were kept going for precisely that purpose. Hong Kong had been Westernized in many ways, but the temples could only belong to the East, providing glimpses of another age.

Tin Hau was just like the others. As Scarlett stepped inside, she found herself facing not one but several altars, surrounded by a collection of life-size statues that could have come out of a bizarre comic book: a cross-legged old man with a beard that was made of real hair, two devil monsters, one bright red, the other blue, both of them more childish than frightening. One of them was crying, wiping its eyes and grimacing at its neighbor. The other stood with a raised hand, trying to calm his friend down. There was a china-doll woman carrying a gift and, in a long row, more than fifty smaller figures, each one a different god, perched on a shelf. The temple was a riot of violent colors, richly patterned curtains, lamps, and flowers. The smoke from the incense was so thick that they'd had to install a powerful ventilation system that droned continuously, trying to clear the air.

Scarlett had arrived on time, but she had no idea what she was looking for. There were about a dozen people in the temple, but they were all busy with their devotions. Nobody so much as turned her way. Was it possible that she had misunderstood the passage in the guidebook? It had definitely told her to be there at five o'clock, and it was already a few minutes past. She waited for someone to approach her, to slip another message into her hand — one of the worshippers, or a tourist perhaps. She even wondered if her father might be there.

Nothing happened. Nobody came close. Scarlett knew she could only pretend to be interested in the place for so long. Mrs. Cheng was watching her with growing suspicion. She certainly hadn't shown much interest in temples the day before — so what was so special about this one?

"Have you had enough, Scarlett?" she demanded.

"Who is that?" Scarlett asked desperately, pointing at one of the statues.

"His name is Kuan Kung, the god of war." Something flickered deep in Mrs. Cheng's eyes. "Maybe you should pray to him."

"Why do you say that, Mrs. Cheng?"

"You never know when another war will begin."

In the end, Scarlett had to leave. She had lingered for as long as she could, but it seemed clear that nobody was going to come. She was hugely disappointed. Of course, the note had given her only a time. It hadn't told her what day to be there. On the other hand, it was unlikely that she would be able to find an excuse to return, and slipping out of Wisdom Court on her own was out of the question. Nine people had died when the office on the waterfront had burned down. Maybe whoever had sent the message had been among them.

It was beginning to get dark when they emerged into the square. Karl was sitting on a bench with his arms folded, looking about as animated as the statues they had just seen. A number of stalls were being set up all around. They didn't look particularly interesting — selling socks, hats, reading glasses, and useless bits of bric-a-brac — but they were attracting quite a crowd.

"Can we look at them?" Scarlett asked.

It had only struck her there and then. The passage in the guidebook had described the Tin Hau Temple. But it had also gone on about the square outside. Maybe her secret messenger would be waiting there. Mrs. Cheng scowled briefly, but Scarlett had already set off. She followed.

Scarlett pretended to browse in front of a stand selling cheap alarm clocks and watches. She was determined to spend as much time here as possible. She noticed that the next stall wasn't selling anything. There was a woman with a pack of tarot cards. In fact, now that Scarlett looked around, she saw that at least half the market was devoted to different methods of fortune-telling.

She walked over to a very old man, a palm reader who was sitting on a plastic stool, close to the ground. His stall was decorated with a banner showing the human hand divided into different segments, each one with a Chinese character. He was examining the palm of a boy of about thirteen, his nose and eyes inches away from the skin as if he really could read something there. Scarlett moved on. There was a woman a little farther along, also telling the future. But in a very different way.

The woman was small and round with long, gray hair. She was wearing a red silk jacket, sitting behind a table, arranging half a dozen packets of envelopes that were stacked up in front of her. On one side, there were three cages, each one containing a little yellow bird — a canary or something like it. On the other, she had a mat with a range of different symbols and a jar of seeds. The woman seemed to be completely focused on what she was doing, but as Scarlett approached, she suddenly reached out with a single, gnarled finger and, without looking up, tapped one of the symbols on the mat.

It was a five-pointed star.

Scarlett had seen exactly the same thing on the door that had led her to the Monastery of the Cry for Mercy. She was careful not to give anything away — Mrs. Cheng was standing right next to her — but she felt a rush of excitement. According to Father Gregory, the doors had been built centuries ago to help the Gatekeepers. They were there to help her. Had the woman sent a deliberate signal? Scarlett examined her more closely. She still didn't look up, busying herself with the envelopes and occasionally muttering at the birds.

Scarlett turned to Mrs. Cheng. "What's this all about?" she asked.

"She uses the birds to tell fortunes," Mrs. Cheng explained.

The old woman had heard the English voices and seemed to notice Scarlett for the first time. She squinted at her and muttered something in Chinese.

"She's offering to tell your fortune," Mrs. Cheng translated. "But it will cost you thirty Hong Kong dollars."

"That's about two pounds."

"It's a complete waste of money."

"I don't care." Scarlett dug in her pocket and took out the right amount. She set it down on the mat and took her place on the plastic seat on her side of the table. The fortune-teller folded the money and transferred it to a little purse that she wore around her neck. Then she reached for a white card and laid it in front of Scarlett. She said something to Mrs. Cheng.

"She wants you to make a choice," Mrs. Cheng explained.

There were a number of categories set out on the card, written in both Chinese and English. Scarlett could choose which part of her life she wanted to know about: family, love and marriage, health, work, business and wealth, or study.

"Maybe I should choose family," she said. "She may be able to tell me what's happened to my dad."

"Your father will be home very soon, Scarlett."

"All right, then. Love and marriage." Scarlett tapped the words on the card and thought briefly of Aidan. She wondered what he was doing right then.

The fortune-teller took the card away and selected one of the piles of envelopes, which she had spread out in front of the three cages. Each cage had a door in the front, and she opened one of them. The little yellow bird hopped out as it had been trained to do, perched on the line of envelopes, then pulled one out with its beak. The old woman rewarded it with a couple of seeds, and the bird obediently hopped back in again. It was all over very quickly.

The woman opened the envelope and handed Scarlett the slip of paper that had been inside.

"Do you want me to translate it for you?" Mrs. Cheng asked.

Scarlett glanced at the sheet. "No, it's okay," she replied. "It's in English."

"Tell me what it says."

"'Good news from Fortune Bird Two.'" Scarlett read out the words. "'You will find your true love in the month of April. Your marriage will be long and happy, and you will travel to many countries. When you are old, you will make a great sum of money. Spend it wisely.'" She folded the page in half. "That's it."

"The note only tells you what you want to hear," Mrs. Cheng remarked.

"The bird chose it for me." She held out the page so that Mrs. Cheng could see it. "There you are. You can see for yourself. I'm going to be rich."

Mrs. Cheng nodded but said nothing. The two of them and Karl walked back to the car. And all the time, Scarlett's heart was racing as she kept the piece of paper close to her. She had folded it quite deliberately. She had only shown Mrs. Cheng half of what had been written.

227

For underneath the printed fortune, there had been another message, written by hand:

Scarlett.

You are in great danger. Do not let the woman read this. Come to The Peak tomorrow afternoon. Follow the path from Lugard Road. We will be waiting.

We are your friends. Trust us if you want to leave Hong Kong alive.

NINETEEN
The Peak

Scarlett knew something was wrong the moment she opened her eyes.

A glance at her bedside clock told her that it was eight o'clock in the morning, but for some reason the sun wasn't reaching her bedroom. It wasn't just cloudy. It was actually dark. What was going on? She turned over and looked at the window. At first she thought that someone had drawn a black curtain across the glass, but then she realized that it wasn't on the inside. It was outside. How was that possible, twelve floors up? She propped herself on one elbow, still half asleep, trying to work it out.

And then the curtain moved. It seemed to fold in on itself, and at the same time Scarlett heard the beating of tiny wings and understood what she was looking at. It was a great swarm of insects, black flies. They had attached themselves to the window like a single living organism.

She lay where she was, staring at them with complete disgust. She had never seen so many flies, not even in the heat of the summer. And this was a cold day in November! What had brought them here? How had they managed to fly across an entire city to come together on a single pane of glass? She could hear their buzzing and the soft tapping as they threw their bodies against the window. She could make out their legs, thousands of them, sticking to the glass. Their wings were blurring as they held themselves in place. Scarlett felt sick. She was suddenly terrified that they would find their way in. She could imagine them swirling around her head, a great black mass, crawling into her nostrils and mouth. On an impulse, she scooped up her pillow and threw it at the window. It worked. As one, the flies peeled away. For a moment they looked like a long silk scarf, hanging in the breeze. Then they were gone.

For about twenty minutes, Scarlett stayed where she was, almost afraid to get up. She didn't like insects at the best of times, but this was something else again. She knew that what she had seen was completely impossible . . . just like the door in the church of St. Meredith's. And that told her what should have been obvious all along.

She had thought that, at the very least, her sudden departure to Hong Kong would be an escape from what had been happening in London — the monastery, the sense of being followed, the restaurant that had blown up. But of course it wasn't. It was a continuation, part of the same thing. The events that had closed in on her in London had followed her here. She was caught in the same trap. And here it was even worse. She was far from her friends and family, alone in a city that seemed to be hostile in every way.

This was all happening because she was a Gatekeeper. She remembered what Father Gregory had told her. He had talked about an ancient evil . . . the Old Ones. Scarlett didn't know exactly what they were, but she could imagine the worst. They were here, in Hong Kong. That would explain everything. The Old Ones were toying with her. They were the ones who were controlling the crowd.

What was she going to do?

She could march into the kitchen and tell Mrs. Cheng that she didn't want to wait for her father, that she was taking the next flight back to London. She could telephone her mother in Australia or Mrs. Murdoch or the headmistress at St. Genevieve's. They would get her out of here. She could even contact the police.

But she knew that none of it would work. The forces ranged against her were too powerful. She could see it every time she went outside. Hong Kong was sick. There was a sort of cancer that had spread through every alleyway and every street and had infected everyone who walked there. Did she seriously think that they were just going to let her walk out of here? So far, they hadn't threatened her directly. That hadn't been part of their plan. But if she challenged them, if she tried to assert herself, they would close in on her, and it would only make her situation worse.

She had just one hope. The people who were trying to reach her — they had to be on her side. *We are your friends.* That was what they had told her. She just had to behave normally until she reached them. Then, once she knew what was really happening, she would be able to act.

She got up and got dressed. The fortune-teller's note was beside the bed, but now she tucked it away beneath the mattress. Whoever her friends were, they were being very careful. They were contacting her in four separate stages: the guidebook hidden in her luggage, the illuminated sign across the harbor, the bird of fortune at Tin Hau, and finally a meeting this afternoon. The question was, how was she going to persuade Mrs. Cheng to take her back to The Peak?

They had already been there once. Victoria Peak was the mountain that rose up behind Hong Kong, a must-see for every tourist. Scarlett had gone there on the second day, taking the old wooden tram — it was actually a funicular railway — up the slope to the top, five hundred yards above the city. The views were meant to be spectacular, but they hadn't seen very much on account of the pollution. Maybe that was the answer. If the weather cheered up, it would give her an excuse to go back.

Mrs. Cheng was in the kitchen, cooking an omelette for Scarlett's breakfast.

"Good morning, Scarlett."

"Good morning, Mrs. Cheng."

"Did you sleep well?"

"Very well, thank you."

As Scarlett sat down, it occurred to her that she had never seen the woman eat — not so much as a mouthful. Even when they went to restaurants together, Mrs. Cheng ordered food only for Scarlett. In fact, she had only ever shown hunger once. That had been at the market when they examined the hideous, sliced-in-half-but-still-living fish.

"So where would you like to go today, Scarlett?" They

were exactly the same words she had used the day before. And she spoke without any real enthusiasm, as if it was simply what she had been programmed to say.

"Why don't we go back to The Peak?" Scarlett suggested. "We didn't see anything very much last time. Maybe we'll get a better view."

Mrs. Cheng looked out of the window. "There's a lot of cloud," she remarked.

"But it's going to cheer up this afternoon," Scarlett said. "I saw the forecast on TV." It was grim outside, with a nonstop drizzle sweeping across the sky. And the forecast had said it would stay the same for the rest of the week. But somehow Scarlett knew she was right.

"I don't think so." Mrs. Cheng shook her head. "Maybe you would like to go to the cinema?"

"Let's see what it's like this afternoon," Scarlett pleaded. "I'm sure it will clear up."

And against all the odds, it did. At around two o'clock, the clouds finally parted and the sun came out, still weak against the ever-present pollution, but definitely there. Even Mrs. Cheng had to agree that it was too nice an afternoon to stay indoors, and so the two of them set out.

The receptionist was in his usual place as they left Wisdom Court, sitting stiffly behind the desk and wearing the same dark suit and white shirt, watching them with no expression at all. As they went past, Scarlett noticed something. The man had a black spot, a mole, on the side of his face. At least, that was what she thought. Then the spot moved. It crawled over his cheek and began to climb up, and she realized that it was actually a fly, one of the fat, black insects that had come to her window that morning. The receptionist didn't move. He didn't try to swat it. He didn't even seem to have noticed it. He did nothing as the creature reached the corner of his eye and began to feed.

Scarlett couldn't get out of the building fast enough. Wisdom Court was only a few minutes from the tram station — they could have walked, but Karl drove them anyway. At least he had decided not to come to the top. Mrs. Cheng bought tickets for the two of them, and she and Scarlett got onto the tram.

Although the station looked new, the tram itself had been built more than a hundred years before. Climbing on board was like stepping back in history. They took their places on the polished wooden seats, and a short while later, with no warning, they set off, trundling up the tracks through thick vegetation with occasional glimpses of the city, ever smaller and more distant as they went. There were about twenty tourists sharing the ride, some of them small children, laughing and pointing. Watching them, Scarlett wished that she could be part of an ordinary family, out here on holiday. She was only a few seats away from them, but they could have been inhabiting a different world. Had they really got no inkling about what was happening in Hong Kong? Was she the only one to feel the all-pervading sense of evil?

We will be waiting.

She focused her mind on what lay ahead. Who would be there and why had they chosen The Peak, of all places? Maybe it was because it was outside the city, away from the buildings. At the summit, there would be no crowds, no surveillance cameras. It was somewhere with room to breathe.

The tram arrived and the passengers poured out, straight into a complex that seemed to have been specially built to make as much money from as many tourists as possible. From the outside, it looked like a bizarre observation tower, like something out of *Star Wars*. Inside, it was full of tacky shops and restaurants with a Madame Tussauds and a Ripley's Believe It or Not with signs inviting visitors to COME AND SEE THE WORLD'S FATTEST MAN. Scarlett couldn't wait to get out.

"Let's go for a walk," she suggested. She was careful to sound as innocent as possible.

Mrs. Cheng looked doubtful. She wasn't dressed for a walk — in a short, gray skirt, black stockings, and high-heeled shoes. "Maybe a short way . . . ," she muttered.

There was a distinct chill in the air as the two of them made their way down a slope, passing a man who was sweeping leaves. Scarlett knew what she was looking for: a path that led off from the Lugard Road. That was what the fortune-teller's note had said. She saw the sign almost at once. Without even waiting for Mrs. Cheng to catch up, she set off.

The path was three miles long, snaking all the way round the mountain, paved all the way. On one side, there was The Peak itself, with a tangle of exotic trees and bushes hanging overhead. On the other was an iron railing, to prevent anyone from falling down the hill. There weren't many other people around. The changing weather must have dissuaded them, and the other tourists who had come up in the tram had all stayed inside. Soon Scarlett found that she and Mrs. Cheng were entirely on their own.

There was a strange atmosphere on The Peak. The mist had returned, hanging in the air, almost blotting out the sun. Everything was washed out, dark green and pale white. There were birds whistling, squawking, and rattling in the undergrowth, but none of them could be seen. The path was lost in the clouds and it was impossible to see more than fifty feet ahead. As she made her way forward, Scarlett found it easy to imagine that she had somehow traveled back in time, that this was some Eastern version of Jurassic Park and that a dinosaur might be waiting for her round the next corner.

But then she arrived at an observation point where the vegetation had been cut back and Hong Kong appeared, sprawled out below. It was incredible to see so many skyscrapers packed together on both sides of the water. There were hundreds of them, every shape and size, made small and insignificant by the distance — with millions of people invisible among them.

Mrs. Cheng plodded along behind, saying nothing. Her face was sullen, her hands — loosely curled into fists — hung by her side. Scarlett was quietly amused. Her guardian clearly wasn't enjoying the visit. She wasn't even bothering to glance at the view.

A couple of people walked past them — a woman pushing an old-fashioned stroller and a man, jogging. The man was wearing a blue tracksuit, and his face was covered by an anti-pollution mask, with only his eyes showing above the white square. Scarlett tensed as each one of them approached. She was waiting for someone to make contact. But neither of them so much as noticed her, both continuing on their way.

They walked for another five minutes, still following the path that curved round the side of The Peak.

"I think we should go back, Scarlett," Mrs. Cheng said.

"But it's a circular walk," Scarlett protested. "If we keep going, we'll find ourselves back anyway."

Three more walkers appeared ahead of them: two men and a woman, all Chinese. They were dressed in much the same way, with jeans, zip-up jackets, and walking shoes. One of the men had a walking stick although he looked young and fit and surely didn't need it. The other man carried a backpack. He was in his thirties, with glasses and a pockmarked face. The two of them were chatting. The woman — she was slim and athletic, her long hair tied back with a pink band — was listening to an iPod. As they drew nearer, they showed no interest in Scarlett at all.

The three of them drew level.

"Scarlett . . . ," Mrs. Cheng began.

She never finished the sentence. The man with the backpack reached behind him and drew out something that was flat and silver. It was a move that he must have rehearsed many times. To Scarlett's eyes, it was as if he had suddenly produced an oversize kitchen knife. Then she realized what it was: a machete. The blade was about two feet long and razor-sharp. At the same time, the other man twisted the handle of his walking stick, revealing the sword that had been concealed inside. Scarlett saw the glint of metal and heard it slice the air as he pulled it free. The woman wasn't armed. She was looking behind her, checking that the path was clear.

Both men plunged their weapons into Audrey Cheng. The Chinese woman screamed — but there was nothing remotely human about the sound. It was a high-pitched howl, almost deafening. Scarlett stared in horror. Mrs. Cheng's face was unrecognizable, her mouth stretched open in a terrible grimace. Blood was pouring in a torrent over her lower lip. Her eyes had clouded over. She hadn't had time to defend herself or react in any way. Scarlett saw her neck open as if it were hinged and she looked away. She heard the thud as Mrs. Cheng's severed head hit the ground. She knew it was a sound that she would never forget.

The woman ran forward and put an arm around Scarlett, comforting her. Some of Mrs. Cheng's blood had splattered onto her. There were flecks of it on her jacket. The very air had gone a hazy red.

"I'm sorry you had to see that, Scarlett," the woman said in perfect English. "Don't look. We had to do it. There was no other way."

"You killed her!" Scarlett was in shock. She had never liked Mrs. Cheng, but she couldn't believe what she had just seen. These people hadn't given her a chance to defend herself. They had murdered her in cold blood.

"Not her. It."

Scarlett stared. "What do you mean?"

"Show her!" one of the men snarled.

"We're your friends," the woman said. "We sent you the message with the fortune-teller. We've come to help you and, believe me, there was no other way." She placed her hands on Scarlett's shoulder. "Turn round and have a look for yourself," she went on. "The woman isn't what you think. She's a shape-changer. We'll show you, but then you have to come with us. They'll know what's happened. They'll have heard her. We don't have much time. . . ."

Scarlett turned round. The man with the sword-stick was already sheathing it. The other was wiping his machete on a piece of cloth. She swallowed hard, not wanting to do this. There was a lot of blood, spreading across the path.

Mrs. Cheng was lying on her back, her legs in their black stockings lying straight out in front of her. There was a dreadful wound in her chest where one of the blades had stabbed her through the heart. The other had decapitated her. Scarlett forced herself to examine the rest of the body. She saw something thick and green coming out of the jacket where Mrs. Cheng's neck should have been. It had been severed halfway up. But it didn't belong to a human body. It looked like part of a snake.

And the head, lying on the path, wasn't human either. It was the head of an oversize lizard, with yellow-and-black diamond eyes, scales, a lolling forked tongue. Scarlett glanced back at the body. Mrs. Cheng had thrown out one of her arms as she fell. It was also covered in scales.

A shape-changer.

That was what they had said. And in the shock of the moment, all Scarlett could think was — Was this the creature she had been living with since she had come to Hong Kong? Audrey Cheng had cooked for her. She had been sleeping in the same apartment. And all the time . . .

She thought she was going to be sick. She couldn't get the hideous images out of her head. But then she heard the sound of an approaching engine, coming down the path toward her. Had they been discovered? The woman and the two men weren't moving. They didn't look alarmed. Scarlett relaxed. Whoever was coming was part of the plan.

A motorbike appeared, speeding round the corner. It was a silver Honda, being ridden by a figure in black leather, gloves, and boots. Scarlett guessed that it was a man, but it was hard to be sure as his head was concealed by a helmet with a strip of mirrored plastic across his face. He stopped right in front of them, the wheels tilting underneath him, one leg stretching out to keep the bike upright.

The woman grabbed hold of Scarlett once again. "We need to get you out of here fast," she said. "We don't have time to explain."

"Where are you taking me?"

"Somewhere safe."

They produced a second helmet. Scarlett hesitated, but only for a few seconds. Audrey Cheng's dead body told her everything she needed to know. She had been living in a nightmare, and these people, whoever they were, were rescuing her from it. She grabbed the helmet and put it on, then climbed onto the bike, putting her arms around the driver. At once they were away. She felt the engine roar underneath her as they shot down the path. She tightened her grip, afraid that she would be blown over backward by the rush of wind.

They shot past a man walking a dog and then a family of local people who had been posing for a photograph but who scattered to get out of the way. They turned another corner. If they went much farther, they would surely arrive back at the tram station where Scarlett had begun. On one side there was a small park, on the other, a driveway leading up to a house, for there were a few private homes scattered along the upper reaches of The Peak. But that wasn't where they were heading. Scarlett saw a parked car with two more men waiting. They skidded to a halt.

She got off, quickly removing her helmet. The two men were young, in their twenties, both wearing jeans and sweatshirts. One was Chinese, but the other was a foreigner, maybe from Japan or Korea. They both hurried over to her, their faces filled with a mixture of determination and fear.

"You have to come with us," the first one said. He had a thin face, and his nose and cheekbones were so sharp-edged that they could almost have been folded out of paper. "We must leave at once."

"Where are we going?"

"Somewhere safe." That was exactly what the woman had said. "Not far. Maybe twenty minutes."

"Wait —"

"No time." He spoke in fractured English, spitting out the words. "You want to die, you stay here. You ask your

241

questions. You want to live, get in the car. Now! They will be coming very soon."

"Who will be coming?"

"Shape-changers. Or worse."

The other man had gone over to the car. But he hadn't opened the door. He had opened the trunk.

"You don't expect me to get in there!" Scarlett said.

"It must be this way," the thin-faced man insisted. "You can't be seen. But you'll be all right. We make airholes. . . ."

"No . . ." It was too much to ask. Scarlett didn't care how many shape-changers there might be, making their way up The Peak. She wasn't going to be locked in the trunk of a car by two people she had never met before and driven off to God knows where. "You can forget it —" she began.

The man had whipped something out of his pocket, and he grabbed her before she knew what he was doing. She felt a handkerchief being pressed against her face. She kicked out, trying to knock him off balance, but he was too strong. The fumes of some sort of chemical, sweet and pungent, crept into her nose and mouth. Almost at once, all the strength drained out of her. She felt her legs fold, and the world spun. And then she was falling, being guided into the trunk, which had become a huge black hole waiting to swallow her up.

The end came very quickly. Darkness. Terror. And then the welcome emptiness of sleep.

TWENTY

Lohan

She was in a cage, not lying down but standing. And there was something strange. The wall was moving. It seemed to be scrolling downward in front of her. Or was it she who was moving up?

As consciousness returned, Scarlett realized what was happening. She was in an elevator, one of the old-fashioned kind with a folding iron gate instead of a door. What she was looking at was the brickwork between floors in what had to be a very tall building. She was pinned between the Japanese man and the one she had decided to call Paper Face. They were supporting her. She could still taste the drug — chloroform or whatever it was — that had knocked her out.

Scarlett groaned and the two men immediately tightened their grip. There was no chance she was going to start a fight in such a confined space, but she had already struggled at the car, and they weren't taking any chances.

"You are safe now," Paper Face said.

"Where am I?"

"You will see . . . very soon."

The elevator slowed down to a stop, and the Japanese man jerked the cage door open. They stepped out into a long, dimly lit corridor with walls that were either grimy or had been deliberately painted the color of grime. There were doors every few feet. The whole place looked like a cheap hotel.

There was a Chinese man guarding the corridor with a machine gun cradled across his chest. The sight of the weapon struck Scarlett as completely bizarre. It was like something out of a gangster film. But the man didn't look anything like her idea of a gangster. He was dressed in jeans and a loose-hanging shirt. He was skinny, with a wispy beard, a tattoo on his neck, and a gold tooth prominent at the front of his mouth. A drug dealer, perhaps? Looking at him, it was hard to believe that he was on her side.

The two men took her to the fourth room along the corridor. Paper Face knocked and the door was unlocked from inside. They entered. Machine Gun stayed where he was, opposite the elevator.

Scarlett found herself in a large, almost empty apartment that looked as if someone had recently moved out . . . or in. There were a few pieces of furniture, some of them covered in dust sheets, and no decoration — no carpet, no lamp shades, no pictures on the walls. The windows had been blanked out with sheets of paper. Scarlett wondered why. They had to be fairly high up, so surely there was no chance of anyone looking in. An archway led into a small kitchen, and there was a corridor on the other side, presumably with a bedroom and bathroom at the end.

Another man had been waiting for her to arrive. He

was Chinese, more smartly dressed than the others — in a gray suit and gray T-shirt — and everything about him radiated confidence and control. Was he the one in charge? He examined Scarlett briefly. His eyes were very dark, almost black, and gave nothing away. There was a thin scar starting high up on his left cheek and then slanting diagonally across his lips so that the two halves of his face didn't quite meet, like a reflection in a broken mirror. But, even so, he was handsome. Scarlett guessed that he was barely more than twenty years old.

"How are you?" he said. "You must have been very frightened by your ordeal. I'm sorry that there was no other way."

"Who are you?" Scarlett demanded. "Where am I, and who are these people? What do you want with me? And what was that with Mrs. Cheng? They said she was a shape-changer. What does that mean?" Once the questions had started, they wouldn't stop.

The man held up a hand. He had long, elegant fingers, like a piano player. "We have a great deal to say to each other," he said. "Would you like a drink?"

"No, thank you."

"But I would." He nodded and Paper Face hurried into the kitchen. The man was obviously used to being obeyed. He turned back to Scarlett. "Please, come and sit down."

Scarlett went over to the sofa. She was surprised how quickly the drug had worn off. She sat down. The man followed her and sat opposite. He moved slowly, taking his time. Everything about him was very deliberate.

"My name is Lohan," he said. "Does that answer your first question? I doubt if my colleagues will have very much to say to you, but I will tell you their names too. The man in the kitchen is called Draco. And this here"—he nodded in the direction of the Japanese man—"is Red. Not their real names, you understand. Just the names they use.

"Your next question — what do we want with you? Very simply, we want to get you out of Hong Kong as quickly as possible. Quite frankly, it would have been better for everyone if you had never arrived, but never mind. We couldn't stop you coming, although we tried. It's remarkable how many people you've already managed to get killed."

He certainly wasn't sparing her feelings. But Scarlett wasn't going to let him intimidate her. "I want to see my father," she said. "Do you know where he is?"

"I'm afraid not," Lohan replied. "I have never even met him. For what it's worth, I would imagine that he is dead. A very great many people have died in Hong Kong in the last weeks. He might have been one of them."

"You're telling me my father's dead! Don't you care? Can't you find out?"

Lohan shrugged. "I've told you. I've never met him. Why should it matter to me whether he is alive or dead?"

Draco came back in from the kitchen, carrying a tray with a small porcelain bowl and a jar of some sort of spirit — vodka or sake. He set the whole thing down in front of Lohan, bowed, and then took his place on a seat beside the front door. Lohan poured himself a drink. He held it briefly between his index finger and his thumb, then threw it back and swallowed. He set the bowl back down.

"You want to know where you are," he continued. "This apartment is in Mong Kok, a couple of blocks north of the Tin Hau Temple, where you had your fortune told. The entire building belongs to us, and with a bit of luck, nobody will come up here. While you remain in this room, you are safe. Every minute you spend outside it, you are in more danger than you can possibly imagine."

"You mean shape-changers."

Lohan ignored her. For a moment he gazed past her, as if focusing on something outside the room. Then he began.

"You have to understand the nature of a city," he said. "You live in London, so maybe what I'm about to say will be obvious to you. All cities are the same. They have an atmosphere. More than that. You might call it a flow. The traffic moves in a certain way. The trains pull in and out of the stations. People go to work, they have their lunch, they go shopping, they go home again. Postmen deliver the post. Policemen patrol the streets. Garbage collectors come out in the evening. The night bus arrives at the right time and picks up the people who are waiting at the stop and takes them where they expect to go. Everyone is obeying the flow, even if they don't realize it, because if they didn't, life would descend into chaos.

"Now, consider Hong Kong. It is one of the most densely populated cities in the world. There are more than seven million people living here. That works out at around 18,000 people per square mile. A few of them are rich. Most of them are very poor. And then there are the millions in between — the doctors and dentists, the shop-keepers, builders, plumbers, teachers —"

"I think I get the point," Scarlett interrupted.

"No, Scarlett — I don't think you do." Lohan hadn't raised his voice. His face was as impassive as ever. But Scarlett realized that she shouldn't have spoken. He wasn't used to being interrupted. "This is the point," he went on. "How many of those people could die, do you think, before you noticed? How many of them could be shot or knifed while they lay in bed before the city seemed any different? Fifty of them? Or five hundred? Or how about five hundred thousand? Can you describe to me, accurately, the man who sold you the ticket when you boarded the tram this morning? Or the driver who took you to The Peak? Or the man who was sweeping the leaves away when you began your walk? Suppose they had all been taken away and replaced with people who looked a little like them but who were not the same? Would you notice? If they and their entire families had been murdered, would you care? We see only what we want to see because that is the way of the city. In a village, in the country, people notice things. But on the streets, we are willfully blind."

"Are you saying that's what's happened?" Scarlett asked. "Ever since I've been here, I've been seeing weird things. And there's nobody living at Wisdom Court. The whole place is empty. Are you saying they were all killed?"

"In the last three months, Hong Kong has been taken over," Lohan replied. "It happened very quickly, like a virus. It is impossible to know how many people have been killed. Anyone who has noticed what has been going on or who has tried to fight it has been removed. What has happened has been so huge, so terrible, that it is almost impossible to understand.

"Of course, some people have guessed, or half guessed, and they have managed to get out, taking their money and their families with them. Ask them why they have gone and they will lie to you. They will say they wanted a change or had new business opportunities. But in truth, they have gone because they are afraid. Other people are aware that Hong Kong has changed. They have stayed here because they have no choice, because they have nowhere else to go. They are frightened too. But they keep their heads down and they go about their daily business in the hope that, if they ask no questions, they will be left alone. If you are poor, Scarlett, if you run a tiny stall in the street, what does it matter who controls the city? All you care about is your next meal. The city can take care of itself."

"Who has taken over Hong Kong?" Scarlett asked, although she already knew the answer.

"They are called the Old Ones," Lohan said. "At least, that is what you call them. In the East, we talk of *gwei*, evil spirits. We have many names for them."

"I know about all this," Scarlett said. "It's what Father Gregory told me."

"Who is Father Gregory?"

"He's a monk. I went through a door in a wall and I met him. . . ."

"This was at the Church of St. Meredith's." Lohan knew the name. Perhaps he had read about it in the newspapers when Scarlett disappeared, but she doubted it. He seemed to know a lot about a lot of things. She wondered how. She still wasn't sure how he fit in. "You have to understand that we have been interested in you for a long time, Scarlett," Lohan said. It was as if he had been reading her thoughts.

"We?"

"I am referring to the organization to which I have the great honor to belong. In fact, we have been watching you since the day you were born." He allowed this to sink in, then went on. "Have you ever wondered how you came to find yourself in the Pancoran Kasih Orphanage in Jakarta? Well, I can tell you. We arranged it. Why were you taken to live in Great Britain, thousands of miles away from your true home? We wanted it."

"Why?"

"To keep you safe. To hide you from the enemies that we knew would one day search for you."

"There was an accident in Dulwich. A white van . . ." Scarlett didn't know why it had come into her mind right then, but she was suddenly sure that it was connected. She had a sense of everything coming together.

Lohan nodded. "It happened when you were thirteen years old," he said. "It was not enough simply to send you far away. My organization had a sacred pledge to protect you, even from your own carelessness. When you stepped in front of the van, one of our people was there to push you out of the way. He was able to save you once. Unfortunately, he was less successful a second time."

"He tried to contact me. In London."

"His task was to give you a message. Under no circumstances were you to come here to Hong Kong. We had hoped to intercept you before you even left for the airport. But by then it was too late. The Old Ones had discovered who you were. They killed him."

"He was waiting for me at the restaurant — the Happy Garden."

Lohan nodded, a tiny spark of anger in his eyes. Perhaps part of him blamed her for the death. "Three people died in the explosion," he said. "And the British authorities didn't even bother to investigate. They just blamed it on us — Chinese gangs fighting each other. What did it matter to them? A few dead *fei jais*." He used the Cantonese slang for petty criminals. "To the police, it just meant more paperwork."

"This all happened because of the church, didn't it?"

It was all making sense. Father Gregory had told her he was going to hand her over to the Old Ones. Scarlett had managed to escape — but not before she had given him her name and address. That had been all he needed. From that moment on she had been in a trap from which there was no escape.

"As soon as you returned, the Old Ones closed in on you," Lohan said. "They knew that they had found one of the Gatekeepers, and they weren't going to let you go. From that moment on, they never let you out of their sight."

Scarlett thought back. She had felt all along that she had been under surveillance, but it was only now that she realized how true that had been. Every movement she had made had been watched. She had been pushed around like a piece on a board game — and the last roll of the dice had brought her here.

"They used my dad to bring me to Hong Kong," she said, and felt a sudden ache of sadness. Where was he?

"We never wanted you to come to this city," Lohan said. "Once you were here, you would be utterly in their power, and you have no idea to what extent that has been true. All day, every day, you have been surrounded by them. Nobody has been allowed to come anywhere near you. Haven't you noticed? Since you have been here, nobody has approached you. Nobody has come near."

"There was a man with a letter . . . ," Scarlett began. "On Queen Street."

Lohan shook his head. "We didn't send him. We knew that it would never have worked." He paused. "The Old Ones control the police, the government, and the civil service. They have made deals with the Chinese authorities — and they have killed anyone who has stood in their way. The hospitals, the fire service, the newspapers, and the television and radio stations all serve them now. They keep constant watch on us through the surveillance cameras in the streets and know what we buy every time we use a credit card. They have taken over the mobile phone network and the Internet. Every call is monitored, every one of the millions of e-mails that are sent every day is read by their spyware. Criticize the government — you die. Even try to tell people what you know — you die. We're back where we started, Scarlett. How many thousands of people can you kill in a city like

252

this without anyone noticing? Only the Old Ones know the answer.

"And they are everywhere. The woman and the driver who pretended to work for your father were both shape-changers. We don't know where they came from or what exactly they are. Many of the crowds that surrounded you were the same. Why do you think Wisdom Court is empty? They wanted to keep you in isolation, and every man, woman, or child who might come into contact with you was either taken away, killed, or replaced."

"Replaced with what?" Scarlett asked.

"With creatures that belong to the Old Ones." Lohan filled the bowl a second time and drank it. The alcohol had no effect on him at all. "The whole city is against you, Scarlett. If you stepped outside now, you would be seen and identified in seconds. That was why you couldn't travel here sitting in a car. It was also why we had to be so careful reaching you. One of my people added the guide-book to your luggage at the airport. Then we bribed the supervisor of an office building and transmitted a message on the screen. The fortune-teller is part of our organiza-tion, and she sent you to The Peak. Four different approaches, and each time we had to be certain that you alone knew our intentions."

"So what am I going to do?" Scarlett couldn't keep the helplessness out of her voice. This is what it came down to. She was stuck in a room in a dirty block of apartment buildings. And outside, a whole city was searching for her. She remembered how the day had begun — even the flies were on their side.

"You must not be weak!" For a moment, Lohan didn't even try to hide his contempt. He spat out the words and his mouth, cut in half by the scar, was twisted into a sneer. "It will not be easy," he said. "The Old Ones chose this city very carefully. You are on an island with only four possible ways out. First, of course, there is the airport, where you arrived. But that is out of the question. Every flight will be watched, and even if we disguise you and give you a false passport, the danger is too great.

"The second possibility would be to travel by Jetfoil to the island of Macao, which is only an hour away. From there you would be able to fly to Singapore or Taiwan. But again there is too much risk. I don't think that you would even get on board before you were spotted. There is a passport control at the terminal, and remember — every single official will be looking for you."

"Can't I go into China?" Scarlett asked.

"It is possible to cross into China at Shenzhen. Many tourists go there to shop because the prices are cheap. But there are police everywhere. The border is well patrolled. And once the Old Ones know you are missing, they will be looking carefully at everyone who crosses."

"So what's the fourth way?"

But she wasn't going to find out. Not then. She hadn't even noticed the telephone in the room, but suddenly it rang. The three men froze, and she saw at once that it wasn't good news. Lohan didn't answer it himself. He gestured at the Japanese man, Red, who snatched up the phone and listened for a moment in silence. He put it down and muttered a few words in Chinese. Scarlett didn't understand what he'd said, nor did she need to. The call was a warning. The Old Ones were here.

Lohan turned to her, examining her as if for the first time. Even now he seemed undisturbed, refusing to panic.

"Have they found us?" Scarlett blurted out the question.

Lohan nodded slowly. "They're outside. The building is surrounded."

"But how . . . ?"

"We seem to have missed a trick." Lohan's eyes were still fixed on her. For a few seconds, he didn't speak. Then he worked it out. "You have something with you," he said. "The woman — Mrs. Cheng or someone at Nightrise — gave you something to wear."

"No —" Scarlett began. But then she remembered. Her hands went to her throat. "The chairman gave me this."

She was still wearing the jade pendant. Now, with trembling fingers, she unhooked it and took it off. The little green stone with the carved insect hung at the end of the chain. She handed it over. "It can't be bugged," she said weakly. "It can't . . ."

Lohan examined it with cold anger. Then he turned it round and dangled it in front of her face.

Scarlett gasped. The creature inside the pendant — the lizard or the locust or whatever it was — was moving. She saw it blink and shift position. Its legs curled up underneath it. One of its wings fluttered. Scarlett cried out in revulsion. The thing was alive. And all this time it had been around her neck. . . .

Lohan laughed briefly and, without humor, closed his fist over the pendant, winding the chain around his wrist.

"What are we going to do?" Scarlett asked.

Before anyone could reply, there was an explosion in the street. It sounded soft and far away, but it was followed at once by screaming and the sound of falling glass. There was the wail of police sirens — not one car but any number of them, closing in from all sides.

Lohan produced an automatic pistol, drawing it out of his back pocket. It was sleek and black, and he handled it expertly, loading it with a clip of ammunition, releasing the safety catch and briefly checking the firing mechanism. "You must do whatever we tell you," he said. "No questions. No hesitation. Do you understand?"

Scarlett nodded.

From somewhere in the building came the first burst of machine-gun fire. Lohan threw the door open, signaled, and together they began to move.

TWENTY-ONE
Across the Roof

Lohan was the first out into the corridor, then Draco and Scarlett, with Red behind. They were all armed, apart from her. The man outside the elevator had unhooked his machine gun and was cradling it in his arms. He didn't look scared. In fact, he was completely relaxed, as if this was all in a day's work.

Scarlett was feeling sick with anger. This was her fault. The jade pendant that she had been given was bugged in every sense of the word — and it had told the chairman exactly where she was. Why had she even worn it? She should have left it beside the bed. But it was too late to think about it now. The Hong Kong police had arrived. They were already on their way up.

Her every instinct would have been to get out of there as quickly as they could, but they were moving slowly, taking it one step at a time. Lohan was listening for any sound, his head tilted sideways, his gun level with his shoulder. Scarlett saw him signal to the man at the elevator, pointing with two fingers, ordering him to stay where he was — probably a death sentence. These people had some sort of code among themselves. They did exactly what they were told no matter what it might cost.

For a brief moment, everything was silent. The police cars had turned off their sirens, and the gunfire had stopped. The corridor was empty. But then, with a surge of alarm, Scarlett saw a blinking light. There were two arrows next to the elevator doors, one pointing up, the other down. One of them was flashing. The elevator was on its way up.

Lohan gestured with the gun. "You follow me. This way."

They set off down the corridor, but it seemed to Scarlett that he was leading them the wrong way. It would obviously have been crazy to have tried taking the elevator, but wouldn't the emergency stairs be somewhere nearby? Lohan was taking them ever farther into the building and away from what was surely the only way out.

But nobody argued. Scarlett still had no idea who Lohan was or what authority he had over the others. He had said that he belonged to an organization that had been looking out for her from the day she had been born, but he hadn't told her what it was called, who ran it, or anything like that. It seemed that he and his people were some sort of resistance, fighting against the Old Ones, the last survivors in a city that had been attacked from within. But they weren't the police. They weren't the army. What did that leave?

It was too late for any more questions. Lohan was moving a little faster, still on tiptoe, making no noise, as if he expected one of the many doors to spring open and someone to jump out. How high up were they? How long did they have before the elevator arrived? The end of the corridor was about a hundred feet away with ten doors on either side. A row of lightbulbs hanging from the ceiling lit the way ahead. Scarlett heard a loud, metallic click and risked a glance back. The man with the machine gun had released the safety catch. Lohan muttered something under his breath.

There was the ping of a bell.

The elevator had arrived.

Scarlett was still watching as the doors opened and yellow light flooded out. The man with the machine gun had positioned himself directly opposite with his shoulders planted against the wall. Without any warning, he opened fire, sending a firestorm of bullets into the elevator. The noise in the confined space was shocking. She could actually feel it, hammering into her ears. But she couldn't see what the man was shooting at. The entire corridor blazed white and red and she heard a high-pitched scream like nothing she had ever heard before, as whatever was inside the elevator was pulverized.

Then something appeared, stretching out of the open doorway. It was impossible to make it out clearly between the gloom of the corridor and the brilliance of the gunfire, the two of them strobing — black, white, black, white — turning everything into slow-motion chaos. Some sort of tentacles, extending themselves into the corridor. They reached the man. One slammed into his face. Another curled around his throat. But it was the third that killed him, punching right through his stomach and dragging him up the wall, a great streak of blood following up behind him. The man was screaming, his legs writhing in agony. But his finger was clenched around the trigger and he was still firing. His last bullets went wild, tearing into the ceiling and floor.

Something spilled out of the elevator. It seemed to be partly human, but there was smoke everywhere now, adding to the confusion. A second creature followed it. The two had come up together. A huge pincer snapped open and shut. Black eyes on stalks. Straight out of a nightmare. It saw Scarlett and the others and began to move with frightening speed.

"Hurry!"

It was the first time that Lohan had raised his voice. He broke into a run. Scarlett followed him, convinced that they didn't have a chance. There was no emergency exit, nowhere else for them to go. Red turned round and fired twice. The bullets had no effect. Then Draco dragged something out of his pocket, brought it to his mouth, and threw it. A hand grenade! The pin was still between his teeth. A door to one of the other apartments opened and Lohan threw himself in, pulling Scarlett with him, just as there was a deafening explosion and an orange ball of flame in the corridor behind.

Scarlett leaned against the wall on the other side of the door. She was choking and there were tears streaming down her face. She wasn't crying. It was the dust and the plaster that had cascaded down, almost blinding her. She wiped a sleeve across her eyes. Red slammed the door shut. It had about half a dozen locks, chains, and bolts, which he fastened, one after another. Lohan snapped out another command. Draco muttered something in reply.

The apartment they were in was very similar to the one they had left but more run-down, with even less furniture. There was a woman living here. She had opened the door to let them in and Scarlett recognized her. It took her a moment to work out where they had met, but then she realized — it was the fortune-teller from the temple. She was standing by the door, blinking nervously. Her three birds were in their cages on a table, hopping up and down, frightened by all the noise.

Lohan hadn't stopped moving. He was heading toward a second door and the kitchen beyond. "This way, Scarlett," he called out.

Scarlett followed him into a room with a fridge and an oven and little else. A large hole had been knocked through the wall. The sides were jagged, with old bits of wire and pipework sticking out. They climbed through the brickwork and into the apartment next door, and then into the one after. Each one had been smashed through to provide a passageway that couldn't be seen from the corridor. The last two apartments were completely abandoned, with dust and rubble all over the floor. They came to a window with a steel structure on the other side. A fire escape. Lohan jerked the window open. They climbed out.

Scarlett found herself standing on a small, square platform with a series of metal ladders zigzagging all the way down to street level, about twenty floors below. It was very cold up there, the air currents rushing between the buildings, carrying the driving rain. She looked down onto the sort of scene she would normally have associated with a major accident. There must have been at least a dozen police cars parked at different angles in the street. They might have turned their sirens off, but their lights were flashing, brilliant even in the daylight. Barricades were still being erected around the building, and all the traffic had been stopped. Men in black-and-silver uniforms were holding the crowds back.

They couldn't go down. The fire escape led into the middle of all the chaos, and the moment they reached the bottom, they would be seized. Worse still, one of the policemen had seen them. He shouted out a warning and pointed. At once a group of armed officers ran forward and began to climb up.

Lohan didn't seem worried. "We don't go down," he muttered. "We go up."

There were just three flights of stairs from the platform to the roof and, aware of the policemen getting nearer all the time, Scarlett made her way up as quickly as she could, keeping close to the wall in case any shots were fired. Draco and Red followed up behind, and a minute later, they had all reached the roof and were squatting there, catching their breath in the shelter of a rusty water tank. The rain was slicing down. Scarlett was already drenched, her hair clinging to her eyes.

Lohan had taken out a phone. He pressed a direct-dial button and spoke urgently into it, then folded it away. The other men hadn't said a word, but they seemed to understand what had been agreed. Then Red muttered something and pointed. Scarlett looked up, wondering what he had seen. And shuddered. She had thought their situation couldn't get any worse . . . but it just had.

There was a cloud of what looked like black smoke in the distance, high above the tower blocks of Kowloon. It was traveling toward them, against the wind. Scarlett knew at once that it couldn't be smoke. It was the swarm of flies. They had come back again. They were heading directly for her.

"Move!"

Lohan set off at once, running across the roof, no longer caring if he was seen or not. He had hung the jade pendant around his neck and Scarlett realized that as long as he was wearing it, the flies would know where he was. That was his plan. It was the reason he had taken it from her. He was protecting her, making himself the target in her place. He leaped over stacks of cable, moving toward the back of the building. Scarlett followed. She still had no idea where they were heading, or how they were going to get down.

They reached the other side and came to a breathless halt. Once again, Scarlett was completely thrown. There was no fire escape, no ladder, no window cleaner's lift. The next apartment block was about fifty feet away and there was no possible means of crossing. Lohan was standing at the very edge of the building. For a moment he looked like a ghost, or maybe a scarecrow with his pale skin and his dark clothes, drenched by the falling rain. His black hair had fallen across his face. The scar seemed more prominent than ever.

"Follow me," he instructed. "Don't look down."

And then he stepped into space.

Scarlett waited for him to fall, to be killed twenty floors below. Instead, impossibly, he seemed to be standing in midair, as if he had learned to levitate. More magic? That was her first thought — but then she looked more closely and saw that it was just an incredible trick. There was a bridge constructed between the two buildings, a strip of almost invisible glass or Perspex — some see-through material strong enough to take his weight. Nobody would have been able to see it from the street or from the air, and even now she might not have been able to make it out but for the rain hitting it and the faint coating of grime that covered the surface. It still looked as if Lohan was suspended between the two buildings. He had walked some distance from the edge of the roof and was standing over the road, the cars and people far below.

It would be Scarlett's turn next.

A door burst open on the roof behind her. Their pursuers had finally reached them, pouring out onto the roof, nine of them, human from the look of them but with dead eyes and pale, empty faces that might have spent years out of the light. Their hair was ragged, their clothes moldering away, and they wore no shoes. Some of them carried long, jagged knives. Others had lengths of chain hanging down to the ground and wooden clubs spiked with nails. Slowly, they began to fan out.

"You — go!" Red pushed Scarlett forward, propelling her toward the glass bridge. "Draco . . ." He finished the sentence in Chinese.

There was no time to argue. The creatures were already getting closer. Red moved toward them, away from the safety of the bridge, his own gun raised in front of him. Scarlett looked down. The bridge had no sides, no safety rails. The surface was wet and slippery. Worse still, because it was transparent, it felt completely insubstantial. She could imagine herself falling through it or losing her balance and plunging over the side. And she could see where she would land. The road was there, waiting for her far below.

Red fired a shot, and the sound of it propelled her forward. She couldn't look back. She couldn't see what was happening behind her. All her concentration was focused on what she had to do. She took one step, then another. Now she was in midair with the wind buffeting her. She felt Draco behind her, urging her on, but fear was paralyzing her. Lohan had told her not to look down — but if she didn't, how could she be sure that her foot was coming down in the right place? The rain sliced into her face, half blinding her. She could feel it running down her cheeks.

There were two more shots, but then they stopped and she heard screaming. Red had been caught, and terrible things were being done to him. Scarlett hated herself for doing nothing to help him. He had stayed behind for her, to give her the time to cross, and she was literally walking out on him. All these people were risking their lives for her. The whole apartment block with its knocked-through walls and this incredible transparent bridge had been prepared for the time she might need it. And the crazy thing was that she still didn't know who they were or why they had decided to help.

Somehow, she got to the other side, taking the last step with a surge of relief. At that exact moment, Red's screams ended and she turned round to see him being held in the air by a group of the creatures who were standing at the edge of the building she had just left. His body was limp. Blood was pouring from a dozen stab wounds in his arms and chest. Then they let him go. He seemed to glide rather than fall through the air, as if he weighed nothing. Finally, he smashed into one of the parked cars, crumpling the roof and shattering the front windshield. An alarm went off. With a screech of triumph, the creatures who had killed him lurched themselves onto the bridge.

Lohan was standing, watching them. He let them get about halfway across before he stretched out a hand and closed it around a lever set in a wall. He smiled briefly, malevolently, and pulled. At once, the bridge collapsed. It was like one of those magic wands used by conjurors at children's parties. The different sections folded, then plunged downward. Five of the creatures went with it, hitting the road in an explosion of bone and blood. The rest were left on the other side, jabbering and shaking their fists, unable to cross.

Behind them, something vague and dark rose up over the side of the rooftop. The swarm of flies had arrived. Lohan signaled and set off across the second apartment block, making for a door on the far side. If he was going to mourn the man who had died, it would have to wait. He went through, waited for Scarlett and Draco, then slammed it shut. There was a flight of stairs on the other side. It led down into a room humming with pipes and banks of machinery. There was a service elevator on the other side. Lohan hit the button and the doors opened at once. The three of them piled in. He pressed two buttons: the ground floor and the basement.

Scarlett stood inside the confined space, panting. Her heart was racing at a hundred miles an hour. It felt unnatural to be suddenly standing still, knowing that there was danger all around, but there was nothing she could do and nowhere she could go as the elevator carried them down. She just hoped there wouldn't be anyone waiting for them at the bottom.

Lohan was completely relaxed, leaning against the back wall, the pendant hanging around his neck. Water was dripping down his forehead, over his eyes. "You are to go with Draco," he said. "I have made arrangements. There are people waiting. You will be safe with them."

"What about you?" Scarlett asked.

"I will lead them away." He lifted the pendant, glanced at it, then let it fall again.

"They'll kill you. . . ."

"If they find me, they will kill me. But my life is not in question here. You are all that matters. You must get away."

"This is my fault." Scarlett felt miserable. She had led the creatures to the apartment. They were only here because of her. "I'm sorry. . . ."

"You are one of the Five!" Lohan stared at her as if he couldn't believe what she had just said. "Do not be sorry. Do not be a little girl. You have the power to destroy them. Use it."

The elevator doors opened. They had arrived at the ground floor. Lohan stepped forward and looked outside. Scarlett could hear the wail of police cars, but there was nobody around, and she guessed that the police hadn't yet worked out that they had crossed from one building to another. But the jade pendant would bring them soon enough. Lohan gave a last instruction in Chinese to Draco and then he was gone. The doors slid shut behind him.

"You stay with me now," Draco muttered.

Red had been killed. The man with the machine gun was dead. Lohan was probably next. But he didn't seem to care.

The elevator continued down to the basement. It opened into an underground parking garage. There was a shiny black car waiting for them, and at first Scarlett couldn't believe what had been arranged for her, what was waiting there beneath the building. But at the same time, she knew it made complete sense. She remembered what Lohan had told her. The entire city was against her. Every policeman, every surveillance camera, every official was looking out for her. How was she meant to get past them all?

The car was a hearse. There was an open coffin in the back, the inside of it lined with cream-colored satin with a pillow at one end. Two men were waiting for her. They were dressed in dark suits, like undertakers, but she recognized them from The Peak. They were the ones who had killed Mrs. Cheng. One of them made a gesture. Scarlett knew what she had to do.

This time she didn't argue. Without hesitating, she climbed into the back of the hearse and lay down. It occurred to her that only a few hours ago, when they had tried to lock her in the trunk of a car, she had thought it would be like being buried alive. And here it was, happening for real.

She laid her head on the pillow. The two men moved toward her. And then once again darkness claimed her as the lid was bolted into place.

TWENTY-TWO

Ocean Terminal

Nobody noticed the hearse as it swung out of the underground parking garage and began to make its way south toward Victoria Harbor. Everyone's attention was on the building where Lohan and his friends had been found. The hearse emerged on the other side, turned left at a set of traffic lights, and set off down the Golden Mile.

It never did more than ten miles an hour. If anyone had been watching it, the fact that it was moving so slowly would only have made it all the more unlikely that it was being used as an escape vehicle. But very soon it had left the crowds and the police cars behind. In the front, the driver and his assistant gazed straight ahead, their grim faces hiding their joint sense of relief.

For Scarlett, it was less easy.

She couldn't see anything. She couldn't do anything. She couldn't even move. She was lying on her back, trapped in a black, airless space with the lid bolted into place only inches above her head. She was completely at the mercy of her own imagination. Every time the car slowed down or stopped, she wondered if they had been discovered. Worse than that, she imagined a nightmare scenario where something had gone horribly wrong and she really was taken to a cemetery and buried alive. Every nerve in her body was screaming. She could hardly breathe.

After what seemed like an hour, she felt the car stop. She heard the doors open and slam shut. A long pause. And then suddenly a crack of daylight appeared, widening as the coffin lid was lifted off. A hand reached out to help her, and gratefully she grabbed hold of it. Gently, she was pulled out like a corpse returning to life. She found herself trembling. After all she had been through, she wasn't surprised.

Where was she? The hearse was parked next to a fork-lift truck in a warehouse filled with pallets and crates. There were skylights in the ceiling, but it was also lit by neon strips, hanging down in glass cages. One of the men had hit a switch that brought a sliding door rumbling down on castors, but before it reached the floor, Scarlett glimpsed water and knew that they were near the harbor. The smell of gunpowder hung in the air. Normally, she might not have recognized it — but there had been plenty of it around in the building she had just left.

The driver was already stripping off his jacket and black tie. The last time Scarlett had seen him, he had been wiping a bloody machete on a cloth up on The Peak. He had been the one with the backpack — long hair and glasses — and he was younger than she had first thought, in his mid-twenties. He was wearing a short-sleeved shirt under the jacket, and she noticed a tattoo on his upper arm, a red triangle with a Chinese character inside.

"My name is Jet," he said. Like all the others, he wasn't bothering with surnames. He spoke hesitant English but with a polished accent. "I will be looking after you now. This is Sing."

The other man came over from the door and nodded.

"Where are we?" Scarlett asked.

"Still in Kowloon. This is our warehouse." Jet walked over to one of the crates and pulled off the tarpaulin that half covered it so that she could read the words stenciled underneath. They were written in Chinese and English.

KUNG HING TAO FIREWORK MANUFACTURERS

"Fireworks?"

"It's good business," Jet explained. "In China, we let off fireworks if someone marries and again when they die. The Bun Festival, the Dragon Boat Festival, the Hungry Ghost Festival, and New Year. Everyone wants fireworks! There are one hundred thousand dollars' worth in this warehouse. I suggest you don't smoke."

"You want Coke?" the man named Sing asked. He still had his walking stick with the sword concealed inside. It had been inside the hearse, but he had yanked it out and carried it with him.

"We have a small kitchen and a toilet," Jet said. "We have to stay here for a while."

"How long?"

"Twenty-four hours. But nobody will find you here. . . ."

"What about Lohan?" Scarlett had been worrying about him. She knew it was her fault that he was in danger.

272

"He will come. You do not need to be afraid. Very soon you will be on your way out of Hong Kong."

Lohan had spoken of four ways to get out of the city, and he had dismissed three of them: the airport, the Jetfoil to Macao, the Chinese border. What did that leave? Scarlett had seen the harbor. Perhaps they were going to smuggle her out on a container ship. First a car trunk, then a coffin. These people wouldn't think twice about packing her into a crate of fireworks and sending her somewhere in time for Bonfire Night.

Sing had gone into the kitchen, and now he came back with three bottles of water and sandwiches on plastic plates. He was still wearing his undertaker's suit, but he had taken off the tie. The three of them ate, sitting cross-legged in a circle on the floor. It was only when she took her first bite that Scarlett realized how hungry she was. She'd had little breakfast, no lunch, and it was now six o'clock.

"It is not possible to take you out on a container ship." Jet had seen her sizing up the crates and must have guessed what was on her mind. "There's too much security. The ports are all watched day and night — and anyway, it will be the first thing that they expect. We will take you out in public, in front of their eyes."

"How?"

He glanced at the other man, who nodded, giving him permission to go on.

"Tomorrow morning, a cruise ship arrives in Kowloon. It will dock at the Ocean Terminal on the other side of Harbor City, just ten minutes from here. It spends a day in Hong Kong on its way from Tokyo to the Philippines and then Singapore. That is where it will take you. The ship is called *The Jade Emperor*, and it will be full of wealthy tourists. You will be one of them."

"How do I get on board?"

"For their own reasons, the Old Ones do not want the world to know that they have taken over this city. That is good. When *The Jade Emperor* ties up, they will have to be careful. There will be security, but it will have to be invisible. They will not want to frighten the tourists. Everything will have to seem normal — and that gives us the advantage. We will smuggle you onto the ship with the other passengers. And once you are there, you will be safe."

"What happens when I get to Singapore?"

Jet shrugged. Sing muttered something in Chinese and laughed. "That is the least of your worries," Jet said. "First of all, you have to survive tomorrow. And remember — there are at least a hundred thousand people who are looking for you. This is a trap, and you walked straight into it. Now that you're here, it's not going to be so easy to get you out."

He wasn't being fair. Scarlett hadn't walked into Hong Kong. She had been deliberately drawn in, and there had been nothing she could have done to avoid it. But she didn't argue. There was no point.

"We will disguise you," he went on. "We will cut your hair and change its color, and we will dress you as a boy. You must learn to walk in a certain way. We will show you. There is a family joining the boat. Their names are Mr.

and Mrs. Soong, and they are part of our organization. Right now, they are traveling with their twelve-year-old son, Eric. You will change places with him and travel on his passport. By midnight tomorrow, you will be in international water and out of danger. Do you understand?"

"How will you make the change?" Scarlett asked.

"We have arranged to meet in a shop in Harbor City. The shop is also owned by us. It pretends to sell tea and Chinese medicine."

"What does it really sell?"

Jet thought for a moment. He was reluctant to answer the question, but for some reason he decided to. "Do you really want to know?" He smiled. "Normally, it sells opium."

• • •

Scarlett spent the night on a mattress behind a row of crates that the two men had arranged to form a private "room." She barely slept at all. It was cold in the warehouse — there wasn't any form of heating — and she had only been given a couple of thin blankets. Every night is trapped between the day before and the day after, and she had never been so torn between the two.

She thought about the creatures she had seen coming out of the elevators, the flies approaching the tower block, and the people — were they actually living people? — who had followed her onto the roof. How could things like that be happening in a modern city — monsters and shape-changers and all the rest of it?

Then she turned her mind to the people she was with. Despite everything that had happened, she still knew almost nothing about them. There were lots of them and they were well organized. Lohan had spoken about them with reverence, almost as if they were a holy order. And yet she had just been told that they sold opium! Opium was a drug that came from the same source as heroin. Could it be that they were some sort of gangsters, after all? They carried machine guns and hand grenades. And although they were helping her, none of them was exactly friendly.

Finally, she thought about the next day and the dangers it would bring, walking onto a cruise ship disguised as a boy. Would it really work — and what would happen to her if it didn't? As far as she could see, the Old Ones didn't want to kill her. Father Gregory could have done that, and he'd made it clear he had other plans. For some reason, they needed her alive.

Lying on her back, gazing at the skylight, she watched night crawl toward day. In the end, she did manage to sleep — but only fitfully. When she woke up, her neck was aching and she felt even more tired than she had been before. Her two bodyguards were already awake. Sing had made breakfast, a plate of noodles, but she hardly ate. Today was her last chance. She knew that if she didn't get out today, she never would.

Nothing happened for the next three hours. Jet and Sing sat silently, waiting, and for some reason Scarlett found herself trying to remember her lines from the school play. She had lost track of the date but guessed that it would be performed — without her — in a couple of weeks' time. All the parents would be there, along with some of the boys from The Hall. She thought of Aidan. And as she sat there, trapped in a warehouse full of fireworks, Dulwich seemed a very long way away. She wondered when, if ever, she would see it again.

Jet's phone rang. He snapped it open and muttered a few words into it, then nodded at Sing, who went and unlocked the door. They opened it just a little bit, enough for Scarlett to see that it had stopped raining outside. Bright sunlight streamed in through the crack, lighting up the dust that hung in the air. Two more people came into the warehouse.

The first of them was Lohan. He went straight over to Scarlett. "Are you okay?" he asked.

Scarlett was relieved to see him. "How about you?" she asked. "What did you do with the pendant?"

"The pendant is on a flight to Australia. Hopefully the Old Ones will follow it there."

"I'm glad you're okay."

"And I will be glad when you have gone."

He gestured at the man who had come with him. The man hurried forward, carrying a canvas suitcase about the size of a weekend bag. This man was quite a bit older than the others, wearing a crumpled cardigan and glasses. He placed the suitcase on the floor and opened it to reveal scissors, hair brushes, lots of bottles, and pads of cotton wool. There were clothes packed underneath.

It was time for Scarlett to change.

Jet dragged one of the crates over and Scarlett sat

down. The older man examined her for a moment, using his fingers to brush her hair back from her face. He nodded as if satisfied, then reached for the scissors.

Scarlett would never forget the way he cut her hair. She wouldn't have said she was particularly vain, but she had always taken care of how she looked. There was something brutal about the way he attacked her, chopping away as if she had no more feelings than a tree. She looked down and saw great locks of her hair hitting the ground, and although she knew that it was necessary and that anyway it would all grow back soon enough, she still felt like a victim, as if she were being assaulted. But the man didn't notice her distress — or if he did, he didn't care.

He kept cutting, and soon she felt something she had never felt before: the cold touch of the breeze against her scalp. He finished her hair with a scoop of gel, then set to work on her face, turning it first one way, then the other, his fingers pressing against her chin. There was absolutely nothing in his eyes. He had done this many times before. It was his business, and he did it well. He just wanted to get it over with as quickly as possible.

He painted her skin with a liquid that smelled of vinegar and stung very slightly, then added a few splotches with a thin brush. After that, he set to work on her eyes. Just when Scarlett thought he had finished, he muttered something to Lohan, the first time he had spoken. His voice was completely flat.

"He wants to put in contact lenses," Lohan explained. "They're going to sting."

They did more than that. The man had to clamp Scarlett's head while he pressed them in, the lens balanced on the end of his finger, and when he backed away, the entire room was out of focus, hidden behind a blur of tears.

"Now you must get dressed," Lohan said.

They didn't allow her any privacy. The four men stood watching as she stripped down to her underwear, and then the man in the cardigan dug a white, padded thing out of his case. Scarlett understood what it was. The boy whose place she was taking must have been quite a bit fatter than her. She slipped the pads over her shoulders and saw at once that she had a completely new body shape and that the slight curve of her breasts had gone. The man handed her a shirt, linen pants, a blazer, and a pair of black leather shoes that added about an inch and a half to her height. Finally he gave her a pair of glasses. The disguise was complete.

"Look in the mirror," Lohan said.

They had brought a full-length mirror out of the kitchen. Scarlett stood in front of it. She had to admit that the transformation was incredible. She barely recognized herself.

Her hair was now short and spiky, held rigidly in place by the gel. Her eyes, which were normally green, were now dark brown, the color magnified by the glasses, which were clumsy and old-fashioned, with plastic frames. There was a touch of acne around her nose. She had become one hundred percent Chinese — a slightly pudgy twelve-year-old who probably went to an expensive private school and dressed like his dad. She even smelled like a boy. Maybe they had put something in all the chemicals they had used.

"Now you must practice walking," Lohan said. "Walk like a boy, not like a girl."

For the next two hours, Lohan kept her pacing up and down with slouching shoulders, hands in her pockets. Scarlett had never really thought that teenage boys were so different in the way they walked, but she was sensible enough not to argue. Finally, Lohan was satisfied. He crouched next to her. "It is time for you to leave," he said. "But there is something I must tell you before you go."

"What?"

She was alarmed, but he held up a hand, reassuring her. "There is a boy who is coming to meet you," he said. "He is on his way already, traveling from England."

Her first thought was that it was Aidan — but that was ridiculous. Aidan knew nothing about what was happening.

"His name is Matt."

The boy in her dream! The boy who had led her through the door at the church of St. Meredith's. Scarlett felt a surge of hope and excitement. She didn't know why, but if Matt was on his way, then she was sure that everything would be all right.

"He is not coming to Hong Kong," Lohan went on. "It is too dangerous here. But he will be in Macao. He is being protected by the Master of the Mountain. He will remain there until he knows that we have been successful and that you have escaped. Then he will follow you, and our work will be done."

"Who is the Master of the Mountain?" Scarlett asked.

"He is a very powerful man." That was all Lohan was

prepared to say. He straightened up. "Don't speak until you are on the boat. If anyone tries to talk to you, ignore them. When you are with your new parents, hold your mother's hand. She alone will talk to you, and you'll smile at her and pretend that you understand. When you are on *The Jade Emperor*, she will take you straight to her cabin. You will remain there until the ship leaves."

"Thank you," Scarlett said. "Thank you for helping me."

Lohan glanced at her, and just for a moment she saw the hardness in his eyes and knew that whatever else he was, he would never be her friend. "You do not need to thank us," he said. "Do not imagine that we are helping you because we want to. We are obeying orders from the Master of the Mountain. You are important to him. That is all that matters. Do not let us down."

They opened the warehouse door and, remembering her new walk, Scarlett went out. She found herself in a concrete-lined alleyway. It was after five o'clock and the light was already turning gray. As she stood there, a car drove past and she flinched, afraid of being seen. But she was a boy now, the son of Chinese parents. Nobody was going to look at her twice. Jet and Sing had joined her. The three of them set off together, making their way toward the main road.

The alleyway came out at the very tip of Kowloon, where the Salisbury Road curved around on its way to the ferry terminals. The harbor was in front of them. Scarlett could see all of Hong Kong on the other side of the water, with The Nail, the headquarters of Nightrise, slanting diagonally out of the very center where it seemed to have been smashed in.

"Walk slowly," Jet whispered. "If you see anyone looking at you, just ignore them. Don't stop . . ."

They walked down the Salisbury Road, passing the Hong Kong Cultural Center, a huge, white-tiled building that looked a little bit like a ski slope. The weather had changed again. The sky was clear and the evening sun was dipping down, the water shimmering silver and blood red. Despite the horror of the last thirty-six hours, everything looked very ordinary. There were several groups of tourists on the promenade, enjoying the view. Crowds of people were pouring out of the terminal for the Star Ferry, on their way home. Young couples walked together, holding hands. Newspaper and food sellers stood behind their stalls, waiting for business. A fleet of ships, all different shapes and sizes, was chugging back and forth.

And all the time Scarlett was thinking: *What is real and what isn't? Which of these people are shape-changers? How many of them are looking for me?* She walked on between Jet and Sing, trying to behave normally but knowing all the time that there were a thousand eyes searching for her. She was already beginning to sweat with all the padding pressing down on her. It made it difficult to breathe.

They passed the Peninsula Hotel. Just a few days before, Scarlett had gone there with Audrey Cheng. They had sat down for tea and sandwiches. It felt like a lifetime ago. They turned into a wide avenue, and she found herself walking past a police station. Two men came out, chatting together in dark blue-and-silver uniforms. Both of them carried guns. Scarlett remembered what Lohan had told her — the Old Ones controlled the police as well as the government and the civil service. These two men would have her description. If they recognized her, it would all be over before they got anywhere near the ship.

But they didn't. They continued past, and it was only when they had gone that Scarlett realized she had stopped breathing. She felt completely defenseless, waiting for someone to shout her name and for the crowd to close in. A few inches of padding and a handful of makeup was all that stood between her and capture. She was terrified that it wouldn't be enough.

Harbor City lay ahead of them. It was just another shopping center, though much bigger than any she had visited with Mrs. Cheng. They strolled in as if that was what they had always intended to do, as if they were just three friends out for an evening's shopping. The interior was very ugly. It was brightly lit with small, boxlike shops standing next to each other in corridors that seemed to go on forever. They were selling the usual goods: jeans and T-shirts and sunglasses and souvenirs, with fewer famous names than could be found in Hong Kong Central and presumably lower prices.

They continued past a luggage store and there, ahead of them, Scarlett saw a neon sign that read TSIM CHAI KEE HERBAL REMEDIES and knew that they had reached the place where the exchange would happen. The shop was directly in front of them. It was filled with cardboard boxes and glass bottles. Three people were standing with their backs to the front door. A man, a woman, and, between them, a boy.

The woman was plump with gray hair, dressed in black. The man was smaller than her, laden down with shopping bags, with a camera around his neck. Their son was dressed exactly the same as Scarlett. They were waiting while the shop assistant wrapped up a packet of tea.

Scarlett walked in. Jet and Sing didn't follow her but continued on their way. At the same time, the boy walked forward, farther into the shop, and disappeared. The man and the woman stayed exactly where they were so that as Scarlett entered, there was a space between them. And that was it. A moment later she was standing between them. The woman paid for the tea. The shopkeeper handed over some change. The three of them left together.

A mother, a father, and a son had gone into the shop. A mother, a father, and a son walked out of it. As they left, Scarlett glanced up and noticed a TV camera in the passageway, trained down on them. She wondered if there was anybody watching and, if so, whether they could possibly have seen anything that might have aroused their suspicions. Still, for the first time, she was feeling confident. She was no longer on her own. She was part of a family now. She would be joining hundreds or even thousands of tourists returning to *The Jade Emperor*. Even the Old Ones with all their agents would be unable to spot her.

The family left Harbor City through a set of huge glass doors that brought them straight out onto Ocean

Terminal. And there was the ship, tied to the quay by ropes as thick as trees. *The Jade Emperor* was massive, with at least a dozen decks, each one laid out on top of the other, with two smoking funnels at the very top. The lower part of the ship was punctuated by a long line of tiny-looking portholes, but farther up there were full-size sliding windows that probably opened onto staterooms for the multimillionaires on board. *The Jade Emperor* was entirely white, apart from the funnels, which were bright green. Crew members, also in spotless white, were hurrying along the corridors, mopping the decks and polishing the brass railings as if it were vital for the ship to look its best before it was allowed to leave.

Scarlett examined her surroundings. The ship was on her left, blocking out the view over to Hong Kong, with a single gangplank, slanting down at its center. On the right, running the full length of the quay, was a two-story building lined with flags. This was the back of Harbor City, the shopping center she had just visited. Between them was a strip of concrete about ten feet wide, which they would all have to walk along if they wanted to go on board.

The way was blocked by a series of metal fences that forced passengers to snake round to a control point where half a dozen men in uniforms were checking passports and embarkation slips. The sun was beginning to set now, and although it still sparkled on the water and glinted off the ship's railings, the actual walkway was in shadow. So this was it. Five minutes and maybe fifty paces separated Scarlett from freedom. Once she was on board

The Jade Emperor, it would be over. Matt was waiting for her. Help had finally arrived. She would set sail, and she would never see Hong Kong again.

The woman acting as Scarlett's mother, Mrs. Soong, said something and reached out for her hand. Scarlett took it, and together they began to walk toward the barrier. Nobody stopped them. Nobody even seemed to glance their way. They passed a restaurant with floor-to-ceiling plate-glass windows and tables and gas umbrellas outside. It was too late for lunch and too early for dinner, so there was hardly anyone there, but as they continued forward, Scarlett noticed a man with gray hair and glasses, sipping a glass of beer. He was partly obscured by the window, but there was something familiar about him, the way he sat, even the way he held his glass. She stopped dead.

It was Paul Adams.

Maybe if she hadn't stopped so abruptly, he wouldn't have noticed her. But now he looked up and stared at her. Even then he might not have recognized her. But they had made eye contact. That was what did it. Even with the spectacles and the contact lenses, the strange clothes and the short hair, the two of them had made the link.

And Scarlett was glad to see him. For the past week she had been worrying about him, wondering if he was dead or alive. She had hated the thought of skulking out of Hong Kong without letting him know, and if there had been any way to warn him what was happening, she would have done so. This was her opportunity. She couldn't just leave him behind.

A second later, he burst out of the restaurant and onto the quay. He still couldn't decide if it was really her. The disguise was that good. But then she smiled at him, and he came over to her, his face a mixture of bafflement and relief.

"Scarly . . . is that you?"

Scarlett felt Mrs. Soong stiffen beside her. Mr. Soong stopped, his face filled with alarm. None of the guards at the passport control had noticed them. Tourists were streaming past on both sides, taking out their documents as they approached the fence. Scarlett knew she would have to be quick. She was risking everything even by talking to him, but she didn't care. She felt a huge sense of relief. Her father was alive.

"Scarly?" Paul Adams spoke her name again, peering at her, trying to see through the disguise.

"Dad," Scarlett whispered. "We can't talk. You have to leave Hong Kong. We're in terrible —"

She didn't finish the sentence.

To her horror, Paul Adams grabbed hold of her, dragging her hand up as if to show her off. His face was flushed with excitement — and something else. He looked demented. There was a sort of terror in his eyes. He was like a man who had just committed murder.

"It's her!" he shouted. "I've got her! She's here!"

"No, Dad!"

But it was already too late. The uniformed policemen had heard. They were already heading toward them. The tourists had stopped moving, and in an instant, Scarlett saw that half of them weren't tourists at all. They began to close in, their faces blank, their eyes shining with triumph. More people appeared, pouring out of the shopping center. Matted hair. Dead, white skin. Their mouths hanging open. Dozens of them. And the flies. They burst into the air like a dark geyser and spread out, swarming overhead.

"Dad . . . what have you done?"

He clung on to her, one hand on her wrist, the other around her neck, strangling her. Mr. and Mrs. Soong stood there, paralyzed, then tried to run. The woman was the first to be brought down. One of the tourists grabbed her. A few seconds earlier he had looked like a grandfather, an Englishman enjoying his retirement. But the mask had slipped. He was grinning and his eyes were ablaze. He was holding her with terrible strength, his hooked fingers gouging into her face, forcing her down to her knees. Then they were all onto her. Mrs. Soong disappeared in a crowd that was moving now like a single creature. Mr. Soong had taken out a gun. He pointed it at one of the approaching policemen and fired. The bullet hit the policeman in the face, tearing a huge hole in his cheek, but he didn't even flinch. He kept on coming. Mr. Soong fired a second time, this time straight into the man's chest. Blood spouted, but still the policeman came. Mr. Soong was trapped. He had nowhere to run. Scarlett saw him push the barrel of the gun into his own mouth. She closed her eyes a moment before he fired.

It was easy to tell the real tourists now. They were screaming, in hysterics, dropping their new purchases and scattering across the quay, unsure what was going on, not wanting to be part of it. A woman in a fur coat slipped and fell. She was immediately trampled underfoot by the rest of the crowd trying to get past. Two men were knocked over the side into the narrow space between the ship and the dock. Scarlett heard them hit the water and doubted that either of them would ever climb out again.

Her father was still holding her. She couldn't believe what he had done. He had deliberately told them she was there. He had been waiting for her all along. And she had helped him. There had been one final trap, and she had fallen into it.

"I'm sorry, Scarly," he was saying. "I had to do it. It was the only way. They've promised that they won't hurt you, and my reward, the reward for both of us — we're going to be rich! You have no idea how much power they have. And we're going to be part of it . . . their new world."

Of course he had been in it all along. He worked for Nightrise. He had invited her here, made her leave school early with no explanation. He had been skulking somewhere nearby, leaving her in their clutches. And finally he had been positioned here, just in case she tried to get onto the ship. . . .

Scarlett thought of all the people who had tried to help her, all the people who had died because of her. Mr. and Mrs. Soong had spent just a few minutes with her, but it had been enough. She had killed them.

She listened to this pathetic man — he was still jabbering at her — and she spat in his face.

Then someone grabbed her from behind. It was Karl. She didn't know where he had come from, but the chauffeur was unbelievably strong. He lifted her into the air, then dashed her down. Her head hit the concrete so hard that she thought her skull must have cracked. A bolt of sheer pain ripped across her vision.

In the final moments of consciousness, she saw a whole series of images, flickering across her vision like an out-of-control slide show. There was Matt, the boy she had never met in the real world, on his way to Macao. There were the other three — Scott, Jamie, and Pedro — gazing at her helplessly. There was the beach where she had found herself night after night. And there, once again, was the neon sign with a symbol that was shaped like a triangle, and two words:

SIGNAL EIGHT

The letters flared in the darkness. Looking through them, she saw the chairman, Audrey Cheng, Father Gregory, and, for one last brief moment, her father.

"It's coming," she managed to whisper to them.

Then the darkness rushed in, slamming into her like an express train, and at that moment she felt something unlock inside her. It was like a window being shattered, and she knew that she would never be the same again.

• • •

Five hundred miles away, in a place called the Strait of Luzon, between Thailand and the Philippines, the dragon heard her. It was there because she had summoned it. The dragon had been sleeping in the very depths of the ocean, but it slowly opened one eye.

SIGNAL NINE

The letters burned in brilliant neon light. There was a symbol beside it, an hourglass, and Scarlett almost wanted to laugh because she knew what it was saying. Time's up. The countdown has begun.

The dragon began to move. Nothing could get in its way.

It was heading for Hong Kong.

TWENTY-THREE

Matt's Diary [3]

I don't think I'm going to be able to write much more of this diary. I don't find it easy, putting all these words together, and anyway, what's the point? Who will ever read it? Richard thought it was a good idea, but really it just fills in time.

I can't believe we've finally made it to Macao. Jamie is asleep, worn out with jet lag after another flight across the world, and Richard is in a room next door. In an hour's time, we're going to meet a man named Han Shan-tung, who can help us get into Hong Kong. We've waited almost a week for him to turn up, and I just hope that we haven't been wasting our time. We have no idea at all what's been happening to Scarlett, whether she is even alive or dead. Harry Foster, the Australian newspaperman who was at the meeting of the Nexus, sent someone to meet her — an assistant from his office. Maybe he managed to track her down, but we never heard. The assistant went missing . . . presumed dead.

The Old Ones are there, waiting for me to arrive. In a way, it's extraordinary that they've managed to keep themselves hidden, but that has always been their way. When I was in Yorkshire, they worked through Jayne Deverill and the villagers who lived at Lesser Malling. In Peru, it was Diego Salamanda. Now it's Nightrise. They like people to do their dirty work for them, and when war finally breaks out, as I know it must, my guess is that they won't reveal themselves until the end. And by then it will be too late. They will have won.

Maybe the five days we had in London were worth it after all. Jamie enjoyed himself, seeing all the sights, and in the end, I enjoyed being with him. Buckingham Palace, the London Eye, Harrods, the London Dungeon. Richard kept us busy, maybe because he wanted to keep our minds off what lay ahead. We also spoke to Pedro and Scott in Vilcabamba, talking on the satellite phone. Pedro is worried about Scott. He still seems far away, as if he isn't even on our side. I know he's angry that I separated him from Jamie, but I still think it was a good idea. He isn't ready yet.

And then the flight. London to Singapore, followed by Singapore to Macao. I'm too tired to sleep. When I've finished this, I'll have another shower. A cold one, this time. Maybe it will wake me up.

I don't know what to make of Macao. If anyone had asked me about it six months ago, I wouldn't even have been able to point to it on a map. I hadn't heard of it. As it turns out, it's a chunk of land, just ten miles from one end to the other. And it's packed with some of the weirdest buildings I've ever seen. Take the ferry terminal. If you're coming in from Hong Kong on the Jetfoil, it's the first building you'll see, and you'd have thought they could have made it a bit welcoming. It's not. It's a slab of white concrete, surrounded by overpasses. It's drab and ugly.

But then you come to the casinos, and you think you must have landed on another planet. Macao makes its money out of gambling . . . horse racing, greyhound racing, blackjack, and roulette. The casinos look like nothing I've ever seen before. One of them is all gold, like a piece of metal bent in the middle. There's another one like a sort of crazy birthday cake. The biggest and the most spectacular reminded me of a giant flower. It was five times taller than anything else in the city. I got a crick in my neck trying to see the top.

The old part of Macao was better. Richard told me that it had once belonged to the Portuguese, and he pointed out their influence in some of the palaces with their pillars, arcades, and balconies jutting out over the street. But it was still a bit of a dog's dinner. The traffic and the crowds were Chinese. The older buildings seemed to be in better condition than the new ones, which were all dirty and falling down. The Portuguese had built pretty squares and fountains. Then the Chinese had come along and added casinos, shops, and apartment buildings, forty or fifty floors high. And now they were all stuck next to each other, like quarreling neighbors.

Jamie was disappointed too. "I once read a book about China," he told me. "It was in the house when we were in Salt Lake City. I never read very much, but it had dragons and magicians, and I thought it must be a really cool place. I guess the book was wrong. . . ."

We were met at the airport by a young Chinese guy

who was carrying a big bunch of white flowers. That was a bit weird, but it was the signal we had been given so we would recognize him. He dumped them straight away. There was a Rolls Royce parked outside, license plate HST 1. I noticed that it had been parked in a no-waiting zone, but nobody had given it a ticket. So that told me something about Han Shan-tung. He likes to show off.

The journey from the airport took about half an hour. It was pouring with rain, which certainly didn't make Macao look any better. Fortunately, it eased off a little by the time we arrived here.

And where are we now?

The driver stopped in front of a wide flight of stairs that climbed up between two old-looking walls that had been painted yellow. The steps were decorated with a black-and-white mosaic, and there were miniature palms growing in neat beds along the side. There were clumps of trees behind the walls. They were still in leaf, filling the sky and blocking out any sight of the shops and apartments. It was like walking through a park. The driver got out of the car and signaled for us to follow him. We grabbed our bags and went about halfway up the stairs, until we came to a metal gate that swung open as we approached.

It wasn't a park on the other side. It was a private garden with a courtyard, a marble fountain that had been switched off, and, beyond, a really amazing house built in a Spanish style. The house was painted yellow, like the wall, with green shutters on the windows and a balcony on the first floor. It looked a bit like an embassy, somewhere you weren't normally allowed. The house seemed to belong to its own world. It was right in the middle of Macao, and yet somehow it was outside it.

"Quite a place," Richard said.

The driver gestured and we went in.

The front door also opened as we walked toward it. A woman was waiting for us on the other side. She was some sort of servant, dressed in a long, black dress with a gray shirt buttoned up to the neck. She bowed and smiled.

"Welcome to the home of Mr. Shan-tung. I hope you had a good journey. Please, will you come this way? I will take you to your rooms. Mr. Shan-tung invites you to join him for dinner at eight o'clock."

It was one of the most beautiful houses I had ever seen. Everything was very simple but somehow arranged for maximum effect so that a single vase on a shelf, sitting under a spotlight, let you know that it was Ming or something and probably worth a million pounds. The floors were polished wood, the ceilings double height, the walls clean and white. As we went upstairs, we passed paintings by Chinese artists. They were very simple and clean, and they probably cost a fortune too.

We all had bedrooms looking out over the garden, on the same floor — Jamie and me sharing, Richard on his own. The beds had already been turned down with sheets that looked brand-new. There was a TV and a fridge filled with Coke and fruit juice. It was like being in a five-star hotel, but (as Richard said) hopefully without the bill.

We were all dirty and tired after so much traveling, and Jamie and I tossed a coin to see who got to shower first. I won and stood naked in a cubicle that would have been big enough to sleep in, with steaming water jetting at me from nine directions. There were robes to put on when we came out. Jamie went next. He was asleep before he was even dry.

I would have liked to have slept.

I've been thinking a lot about the library that I visited. Did I make the right decision? I didn't read the book, and I'm beginning to wish I had. Right now I'm just a forty-five-minute journey away from Hong Kong, and I have no idea what I will find there. The book would have told me. It might have warned me not to go.

But it might also have told me when and how my life will end — and who would want to read that?

It makes me think of a computer game that I used to play when I was living in Ipswich. It was an adventure, a series of puzzles that took you through a whole set of different worlds. Shortly after I met Kelvin, he showed me how to download a cheat. It gave me all the answers. It took away the mystery. Suddenly I knew everything I wanted — but here's the strange thing. I never played the game again. I just wasn't interested.

Why did the Librarian show it to me? What was the point he was trying to make? And for that matter, who was he? He never even told me his name. When I think about it, the dreamworld really annoys me. It's supposed to help us, but all it ever gives us is puzzles and clues. I know that it's important to what's going to happen, that it's there for a reason. One day, perhaps, I'll find out what that reason is.

I've written enough. It's twenty to eight. Time to wake Jamie and to meet our host. Han Shan-tung.

Hong Kong is waiting for us. It's out there in the darkness, but I can feel it calling.

Very soon now, I will arrive.

TWENTY-FOUR
Master of the Mountain

Han Shan-tung was one of the most impressive men Matt had ever seen. He was like a bronze Buddha in a Chinese temple. He had the same presence, the same sense of power. He wasn't exactly fat, but he was very solid, built like a sumo wrestler. You could imagine him breaking every one of your fingers when you shook hands.

His hair was black. His face was round, with thick lips and hard, watchful eyes. He was elegantly dressed in a suit that was obviously expensive, possibly silk. His fingers, resting on the table in front of him, were manicured, and he wore a slim, silver wedding ring. There was a packet of cigarettes and a gold lighter on the table next to him . . . his one vice perhaps. But none of his guests was ever going to give him a lecture on smoking. Everything about the man, even the way he sat there — still and silent — suggested that he wasn't someone to be argued with. He was someone who was used to being obeyed.

And yet his manner was pleasant enough. "Good evening," he said. "Please come and sit down." His English was perfect. Every word was well modulated and precise.

He was sitting in the dining room, at the head of a long table that could have seated ten people but which had been laid for only four. The room was as elegant as the rest of the house, with floor-to-ceiling windows looking out onto a wooden terrace and views of the garden beyond. Richard, Matt, and Jamie took their places. At once, a door at the side slid open and two women appeared, pouring water and shaking out the napkins.

The man waited until they had gone. "My name is Han Shan-tung," he announced.

"I'm Richard Cole." Richard introduced himself, then the boys. He had already decided he was going to use the names that were on their passports. "This is Martin Hopkins. And Nicholas Helsey."

"I would have said that this was Matthew Freeman and Jamie Tyler," Shan-tung muttered. "And I would add that it is discourteous to lie to a man in his own home — but I will overlook it, as I can understand that you are nervous. Let me assure you, Mr. Cole, that I know everything about all three of you. More, in fact, than you perhaps know about yourselves. Otherwise you would not be here."

"And we know nothing about you," Richard replied. "That's why we have to be careful."

"Very wise. Well, it will be my pleasure to enlighten you. But first we should eat."

As if on cue, the two women returned, carrying plates of food. Silently, they laid out a Chinese dinner. It was a world apart from the sweet-and-sour, deep-fried grease balls that Matt had once purchased at his local takeaway in Ipswich. The dinner came in about a dozen china bowls — fish, meat, rice, noodles — and it had obviously been cooked by a world-class chef. Matt was glad to see that he had been provided with a spoon and fork. Han Shan-tung ate with chopsticks.

"I must apologize to you," he began. There was no small talk. He didn't ask them about their journey or what they thought of their rooms. "Urgent business took me to America. It was badly timed because it delayed your arrival here. And I'm afraid I have bad news. I had hoped that the object of your journey would have been sitting here with us tonight. I am referring to the girl, Lin Mo." He continued quickly, before Richard could interrupt. "You call her Scarlett Adams. But I refer to her by the name she was given before she was adopted and taken to the West."

"How do you know about Scarlett?" Richard asked.

Shan-tung leaned forward and plucked a prawn off one of the dishes. Despite his large hands, he used the chopsticks very delicately, like a scientist handling a specimen. "I know a great deal about the girl," he replied. "The fact of the matter is that she was with my agents in Hong Kong only yesterday. I have spent a great deal of time and money — not to mention human life — trying to remove her from the city."

Matt played back what Shan-tung had just said and realized that it confirmed exactly what he had thought. "The Old Ones are in Hong Kong," he said.

"The Old Ones *have taken over* Hong Kong," Shan-tung replied. "They control almost every aspect of the city. From the government and the police to the street cleaners. I do not know how many people they have killed, but the number must run into thousands. My people have been fighting them on your behalf. We are the only remaining resistance."

"Who are your people?" Richard asked.

Shan-tung sighed. "It is unnecessary to keep asking me these things. I am about to tell you anyway."

"I'm sorry." Richard realized his error. "I suppose it's a habit. I used to be a journalist."

"I do not like journalists. It is nothing personal — but they have caused me trouble in the past. I suggest you continue eating. I will tell you everything you need to know."

Han Shan-tung had barely eaten anything. But he laid down his chopsticks and continued to speak.

"I have the very considerable honor to be a member of an organization called the *Pah Lien*. This translates as the White Lotus Society. You might have remarked upon a clue that I sent you at the airport. The man who met you was carrying a bunch of lilies. The lily is part of the lotus family. My society is a very old one. It was founded in the fourth century to resist the foreign invaders known as the Mongols who then ruled over China. The aim of White Lotus remained the same over the next four centuries: to help the Chinese people fight against tyranny and oppression.

"But over the years, something very interesting happened. The White Lotus Society changed. It will be difficult for you to understand the nature of this change, so let me explain it to you by referring to a character from your own history. You will, I am sure, know Robin Hood. He stole from the rich and gave to the poor. He was a hero to the peasants in Sherwood Forest. But to the authorities, he was an outlaw, a criminal. They would have hanged him if they could.

"In the early days, the White Lotus Society operated in much the same way. Indeed, it might interest you to know that the society had a motto: *Ta fu — chih p'in.* This translates as 'strike the rich and help the poor.' But here was the crucial difference: As the years passed, White Lotus found that it was enjoying and benefiting from the criminal nature of its activities. It was also remarkably successful in the world of organized crime. It continued to steal from the rich but, as its members became richer themselves, it found itself giving rather less to the poor. It also changed its name. It became known as the Three United Society. There was a reason for this. White Lotus believed that the world was made up of three different parts: heaven, earth, and mankind. Its members therefore had a triangle tattooed onto their body. The triangle also appeared on their flags. And in the end, they became known simply as the Triads."

There was a long silence. Matt had heard of the Triads, the criminal gangs that were active all over Asia. They were drug dealers. They were involved in people-smuggling, extortion, and murder. They would torture or kill anyone who got in their way. They were as brutal as they were powerful. And this man was calmly admitting that he was one of them! He glanced at Jamie. The American boy was listening politely. He didn't seem shocked by what he had just heard. Richard, on the other hand, was staring openmouthed.

"I can see that you are dismayed," Shan-tung remarked. "And before you ask me one of your inane questions, Mr. Cole, I will answer you. Yes. I am a criminal. More than that, I am what is known as Shan Chu, the Master of the Mountain. This means that I am the supreme leader of my own Triad. I cannot tell you how many people I have murdered to get to where I am today, but a conservative guess would be about twenty-five. I do know that I am wanted in exactly nine countries, including the United Kingdom and the United States — and I would have been arrested a long time ago if I hadn't paid the right people a great deal of money to leave me alone.

"You are now wondering if you should be sitting at my table, eating my food. You are asking yourself why I should wish to help you in your struggle against the Old Ones. You are thinking, perhaps, that it would be more natural for me to be on their side. But you would be wrong.

"Until very recently, I controlled all the crime in Hong Kong. I have, for example, drug laboratories in Kowloon and the New Territories. I have illegal casinos and betting shops throughout the island. Immigrants from China were paying five thousand dollars a time for me to help them cross the border illegally. The arrival of the Old Ones has changed everything. They have no interest in profit. They do not want to do business. They want only to destroy everything around them — and that includes the Triads. They are as much my enemy as anyone's, the only difference being that I have the means to fight back. And that is what I have been doing. There is a certain irony, don't you think? I am undoubtedly a bad man. But a greater evil has come my way, and now I am forced to do good.

"And so I have used all my resources within Hong Kong to set up a resistance. I have buildings. I have people. I have weapons — not that they are of much use against creatures that can form themselves out of flies. Above all, I have determination. I will not be defeated by the Old Ones. They can destroy the world — but they will not destroy me."

"I'm surprised they didn't ask you to work for them," Richard said.

"As it happens, they did indeed ask me to serve them. The Nightrise Corporation approached me exactly a year ago. But the Master of the Mountain does not serve any-one. I mentioned twenty-five victims. The man who put that question to me was the twenty-fifth."

"May I ask a question?" Matt asked.

"You have my permission," Han Shan-tung replied. "But I should warn you that soon I have a question to put to you, and I very much hope you will be able to provide me with the right answer."

Matt didn't like the sound of that, but he went on any-way. "How do you know about Scarlett?" he asked. "And why did you call her Lin Mo?"

"The White Lotus Society has always known about the Gatekeepers. You must remember that in our early days, almost two thousand years ago, we were to all intents and purposes a religious order. We still are. That means we are the keepers of many secrets . . . sacred texts and ancient beliefs. Even when we began to devote ourselves exclusively to crime, we stayed true to ourselves. The secrets were passed on from generation to generation. And I think we always knew that one day we would be called upon to return to our origins, to take up the sword once again.

"As to the second part of your question, regarding Lin Mo, that I am not yet prepared to tell you. I need to be persuaded that I can trust you, and that is still not the case.

"However, I can say that she was born in a place called Meizhou. We always knew that the Old Ones would return and look for her . . . that she was one of the Gatekeepers. We therefore arranged for her to be adopted and taken to the West. We wanted her to be as far away from here as possible. We hoped that she would be safe."

"It didn't work."

Shan-tung shrugged. "We did everything we could to protect her. It was not our fault that the Old Ones found her. In fact, if anyone is to blame, it is her. Nonetheless, you are right. The Old Ones found her and brought her back."

"You tried to get her out of Hong Kong," Jamie said. He hadn't eaten very much, absorbed in what he was being told.

"Scarlett was kept under guard from the moment she arrived," Shan-tung explained. "With great difficulty, we managed to get a message to her. My most trusted agent in Hong Kong, a man called Lohan, contacted her and arranged for the shape-changer who had been guarding her to be killed. He took her to a safe place where we hoped to keep her hidden, but unfortunately — and again through no fault of our own — she was found again. As I mentioned to you, several of my people died. However, Lohan managed to move her to one of our warehouses and had planned to smuggle her out on a cruise liner. That was yesterday. The plan failed for reasons that are not yet clear. She is now their prisoner."

"So what do we do now?" Jamie asked. "How do we get her back again?"

The Master of the Mountain poured himself a glass of water from a crystal jug and drank it.

"Jamie and I can go into Hong Kong," Matt said. "We can find her. . . ."

"If you go into Hong Kong, you will be doing exactly what they want you to do. They will be waiting for you, and although they will not kill you — that is not part of their plan — they will keep you in so much pain that you will wish constantly for death."

"We can't just leave her."

"You may have no choice."

"No, Mr. Shan-tung," Matt said. "You don't believe that. Otherwise, why would you have invited us here?" Matt looked him straight in the eyes. "You're going to help us get into Hong Kong. You've already told us. You've got people over there. You can smuggle us in. We can find Scarlett. And we can be out of there before the Old Ones know what's happened."

Han Shan-tung set his glass down. "I might help you," he said. "But as I mentioned to you earlier, there is still a question you have to answer for me."

"And what is that?"

"I am, by nature, a very careful man. I have told you that I have killed twenty-five times. What I should have added is that there have been as many attempts on my own life. You are here in my house on the recommendation of my friend, Mr. Lee. I trust him. He has been useful to me in the past, and he definitely believes that you and the American boy are who you say you are."

"Is that your question?"

"It is exactly that. How can I be sure that you are one of the Five?"

Matt thought for a moment. Then he pointed at the crystal jug. He didn't even need to think about it any more. The jug was swept, instantly, off the table. It fell to the floor and smashed. Shan-tung blinked. It was his only reaction. But then he slowly smiled. "An amusing conjuring trick. But it is still not enough. I do not question your abilities. It is your identity I wish to know."

"I'll read your mind," Jamie said. "You say you know everything about us. In ten seconds I can tell you even more about you."

"I would recommend that you stay out of my mind," Han Shan-tung said. He turned to Matt. "There is a test, a trial you might say, that will prove to me beyond any doubt that you are who you say you are. Only one of you needs to take part in it. But I should warn you, though, that to fail will cause you great pain and perhaps even death. What do you say?"

Matt shrugged. "We need your help," he said. "We've flown a long way to get it. If there is no other way —"

"There isn't."

"Matt . . . ," Richard muttered.

"Then let's go ahead," Matt said. "What test do you have in mind?"

Han Shan-tung got to his feet. "It is called the sword ladder," he said. He gestured toward a door at the back of the room. "Please . . . will you come this way?"

TWENTY-FIVE

The Sword Ladder

Matt stood up and followed Han Shan-tung. Richard and Jamie came behind. They went through the door into a long corridor, all polished wood but otherwise undecorated. There was a second door at the far end.

It opened into a large, square room that didn't seem to belong to the rest of the house. It reminded Matt of a chapel, or perhaps a concert hall that might comfortably seat fifty or sixty people. The walls were plain and wood-paneled, matching the corridor outside, and there were pews arranged around three of the sides. The fourth was concealed by a dark red curtain that had been pulled across, perhaps concealing a stage. There was a gallery above the curtain, but it was high up, arranged in such a way that it was impossible to tell from floor level what it might contain.

"You are inside a Triad lodge," Mr. Shan-tung explained. "And you should consider yourselves very privileged. Only Triad members and initiates are allowed in here — normally any outsiders would be instantly killed. We meet in this place on the twenty-fifth day of each Chinese month. There is a separate entrance from the street. You might be interested to know that an initiation ceremony lasts six hours. A new recruit is expected to answer three hundred and thirty-three questions about the society. He learns secret handshakes and recognition signals. A lock of his hair is taken, and he signs his name in blood."

"Actually, I wasn't thinking of joining," Richard muttered.

Fortunately, Shan-tung didn't appear to have heard. "I speak of our rituals to remind you that the White Lotus Society is very old," he went on. "Things have, of course, changed with modern times. Nine hundred years ago, initiates would have drunk each other's blood, mixed with wine. And there is another part of the ceremony that has fallen out of use. When China was enslaved by Kublai Khan, it is said, the society searched for a leader, the one man who might liberate them. That man would be known as the Buddhist Messiah, and he would show himself by a sign. . . ."

He crossed the room and pulled on a cord that drew back the curtain. Jamie gasped. Matt stepped forward. At first he thought he was looking at a strange ladder leading up to the balcony above, but then he realized that it was actually made up of antique swords, each one polished until it shone, lashed together in a wire frame with the edges of the blades facing upward. Theoretically, it might be possible to climb. But he doubted it. As soon as you rested your body weight on one sword, you would cut your foot in half. Even if you were light enough, the climb to the top would be agony. It was a long way to the balcony. Matt counted nineteen steps. Nineteen chances to slice yourself apart.

"In my time as Master of the Mountain, three initiates

have claimed to be the Buddhist Messiah," Shan-tung explained. "They asked my permission to be allowed to climb the ladder, and I was glad to give it. Watching their attempts was a fascinating experience. One of them almost made it to the top before he fainted. Sadly, he broke his neck in the fall."

"What about the other two?" Matt asked.

"One cut off the fingers of his left hand on the first step and chose not to continue. The other bled to death."

"This is insane!" Richard couldn't restrain himself anymore. "Matt isn't claiming to be your Buddhist Messiah or whatever you want to call it."

"He is claiming to be one of the Gatekeepers. If he is who he says he is, he has nothing to fear."

"And if we say no? If we refuse to perform your little party trick?"

"Then I will not help you. You will leave Macao. And the girl will die, slowly, on her own."

Richard swore under his breath. Jamie came forward and stood next to Matt. "I don't mind giving it a try," he said quietly.

"Thanks, Jamie," Matt replied. "But I brought us here. I think this one's down to me."

He took a step closer, but Richard held out a hand. "Forget it, Matt!" he said. "You don't need to do this. There are plenty of ways we can get into Hong Kong without this maniac's help."

"We can't go in on our own," Matt said. "One of us has to try."

"You're going to cut yourself to pieces."

"After the first finger, I promise I'll stop."

He went over to the ladder. Any hope that it might not be as dangerous as it looked vanished at once. The swords were fixed rigidly in place by the wires. The blades were pointing toward each other so that as he climbed up, the hilts and the points would be on alternate sides. The swords had been sharpened until they were razor-thin. He rested a finger on one and almost cut through the skin just doing that. If he had dropped an envelope onto it, he would have sliced it in two.

Could he do it? Every instinct told him that he couldn't, that it was impossible, that he was being asked to mutilate himself. He closed his eyes. Was there any way out of this? Did they really need this man's help? Hong Kong was only fifty miles away. They could get on a Jetfoil and take their chances. Why would they want to involve themselves with gangsters anyway?

But he knew he was fooling himself. Scarlett was in trouble. If he'd wanted to go into Hong Kong on his own, he could have done it a week ago. There was no other way. He opened his eyes. "All right," he said.

"Remove your shoes," Shan-tung commanded.

"Sure," he muttered. "Shame to waste good leather." Right then, he was wondering if he would ever wear shoes again. He took them off, and his socks as well, for good measure. He could feel the wooden floor, cool against the soles of his feet. He flexed his toes.

"Matt . . . ," Richard tried one last time.

"It's okay, Richard."

Matt didn't look at him. He didn't look at any of them. He knew there was only one way this was going to work. He had to focus completely on the task ahead of him. Nineteen steps. He had once seen people walking on hot coals on television. And in India, fakirs did incredible things with their bodies. Matt remembered what he had done in the Nazca Desert. He had taken a bullet in full flight and turned it back on the person who had fired it. Mind control. That was what this was all about.

He reached out and gently took hold of one of the swords. He felt the blade cut through his skin. It hurt. Blood welled out of the palm of his hand.

"That's enough!" Richard exclaimed. "You can't do this."

"Yes. I can."

Matt gritted his teeth. He knew the mistake he had made. He had been thinking too much about the impossibility of what he was supposed to do. When he moved things without touching them, it never occurred to him that he couldn't do it. That was how the power worked. It was part of him, and he could use it anytime. This task might seem different, but the principle was just the same. Nineteen steps. He wasn't going to hurt himself a second time. He was a Gatekeeper. He had nothing to fear.

He forgot Richard. He forgot where he was. The balcony above him — that was all that mattered. He let the swords blur in front of him. They were no longer there. He reached out with one hand. At the same time, he lifted his left foot and rested his bare sole on the first blade. There was no going back now.

Richard had seen many unforgettable things in his time with Matt, but this was the most incredible of all. He watched Matt begin to climb, one sword at a time, resting his entire weight on edges that were clearly razor sharp. He seemed to be in a self-induced trance, moving steadily upward as if he were levitating. Already he was halfway up, and he hadn't cut himself at all. Next to Richard, Jamie stared in wonderment. Even Han Shan-tung looked quietly impressed.

He reached the top. He climbed off the ladder and stood on the balcony. Nobody spoke. Shan-tung hurried to the side of the room and took a staircase that also led up. Matt waited for him. There was a single wound on his right palm, the result of his false start, but otherwise he was unharmed.

The Master of the Mountain reached him. He was holding a bandage. He bowed low, then handed it over. "I apologize for questioning you, Matthew," he said — and he sounded completely sincere. "You are indeed one of the Five, and it is my honor to be able to help you."

Matt took the bandage and wrapped it round his hand. At the same time, he noticed an altar on the far side of the balcony, hidden from the room below. There were several gold bowls, incense sticks, two crouching Buddhas, and, between them, a jade figure of a young girl, slim with long hair falling in waves around her shoulders.

"That is Lin Mo," Han Shan-tung said. "It is the answer to the question that you asked me earlier. Lin Mo is the name of a young girl in Chinese legend. She was born in Meizhou, in the eastern Guangdong province. She had the power to forecast the weather. And she grew up to become the goddess of the sea, very important to the sailors who explored these uncharted waters. She is still worshipped in Macao."

He moved over to the altar and bowed in front of it.

"This figure is very precious to me," he continued. "It is Ming dynasty. From the seventeenth century. It is said to be a true representation of Lin Mo, copied from an earlier work."

Matt recognized the face. He remembered the picture he had seen in the newspaper. "It's Scarlett, isn't it?" he said.

"The girl that you know as Scarlett was also born in Meizhou. It was always our belief that she was the reincarnation of Lin Mo. And it is true, yes, that in appearance the two are identical."

"So you're going to help us."

Shan-tung nodded. "You must leave very soon," he said. "Come now with me to my study and we will make the final preparations."

He led Matt over to the staircase, and the two of them made their way down. Richard and Jamie were waiting for him.

"That was quite a trick," Richard muttered through clenched teeth.

Jamie said nothing. He rested a hand briefly on Matt's shoulder. He was glad that it hadn't been him.

They followed Shan-tung back down the corridor and into a study that also overlooked the garden. It was an austere room with a large desk, a few shelves of books, and little else. His whole manner had changed. He was still in command, a man who was used to being obeyed instantly, but he was being a little quieter about it. Had he really expected Matt to climb the sword ladder? He seemed shaken by what he had seen.

He took out a map and laid it on his desk. Matt glanced at his watch, wondering how long this would take. It was already ten o'clock.

"The Old Ones may control the city," Shan-tung said, "but if they have underestimated the size and extent of the Triads, then they have made a fatal mistake. I have a thousand foot soldiers that I can place at your service. If called to do so, they will not hesitate to lay down their lives for you. That is our way. The man who commands them is called Lohan. His rank is 438, which we also call Incense Master. He will meet you when you arrive in Hong Kong."

"How do we know we can trust him?" Richard asked.

"Very simply, Mr. Cole. He is my eldest son. You will recognize him because his face is scarred." Shan-tung drew a line with his finger, starting on his left cheek and crossing his mouth. "A man was sent to kill me with a *jian*, a Chinese sword. Lohan got in his way. If it were not for him, I would be dead. This is where you will meet. . . ."

His finger stabbed down on the map, at a point close to the waterside.

"I have a legitimate business delivering fireworks to Kowloon. There is a warehouse next to the Salisbury Road, and it is there you will be taken. Scarlett was also there before she was captured. You don't need to worry — the location is still secure.

"We are trying to discover where Scarlett is being held

317

prisoner, but so far we've had no luck. It is possible that she is here." He pointed again, this time to a street on the other side of the water. "This is The Nail. It is on Queen Street, and it is the headquarters of the Nightrise Corporation. If the girl is there, Lohan will lead an assault on the building. You will be with him.

"The Tai Shan Temple with the door that you were seeking is also on Queen Street." He pointed to a crossroads close to a patch of green with what might be a lake in the middle. "You would be wise not to go there, as it is almost certainly being watched. But once you have the girl, the rules will change. It is less than a quarter of a mile away, close to Hong Kong Park. Lohan will help you enter the compound. He will kill anyone who gets in your way. You will enter the temple, and the door will take you wherever you want to go."

"But what if Scarlett isn't at The Nail?" Richard asked.

"Then you will have to search for her. Perhaps her father will be able to help you." The finger slid across the page. "Paul Adams has returned to Wisdom Court, the apartment block where he lives. It is here, on Harcourt Road. Be warned: He was with her when she was captured and may have had a hand in what took place. We can't trust him. Even so, he may know where she is."

"And you think he'll tell?" Matt asked.

"We will make him tell us." Han Shan-tung muttered the words casually, but there was something about the way he spoke that made the skin crawl.

He seemed to have finished. Matt was exhausted. He was looking forward to getting to bed. But then Han Shan-tung went over to the desk and took a mobile phone out of one of the drawers. He handed it to Richard. "You can use this to contact me at any time of the day or night," he explained. "The speed dial is already set. Just press one, and it will connect you directly."

"So when are we leaving?" Jamie asked.

Shan-tung turned and looked at him. There was no expression on his face. "The boat is already waiting for you," he said. "You must enter Hong Kong under cover of darkness. You leave tonight."

TWENTY-SIX
Into Hong Kong

The boat was tied up at Porto Exterior, the outer port of Macao. Han Shan-tung had said a brief good-bye in the hallway of his home, and now Matt, Jamie, and Richard were being driven across the city through half-empty streets. It was raining again, and the sidewalks, black and glistening, had been deserted by the crowds, many of them sheltering in the casinos, throwing their money after dice and cards in the artificial glare of the chandeliers.

They were all tired. Jamie was half asleep, his head resting on the window, his long hair falling across his face. Richard was sitting next to him. Matt could tell that he was angry — with Shan-tung for arranging the ordeal of the sword ladder and with himself for allowing it. Matt was in the front, beside the driver. The speed of events had taken him by surprise. He had only just arrived in Macao and already he was leaving. He thought about what might lie ahead of him in Hong Kong and wondered if he was doing the right thing. It was obvious now that the whole place was a trap, set up by the Old Ones. And yet, he was walking straight into it.

But they wouldn't be expecting him . . . not like this. That was what he told himself. And there was no other way. He couldn't leave Scarlett on her own any longer. It had already been too long. It was his responsibility to find her and bring her out. He was a Gatekeeper. It was time to take control.

The ferry terminal was ahead, but they didn't drive into it. Instead, the driver took them down a narrow road that led to the water's edge and stopped. They got out, bracing themselves against the cold night air.

For a moment, Matt and Richard found themselves standing next to each other. "Do you really think we should trust these people?" the journalist muttered, putting into words what he had been thinking all along. "They're Triads. Do you know what that means? Drugs and guns. Gambling. They'll chop up anyone who gets in their way — including you and me. Between them and the Old Ones, I wouldn't have said there was a lot to choose."

A few hours ago, Matt might have agreed. But he remembered how Han Shan-tung had looked at the statue of Scarlett, or Lin Mo, as he preferred to call her. "I think they're on our side," he said.

"Maybe." Richard reached out for Matt's injured hand and turned it over. There was a dark stain seeping through the bandage. "But he still shouldn't have done that to you."

"I did it to myself," Matt said. "I wasn't concentrating."

Jamie came over to them. "I think he wants us to go with him," he said, glancing at the driver. He yawned. "I just hope this boat has got a decent bed."

There wasn't much to the port: a stretch of white

concrete, a couple of gantries, and arc lamps spreading a hard, electric glow that only made everything look more unwelcoming. Once again the rain had eased off, but a thin drizzle hung in the air. The driver led them over to a boat, moored along the quayside. This was going to take them across.

It was an old, hardworking cargo boat with just two decks. The lower of them had a cargo hold that was open to the elements. Looking into it, Matt saw that it was filled with wooden crates, each one marked with a name that had been stenciled in black letters: KUNG HING TAO. The cabin was on the upper deck. It was shaped like a greenhouse and not much bigger, with windows all the way round. There were two radio masts jutting into the air, a radar dish, and a funnel that was already belching black smoke. The boat was completely ringed with car tires to stop it from colliding with the dock; this, along with the flaking paint and patches of rust, made it look as if it had been rescued from a junkyard. Matt just hoped the sea would be calm.

"We've got company," Richard said.

A man had appeared, climbing down from the cabin, his feet — in Wellington boots — clanging against the metal rungs. As he stepped into the light, it became clear that he wasn't Chinese. He was a European, a big man with a beard, dark eyes, and curly, black hair. His whole face looked beaten about — cracked lips, broken nose, veins showing through the skin. Either the weather had done it, too many years at sea, or he had once been a boxer . . . and an unsuccessful one. He was wearing jeans, a thick knitted jersey, and a donkey jacket, dark blue, with the rain sparkling on his shoulders. His hands were huge and covered in oil.

"Good evening, my friends," the man said. "You are welcome to *Moon Moth*." He had introduced his ship but not himself. He had a deep voice and a Spanish accent. The words came from somewhere in his chest. "Mr. Shantung has asked me to look after you. Are you ready to come on board?"

"How long will the journey take us?" Richard asked. He sounded doubtful.

"Three hours, maybe longer. We don't have the power of a Jetfoil, and the weather's strange. All this rain! It may hold us up, so the sooner we get started, the better." The man took out a pipe and tapped it against his teeth as if checking them for cavities. "I often make the journey at night, if that's what's worrying you," he went on. "Nobody's going to take any notice of us. So let's get out of this weather and be on our way."

He turned and climbed back onto the boat. Richard glanced at Matt. Matt shrugged. The captain hadn't been exactly friendly, but why should they have expected otherwise? These people were criminals. They were only obeying orders. They had no interest in the Gatekeepers or anybody else, so it was pointless to expect first-class comfort and smiles.

Richard had brought his backpack with them — it was their only luggage. He picked it up and they followed the man on board. They reached the ladder, and Matt was grateful that this one had ordinary rungs instead of swords.

As he began to climb, he noticed a Chinese man in filthy jeans and an oil-skin jacket drawing a tarpaulin over the crates. For a moment, their eyes met and Matt found himself being studied with undisguised hostility. The man spat, then went back to work. He seemed to be the only crew.

There wasn't much room in the cabin, which looked even older than the ship, with equipment that wouldn't have been out of place in a Second World War film. The captain was sitting on a stool in front of a steering wheel, surrounded by switches and gauges with markings that had largely faded away. The rain had picked up. It was streaming down the windows, and the world outside was almost invisible, broken up into beads of water that clung in place, reflecting everything but showing very little. The engines were throbbing sullenly below. The whole cabin was vibrating. It smelled of salt water, diesel fuel, and stale tobacco.

There was a low sofa and a couple of chairs for the three passengers. All the furniture was sagging and stained. Richard, Matt, and Jamie took their places. The captain sat at the wheel, flicking on a pair of ancient windshield wipers that began to swing from left to right, clearing the way in front of them. The Chinese crewman cast off, and the boat slipped away, unseen, into the night.

A single row of lights shone ahead. There was a road bridge, at least half a mile long, snaking across the entire length of the harbor. But once they had passed underneath it, there was nothing. *Moon Moth* had its own spotlights mounted on the bow and the cabin roof, but they barely penetrated the driving rain and showed nothing more than a circle of black water a few feet ahead.

The captain switched on the screens, and the cabin glowed green with a soft beeping sound that divided up the silence like commas in a sentence. For about ten minutes nobody said anything, but then the crewman appeared, carrying a battered tray with four tin mugs of hot chocolate that he had brought up from a galley somewhere below.

"You haven't told me your names," the captain said. He lit his pipe and blew smoke into the air, making the cabin feel closer and snugger than ever. It was very warm inside, presumably from the heat of the engines below.

Richard introduced them. "I'm Richard. This is Matt and Jamie." They were being smuggled into Hong Kong illegally, and Han Shan-tung already knew who they were. There was no need for false names.

"And I am Hector Machado. But you can call me Captain. That is what everyone calls me — even when I am not on the ship."

"Are you Spanish?" Richard asked.

"Portuguese. I was born in Lisbon. Have you been there?"

Richard shook his head.

"I'm told that it's a beautiful city. I left there when I was three. My father came to Hong Kong to fight against the communists. This was his boat." Machado sucked on his pipe, which glowed red. He blew out smoke. "He was shot dead in the very seat where I am sitting now. And the boat is mine."

"How many crew do you have?" Matt was thinking

of the man he had seen. Why had he appeared so unfriendly?

"Just Billy. No need for anyone else."

"What's in the crates?"

Machado hesitated, as if afraid of giving too much away. Then he shrugged. "Fireworks. A lot of fireworks. Mr. Shan-tung has a business selling them to mainland Hong Kong."

"And what do you carry when you're not delivering fireworks?" Richard asked. His voice was hostile. It clearly bothered him, being with these people.

"I've carried all sorts of things, Richard. Stuff that maybe it would be better you didn't know about. I've smuggled people in, if that's what you want to know. And maybe you should be grateful. I know the ins and outs. *Moon Moth* may not be much to look at, but she'll outrun the Hong Kong harbor patrols anytime — not that they'll bother themselves about us. Everyone knows me in these parts. And they leave me alone."

"So how long have you worked for the Triads?"

"You think this is an interview? You want to write about me?" Machado gestured with the pipe. "I'd get some rest, if I were you. It could be a long night." He slipped the pipe between his teeth and said no more.

They cruised on into the darkness, guided by the strange, green light of the radar system. The night was so huge that it swallowed them completely. There was no moon or stars. It was impossible to tell if it was still raining as the windows were being lashed by sea spray. Machado sat where he was, smoking in silence. Richard, Matt, and

Jamie sat at the back of the cabin, out of his way. All three of them were tense and nervous. They hadn't discussed what they might find in Hong Kong, but now that they were finally on the way, they could imagine what they might be up against. A whole city, millions of people . . . and the Old Ones infesting everything. They had to be mad to be going in there. But there seemed to be no other way to get Scar out.

Jamie finished his hot chocolate and dozed off. Richard opened his backpack and began to go through his things. He had brought maps, money, a change of clothes. The precious diary was also there, sealed in plastic to keep it protected. Matt noticed a glimmer of gold and realized that he was carrying the tumi — the Inca knife.

Richard glanced up. "You never know when it may come in handy," he said. "Anyway, I didn't like leaving it behind with that bunch of crooks." He zipped the backpack shut, then lowered his voice. "What do you think?" he asked.

He was referring to Hector Machado, although he didn't need to whisper, as the captain would never have heard him above the noise of the engines.

"Shan-tung trusts him," Matt said.

"He doesn't seem to be exactly friendly."

"He doesn't have to be friendly. He just has to get us there."

"Let's hope he does."

The two of them fell silent and soon they were both asleep. But then — it felt like seconds later — Matt found himself being woken by something. It was the boat's engine, which had changed tempo, slowing down. He opened his eyes. It was still dark, still raining. But there were lights ahead.

"You can wake up your friends," Captain Machado said. "We're here."

Matt stood up and went over to the window.

And there it was. It was two o'clock in the morning, but a city like Hong Kong never really slept. Matt could make out the skyscrapers by the lights that burned all around them, picking out their shapes in brilliant green, blue, and pink neon. It was as if someone had drawn the city onto the darkness with a vast, fluorescent crayon. There were advertisements — PHILIPS, SAMSUNG, HITACHI — burning themselves onto the night sky, the colors breaking up in the water, being thrown around by the choppy waves. There were signs in Chinese too, and they reminded him how very different this city would be from London or Miami. This was another world.

It was very misty. Maybe it was an illusion caused by all the neon, but the mist was a strange color, an ugly, poisonous yellow. It was rolling across the harbor toward them, reaching out to surround them as if it were a living thing and knew who they were. As they continued forward, it pressed itself against the glass of the cabin, and the sound of the engines became even more distant.

Richard had joined the captain at the steering wheel. "Why are we going so slowly?" he asked. It was a good question. They were barely moving at all.

"We don't want to draw attention to ourselves," Machado replied.

"I thought you said nobody cared about you anyway."

"There's still no reason to make too much noise."

Another minute passed.

"I thought we were going to Kowloon," Richard said.

"We are."

"But isn't Kowloon on the other side?"

Machado grinned in the half-light. He had put the pipe away. "The current will carry us over," he said, and at that moment Matt knew that he wasn't telling the truth and felt the familiar tingle of imminent danger. For what seemed like an age, nothing happened. They weren't moving. Machado was standing there, almost daring them to challenge him — to do anything. But there was nothing they could do. They were trapped on board his boat, completely in his power.

And then a searchlight cut through the darkness, pinning *Moon Moth* in its glare. The entire cabin seemed to explode with dazzling light. A second beam swung across. Two boats. They were still some distance away, but they were rapidly closing in. They must have been waiting there all the time.

At the same moment, Machado swung his hand, crashing it into the side of Richard's head and then bringing it around on Matt. He was holding a gun. Richard fell. Machado's lips curled in an unpleasant smile. "If you move, I will kill you," he said.

He had betrayed them. He had known the boats were coming. He had led them straight to them.

"The Triads will kill you for this," Richard muttered. He had pulled himself onto one knee and was cradling his head in his hand. Blood was trickling from a wound just above his eye.

"The Triads are finished," Machado replied. "They're nothing anymore."

"So who's paying you?" Matt asked.

"There's a big reward out for you, boy. Two million Hong Kong dollars. More than I've earned with Shan-tung and his friends in ten years. They want you very badly. And they warned me about you. If you even blink, I'll shoot you."

Matt looked out of the window. The boats were getting closer, and they had been joined by three more, making five in all, moving in from every side. They were police launches — gray, solid steel with identifying numbers printed on the side. They were coming out of the night like miniature battleships, with bulletproof windows and bows shaped like knives.

Richard pulled himself to his feet. Machado aimed the gun at him. "Nightrise doesn't want you," he said. "So I hope you don't mind a burial at sea." He was about to fire at point-blank range. He licked his lips, enjoying himself. Richard stared at him helplessly.

"Put the gun down," Jamie said.

Machado didn't hesitate. He laid the gun on the floor, although his face was filled with puzzlement. He had no idea why he'd done it. But Matt did. In his moment of triumph, the captain had forgotten Jamie. He'd thought he was still asleep . . . but he'd been wrong. Jamie had seen what was happening and had used his power. If he'd told Machado to stop breathing, the man would have stood there until he died. And, Matt reflected, maybe that was what he deserved.

"This is the Hong Kong police. Heave to . . ."

The voice echoed out of the water, amplified through a megaphone. There was a man standing on the bow of the nearest boat — except he looked far too tall to be human. He was black and was dressed in the uniform of a senior officer in the Hong Kong police. But it was obvious he was no policeman. He was like something out of a nightmare, with his bald head and empty, staring eyes. It was freezing cold out on the water, but he wasn't shivering. He showed no feeling or emotion at all.

Richard lunged forward, grabbed hold of the steering wheel, and slammed down the throttle. Matt felt the floor tilt beneath him as the cargo boat surged forward. Captain Machado had been standing there, dazed, as if unsure what to do, but now he seized hold of Richard, and the two of them began to grapple for the steering wheel.

"Get rid of him, Jamie," Matt said.

"Jump overboard," Jamie commanded.

Machado let go of Richard and lurched out of the cabin, moving in a trance. There was shouting, a shot, then a splash as Machado was gunned down even as he hit the sea. The Hong Kong police had assumed he was trying to escape. Or maybe they knew who he was but had decided to kill him anyway. Machado floated facedown in the water. He didn't move.

Richard had control of the cargo boat. He spun it round, taking the police by surprise. Seconds later, he burst through them, weaving round one of their boats, heading for the central side of Hong Kong.

"The gun!" Richard shouted.

Matt snatched it up and handed it to him. Then Jamie shouted and pointed. "Watch out!"

A face had appeared at the window, glaring at them with furious eyes. For a moment, Matt thought one of the policemen had somehow boarded *Moon Moth.* Then he remembered the single crewman — Billy — who had sailed with them from Macao. He was holding a gun, bringing it round to aim at the cabin. Richard shot him through the window, a single bullet between the eyes. The boat lurched crazily. The wheel spun. The crewman disappeared.

Then the nearest police launch opened fire. The noise was deafening as the bullets smashed into the metal plates of the cargo boat, cutting a line along the bow and ricocheting back into the water. One of the windows shattered and Richard ducked as tiny fragments of glass showered down onto his shoulders and back. The cold night air rushed into the cabin, carrying with it the spray of water and the foul, decaying smell of the pollution. *Moon Moth* surged forward. Richard was fighting with the wheel, trying not to be shot. Matt looked back. The police launches were regrouping, preparing to come after them. The man at the front suddenly opened his mouth and howled, a sound that split the night, louder than all the boats put together. Matt knew at that moment that he wasn't a man at all.

"We're going to have to jump!" Richard shouted above the roar of the engines and the raging wind. "Jamie, can you swim?"

Jamie nodded.

"I'm going to take us in as close as I can." He turned to Matt. "If we get separated, meet at —"

But Matt didn't hear the rest of the sentence. There was another burst of gunfire, this time strafing the stern and the cargo hold where the fireworks were packed.

"Now!"

Richard abandoned the wheel, and the boat began to zigzag. Matt needed to ask him what he had just said, but everything was happening too quickly. Richard snatched up his backpack and forced it over his shoulders. Jamie was right next to him. The five police boats were getting closer, only a few yards behind.

"Go!" Richard shouted.

Jamie hurried out to the deck and disappeared over the side of the boat. But Richard hadn't followed. He had climbed down from the cabin and was balancing himself, clinging to a handrail as *Moon Moth*, its engines screaming on full power, swerved drunkenly through the sea. Blood and water streamed down his face and his eyes were wild. Matt had never seen him like this before. Gritting his teeth, he brought the gun up and fired into the crates of fireworks, again and again, emptying the chamber into the same spot.

Nothing happened until the final shot. Then there was a flare of magnesium, burning through the tarpaulin. Richard noticed that Matt was still there, that he hadn't jumped overboard. "Jump!" he pleaded.

Matt jumped.

Even as his feet left the deck, the fireworks went off. There were thousands of pounds worth in the hold. A ton of gunpowder. But there was nothing beautiful about the explosion. It was just a blinding, burning wheel of fire that seemed to take Richard and hurl him into the air. That was the last thing Matt saw before he hit the water. For a moment everything was panic. The sea was black and freezing. He was still wearing his clothes and sneakers. He was being sucked down. He had to fight with all his strength just to get back to the surface.

He emerged, gasping for air, into a brilliant, blazing nightmare. It was as if the whole night was on fire. *Moon Moth* was alight. The fire was burning so intensely that the metal plates would surely melt away. With no one to steer it, the boat had turned a full circle and was plowing into the police launches that had been too slow to get out of the way. It was right in the middle of them, and Matt could just make out figures in helmets and full riot gear staring at the destruction, knowing that they were too close, that they were part of it. One of their boats was already on fire. The tall man was still howling — but this time in agony. Every part of him was on fire. His suit and the skin beneath it were peeling away. At the very end, his head split open and something began to snake out of it — a second head, not a human one. Then there was a great rush of white flame as more of the fireworks exploded and he was blown out of sight.

Individual fireworks were going off, one after another, and Matt saw cascades of red, blue, white, green, and yellow as blazing missiles were shot into the air, reflecting in the water below. About fifty rockets screamed out at once, some of them twisting into the sky, others slamming into the police boats. One of them spluttered across the water and plunged down in front of Matt, missing his head by inches. He saw a policeman on fire, jumping into the water to save himself. Another was less lucky. He seemed to be holding a spinning Catherine wheel, unable to let go of it even though it was burning into his chest. Fireworks were cracking and buzzing and whining all around him. He didn't make it into the sea. He died where he stood.

Matt was treading water, forcing himself to breathe. He was so cold that his lungs had shut down. He knew that he couldn't stay out here much longer. Two of the police boats were undamaged. Very soon they would be looking for him. But where was Richard? Where was Jamie? The surface of the water was like a black mirror, reflecting the light, but he couldn't see them anywhere. He wanted to shout out for them but he didn't dare. The policemen would have heard him.

There was only one thing he could do. The edge of the water was about two hundred feet away. He had to get to dry land and hope to find them there. He took one last look and then turned round and began to swim, slowed down by his clothes. The glow from the flames spread out over his shoulders, helping to light the way, and there were more bangs and fizzes as the last fireworks went off. He heard someone shouting an order in Chinese but doubted that they'd seen him. He was wearing dark clothes. His hair was dark. The currents were carrying him away.

He reached land without even realizing it. Suddenly there was a slimy concrete slope under his knees. He crawled onto it and pulled himself out. He was on a building site. That was what it looked like. It was hard to tell as he squatted in the darkness, shivering, filthy water dripping out of his hair.

"Richard? Jamie?"

He didn't dare call too loudly. The whole city — anyone who was awake — must have seen the firework display. The Old Ones knew he was there. They would already be searching.

"Richard? Jamie?"

There was no reply.

He waited ten minutes before he made a decision and set off, moving while he still could. If he stayed in one place much longer, he would freeze.

It was three o'clock in the morning. He had entered the enemy city. He had no idea where he was going. He was dripping wet. He was unarmed.

And he was alone.

TWENTY-SEVEN
Necropolis

Leaving the water behind him, Matt made for the wall of light that defined the edge of Hong Kong. He came to a main road, empty at this time of the night, with a block of luxury hotels and shopping centers on the far side. The smog was worse than ever. The entire city reeked of it, like a chemical swamp. He had only been there for a few minutes, but he already had a nagging headache and his eyes were killing him.

Where were Richard and Jamie? He had to find them. He was lost without them. Jamie had been the first off the boat, and although Matt hadn't seen Richard jump, he must surely have followed moments later. The two of them must have swum ashore — unless the police had managed to find them first. The thought of his friends in captivity sickened him.

He tried to shake off the sense of hopelessness. He had to work out what to do. First he had to get in touch with the Triads. There were a thousand of them, waiting to help him, but the way things had turned out, it wasn't going to be so easy after all. Han Shan-tung had given them a phone with a direct dial. Richard had been carrying it. But it would have been made useless the moment it hit the water. And then there was Shan-tung's son, Lohan. He would already know that something had gone wrong. Presumably his men would be searching for them all over the city.

But Matt had no way of contacting them. He remembered the address of the place where they were supposed to be going, a warehouse on Salisbury Road. But that was on the other side of the harbor, in Kowloon. Matt had no map and no money. He was soaking wet. It was the middle of the night. How was he supposed to get there?

He was already finding it hard to walk. Every time his foot came down, his shoes squelched and he felt the water rise over his foot. His shirt and pants were clinging to him, digging in under his arms and between his legs. As he crossed the road and passed between the first of the buildings, he wondered if it wasn't a little warmer here than it had been in the harbor. But it was only a matter of degrees. He was soaked and shivering, and if he didn't want to catch pneumonia, he was going to have to find a change of clothes.

He stopped. A man had appeared, coming toward him from round the corner of a building. At first Matt assumed he was drunk, on his way home from a late-night party. The man was wearing a crumpled suit with a tie hanging loosely from his neck, dragged round one side, and he was staggering. Matt thought about hiding, but the man obviously had no interest in him. And he wasn't drunk. He was ill. As he drew nearer, Matt saw that his suit was stained with huge sweat patches, and his face was a sickly white. He almost fell, propped himself against a lamppost, then threw up. Matt turned away, but not before he saw that whatever was coming out of his mouth was mixed with blood. The man was dying. He surely wouldn't last the night.

Slowly, the city began to reveal itself. Matt wasn't completely on his own, after all. There were street cleaners out, sweeping the sidewalks, their faces covered by white cloth masks. He saw security men sitting on their own in the neon glare behind the windows, only half awake as they counted the long minutes until dawn. He passed the entrance of a subway station, closed for the night — but there was a woman sitting on the steps, a vagrant, her whole body completely wrapped in old plastic bags. She saw him and laughed, her eyes staring, as if she knew something he didn't. Then she began to cough, a dreadful racking sound. Matt hurried on.

An ambulance raced past, its siren off but its lights flashing, throwing livid blue shadows across the shop windows. It pulled in ahead of him, and he saw that a small crowd had gathered round a man lying unconscious on the sidewalk. The ambulance doors were thrown open and two men climbed out, also wearing white masks. Nobody spoke. The man on the ground wasn't moving. The ambulance men scooped him up like a sack of meat and threw him into the back. He was either dead or dying and they didn't care. There were other bodies in the back, lots of them, piled one on top of the other. The ambulance men slammed the doors, then got back in. A moment later, they drove away.

The city was huge, silent, threatening. It seemed to be

entirely in the grip of the night, as if the morning would never come. Bald-headed mannequins in furs and diamonds stared out of the shop windows as Matt hurried past. Hundreds of gold and silver watches lay ticking quietly behind armor-plated glass. In the day, in the sunshine, Hong Kong might be a shopper's paradise. But at three o'clock in the morning with the pollution rolling in and the inhabitants sick and dying in the streets, it was something close to hell.

They were looking for him.

He heard the sound of a car approaching, and the very speed of it, the angry roar of the engine at this time of the night, told Matt that its journey was urgent and that he should get out of its way. Sure enough, just as he threw himself into a doorway, a police car shot past, immediately followed by a second, both of them heading the way he had just come. He knew that he had to get out of sight before any more arrived. He crossed another wide avenue and began climbing uphill.

And then he heard something coming through the darkness. It was the last thing he would have expected in a modern city, and at first he thought he must be mistaken. The clatter of metal against concrete. Horse's hooves . . .

A man appeared, riding a horse through a set of red traffic lights. The hooves were striking the surface of the road with that strange, unmistakable rhythm, and the echo was being trapped, thrown back and forth between shop windows. The horse paused under a streetlamp, and in the yellow glare, Matt saw that it was even more horrible than he had imagined. It was skeleton-thin, and in an act of dreadful cruelty, someone had driven a knife into its head, the blade pointing outward, so that it looked like a grotesque version of a unicorn.

Matt saw it and remembered Jamie telling him about the fire riders who had taken part in the battle ten thousand years before. Was this one of them? As the man and the beast went past, he ducked behind a parked car, watching them in the side mirror until they had disappeared from sight.

He was about to stand up, then froze as something huge fluttered through the darkness, high above the skyscrapers. Matt didn't see what it was but guessed that it was some sort of giant bird, maybe even the condor that had been part of the Nazca Lines. It was there, a sweeping shadow, and then it had gone. He knew now that the whole city was possessed: the roads, the water, the very air. It could only be a matter of time before he was seen and captured. Every moment he was on the street, he was in terrible danger.

He waited until he was sure there was no one around, then straightened up and hurried on his way, keeping close to the buildings so that he could throw himself into the shadows if anyone approached. He came to a junction. A car had swerved and crashed into a post. It was completely smashed up, its horn blaring. Matt could see the driver, half hanging out of the front door, pinned in place by his seat belt, his head and chest covered in blood. No one was coming to help.

A street sign. Matt looked up and read two words directly above him. HARCOURT ROAD. The name meant something.

"Paul Adams has returned to Wisdom Court. . . . It is here, on Harcourt Road."

He remembered Han Shan-tung, talking to him in the study, pointing it out on the map. Suddenly he knew what he had to do. Somehow he had stumbled onto the right road. If Paul Adams was at the flat, maybe he would let him in. At the very least, he would have somewhere to stay until the break of day.

"Help me. . . ."

The man in the car wasn't dead. His eyes, very white, had flicked open. He seemed to be crying, but the tears were blood. There was nothing Matt could do for him. He turned away and began to run.

The road seemed to go on forever. Matt went past more shopping malls, a hospital, a huge conference center. He didn't see any more police cars, but he heard them in the distance, their sirens slicing through the air. At one point, a taxi rushed past, zigzagging crazily on the wrong side of the road. He turned a corner and came upon a tram, parked in front of an office building. It was an old-fashioned thing. Apart from the Chinese symbols, it was like something that might have driven through London during the Second World War. And it was full of people. They were just sitting there, slumped in their seats, unmoving. Matt didn't know if they were alive or dead, and he didn't hang around to find out. He guessed they were a mix of both.

Somehow he found his way to Wisdom Court. He had only glanced at the map when he was in Macao and he'd gotten no more than an overview of the city. But there it was, suddenly in front of him, the name on a block of stone and behind it a driveway leading up to a fountain, a wide entrance, and, on each side, a statue of a snarling lion. The building was very ordinary, shrouded in darkness, but there was one light burning on the twelfth floor — Matt counted the windows — and he thought he saw a curtain flicker as somebody moved behind.

The driveway hadn't been swept. It was strewn with dead leaves and scraps of paper. The fountain had been turned off. As he walked up to the door, Matt got the feeling that the whole place, apart from that one room on the twelfth floor, might be deserted. There were no cars parked outside. He put his face against the glass door and looked into the reception area. It was empty. The door was locked, but there was a panel of buttons next to it, more than a hundred of them, numbered but with no names.

Was this really a good idea? He stood there for a few seconds, cold and wet, and tried to work out his options. Han Shan-tung had suggested that Paul Adams might have been working with the Old Ones. He had been there when Scarlett was taken prisoner. But could he really have sentenced his own daughter to death? Surely not.

At the end of the day, it didn't make any difference if Matt trusted him or not. He was freezing. He had to get inside, off the street. He had nowhere else to go.

He began to ring the bells, one after another, beginning with 1200 and moving along, waiting briefly for each one to reply. There was silence until he reached 1213, then a crackle as a voice came over the intercom.

"Yes?"

"Mr. Adams?"

"Who is this?"

"I know it's very late, but I'm a friend of Scarlett's. I wonder if I could talk to you."

"Now?"

"Yes. Could you let me in?"

A pause. Then a buzz, and the door opened.

As Matt walked into the reception area, he became aware of a stench — raw sewage. A pipe had burst — he could hear it dripping, and the floor was wet underfoot. There was just enough light to make out a staircase leading up, but once he began to climb, he had to feel his way in total darkness. He counted twelve floors, sliding his hand along the banister, pressing his shoulder against the wall as he turned each corner. It really was like being blind, and he felt smothered, afraid that at any moment something would jump out and grab hold of him. But at last he arrived at a swing door, pushed it open, and found himself at the beginning of a long corridor. Light spilled out from an open door about halfway down. Scarlett's father was waiting for him, but Matt couldn't make him out because the light was behind him and he was in silhouette.

"Who are you?" Paul Adams called out.

"My name is Matt."

"You're a friend of Scarly's?"

"I want to help her."

"You can't help her. You're too late."

Matt walked down the corridor, afraid that Paul Adams would go back in and close the door before he could reach him. But Adams waited for him. Matt reached the door and saw a small, unhappy man with gray hair and glasses. Scarlett's father hadn't shaved for a couple of days, nor had he washed. He was wearing a blue shirt that might have been expensive when he had bought it but now hung off him awkwardly, as if he had been sleeping in it. And he had been drinking. Matt could smell the alcohol on his breath and saw it in the eyes behind the glasses. They were red with exhaustion and self-pity.

"Mr. Adams . . . ," Matt began.

"I don't know you." Paul Adams looked at him blankly.

"I told you. My name is Matt."

"You're soaking wet."

"Can I come in?"

Matt didn't wait for an answer. He pushed his way past and entered the flat. The place was a mess. There were dirty plates stacked in the sink and on the kitchen counter. Everything smelled stale and airless with the sewage creeping up from below. It was as if someone had died there . . . or maybe it was the place itself that had died. Once it had been luxurious. Now it was sordid and sad.

Paul Adams closed the door. "Do you want something to eat?" he asked.

"I'd like some tea," Matt said. The man didn't move, so he went into the kitchen and began to make it himself. He looked in the fridge for some food. There were only leftovers, but he helped himself anyway. It was only now that he realized how hungry he was. A clock on the oven showed twenty past four. Six hours had passed since he had left Macao.

Paul Adams sat down. He had a glass of whiskey and he drank it in one swallow, then refilled it. "You're English," he said.

"I was at your home in Dulwich," Matt said. He was rummaging through a cupboard for a tea bag. "I tried to find Scarlett there. But she'd gone."

"They've taken her."

"Do you know where she is?"

"No." He drank again. "I know who you are!" he exclaimed. He had only just worked it out. "You're the boy they're all looking for. You're the reason why they wanted Scarlett."

Matt didn't say anything. The kettle boiled and he made himself the tea, adding two spoons of sugar.

"Matt Freeman. That's who it was. Matt Freeman!" Scarlett's father got up and went over to the kitchen, weaving his way across the carpet. Matt didn't know whether to be saddened or disgusted. He had never seen anyone so utterly lost. Paul Adams leaned heavily against the side of the counter, and suddenly there were tears in his eyes. "They lied to me," he said. "They told me she'd be all right if I helped them. I was the one who caught her! She'd have gotten away if it hadn't been for me. But I only did it to protect her. They said they'd kill her if I didn't help them."

"Did they take her to The Nail?" Matt asked.

Paul Adams shook his head. "She's not there."

"Is she still in Hong Kong?"

"Somewhere. They won't tell me." He paused and looked out the window. The first streaks of morning were beginning to bleed through the night sky. "I thought they'd be grateful for what I did, but they said I'd never see her again. They were mocking me. I'd helped them, and it was all for nothing. They wanted me to know that." He took off his glasses and wiped his eyes with the back of his hand. "I don't understand what they want, Matt. I don't understand anything anymore. This whole city . . ." His voice trailed away.

"Mr. Adams, I can help you," Matt said. "I can find her and get her out of here."

"How? You're just a kid."

"I need to have a shower and get changed." Matt was still dripping water onto the expensive carpet. "Do you have spare clothes?"

"I don't know. . . ." He waved vaguely in the direction of the bedroom.

Matt drew on the last of his strength, forcing his mind into gear. He had to find Scarlett. That was the reason he was here. But that wasn't going to be possible, not if she had been taken to some secret location. Was she even still in Hong Kong? He guessed that she would have to be. The Old Ones were using her to get at him. Surely they would keep her there until he arrived.

How to find her? Matt's eyes were desperately heavy. All he wanted to do was go to bed. But somehow he knew that this was his last chance. He had to bring all the pieces together, here in this room. First there was Paul Adams, destroying himself, wracked with guilt and misery. Then there was the man called Lohan, somewhere in Hong Kong with his thousand foot soldiers. Richard and Jamie. Maybe they had found their way over to them. And the fireworks. What was the name he had seen, stenciled on the crates?

And suddenly he had it.

"Listen to me," he said. "I may be able to find Scarlett, but you're going to have to help me. Will you do that?"

"I'll do anything."

"Does your telephone work here? And do you have a phone book?"

Paul Adams had been expecting something more. How would a simple phone call save his daughter? "It's over there." He gestured with the hand that was still holding the whiskey glass.

Matt went over to the telephone. It was a desperate plan. But he could think of no other way.

He picked it up and began to dial.

• • •

They came for him just after seven o'clock.

Matt was asleep on the sofa, dressed in jeans and a sweater that didn't really fit but were a lot better than the ones he had dumped in the bathroom. He had taken a hot shower, washing the smell of the harbor off his skin and out of his hair. And then he had fallen into a deep, dreamless sleep.

He hadn't heard the police arrive. They had driven down Harcourt Road and turned into Wisdom Court without sirens. He was woken by the sound of the door being smashed open and the shouts of a dozen men as they poured into the flat. Some of them were carrying guns. It was hard to say who was in charge. Suddenly, they were everywhere and Matt was surrounded.

He started to get up, but something hit him in the chest. It was a dart, fired from what looked like a toy gun, trailing wires behind it. But the next thing he knew, there was an explosion of pain and he was literally thrown off his feet as a bolt of electricity seared through him. He had been hit with a Taser, a weapon used by police forces all over the world. Despite its appearance, it had fired an electrical charge that had resulted in the total loss of his neuromuscular control. Matt had never felt pain like it. It seemed to shatter every bone in his body. He heard an animal whimper and realized it was him.

Matt collapsed to the ground, unable to move. The policemen weren't taking any chances. They had deliberately neutralized him before he could use his power against them.

A moment later, two of them fell on him. They twisted his arms behind his back and he felt cold steel against his wrists as a pair of handcuffs were locked into place. One of the policemen grabbed him by the hair and twisted him round so that he was in a kneeling position.

Another man appeared at the door.

"So this is Matthew Freeman," he said.

The chairman of the Nightrise Corporation had wanted to make sure that everything was safe before he came in. Now he strutted forward and stood over Matt, looking down at him with a smile on his face. Although he had been hastily summoned out of bed, he was as impeccably dressed as always, in a new suit and polished shoes. "What a great pleasure to meet you," he added.

Matt ignored him. He twisted round so that he was facing Paul Adams. His eyes were filled with anger. "What have you done?" he yelled.

"I called them while you were in the shower." Adams went over to the chairman. It was clear he was afraid of him. He stood there, wringing his hands together as if trying to wash them clean. "This is the boy, Mr. Chairman," he muttered. "He came to the flat in the middle of the night. I called you the moment I could."

"You've done very well," the chairman muttered. He was still gazing at Matt. "I never thought it would be this easy," he said.

Matt swore at him.

"I knew you were looking for him, Mr. Chairman," Paul Adams went on. "And now you have him. So you don't need Scarly. Tell me you'll let Scarly go."

The chairman turned his head slowly and examined Scarlett's father as if he were a doctor about to break bad news. "I will not let Scarly go," he said. "I will never let Scarly go."

"Then at least let me see her. I've given you the boy. Don't I deserve a reward?"

"You most certainly do," the chairman said.

He nodded at one of the policemen, who shot Paul Adams in the head. Matt saw the spray of blood as the back of his skull was blown off. He was dead instantly. His knees buckled underneath him, and he fell to one side.

"A quick death," the chairman remarked. He nodded at Matt. "Soon you'll be wishing you could have had one too."

He turned and walked out of the room. Two of the policemen reached forward and jerked Matt to his feet. Then they dragged him out, along the corridor and down to the city below.

TWENTY-EIGHT

Tai Fung

T

SIGNAL ONE

The dragon was moving toward Hong Kong, closing in with deadly precision, gaining strength as it crossed the water. Scarlett had summoned it, and it had heard. Even she couldn't turn it back now.

It had begun its life as nothing more than a front of warm air, rising into the sky. But then, very quickly, a swirl of cloud had formed, spinning faster and faster with a dark, unblinking eye at the center. By the time the weather satellites had transmitted the first pictures from the Strait of Luzon, it was already too late. The dragon was awake. Its appetite was as big as the ocean where it had been born, and it would destroy anything that stood in its path.

The dragon was a typhoon.

Tai fung.

The words meant "big wind," but they went nowhere near describing the most powerful force of nature — a storm that contained a hundred storms within it. The typhoon would travel at over two hundred miles an hour.

Its eye might be thirty miles wide. The hurricane winds around it would generate as much energy in one second as ten nuclear bombs. To the Chinese, typhoons were also known as "the dragon's breath," as if they came from some terrible monster living deep in the sea.

Since 1884, the Hong Kong Observatory had put out a series of warnings whenever a typhoon had come within five hundred miles of the city, and each warning had come with a beacon, or a signal, attached. Signal One was shaped like a letter T and warned the local populace to stand by. Signal Three, an upside-down T, was more serious. Now people were told to stay at home, not to travel unless absolutely necessary. Later on came Signal Eight, a triangle, Signal Nine, an hourglass, and finally, most terrifyingly, Signal Ten. Perhaps appropriately, this took the shape of a cross. Signal Ten meant devastation. It would almost certainly bring wholesale loss of life.

And that was what was on its way now.

But there were no warnings. Nobody had been prepared for a typhoon in November, which was months after the storm season should have ended. And anyway, no typhoon could possibly have formed so quickly. It would normally take at least a week. This one had reached its full power in less than a day. The whole thing was impossible.

Nor was there anyone left to send out the signals. Hong Kong Observatory had been abandoned. Many of the scientists had left. The others were too scared to come to work as the city continued its descent into sickness and death.

Unseen, the dragon rushed toward them. The skyscrapers were already in its sight. Suddenly they seemed tiny and insubstantial as, with a great roar, it fell on them. By the time anyone realized what was happening, it was already far too late.

=

SIGNAL TWO

The chairman of the Nightrise Corporation was wondering how many people had died in the last twenty-four hours and how many more would die in the next. He could imagine them, sixty-six floors below, crawling over the sidewalks, begging for help that would never come, finally losing consciousness in a cloud of misery and pain. He himself would leave Hong Kong very soon. His work here was almost finished. It was time to claim his reward.

The Old Ones were going to give him the whole of Asia to rule over in recognition of what he had achieved. Even Genghis Khan hadn't been as powerful as that. He would live in a palace, an old-fashioned one with deep, marble baths and banquet rooms and gardens a mile long. The world leaders who survived would bow in front of him, and anyone who had ever offended him, in business or in private life, would die in ingenious ways that he had already designed. He would open a theatre of blood and they would star in it. Anything he wanted, he would have. The thought of it made his head spin.

He was behind his desk in his office on the executive floor of The Nail, and he was not alone. There was a man sitting on the same leather sofa that Scarlett Adams had occupied just a week before. The man had traveled a very long way, and he was still looking crumpled from his flight. He was elderly, dressed in a shabby, brown suit that didn't quite fit him. It was the right size, but it hung awkwardly. The man was bald, with white eyebrows and two small tufts of white hair around his ears. He looked ill at ease in this impressive office. He was out of place, and he knew it. But he was glad to be here. It had been a journey he had been determined to make.

His name was Gregor Malenkov. For many years he had been known as Father Gregory, but he planned to put that behind him now. He had left the Monastery of the Cry for Mercy for good. He too had come for his reward.

"So how do you like Hong Kong?" the chairman asked.

"It's an extraordinary city," Father Gregory rasped. "Quite extraordinary. I came here as a young man, but it was much smaller then. Half the buildings weren't here, and the airport was in a different place. All these lights! All the traffic and the noise! I have to say, I hardly recognized it."

"A week from now, it will be completely unrecognizable," the chairman said. "It will have become a necropolis. I'm sure you will understand what that means, a man of your learning."

"A city of the dead."

"Exactly. The entire population has begun to die. In just a matter of days, there will be no one left. The corpses are already piling up in the street. The hospitals are full — not that they would be of any use as the doctors and the nurses are dying too. Nobody even bothers to call the cemeteries. There's no room there. And soon things will get much, much worse. It will be interesting to watch."

"How are you killing them?" Father Gregory asked. "Would I be right in thinking it is something to do with the pollution?"

"You would be entirely correct, Father Gregory. Although perhaps I should not call you that, as I understand you are no longer in holy orders." The chairman stood up and went over to the window, but the view was almost completely obliterated by the mist that swirled around the building, chasing its own tail. There was going to be a storm. He could just make out the water down in the harbor. The water was choppy, rising into angry waves.

"There has always been pollution, blowing in from China," he continued. "And the strange thing is that the people here have tolerated it. Coal-fired power stations. Car exhausts. They have always accepted that it's a price that has to be paid for the comforts of modern life."

"And you have made it worse?"

"The Old Ones have added a few extra chemicals — some very poisonous ones — to the mix. You've seen the results. The elderly and the weak have been the first to go, but the rest of the city will follow if they are exposed to it for very much longer. Which they will be. An unpleasant death. We are safe, of course, inside The Nail. The air is filtered. We just have to be careful not to spend too long in the street."

Father Gregory pressed his fingers together. His sty had gotten much worse. The eyeball was jammed, no longer able to move. Only his good eye watched the chairman. "I have to say, I'm disappointed," he said. "I was looking forward to meeting — to actually seeing — the Old Ones."

"The Old Ones have left Hong Kong. They have a great deal of work to do, preparing for a war that will be starting very soon. As soon as they heard that Matthew Freeman had been taken, they went."

"I don't understand why they don't show themselves to the world," Father Gregory said. "You have two of the Gatekeepers. So surely nothing can stop them. . . ."

"It's not the way they work. If the Old Ones told the world that they existed, people would unite against them. That would defeat the point. By keeping themselves hidden, they can let humanity tear itself apart. That is what they enjoy."

There was a moment's silence. Father Gregory licked his lips, and something ugly came into his eyes. "I want to see the girl," he said. "I still can't believe that she managed to break free when I had her. I had plans. . . ."

"Yes, that was most unfortunate," the chairman agreed. "Well, right now they are together. The boy came all this way to find her, so I thought it would be amusing to let them spend one day in each other's company."

"Is that safe?"

"The two of them are locked up very securely, and nobody knows where they are. The boy has certain abilities that make him dangerous. But as for the girl . . ."

"What is her power?"

"It seems that she drew the short straw. I'm afraid Scarlett Adams is not quite the superhero one might have imagined." The chairman smiled. "She has the ability to predict the weather. That's all. She can tell if it's going to rain or if the sun is going to shine. As she will never see either of these things again, it will not do her very much good. We are sending her away tonight. To another country."

"You can't kill her, of course."

"It's vital that both children are kept alive. In pain, but alive. We are going to bury them in separate rooms, many thousands of miles apart. They will be given limited amounts of food and water, but no human contact. The Old Ones have asked me to blind Matt Freeman, and that will be done just before Scarlett leaves. We want her to take the horror of it with her. In the end, she will probably go mad. It will be one of the last memories that she has."

"Excellent. I'd like to be there when it happens."

"That may not be possible."

Father Gregory was disappointed. But he continued anyway. "What about the other boy?" he asked.

"Jamie Tyler?" The chairman was still standing at the window. "He is somewhere here in Hong Kong. We haven't yet been able to find him."

"Have you looked for him?"

The chairman blinked slowly. Far below, two Star Ferries were crossing each other's paths, fighting the storm as they made their way across the harbor. Where had the storm come from? It seemed to be getting stronger. He was surprised the ferries were still operating and looked forward to the time when they finally stopped. It had always annoyed him, watching them go back and forth.

A boat will be the death of you. And it will happen in Hong Kong.

A prophecy that had been made by a fortune-teller. Well, soon there would be no more boats. There would be no more Hong Kong.

"Jamie Tyler can't leave the city," he said. "Unless, of course, he dies in the street and gets thrown into the sea. Either way, he is of no concern to us."

There was another silence.

"But now, my dear Father Gregory," the chairman said. "It is time for you to go."

"I am a little tired," Father Gregory admitted.

"It has been a pleasure meeting you. But — please — let me show you out. . . ."

There was a handle on the edge of one of the windows, and the chairman seized hold of it and pulled. The entire window slid aside and the wind rushed in, the mist swirling round and round. Papers fluttered off the desk. The stench of the pollution filled the room.

Father Gregory stared. "I don't understand —" he began.

"It's perfectly simple," the chairman said. "You said it yourself. You let the girl escape. You let her slip through your hands. You don't really think that the Old Ones would let that go unpunished?"

"But . . . I found her!" Father Gregory was staring at the gap. "If it hadn't been for me, you would never have known who she was!"

"And that is why they have granted you an easy death." The chairman had to shout to make himself heard. "Please don't waste any more of my time, Father Gregory. It's time for you to go!"

Father Gregory stared at the open window, at the clouds rushing past outside. A single tear trickled from his good eye. But he understood. The chairman was right. He had failed.

"I've enjoyed meeting you," he said.

"Good-bye, Father Gregory."

The old man walked across the room and stepped out of the window. The chairman waited a moment, then slid it shut behind him. It was good to be back in the warmth again. He wiped some raindrops off his jacket.

The storm was definitely getting worse.

$$\perp$$

SIGNAL THREE

The Tai Shan Temple was very similar to all the other temples in Hong Kong.

It was perhaps a little larger, with three separate chambers connected by short corridors, but it had the same curving roof made of dark green tiles, and it was set back behind a wall, on the edge of a park, in its own private world. Inside, it was filled with smoke, both from the coils of incense that hung from the ceiling and from the oven, which was constantly burning bundles of paper and clothes as sacrifices to the Mountain of the East. There were several altars dedicated to a variety of gods who were represented by standing, sitting, and kneeling statues — a whole crowd of them, brilliantly colored, staring out with ferocious eyes.

Despite the bad weather, there were about fifteen people at prayer in the main chamber, bowing with armfuls of incense, muttering quietly to themselves. They were many different ages, men and women, and to all appearances they looked exactly the same as the people who came daily to Man Mo or Tin Hau. And yet there was something about them that suggested that religion was not, in fact, the first thing on their minds. They were too tense, too watchful. Their eyes were fixed on a single entrance at the back of the building — a low, wooden door with a five-pointed star cut into the surface.

The worshippers — who were, in fact, no such thing — had very simple instructions. Any child who passed through that door was to be seized. If they resisted, they could be hurt badly but preferably not killed. The same applied to any young person coming in from the street. They were to be stopped before they got anywhere near the door. The people in the temple were all armed with guns and knives, hidden beneath their clothes. They were in constant touch with The Nail and could call for backup at any time.

This was the ambush that Matt had feared. It was the reason he had refused to take the shortcut to Hong Kong. He had been right from the very start.

The fifteen of them stood there, muttering prayers they didn't believe and bowing to gods they didn't respect. And outside, gusts of wind — growing stronger by the minute — hurled themselves at the temple walls, battering at them as if trying to break through, tearing up the surrounding earth and the grass, whistling around the corners. A tile slid off the roof and smashed on the ground. A shutter came loose and was instantly torn away. The rain, traveling horizontally now, cut into the brickwork. The traffic in the street had completely snarled up. The drivers couldn't see. There was nothing they could do.

The wind rushed in, and the flames inside the temple furnace bent, flickered, and were suddenly extinguished. Nobody noticed. All their attention was fixed on the doorway. That was what they were there for. Ignoring the storm, they waited for the first of the Gatekeepers to arrive.

↑

SIGNAL FOUR

Scarlett was in a dark place, but someone was nudging her, trying to draw her back into the light. Unwillingly, she opened her eyes to find a boy leaning over her, shaking her awake. She recognized him at once and knew that the fact that he was with her, that he was bruised and disheveled, could mean only one thing . . . and it was the worst news of all. He was here because of her. The Old Ones must have tricked him into coming to Hong Kong, and now the two of them were prisoners. Scarlett felt a sense of great anger and bitterness. She had been drawn into this against her will. And it was already over. She had never been given a chance.

"Matt. . . ." she said.

At last the two of them were together. But this wasn't

how she had hoped they would meet. She drew herself into a sitting position and rubbed her eyes. They had given her back her own clothes, but her hair, cut so short, still felt unfamiliar to her. At least she had lost the contact lenses. She had taken them out the moment she had been left to herself.

"Are you okay?" Matt asked.

"No." She sounded miserable. "How long have I been asleep?"

"I don't know. They only brought me here an hour ago."

"When was that?"

"About eight o'clock."

"Night or day?"

"Day."

Matt examined his surroundings. They were in a bare, windowless room with brick walls and a concrete floor. The only light came from a bulb set in a wire mesh cage. From the moment the solid steel door had been closed and locked, he'd had to fight a sense of claustrophobia. They were deep underground. The policemen who had brought him here had forced him down four flights of stairs and then along a corridor that was like a tunnel. Ordinary policemen. The same as the ones who had arrested him. It seemed that the shape-changers, the fly soldiers, and all the other creatures of the Old Ones had decided to leave Hong Kong. He wondered why.

Despite everything, he had been relieved to find Scarlett. She looked very different from the photograph he had seen of her. He couldn't imagine what it must have been like for her, being stuck here on her own.

"Why are you here?" Scarlett asked. She still couldn't keep the disappointment out of her voice.

"I came for you," Matt said. He wanted to tell her more, but he didn't dare. There was always a chance that they were being listened to.

"You shouldn't have. I've ruined everything. I'd have got away if I hadn't . . ." Scarlett stopped herself. She couldn't bring herself to talk about her last meeting with her father.

Matt sat next to her so that they were shoulder to shoulder with their legs stretched out on the floor. From the way he moved, she could see that he had been hurt. He looked pale and exhausted. "Why don't you tell me everything that happened to you?" he suggested. "You could start by telling me where we are. Do you know?"

She nodded. "The chairman came to see me. . . ."

"Who is the chairman?"

"Just some creep in a suit."

"I think I may have met him."

"He wanted to gloat over me," Scarlett continued. "He told me that you were on your way, but I'd hoped he was lying. This is an old prison. We're right in the middle of Hong Kong. It was left over from Victorian times."

"So when do they serve breakfast?"

"They don't. It's bread and cold soup, and they bring it once a day."

Matt lowered his voice. "Hopefully we won't be here that long," he said. It was as much as he dared tell her, but even so, Scarlett felt a glimmer of hope. "You know I went to your home in Dulwich," he said, changing the subject.

"Was that you in the car? There was an accident —"

364

"It was no accident."

"I knew it had to be you," Scarlett said. "They planned it all very carefully, didn't they? Using me to get you here. Are any of the others with you?"

Matt nodded briefly and Scarlett understood. They both had to be careful what they said. She gazed at him as if seeing him for the first and the last time. "I can't believe you're here. I can't believe I'm really talking to you. Do you know, I've even dreamed about you."

"Don't worry about it," Matt said. "We all dream about each other. It's how it works."

"There's so much I don't understand."

"Join the club."

"It looks like I already have." She took a deep breath. "I don't know where my story even begins, but I suppose I'd better start with St. Meredith's. . . ."

She told him — briefly and without fuss — and as she spoke, Matt knew that he was going to like her. She had been through so much, and in a way her experiences reminded him of his own at Lesser Malling, the way she had been reeled into something so completely beyond her understanding. And yet she had coped with it. She had been brought here. She had been locked in this room for three days. But she hadn't cracked. She was ready to fight back.

She finished talking, and it seemed to Matt that just for a moment the building trembled as something, a shock wave, traveled through the walls. Scarlett looked up, alarmed. Part of her knew what was happening and had even been expecting it.

"What?" Matt began.

"It was nothing." She said it so hastily that he could see she didn't want to talk about it, didn't even want to imagine what might be happening outside. "Tell me about yourself," she went on quickly. "Tell me how you got here. Did you go to the temple? They've got people there waiting for you. They thought you'd come through one of the doors."

"I didn't."

He told her his own story, or part of it, starting in Peru. It would have taken too long to tell her the whole thing, and he was still afraid of being overheard. From Nazca to London to Macao . . . It had been a long journey, and it was only now that they both saw how closely they had been following each other's paths.

Matt finished by explaining how he had found his way to Wisdom Court. This was the difficult part. He had seen Scarlett's father die, and he had been at least in part responsible. How was he going to break the news?

But she was already ahead of him. "That shirt you're wearing," she said. She had suddenly realized. "It's his."

"Yes," Matt admitted.

"Where is he now?" Matt didn't answer and she continued. "They've killed him, haven't they?"

Matt nodded. He didn't want to remember what he had seen in the last moments before he had been taken out of Wisdom Court.

Scarlett's face didn't change, but suddenly there were tears in her eyes. "It was all his fault," she said. "He thought he could make a deal with the Old Ones." She paused. "I don't know, Matt. I suppose that's the way they work. They get ordinary people to do evil things for them. They used him. He really thought he was helping me."

The building shivered a second time. It wasn't as strong as it had been before, but they both felt it.

"You know that Hong Kong is dying," Scarlett said. "The chairman told me. They're doing it deliberately. They want to turn it into what they call a necropolis. A city of the dead."

"I saw some of it last night," Matt said. "It was horrible."

"Don't tell me. I lived in it. I can't believe I didn't see what was going on." She sighed. "What will happen to us, Matt? Are we going to be killed?"

"They don't want to kill us," Matt said. "It's complicated. But killing us doesn't really help."

"Then what?"

"They think they've beaten us, but they haven't. The others are still out there. And you and me . . ."

"What about us?"

"They put us together because they want to crow over us. But that's their mistake. Because —"

He didn't finish the sentence.

There was an explosion. It was loud and immediate — and it came from somewhere inside the building.

"What — ?" Scarlett began.

Then the light went out.

↓

SIGNAL FIVE

Lohan had used the storm as cover, closing in on the prison through streets that had quickly emptied as

367

the weather had become more intense. He had only been given one night to prepare the attack, but he had still managed to assemble a small army. He had a hundred men with him, all of them well armed. The Triads had been smuggling weapons across Asia for many years, supplying anyone from terrorists to mercenaries. Lohan had simply taken what he needed. He had plenty of choice.

Meanwhile, Jet and Sing would be arriving at the Tai Shan Temple. They both had the rank of 426, Red Pole, making them fighting unit lieutenants. They had another fifty men with them, and both operations were to begin at the same moment. There was one door out of Hong Kong. The way there had to be cleared.

Lohan knew where Matt had been taken because he had followed him. This was what Matt had been unable to tell Scarlett. He had played a trick on the chairman. Just for once, he was the one pulling the strings.

Matt had contacted Lohan the night before, the call forwarded through the Kung Hing Tao firework company. The Triad leader already knew what had happened. Richard and Jamie were with him. The two of them had made it out of the water and over to Kowloon. They were standing next to him, worrying desperately about Matt, when the phone rang.

"We have to find Scarlett," Matt had said. "And there's only one way to do it. We have to let the Old Ones capture me."

"How will you do that?"

"Paul Adams — Scarlett's father — will call them and tell them I'm at Wisdom Court. They won't suspect anything. They know that he wants Scarlett back, and they'll think he's still trying to help them."

"And then?"

"You have your men outside. You follow me wherever they take me."

"How do you know they'll take you to Scarlett?"

"I don't — not for sure. But my guess is they'll probably hold us together. I know the way these people think. They'll want to parade us, to boast about how they've beaten us. Having the two of us together will make it more fun for them. Anyway, I haven't got any other ideas, so we'll just have to risk it."

Richard had come onto the phone. He had heard what Matt was suggesting. "You can't do this," he pleaded. "It's too dangerous. Please, Matt, think what could go wrong."

"We don't know where she is, Richard. There's no other way we'll find her."

"What about Paul Adams? Once they have no further use for him, you know they'll kill him."

"He's prepared to risk it. He knows what he's done. And he'll do anything to get Scarlett freed."

Six police cars had arrived at Wisdom Court just after seven o'clock. Lohan — with Richard and Jamie crouching next to him — had watched the police go in. They had seen the chairman arrive and leave, and they were still there when Matt, semiconscious and in pain, had been dragged out. Jamie had started forward at that moment, wanting to go to him. But Richard had grabbed hold of him, forcing him to remain still. This was Matt's plan. It was all or nothing.

Matt had been driven across the city, never out of sight of Lohan's men. They had seen him disappear into the prison close to Hollywood Road. So now they knew where he was being held. Hopefully, Scarlett would be there too. As the storm had worsened, Lohan had surrounded the prison, his men closing in from all sides.

The storm.

Lohan was beginning to think that it was getting out of control. In all the years that he had been in Hong Kong, he had never experienced anything like it. When he stood up, he could feel the wind trying to batter him down again. Dust and dead leaves whipped into his face. He could hear the air currents howling as they rushed through the streets. If it got any worse, it would be dangerous out here. But then, of course, it was dangerous anyway. If the storm destroyed the city, it would only be finishing what the Old Ones had already begun.

A crash of thunder. Rain lashing down so hard that he could see it bouncing off the parked cars, turning into miniature rivers that coursed along the side of the road. In seconds, he was soaked. Richard was next to him. "What's going on?" Richard muttered.

"We must move now," Lohan said.

Victoria Prison was a huge building with barred windows and a single, massive door — the only way in. Six armed guards stood outside it in the rain, dressed in uniforms, with their faces partly obscured by their caps. Lohan, Richard, and Jamie were watching from the doorway of an antique shop across the road. Lohan's strategy was simple. There was no time to be clever. He knew he had to break in as quickly and as decisively as possible. Once the enemy knew they were there, they would fight back.

He gave the signal.

There was an explosion — the same explosion that Matt had heard — as a rocket launcher, concealed in a parked van, fired a 40mm shell at the main door. The prison hadn't been built to withstand such an attack. The doors were blown apart in a ball of flame. Half the guards were killed instantly. The rest were cut down by a burst of machine-gun fire as the Triad fighters surged forward, pouring out of alleyways and rising up from behind parked cars. Farther down the road, two of Lohan's men, disguised as construction workers, cut off the main power supply, isolating the prison and short-circuiting the alarms.

"Move!" Richard and Jamie were unarmed, but they ran forward with Lohan and in through the shattered doors.

And then they were inside the prison. Lohan's people were spreading in every direction, through the upper floors, smashing open the doors to reveal the empty cells behind them. Some of them were armed with guns and grenades. Others carried swords and chain-sticks. It was pitch-black inside the building now that the electricity had been cut, but they had brought flashlights with them, strapped to their shoulders, the beams slicing through the dark and showing the way ahead. Lohan's orders were clear: Kill anyone who gets in your way. Find Matt and Scarlett. We have only minutes to get them out.

There were more guards on the upper levels. Although the building held only two prisoners, the chairman had taken no chances. Now they opened fire on the invaders.

Lohan saw the flash of bullets, heard some of the Triad men cry out. A few bodies fell. Then someone threw a grenade. Another fireball, and one of the guards pitched forward as if diving into a swimming pool, disappearing into the darkness below.

Lohan himself led a group of fighters four floors down into the basement, Richard and Jamie close behind him. Only now was Richard beginning to see the hopelessness of the task. There had to be at least two hundred cells in the prison. Were they really going to blow every one of them open? They came to a corridor with more steel doors set at intervals. A guard ran toward them, bringing his machine gun round to aim.

"Drop the gun!" Jamie said. "Lie on the floor."

The guard did as he was told. A second guard appeared. He was less fortunate. Lohan shot him down. They had been in the prison for less than three minutes, but they knew that reinforcements would already be on the way. There was another explosion upstairs, a scream, the clatter of bullets hitting metal.

Thirty doors stretched out in front of them. There was no point looking for bolts or keys. Lohan rapped out an order and his men blew them open, one at a time, using balls of plastic explosive. Richard and Jamie continued forward as, one after another, the doors were smashed out of their frames, orange flames briefly flaring up. The corridor stank of cordite. Smoke and brick dust filled the air. But every cell was empty. How much more time did they have?

"They're at the end," Jamie said suddenly. "The last door on the left."

Lohan stared at him. But Richard nodded, relief surging through him. Somehow Jamie had managed to connect with them in his own way . . . telepathically. Lohan shouted something, and his men ran down to the door he had indicated. A final blast. It swung open. Two figures came out into the corridor, choking and covered in dust. It was Matt and Scarlett.

"Matt!" Richard grabbed hold of his friend and embraced him. The night before, when he had pulled himself out of the water, he had been afraid that he would never see him again. "Are you okay?"

Matt nodded. "This is Scarlett."

"I'm delighted to meet you." Richard didn't know what else to say. He examined the girl with the close-cropped hair. She looked worn out.

Jamie said nothing, but he went over to her so that the three Gatekeepers were together.

"We have to get to the Tai Shan Temple," Matt said.

Lohan was impressed. The boy was only fifteen, but already he had assumed command. The experiences of the past twenty-four hours didn't seem to have had any effect on him. But there was still more trouble to come. Quickly, Lohan took out his mobile phone, pressed a button, and spoke a few words. He waited until he had heard what he wanted, then he turned to Matt. "The temple is safe now," he said. "But we have another problem, and it may be more serious. There is a storm. In fact, my people are saying that it may be something worse. . . ."

But they had all become aware of it. Above the gunfire and the explosions, beyond the battle that was taking place inside the prison, the wind was screaming. The whole building was shuddering. The full force of the typhoon had fallen on Hong Kong, and its total destruction had begun.

SIGNAL SIX

The sun was setting in Cuzco, the ancient city of the Incas, in Peru. There was a band playing, and the sound of panpipes and the throb of drums rose up into the evening air. The shadows were stretching out over the foothills. The restaurants and cafés were beginning to fill up at the end of another day.

Pedro knew that they shouldn't be here. This wasn't Matt's plan. He wished that they had been able to speak over the satellite telephone, but for the past forty-eight hours there had been only silence. A whole world separated them. They were thousands of miles apart. But he was about to take the single step that would bring them together. He wondered if it was a good idea.

Not that he had been given any choice.

The night before, Pedro had woken up to find Scott leaning over him. The two boys were sharing a stone house in Vilcabamba, high up in the Andes. This was the lost city where Pedro had gone with Matt when they were hiding from Diego Salamanda. It was hidden above the cloud forest in an extraordinary location, a mountain peak that couldn't be seen by anyone. Getting there had involved a helicopter ride and then a one-day hike from

Cuzco. The city itself could only be reached by a stone staircase that could vanish in a single moment.

"Scott? What is it?"

Scott was deathly pale, and his eyes were full of worry. Pedro had never seen him like this before. "Jamie's in trouble," he said. "We have to go to Hong Kong."

"We can't —"

"Pedro. You don't understand. We have to go straight away. I have to go to Jamie. I've had a dream."

The dreamworld. All of them had been there. They all knew its significance. They had talked about it often enough. Pedro knew that he couldn't argue. If Scott had been sent a message, they couldn't ignore it — particularly if it involved his brother. And yet the doors were supposed to be too dangerous. It was the whole reason Matt and Jamie had flown to Europe, and why the two of them had been left behind.

"Are you sure . . . ?" he began.

Scott wasn't in the mood for an argument. "I'm leaving as soon as it's light," he said. "You can come with me or you can stay behind."

The next morning, they left together. One of the Incas escorted them down to the clearing where the helicopter was waiting, and then it was a two-hour flight to the Cuzco airport. All the time, Scott had been silent and intense. He still hadn't explained what he had seen. He was often reserved, but now he seemed miles away, staring ahead with empty eyes. Pedro was trying not to think what they were letting themselves in for. Of all the Gatekeepers, he alone had never been through one of the doors, and the thought of transporting himself halfway round the world filled him with dread.

And here they were now in Cuzco. It was a beautiful evening with hundreds of tourists milling around the brightly colored stalls that were spread out in front of them. The cathedral would be closing soon. The last visitors were coming out, surrounded by street children begging for money and sweets. Taxis, like wind-up toys made out of tin, were buzzing around the main square.

Pedro was hungry, but he didn't dare suggest that they stop and eat. He knew what the answer would be.

"There it is." Scott pointed at a great pile of bricks and ornate windows, a Spanish church built on the site of a place of worship that had been there centuries before. The Temple of Coricancha. It was where he and Jamie had found themselves when they first arrived in Peru. Inside was the doorway that had brought them from a cave in Nevada.

Neither of them spoke again. Pedro shook his head and followed as, with grim determination, Scott began to walk across the square.

$\rightarrow$

SIGNAL SEVEN

Matt and Scarlett stood in the shelter of the prison, knowing that they couldn't leave. Hong Kong was being torn apart by a force so devastating it was as if they had arrived at some chapter in the Bible when all the old prophecies happened and Judgment Day finally arrived.

Smashed buildings and debris were being flung along the street as if they weighed nothing. As they looked out of the broken doorway, a huge neon sign spun past like an oversize playing card. It was followed by a table, several crates, a lawn mower, part of a piano — they had somehow been sucked out of the shops and sent on their way as if they were prizes in some insane TV game show. Matt could actually see the air currents. Mixed with the rain, they had become a thousand gray needles that raced along the streets, slamming into cars and tipping them over, flattening everything in their path.

He looked up and saw two clouds rushing together, moving faster than he could have believed. They hit and there was a massive burst of thunder. A bolt of electricity, so bright that it hurt his eyes, crackled down and smashed into a skyscraper half a mile away, cutting it in two. Shards of glass and pieces of broken metal burst outward as the top seven floors of the building leaned over and then fell, trailing wires and pipes. Matt didn't see where they landed or how many people were killed, but he heard the massive explosion as they hit the street below. Despite the rain, what remained of the building caught fire. The orange flames licked at the falling water, desperately trying to climb into the air.

"We must wait." Lohan was right next to him. Matt understood what he meant. If they took so much as one step forward out of the protection of the walls, they would be whisked away. He was having to shout the words to make himself heard.

"We can't wait!" Matt shouted back. "We only have this one chance. We must leave Hong Kong now."

Scarlett was behind him with Richard and Jamie. Matt turned round and their eyes met. In that moment, they both understood what was happening. They could have no secrets from each other. "This is you!" he shouted at her. The wind was still howling. A window on the other side of the road was suddenly torn out, the glass leaping away. "You've done this!"

"No!" Scarlett shook her head, trying to deny it.

"We all have powers. All five of us. This is yours."

And Scarlett knew he was right. In a way, she had known it all along.

Her real name wasn't Scarlett Adams. White Lotus believed that she was a reincarnation of Lin Mo, a figure out of Chinese mythology, a goddess of the sea. And if she had once been a goddess, then she would have a power that went far beyond anything humanly possible. The chairman of Nightrise had made another mistake: He had thought she could only predict the weather. In fact, she could control it.

The evidence had always been there. At school in Dulwich, when Scarlett had wanted to go on a history trip, the weather had cleared up against all expectations. The same thing had happened again in Hong Kong when she'd needed to get to The Peak. Against all the forecasts, the rain had stopped and the sun had suddenly come out.

She had even used the same power at the battle, ten thousand years before. Jamie had once described it to Matt. Just as Pedro had appeared with his reinforcements, a storm had started, the rain coming down so violently that the Old Ones had been unable to see him.

It hadn't been a coincidence.

It had been her.

The chairman had claimed that she was the weakest of the Five. He had been wrong. She was by far the most powerful.

"You can stop it!" Matt shouted.

"I can't!" Scarlett shook her head. She had brought the dragon. She accepted that much. But looking inside herself, after three days in prison, after all she had been through, she knew that she didn't have the strength to turn it back.

"Then you can protect us. You can keep it away."

Scarlett looked out into the road, at the crashing rain, the buildings being scattered like confetti, cars spinning crazily, broken pieces of wood and metal hurtling past. Had she really done this, brought destruction on an entire city? How many people would she have killed? The thought terrified her more than anything else she had seen. Was she really responsible for this?

"I can't do it, Matt. . . ."

"You have to! We have to reach the temple."

Lohan understood. "It's not so far from here," he shouted. "I can show you."

"Scar?" Matt looked at her.

And maybe it was simply the fact that he had used that name, a name from ten thousand years ago. Maybe that was the trigger. But in that second, something changed. Scarlett took a deep breath. For too long she had been a victim, pushed around by the chairman, by the Old Ones, even by the Triads. It was time to put that behind her. She was a Gatekeeper. That was what had brought her into all this, and suddenly she felt a great anger for everything she had lost — her friends, her home — even her father. And with the anger came the full knowledge of her own strength. She knew what she had to do.

"Follow me," she said.

They left the prison. First Lohan, then Scarlett and Matt, with Richard and Jamie behind. They stepped outside into the rain, into the wind, into an endless explosion as nature pounded the city with all its strength. They should have been thrown off their feet instantly, or battered senseless to the ground. But the wind spun around them. The rain was lashing everything, but they remained dry. They walked into the heart of the typhoon, and it swallowed them up without touching them. It was as if they were inside a glass ball that surrounded and protected them. They could barely see. Everything was chaos. But while they stayed together, they were safe.

Lohan led the way, but it was Scarlett who made it possible. She seemed to be in a trance, gazing straight ahead, her arms by her side. Matt kept close to her, knowing that his life depended on her protection. All around them, everywhere he looked, brick walls crumbled, buildings fell, windows shattered, and, spinning in the rain, lethal shards of broken glass came slashing down. Again and again the thunder sounded. The clouds were a boiling mass.

They didn't hurry. There was no need to. No living thing was going to come out in the typhoon, and the five of them were completely invisible. Scarlett was more confident now. She looked almost relaxed. Walking next to her, Matt was amazed by the extent of her power. He could feel it flowing out of her. She was a girl and she was fifteen years old. But she could destroy the entire world.

Another building fell behind them, crumbling in on itself as if it had simply lost the will to live. Bricks showered down, slamming into the pavement, but not near them. The road continued straight ahead. They could see the park. Most of the trees had been uprooted and turned into flying battering rams. The few that remained were bending over, kissing the ground. The Tai Shan Temple was on the other side. Matt was surprised that it was still standing, but perhaps the wall that surrounded it had protected it from the worst of the weather.

Lohan pointed. Scarlett nodded. There was no need for any of them to speak. They had made it. They had crossed Hong Kong in the middle of a typhoon, and they had survived.

Moving faster now, they crossed what was left of the park and went in.

▲

SIGNAL EIGHT

The chairman of the Nightrise Corporation was watching the final destruction of his necropolis. He was back in his office on the sixty-sixth floor of The Nail, and he could feel the whole building trembling as it was buffeted again and again by the storm. Every now and then there was a grinding sound followed by an explosion of breaking glass as another window burst out of its frame. The lights had long ago flickered and gone out. There was no power in the office. Nor were there any people. The staff had all evacuated, fighting and clawing their way down sixty-six flights of stairs. Some of them might have made it to the basement and would be huddled there now, but he suspected that many more of them would have been killed on the way down — pushed down the stairs or trampled in the general panic. The chairman certainly had no intention of joining them. He was safe here. The Nail could stand up to anything. And it was a spectacular view.

It did trouble him that his plans had somehow gone wrong. The city had been meant to die. That had been the whole idea. But not like this. Indeed, the typhoon might well end up saving many more people than it actually killed because there had been a side effect: The poisonous gases put in place by the Old Ones had been dispersed. The pollution had been swept away. When the storm finally eased off, the people would be able to breathe again.

He didn't know what had happened at Victoria Prison. All the telephone lines were down, and even his mobile didn't work. The whole network must have collapsed. But this devastation couldn't be a coincidence. The girl must have brought it. She was able to predict the weather, so at the very least she must have known it was coming. He had put the boy in with her to taunt her, to show her how completely defeated she had been. Perhaps, all in all, it had been a mistake.

He was holding a bottle of cognac. It had a price tag that made it one of the most expensive in the world, and it had always amused him that there were people dying in some countries because they had no water while he could afford to spend five thousand dollars on a drink he didn't even enjoy. Over the years, most of the chairman's taste buds had died. Nothing he ate or drank had any flavor. If he was killed now, it would hardly matter. Most of him was dead anyway.

But he wasn't going to die. Even if Matt and Scarlett had escaped, there was nowhere for them to go. The Tai Shan Temple was protected. They wouldn't be able to reach the door. And soon the typhoon would pass. He would begin the search through the wreckage immediately, turning it over brick by brick, and next time he would deal with them at once.

He noticed something out of the corner of his eye. It was a speck in the window. At first he thought it was a bird. No. It was extraordinary. As the chairman watched, it grew larger and larger. It was heading toward him.

It was a ship.

Not a huge ship. A wooden sampan, one of the Chinese sailing boats that were kept moored up in the harbor, to be photographed by tourists. The wind had grabbed it and torn it free. Even as the chairman watched, it was getting closer, rapidly filling up the window frame. He stood there, transfixed by the sight. He thought about running. Perhaps he could still make it to safety. But what was the point? How could he escape something that had been predicted so many years ago?

He would die in an accident that involved a ship.

He died now.

The sampan was thrown at The Nail as if it were a paper dart that had been deliberately aimed. It smashed through the window on the sixty-sixth floor and into the man who stood behind it. At the same time, the wind howled in, scooping up the contents of the room and throwing them out, the files and papers rattling with a sound that was very like applause. The broken body of the chairman went with them, spun once in the air, then plunged down to the pavement below.

Bloodstains on the carpet. A bottle of cognac with its contents gurgling out. A scattering of broken glass. In the end, that was all that was left.

▼
▲

SIGNAL NINE

There had been a bloody battle inside the Tai Shan Temple. All the bodies had been taken into one of the other chambers, but the evidence was still there in the bullet holes across the walls, rubble and scorch marks from a grenade, a puddle of blood in front of the main altar. One of the porcelain gods was standing with his arms outstretched, but his body now ended at his neck, which was jagged and hollow. His head was in pieces all around him. Another had lost a hand. It was as if they had tried to take part in the fight and had been crippled as a result.

Jet and Sing had been on their own, waiting for Scarlett and the others to arrive. They had no idea how she had managed to cross Hong Kong — it would have been impossible now to leave the building — but they were glad to see her when she walked in. Jet had been wounded. He was holding a dressing against his neck, and his shirt was soaked in blood. Sing was still holding the sword stick that he had used to kill Audrey Cheng. He seemed to be unhurt.

Neither of them had noticed that there was another man in the chamber, hiding underneath the altar. He was one of the chairman's men, and he had been shot twice. It was his blood that was pooling out. He knew he didn't have very long. There was a gun inches from his outstretched hand.

Speaking in Chinese, Lohan demanded a report from his two lieutenants. Quickly, they told him what he wanted to know, and he translated for Matthew and Richard.

"There were many people waiting here," he said. "They would have killed you if you had tried to reach the door. But they have all been dealt with."

"Then let's get out of here," Richard said. He turned to Matt. "It's time to go."

Lohan walked forward and shook Scarlett's hand. "Good luck," he said. "The journey that we made together just now is something that I will never forget."

"I'm glad I met you, Lohan," Scarlett said. "Thank you for helping me." She had relaxed a little, but Matt could see that she was still concentrating, keeping the typhoon at bay. She had to stay in control. While she was inside the temple, the wind and the rain were barely touching its walls.

The door with the five-pointed star was in front of

them. It seemed so small and ordinary that it was hard to believe that it would lead them, not outside and into the storm but to anywhere in the world.

"So where are we going, Matt?" Jamie asked.

The dying man had fumbled for the gun. From where he was lying, he could only see the two boys and the Chinese man who had arrived with them. The girl was standing right behind and the other man was somewhere out of sight. He could probably take out at least two of them before he was killed himself. He had decided that was what he would do. After all, it was the reason he was here.

Which one first?

The boy who had just asked the question — the one with the long hair and the American accent — was directly in his sight. Slowly, the man took aim. The boy was only a few steps away. The man's hand was sticky with his own blood. The gun was covered in it. But he knew exactly what he was doing. There was no way he was going to miss. . . .

The door with the five-pointed star opened.

Scott, with Pedro right behind him, burst into the temple. Jamie opened his mouth to speak. Matt was gazing in surprise. What had seemed impossible for so long had finally happened. The Gatekeepers had come together. They were all here, in the same space.

Scott. Jamie. Matt. Pedro. And Scarlett.

The Five.

But Scott hadn't stopped. He ran forward and threw himself at his brother, knocking him aside.

A second later, there was a gunshot.

Lohan acted with lightning speed. His own gun was in his hand instantly and he fired five times, the bullets strafing underneath the altar. The man who had been concealed there was killed before he could fire again.

Richard saw that Jamie was all right. Somehow Scott had known and had arrived in time to save him. But then Matt cried out.

The shot had missed Jamie, but Scarlett had been standing right behind him. She had been hit in the head and the wound was a bad one. Blood was pouring down the side of her neck. She toppled sideways. Richard caught her before she hit the floor.

As she lost consciousness, the whole world exploded.

The typhoon had been kept at bay for too long. Now, as if recognizing what had happened, it fell on the Tai Shan Temple with all its strength. It was like being hit by a bomb, but in slow motion. As the nine of them stood there — the five Gatekeepers with Richard, Lohan, Jet, and Sing — the whole building disintegrated around them. The roof was the first to go, torn off as if by a giant hand. Green tiles came crashing down. The wind roared in. Then one of the walls buckled and collapsed, the huge stones toppling forward. For centuries, the gods inside the temple had never seen daylight. Now they were flooded in it as the outside world burst in.

"The door!" Matt shouted.

It was still standing, but it wouldn't be there for long. Once the walls were destroyed, it would all be over. The door would go with them. Even now it might be too late. Jamie had joined his brother. The two of them had already turned toward it. Pedro seemed to be confused, frozen to the spot. Matt reached him and spun him round. Richard was hurrying forward, carrying Scarlett in his arms, limp, her eyes closed. Lohan followed. One of the spinning tiles had hit him and he was cradling his arm. There was no sign now of Jet and Sing. They had disappeared beneath the broken wall.

The door had been built for the Gatekeepers, but each of them could take one companion with them. Richard was with Scarlett. Lohan was with Matt. There was still a chance they could all get out alive.

There was another explosion, and a great hole suddenly appeared, punched into the wall. Rain and daylight came shafting through. The whole temple was shaking. Scott was the first to reach the door and threw it open. Behind him, the remaining gods were toppling and smashing to pieces on the hard floor. Pedro was next to him. The others were right behind.

They plunged through just as a last bolt of lightning struck the temple, pulverizing it. The remaining walls were swept away and scattered. Moments later, there was nothing left. Hong Kong Park was empty. And beyond it, Hong Kong itself lay in ruins as the clouds finally parted and the first, small ray of sunlight was allowed through.

SIGNAL TEN

The Necropolis was finished.

Much of it had been destroyed. More than half the skyscrapers had collapsed. Whole streets were buried beneath piles of twisted metal and brickwork that would take years to remove. Scavengers were already hard at work, burrowing into the rubble to find the jewelry — the diamond necklaces and the watches — that must surely lie beneath.

All over the world, people were waking up to the fact that a catastrophe on a massive scale had occurred. Twenty-four-hour television news programs were running the first pictures. There would be thousands dead, but at least the survivors would be able to breathe. The poisonous smog that had been suffocating them for so long had been completely swept aside.

Far away, sitting in the ice palace that he had made his home, the King of the Old Ones saw what had happened. He knew that the chairman had failed him. He knew that the Gatekeepers had escaped.

But it didn't matter.

The Five had entered the door without knowing where they were going, so none of them would have arrived in the same place. They would be as far apart now as they had ever been. Worse than that, the door had been disintegrating even as they had passed through it, and the final blast had played one last trick on them. If the five of them had survived the journey, they would find out very soon.

It would be a very long time before they found each other again.

It was enough.

The King of the Old Ones reached out and gave the order that his disciples had been waiting for. He had made the decision. It was time for the end of the world to begin.

Galería Hispánica

THIRD EDITION

Margaret Adey
Louis Albini
Robert Lado
Joseph Michel
Hilario S. Peña

McGRAW-HILL BOOK COMPANY

New York   St. Louis   San Francisco   Auckland   Bogotá   Düsseldorf
Johannesburg   London   Madrid   Mexico   Montreal   New Delhi
Panama   Paris   São Paulo   Singapore   Sydney   Tokyo   Toronto

CREDITS

Editor: Joan Saslow
Editing Supervisor: Lois Kierstead-Lapid
Design Supervisor: Jim Darby
Production Supervisor: Angela Kardovich

Copy Editing: Suzanne Shetler
Photo Editor: Suzanne Volkman
Illustrations: Claudia Karabaic Sargent
Text Design: Graphic Arts International
Cover photo by George Holton/Photo Researchers, is a *mola*—a good example
 of Panamanian folk art.

Library of Congress Cataloging in Publication Data
Galería hispánica.

First-2d ed. by R. Lado.
Includes index.
1. Spanish language—Grammar—1950-   I. Adey,
Margaret. II. Lado, Robert, date   Galería
hispánica.
PC4112.G35 1979   468'.2'421   78-14538
ISBN 0-07-000361-0

ABOUT THE AUTHORS

Margaret Adey teaches Spanish at David Crockett High School in Austin, Texas, where she introduced language laboratory instruction. She organized and directed the Spanish Workshop for High School Students in Guanajuato, Mexico (formerly of Monterrey), for eighteen years, and is a past president of the Austin Chapter of the American Association of Teachers of Spanish and Portuguese.

Louis Albini is Chairman of the Foreign Language Department of Pascack Hills High School, Montvale, New Jersey. He taught methods and demonstration classes at the University of Puerto Rico for the NDEA Institute for three summers. Mr. Albini has been a pioneer in the use of the language laboratory in New Jersey.

Robert Lado, Professor of Linguistics and former Dean of the School of Languages and Linguistics at Georgetown University, is a well-known author in the field of linguistics and language teaching. Dr. Lado is the author of *Language Teaching: A Scientific Approach*, *Language Testing*, and *Linguistics Across Cultures*.

Joseph Michel is Professor of Spanish and Dean of the College of Multidisciplinary Studies at the University of Texas at San Antonio. He was founder of the Foreign Language Education Center at the University of Texas at Austin. From 1964 to 1965 he was a Fulbright lecturer on foreign language teaching at the University of Madrid, and he taught Spanish in Monterrey, Mexico, for seven years.

Hilario S. Peña was a teacher of Spanish and French for twenty-two years and was a junior high school principal in the city of Los Angeles. Dr. Peña was Assistant Director of the NDEA Spanish Institute at the University of Southern California for six consecutive years and is a member of the California Advisory Council of Educational Research.

ACKNOWLEDGMENTS

The authors would like to thank the following publishers, authors, and holders of copyright for their permission to reproduce the following literary works:

"Una Carta a Dios" by Gregorio López y Fuentes, from *Cuentos campesinos de México*, published by Editorial Cima, Mexico, D.F., courtesy of Gregorio López y Fuentes.

"El Gato de Sèvres" by Marco A. Almazán, from *El Libro de las comedias*, 1976, published by Editorial Jus, S.A., Mexico, D.F.

"Signos de puntuación" by M. Toledo y Benito, from *Repaso y composición*, 1947, published by D.C. Heath and Company, Boston, Massachusetts.

"El Mensajero de San Martín" from *Segundo curso progresando*, published by D.C. Heath and Company, Boston, Massachusetts.

"El Alcázar no se rinde" by Carlos Ruiz de Azilú, from *Temas españoles*, published by Publicaciones Españolas, Madrid, Spain.

"Una Medalla de bronce" by Alvaro de Laiglesia, from *Medio muerto nada más*, 1962, published by Editorial Planeta, S.A., Barcelona, Spain.

"El Indio del Mayab" by Antonio Médiz Bolio, from *Lectura en voz alta*, 1972, published by Editorial Porrua, S.A., Mexico, D.F.

"La Yaqui hermosa" by Amado Nervo, from *Obras completas*, Vol. 20, *Cuentos misteriosos,* published by Ruiz-Castilla y Cía., S.A., Editorial Biblioteca Nueva, Madrid, Spain.

"Manuel" by Pedro Villa Fernández, from *Por esas Españas*, 1945, published by Holt, Rinehart and Winston, New York, New York.

"El Lago encantado" from *Cuentos contados*, edited by Pittaro and Green, published by D.C. Heath and Company, Boston, Massachusetts.

"La Vieja del Candilejo" by Antonio Jiménez-Landi, from *Leyendas de España*, 1967, published by Aguilar S. A. de Ediciones, Madrid, Spain.

"La Camisa de Margarita" by Ricardo Palma, from *An Anthology of Spanish American Literature*, Vol. I, edited by Englekirk, Leonard, Reid, and Crow, 1968, published by Appleton-Century-Crofts, New York, New York, reprinted by permission of Prentice-Hall, Inc., Englewood Cliffs, New Jersey.

"El Abanico" by Vicente Riva Palacio, from *Cuentos del general*, 1929, published by Editorial "Cultura", Mexico, D.F.

"El Padre" by Olegario Lazo Baeza, from *Cuentos hispanoamericanos*, 1970, published by Editorial Universitaria, Santiago, Chile.

"La Pared" by Vicente Blasco Ibáñez, from *La Condenada*, 1919, published by Prometeo, Sociedad Editorial, Valencia, Spain.

"Una Esperanza" by Amado Nervo, from *Obras completas*, Vol. 5, *Cuentos misteriosos*, published by Ruiz-Castilla y Cía., S.A., Editorial Biblioteca Nueva, Madrid, Spain.

"Mejor que perros" by José Mancisidor, from *Escritores contemporáneos de México*, 1949, edited by Paul Patrick Roger, published by Houghton Mifflin Company, Boston, Massachusetts, courtesy of Dolores Varela de Mancisidor.

"En el Ford azul" by Lizandro Otero, from *El Cuento actual latinoamericano*, 1973, published by Librería Porrua Hnos., S.A., Mexico, D.F.

"La Lechuza" by Alberto Gerchunoff, from *Los Gauchos judíos*, 1910, published by EUDEBA, Buenos Aires, Argentina, courtesy of Ana María Gerchunoff de Kantor.

"En el fondo del caño hay un negrito" by José Luis González, from *En este lado*, published by Los Presentes, Mexico, D.F.

"La Muerta" by Carmen Laforet, from *La Niña y otros relatos*, published by Editorial Magesterio Español, S.A., Madrid, Spain.

"A la deriva" by Horacio Quiroga, from *Biblioteca Roda*, published by Claudio García y Cía., Editores, Montevideo, Uruguay.

"La Cita" by Raquel Banda Farfán, from *Siglo veinte*, 1968, edited by Leal and Silverman, published by Holt, Rinehart and Winston, New York, New York.

"El Diente roto" by Pedro Emilio Coll, from *Siglo veinte*, 1968, edited by Leal and Silverman, published by Holt, Rinehart and Winston, New York, New York.

"Narración personal de Elías Garza" by Elías Garza, from *El Inmigrante mexicano: la historia de su vida*, 1969, edited by Manuel Gamio, published by the Universidad Nacional Autónoma de México, Mexico, D.F.

"Día 50" by Luis Ricardo Alonso, from *El Candidato*, 1970, published by Ediciones Destino, Barcelona, Spain.

"En Nueva York" by José Luis González, from *En Nueva York y otras desgracias*, 1973, published by Siglo Veintiuno editores S.A., Mexico, D.F.

"Cuando las nubes cambian de nariz" by Eduardo Criado, from *Teatro español*, 1960–61, published by Aguilar S.A. de Ediciones, Madrid, Spain, courtesy of Eduardo Criado.

"Acabo de alistarme . . ." by José Corrales Egea, from *La otra cara*, 1962, published by George G. Harrap & Co., Ltd., London, England.

"Moda masculina" by Francisco Baeza Linares, from *Al otro lado de la montaña*, 1968, published by George G. Harrap & Co., Ltd., London, England.

The authors are also indebted to the following persons and organizations for permission to include the following photographs: Pages 5, 18: Robert Doisneau/Photo Researchers; 10, 84, 283: Marilu Pease/Monkmeyer; 20: Margaret Durrance/Photo Researchers; 25: George Zimbel/Monkmeyer; 38, 130: Nat Norman/Photo Researchers; 44: Spanish National Tourist Office; 49: Museum of Modern Art, New York, from the artist; 50: Christa Armstrong/Photo Researchers; 61: Bernard Silberstein/Monkmeyer; 71, 79, 357: Bettmann Archive; 75: Fritz Henle/Photo Researchers; 88, 92: Carl Frank/Photo Researchers; 87: John L. Stage/Photo Researchers; 93: Braniff Airways; 106: Tom Hollyman/Photo Researchers; 116: Inge Morath/Magnum; 125: Dieter Grabitzky/Monkmeyer; 141: Aspect/Wallace Collection, London; 151: National Gallery of Art, Washington, D. C., Chester Dale Collection; 152, 277: Ernest Haas/Magnum; 161: Roger Malloch/Magnum; 179: Collection, the Museum of Modern Art, New York; Commissioned by Mrs. John D. Rockefeller, Jr., for the Rivera Exhibition; 181: Prado—Art Reference Bureau; 188: Robert Capa/Magnum; 195, 205: Leonard Freed/Magnum; 197: J. K./Magnum; 223: Collection, the Museum of Modern Art, New York, Inter-American Fund; 229: Arthur W. Ambler/Photo Researchers; 232, 248: Collection, the Museum of Modern Art, New York; 236, 311: Freda Leinwand/Monkmeyer; 242: Guy Le Guerrec/Magnum; 263: Roger Coster/Monkmeyer; 269: Yvonne Freund/Photo Researchers; 279: George Holton; 297, 300, 305: Michal Heron/Monkmeyer; 303, 315: Paul Conklin/Monkmeyer; 310: Danny Lyon/Magnum; 328: Robert J. Capece/McGraw-Hill; 326: Toge Fujihira/Monkmeyer; 343: Mimi Forsyth/Monkmeyer; 350: Rhoda Galyn/Photo Researchers; 351: Wide World Photos; 352: Warren Uzzle/Photo Researchers; 356: Culver Pictures.

PREFACE

El Prado, the famous museum in the heart of Madrid, houses a collection of art treasures from the entire world. Captured on canvas in vivid hues or sculptured from stone in quiet gray, the creative fancy of the great artists is on display for all the world to see.

The visitor who wanders through the silent exhibition rooms pauses to admire the strength of Goya, the majesty of Velázquez, the sensitivity of El Greco, or the warmth of Murillo. On every wall and in every niche there is an artistic creation that opens the way to a reflection on life, both past and present.

Galería Hispánica, Third Edition, also houses a rich collection of pictures from the Spanish-speaking world. The student of Spanish is invited to wander through the "gallery," read the diverse selections, and reflect upon the "pictures" of Hispanic life.

Each theme in *Galería Hispánica*, Third Edition, is familiar to all. Humor, heroism, sentiment, death, whims of fate, and roots are aspects of life with which students of all ages can readily identify. As the students read, not only will they make the acquaintance of modern authors of Spain and Spanish America, but also they will be naturally exposed to the similarities and differences in the cultures of the people who speak the Spanish language.

Included in this Hispanic gallery are selections representing many literary genres. Short stories, excerpts from novels and plays, and articles from newspapers and magazines offer students an opportunity to increase their ability to read with understanding, gain greater insight into the structure of the Spanish language, appreciate contemporary Spanish writing, and lay the foundation for discussion of style and literary analysis.

As emphasis shifts to reading and writing, it is important that students maintain and develop their listening and speaking skills. To continue learning Spanish in this effective way, there are detailed questions that accompany each selection, structure drills and patterns for oral practice, unique treatment of new vocabulary, and creative exercises.

Galería Hispánica, Third Edition, reproduces for us *cuadros de la vida hispánica*.

FORMAT

This book is designed to carry students further in their development of the four language skills while deepening their insight into Hispanic culture through an exposure to the works of modern writers of the Spanish-speaking world.

Each of the ten units of *Galería Hispánica*, Third Edition, is called a *cuadro* because it presents a picture of a phase of the cultures of Spain, South America, Central America, Mexico, or the Caribbean area. Each *cuadro* is composed of three literary selections.

Vocabulary and structure concepts are taught through contextual drills stimulated by the literary selections.

All *cuadros* are developed in the following manner:

PARA PREPARAR LA ESCENA. Each *cuadro* is presented to the students through an illustration and a thematic introduction.

PARA PRESENTAR LA LECTURA. A short statement about the literary selection and the author precedes each selection.

PARA APRENDER VOCABULARIO is made up of two features:

Palabras Clave. Key words from the literary selection are presented and defined in Spanish so that the students may comprehend the reading without difficulty. Words have been chosen because of their high frequency in spoken and written Spanish. Each word is defined in the context in which it is used in the selection that follows. English is used only where necessity dictates. The definition for each word is followed by a contextual sentence which illustrates for the student the way the new word is frequently used.
Práctica. This exercise reinforces the meaning and use of the *Palabras clave.*

SELECCIÓN. The literary pieces are representative of authors of the Spanish-speaking world. Authors of the nineteenth and twentieth centuries predominate in the text.

PARA APLICAR is made up of the following three sections:

Comprensión. Questions guide the students to discuss what they have read and provide an effective tool for the teacher to check comprehension. In addition to the questions, a variety of true-false, vocabulary-in-context, sentence-completion, and matching exercises is provided to reinforce reading comprehension skills.
Más práctica. Vocabulary exercises are provided in this section. These exercises give students an opportunity to practice in a variety of contexts those words that should become an active part of their vocabulary. The *Más práctica* section can be considered an optional extension activity.
Ejercicios creativos. Each literary selection is accompanied by creative exercises which provide challenging written assignments and discussion topics for a variety of ability levels.

ESTRUCTURA. Both simple and challenging drills in each *cuadro* present in an interesting manner a complete review of the important concepts of Spanish structure.

In keeping with its title, *Galería Hispánica,* Third Edition, contains reproductions of Hispanic art, photographs from all over the Spanish-speaking world, and sixteen pages of Hispanic masterpieces in full color.

CONTENTS

Cuadro 4 La Leyenda

Cuadro 5 Sentimientos y Pasiones

Cuadro 6 La Revolución

Cuadro 7 La Muerte

El Humorismo

Las burlas son víspera de las veras.

PARA PREPARAR LA ESCENA

Los españoles y los latinoamericanos son muy amantes del humor. Su humorismo es una mezcla de lo chistoso con lo trágico y con lo irónico, como en El Quijote. Los ricos y los pobres, los nobles y los campesinos, todos tienen una inclinación natural por el humorismo. Por eso Gómez de la Serna, un escritor español, dijo que lo que se apoya en el aire claro de España es lo humorístico.

Una Carta a Dios

Gregorio López y Fuentes

PARA PRESENTAR LA LECTURA

El cuento que sigue fue escrito por Gregorio López y Fuentes, autor mexicano, y demuestra el humor irónico mexicano. Además del humorismo que se ve en este cuento, se puede ver la fe de un campesino pobre. Es esta fe la que sirve de ímpetu para escribir *Una Carta a Dios*.

El campesino mexicano de este episodio también nos revela la sencillez de toda cosa complicada. A la vez podemos comprender con mejor claridad el problema de ganarse la vida con las manos y luchar contra los caprichos de la naturaleza.

PARA APRENDER VOCABULARIO

Palabras Clave   I

1. **aguacero**   lluvia fuerte de poca duración
   Un aguacero inundó la calle.

2. **cortina**   lo que cubre y oculta algo, como la tela que cubre una ventana *(curtain)*
   Me gusta la cortina que tienes en la sala.

3. **cosecha**   acto de recoger los frutos del campo *(harvest)*
   La cosecha del maíz es en septiembre.

4. **darse el gusto**   hacer algo con placer y en beneficio propio
   Elena quiere darse el gusto de comprarse un automóvil nuevo.

5. **gotas**   partículas de un líquido
   Las gotas de agua caen de las nubes.

6. **granizos**   hielo que cae del cielo, lluvia helada
   Cayeron granizos muy grandes que destruyeron la cosecha.

7. **maduro**   listo para comer *(ripe)*
   El maíz estaba maduro.

8. **soplar**   hacer viento
   Un fuerte viento comenzó a soplar.

Práctica

Complete con una palabra de la lista.

cosecha   gotas   soplar
granizos   maduro   aguacero
darse el gusto   cortina

1   Una brisa fresca comenzaba a _____ las hojas.
2   Le gustaba sentir las _____ de lluvia en la cara.
3   La luz no puede penetrar la _____ en la sala.
4   Comenzaron a caer _____ tan grandes que destruyeron la cosecha.
5   El campesino esperaba que el _____ pudiera salvar la cosecha de maíz maduro y las flores del frijol.
6   Con bastante lluvia tendremos buena _____ en el otoño.
7   El melón duro no está todavía _____.
8   Quiere _____ de ver a sus niños.

Palabras Clave   II

1   **aflijas (afligirse)**   te preocupes
    No vale afligirse cuando el mal no tiene remedio.

2   **buzón**   cajón para las cartas
    Mariana echó la carta en el buzón.

3   **esperanza**   fe, confianza que ha de pasar una cosa *(hope)*
    Juan todavía tenía esperanza de recibir una respuesta.

4   **fondo**   parte más baja de una cosa
    Hay leche en el fondo del vaso.

5   **huerta**   lugar donde hay árboles frutales
    La huerta estaba llena del aroma de manzanas y peras.

6   **mortificado**   muy preocupado
    Jaime estaba mortificado por las malas noticias.

7   **rudo**   áspero, sin educación
    La pescadora era una persona muy ruda.

8   **sello**   estampilla para mandar cartas
    Las cartas necesitan sello.

9   **sobre**   papel doblado dentro del cual se mandan las cartas
    Mi hermana puso la dirección en el sobre.

10   **tempestad**   tormenta *(storm)*
    Pepe se asustó con la tempestad.

11   **tristeza**   infelicidad, pena
    Los padres se consumían de tristeza al ver que su hija no mejoraba.

Práctica

Complete con una palabra de la lista.

fondo   sobre   tempestad
sello   aflijas   tristeza
buzón   ruda   esperanza
huerta   mortificado

1   Ana escribió «por avión» en el _____ antes de mandar la carta.
2   La familia sintió _____ al ver que la cosecha estaba arruinada.
3   No te _____ tanto, aunque el mal sea muy grande.
4   En su _____ mi tía tiene perales, manzanos y cerezos.
5   Para mandar una carta por correo aéreo a España hay que ponerle un _____ de treinta y un centavos.
6   La llave había caído al _____ de su bolsillo.
7   La _____ de granizos destruyó la cosecha del campesino.
8   Tenemos la _____ de ver paz en la tierra.
9   Eche estas tarjetas postales en el _____, por favor.
10   El hijo del campesino era una persona _____.
11   El campesino se sintió _____ al ver el granizo.

Palabras Clave   III

1 **arrugando (arrugar)**   haciendo pliegues (*wrinkling*)
   Con tanta humedad toda mi ropa quedó arrugada.

2 **enfadó (enfadarse)**   se enojó
   Al enterarse de lo que había sucedido, la doctora no pudo menos que enfadarse.

3 **equivocado (equivocarse)**   que no tiene razón, que ha errado
   Perdone, señora. Yo estoy equivocado.

4 **firma**   nombre de una persona puesto al pie de algo escrito
   El contrato tenía la firma de la abogada.

5 **golpecitos**   choquecitos,   palmaditas (*little taps*)
   Sentí unos golpecitos pero no sabía de dónde venían.

6 **ladrones**   los que roban
   Anoche entraron unos ladrones y nos robaron todo.

7 **mojó (mojar)**   humedeció con un líquido
   La lluvia mojó la camisa de Roberto.

8 **puñetazo**   acto de pegar con el puño
   Sara le dio a Juan un puñetazo.

9 **seguridad**   certidumbre
   Rosa tenía la seguridad de que iba a ganar el juego.

Práctica

Complete con una palabra de la lista.

firma	golpecitos	mojó
ladrones	arrugando	equivocado
enfadó	seguridad	puñetazo

1 Al ver que le dieron poco dinero, el carpintero se _____.

2 Había unos _____ en la puerta.

3 El chico estaba _____ el papel.

4 La reunión tendrá lugar el dos de julio, no el tres; yo estaba _____.

5 El empleado _____ el sobre para cerrarlo.

6 Hay que poner su _____ en el contrato.

7 El campesino tenía la _____ de ser oído.

8 La policía encontró a los _____ que habían robado el banco.

9 La directora dio un _____ en la puerta.

Una Carta a Dios

Gregorio López y Fuentes

I

La casa . . . única en todo el valle . . . estaba en lo alto de un cerro bajo. Desde allí se veían el río y, junto al corral, el campo de maíz maduro con las flores del frijol que siempre prometían una buena cosecha.

Lo único que necesitaba la tierra era una lluvia, o a lo menos un fuerte aguacero. Durante la mañana, Lencho . . . que conocía muy bien el campo . . . no había hecho más que examinar el cielo hacia el noreste.

—Ahora sí que viene el agua, vieja.

Y la vieja, que preparaba la comida, le respondió:

—Dios lo quiera.

Los muchachos más grandes trabajaban en el campo, mientras que los más pequeños jugaban cerca de la casa, hasta que la mujer les gritó a todos:

—Vengan a comer . . .

Fue durante la comida cuando, como lo había dicho Lencho, comenzaron a caer grandes gotas de lluvia. Por el noreste se veían avanzar grandes montañas de nubes. El aire estaba fresco y dulce.

El hombre salió a buscar algo en el corral solamente para darse el gusto de sentir la lluvia en el cuerpo, y al entrar exclamó:

—Éstas no son gotas de agua que caen del cielo; son monedas nuevas; las gotas grandes son monedas de diez centavos y las gotas chicas son de cinco . . .

Y miraba con ojos satisfechos el campo de maíz maduro con las flores del frijol, todo cubierto por la transparente cortina de la lluvia. Pero, de pronto, comenzó a soplar un fuerte viento y con las gotas de agua comenzaron a caer granizos muy grandes.

Lencho sobrenombre de Lorenzo

Esos sí que parecían monedas de plata nueva. Los muchachos, exponiéndose a la lluvia, corrían a recoger las perlas heladas.

II

—Esto sí que está muy malo—exclamaba mortificado el hombre—, ojalá que pase pronto . . .

No pasó pronto. Durante una hora cayó el granizo sobre la casa, la huerta, el monte, el maíz y todo el valle. El campo estaba blanco, como cubierto de sal. Los árboles, sin una hoja. El maíz, destruido. El frijol, sin una flor. Lencho, con el alma llena de tristeza. Pasada la tempestad, en medio del campo, dijo a sus hijos:

—Una nube de langostas habría dejado más que esto . . . El granizo no ha dejado nada: no tendremos ni maíz ni frijoles este año . . .

La noche fue de lamentaciones:

—¡Todo nuestro trabajo, perdido!

—¡Y nadie que pueda ayudarnos!

—Este año pasaremos hambre . . .

Pero en el corazón de todos los que vivían en aquella casa solitaria en medio del valle había una esperanza: la ayuda de Dios.

—No te aflijas tanto, aunque el mal es muy grande. ¡Recuerda que nadie se muere de hambre!

—Eso dicen: nadie se muere de hambre . . .

Y durante la noche, Lencho pensó mucho en su sola esperanza: la ayuda de Dios, cuyos ojos, según le habían explicado, lo miran todo, hasta lo que está en el fondo de las conciencias.

Lencho era un hombre rudo, trabajando como una bestia en los campos, pero sin embargo sabía escribir. El domingo siguiente, con la luz del día, después de haberse fortificado en su idea de que hay alguien que nos protege, empezó a escribir una carta que él mismo llevaría al pueblo para echarla al correo.

No era nada menos que una carta a Dios.

«Dios», escribió, «si no me ayudas, pasaré hambre con toda mi familia durante este año. Necesito cien pesos para volver a sembrar y vivir mientras viene la nueva cosecha, porque el granizo . . .»

Escribió «A Dios» en el sobre, metió la carta y, todavía preocupado, fue al pueblo. En la oficina de correos, le puso un sello a la carta y echó ésta en el buzón.

III

Un empleado, que era cartero y también ayudaba en la oficina de correos, llegó riéndose mucho ante su jefe, y le mostró la carta dirigida a Dios. Nunca en su existencia de cartero había conocido esa casa. El jefe de la oficina . . . gordo y amable . . . también empezó a reir, pero muy pronto se puso serio y, mientras daba golpecitos en la mesa con la carta, comentaba:

—¡La fe! ¡Ojalá que yo tuviera la fe del hombre que escribió esta carta! ¡Creer como él cree! ¡Esperar con la confianza con que él sabe esperar! ¡Empezar correspondencia con Dios!

Y, para no desilusionar aquel tesoro de fe, descubierto por una carta que no podía ser entregada, el jefe de la oficina tuvo una idea: contestar la carta. Pero cuando la abrió, era evidente que para contestarla necesitaba algo más que buena voluntad, tinta y papel. Pero siguió con su determinación: pidió dinero a su empleado, él mismo dio parte de su sueldo y varios amigos suyos tuvieron que darle algo «para una obra de caridad».

Fue imposible para él reunir los cien pesos pedidos por Lencho, y sólo pudo enviar al campesino un poco más de la mitad. Puso los billetes en un sobre dirigido a Lencho y con ellos una carta que tenía sólo una palabra como firma: DIOS.

Al siguiente domingo, Lencho llegó a preguntar, más temprano que de costumbre, si había alguna carta para él. Fue el mismo cartero quien le entregó la carta, mientras que el jefe, con la alegría de un hombre que ha hecho una buena acción, miraba por la puerta desde su oficina.

Lencho no mostró la menor sorpresa al ver los billetes . . . tanta era su seguridad . . . pero se enfadó al contar el dinero . . . ¡Dios no podía haberse equivocado, ni negar lo que Lencho le había pedido!

Inmediatamente, Lencho se acercó a la ventanilla para pedir papel y tinta. En la mesa para el público, empezó a escribir, arrugando mucho la frente a causa del trabajo que le daba expresar sus ideas. Al terminar, fue a pedir un sello, que mojó con la lengua y luego aseguró con un puñetazo.

Tan pronto como la carta cayó al buzón, el jefe de correos fue a abrirla. Decía:

«Dios: Del dinero que te pedí, sólo llegaron a mis manos sesenta pesos. Mándame el resto, como lo necesito mucho; pero no me lo mandes por la oficina de correos, porque los empleados son muy ladrones. —Lencho».

PARA APLICAR

Comprensión   I

A   Conteste a las siguientes preguntas.

1   ¿Dónde estaba la casa?
2   ¿Qué se veía desde allí?
3   ¿Qué necesitaba la tierra?
4   ¿Qué hacía la vieja?
5   ¿Cuándo comenzaron a caer grandes gotas de lluvia?
6   ¿Cómo estaba el aire al comenzar la lluvia?
7   ¿Qué parecían monedas nuevas?

B   ¿Verdadero o falso?

1   Había muchas casas en el valle.
2   Parecía que la cosecha sería abundante.
3   Lencho no había hecho nada durante toda la mañana.
4   Los muchachos más grandes ayudaban a su papá.
5   Mientras comían comenzó a llover muy fuerte.
6   Las montañas avanzaban hacia ellos.
7   Lencho declaró que no caían gotas de agua sino maíz maduro.
8   Al principio llovió poco.
9   Los niños se divertían recogiendo el dinero.
10   Lencho se preocupó cuando empezó a caer el granizo.

Comprensión   II

A   Conteste a las siguientes preguntas.

1   ¿Cuánto tiempo cayó el granizo?
2   ¿Cómo estaban los árboles después de caer el granizo? ¿Y el maíz? ¿Y el frijol?
3   ¿En qué pensó Lencho durante la noche?
4   ¿A quién escribió Lencho una carta?
5   ¿Por qué necesitaba Lencho los cien pesos?

B   Complete las siguientes oraciones con una palabra o una expresión apropiada.

1   El granizo cayó durante una hora sobre la _____, la _____, el _____, el _____ y todo el _____ .
2   El campo quedó blanco como _____ .
3   Lencho ya no sentía alegría sino _____ .
4   El _____ no dejó nada en las plantas.
5   Pasaron la noche muy tristes pero en sus corazones guardaban una _____ .
6   No se afligieron demasiado porque recordaron que nadie _____ .
7   Lencho pasó la noche pensando en la _____ .
8   Aunque Lencho era hombre de poca educación, sabía _____ .
9   En su carta a Dios pidió _____ para _____ y _____ .
10   Después de poner el _____ a la carta, la echó en el _____ .

Comprensión   III

A   Conteste a las siguientes preguntas.

1   ¿Quién le mostró la carta al jefe de la oficina?
2   ¿Qué dijo el jefe de la oficina después de leer la carta?
3   ¿Qué idea tuvo el jefe de la oficina?
4   ¿A quiénes les pidió dinero?
5   ¿Fue posible reunir todo el dinero pedido por Lencho?
6   ¿En dónde puso los billetes?
7   ¿Cómo reaccionó Lencho al recibir la carta?
8   ¿Qué pidió Lencho en la ventanilla?
9   ¿Dónde escribió Lencho su segunda carta?
10   ¿Cómo mojó Lencho el sello?
11   Según Lencho, ¿cómo eran los empleados de la oficina de correos?

B ¿Verdadero o falso?

1 Al ver la carta a Dios un empleado llegó muy triste ante su jefe.
2 El jefe se rió mucho y después se puso triste.
3 Los dos se sorprendieron de que alguien tuviera tanta fe en Dios.
4 El jefe no quería desilusionar al hombre de tanta fe.
5 Decidió mandar la carta a Dios por un mensajero especial.
6 Tuvo mucha suerte y reunió los cien pesos que necesitaba Lencho.
7 Lencho estaba sorprendido al recibir una respuesta a su carta.
8 Cuando contó el dinero se enojó.
9 Le fue fácil escribir otra carta.
10 Lencho creyó que los empleados de la oficina de correos eran ladrones.

Más Práctica

A Reemplace el verbo *afligirse* por *preocuparse*.

1 No te aflijas.
2 ¿Por qué andas tan afligida?
3 ¿Tiene Ud. motivo para afligirse?

B Reemplace el verbo *enojarse* por *enfadarse*.

1 No comprenden por qué nos enojamos tanto.
2 Cuando caen granizos, los labradores se enojan.
3 ¿Por qué te enojaste cuando te lo dije?

C Reemplace la palabra *nombre* por *firma*.

1 Antes de mandar la carta, tienes que poner tu nombre.
2 El nombre aparece en la carta, no en el sello.
3 Pon tu nombre, y luego al buzón.

D Complete las siguientes oraciones con una palabra apropiada.

1 De repente empezó a ———— un viento fuerte.
2 Este año habrá buena ————. Los labradores serán ricos.
3 ¡Qué ———— es él! Le roba a cualquiera.
4 Tan pobre es que no tiene la ———— de ver mejorar su situación.
5 Echa la carta en el ————.
6 Hay tantas nubes. Me parece que habrá un ————.
7 No comas el tomate. No está ————.
8 No te olvides de poner el ———— en el sobre antes de mandarlo.
9 Hay un montón de árboles frutales en la ————.

E Dé un antónimo de las siguientes palabras.

1 la alegría
2 secar
3 la incertidumbre
4 tener razón
5 verde

F Dé un sinónimo de las siguientes palabras.

1 la fe
2 la infelicidad
3 la estampilla
4 el jardín
5 enojarse
6 áspero
7 humedecer
8 la tormenta
9 el socorro
10 los choquecitos

Ejercicios Creativos

1 Escriba una descripción del campo después de la caída del granizo.
2 Escriba sobre la reacción del empleado al ver la carta de Lencho.
3 Ud. es empleado(a) de correo y recibe la carta de Lencho. Conteste por escrito.
4 Si Ud. fuera Lencho, ¿dónde buscaría Ud. ayuda? Discuta las varias maneras de obtener ayuda que existen hoy día para los campesinos y la gente pobre.

El Gato de Sèvres

Marco A. Almazán

PARA PRESENTAR LA LECTURA

Sèvres es un pueblo del norte de Francia. Este pueblo es conocido por la hermosa porcelana que produce desde el siglo dieciocho. La porcelana de Sèvres, delicada y translúcida, tiene fama internacional como el mejor ejemplo del arte en dicho material.

Recientemente ha surgido gran interés en toda clase de antigüedades. Los coleccionistas, según el gusto personal, compran y venden preciosos objetos de arte. Van de tienda en tienda buscando curiosidades, y cuando por fin encuentran algo auténtico, pues, ¿quién sabe lo que harían para conseguírselo?

Marco A. Almazán, el maestro mexicano del humorismo, nos presenta un cuento que demuestra con humor que a los propietarios no se les engaña fácilmente.

PARA APRENDER VOCABULARIO

Palabras Clave   I

1 **antigüedades**   objetos de arte antiguos
   Su casa está llena de antigüedades.

2 **aparentando (aparentar)**   manifestando una actitud que uno no siente
   Mi hermana tenía que aparentar gran satisfacción con ese regalo ridículo.

3 **desdeñosamente**   con indiferencia que insulta
   Me ofendes hablándome desdeñosamente.

4 **escaparate**   ventana de una tienda donde se exhiben cosas para vender
   ¿Cuánto cuesta esa camisa en el escaparate?

5 **no cabía (caber) duda**   había seguridad
   No cabía duda que Lencho iba a sufrir.

6 **pedazos**   partes pequeñas de algo *(pieces)*
   El plato se cayó y se quedó en pedazos.

7 **vistazo**   mirada *(glance)*
   Vio todo de un vistazo.

Práctica

Complete con una palabra de la lista.

antigüedades   *escaparate*   *vistazo*
aparentando   *no cabía duda*   *pedazo*
desdeñosamente

1 Quiere comprar los zapatos que vio en el
    _____.
2 _____ que ése era el ladrón.
3 Estoy arreglando este plato, pero me falta
    un _____.
4 Dio un _____ al periódico y luego lo dejó
    en la silla.
5 El capitán se enojó cuando el sargento le
    saludó _____.
6 Compré unas estatuas en esa tienda de
    _____.
7 Aunque se sentía muy triste, Roberto entró
    _____ alegría.

Palabras Clave   II

1 **acariciar**   tratar con amor y ternura, mostrar afecto con la mano *(to caress, to pet)*
    El perro no nos dejó en paz hasta que lo acariciamos.

2 **adquirir**   obtener o ganar una cosa
    En esa tienda Ud. puede adquirir lo que busca.

3 **agachó (agacharse)**   inclinó o bajó una parte del cuerpo
    María se agachó para poder ver el insecto en el suelo.

4 **cazador**   persona que caza, que busca animales para matarlos
    El cazador regresó del monte con el animal que había matado.

5 **cola**   extremidad del cuerpo de un animal opuesta a la cabeza, rabo
    El perro movía la cola de pura alegría.

6 **hombro**   parte superior del tronco de donde sale el brazo *(shoulder)*
    Después de tanto trabajo me duele el hombro.

7 **incorporándose (incorporarse)**   levantándose de posición horizontal
    El enfermo estaba incorporándose en la cama para poder comer.

8 **obsequiaron (obsequiar)**   regalaron, dieron algo de regalo
    Yo quiero obsequiar el plato de porcelana a los recién casados.

9 **palmada**   golpe que se da con la palma de la mano
    Le di una palmada al perro para mostrarle que no le tenía miedo.

10 **pleito**   disputa, lucha
    Roberto siempre está de pleito con su hermana.

Práctica

Complete con una palabra de la lista.

acariciar   *cola*   *obsequiar*
adquirir   *hombros*   *palmada*
agachó   *incorporándose*   *pleito*
cazadores

1 El perro perdió la mitad de su _____ en
    la batalla.
2 ¿Qué vas a _____ a tu padre el día de
    su santo?
3 Tengo que _____ una buena calculadora
    para hacer mis ejercicios de matemáticas.
4 Perdió toda su fortuna en un _____ legal.
5 Al ver a su papá regresar a casa, el niño le
    dio una _____ de alegría.
6 El campesino se _____ para examinar el
    daño a las plantas.
7 Los _____ tienen que salir muy temprano.
8 _____, María se dio cuenta de que se
    había despertado tarde.

9 Ven, michito, quiero _____ tu pelo tan suave.

10 Durante el desfile, el padre sentó al niño en sus _____.

Palabras Clave   III

1 **ademán**   movimiento del cuerpo con que se expresa un sentimiento, gesto
Al ver su ademán de sorpresa, supe que hacía algo incorrecto.

2 **advierto (advertir – ie, i)**   aconsejo, llamo la atención sobre una cosa, hago saber
Le advertí que no lo hiciera para no sufrir las consecuencias.

3 **cartera**   bolsa portátil para llevar billetes y documentos, billetera
La mujer sacó treinta pesos de su cartera y pagó la cuenta.

4 **retirarse**   irse, marcharse
Antes de retirarse le pagó cuarenta pesos más.

Práctica

Complete con una palabra de la lista.

ademán	cartera
advierto	retirarse

1 Disculpe a la niña. Es tarde y tiene que _____.

2 Mi hermana guardaba sus llaves en la _____.

3 Te _____ ahora del peligro de ir tan rápido.

4 Marlena hizo un _____ de disgusto.

El Gato de Sèvres

Marco A. Almazán

I

El coleccionista de cerámica sintió que el corazón le daba un vuelco. Al pasar frente a la pequeña tienda de antigüedades—en realidad de baratijas, según la había catalogado al primer vistazo—observó que un gato escuálido y roñoso bebía leche pausadamente en un auténtico plato de Sèvres, colocado en la entrada del establecimiento.

El coleccionista llegó hasta la esquina y después volvió sobre sus pasos, aparentando fastidio e indiferencia. Como quien no quiere la cosa, se detuvo frente al escaparate de la tienda y paseó la mirada desdeñosamente por el amontonamiento de cachivaches que se exhibían: violines viejos, mesas y sillas cojas, figurillas de porcelana, óleos desteñidos, pedazos de cacharros supuestamente mayas o incaicos y, en fin, las mil y una menudencias que suelen acumularse en tiendas de esta especie. Con el rabillo del ojo, el coleccionista atisbó una vez más el plato en que bebía leche el gato. No cabía duda: Sèvres legítimo. Posiblemente del segundo tercio del siglo XVIII. Estos animales—pensó el experto, refiriéndose a los dueños . . .—no saben lo que tienen entre manos . . .

II

Venciendo la natural repugnancia que le inspiraban los felinos, se agachó para acariciar al gato. De paso, examinó más de cerca la pieza de cerámica. El coleccionista se dio mentalmente una palmada en el hombro: no se había equivocado. Sin lugar a dudas, Sèvres, 1750.

—Michito, michito—ronroneó el coleccionista, al ver que se acercaba el propietario de la tienda.

el corazón le daba un vuelco *his heart was skipping a beat*
baratijas mercancías baratas
escuálido y roñoso flaco y sucio

fastidio falta de interés

amontonamiento de cachivaches monte de utensilios viejos
cojas rotas
óleos desteñidos *faded oil paintings*
cacharros fragmentos de cerámica
menudencias cosas de poco valor
Con el rabillo del ojo *Out of the corner of his eye*
atisbó observó

Michito Gatito
ronroneó *purred*

de casta puro (pedigreed)
ribetes de Manx markings
of a Manx (gato sin cola)

linaje familia
callejero de la calle

enguantada llevando
guantes
lomo espalda (back)

—Buenas tardes. ¿Puedo servirle en algo?

—En nada, muchas gracias. Sólo acariciaba al animalito.

—¡Ah, mi fiel Mustafá . . . ! Está un poco sucio, pero es de casta: cruce de persa y angora, con sus ribetes de Manx. Observe usted qué cola tan corta tiene. Eso lo distingue.

El gato, efectivamente, tenía sólo medio rabo; pero no por linaje, sino porque había perdido la otra mitad en un pleito callejero.

—Se ve, se ve—dijo el coleccionista, pasándole una mano enguantada por encima del lomo—. ¡Michito, michito mirrimiáu . . . ! Me encantaría tenerlo en casa para que hiciera pareja con una gatita amarillo limón que me obsequiaron. ¿No me lo vendería?

—No, señor. Mustafá es un gran cazador de ratones y sus servicios me son indispensables en la tienda.

—¡Lástima!—dijo el coleccionista, incorporándose—. Me hubiera gustado adquirirlo. En fin, que tenga usted buenas tardes.

III

El coleccionista hizo ademán de retirarse.

—¡Un momento!—lo llamó el propietario—. ¿Cuánto daría por el gato?

—¿Cuánto quiere?—le devolvió la pelota el coleccionista, maestro en el arte del trapicheo.

—Cincuenta pesos.

—No, hombre, qué barbaridad. Le doy treinta y ni un centavo más.

—Ni usted ni yo: cuarenta morlacos y es suya esta preciosidad de morrongo.

El coleccionista lanzó un suspiro más falso que un manifiesto político, sacó la cartera, contó los billetes y se los entregó al dueño de la tienda. Éste a su vez los contó y se los guardó en el bolsillo. El coleccionista, siempre aparentando una sublime indiferencia, señaló el plato con la punta del bastón.

—Imagino que el animalito estará acostumbrado a tomar su leche en ese plato viejo, ¿no? Haga el favor de envolvérmelo.

—Como el señor disponga—repuso el anticuario—. Sólo que le advierto que el plato cuesta diez mil pesos . . .

—¡Diez mil pesos!—aulló el coleccionista.

—Sí, señor. No sólo es un auténtico Sèvres, 1750, sino que además me ha servido para vender trescientos veinticinco gatos desde que abrí mi modesto establecimiento . . .

trapicheo regateo
(bargaining)

morlacos pesos
morrongo gato

bastón palo que ayuda al
andar

Como el señor disponga
Como el señor quiera
anticuario experto en
antigüedades
aulló gritó

PARA APLICAR

Comprensión   I

A   Conteste a las siguientes preguntas.

1   ¿Quién pasó por delante de la tienda de antigüedades?
2   ¿Cómo había clasificado esa tienda?
3   ¿Qué sorpresa tuvo?
4   ¿Se quedó allí mirando?
5   Al regresar, ¿cómo parecía?
6   ¿Cómo observó el objeto de su deseo?
7   ¿De qué estaba seguro?

B   ¿Verdadero o falso?

1   El coleccionista se enfermó en la calle.
2   Se vendían cosas valiosas en la tienda de antigüedades.
3   El gato que bebía leche estaba limpio y bien cuidado.
4   El coleccionista no quería parecer interesado en el plato que miraba en el escaparate.
5   Observó directamente el plato.
6   Según el coleccionista, el dueño no se dio cuenta del tesoro que poseía.

Comprensión   II

A   Conteste a las siguientes preguntas.

1   ¿Al coleccionista le gustaban los gatos?
2   ¿Qué hizo para acercarse al gato?
3   ¿Tenía razón o estaba equivocado?
4   ¿Qué hizo cuando se acercaba el dueño?
5   ¿Cómo describe el dueño al gato?
6   ¿Qué distingue a un gato Manx?
7   ¿Por qué le encantaría al coleccionista tenerlo en casa?
8   ¿Qué servicio importante ofrece Mustafá?
9   Al coleccionista, ¿qué le hubiera gustado?

B   Complete las siguientes oraciones con una palabra o una expresión apropiada.

1   Decidió agacharse para _____ al gato.

2   Se contentó de su observación y se dio mentalmente una _____ en el _____.
3   El propietario estaba orgulloso del gato porque era de _____.
4   Al gato Manx le falta la _____.
5   Mustafá perdió la cola en un _____.
6   En casa el coleccionista tiene una gatita que unos amigos le _____.
7   El dueño no quiere vender el gato porque es un gran _____ de ratones.
8   El señor se sentía triste porque quería _____ al gato.

Comprensión   III

A   Conteste a las siguientes preguntas.

1   ¿Cuánto dinero pide el dueño por el gato?
2   ¿Cuánto le ofrece el señor?
3   ¿Cuánto acepta el dueño?
4   ¿Qué quiere incluir el coleccionista en el precio?
5   ¿Qué le advierte el dueño?
6   ¿Cómo le ha ayudado el plato?
7   ¿Cuál de los dos es el más astuto?

B   ¿Verdadero o falso?

1   El coleccionista se marchó.
2   Los dos señores jugaron a la pelota.
3   El coleccionista era listo en el regateo.
4   Fingió insatisfacción con el precio.
5   Resultó que el dueño sabía el valor del plato.

Más Práctica

A   Dé un sinónimo de las siguientes palabras.

1   levantarse
2   obtener
3   rabo
4   lucha
5   mirada
6   billetera
7   regalar
8   irse
9   gesto

B Complete las siguientes oraciones con una palabra o una expresión apropiada.

1 El que colecciona algo es _____.
2 Hacer algo con indiferencia es hacerlo _____.
3 Aconsejar es _____.
4 Un golpe que se da con la mano es _____.
5 Una parte pequeña de algo es un _____.
6 Bajarse hacia los pies es _____.
7 Un gesto que expresa una actitud es _____.
8 _____ son objetos viejos de mucho valor.

Ejercicios Creativos

1 Prepare una lista de objetos que se podrían encontrar en una tienda de antigüedades. Antes de entregar la lista, póngala en orden alfabético.

2 Ud. tiene un objeto de arte valioso que desea vender. Tiene que ser catalogado detalladamente como lo hacen todos los coleccionistas. Incluya en su descripción los siguientes detalles:
   a. identificación del objeto
   b. medidas exactas empleando el sistema métrico
   c. período a que pertenece (¿barroco? ¿colonial? ¿renacentista?)
   d. lugar y año de fabricación y nombre del artesano si es posible

3 Haga un dibujo de un objeto de arte. Prepárese para describirlo oralmente ante la clase.

4 Prepare una breve conversación entre el dueño de una tienda de antigüedades y un coleccionista. Acuérdese que el regateo es parte integral de los negocios de ese tipo.

Signos de puntuación

M. Toledo y Benito

PARA PRESENTAR LA LECTURA

En la pequeña escena que sigue, el autor nos enseña la importancia de los signos de puntuación, manteniendo a la vez un tono ligero y alegre. Varios personajes se presentan delante del juez para saber los detalles del último testamento del señor Álvarez. Entre ellos hay un maestro, un sastre, un mendigo, el hermano y el sobrino del difunto. ¡Qué listos son todos! Cada uno de los personajes tiene su propia interpretación del testamento. La conclusión contiene una sorpresa para los lectores y para todos los personajes también.

PARA APRENDER VOCABULARIO

Palabras Clave   I

1   **mendigo**   persona indigente que pide limosna

    El mendigo me pidió diez centavos.

2   **puntúa (puntuar)**   pone puntuación en la escritura

    Los niños tienen que aprender a puntuar.

3   **sastre**   persona que cose y arregla trajes y vestidos

El sastre dice que no puede arreglar el saco.

4   **testamento**   documento en que uno declara su última voluntad y dispone de sus bienes

    Mi amiga se murió antes de escribir su testamento.

Práctica

Complete con una palabra de la lista.

> *puntúa*   *testamento*
> *mendigo*   *sastre*

1 Dale una moneda a ese pobre _____.
2 Poco después del funeral se juntaron para leer el _____.
3 Roberto _____ muy mal. Nadie entiende lo que escribe.
4 ¡Mira este traje tan bonito que me hizo el _____!

Palabras Clave   II

1 **herederos**   personas que reciben lo que alguien les deja en un testamento
    Hay tantos herederos que ninguno va a recibir mucho.

2 **herencia**   bienes y derechos dejados o recibidos en un testamento
    La herencia que recibió Julia le permite vivir sin trabajar.

3 **juicio**   proceso que tiene por objeto la liquidación y partición de una herencia
    El juez declaró terminado el juicio.

4 **me toca a mí (tocarle a uno)**   me llega a mí el turno
    Ahora a mí me toca dar la interpretación.

Práctica

Complete con una palabra de la lista.

> *herederos*   *juicio*
> *herencia*   *le toca*

1 ¿Cuál de los _____ recibirá la casa del difunto?
2 Ahora, ¿a quién _____ hablar?
3 ¿Es grande la _____ del señor Álvarez?
4 El _____ duró poco tiempo.

Signos de puntuación

I

Personajes

El juez	El mendigo
El maestro	El hermano
El sastre	El sobrino

Escena

(Una sala. Los personajes están sentados delante de una mesa. Habrá una pizarra colocada frente al público.)

El juez: Y ya, señores, para que todos aprecien las diversas interpretaciones del testamento que dejó nuestro buen amigo, el señor Álvarez, vamos a copiar en esa pizarra la forma en que lo dejó. *(al maestro)* Hágame el favor de copiarlo usted, señor maestro, que sabe usar la tiza con más soltura que cualquiera de nosotros . . .

soltura agilidad

El maestro: Permítame el original, señor juez.

El juez: *(dándoselo)* Sírvase.

El hermano: *(mientras el maestro copia en la pizarra el testamento que dice: «Dejo mis bienes a mi sobrino no a mi hermano tampoco jamás se pagará la cuenta del sastre nunca de ningún modo para los mendigos todo lo dicho es mi deseo yo Federico Álvarez».)* Señor juez, como hermano, quisiera hacer la primera interpretación.

El juez: Puede hacerla, señor.

El hermano: *(Puntúa el testamento y lo lee en la siguiente forma:)* «¿Dejo mis bienes a mi sobrino? No: a mi hermano. Tampoco jamás se pagará la cuenta del sastre. Nunca, de ningún modo para los mendigos. Todo lo dicho es mi deseo. Yo, Federico Álvarez».

El sobrino:	Está equivocado, completamente equivocado, señor juez. La verdadera intención de mi tío fue otra, como les puedo demostrar. *(Puntúa el testamento y lee.)* «Dejo mis bienes a mi sobrino, no a mi hermano. Tampoco jamás se pagará la cuenta del sastre. Nunca de ningún modo para los mendigos. Todo lo dicho es mi deseo. Yo, Federico Álvarez».

II

El sastre:	Y ahora, señor juez, me toca a mí demostrar la intención del señor Álvarez. *(Puntúa el testamento y lo lee.)* «¿Dejo mis bienes a mi sobrino? No. ¿A mi hermano? Tampoco, jamás. Se pagará la cuenta del sastre. Nunca de ningún modo para los mendigos. Todo lo dicho es mi deseo. Yo, Federico Álvarez».
El mendigo:	Permítame, señor juez, puntuar el testamento como lo habría querido el señor Álvarez. *(Puntúa el testamento y lo lee.)* «¿Dejo mis bienes a mi sobrino? No. ¿A mi hermano? Tampoco jamás. ¿Se pagará la cuenta del sastre? Nunca, de ningún modo. Para los mendigos todo. Lo dicho es mi deseo. Yo, Federico Álvarez». Esto y nada más es lo que quiso mandar el señor Álvarez, téngalo por seguro.
El maestro:	Yo no lo creo. El señor Álvarez habría querido que yo puntuara el testamento para él. *(Lo hace y lee este testamento en esta forma.)* «¿Dejo mis bienes a mi sobrino? No. ¿A mi hermano? Tampoco. Jamás se pagará la cuenta del sastre. Nunca, de ningún modo para los mendigos. Todo lo dicho es mi deseo. Yo, Federico Álvarez».
El sastre:	En esa forma el señor Álvarez no habría dejado herederos.
El juez:	Así es, en efecto, y, visto y considerando que esta última interpretación es correcta, declaro terminado el juicio, incautándome de esta herencia en nombre del Estado.

adaptado de M. Toledo y Benito

incautándome tomando posesión

PARA APLICAR

Comprensión I

A Conteste a las siguientes preguntas.

1 ¿Por qué van a copiar el testamento en la pizarra?
2 ¿Quién va a copiarlo?
3 ¿En qué forma va a copiarlo?
4 Mientras el maestro copia el testamento en la pizarra, ¿qué le pide el hermano al juez?
5 Conforme a la puntuación del hermano, ¿qué recibirá el sobrino?
6 ¿Quién recibirá todos los bienes, según el hermano?
7 ¿Qué dice el sobrino de la puntuación del hermano del difunto?
8 Cuando el sobrino puntúa el testamento, ¿quién recibirá los bienes?

B Termine las oraciones poniendo en orden las palabras entre paréntesis.

1 El juez quiere que todos (interpretaciones/del/aprecien/diversas/testamento/las).
2 Van a copiar en esa pizarra (dejó/que/lo/la/en/forma).
3 El señor maestro va a copiarlo porque (soltura/más/la/usar/con/sabe/tiza).
4 Mientras el maestro copia en la pizarra el testamento, el hermano (primera/permiso/de/pide/interpretación/la/hacer).
5 El hermano declara que (nada/no/sobrino/el/recibe).
6 La interpretación del sobrino dice que (tío/todos/él/le/deja/a/bienes/sus/su).

Comprensión II

A Conteste a las siguientes preguntas.

1 Ahora, ¿a quién le toca demostrar la verdadera intención del señor Álvarez?
2 Según el sastre, ¿deja el señor Álvarez sus bienes a su hermano?

3 ¿Qué beneficio recibirá el sastre?
4 ¿A quiénes les dará todo el mendigo?
5 ¿Qué hace el maestro?
6 ¿Qué problema comprende el sastre?
7 En vista de eso, ¿qué declara el juez?

B ¿Verdadero o falso?

1 El sastre tocó al juez.
2 El sastre dividió los bienes entre todos.
3 Según la puntuación del sastre, él recibirá el pago por su trabajo.
4 El mendigo no quiere dar nada a los demás.
5 El maestro sabe la manera en que el señor Álvarez quería distribuir sus bienes.
6 Según la puntuación del maestro, él mismo recibirá mucho dinero.
7 El sastre se da cuenta de que el señor Álvarez no dejó nada a ningún heredero.
8 El juez quiere dar su interpretación personal al testamento.
9 El juez declara terminado el juicio.
10 El Estado recibe la herencia.

Más Práctica

A ¿Verdadero o falso?

1 Copiar es reproducir algo.
2 Los herederos son los heridos en algún conflicto.
3 Un mendigo da dinero o comida a otros.
4 Un sastre trabaja con telas y una máquina de coser.
5 Un juez dirige una defensa legal.
6 Van a leer el testamento para ver quién ganó el partido de fútbol.
7 Es importante puntuar claramente todo lo escrito.
8 Puso un sello en la carta y la echó en el juicio.
9 Se hizo rico con la herencia de su abuelo.

B Complete las siguientes oraciones con una palabra o una expresión apropiada.

1 El _____ aceptó la interpretación del maestro.
2 Al escribir el contenido del documento en la pizarra, el maestro no _____ ningún signo de puntuación.
3 El señor Álvarez dejó un _____ que podía ser interpretado de varias maneras.
4 Lo único que deseaba el _____ fue que le pagara la cuenta.
5 No pide limosna el maestro sino el _____ .
6 El maestro no es uno de los _____ .
7 El _____ fue concluido en poco tiempo.
8 Con la _____ de mi abuela abrí una tienda de antigüedades.
9 A ti _____ hablar después.
10 El maestro _____ el testamento porque sabía usar la tiza con más soltura.

Ejercicios Creativos

1 Relate el cuento en sus propias palabras.
2 Escriba un testamento en el cual Ud. deja algo a dos o tres compañeros de la clase de español. Más tarde, en clase, se leerán todos los testamentos sin dejar saber quién los escribió. Todos tratarán de adivinar quién escribió el testamento.
3 Cite los elementos humorísticos. Explique el tipo de humor que se explota en cada cuento. ¿Es exagerado? ¿Educado? ¿Irónico? ¿Satírico?
4 ¿Es importante dejar un testamento bien preparado? ¿Qué puede suceder si hay conflictos o malos entendidos? Cite ejemplos de testamentos famosos que estaban en litigio por mucho tiempo.

El Pretérito—Verbos Regulares

Verbos de la Primera Conjugación

Estudien las formas del pretérito de los verbos regulares de la primera conjugación.

mirar			
(yo)	miré	(nosotros)	miramos
(tú)	miraste	(vosotros)	mirasteis
(Ud., él, ella)	miró	(Uds., ellos, ellas)	miraron

A Sustituyan según el modelo.

> La mujer les gritó a todos.
> Lencho/
> Lencho les gritó a todos.

1 La mujer les gritó a todos.
el campesino/las muchachas/yo/los empleados y yo/tú/

2 El hombre rudo se acercó a la ventanilla.
los ladrones/yo/la vieja/tú/la jefa y yo/

3 Cuando comenzó a llover, el campesino se mojó.
las trabajadoras/yo/el empleado y yo/tú/la más pequeña/

4 No pasaron hambre porque sembraron otra vez.
su familia/yo/los afligidos/tú/nosotros/

5 Lencho echó la carta en el buzón.
la mujer de fe/yo/mi amigo y yo/tú/la abogada/

B Contesten a las siguientes preguntas según el modelo.

> ¿Dónde trabajaste ayer?
> Trabajé en la casa de Lencho.

1 ¿Dónde cenaste ayer?

2 ¿Dónde jugaste ayer?
3 ¿Dónde estudiaste ayer?
4 ¿Dónde empezaste a escribir ayer?
5 ¿Dónde esperaste ayer?
6 ¿Dónde pagaste ayer?

C Contesten a las siguientes preguntas según el modelo.

> ¿Quiénes buscaron la carta?
> Nosotros la buscamos.

1 ¿Quiénes encontraron la carta?
2 ¿Quiénes miraron la carta?
3 ¿Quiénes escucharon la carta?
4 ¿Quiénes empezaron la carta?
5 ¿Quiénes mandaron la carta?
6 ¿Quiénes esperaron la carta?
7 ¿Quiénes llevaron la carta?
8 ¿Quiénes echaron la carta?

D Contesten a las siguientes preguntas según la indicación.

1 ¿Qué exclamaste? —Ojalá que pase pronto.
2 ¿Qué gritaste a todos? —Vengan a comer.

3 ¿Qué observaste? *un fuerte aguacero*
4 ¿A quién ayudaste? *al pobre labrador*
5 ¿Dónde echaste la carta? *al correo*
6 ¿En qué pensó Lencho? *en su única esperanza*
7 ¿Cómo trabajó Lencho? *como una bestia de campo*
8 ¿Qué sembró Lencho? *maíz y frijoles*

9 ¿Cómo pasaron Uds. la noche? *llorando y lamentando la mala suerte*
10 ¿Qué enviaron Uds. al campesino? *poco más de cincuenta pesos*
11 ¿Cuándo llegaron Uds.? *un poco más temprano que de costumbre*
12 ¿Para qué contestaron Uds. la carta? *para no desilusionar a la mujer de fe*

Verbos de la Segunda Conjugación

Estudien las formas del pretérito de los verbos regulares de la segunda conjugación.

comer			
(yo)	comí	(nosotros)	comimos
(tú)	comiste	(vosotros)	comisteis
(Ud., él, ella)	comió	(Uds., ellos, ellas)	comieron

E Sustituyan según el modelo.

> *El empleado vendió el sello.*
> *Ud./*
> *Ud. vendió el sello.*

1 La empleada vendió el sello.
todas nosotras/los carteros/yo/el jefe de la oficina/tú/
2 Lencho y su mujer vieron el aguacero.
yo/el pobre/tú/las trabajadoras/nosotros/
3 La mujer no conoció a la jefa.
los amigos nuestros/yo/la autora y yo/tú/Uds./
4 La campesina perdió su dinero.
yo/mi hermano/tú/los carteros/tú y yo/

F Contesten a las siguientes preguntas según el modelo.

> *¿Vas a comer?*
> *No, ya comí.*

1 ¿Vas a beber?
2 ¿Vas a responder?
3 ¿Vas a leer?
4 ¿Vas a vender?
5 ¿Vas a escoger?
6 ¿Van Uds. a comer?
7 ¿Van Uds. a responder?
8 ¿Van Uds. a leer?
9 ¿Van Uds. a vender?
10 ¿Van Uds. a escoger?

G Cambien las siguientes oraciones al pretérito.

1 Recogen las perlas heladas.
2 Las gotas de agua parecen monedas de plata.
3 Una nube negra aparece sobre el valle.
4 ¿No reconoces al jefe?
5 ¿Por qué escoges este cuento?
6 ¿Por qué rompes el vaso?
7 Prometo ayudarle.
8 No debo reir ante la jefa.
9 Comprendo la fe de Lencho.
10 ¿Quiénes venden los sellos?
11 Los empleados comen a la una.
12 Las carteras meten la carta en la bolsa.

H Contesten a las siguientes preguntas según la indicación.

1 ¿Cuántos huevos comiste anoche? *dos*

2 ¿Adónde corriste? *a buscar un carpintero*
3 ¿Qué perdiste? *todo lo que tenía*
4 ¿Qué leíste? *el testamento sin puntuación*
5 ¿Cómo les pareció la carta? *bien escrita*
6 ¿A quién vieron Uds. llorando y sollozando? *al pobre viudo*
7 ¿Qué aprendieron Uds. del empleado? *que es ladrón*
8 ¿Qué comprendieron las hermanas? *el problema*
9 ¿Cuándo corrieron del parque? *cuando empezó el aguacero*
10 ¿Quiénes escogieron el plato de Sèvres? *los gatitos*
11 ¿Qué vieron los asistentes? *un regateo impresionante*

Verbos de la Tercera Conjugación

Estudien las formas del pretérito de los verbos regulares de la tercera conjugación.

abrir			
(yo)	abrí *é*	(nosotros)	abrimos *amos*
(tú)	abriste *aste*	(vosotros)	abristeis
(Ud., él, ella)	abrió *ó*	(Uds., ellos, ellas)	abrieron *aron*

I Sustituyan según el modelo.

El juez permitió la puntuación del testamento.
los asistentes/
Los asistentes permitieron la puntuación del testamento.

1 El juez permitió la puntuación del testamento.
yo/el sastre/el sobrino y el hermano/ tú/el mendigo/nosotros/

2 Todos exigieron la puntuación correcta.
el maestro/los señores/yo/tú/el juez/ellos/Uds./

3 El juez decidió pedir ayuda a los otros.
yo/los mendigos/la prima/tú/el hermano y yo/Ud./

4 El sastre recibió una sorpresa.
tú/todas/él/el juez y yo/los personajes/ el público/

J Contesten a las siguientes preguntas según el modelo.

> *¿Fue aconsejable abrir la carta?*
> *No, pero la abrí.*

1 ¿Fue fácil escribir la carta?
2 ¿Fue difícil subir aquella montaña?
3 ¿Fue divertido asistir a esa función?
4 ¿Fue aconsejable exigir esa cantidad?
5 ¿Fue correcto interrumpir la conversación?
6 ¿Fue necesario recibir la noticia?

K Contesten a las siguientes preguntas según el modelo.

> *¿Fue necesario abrir la carta?*
> *No, y por eso no la abrieron.*

1 ¿Fue aconsejable escribir una carta sin puntuación?
2 ¿Fue fácil subir aquel cerro?
3 ¿Fue importante escribir la carta?
4 ¿Fue correcto exigir su presencia?
5 ¿Fue necesario interrumpir la conversación?
6 ¿Fue posible recibir la noticia?

L Contesten a las siguientes preguntas según el modelo.

> *El sastre no recibió el dinero. ¿Y tú?*
> *Yo no recibí el dinero tampoco.*

1 La mujer no asistió a la función. ¿Y tú?
2 El juez no subió a su asiento. ¿Y tú?
3 Ella no insistió en puntuar el testamento. ¿Y tú?
4 El sobrino no describió bien su problema. ¿Y tú?
5 La señora González no escribió bien el testamento. ¿Y tú?
6 Los asistentes no interrumpieron la conversación. ¿Y Uds.?
7 Los personajes no recibieron dinero. ¿Y Uds.?
8 Las profesoras no abrieron el sobre. ¿Y Uds.?
9 Los otros no asistieron a la función. ¿Y Uds.?
10 Los empleados no exigieron mucho. ¿Y Uds.?

El Pretérito—Verbos Irregulares

Las terminaciones de la mayoría de los verbos irregulares en el pretérito son *–e, –iste, –o, –imos, –isteis, –ieron*. Los siguientes verbos tienen una raíz irregular.

infinitivo	raíz	pretérito
andar	anduv-	anduve
caber	cup-	cupe
estar	estuv-	estuve
hacer	hic-	hice (hizo)
poder	pud-	pude
poner	pus-	puse
querer	quis-	quise
saber	sup-	supe
tener	tuv-	tuve
venir	vin-	vine

Si una jota precede a la terminación, se omite la *i* en la terminación de la tercera persona plural.

infinitivo	raíz	pretérito
decir	dij-	dijeron
traer	traj-	trajeron

(Otros verbos semejantes son *conducir, producir* y *traducir*.)

Los siguientes verbos tienen una *y* en la tercera persona singular y plural. Noten los acentos.

infinitivo	pretérito
caer	caí, caíste, cayó, caímos, caísteis, cayeron
creer	creí, creíste, creyó, creímos, creísteis, creyeron
leer	leí, leíste, leyó, leímos, leísteis, leyeron
oir	oí, oíste, oyó, oímos, oísteis, oyeron

Los verbos *dar, ser* e *ir* también son irregulares en el pretérito.

infinitivo	pretérito
dar	di, diste, dio, dimos, disteis, dieron
ser e ir	fui, fuiste, fue, fuimos, fuisteis, fueron

El Pretérito—Verbos de Cambio Radical

Verbos con el Cambio e → i

Los verbos *pedir, mentir, rendir, despedir, conseguir, seguir, reir, repetir, sentir, preferir* y *sugerir* tienen una *i* en la tercera persona singular y plural.

infinitivo	pretérito
pedir	pedí, pediste, pidió, pedimos, pedisteis, pidieron

Verbos con el Cambio o → u

Los verbos *dormir* y *morir* tienen una *u* en la tercera persona singular y plural.

infinitivo	pretérito
dormir	dormí, dormiste, durmió, dormimos, dormisteis, durmieron
morir	morí, moriste, murió, morimos, moristeis, murieron

M Reemplacen el verbo con la forma correspondiente del infinitivo indicado.

1 Recibiste una carta.
traer/dar/tener/leer/
2 No hicimos nada ayer.
dar/oir/decir/tener/
3 Escribió de la gran tempestad.
saber/querer hablar/leer/oir/

4 Yo estudié demasiado.
oir/saber/traer/hacer/
5 ¿Qué recibieron?
querer/decir/hacer/dar/
6 Yo hablé con el juez.
venir/ir/andar/estar/

N Contesten a las siguientes preguntas según el modelo.

> *¿Qué leíste?*
> *No leí nada, pero la jefa leyó algo.*

1 ¿Qué hiciste?
2 ¿Qué dijiste?
3 ¿Qué oíste?
4 ¿Qué supiste?
5 ¿Qué quisiste?
6 ¿Qué tuviste?
7 ¿Qué trajiste?

O Contesten a las siguientes preguntas según el modelo.

> *¿Salió el sobrino esta mañana?*
> *Él salió ayer. Los otros salieron hoy.*

1 ¿Vino el sobrino esta mañana?
2 ¿Se fue el sobrino esta mañana?
3 ¿Lo supo el sobrino esta mañana?
4 ¿Estuvo el sobrino esta mañana?
5 ¿Se detuvo el sobrino esta mañana?
6 ¿Se despidió el sobrino esta mañana?

P Sigan el modelo.

> *Las maestras no lo creyeron.*
> *Nosotros sí lo creímos.*

1 Las ladronas no lo supieron.
2 Los coleccionistas no lo quisieron.
3 Los jueces no lo oyeron.
4 Las doctoras no lo leyeron.
5 Las mendigas no lo tuvieron.
6 Los sastres no lo hicieron.
7 Las propietarias no lo consiguieron.
8 Los hermanos no lo pidieron.

Q Cambien las siguientes oraciones al pretérito.

1 Estoy cerca de la ventanilla.
2 Tengo que puntuarlo.
3 Teresa no duerme bien.
4 No voy a la tienda de antigüedades.
5 ¿Por qué te vas?
6 ¿Oyes al juez?
7 ¿Dices que me dejas tus bienes?
8 ¿Sabes de su tristeza?
9 La carta cae al buzón.
10 Ella le pone la puntuación al testamento.
11 La mendiga pide limosna.
12 No podemos puntuar el documento.
13 No producimos una buena cosecha.
14 No traducimos las oraciones fácilmente.
15 Andan despacio hacia la ventanilla.
16 Están en la tienda de antigüedades.
17 Van tranquilamente a la esquina.
18 Prefieren oir chistes.
19 Sugieren una puntuación diferente.
20 Piden tiza para escribir en la pizarra.

R Cambien las siguientes oraciones al pretérito.

1 La propietaria se ríe de su burla.
2 No quepo en este pequeño espacio.
3 Pongo el testamento en tus manos.
4 Sirvo una comida buena.
5 Haces una buena interpretación.
6 Andas por las calles con tus amigos.
7 Estás en el centro de la ciudad.
8 Vamos a la tienda con el coleccionista.
9 Le decimos la pura verdad.
10 Mueren valientemente.
11 No pueden hacerlo.
12 ¿Vienen temprano?
13 Ellas repiten los mismos chistes.
14 El sobrino no miente.
15 La empleada no sabe qué decir.

S Sigan el modelo.

Pregúntele a Luis si tuvo que venir temprano hoy.
Luis, ¿tuviste que venir temprano hoy?

1 Pregúntele a una amiga   si oyó la interpretación del maestro.
                             si oyó la respuesta de la jefa.
                             si oyó el chiste.

2 Pregúntele a un amigo   si fue a la tienda de antigüedades.
                             si fue a la oficina de correos.
                             si fue solo.

3 Pregúntele a un amigo   si hizo la tarea para hoy.
                             si hizo su cama antes de salir de la casa.
                             si hizo algo interesante ayer.

4 Pregúntele a una amiga   si trajo su libro a clase.
                             si trajo dinero para comprar el almuerzo.
                             si trajo un sello para mandar la carta.

CUADRO 2

El Heroísmo

Quien no se aventura no pasa la mar.

PARA PREPARAR LA ESCENA

En la literatura universal hay miles de cuentos que tratan de la conducta heroica y los personajes valientes. Estos cuentos perduran, aumentando en popularidad, no sólo porque son muy emocionantes sino porque también tienen valor inspirativo.

En los anales del heroísmo uno puede encontrar muchos nombres españoles inmortalizados en canción y cuento. Mientras que algunos han ganado fama mundial a causa de su valor, otros, igualmente valerosos, han muerto en la oscuridad, desconocidos y olvidados.

El Mensajero de San Martín

PARA PRESENTAR LA LECTURA

El Mensajero de San Martín es el cuento de un joven que se muestra muy valiente. Aunque no lucha en el campo de batalla, ni siquiera lleva armas, su acto es digno de un verdadero patriota.

En la tierra de nuestros vecinos sudamericanos tuvo lugar una insurrección tan dramática como la de los colonos norteamericanos a fines del siglo dieciocho. Hubo numerosas batallas, mucho sufrimiento y muchos sacrificios, inmensurables conspiraciones e intrigas, el heroísmo en todas sus formas. Ambos lados, las fuerzas realistas así como las patriotas, querían conseguir la victoria, haciendo del movimiento independista una lucha larga y sangrienta. Muchos soldados y hombres de estado figuraron de un modo prominente en la guerra — héroes como Bolívar, Sucre, Miranda, O'Higgins, Artigas, San Martín, y otros menos conocidos, como el mensajero de San Martín.

PARA APRENDER VOCABULARIO

Palabras Clave   I

1 **castigo**   pena o sufrimiento impuesto por alguna falta
   Le van a dar un castigo fuerte por ese crimen.

2 **despacho**   oficina, lugar donde una persona trabaja
   La abogada trabajaba en su despacho.

3 **enviar**   mandar a una persona o cosa a alguna parte

   Roberto le va a enviar ese regalo a su primo.

4 **fusilarán (fusilar)**   matarán con una descarga de escopeta o fusil
   Han capturado al espía y mañana lo van a fusilar.

5 **halló (hallar)**   encontró
   La profesora te buscaba ayer, pero no te podía hallar.

6 **huir**　　escaparse rápidamente para no sufrir algo malo

En circunstancias especiales aun una persona fuerte puede huir.

7 **paisaje**　　vista del campo considerada desde el punto de vista artístico (landscape)

Las montañas y los valles formaban un paisaje mágico.

Práctica

Complete con una palabra de la lista.

fusilar	paisajes	castigo
halló	enviar	despacho
huir		

1 Al ver a los soldados la familia cometió el error de _____ .
2 La secretaria trabajaba en el _____ cuando recibió la noticia.
3 Si confiesas quizá puedas evitarte el _____ .
4 Creo que van a _____ a los culpables.
5 Inés buscó sus llaves pero no las _____ .
6 Este artista es especialista en _____ .
7 Quiero _____ el paquete por correo aéreo.

Palabras Clave　　II

1 **choza**　　casa pequeña y pobre (hut)
　　El pobre tiene que vivir en aquella choza.

2 **encierren (encerrar – ie)**　　contengan a una persona o cosa en una parte de donde no es posible salir (lock up)
　　Llévenlo a la policía y enciérrenlo esta noche.

3 **golpearon (golpear)**　　dieron golpes (struck repeatedly)
　　El boxeador golpeó a su rival sin piedad.

4 **jurado (jurar)**　　prometido solemnemente

Juan le había jurado amor eterno, y ya cambió de opinión.

5 **puñado**　　lo que cabe en la mano, cantidad pequeña
　　De toda la fortuna, sólo quedó un puñado de monedas.

6 **sombras**　　imágenes oscuras por interrupción de luz (shadows)
　　La sombra se movía misteriosamente en la noche.

7 **valiente**　　que no tiene miedo, que muestra coraje
　　La enfermera fue muy valiente durante la batalla.

8 **velaban (velar)**　　pasaban la noche sin dormir
　　Las tropas velaban de noche para prevenir un ataque por sorpresa.

Práctica

Complete con una palabra de la lista.

choza	puñado	sombra
jurado	golpearon	valiente
velaban	encierren	

1 Dos soldados lo _____ hasta que perdió el conocimiento.
2 Algunos _____ , pero otros estaban dormidos.
3 No quiero decirte el nombre porque he _____ guardar el secreto.
4 La ladrona andaba como una _____ en la noche oscura.
5 En el invierno esos pobres niños tienen frío en la _____ en que viven.
6 El ladrón no quiere que ellos lo _____ , pero sabe que lo tienen que castigar.
7 En todo el ejército sólo un _____ de soldados se escapó.
8 El coronel vio que la madre era muy _____ .

El Mensajero de San Martín

I

El general don José de San Martín leía unas cartas en su despacho. Terminada la lectura, se volvió para llamar a un muchacho de unos dieciséis años que esperaba de pie junto a la puerta.

—Voy a encargarte una misión difícil y honrosa. Te conozco bien; tu padre y tres hermanos tuyos están en mi ejército y sé que deseas servir a la patria. ¿Estás resuelto a servirme?

—Sí, mi general, sí—contestó el muchacho.

—Debes saber que en caso de ser descubierto te fusilarán—continuó el general.

—Ya lo sé, mi general.

—Entonces, ¿estás resuelto?

—Sí, mi general, sí.

—Muy bien. Quiero enviarte a Chile con una carta que no debe caer en manos del enemigo. ¿Has entendido, Miguel?

—Perfectamente, mi general—respondió el muchacho.—Dos días después, Miguel pasaba la cordillera de los Andes en compañía de unos arrieros.

Llegó a Santiago de Chile; halló al abogado Rodríguez, le entregó la carta y recibió la respuesta, que guardó en su cinturón secreto.

—Mucho cuidado con esta carta—le dijo también el patriota chileno—. Eres realmente muy joven; pero debes ser inteligente y buen patriota.

Miguel volvió a ponerse en camino lleno de orgullo. Había hecho el viaje sin dificultades, pero tuvo que pasar por un pueblo cerca del cual se hallaba una fuerza realista al mando del coronel Ordóñez.

encargarte darte

resuelto listo, decidido

cordillera cadena de montañas
arrieros *mule drivers*

entregó dio

—Cordillera de los Andes

Alrededor se extendía el hermoso paisaje chileno. Miguel se sintió impresionado por aquel cuadro mágico; mas algo inesperado vino a distraer su atención.

Dos soldados, a quienes pareció sospechoso ese muchacho que viajaba solo y en dirección a las sierras, se dirigieron hacia él a galope. En la sorpresa del primer momento, Miguel cometió la imprudencia de huir.

—¡Hola!—gritó uno de los soldados sujetándole el caballo por las riendas—. ¿Quién eres y adónde vas?

Miguel contestó humildemente que era chileno, que se llamaba Juan Gómez y que iba a la hacienda de sus padres.

Lo llevaron sin embargo a una tienda de campaña donde se hallaba, en compañía de varios oficiales, el coronel Ordóñez.

—Te acusan de ser agente del general San Martín—dijo el coronel—. ¿Qué contestas a eso?

Miguel habría preferido decir la verdad, pero negó la acusación.

—Oye, muchacho—añadió el coronel—, más vale que confieses francamente, así quizá puedas evitarte el castigo, porque eres muy joven. ¿Llevas alguna carta?

—No—contestó Miguel, pero cambió de color y el coronel lo notó.

Dos soldados se apoderaron del muchacho, y mientras el uno lo sujetaba, el otro no tardó en hallar el cinturón con la carta.

—Bien lo decía yo—observó Ordóñez, disponiéndose a abrirla.—Pero en ese instante Miguel, con un movimiento brusco, saltó como un tigre, le arrebató la carta de las manos y la arrojó en un brasero allí encendido.

II

—Hay que convenir en que eres muy valiente—dijo Ordóñez.— Aquél que te ha mandado sabe elegir su gente. Ahora bien, puesto que eres resuelto, quisiera salvarte y lo haré si me dices lo que contenía la carta.

—No sé, señor.

—¿No sabes? Mira que tengo medios de despertar tu memoria.

—No sé, señor. La persona que me dio la carta no me dijo nada.

El coronel meditó un momento.

---

mas pero

se dirigieron fueron hacia

sujetándole holding
riendas reins

tienda de campaña tent

más vale es mejor
evitarte avoid

se apoderaron held

brusco repentino
arrebató snatched, took away
brasero small charcoal stove

convenir admitir

—Bien—dijo—te creo. ¿Podrías decirme al menos de quién era y a quién iba dirigida?

—No puedo, señor.

—¿Y por qué no?

—Porque he jurado.

El coronel admiró en secreto al niño pero no lo demostró. Abriendo un cajón de la mesa, tomó un puñado de monedas de oro.

—¿Has tenido alguna vez una moneda de oro?—preguntó a Miguel.

—No, señor—contestó el muchacho.

—Bueno, pues, yo te daré diez. ¿Entiendes? Diez de éstas, si me dices lo que quiero saber. Y eso, con sólo decirme dos nombres. Puedes decírmelo en voz baja—continuó el coronel.

—No quiero, señor.

azotes *lashes*

—A ver—ordenó—unos cuantos azotes bien dados a este muchacho.

En presencia de Ordóñez, de sus oficiales y de muchos soldados, dos de éstos lo golpearon sin piedad. El muchacho

apretó *tightened, pressed, gritted*

perdió el conocimiento se desmayó

apretó los dientes para no gritar. Sus sentidos comenzaron a turbarse y luego perdió el conocimiento.

—Basta—dijo Ordóñez—, enciérrenlo por esta noche. Mañana confesará.

Entre los que presenciaron los golpes se encontraba un soldado chileno que, como todos sus compatriotas, simpatizaba con la causa de la libertad. Tenía dos hermanos, agentes de San Martín, y él mismo esperaba la ocasión favorable para abandonar el ejército real. El valor del muchacho lo llenó de admiración.

A medianoche el silencio más profundo reinaba en el campa-

centinelas guardias

mento. Los fuegos estaban apagados y sólo los centinelas velaban con el arma en el brazo.

Miguel estaba en una choza, donde lo habían dejado bajo

cerrojo *bolt, lock*

cerrojo, sin preocuparse más de él.

Entonces, en el silencio de la noche, oyó un ruido como el de un cerrojo corrido con precaución. La puerta se abrió despacio y apareció la figura de un hombre. Miguel se levantó sorprendido.

¡Quieto! ¡Quédate calmo!
cansancio fatiga

—¡Quieto!—murmuró una voz—. ¿Tienes valor para escapar?

De repente Miguel no sintió dolores, cansancio, ni debilidad; estaba ya bien, ágil y resuelto a todo. Siguió al soldado y los dos andaban como sombras por el campamento dormido, hacia un corral donde se hallaban los caballos del servicio. El pobre animal de Miguel permanecía ensillado aún y atado a un poste.

ensillado *saddled*

—Éste es el único punto por donde puedes escapar—dijo el soldado—, el único lugar donde no hay centinelas. ¡Pronto, a caballo y buena suerte!

El joven héroe obedeció, despidiéndose de su generoso salvador con un apretón de manos y un ¡Dios se lo pague! Luego, espoleó su caballo sin perder un minuto y huyó en dirección a las montañas.

apretón de manos *strong handshake*
espoleó *spurred*

Huyó para mostrar a San Martín, con las heridas de los golpes que habían roto sus espaldas, cómo había sabido guardar un secreto y servir a la patria.

PARA APLICAR

Comprensión   I

A   Conteste a las siguientes preguntas.

1   ¿Qué estaba haciendo San Martín en su despacho?
2   ¿Qué misión difícil le encargó al joven?
3   ¿Qué podría pasar si lo descubrieran?
4   ¿Qué le entregó a Rodríguez?
5   ¿Dónde guardó la respuesta?
6   ¿Qué le dijo el patriota chileno?
7   ¿Qué vino a distraer la atención de Miguel al contemplar el paisaje chileno?
8   ¿Por qué les pareció sospechoso el muchacho?
9   ¿Adónde lo llevaron?
10 ¿Cómo notó el coronel Ordóñez que Miguel tenía un secreto?
11 ¿Cómo evitó Miguel que el coronel Ordóñez leyera la carta?

B   ¿Verdadero o falso?

1   San Martín llamó al joven que descansaba cerca de la puerta.
2   San Martín le tenía confianza porque conocía a varios parientes suyos.

3   El encargo que el general le dio era peligroso.
4   Miguel entendió que si lo descubrieran lo fusilarían.
5   Miguel tenía diecisiete años de edad.
6   Halló al abogado en la capital de Chile.
7   En el pueblo cerca del cual tuvo que pasar Miguel había un ejército español.
8   Cuando los soldados le llamaron, Miguel se entregó humildemente.
9   El joven convenció a los soldados realistas con sus mentiras inocentes.
10 Miguel se apoderó del coronel y lo sujetó con su cinturón.

Comprensión   II

A   Conteste a las siguientes preguntas.

1   ¿Cómo intentó el coronel persuadir a Miguel de que le dijera el contenido de la carta?
2   ¿Cómo intentó que le dijera a quién iba dirigida?
3   ¿Qué sentimiento tuvo el coronel hacia el muchacho?
4   ¿Cuándo se abrió la puerta de la choza de Miguel?

5 ¿Cómo se escapó Miguel?
6 ¿Dónde se quedó el soldado chileno?
7 ¿Adónde huyó Miguel?
8 ¿A quién fue a mostrar cómo había sabido guardar el secreto para servir a la patria?

B ¿Verdadero o falso?

1 El coronel sigue insistiendo en que Miguel le diga el contenido de la carta.
2 El coronel cree que Miguel le miente otra vez.
3 Miguel juró no revelar nada acerca de la carta.
4 Las monedas de oro le interesaron a Miguel.
5 Todos los compatriotas chilenos querían la libertad.
6 San Martín tenía dos hermanos que eran agentes de la causa de la libertad chilena.
7 El coronel Ordóñez quería abandonar las fuerzas de España.
8 La choza estaba cerrada con llave.
9 Miguel y el soldado caminaban por el campamento con mucha precaución.
10 Miguel no quería que San Martín supiera de sus heridas y cómo había sufrido.

Más Práctica

A Complete las siguientes oraciones con una palabra o una expresión de la lista.

servirme, arrieros, cerrojo, medianoche, de pie, corrido, espoleó su caballo, atado, dolores, misión, admiración, buena suerte, huyó, generoso salvador, sombras, apoderaron, despacho, cordillera, choza, manos del enemigo

1 El general leía unas cartas en su _____ .
2 El muchacho esperaba _____ junto a la puerta.
3 Voy a encargarte una _____ difícil.
4 ¿Estás resuelto a _____?
5 La carta no debe caer en _____ .
6 Miguel pasaba la _____ de los Andes.

7 Iba en compañía de unos _____ .
8 El valor del muchacho lo llenó de _____ .
9 Dos soldados se _____ del muchacho.
10 A _____ el silencio más profundo reinaba.
11 Miguel estaba en una _____ .
12 Lo habían dejado bajo _____ .
13 Oyó el ruido de un cerrojo _____ .
14 De repente no sintió _____ .
15 Los dos andaban como _____ .
16 El animal permanecía _____ a un poste.
17 ¡Pronto, a caballo y _____!
18 Se despidió de su _____ con un apretón de manos.
19 Luego _____ sin perder un momento.
20 _____ en dirección a las montañas.

B Dé un antónimo de las siguientes palabras.

1 un palacio   4 dormir bien
2 perder   5 cobarde
3 poner en libertad

C Conteste a las siguientes preguntas.

1 ¿Qué hace la policía con un criminal?
2 ¿Qué hay en un ejército?
3 ¿En qué tienen que vivir los pobres?
4 ¿Qué lleva una persona para que no se le caigan los pantalones?
5 ¿Qué reciben los soldados en una batalla cruel?

Ejercicios Creativos

1 Imagine que Ud. es director de escena de un estudio cinematográfico. Ud. tiene que repartir papeles para una película titulada *El Mensajero de San Martín*. ¿Qué características tendrían los actores que Ud. escogería para desempeñar los siguientes papeles?
   a. San Martín
   b. Luis
   c. el coronel Ordóñez
   d. el soldado que simpatizaba con la causa de la libertad

2 Mencionados en la selección figuran «el hermoso paisaje chileno» y «una cordillera de los Andes». Prepare un breve informe sobre la topografía de Chile. Use un mapa en su presentación.

3 Haga una lista de palabras y expresiones «militares» que se encuentran en el cuento. Luego, escriba un párrafo usando por lo menos cinco palabras de la lista (por ejemplo: *soldado, luchar, ejército, fusilar, herida*).

El Alcázar de Toledo

El Alcázar no se rinde

Carlos Ruiz de Azilú

PARA PRESENTAR LA LECTURA

Durante la Guerra Civil en España las fuerzas republicanas se habían apoderado de la ciudad de Toledo. Asediados en el Alcázar de Toledo había algunos insurgentes quienes se habían negado a entregar el armamento y las municiones de este centro militar a los republicanos. El contingente, bajo las órdenes del comandante militar, coronel Moscardó, había jurado morir si fuera preciso antes que rendirse.

Para ser héroe, muchas veces es necesario sacrificar algo. Hay dos héroes identificados en este cuento del Alcázar de Toledo. ¿Quiénes son? ¿Por qué lo son?

PARA APRENDER VOCABULARIO

Palabras Clave   I

1 **alcázar**   fortaleza, palacio árabe
El Alcázar de Sevilla es un edificio magnífico.

2 **aparato**   instrumento para ejecutar una cosa; máquina, teléfono
El aparato no funciona.

3 **detenido (detener)**   parado, arrestado
Tenemos que detener a todos los criminales.

4 **rinde (rendirse – i)**   se entrega, se sujeta al dominio de otros
Prefieren morir antes que rendirse.

5 **sonó (sonar – ue)**   hizo ruido una cosa
(sounded, rang)
El niño se despertó al sonar el teléfono.

Práctica

Complete con una palabra de la lista.

sonó	rendirse	detenido
Alcázar		aparato

1 Han _____ al asesino hasta que vengan los demás.

2 Es un acto de coraje no _____.

3 Creo que _____ el teléfono durante la noche.
4 ¿Dónde está el _____ de radio?
5 El _____ de Sevilla es un palacio magnífico.

Palabras Clave   II

anguish **angustia**   dolor moral profundo
El padre no podía disimular la angustia que sentía cuando perdió a su hijo.

want 2   **atrevía (atreverse)**   quería, osaba
Nadie se atrevía a hablarle de la muerte de su padre.

3   **colgó (colgar – ue)**   suspendió una cosa en otra; cortó una comunicación telefónica *(hung up)*
Tengo que colgar. Mi padre quiere usar el teléfono.

4   **entristecidos**   tristes *(saddened)*
Todos quedaron entristecidos al despedirse en el aeropuerto.

exceed 5   **sobran (sobrar)**   exceden, están unas cosas de más, hay más de lo necesario de una cosa
Como no vienen nuestras amigas, sobran tres asientos.

Práctica

Complete con una palabra de la lista.

angustia	entristecidos	atreverse
colgó	sobran	

1 Elena _____ su abrigo en este clavo.
2 Veo por la lista de los invitados que _____ hombres.
3 Todos podían comprender la _____ que sentía el viudo.
4 Pablo tenía los ojos _____ por la profunda emoción que sentía.
5 El niño ha aprendido una buena lección. La próxima vez no va a _____ a hacer tal cosa.

El Alcázar no se rinde

Carlos Ruiz de Azilú

I

Eran aproximadamente las diez de la mañana del día veintitrés de julio de 1936 cuando sonó el teléfono del despacho del coronel Moscardó. Se hallaba éste rodeado de varios de los jefes del Alcázar y otros oficiales, organizando la defensa exterior y la acomodación del personal refugiado. Pausadamente se levantó el coronel y se dirigió al teléfono.

personal refugiado gente sin hogar

La conversación de aquella llamada telefónica ha de contarse entre los diálogos más heroicos de nuestros días:

ha de contarse *has to be considered*

—¿Quién está al aparato?

—Soy el jefe de las milicias socialistas. Tengo la ciudad en mi poder, y si dentro de diez minutos no se ha rendido Ud., mandaré fusilar a su hijo Luis, que lo he detenido; y para que vea que es así, él mismo le hablará. «A ver, que venga Moscardó».

En efecto, el padre oye a su hijo Luis, que le dice tranquilamente por el aparato:

—Papá, ¿cómo estás?

—Bien, hijo mío. ¿Qué te ocurre?

—Nada de particular. Que dicen que me fusilarán si el Alcázar no se rinde, pero no te preocupes por mí.

encomienda confía, da

—Mira, hijo mío; si es cierto que te van a fusilar, encomienda tu alma a Dios, da un ¡Viva Cristo Rey! y otro ¡Viva España! y muere como un héroe y mártir. Adiós, hijo mío; un beso muy fuerte.

—Adiós, papá; un beso muy fuerte.

II

A continuación se oye nuevamente la voz del jefe de milicias, preguntando:

—¿Qué contesta Ud.?

El coronel Moscardó pronuncia estas sublimes palabras:

—¡Que el Alcázar no se rinde y que sobran los diez minutos!

A los pocos días fue asesinado vilmente don Luis Moscardó Guzmán, joven de diecisiete años, nuevo mártir de la Cruzada.

auricular *receiver*

Cuando el coronel Moscardó colgó el auricular, un silencio impresionante que nadie se atrevía a romper reinaba en su despacho. Todos comprendían la magnitud del sacrificio ofrecido a la Patria y la singular heroicidad del gesto. Intensamente pálido y con los ojos entristecidos por la angustia de su drama interior, el coronel Moscardó rompió el silencio, dirigiéndose a sus colaboradores:

—Y bien, señores, continuemos . . .

PARA APLICAR

Comprensión   I

A   Conteste a las siguientes preguntas.

1   ¿Quién es el coronel Moscardó?
2   ¿Quién le llamó por teléfono?
3   ¿Qué le dijo?
4   ¿Con quién habló el coronel entonces?
5   ¿Qué consejo le dio a su hijo el coronel?

B   ¿Verdadero o falso?

1   Este incidente tiene lugar exactamente a las diez de la mañana.
2   Era el veintitrés de junio de 1936.
3   El coronel Moscardó estaba en un rodeo.
4   Algunos oficiales estaban organizando la defensa de la fortaleza.
5   Las milicias socialistas tenían el control de la ciudad.
6   Si el coronel no se rinde inmediatamente, los socialistas van a matar a Luis Moscardó.
7   Luis parecía nervioso cuando habló con su padre.

8   Luis no quiere que su padre se preocupe por él.
9   El padre quiere que su hijo muera como un héroe.

Comprensión   II

A   Conteste a las siguientes preguntas.

1   ¿Con quién volvió a hablar el coronel?
2   ¿Qué le dijo?
3   ¿Qué pasó a los pocos días?
4   Cuando el coronel Moscardó colgó el auricular del teléfono, ¿qué reinaba en su despacho?
5   ¿Qué comprendían los que habían escuchado la conversación entre el padre y su hijo?
6   ¿Quién rompió el silencio por fin?
7   ¿Qué dijo él?
8   ¿Por qué podemos llamarles héroes al coronel y a su hijo?

B ¿Verdadero o falso?

1 Luis es valiente, aun sabiendo que lo van a matar.
2 El coronel decide rendirse.
3 Mataron en seguida a Luis.
4 Todos comenzaron a hablar cuando el coronel colgó el aparato.
5 Todos simpatizaban con el coronel.
6 Tuvieron que suspender el trabajo por varios días.

Más Práctica

A Reemplace la palabra en letra bastardilla con la palabra indicada.

1 Soy el *jefe* de las milicias nacionales. *general*
2 Si no se rinde, mandaré *fusilar* a su hijo. *matar*
3 Sonó el teléfono en *el despacho* del presidente. *la oficina*
4 Fue asesinado *vilmente*. *cobardemente*

5 Hizo un *gesto* de desesperación. *ademán*
6 Esperamos que se *rinda* el enemigo. *entregue*
7 Oye, Carmen, ¿qué te *ocurre*? *sucede*
8 ¿Es *cierto* que te van a fusilar? *seguro*

B Complete las siguientes oraciones con una palabra de la lista.

pausadamente, rendido, fortaleza, detención, preciso, aparato, poder

1 Era _____ acabar lo que se había empezado.
2 Por infracción de la ley, lo habían puesto en _____ .
3 Cuando quiso hablar por el _____, no funcionaba.
4 Cayó en _____ del enemigo.
5 Siempre hablaba _____ .
6 Después de un asedio largo, la _____ cayó en manos del enemigo.
7 Después de luchar por semanas, la fortaleza se había _____ .

Picasso: *Guernica*

On extended loan to the Museum of Modern Art, New York, from the estate of the artist

C Dé un antónimo de las siguientes palabras.

1	la mañana	6	vivir
2	la noche	7	preguntar
3	hablar	8	oscuro
4	exterior	9	el silencio
5	impersonal	10	guardar silencio

Ejercicios Creativos

1 Una guerra civil casi siempre resulta en tragedia. En un párrafo en español explique por qué.

2 Cada guerra produce sus héroes. Escoja una figura heroica de una de las muchas guerras que la historia nos revela. En un párrafo, explique por qué merece el título de héroe.

3 En su opinión, ¿cuál es la diferencia entre un héroe y un mártir?

4 Examine la pintura de la destrucción de Guernica en la página 49. Luego, haga la siguiente tarea:

   a. Prepare una lista de cosas que Ud. puede identificar en el cuadro.

   b. Escriba algunas líneas indicando sus impresiones o reacciones personales al examinar la reproducción de la pintura.

   c. En su opinión, ¿qué es lo que Picasso trata de decirnos a propósito de la Guerra Civil en España?

5 Compare o contraste el cuento El *Alcázar no se rinde* con *El Mensajero de San Martín*, poniendo atención a los siguientes puntos:

   a. lugar de la acción

   b. tiempo de la acción

   c. personajes valientes

Amor paternal: abuelo y nietos

Una Medalla de bronce

Álvaro de Laiglesia

PARA PRESENTAR LA LECTURA

África ha sido, durante la historia, un campo de batalla permanente. Miguel, protagonista del cuento que vamos a leer, había luchado en una de las muchas batallas africanas y había regresado de la guerra con una medalla de bronce como héroe de la campaña.

No nos interesa la guerra en la cual Miguel se había distinguido, ni la batalla específica, ni el continente misterioso en que tuvo lugar, ni siquiera la medalla misma. Lo que nos llama la atención son los sorprendentes detalles de cómo Miguel había recibido su condecoración y las varias transformaciones de la historia de la medalla a lo largo de la vida de Miguel. ¡Somos héroes todos!

PARA APRENDER VOCABULARIO

Palabras Clave   I

1 **al principio**   al empezar
   Al principio no me di cuenta de las complicaciones.

2 **derrotado (derrotar)**   hecho huir el ejército contrario
   El general había derrotado al enemigo en una batalla muy larga.

3 **nos enteramos (enterarse)**   informarse
   Cuando Isabel regresó, nos enteramos de la situación.

4 **huesos**   partes duras y sólidas que forman la estructura del cuerpo *(bones)*
   Dieron los huesos al perro.

5 **medalla**   pieza de metal hecha para conmemorar una acción o personaje ilustre
   Le presentaron una medalla por sus acciones heroicas.

6 **pecho**   parte del cuerpo desde el cuello hasta el abdomen
   Al saludar la bandera ella puso la mano sobre el pecho.

Práctica

Complete con una palabra de la lista.

> al principio   hueso   derrotar
> pecho   enteramos   medalla

1 No, nadie pudo creerlo _____.
2 El soldado recibió la _____ del general.
3 No la llamamos antes porque no nos _____ hasta esta mañana.
4 Lorenzo tiene una fractura en un _____ del brazo.
5 Nuestro equipo no puede _____ al otro.
6 ¿No sabes el nombre del pájaro que tiene el _____ de color rojo?

Palabras Clave   II

1 **agotaron (agotar)**   consumieron, usaron todo (fuerzas, energías, dinero, etc.)
    Luchamos tanto tiempo que se nos agotaron las balas.

2 **aprovechando (aprovechar)**   sirviendo de buen uso alguna cosa
    Vamos a la playa. Hay que aprovechar el buen tiempo.

3 **balazo**   golpe o herida de un arma de fuego
    Murió de un balazo en el corazón.

4 **cicatriz**   marca permanente dejada por una herida
    Después del accidente quedó una cicatriz larga en la cara de la joven.

5 **hazañas**   hechos ilustres o célebres
    Todo el mundo queda impresionado por las hazañas de los astronautas.

6 **rechazar**   resistir, no aceptar
    Los soldados lucharon con valentía para rechazar el ataque.

7 **socio**   persona asociada con otras, miembro de un club
    Mi tía es socia del club de tenis.

Práctica

Complete con una palabra de la lista.

> agotado   rechazan   cicatriz
> balazo   hazañas   aprovechando
> socio

1 La mujer recibió un _____ en el hombro.
2 Señor, lo siento, pero no puede entrar en el club porque Ud. no es _____.
3 Desgraciadamente, la herida le dejó una _____ muy fea.
4 Recibieron poco de herencia porque ellos ya habían _____ el dinero de su papá.
5 Se conocen a los héroes por sus _____.
6 _____ la ausencia de sus padres, los jóvenes dieron una fiesta.
7 Benjamín es muy desafortunado en el amor. Todas las mujeres lo _____.

Palabras Clave   III

1 **apoyando (apoyar)**   se dice de una cosa descansando sobre otra   *(leaning, resting)*
    Lorenzo lloraba en el sillón, apoyando la cabeza en las manos.

2 **arrancó (arrancar)**   sacó con violencia
    Ayer el dentista me arrancó una muela.

3 **bata**   ropa larga y cómoda que se usa para estar en casa   *(bathrobe)*
    Enrique colgó su bata en el clavo cerca de la puerta.

4 **disparaban (disparar)**   fusilaban
    Las tropas disparaban contra la gente, matando a varios.

5 **realizado (realizar)**   hecho efectivo algo, cumplido
    Realizado el triunfo, se acabó la guerra.

6 **vacuna**   inmunización contra una enfermedad determinada
    ¿Quién descubrió la vacuna contra la viruela?

7 **zapatillas** zapatos ligeros que se usan por comodidad en casa
   Bárbara siempre lleva zapatillas en casa.

Práctica

Complete con una palabra de la lista.

disparar	zapatillas	realizado
arrancó	bata	vacuna
apoyaron		

1 Una vez _____ su plan, María se quedó contenta.
2 La propietaria se enojó cuando los niños _____ sus bicicletas contra la pintura fresca.
3 Por la mañana la autora trabaja vestida con _____ .
4 Este certificado de _____ te permitirá entrar en los Estados Unidos.
5 La señora López _____ la pistola de la mano del ladrón y llamó a la policía.
6 Después de suficiente práctica, uno puede _____ una pistola con confianza.
7 Bajaré a desayunar cuando encuentre mis _____ .

Palabras Clave IV

1 **cintas** tejidos largos, planos y angostos, *(ribbons, tapes)*
   La niña se sujeta el pelo con una cinta graciosa.

2 **opinó (opinar)** tuvo opinión sobre una cosa
   No me digas lo que debo opinar de él.

3 **padezco (padecer)** sufro, siento un daño o dolor
   Padecieron mucho después de la tempestad.

4 **tirada (tirar)** lanzada, arrojada, botada *(thrown)*
   Encontré tu bata tirada en el piso.

Práctica

Complete con una palabra de la lista.

padecer	tirada
opinar	cintas

1 En el laboratorio de idiomas se usan _____ magnéticas en la práctica oral.
2 ¡Doctora! Mándeme algo para aliviar este dolor. No quiero _____ toda la noche.
3 Soy imparcial. No quiero _____ nada sobre esa situación.
4 La blusa fue _____ en la basura.

Una Medalla de bronce

Álvaro de Laiglesia

I

Miguel había hecho una guerra en África. Una de tantas. No sé cuál, ni me importa, porque todas son iguales.

* * *

África ha sido, es, y quizá lo siga siendo durante muchos años, un campo de batalla permanente. Situado en las afueras de la civilización, viene a ser algo así como esos «clubs» que hay en los alrededores de las ciudades para practicar algunos deportes.

La guerra en cierto modo es un deporte también, y el inmenso «club» africano dispone de muchas pistas para que puedan practicarlo varios ejércitos a la vez. Las tropas con sus pertrechos embarcan para combatir en África, lo mismo que los «tenistas» con sus raquetas suben al coche para jugar unos «sets» en el Club de Campo.

Miguel, como dije al principio, hizo una guerra de ésas. Y al terminarla regresó muy contento a su casa, porque su equipo había derrotado al enemigo.

—¿Qué tal lo pasaste? —le preguntaron sus padres mientras él, después de quitarse el uniforme, se duchaba para refrescarse y vestirse de paisano.

—Bien —contestó él—. Los primeros asaltos fueron duros, pero ganamos.

Y se incorporó a la vida civil.

Miguel había vuelto del campo africano con cinco kilos menos sobre los huesos y una medalla más encima del pecho. Los kilos los perdió en los seis meses de duración de la campaña; pero la medalla la ganó en veinticuatro horas.

Es la historia de esta medalla la que voy a contar. O mejor dicho, las sucesivas transformaciones que fue sufriendo la historia de esta medalla, a lo largo de la vida de Miguel. Porque ni el

pertrechos municiones y armas

se duchaba *was taking a shower*
paisano *civilian*

se incorporó a entró en

campaña expedición militar

bronce en que estaba fundida, ni las alegorías que figuraban en su anverso y reverso, sufrieron con los años ninguna transformación. Pero sí los pormenores de la acción bélica que motivó su concesión al soldado que la ostentaba.

*   *   *

Recién llegado de la guerra, con veinticuatro años de edad recién cumplidos, Miguel contó así a sus padres la historia de esta condecoración:

—Una noche, después de avanzar durante todo el día sin encontrar resistencia, mi pelotón se refugió en una casucha abandonada. Éramos seis hombres al mando de un cabo. Estábamos cansadísimos y nos quedamos profundamente dormidos. Tan profundamente, que al amanecer nuestra compañía recibió la orden de retirarse y nosotros no nos enteramos. A la mañana siguiente, nos despertó un tiroteo: estábamos aislados del resto de nuestras fuerzas y el enemigo había rodeado la casucha. Nos defendimos disparando desde las ventanas durante todo el día. Por fortuna, los atacantes eran escasos y malos tiradores. Al anochecer una patrulla llegó a liberarnos, y el capitán nos echó una bronca por habernos dormido. Pero como luego resultó que aquella casucha era un punto estratégico, el propio capitán no tuvo más remedio que condecorarnos por haberla defendido.

*   *   *

<h1 style="text-align:center">II</h1>

Tres años después, al cumplir los veintisiete, Miguel se echó novia formal. Se la echó al brazo, y con ella paseaba por las tardes planeando la fundación de un hogar. Ya tenía él una pequeña posición en la vida, y ella algún dinerito en el banco. Dos motivos importantes para que un hombre se preste a uncirse al yugo matrimonial.

A su novia, en uno de aquellos paseos preparatorios, le contó así la historia de la medalla:

—No tuvo ninguna importancia. Después de un combate que duró varias horas, mi sección logró conquistar un polvorín enemigo. Yo era cabo y mandaba seis hombres. Nos fortificamos en el polvorín aprovechando las sombras de la noche, pues mi compañía sufrió muchas bajas y no podía enviarnos refuerzos. Al amanecer,

el enemigo inició el contraataque con fuerzas nutridas y bien
armadas. Teníamos orden de defender el polvorín, y lo defendimos
durante todo el día hasta que se nos agotaron las municiones. Y
cuando nos disponíamos a calar las bayonetas para continuar
la defensa, nos llegó una columna de socorro para romper el cerco.
Todos los supervivientes fuimos condecorados por el comandante
del batallón.

calar poner en posición
cerco *fence*
supervivientes los que no
murieron

*   *   *

Casado ya, con más de treinta años y más de tres niños
(el cuarto estaba en camino), Miguel se hizo socio de un casino.
Y todas las tardes, en uno de sus salones, tomaba café con un
grupo de amigos.

En estas tertulias, como los cafés que se toman son cortos
y las horas para tomarlos muy largas, cada tertuliano va
desembuchando todas las hazañas de su vida. Y cuando le llegó
el turno a Miguel, contó así la historia de su medalla:

—Fue bastante desagradable. Dos días luchó mi compañía
sin poder tomar aquel fortín. Al final, gracias a un puñado de
voluntarios entre los cuales estaba yo, lo conquistamos en un
audaz golpe de mano. Habíamos sufrido tantas bajas que yo,
aunque sólo era sargento, tuve que tomar el mando de una
sección. El enemigo recibió refuerzos durante la noche, con los
cuales desencadenó al amanecer una furiosa contraofensiva.
Incluso emplazaron un cañón, con el cual abrieron varias brechas
en los muros del fortín. A primeras horas de la tarde, como las
municiones se nos habían agotado, hasta los heridos tuvieron que
empuñar las bayonetas para rechazar a los asaltantes. Cuando
llegó la columna blindada que nos enviaron para socorrernos,
quedábamos en pie tres docenas de hombres. Yo apenas podía
sostenerme, porque me habían pegado un balazo en un muslo.
Aquí exactamente. No os enseño la cicatriz porque tendría que
quitarme los pantalones. Nos condecoró el teniente coronel del
regimiento, después de pronunciar unas palabras conmovedoras.

tertulias reuniones sociales

desembuchando contando

fortín pequeña fortaleza

desencadenó empezó
emplazaron pusieron en su
lugar
brechas aberturas que
hace la artillería
empuñar tomar con la
mano
blindada armada

muslo parte superior de la
pierna

conmovedoras emocionantes

*   *   *

III

Los hijos de Miguel fueron creciendo hasta alcanzar el uso de
razón. Él por su parte alcanzó la cuarentena, y la rebasó en más
de un lustro.

la . . . lustro ya tenía más
(de cuarenta y cinco años)

estufa aparato de calefacción

veladas invernales períodos de invierno

diezmado *decimated*
palmo a palmo poco a poco
penosísima muy triste
extenuados fatigados

derribadas arruinadas
se apostaron tomaron sus posiciones
víveres comidas, alimentos

ametralladoras *machine guns*

suplirlas añadir lo que faltaba
culata *rifle butt*

cartucho *cartridge*

al arma blanca con cuchillos
enardecidos llenos de emoción

muelas postizas dientes falsos
casco de metralla *exploding shell*

Con cuarenta y seis años de edad y noventa kilos de peso, toda la gente antepuso el «don» a su nombre. Y don Miguel, cuando apretaba el frío, no salía de su casa por las noches. Se quedaba junto a la estufa en bata y zapatillas, charlando con su familia hasta la hora de dormir.

Fue en una de estas veladas invernales cuando a sus hijos, ya mayorcitos, les contó así la historia de su medalla:

—Fueron unos días que no olvidaré nunca. Mi batallón, diezmado por el fuego incesante de la artillería, logró avanzar palmo a palmo durante una penosísima semana. Llegamos extenuados junto a las murallas de una fortaleza, objetivo primordial de aquella ofensiva. El coronel del regimiento, comprendiendo que habíamos realizado un esfuerzo sobrehumano, ordenó que nos retirásemos a posiciones más seguras. Pero nosotros, sabiendo que aquel día era el cumpleaños del coronel, quisimos hacerle un regalo. Y tomamos la fortaleza a sangre y fuego. La noche cayó sobre las murallas medio derribadas, entre cuyas ruinas los restos de mi batallón se apostaron para defenderlas. No teníamos agua, ni víveres, ni municiones . . . Bueno; municiones sí, pero pocas. Como casi todos los oficiales habían muerto, yo tuve que tomar el mando de una compañía. Muchas horas antes del amanecer, las ametralladoras enemigas nos sometieron a un fuego mortífero. Nuestras bajas eran tan numerosas que, para suplirlas, muchos soldados disparaban con dos fusiles a la vez, apoyando una culata en cada hombro. Desfallecidos de cansancio, hambrientos y sedientos, resistimos hasta agotar el último cartucho. La batalla había durado todo el día. A partir de entonces, protegidos por las sombras de la noche luchamos al arma blanca. «¡Resistir hasta morir!», gritábamos enardecidos, repartiendo bayonetazos y cuchilladas. Una división, perforando trabajosamente las compactas líneas enemigas, nos salvó. Del batallón sólo quedábamos un puñado de supervivientes, de los cuales ninguno estaba intacto. ¿Veis este circulito que tengo en el brazo, y que a primera vista parece una vacuna? Pues en realidad es la cicatriz de una bala de máuser. ¿Y os habéis fijado en todas estas muelas postizas que llevo de oro? Pues las auténticas me las arrancó un casco de metralla. Aún recuerdo el día en que nos condecoraron. Mi regimiento formó en el patio del cuartel, con uniforme de gala. Y mientras la banda interpretaba el himno nacional, el general que mandaba la división nos impuso esta medalla.

* * *

IV

Un cuarto de siglo después, el tiempo operó una profunda transformación en el aspecto físico de don Miguel. La Muerte había comenzado a cobrarle algunos anticipos y se llevó los pelos de su cabeza, todos los dientes de su boca y algunos kilos de su esqueleto. Eran los tres avisos anunciadores de que pronto volvería a llevarse el resto.

En espera de esa recogida final, el antiguo soldado se convirtió en «el abuelito». Parece mentira, pero siempre ocurre lo mismo: los hijos se hacen hombres y llenan la casa de nietos. Los abuelitos quedan en un rincón, mientras sus familiares esperan con más o menos impaciencia que dejen libre el lugar que ocupan.

El abuelito Miguel, jubilado de todas las actividades propias de su sexo, vegetaba en la casa que fue suya y que había pasado a ser de su hijo mayor . . . Y a sus numerosos nietos, cuando regresaban del colegio, solía contarles así la historia de su medalla:

—En la Historia se hablará algún día de aquella batalla memorable. Casi un mes tardó mi división en tomar aquella ciudad amurallada. El enemigo, bien armado y adiestrado por instructores extranjeros, se defendía casa por casa. Yo, al frente de la compañía que mandaba (me ascendieron por méritos de guerra), conseguí izar nuestra bandera en la torre más alta de la ciudad. Una ráfaga de ametralladora me perforó varias veces el estómago (de ahí me vienen las úlceras que padezco) . . . Aquella misma noche tres divisiones enemigas, con carros de combate y artillería pesada, iniciaron un movimiento envolvente y nos coparon. Combatimos sin interrupción durante varios días y algunas noches . . . Sin víveres, sin pólvora, sin botiquines, sin nada de nada, nos mantuvimos en nuestros puestos. La batalla era decisiva para el futuro de la guerra, pues aquella ciudad era un nudo de comunicaciones fundamental. A mi alrededor caían los soldados a centenares, y sus cuerpos nos servían de parapeto para seguir resistiendo. Recuerdo que de mi compañía sólo quedamos yo y un soldado . . . Las fuerzas que acudieron a liberarnos, al ver el espectáculo dantesco de nuestra resistencia, se echaron a llorar. Pero la patria nunca olvida a sus héroes. Y fuimos condecorados por el entonces Ministro de la Guerra . . .

* * *

Unos años más tarde el abuelo Miguel murió tranquilamente, como mueren todos los viejecitos que han vivido en paz. El

---

jubilado *retired*

solía tenía costumbre

adiestrado enseñado

izar subir
ráfaga *burst*

coparon encerraron

pólvora *gunpowder*
botiquines *first-aid kits*
nudo centro

a centenares *by the hundreds*

acudieron vinieron
dantesco infernal

rincón que ocupaba en la casa fue convertido en cuarto de jugar los niños . . .

*   *   *

chucherías cosas de poco valor

borrosas difíciles de leer

Un día, el más joven de los nietos del fallecido Miguel jugaba en la que fue su habitación con unas chucherías: viejas monedas, algunas cintas y los restos de un pequeño tren metálico. Entre las monedas había una de diámetro algo mayor, fundida en bronce, con unas alegorías ya borrosas en su anverso y reverso.

—¿De qué país es esta moneda, mamá? —preguntó el niño a su madre, mostrándole la medalla de bronce, que ya había perdido la cinta . . .

—¿Dónde la encontraste? —preguntó la madre, examinándola con poco interés.

—Tirada en un rincón.

—Parece una medalla —opinó la madre—, pero no debe de serlo porque no tiene ningún santo. Quizá sea una moneda . . . que trajo alguien como recuerdo de algún viaje. De todas formas, puedes seguir jugando con ella, porque no creo que valga nada.

PARA APLICAR

Comprensión   I

Escoja la respuesta apropiada.

1   ¿Qué ha sido África durante la historia?
   a.   buen lugar para practicar los deportes
   b.   sitio de gran número de conflictos
   c.   un club de campo para los tenistas

2   ¿Por qué fue Miguel a ese sitio de conflictos?
   a.   para ser espectador de su partido favorito
   b.   para participar en un partido de tenis
   c.   para luchar en una guerra

3   Después de regresar de la guerra, ¿qué hizo Miguel?
   a.   Contestó a las preguntas modestamente.
   b.   Preguntó a sus padres si podía bañarse.
   c.   Siguió usando su uniforme militar.

4   ¿De qué trata la selección?
   a.   de cómo se hacen las medallas
   b.   de los cambios en la historia de la medalla
   c.   de las alegorías representadas en la medalla

5   Miguel relató a sus padres que
   a.   por estar fatigados durmieron profundamente.
   b.   se quedaron despiertos en espera de un ataque por el enemigo.
   c.   estaban listos para salir cuando llegó la orden de retirarse.

6   Le dieron la medalla porque
   a.   el capitán estaba orgulloso de él.
   b.   su pelotón libertó a la patrulla.
   c.   el capitán no tuvo más remedio que condecorarlo por haber defendido un punto estratégico.

Comprensión   II

Escoja la respuesta apropiada.

1   ¿Qué hizo Miguel al cumplir los veintisiete?
   a.   Se casó y estableció un hogar.
   b.   Llevó a su novia a un baile formal.
   c.   Se quebró el brazo.
2   ¿Qué hizo Miguel una tarde en el paseo?
   a.   Se unció al yugo matrimonial.
   b.   Relató a su novia cómo había ganado la medalla.
   c.   Preparó un paseo.
3   ¿Cómo ha cambiado el relato?
   a.   Es casi igual al relato contado a sus padres.
   b.   Miguel no cambió nada.
   c.   El comandante del batallón les presentó las medallas a los que no murieron.
4   Cuando tenía más de treinta años y se hizo socio de un club, ¿cómo exageró el cuento a los otros socios?
   a.   El relato no había cambiado.
   b.   Los soldados de su pelotón durmieron toda la noche.
   c.   Dijo que durante la noche el enemigo recibió refuerzos para comenzar un contraataque.
5   ¿Por qué no les enseñó la cicatriz que llevaba en el muslo?
   a.   Tendría que quitarse los pantalones.
   b.   No tenía tal cicatriz.
   c.   Era el coronel quien tenía una cicatriz.

Comprensión   III

Conteste a las siguientes preguntas.

1   ¿Cuánto pesaba Miguel a los cuarenta y seis años?
2   ¿Cuándo no salía de casa?
3   ¿Cómo se vestía de noche durante la época de frío?
4   ¿Cómo relató la historia de la medalla?
5   ¿Por qué no obedecieron la orden de retirarse?

6   ¿Qué les faltaba esa noche?
7   Después de agotar el último cartucho, ¿con qué pelearon?
8   ¿Qué causó ese circulito en el brazo que parecía una vacuna?
9   ¿Por qué llevaba muelas postizas?
10   ¿Cómo les describió a sus niños el día de la condecoración?

Comprensión   IV

¿Verdadero o falso?

1   Los tres avisos que anuncian que pronto vendrá la muerte son menos peso, menos pelo y menos dientes.
2   Los últimos años de los abuelos son alegres porque nadie quiere estar en su rincón.
3   El abuelito cultivaba vegetales en un rincón de la casa.
4   La casucha abandonada se transformó en una ciudad con murallas.
5   Los extranjeros izaron la bandera.
6   La lucha duró un día y una noche.
7   Los seis hombres de la versión original se habían transformado en cientos.
8   El nieto mayor encontró la medalla entre varias cosas de poco valor.
9   La madre reconoció el valor de la medalla.

Más Práctica

A   Reemplace las palabras en letra bastardilla con una de las palabras de la lista.

agotados, aprovechando, un balazo, hazañas, la muralla, el muslo, puñado, rechazaron, socios, socorro

1   Recibió *una bala* en *la pierna.*
2   Relató sus grandes *actos* a sus *compañeros.*
3   Pidieron *ayuda usando* sus últimas municiones.
4   Cruzaron *el cerco* con un *pequeño grupo* de hombres.
5   Aunque *terminados* sus recursos *no se rindieron* al enemigo.

Nuestro abuelito es un verdadero héroe.

B Dé una palabra o una expresión equivalente a cada una de las siguientes.

1 ropa larga y cómoda
2 alimentos
3 inmunización
4 marca permanente en la piel
5 zapatos cómodos
6 carabina
7 inclinar sobre algo
8 sacar

Ejercicios Creativos

1 ¿Le gustó este cuento? ¿Por qué? Cite por lo menos dos razones.
2 Prepare una lista de los incidentes del primer episodio que relata Miguel. Compare estos detalles con el último.
3 Haga una comparación entre el Miguel de *El Mensajero de San Martín* y el Miguel de *Una Medalla de bronce*.

ESTRUCTURA

El Imperfecto

Verbos Regulares

Estudien las formas del imperfecto de los verbos regulares.

mirar	comer	vivir
miraba	comía	vivía
mirabas	comías	vivías
miraba	comía	vivía
mirábamos	comíamos	vivíamos
mirabais	comíais	vivíais
miraban	comían	vivían

Verbos Irregulares

Los verbos *ser*, *ver* e *ir* son irregulares en el imperfecto. Estudien las siguientes formas.

ser	ver	ir
era	veía	iba
eras	veías	ibas
era	veía	iba
éramos	veíamos	íbamos
erais	veíais	ibais
eran	veían	iban

A Sustituyan según el modelo.

Sus padres siempre le daban algo.
los otros/
Los otros siempre le daban algo.

1 Sus padres siempre le daban algo.
yo/su hermana/su esposo y yo/tú/

2 El abogado se refería a la carta.
las abogadas/yo/varios oficiales y yo/tú/

3 En los conflictos los soldados eran valientes.
yo/la jefa/tú/los jóvenes y yo/

4 Iban por la cordillera de los Andes.
tú/Miguel y yo/los arrieros/yo/

5 Veíamos el paisaje impresionante.
yo/la joven/tú/las escritoras/

B Cambien las siguientes oraciones al imperfecto.

1 La joven quiere servir a su patria.
2 El general hace el viaje sin dificultades.
3 Creo que es agente del general San Martín.

4 Yo trato de ser valiente.
5 Los arrieros y yo vemos el paisaje hermoso.
6 Mis compañeros y yo insistimos en guardar el secreto.
7 ¿Tienes miedo de rechazar a los otros?
8 No vas a negar la acusación.

C Contesten a las siguientes preguntas dos veces según el modelo.

> *Cuando llovía, ¿jugaban Uds. en casa o iban al parque?*
> *Cuando llovía, jugábamos en casa.*
> *Cuando llovía, íbamos al parque.*

1 Cuando estabas en Toledo, ¿ibas al Alcázar o te quedabas en casa?
2 Cuando estabas en Toledo, ¿trabajabas mucho o descansabas mucho?

3 Cuando estabas en Toledo, ¿comías en el hotel o preferías comer en los restaurantes?
4 Cuando llovía, ¿jugaban Uds. en casa o iban al parque?
5 Cuando llovía, ¿tenían Uds. que ayudar en casa o podían tener un día de descanso?
6 Cuando llovía, ¿tenían Uds. largas conversaciones por teléfono o pasaban el día sin hacer nada?
7 Mientras hablaba de la medalla, ¿querían Uds. escucharlo o deseaban irse?
8 Mientras hablaba de la medalla, ¿escuchaban Uds. atentamente o salían del cuarto?
9 Mientras hablaba de la medalla, ¿mostraban Uds. interés o no le prestaban atención?

Usos del Imperfecto y del Pretérito

Una Acción No Terminada

Se usa el imperfecto para expresar acciones en progreso en el pasado. En estas oraciones no importa cuándo empieza ni cuándo termina la acción. Lo importante es la acción misma.

> Abría la carta lentamente.
> Durante aquellos días, nos quedábamos callados.

D Sigan el modelo.

> *Estaban comiendo entonces.*
> *Comían entonces.*

1 Yo estaba regresando a casa.
2 La propietaria estaba hablando tranquilamente.

3 Ellos estaban guardando silencio.
4 Estábamos insistiendo en la verdad.
5 Estaba aburriendo a los demás.
6 Los españoles estaban peleando en África.
7 Los indios estaban viviendo en aquella región.

Una Acción Repetida

Se usa el imperfecto para expresar una acción repetida o habitual en el pasado.

> Todas las mañanas me levantaba a las seis.

E Cambien las siguientes oraciones al imperfecto.

1 Muchas veces relata la historia de la medalla.
2 Cada día repite cómo ganó la medalla.
3 Cada vez exagera más sus hazañas.
4 En el invierno hace frío en el valle.
5 El general siempre insiste en la fidelidad.
6 La doctora pasa por aquí con frecuencia.

La Descripción

Se usa el imperfecto para expresar descripciones en el pasado.

> Estaba alegre.
> Hacía un día magnífico.

F Cambien las siguientes oraciones al imperfecto.

1 La casa está en un valle hermoso.
2 Desde allí se ven el río y el campo de maíz.
3 La muchacha tiene dieciséis años.
4 Es una noche triste.
5 Hace buen tiempo y brilla el sol.
6 El padre habla tranquilamente por teléfono.
7 Son las seis en punto.
8 Es la una y quince.
9 Teresa tiene muelas postizas.
10 La cicatriz es larga y fea.

Estado Mental o Emocional

Con ciertos verbos como *tener, creer, querer, pensar, dudar* y *saber*, que expresan un estado mental o emocional, se usa el imperfecto en el pasado.

> El soldado tenía miedo de perder la carta.
> La señora López quería decir la verdad.

G Cambien las siguientes oraciones al imperfecto.

1 La hermana de Susana quiere salir.
2 El patriota quiere protegerlo.
3 Creen todo el relato.
4 Ellas piensan en su obligación.
5 El capitán sabe lo que realmente pasó.
6 La estudiante tiene sólo dieciséis años.
7 El coronel está seguro de haberlo conocido.
8 La señora piensa que la medalla no vale nada.

Una Acción Empezada o Terminada en el Pasado

Se usa el pretérito para expresar una acción empezada o terminada en el pasado.

> Comenzó a hablar de su valentía.
> Los soldados capturaron al mensajero.
> Ayer murió la abuela.

H Cambien las siguientes oraciones al pretérito.

1 Mariana se levanta sorprendida.
2 El mensajero espolea su caballo.
3 Las enfermeras sirven bien a su pueblo.
4 El coronel se dirige al teléfono.
5 Marisol no ofrece ayudar a la niña.
6 El Alcázar no se rinde.
7 Oye la voz de la profesora.
8 Saca unas monedas de oro.
9 Se quedan en las sombras.
10 Salen de la casa oscura.

I Sustituyan según los modelos.

> *Fusilan a los enemigos.*
> *ayer/*
> *Ayer fusilaron a los enemigos.*
>
> *siempre/*
> *Siempre fusilaban a los enemigos.*

1 Me preocupo por él.
   con frecuencia/anoche/
2 Se despiden con mucha emoción.
   el sábado pasado/siempre/
3 Vienen al casino a tomar café.
   la semana pasada/todos los días/
4 Van a la plaza a pasear.
   una vez/todas las tardes/

Los Sufijos

Diminutivos

Se puede variar el significado de muchas palabras agregando un sufijo al final o a la raíz de la palabra. Entre los sufijos más comunes son los diminutivos y los aumentativos. Los sufijos diminutivos expresan la idea de disminuir el tamaño de una persona, un objeto o una calidad. A veces se usan para expresar cariño.

Los sufijos diminutivos más comunes son -*ito(a)(s)*, -*cito(a)(s)*, -*ecito(a)(s)*. Se oyen también -*cillo(a)(s)*, -*ecillo(a)(s)* e -*ico(a)(s)*.

Miguelito   (Miguel)
mesita   (mesa)
poquito   (poco)
afuerita   (afuera)

Algunas reglas generales pueden ayudar con la formación.

1   A las palabras que terminan en *r* o en *n* se agregan -*cito(a)(s)*. También se agregan -*cito(a)(s)* a las palabras de dos sílabas que terminan en e.

doctorcito   (doctor)
limoncito   (limón)
madrecita   (madre)

2   Si el énfasis no cae en la última sílaba de una palabra que termina en vocal, se agrega -*ito(a)(s)* directamente a la raíz.

mesita   (mesa)
copitas   (copas)
gatito   (gato)
solita   (sola)

3   A las palabras que terminan en *l* o en *j* se agregan el sufijo -*ito(a)(s)* directamente a la palabra entera.

papelito   (papel)
relojito   (reloj)
Miguelito   (Miguel)

4   Las palabras de una sola sílaba usan el sufijo -*ecito(a)(s)*.

florecita   (flor)
panecito   (pan)

J Usen las siguientes palabras en una oración original.

1 casita
2 abuelita
3 hombrecito
4 cafecito
5 bajita
6 pobrecito

Aumentativos

Para hacer parecer más grande o más impresionante una persona o una cosa, se agregan los sufijos aumentativos *-ón (-ona)*. Los sustantivos femeninos suelen usar la terminación masculina.

sillón	(silla)
cucharón	(cuchara)
zapatones	(zapatos)
hombrón	(hombre)

Se oyen también las terminaciones *-azo(a)(s), -ote(s), (-ota)(s)* como sufijos aumentativos.

perrazo	(perro)
librote	(libro)
palabrota	(palabra)

K Usen las siguientes palabras en una oración original.

1 borrachón
2 gigantón
3 callejón
4 hombrazo
5 mangotes
6 feote

El Indio

Agua que no has de beber, déjala correr.

PARA PREPARAR LA ESCENA

Es difícil definir al indio. Es un enigma y es casi imposible clasificarlo. ¿Pobre? ¿Sufrido? ¿Humilde? ¿Melancólico? ¿Rico? ¿Afortunado? ¿Orgulloso? ¿Feliz?

Hoy día el indio puede ser una persona que vive como vivían sus antecesores, o alguien que ha logrado éxito en la sociedad moderna. Quizás es descendiente de una civilización bien desarrollada; quizás la sangre de muchas razas corre en sus venas.

Sin hacer caso de su herencia, hay una atracción misteriosa al considerar su historia, una historia tan antigua que mucha de ella se saca de la tierra misma.

El Indio del Mayab

Antonio Médiz Bolio

PARA PRESENTAR LA LECTURA

Se ha dicho que la tierra del Mayab es santa, que es poderosa, que es iluminada por una luz misteriosa, que es solitaria y silenciosa. Pero el que camina por esa tierra se llena de cierto espíritu que le da esperanza porque va acompañado del recuerdo de sus antepasados. Oye el leve canto de una brisa por las ramas de los árboles que le da serenidad y le quita por el momento las preocupaciones de la vida.

La selección que sigue nos presenta al indio que pasa por un camino del Mayab, callado, misterioso, solitario, melancólico — como la tierra misma.

PARA APRENDER VOCABULARIO

Palabras Clave   I

1 **amanecer**   la hora en que empieza la mañana
   Al amanecer los niños saldrán para el campo.

2 **ciervo**   animal de cuernos grandes y ramosos (*deer*)
   El ciervo sintió el peligro y vaciló un instante.

3 **doradas**   del color del oro
   Las playas doradas por el sol siempre son una atracción turística.

4 **grabado (grabar)**   trazado en metal, en cinta magnética o en la memoria (*engraved, recorded*)
   El poema fue grabado en cinta por el autor.

5 **grutas**   cavidades abiertas en la tierra, cuevas, cavernas
   La exploración de las grutas es un pasatiempo muy agradable para muchos.

Práctica

Complete con una palabra de la lista.

grutas   *amanecer*   *doradas*
ciervo   *grabado*

1 Por la tarde las nubes parecían _____ por el sol.
2 El gallo cantó antes del _____.
3 Su nombre fue _____ en la medalla.
4 Le interesa explorar lo desconocido de las _____.
5 El _____ es un animal hermoso y tímido.

Palabras Clave   II

1 **adivinar**   descubrir lo desconocido *(to guess)*
No puedo adivinar. Dime quién es.

2 **alumbra (alumbrar)**   da luz o claridad
De noche parece que una luz divina alumbra la ciudad.

3 **arda (arder)**   queme, lo que hace un fuego o calor intenso
¡Cuidado! No quiero que por la luz te ardan los ojos.

4 **averiguar**   descubrir la verdad, asegu-
rarse de la verdad
Quiero averiguar el misterio sin la ayuda
de nadie.

5 **chispa**   partícula encendida que salta
del fuego   (spark)
Una chispa del cigarrillo me quemó la
mano.

6 **encendió (encender – ie)**   iluminó   (lit,
turned on)
¿Quién encendió tantas luces aquí?

7 **fijos**   firmes, seguros, que no se mueven
No trates de mover los bancos. Están fijos
en su lugar.

Práctica

Complete con una palabra de la lista.

fijos	*averiguar*	*alumbra*
ardiendo	*encendió*	*adivinar*
chispa		

1 No trates de regatear en esta tienda porque
aquí los precios son _____.
2 Veo una luz. Algo _____ el camino.
3 Saltó una _____ de la chimenea.
4 Vamos a la estación. Tengo que _____
el horario.
5 Tú eres listo en estos juegos y siempre
puedes _____ la respuesta.
6´ Aquella casa está _____ desde hace una
hora. Está completamente quemada.
7 El presidente _____ las luces del árbol
de Navidad.

El Indio del Mayab

Antonio Médiz Bolio

I

Sin que nadie se las haya dicho, el indio sabe muchas cosas.

El indio lee con sus ojos tristes lo que escriben las estrellas que pasan volando, lo que está escondido en el agua muerta del fondo de las grutas, lo que está grabado sobre el polvo húmedo de la sabana en el dibujo de la pezuña del ciervo fugitivo.

El oído del indio escucha lo que dicen los pájaros sabios cuando se apaga el sol, y oye hablar a los árboles en el silencio de la noche, y a las piedras doradas por la luz del amanecer.

Nadie le ha enseñado a ver ni a oir ni a entender estas cosas misteriosas y grandes, pero él sabe. Sabe, y no dice nada.

El indio habla solamente con las sombras.

Cuando el indio duerme su fatiga, está hablando con aquéllos que le escuchan y está escuchando a aquéllos que le hablan.

Cuando despierta, sabe más que antes y calla más que antes.

sabana *savanna*
pezuña pata dura de un animal

II

De día, el indio camina con los ojos fijos en la tierra y deja que el sol arda sobre su cabeza y tueste su espalda desnuda.

De noche, el indio levanta la frente y mira las estrellas, que caen dentro de sus ojos, y, entonces, lo que hay en lo más profundo de su pecho se llena todo de luz.

Si tú puedes alguna vez mirar largamente al fondo de sus ojos, verás cómo allí hay escondida una chispa que es como un precioso lucero y que arde hacia adentro de la sombra. Esa luz le alumbra y le enseña los caminos. Pero nadie, ni él mismo, sabe quién la encendió.

tueste haga más oscura
desnuda sin ropa

lucero estrella

Envuelto en su triste oscuridad va por todas partes, y ve. Ve lo que todo el mundo puede ver, y algo más. No se lo preguntes, porque no ha de decírtelo.

El viento de las tardes y la brisa de la alta noche hablan con el corazón del indio, como si fueran ecos de voces que sólo él comprende en el silencio.

Cuando el indio se inclina sobre la tierra, oye una voz dulcísima, como la música de la canción de una madre que adormece a su hijo. Y si pudieras verlo entonces, le verías sonreir como un niño pequeño.

Y mientras pone las semillas en el agujero, su mano acaricia la tierra y sus miradas se llenan de ternura. Luego, el indio se marcha y se tiende a descansar sobre la tierra, que es para él como un regazo de mujer querida.

El amor que hay en las noches del indio que duerme abrazado a la tierra, envuelto en el aire y cubierto por las estrellas del cielo, es lo que él sólo sabe y lo que a nadie dice.

Y así de muchas cosas que son solamente para él. Si no tuviera estas cosas, ¿qué tendría?

Piensa de esto lo que quieras, pero si algo de él mismo necesitas averiguar, procura adivinarlo y no se lo preguntes.

adormece hace dormir *(lulls)*

agujero hoyo, abertura

regazo lap

procura trata de

PARA APLICAR

Comprensión   I

A   Conteste a las siguientes preguntas.

1   ¿Cómo son los ojos del indio?
2   Cite los misterios que él sabe interpretar. Explique lo que ellos significan.
3   ¿Cuáles misterios oye? ¿Qué quieren decir?
4   ¿Quién le enseñó esas cosas?
5   ¿Con quiénes habla mientras duerme?
6   ¿Qué beneficio recibe de ellos?

B   Escoja la respuesta apropiada.

1   El indio es
   a.   sabio.
   b.   ignorante.
   c.   indiferente.

2   El indio comprende los misterios de la naturaleza
   a.   con su pezuña.
   b.   con los ojos.
   c.   con la ayuda de alguien.
3   Al terminar el día el indio duerme
   a.   mal.
   b.   comunicándose con otros.
   c.   olvidándose de sus antepasados.

Comprensión   II

A   Conteste a las siguientes preguntas.

1   De día, ¿cómo camina el indio?
2   De noche, ¿cómo camina el indio?

3 ¿Qué hay escondido en los ojos del indio?
4 ¿Con qué habla el corazón del indio?
5 ¿Cómo duerme el indio?
6 ¿Qué tienes tú que hacer para enterarte de sus secretos?

B ¿Verdadero o falso?

1 Al caminar el indio lo observa todo alrededor de él.
2 Cuando mira las estrellas algo misterioso entra en lo más profundo de su ser.
3 Él ve cosas que lo ponen triste.
4 Todos pueden ver lo que él ve.
5 El indio está contento labrando la tierra.
6 Trata a la tierra como a una persona.
7 Si el indio no tuviera la naturaleza, estaría contento con sus otras posesiones.
8 Si no entiendes este cuento, el indio te lo explicará.

Más Práctica

Reemplace las palabras en letra bastardilla con una de las palabras de la lista.

averiguar, grabada, fijos, gruta, ciervo,
alumbran, arde, procura, dorado

1 El *animal* se acercó con precaución al lago.
2 Vieron formaciones raras y misteriosas en la *cueva*.

3 *Trata de* entender lo que te digo.
4 ¿Por qué tienes los ojos *puestos* en aquella planta?
5 Me *quema* el sol.
6 ¡Tengo su expresión *trazada* en mi memoria!
7 Las linternas *iluminan* el patio.
8 Esa chica de pelo *de oro* es mi prima.
9 Debemos *determinar* si él nos esconde los detalles importantes.

Ejercicios Creativos

1 Con el libro cerrado, escriba una descripción del indio parecida a lo que dice Antonio Médiz Bolio. Incluya lo siguiente:
   a. sus ojos
   b. sus oídos
   c. con quién habla
   d. su amor por la tierra
2 Antonio Médiz Bolio se refiere indirectamente a ciertas injusticias y malos entendidos que ha sufrido el indio. Identifique algunos de éstos.
3 Después de haber leído esta descripción del indio, ¿puede pensar en otros grupos en términos poéticos? Describa en un párrafo a otro grupo.

La Yaqui hermosa

Amado Nervo

PARA PRESENTAR LA LECTURA

En el estado de Sonora, México, viven los indios yaquis. Después de ser conquistados por los españoles, muchos de ellos fueron explotados. Los colonos criollos los usaban en las faenas agrícolas. Algunos de los indios se adaptaron fácilmente a su nueva vida; algunos resistieron hasta la muerte.

El cuento que sigue nos indica la reacción de «la yaqui hermosa». Fue escrito por el mexicano Amado Nervo (1870–1919).

Los yaquis son belicosos y orgullosos. Siempre se han dedicado a la guerra. Los conquistadores españoles también eran belicosos y orgullosos. Imagínese el choque de culturas cuando estos dos grupos, uno vencedor, el otro vencido, trataron de vivir juntos, adaptándose a una vida nueva.

En este cuento la yaqui hermosa representa el espíritu indomable de la raza.

PARA APRENDER VOCABULARIO

Palabras Clave   I

1 **colonos**   habitantes de una colonia
Los colonos no son nativos del país.

2 **coraje**   irritación, ira
Me dio coraje saber de estas injusticias.

3 **faenas**   trabajos, labores
Es una faena difícil.

4 **fierezas**   ferocidades, salvajismos, bestialidades
La fiereza de los animales es el producto de la región donde habitan.

5 **huérfanas**   muchachas que han perdido a sus padres
Una familia bondadosa crió a las huérfanas.

6 **ni siquiera** (conjunción negativa) (*not even*)

Juana quiere jugar al béisbol, pero ni siquiera tiene una pelota.

7 **repartidos (repartir)** divididos entre varias personas

Los dulces fueron repartidos entre todos los niños.

8 **riberas** márgenes de un río, bordes, orillas

Acostada en la ribera del río, la niñita, fascinada, se miraba en el agua.

9 **suavidad** cualidad de suave, blando, tierno

Me gustó sentir la suavidad de sus manos.

Práctica

Complete con una palabra de la lista.

fiereza	ribera	huérfanas
coraje	faenas	suavidad
colonos	repartidos	ni siquiera

1 Después de la tragedia las niñas quedaron _____.

2 Don Luciano descansó en la _____ del Río Bravo.

3 Las _____ del rancho mantenían ocupada a la dueña.

4 Lo que le gustaba a Jorge era la _____ de esa lana.

5 Los _____ se establecieron hace siglos en el Nuevo Mundo.

6 No pudo dominar el _____; le volvía loco.

7 Esa niña no tiene _____ siete años y ya está leyendo el diario.

8 Los premios fueron _____ entre los ganadores.

9 La gente de la ciudad no sabe nada de la _____ de la gente de la selva.

Palabras Clave II

1 **barro** masa que forma la tierra con agua (*clay, mud*)

Había mucho barro en el camino después de la lluvia.

2 **caza** la búsqueda y matanza de animales que sirven de comida; los animales mismos

En aquellas montañas la caza es abundante.

3 **enternecido (enternecer)** movido por la compasión (*moved to compassion*)

La abogada se sintió enternecida al ver a las pobres prisioneras.

4 **esbelta** bien formada, delgada

Aunque pasaron largos años, doña Luz se mantuvo esbelta.

5 **madrugó (madrugar)** se levantó temprano

El día de su santo, la chica madrugó con entusiasmo, pero se quedó dormida durante su fiesta por la tarde.

6 **quejas** lamentos, protestas, clamores

En esa escuela hay alumnos contentos que nunca tienen una queja.

7 **tamaño** dimensión

Ya que Roberto ha aumentado de peso, tiene que comprarse ropa de mayor tamaño.

Práctica

Complete con una palabra de la lista.

enternecido	barro	quejas
caza	esbelto	madrugó
tamaño		

1 El hombre, _____, ayudó al niño perdido.

2 La olla está hecha de _____.

3 El dueño tenía que escuchar todas las _____ de sus clientes que no estaban contentos.

4 La señora López tiene una casa del _____ de un hotel.

5 La india _____ el lunes para el viaje largo a su hogar.

6 José se siente mejor cuando no pesa tanto. Prefiere estar _____.

7 Con los perros, uno puede ir a la _____ .

La Yaqui hermosa

Amado Nervo

I

yaquis *a Native American people named after the Yaqui River in the state of Sonora in northern Mexico* **comarca** región

Los indios yaquis . . . casta de los más viriles entre los aborígenes de México . . . habitan una comarca fértil y rica del estado de Sonora; hablan un raro idioma que se llama el «cahita»; son altos, muchas veces bellos, como estatuas de bronce, duros para el trabajo, buenos agricultores, cazadores máximos . . . y, sobre todo, combatientes indomables siempre.

Su historia desde los tiempos más remotos puede condensarse en esta palabra: guerra.

Jamás han estado en paz con nadie. Acaso en el idioma cahita ni existe siquiera la palabra «paz».

No se recuerda época alguna en que los yaquis no hayan peleado.

Benvenuto Cellini *an Italian Renaissance goldsmith, sculptor, and author, who was famous for his quarrels* **la espuma en la boca** *like the foam at the mouth of a mad dog*

De ellos puede decirse lo que de Benvenuto Cellini se dijo: «que nacieron con la espuma en la boca», la espuma de la ira y del coraje.

La historia nos cuenta que Nuño de Guzmán fue el conquistador que penetró antes que nadie en Sinaloa y Sonora, y llevó sus armas hasta las riberas del Yaqui y del Mayo. El primer combate que los yaquis tuvieron con los españoles fue el cinco de octubre de 1535. Comandaba a los españoles Diego Guzmán, y fueron atacados por los indios, que esta vez resultaron vencidos, pero tras un combate muy duro. Los españoles afirmaron después que nunca habían encontrado indios más bravos.

para dominar . . . medidas radicales *in order to tame their fierce, almost epic tenacity, had to resort to extreme measures* **descepar** *to uproot*

Recientemente el gobierno federal inició nueva acción contra las indomables tribus, y para dominar su tenacidad bravía, casi épica, hubo de recurrir a medidas radicales: descepar familias enteras de la tierra en que nacieron, y enviarlas al otro extremo de la república, a Yucatán y a Campeche especialmente. Lo que

terruño tierra natal
entereza *integrity*

criollos hijos de españoles,
nacidos en América
dada la falta . . . se adolece
*owing to the shortage of
help they suffered from*
terrateniente dueño de
tierra

acurrucadas *huddled up*

hoscas *dark-colored,
gloomy*

ese fiel y conmovedor culto
del indígena *that faithful
and moving respect that the
Indian has*

el yaqui ama más es su terruño. La entereza de raza se vio, pues, sometida a durísima prueba.

En Campeche los desterrados fueron repartidos entre colonos criollos, que se los disputaban ávidamente, dada la falta de brazos de que se adolece en aquellas regiones para las faenas agrícolas.

Un rico terrateniente amigo mío recibió más de cien indios de ambos sexos.

Separó de entre ellos cuatro niñas huérfanas y se las envió a su esposa, quien hubo de domesticar a fuerza de suavidad sus fierezas. Al principio las yaquitas se pasaban las horas acurrucadas en los rincones. Una quería tirarse a la calle desde el balcón. Negábanse a aprender el castellano, y sostenían interminables y misteriosos diálogos en su intraducible idioma, o callaban horas enteras, inmóviles como las hoscas piedras de su tierra.

Ahora se dejarían matar las cuatro por su ama, a la que adoran con ese fiel y conmovedor culto del indígena por quien lo trata bien.

Entre los ciento y tantos yaquis, sólo una vieja hablaba bien el castellano. Era la intérprete.

II

Cuando mi amigo les recibió, hízolos formar en su hacienda, y dirigióse a la intérprete en estos términos:

—Diles que aquí el que trabaje ganará lo que quiera. Diles también que no les tengo miedo. Que en otras haciendas les prohiben las armas; pero yo les daré carabinas y fusiles a todos . . . porque no les tengo miedo. Que la caza que maten es para ellos. Que si no trabajan, nunca verán un solo peso. Que el Yaqui está muy lejos, muy lejos, y no hay que pensar por ahora en volver . . . Que por último, daré a cada uno la tierra que quiera: la que pueda recorrer durante un día.

—¿De veras me darás a mí toda la tierra que pise en un día?—preguntó adelantándose un indio alto, cenceño, nervioso, por medio de la intérprete.

—¡Toda la que pises!—le respondió mi amigo.

Y al día siguiente, en efecto, el indio madrugó, y cuando se apagaba el lucero, ya había recorrido tres kilómetros en línea recta, y en la noche ya había señalado con piedras varios kilómetros cuadrados.

cenceño delgado, esbelto

cuando se apagaba el
lucero *by the time the
morning star was gone*

—¡Todo esto es tuyo!—le dijo sencillamente el propietario, que posee tierras del tamaño de un pequeño reino europeo.

El indio se quedó estupefacto de delicia.

Diariamente iba mi amigo a ver a la indiada, y la intérprete le formulaba las quejas o las aspiraciones de los yaquis.

Un día, mi amigo se fijó en una india, grande, esbelta, que tenía la cara llena de barro.

—¿Por qué va esa mujer tan sucia?—preguntó a la intérprete.

Respondió la intérprete:

—Porque es bonita; dejó al novio en su tierra y no quiere que la vean los «extranjeros».

La india, entretanto, inmóvil, bajaba obstinadamente los ojos.

—¡A ver!—dijo mi amigo—que le laven la cara a ésta. ¡Traigan agua!

Y la trajeron y la intérprete le lavó la cara.

Y, en efecto, era linda como una salambó.

salambó *a character of exceptional beauty in a novel*
tuna *prickly pear or Indian fig*
relumbrosos *brillantes*
que no acababan nunca *which never ended (she had very big, dark eyes)*
lóbregas *murky*

Su boca breve, colorada como la tuna; sus mejillas mate, de una carnación deliciosa; su nariz sensual, semiabierta; y, sobre todo aquello, sus ojos relumbrosos y tristes, que no acababan nunca, negros como dos noches lóbregas.

El colono la vio, y enternecido le dijo:

—Aquí todo el mundo te tratará bien, y si te portas como debes, volverás pronto a tu tierra y verás a tu novio.

tenazmente *determinadamente*
enclavijaba sus manos sobre el seno *clasped her hands over her bosom*

La india, inmóvil, seguía tenazmente mirando al suelo, y enclavijaba sus manos sobre el seno.

Mi amigo dio instrucciones para que la trataran mejor que a nadie. Después partió para México.

*   *   *

Volvió a su hacienda de Campeche al cabo de mes y medio.

—¿Y la yaqui hermosa?—preguntó al administrador.

—¡Murió!—respondió éste.

Y luego, rectificando:

encogida *shrunk, curled up*
Le recetó quinina *he prescribed quinine for her*
quincena pasada *last half month*
peñas *rocas grandes*
amapolas *poppies*

—Es decir, se dejó morir de hambre. No hubo manera de hacerla comer. Se pasaba los días encogida en un rincón, como un ídolo. No hablaba jamás. El médico vino. Dijo que tenía fiebre. Le recetó quinina. No hubo forma de dársela. Murió en la quincena pasada. La enterramos allí.

Y señalaba un sitio entre unas peñas, con una cruz en rededor de la cual crecían ya las amapolas.

PARA APLICAR

Comprensión   I

A   Conteste a las siguientes preguntas.

1   ¿Dónde habitan los yaquis?
2   ¿Qué idioma hablan los yaquis?
3   Describa a los yaquis.
4   ¿En qué palabra puede condensarse la historia de los yaquis?
5   ¿Quién fue el primer conquistador que penetró la tierra de los yaquis?
6   ¿Hasta dónde penetró él?
7   ¿Cuándo fue el primer combate que tuvieron los yaquis con los españoles?
8   ¿Qué hizo el gobierno federal contra los yaquis?
9   ¿Adónde mandaron a los pobres yaquis?
10   ¿Fue fácil para el yaqui este cambio?
11   ¿Qué hizo el gobierno con los yaquis en Campeche?
12   ¿A cuántos indios recibió el rico terrateniente?
13   ¿Qué hizo él con cuatro niñas huérfanas?
14   ¿Qué hacían las yaquitas al principio?
15   ¿Cuántos de los yaquis hablaban bien el castellano?
16   ¿Quién servía de intérprete?

B   Termine las oraciones según la selección.

1   Los yaquis son
2   Viven en
3   Hablan
4   En la guerra son
5   En su idioma no existe la palabra
6   Los yaquis fueron conquistados por
7   Para dominarlos el gobierno tuvo que
8   Los mandó a
9   En Campeche los indios fueron
10   Un rico terrateniente recibió
11   Envió a cuatro niñas a
12   Al principio ellas se pasaban las horas
13   Una quería tirarse

14   Sostenían diálogos
15   Una vieja

Comprensión   II

A   Conteste a las siguientes preguntas.

1   Relate las cosas que les prometió el terrateniente por medio de la intérprete.
2   ¿Qué le preguntó al rico el indio alto?
3   ¿Qué le respondió el terrateniente?
4   ¿Qué hizo el indio al día siguiente?
5   ¿Cumplió su promesa el propietario?
6   ¿Cada cuándo iba el propietario a ver a la indiada?
7   ¿En quién se fijó un día?
8   ¿Por qué andaba sucia la india?
9   ¿Qué ordenó el propietario?
10   Describa a la yaqui hermosa.
11   ¿Qué instrucciones dejó el terrateniente al salir para México?
12   ¿Por quién preguntó al regresar a la hacienda?
13   ¿Cómo murió la yaqui hermosa?
14   Describa el lugar donde la enterraron.

B   ¿Verdadero o falso?

1   El terrateniente les habló directamente a los indios.
2   Él tiene miedo de los indios.
3   Él les permite tener armas.
4   Cuando los indios matan un animal tienen que entregárselo al dueño.
5   Un indio no puede creer que el dueño sea tan generoso.
6   El terrateniente se fijó en una india hermosa y limpia.
7   Ella no quería que los blancos la vieran.
8   El dueño le tuvo compasión y la envió a ver a su novio.
9   Después que el terrateniente se fue, la trataron mal.
10   La yaqui hermosa se murió de hambre.

Más Práctica

A Dé un sinónimo de las palabras en letra bastardilla.

1 *Viven en* una comarca fértil.
2 Fue una *pelea* dura.
3 Era una raza *conquistada*.
4 El yaqui ama a su *tierra*.
5 Era la *traductora*.
6 La india era *esbelta*.
7 Se quedó *quieto*.
8 *Las faenas* son difíciles.

B Complete las siguientes oraciones con una palabra apropiada.

1 Es una india fuerte y _____.
2 Él nunca se levanta tarde; siempre _____.
3 Los dos indios se sentaban a la _____ del río.
4 Van a la _____. ¿Con cuántos conejos van a volver?
5 La india joven tiene una forma _____.
6 No está limpio; está _____.
7 Los padres del _____ murieron hace dos años.
8 El jefe siempre tiene una _____. Nunca está satisfecho.
9 Tenemos que _____ esta comarca.
10 Es una _____ que cuesta mucho trabajo.

C ¿Verdadero o falso?

1 La faena es un animal de las montañas.
2 El huérfano es un chico sin padres.
3 Han peleado mucho durante la guerra.
4 Se sintió enternecida al ver al pobre huérfano.
5 Es tan débil que su fiereza le ha dado fama.
6 Con el barro se puede hacer ollas.
7 Los criollos nacieron en España.
8 Ella madrugó porque tenía cita a las ocho de la mañana.

9 Está sucio porque siempre se lava.
10 Como son tan fuertes son fácilmente vencidos.

D Dé una palabra equivalente a cada una de las siguientes.

1 el niño sin padres
2 el que tiene tierra
3 el que habita una colonia

Ejercicios Creativos

1 El *cuento corto* se divide básicamente en tres partes: la exposición, el desarrollo y el desenlace: (a) *La exposición* (o introducción) le presenta al lector la información necesaria para comprender lo que sigue. Generalmente hay información sobre algunos personajes, el tiempo, el lugar y los sucesos anteriores a la acción. (b) *El desarrollo* consiste en el desenvolvimiento progresivo de la acción hasta llegar al punto culminante. (c) *El desenlace* es sencillamente la solución, o cómo se resuelven los problemas y los conflictos. Ya que ha leído *La Yaqui hermosa*, trate de dividir el cuento en las tres partes fundamentales, indicando la línea en que empieza cada parte.

2 Haga un dibujo del mapa de México, colocando en él el estado de Sonora, Sinaloa, Campeche, Yucatán, el río Yaqui, el Mayo y la Ciudad de México.

3 Escriba un poema breve de cuatro u ocho líneas en que Ud. relata algo de un aspecto de la vida de la yaqui hermosa. Por ejemplo:

> Triste va la yaqui a Campeche,
> Dejando en Sonora a su amor.
> ¿Qué le espera en tierra nueva?
> ¿Vida alegre o vida de dolor?

Manuel

Pedro Villa Fernández

PARA PRESENTAR LA LECTURA

El joven Manuel vivía en un pueblecito indígena escondido entre las
montañas. Aunque le rodeaban la pobreza y la miseria, que
desgraciadamente caracterizan a tales pueblos andinos, Manuel
parecía diferente. Se destacaba entre los demás, no sólo por su
aspecto físico sino también por su inteligencia y sus ambiciones. Solía
llevar las cosas hechas a mano por los aldeanos a la ciudad para
venderlas y volver con el dinero al pueblo donde divertía a los otros,
contándoles detalles de la vida fuera del pueblecito. Sus viajes a la
ciudad duraban cada vez más tiempo hasta que un día cambiaron
las cosas para todos.

PARA APRENDER VOCABULARIO

Palabras Clave

1 **a menudo**   con frecuencia
   En esos años sus amigos iban a menudo
   al cine.

2 **cestas**   utensilios portátiles de mimbre o
   junco que sirven para llevar o guardar
   cualquier cosa *(baskets)*
   El señor Gómez es un gran colector de
   chucherías que guarda en una cesta de
   mimbre en el garaje.

3 **collares**   adornos que se llevan alrededor
   del cuello
   La señora Pérez le trajo a su hija un collar
   de coral de Acapulco.

4 **daba (dar) rienda suelta**   daba   libre
   curso *(freed, cut loose)*
   Al componer sus canciones la mujer daba
   rienda suelta a su talento artístico.

5 **follaje**   hojas de los árboles
   Los pájaros se esconden entre el follaje.

6 **paraguas**   aparato que sirve para proteger a una persona de la lluvia
   Pensando que iba a hacer buen tiempo,
   la doctora Madero dejó el paraguas en
   la oficina.

7 **pescaban (pescar)**   cogían peces con
   redes o cañas
   Tom Sawyer y Huck Finn pescaban en
   el gran río.

En un pueblo indio

8 **tela**   tejido de lana, seda, algodón, etc.
   Con esta tela voy a hacerme un vestido.

9 **tontería**   estupidez, acción o palabras tontas, cosa de poco valor
   Era tal su coraje que Anita dijo muchas tonterías.

Práctica

Complete con una palabra de la lista.

a menudo	*tontería*	*cestas*
pescaban	*daba rienda suelta*	*collares*
follaje	*tela*	*paraguas*

1 Recogieron la fruta y se la llevaron en _____ .

2 En la selva el _____ es abundante y siempre es verde.

3 ¿De qué te ríes? ¿Quién te contó esa _____ ?

4 A todos les encantan los _____ de oro.

5 Veo mucho a mi prima. Viene a mi casa _____ .

6 Al escribir cartas, la autora _____ a su pluma y escribía verdaderas obras de literatura.

7 _____ en alta mar a pesar del peligro.

8 Juan se compró una _____ de lana y la llevó al sastre.

9 No te olvides de llevar tu _____ . Dijeron que iba a llover.

Viaje al mercado

Manuel

Pedro Villa Fernández

Manuel era el indio más popular de un pequeño pueblo que se hallaba entre las montañas a unas cien millas al sur de Ciudad Bolívar. Allí vivía con un pequeño grupo de seres humanos inconscientes todos de su pobreza, rodeados de relativa libertad y abundancia de miseria, hablando una mezcla de español e indio, medio desnudos, con el pelo y las uñas largas, los pies grandes y duros como piedras, los labios secos, la inteligencia atrofiada y el instinto tan despierto como el de un animal de la selva.

Todos se parecían, física y psicológicamente, todos menos Manuel, quien tenía algo diferente. Había más luz en sus ojos y en su mente. Parecía menos indio que los demás. Su piel era más blanca. Era más alto. Hablaba español mucho mejor. Tenía una imaginación viva. Manuel tocaba una pequeña guitarra que siempre llevaba consigo, y cantaba canciones que los demás indios jamás habían oído. Había venido al pequeño pueblo cuando tenía unos catorce años. ¿De dónde? «De allá», era todo lo que les decía. Cuando le preguntaron dónde estaba ese «allá» les decía que muy lejos. ¿Quiénes eran sus padres? No lo sabía. Así fue que el chico vino a formar parte del pequeño grupo de indios que lo recibieron con gusto, pues traía una guitarrita y cantaba como un ángel. Además, en su cara se veía siempre una sonrisa muy simpática, y contaba muchas cosas interesantes de «allá» y sabía mucho de todo.

Aquellos indios cazaban, pescaban, plantaban algo. Hacían cestas, collares, bastones pintados, adornos con plumas de ave y objetos de madera. De vez en cuando bajaban a uno de los pueblos grandes y vendían lo que habían hecho. Con el dinero compraban cerillas, cuchillos, agujas, hilo—simples necesidades sin las cuales era difícil continuar la vida diaria. Algunas veces cuando les era posible compraban sal, y en muy raras ocasiones un poquito de azúcar o alguna tontería que les llamaba la atención y que no les servía para nada. En sus viviendas no había sillas,

uñas *fingernails*

atrofiada *degenerated from disuse*

cerillas *matches*
agujas *needles*
hilo *thread*

agujeros aberturas

ni mesas. No había cocina, ni puerta, ni ventana. Había una entrada y bastantes agujeros por donde entraba el aire, la luz y el agua. Dormían en el suelo. Cocinaban entre unas piedras y comían con las manos. Si se lavaban, que no era a menudo, lo hacían en el río. Creían en Dios, un Dios indio con ciudadanía católica, y los santos de esta religión estaban tan mezclados con las deidades indígenas que no había manera de separarlos. En la vida de la pequeña comunidad no había más que las pequeñas cosas de todos los días: nacían indios, morían indios; se enfermaban, o se ponían bien. En fin, que todo lo que allí pasaba tenía una base fisiológica o biológica. Después venía la cuestión del tiempo. Llovía o hacía sol. Había o no había luna. Esto era todo o casi todo lo que pasaba en su vida.

Pero Manuel trajo un nuevo interés al pequeño pueblo, y empezó a bajar a los otros pueblos para vender lo que hacían los otros indios. Obtenía más dinero que los demás, y volvía no sólo con más dinero, sino con historias muy interesantes de lo que pasaba durante su ausencia. Cuando llegaba se sentaban todos en un círculo; entonces él, en el centro, les contaba los detalles de su viaje. Daba rienda suelta a su imaginación y adornaba cada historia con todo lo que se le ocurría. Los indios le escuchaban con gran interés. Si la historia era triste, se ponían tristes; si era alegre, se alegraban; si era cómica, se reían; si era trágica, lloraban; y si era fantástica, se maravillaban. Cuando Manuel hablaba del gran calor de allá abajo, sentían calor. Si hablaba del fresco de la noche, sentían fresco. Luego que terminaba, uno de ellos le contaba a Manuel lo que había pasado en el pueblo durante su ausencia, porque los viajes del muchacho siempre duraban días, y como inspirado por las historias de Manuel, el narrador contaba también las cosas tristes y alegres, cómicas y trágicas, que habían pasado en el pueblo, y lo hacía lo más dramáticamente posible. Volvían todos a ponerse tristes o alegres; se reían o lloraban. Entonces Manuel entregaba el dinero, y hasta que se iba de nuevo se veía obligado a contar las mismas cosas una y otra vez, lo cual hacía con gusto, y con nuevas versiones de los mismos incidentes.

En busca de nuevas experiencias, Manuel empezó a hacer viajes más largos. Sus ausencias se fueron prolongando. Salía del pueblo muy de mañana con su carga y con su guitarra; jamás se iba sin su guitarra, y trotaba más bien que caminaba pueblo abajo. Los indios le veían alejarse tocando y cantando. Cuando

alejarse irse lejos

le perdían de vista podían oir aún entre el follaje su guitarra y su voz. Con él se iba la alegría, se iba la vida, y el pueblo se quedaba triste.

Cuando los viajes se fueron haciendo más largos los incidentes del viaje aumentaron. Cuanto más lejos iba más fantásticos eran sus cuentos. Ya empezaba a tardar semanas. En uno de sus viajes llegó hasta Ciudad Bolívar y no volvió hasta cuarenta días después, pero trajo cosas increíbles que contar, y nuevas canciones, y muchas cosas bonitas; cintas de colores, una corbata, botones verdes y rojos, un paraguas, un espejo y unos lentes azules. Había visto un barco y mujeres muy bonitas con labios rojos y trajes de seda, y Manuel les contó cosas admirables de todo. Les habló de una casa muy grande que se llamaba un cine donde mucha gente miraba unos fantasmas que caminaban y hasta hablaban en una «tela».

Después les entregó el dinero. Los indios se miraron asombrados. A pesar de que había comprado tantas cosas traía más dinero que nunca. Les dijo que la gente le daba dinero en los cafés, porque cantaba y tocaba la guitarra.

Del próximo viaje no volvió en tres meses. Traía más dinero y más cosas que en el viaje anterior, pero sus historias eran más cortas. Parecía que había dejado el alma allá muy lejos en aquella ciudad maravillosa de que les había hablado y donde había cines y cafés y mujeres bonitas de labios rojos y trajes de seda. Luego se fue otra vez, y el pueblo esperó meses, un año, triste y ansioso. Tenían muchas cosas que contarle. Habían muerto cuatro indios. Habían nacido seis. Había muchos enfermos de una enfermedad que no conocían. Pero Manuel jamás volvió. La civilización lo había reclamado; Ciudad Bolívar primero, Caracas después, y más tarde, ¿quién sabe?

lentes anteojos

«tela» Manuel doesn't know the word **pantalla** *(movie screen)*
asombrados *sorprendidos*

PARA APLICAR

Comprensión

A   Conteste a las siguientes preguntas.

1   ¿Cómo vivía la gente del pueblo?
2   ¿Se dieron cuenta de las condiciones desafortunadas en que vivían?
3   Describa su aspecto físico.
4   ¿Cómo se distinguía Manuel de los demás?
5   ¿Cómo divertía Manuel a la gente?
6   ¿Cómo se ganaban la vida aquellos indios?
7   Con el poco dinero que ganaban, ¿qué compraban los indios?
8   Describa sus casas.
9   ¿En qué se basaba todo lo que sucedía allí?
10   ¿Qué nuevo interés trajo Manuel al pueblo?
11   ¿Cómo reaccionaban a los relatos que les traía Manuel de la ciudad?

«Aquella ciudad me fascina—allá voy».

12 Cite los cambios en las costumbres de Manuel.
13 Cite los nuevos relatos fantásticos que trajo de Ciudad Bolívar.
14 ¿Qué cambios se notaban en él en su última visita?
15 ¿Por qué estaba triste el pueblo?

B Termine las oraciones según la selección.

1 Manuel era de
2 La gente de su pueblo ignoraba
3 Hablaban
4 Comparado con los otros, Manuel era
5 De vez en cuando bajaban
6 Cuando Manuel regresaba del pueblo
7 Al escuchar los relatos de Manuel los indios
8 Con los viajes más largos Manuel les trajo
9 Los indios se maravillaron de
10 Un día Manuel

Más Práctica

¿Verdadero o falso?

1 Los indios usaban collares en los pies.
2 Pescaban dinero en el Banco Central.
3 Manuel daba rienda suelta a su imaginación.
4 Trae follaje del mercado en una cesta encima de la cabeza.
5 Les relató una tela fantástica.
6 Sólo los tontos dicen tonterías.
7 No lo conozco. Nos visita a menudo.

Ejercicios Creativos

1 Esta selección sencilla toca algunos de los muchos problemas que han persistido en la convivencia del indio con la sociedad hispana moderna: el aislamiento, la inclinación a permanecer aparte con gente de su propia cultura, la falta de líderes con contacto exterior y, sobre todo, la pérdida de los más listos a las ciudades. ¿Qué cualidades de buen líder tenía Manuel? ¿Cómo les sirvió a los otros indios? ¿Cómo les faltó?

2 Se hallan en esta historia las razones por las cuales mucha gente de las regiones rurales ha ido a la ciudad. Trate de hacer una comparación entre la historia de Manuel y el movimiento hacia las ciudades en nuestra propia historia.

3 Compare el indio de *Manuel* con *El Indio del Mayab*.

4 ¿Cómo cree Ud. que la pérdida de Manuel realmente afectó al pueblo?

Indias de San Blas

Verbos Reflexivos

Los Pronombres Reflexivos

Si el sujeto y el complemento del verbo se refieren a la misma persona, el verbo es reflexivo. Es decir, el sujeto hace la acción a sí mismo. Los verbos reflexivos van acompañados de un pronombre reflexivo. Estudien las siguientes formas.

lavarse	**acostarse**
me lavo	me acuesto
te lavas	te acuestas
se lava	se acuesta
nos lavamos	nos acostamos
os laváis	os acostáis
se lavan	se acuestan

Se notará que el pronombre reflexivo precede al verbo.

Me lavo las manos.
Carlos se levanta temprano.

A Sustituyan según el modelo.

> Mariana se pone los zapatos.
> Felipe y Manuel/
> Felipe y Manuel se ponen los zapatos.

1 Carla se pone los zapatos.
   nosotros/tú/Teresa/yo/María y yo/Uds./
2 El indio se acostó en la tierra.
   ellos/tú/las huérfanas/mi amiga y yo/ Uds./Ud./yo/
3 Al amanecer él se marchó hacia la ciudad.
   la yaqui hermosa/yo/los colonos/Uds./ tú/nosotros/
4 Mañana ella se levanta temprano.
   yo/el coronel/tú/Marta/las indias/

B Contesten a las siguientes preguntas según el modelo.

> ¿Te sientes bien?
> Sí, me siento bien.

1 ¿Te levantas temprano?
2 ¿Te dedicas a los estudios?
3 ¿Te ríes de esas tonterías?
4 ¿Te diviertes en las fiestas?
5 ¿Te despiertas tarde los sábados?
6 ¿Te portas bien en la clase?
7 ¿Te adaptas fácilmente a nuevas situaciones?
8 ¿Te detienes para admirar el follaje?
9 ¿Te acuestas tarde?
10 ¿Te duermes en seguida?

C Contesten a las siguientes preguntas según el modelo.

> *¿Se sienten bien?*
> *No, no nos sentimos bien.*

1 ¿Se sienten tristes?
2 ¿Se ríen de los problemas?
3 ¿Se alegran de visitar a los amigos?
4 ¿Se van de aquí?
5 ¿Se callan en clase?
6 ¿Se enferman al comer demasiado?
7 ¿Se quedan mucho tiempo después de las clases?
8 ¿Se sientan en los mismos asientos?
9 ¿Se lavan antes de comer?
10 ¿Se acuestan después de cenar?

El Pronombre Reflexivo con Infinitivo

El pronombre reflexivo puede añadirse al infinitivo o puede preceder al verbo auxiliar.

> Me tengo que levantar. ↔ Tengo que levantarme.
> Él se va a enfadar. ↔ Él va a enfadarse.

D Sigan el modelo.

> *Me voy a levantar.*
> *Voy a levantarme.*

1 Me tengo que arreglar.
2 Nos queremos sentar aquí.
3 ¿Te puedes reconocer en esa fotografía?
4 Los novios se quieren casar.
5 No me voy a reir de tus preguntas.

E Sigan el modelo.

> *No se ríe de su compañero.* va a
> *No va a reirse de su compañero.*

1 No se levanta. *quiere*
2 No se fija en nada. *puede*
3 Se va de aquí. *quiere*
4 Se acuesta poco después de las once. *puede*
5 Se duerme en seguida. *puede*
6 No se aleja esta vez. *debe*
7 Se levanta después del trabajo. *va a*

F Sigan el modelo.

> *Me olvidé de lo triste.* tuve que
> *Tuve que olvidarme de lo triste.*

1 No me quedé con poco dinero. *quise*
2 Me puse a sus órdenes. *ofrecí*
3 Me acerqué a la ribera. *traté de*
4 Me preocupé de los indios. *fue natural*
5 No me acordé de las reglas. *pude*
6 Me adelanté con cuidado. *prometí*
7 Me acosté temprano. *fue importante*

La Voz Pasiva

Con *Se*

Se expresa la voz pasiva con el pronombre reflexivo *se* y la tercera persona del verbo. El verbo concuerda con el sujeto. La voz pasiva indica que el sujeto es indefinido o general. Esta construcción se usa con frecuencia.

Aquí se habla español.
Se venden corbatas aquí.
Se graban las cintas en el laboratorio.

G Sigan el modelo.

Nunca dicen eso.
Nunca se dice eso.

1 Arreglan el documento en esa oficina.
2 Venden revistas.
3 Resuelven el problema decisivamente.
4 Abren las puertas a las diez.
5 Celebran los días de fiesta.
6 No hablan inglés aquí.
7 Acaban el trabajo.
8 Echan las cartas al buzón.
9 Hacen todo aquí.
10 Averiguan el misterio sin la ayuda de nadie.

H Cambien las siguientes oraciones al plural.

1 Se consideró la posibilidad.
2 Se inicia la nueva acción.
3 Se apaga la luz aquí.
4 Se termina la faena.
5 Se compra la tela en esa tienda.
6 Se prepara la comida a la hora fija.

I Sigan el modelo.

Yo interrumpo la conversación.
Se interrumpe la conversación.

1 Hacemos una comida especial los domingos.
2 No pongo la fruta en aquella cesta.
3 Venden tacos deliciosos en este restaurante.
4 Ud. llega al centro por esta calle.
5 Doblo la carta antes de ponerla en el sobre.
6 Compramos el periódico todos los días.
7 Oyeron un ruido desagradable.
8 Cultivan maíz y frijoles en México.
9 Celebran las fiestas en diciembre.
10 Honran a los hombres valientes.

Con *Ser*

La voz pasiva, que se emplea con menos frecuencia que la voz activa, se forma con el verbo *ser* y el participio pasado. El participio concuerda en número y género con el sujeto.

El agente (el que ejecuta la acción) generalmente se introduce con la preposición *por*. Si el verbo indica sentimiento o emoción se emplea la preposición *de*.

> El poema fue escrito por Luis Llorens Torres.
> La doctora Ramos es amada de todos.

J Sustituyan según el modelo.

> *La tierra fue repartida por los colonos.*
> *el país/*
> *El país fue repartido por los colonos.*

1 El territorio fue repartido por los colonos.
la comarca/las regiones/la provincia/las sabanas/los trabajos/las faenas/el terruño/

2 La maestra es admirada de sus alumnos.
amada/respetada/venerada/envidiada/odiada/temida/

K Sigan los modelos.

> *Raúl llevó la bolsa al pueblo.*
> *La bolsa fue llevada al pueblo por Raúl.*

1 La autora grabó en cinta su poema.
2 Los indios hacían cestas.
3 Todo el pueblo admiraba a Manuel.
4 El hombre mató el ciervo en el monte.
5 La india vendía un collar de oro.

6 La señora Santos me recibió cordialmente.
7 En raras ocasiones los indios compraban azúcar.
8 La mujer contó los detalles de su viaje.
9 Todos respetaban al guitarrista.
10 El sastre hizo el vestido con tela bonita.

> *Sara ha escrito las cartas.*
> *Las cartas han sido escritas por Sara.*

11 El aguacero ha destruido todo el follaje.
12 El terrateniente ha repartido toda la tierra.
13 Los españoles han dominado a los yaquis.
14 El gobierno federal ha iniciado nueva acción contra las tribus.
15 Muchos turistas han visitado las grutas en Nuevo México.
16 El sol fuerte ha quemado todas las plantitas.

Estar con el Participio Pasado

En español se usa la tercera persona singular o plural de *estar* con el participio pasado de otro verbo para indicar una condición que resulta de un acto previo. El participio pasado concuerda en número y género con el sujeto. Esta construcción no expresa la acción sino el resultado de la acción.

L Sigan el modelo.

Prendí la estufa.
La estufa está prendida.

1 Manuel abrió la cesta.
2 Cerraron las tiendas.
3 Sirvió la comida.
4 Escogieron la tela.
5 Alumbró la sala.
6 Los novios se casaron.
7 Él puso la mesa.
8 La niña se sentó.
9 Grabaron la cinta.
10 Averiguaron los detalles.

Comparaciones

Los dos comparativos más comunes son *más . . . que* y *menos . . . que*.

> Mi hermana es más alta que Carlos.
> Carlos es más gordo que mi hermana.
> Felipe es menos inteligente que Ana.

M Sigan los modelos.

Carla es fuerte. Ana es fuerte también.
Carla es más fuerte que Ana.

1 Mi abuelo es viejo. Tu abuelo es viejo también.
2 Mis padres son liberales. Sus padres son liberales también.
3 Su coche es nuevo. Mi coche es nuevo también.
4 Nuestro colegio está cerca del centro. Tu colegio está cerca también.

Dina es lista. Ricardo es menos listo.
Ricardo es menos listo que Dina.

5 El libro es interesante. La película es menos interesante.
6 Las joyas son caras. Las flores son menos caras.
7 El niño es tímido. La niña es menos tímida.
8 Mi padre es guapo. El padre de Luis es menos guapo.

Formas Irregulares

El inglés tiene algunos comparativos irregulares como *bad → worse*, *good → better*; el español los tiene también.

> más joven — menor
> más viejo — mayor
> más bueno — mejor
> más malo — peor

Nótese que *mayor* significa *más edad* que otra persona o cosa, pero no indica vejez. Así que *más viejo* y *mayor* no son exactamente sinónimos.

Comparaciones con Números

Generalmente se dice *de* delante de los números.

> Gasté más de mil pesos.

En una oración negativa se usa *que*.

> No gasté más que mil pesos.

N Contesten a las siguientes preguntas según el modelo.

> *Este coche es bueno. ¿Y el otro?*
> *Es mejor.*

1 Este muchacho es joven. ¿Y el otro?
2 Esta comida está mala. ¿Y la otra?
3 Estos pasteles son buenos. ¿Y los otros?
4 Estas señoras son viejas. ¿Y las otras?
5 Este regalo es bueno. ¿Y el otro?
6 Esta descripción es mala. ¿Y las otras?
7 Estos guías son jóvenes. ¿Y los otros?
8 Estos indios son viejos. ¿Y el otro?

Comparaciones de Igualdad

Las comparaciones de igualdad se expresan con *tanto . . . como*. *Tanto* con un sustantivo se trata como adjetivo y concuerda en género y número.

> Tengo tanto entusiasmo como tú.
> Siento tanta emoción como ellos.
> Veo tantos errores como la maestra.
> Repito tantas veces como él.
> ¡Mil libros! No creía que tenías tantos.

En otros casos *tanto* es adverbio y pierde la última sílaba.

> Tu hermana es tan alta como la mía.
> Los jóvenes son tan respetados como sus padres.

O Sigan el modelo.

> *Leíste muchos libros. Yo también.*
> *Leíste tantos libros como yo.*

1 Recibí muchos regalos. Tú también.
2 Vimos muchas luces. Él también.
3 Oímos mucha música. Juanito también.
4 Oíste mucho ruido. Yo también.
5 Comió muchos dulces. Los otros también.

P Sigan los modelos. Nótese la secuencia de tiempos.

> *¡Tienes mil libros en tu biblioteca!*
> *No sabía que tenías tantos.*

> *¡Escribiste tres cartas ayer!*
> *No sabía que habías escrito tantas.*

1 ¡Lees un libro cada semana!
2 ¡Recibiste veinte regalos el Día de los Reyes!
3 ¡Sales dos o tres veces cada semana!
4 ¡Comiste todo el pastel!
5 ¡Encontraste cinco blusas!
6 ¡Tienes dos mil rosas en tu jardín!
7 ¡Cultivas todo este campo!
8 ¡Guardaste toda la fortuna!

El Superlativo

El grado más alto, el superlativo, se expresa con el artículo definido con *más, menos* o con una de las formas irregulares. Nótese el uso de *de*.

> Ese festival es el más importante de todos.
> Esas manzanas son las más bonitas del valle.
> La primavera es la mejor estación del año.
> Teresa es la mayor de su grupo.

Q Sigan el modelo.

> *En su grupo Ana es alta.*
> *Ana es la más alta de su grupo.*

1 En nuestra clase Jorge es guapo.
2 En tu familia tu hermana es inteligente.
3 En su club Marcos es popular.
4 En el equipo Marta es buena jugadora.
5 En el coro Esperanza canta bien.
6 Entre mis parientes mi abuelo es viejo.
7 Entre mis tíos mi tío Andrés es joven.

La Leyenda

Del dicho al hecho hay gran trecho.

PARA PREPARAR LA ESCENA

Las leyendas son narraciones en las que se mezcla un poco de verdad con grandes dosis de ficción. La imaginación y la fantasía juegan un papel muy importante en las leyendas, puesto que lo que comenzó como historia acaba por perder de vista la realidad.

Las leyendas tratan de hechos de un pasado remoto y los personajes demuestran cualidades notables. Frecuentemente son personajes históricos.

Las tres selecciones que siguen son del mundo hispánico pero el tema de cada una es distinto. Las leyendas son productos de la tradición y, por consiguiente, tienen rara vez un autor conocido, sino alguien que las colecciona.

El Lago encantado

PARA PRESENTAR LA LECTURA

La primera leyenda en este cuadro viene del Perú y se refiere a los incas, una de las civilizaciones indias del Nuevo Mundo, cuya riqueza y cultura son muy famosas. Algunos de los personajes son históricos y otros ficticios. El conflicto que surge entre conquistadores e indios es un relato poético de la conquista con todas sus hazañas, trágicas y nobles. La leyenda sale de una colección de Alejandro Sux.

Lea esta leyenda y deléitese con su belleza. Luego fíjese en cuáles de los personajes son históricos y cuáles son probablemente legendarios. Examine la narración para ver si reconoce los hechos históricos y los lugares geográficos que verdaderamente existen. La leyenda presenta la conquista bajo un aspecto diferente de como fue en la realidad, porque, como todas las leyendas, quiere filtrar los acontecimientos a través de la fantasía.

PARA APRENDER VOCABULARIO

Palabras Clave   I

1 **atrevidos**   audaces, intrépidos
   Los indios creían que los conquistadores españoles eran muy atrevidos.

2 **desafiando (desafiar)**   confrontando, afrentando
   Susana andaba sola de noche a casa, desafiando el peligro de las calles.

3 **perecía (perecer)**   moría, sucumbía, expiraba
   En las civilizaciones indígenas, cuando perecía una dinastía, nació otra.

4 **pisaban (pisar)**   ponían el pie sobre alguna cosa
   Los niños pisaban las flores cuando el vecino les gritó.

5 **quebrada**   abertura estrecha entre dos montañas, cañón
   Hay una quebrada muy pintoresca cerca de la ciudad.

6 **reinarían (reinar)**   gobernarían (como rey), dominarían
   Creían que los Incas reinarían en paz.

7 **superficie**   parte exterior de un cuerpo plano, especialmente del agua
Se reflejan los rayos del sol sobre la superficie del agua.

Práctica

Complete con una palabra de la lista.

quebrada   atrevidos   superficie
desafiando   reinarían   pisaban
perecía

1 Los tíos de María tienen una casa cerca de la _____.
2 Prometieron que _____ con justicia y compasión.
3 Los indígenas observaban cómo los caballos _____ el maíz que crecía en los campos.
4 Don Ramón era un hombre valiente. Su hijo también era intrépido. Los dos eran muy _____.
5 Juana se echó al lago para salvar al chiquillo, _____ el peligro.
6 Cuando no hay viento la _____ del agua parece un espejo.
7 En la ley de los indígenas, cuando _____ el jefe de la tribu, su hijo le reemplazaba.

Palabras Clave   II

1 **agüero**   anuncio, señal, pronóstico
Algunos creen que es mal agüero encontrarse con un gato negro en el camino.

2 **arroja (arrojar)**   tira un objeto, lanza
Es mala costumbre arrojar basura en la calle.

3 **disimuló (disimular)**   escondió, ocultó, aparentó
El soldado disimuló su temor y siguió la marcha, obedeciendo a su capitán.

4 **engañan (engañar)**   hacen creer a otro u otros lo que no es verdad (*deceive, trick*)

¡Cuidado que esos comerciantes no te engañen!

5 **oculto**   escondido
Hay un edificio oculto entre los árboles al otro lado del río.

6 **rumor**   murmullo, ruido
Cuando uno está en la quebrada, a lo lejos se oye el rumor de las olas del mar.

7 **sacerdote**   cura, ministro de la religión, padre
Los sacerdotes enseñan los misterios de la religión.

8 **sordo**   que no oye u oye mal, que hace muy poco ruido
La india anciana estaba sorda y la gente le tenía que hablar por medio de señas y gestos.

9 **veloces**   rápidos
Hoy día hay aviones muy veloces que transportan a la gente de un sitio a otro en muy poco tiempo.

Práctica

Complete con una palabra de la lista.

arrojes   oculto   sacerdote
agüero   disimuló   rumor
sordo   veloces   engaña

1 En la Sierra Madre hay un lago _____ que es poco conocido.
2 En el pueblo se oía un _____ murmullo de ansiedad y temor.
3 La señora Perales _____ su temor durante toda la interrogación.
4 ¿Qué _____ dijo misa esta mañana?
5 ¡No _____ tus cosas en el suelo!
6 Ese millonario colecciona coches _____.
7 Los vientos fuertes comenzaron a traer el mal _____ de que venía la tempestad.
8 Una buena persona nunca _____ a los demás.

Un lago encantado

9 De la casa se oye el _____ de las personas en la calle.

Palabras Clave   III

1 **atrajo (atraer)**   trajo hacia algo o alguien *(attracted, drew)*
   Cuando el presidente habló en la escuela, atrajo a mucha gente.

2 **lisa**   sin aspereza, suave *(smooth)*
   La gatita era preciosa, de colores brillantes y pelo espeso y liso.

3 **opaca**   no transparente
   Estaba cerrada la cortina opaca y por eso no entraba la luz del día en el salón oscuro.

4 **repentino**   impensado, que pasa de repente *(sudden)*
   El ladrón hizo un movimiento repentino y corrió.

Práctica

Complete con una palabra de la lista.

   repentino   lisa   opaca   atrajo

1 ¿Qué te _____ a estudiar idiomas?
2 El agua del lago es _____.
3 La superficie del agua en la piscina estaba _____.
4 Hubo un cambio _____ en el tiempo y todos tuvieron que volver a casa.

El Lago encantado

I

En el norte de la república Argentina hay un lago tranquilo, circular y rodeado de montañas cubiertas de vegetación. Los habitantes de aquella región lo llaman el Lago Encantado. El paraje sólo es accesible por una estrecha quebrada.

Durante gran parte del día el lago queda en las sombras. Sólo por pocos minutos llegan los rayos del sol a la superficie del agua.

Muchos años antes de la conquista española habitaban aquellas regiones unas tribus de indios, vasallos de los incas. En aquel tiempo vivía un «curaca» muy rico, respetado y querido de su pueblo. Poseía objetos de oro, trabajos de plumas y otras muchas cosas de valor inestimable.

Entre sus tesoros había una urna de oro que uno de los reyes incas había regalado a su abuelo en señal de gratitud por un importante servicio. La urna tenía maravillosas virtudes: mientras estaba en poder de esa nación, los curacas gobernaban en paz y el pueblo vivía tranquilo y feliz; pero si caía en manos enemigas, perecía la dinastía y reinarían poderosos conquistadores.

Todos los años en la gran Fiesta del Sol, la urna sagrada era puesta en exhibición. De todas partes venían los indios para adorarla.

* * *

Las razas indias tenían una tradición común. Era que un día debían llegar al continente hombres de lengua desconocida, de piel blanca y de costumbres extrañas. Estos extranjeros iban a conquistar a los indios. Según unos, un dios iba a anunciar su llegada; según otros, un espíritu malo iba a traer consigo la muerte. Los pueblos que vivían cerca del mar esperaban a los forasteros del otro lado del mar; para las naciones del interior, los forasteros iban a venir de allende las montañas, de los desiertos o de las selvas. El fondo de la leyenda era siempre el mismo.

paraje lugar

vasallos esclavos
curaca jefe

forasteros extranjeros

allende otra parte de

Los años pasaron y la antigua leyenda se convertía en realidad. Los forasteros pisaban las costas del continente. Hombres atrevidos cruzaban las selvas, desafiando todos los obstáculos.

Cierto día un «chasqui» del Cuzco llevó la noticia que del norte venían hombres de aspecto nunca visto.

chasqui mensajero inca

II

En el país hubo un sordo rumor de inquietud. Los habitantes ofrecieron sacrificios humanos al Sol para aplacar su ira.

Poco después se supo que el Inca Atahualpa había caído prisionero en poder de los invasores. Todo el país estaba en conmoción y los guerreros marchaban a defender a su rey.

* * *

La esposa del curaca se llamaba Ima. El noble amaba a Ima con ternura y pasión. Cuando se recibieron las primeras noticias del Cuzco acerca de los invasores, la frente de la joven india se nubló y tuvo sueños de mal agüero.

—Tú estás inquieta—le dijo su marido—; la mala noticia te ha alarmado, pero de todas partes llegan guerreros y pronto el Inca estará libre de los invasores.

—Yo he soñado que las hojas de los árboles caían—contestó Ima—y eso significa desgracia.

—Los sueños engañan muchas veces, mi querida; no todos son enviados por los dioses.

—Pero éste sí, esposo mío—insistió Ima—. Y ayer, vi una bandada de pájaros que volaba hacia el norte. Un sacerdote me explicó que eso también indica calamidad.

El curaca disimuló su propia inquietud y se preparó a partir con sus tropas. Antes de partir llamó a Ima, y dándole la urna sagrada, le dijo:

—Antes de dejarla caer en manos de los enemigos, arrójala al lago sombrío, oculto en medio de la sierra.

sombrío en sombra

Ima prometió hacer lo que mandaba su esposo. A los pocos días el curaca partió con sus guerreros.

* * *

Un día llegaron a la lejana provincia unos veloces chasquis. Anunciaron que el Inca Atahualpa había prometido al jefe de los invasores, en cambio de su libertad, una sala llena de oro y dos piezas más pequeñas llenas de plata. En todas partes del imperio mandaron recoger todos los metales preciosos.

rescatar libertar pagando
(to ransom)

Nadie rehusó, nadie murmuró cuando vino la orden de entregar los tesoros para rescatar al Hijo del Sol. Caravanas de riquezas maravillosas cruzaban el país por bosques, montañas, desiertos y ríos. Una de las caravanas paró en casa del curaca, donde recibió muchos objetos de oro y de plata.

apartaba retiraba

El jefe que recogía los objetos de valor notó que Ima apartaba la urna. Como nunca había estado en aquella región, ignoraba las propiedades maravillosas de la urna sagrada.

—¿Por qué aparta Ud. eso?—preguntó a la mujer del curaca.

Ima le explicó el motivo por qué guardaba la urna. Al guerrero no le interesó eso. Él había recibido orden de recoger todos los objetos de oro y de plata.

—Lo que Ud. dice no me importa—dijo a Ima—, ¡déme la urna!

—No; tome todo lo demás para el rescate del Inca, nuestro señor. Pero la urna he prometido no entregarla jamás.

—En nombre del Inca, ¡déme la urna!

—¡Jamás!

III

Viendo que Ima no consentía, el guerrero quiso quitarle el objeto sagrado por la fuerza. Los criados de la casa acudieron y hubo una lucha. El ruido del combate atrajo gente que tomó parte en favor de Ima. En la confusión del combate, Ima se escapó con el tesoro; iba a cumplir su promesa de arrojar la urna al lago y no dejarla caer en manos de los forasteros.

El jefe había visto huir a Ima y la siguió. Ésta corría con tal velocidad a través del valle que su perseguidor varias veces la perdió de vista. Luego apareció a los ojos del jefe indio la superficie lisa y opaca del lago encantado.

Allí alcanzó a Ima cuando ésta levantaba los brazos con la urna. Los dos lucharon unos instantes. La mujer del curaca, que no podía sostener con éxito una lucha desigual, tomó una resolución suprema. Con un movimiento repentino se libró de las manos del guerrero, y alzando la urna sagrada, se arrojó con ella al agua.

alzando levantando

El agua se agitó con un rumor de voces bajas y excitadas. El lago se iluminó pronto con una luz color de oro. El mágico espectáculo duró algunos instantes. El resplandor se apagó y el guerrero vio otra vez el lago tranquilo en la sombra. Tenía por cierto que el fenómeno extraordinario provenía de la urna sagrada, y que los dioses iban a castigarle. Lleno de espanto, olvidando su altivez

altivez orgullo

de guerrero, volvió la espalda al lago misterioso, y huyó como un loco a través de las selvas.

Al día siguiente hallaron el cuerpo sin vida del indio . . . Y la urna no cayó en manos de los conquistadores.

PARA APLICAR

Comprensión   I

A   Conteste a las siguientes preguntas.

1   ¿De qué trata esta leyenda?
2   Describa el lago y el paraje donde se encuentra.
3   ¿Cómo se llega a ese lugar?
4   Antes de la conquista española, ¿quiénes habitaban esa región?
5   ¿Cómo era el curaca de ese pueblo?
6   ¿Qué objeto especial tenía él entre sus tesoros?
7   ¿De dónde vino esa urna?
8   ¿Tenía alguna virtud esa urna?
9   ¿Por qué era necesario cuidar mucho esa urna?
10   ¿Cuándo se exhibía la urna?
11   Cuente algo de la tradición común que tenían las razas indias.
12   ¿Qué diferencia había entre la leyenda de los indios que vivían cerca del mar y los que vivían en las montañas?
13   ¿Qué noticia llevó cierto día un chasqui?

B   Escoja la respuesta apropiada.

1   Es difícil llegar al lago encantado porque
  a.   está en el norte de Argentina.
  b.   está rodeado de montañas cubiertas de mucha vegetación.
  c.   hay sólo una entrada estrecha.
2   Los habitantes allí
  a.   eran vasallos de los incas.
  b.   conquistaron a los españoles.
  c.   conquistaron a los incas.

3   La urna que tenían los indios
  a.   cayó en manos enemigas.
  b.   poseía maravillosas virtudes.
  c.   fue un regalo del abuelo del curaca.
4   La urna fue puesta en exhibición
  a.   cuando reinaban los conquistadores.
  b.   cuando llegaron hombres de lengua desconocida.
  c.   cada año en la Fiesta del Sol.
5   Existían varias teorías acerca de
  a.   dónde vivían los forasteros.
  b.   los resultados de la llegada de los blancos.
  c.   cómo llegarían los forasteros.
6   Resultó que
  a.   la leyenda se convertía en realidad.
  b.   los forasteros se quedaron en las costas.
  c.   los forasteros temían entrar en las selvas.

Comprensión   II

A   Conteste a las siguientes preguntas.

1   ¿Cómo reaccionó el pueblo a esta noticia?
2   ¿Qué le pasó a Atahualpa poco después de esto?
3   ¿Cómo se llamaba la esposa del curaca?
4   ¿Cómo afectaron las noticias del Cuzco a Ima?
5   Relate algo del diálogo que tuvieron ellos sobre los sueños.
6   Antes de partir el curaca, ¿qué le dijo a Ima?
7   ¿Cuánto valoraba Atahualpa su libertad?

8 ¿Qué hicieron los incas para rescatar al Hijo del Sol?

9 ¿Qué sucedió cuando llegó una de las caravanas a la casa del curaca?

10 ¿Por qué se dirigió el jefe de la caravana a Ima?

11 ¿Qué orden había recibido el guerrero?

B Escoja la expresión de la segunda lista (2) que completa la idea empezada en la primera lista (1).

1

1 El noble curaca amaba
2 Cuando recibieron las primeras noticias del Cuzco
3 El curaca confiaba que el Inca estaría libre
4 Ima opinaba distinto porque
5 Muchas veces los sueños engañan
6 La bandada de pájaros que volaba hacia el norte
7 Antes de irse el curaca le dio a su esposa la urna
8 Más tarde llegaron unos chasquis anunciando
9 Nadie rehusó la orden de entregar sus objetos valiosos de oro y plata
10 El guerrero ignoraba las propiedades maravillosas de la urna

2

a. porque dijo que llegarían guerreros de todas partes a rescatarlo.
b. porque no todos son enviados por los dioses.
c. y caravanas de riquezas fueron mandadas al Cuzco.
d. también indicaba calamidad.
e. a Ima con ternura y pasión.
f. soñaba que las hojas caían de los árboles— señal de desgracia.
g. y exigió que Ima se la diera.
h. Ima tuvo sueños de mal agüero.
i. que Atahualpa, prisionero de los invasores, había prometido grandes cantidades de oro y plata por su libertad.
j. que no debía caer en manos del enemigo.

Comprensión   III

A Conteste a las siguientes preguntas.

1 Viendo que Ima no consentía en darle la urna, ¿qué hizo el guerrero?
2 ¿Por qué se escapó Ima? ¿Qué iba a hacer?
3 ¿Quién la vio huir?
4 ¿Qué hizo él?
5 ¿Dónde alcanzó el jefe a Ima?
6 ¿Qué resolución suprema hizo ella?
7 Describa lo que ocurrió en el lago cuando se arrojó Ima en el agua.
8 ¿Cómo afectó todo esto al guerrero?

B ¿Verdadero o falso?

1 Ima se negó a entregarle al guerrero la urna.
2 El guerrero era más fuerte y le quitó la urna a la mujer.
3 Muchos acudieron a luchar en favor de Ima.
4 En toda la confusión que resultó el guerrero se escapó.
5 Ima temía caer en manos de los forasteros.
6 El guerrero alcanzó a Ima cuando estaba para tirar la urna al lago.
7 La mujer no podía luchar mucho tiempo con el guerrero.
8 De repente Ima arrojó al guerrero al lago.

9   El indio temía un castigo de los dioses y huyó por la selva.
10 Más tarde los indios encontraron la urna en el lago.

Más Práctica

A   Complete las siguientes oraciones con una palabra apropiada.

1   Una extensión de agua rodeada de tierra es un _____.
2   Los _____ vencieron a los indios.
3   El lago estaba rodeado de _____ altas.
4   Un sinónimo de *extranjero* es _____.
5   El cuento que se repite durante varias generaciones es una _____.
6   Un lugar seco donde no hay agua es un _____.
7   El que sirve a otro es _____.
8   *Esposo* es lo mismo que _____.
9   La _____ tiene muchos árboles y vegetación.
10 La sucesión de reyes de una familia forma una _____.

B   Dé una definición de las siguientes palabras.

1   el lago
2   la leyenda
3   el sueño
4   la isla
5   el combate
6   el oro
7   la selva
8   atrevido
9   alcanzar
10 disimular

Ejercicios Creativos

1   Prepare un informe en español sobre la vida de los incas antes de la conquista, como se ve en esta leyenda.
    a. ¿Qué personajes son verdaderamente históricos?
    b. ¿Qué personajes son ficticios?
    c. ¿A qué sucesos históricos se refiere la leyenda?
2   Mencione algunos personajes legendarios de nuestra propia historia, y describa sus hazañas.

La Vieja del Candilejo

Antonio Jiménez-Landi

PARA PRESENTAR LA LECTURA

Cada región de España tiene su bello tesoro de leyendas. Algunas tienen antiguos temas que recorrieron el mundo medieval; otras están inspiradas en mitos locales o en algún suceso histórico. La que sigue es una leyenda andaluza, tal vez disfigurada durante los años, que evoca el nombre de una calle de Sevilla, la de la cabeza del Rey don Pedro, y un extraño suceso de la época del rey del mismo nombre. La leyenda viene de una colección reunida por Antonio Jiménez-Landi.

Don Pedro I, hijo de Alfonso XI, fue rey de Castilla de 1350 hasta 1369. No le interesaba la doctrina caballeresca ni las maniobras políticas de la gente que le rodeaba. Fue hombre de acción, a veces demasiado dispuesto a matar primero y juzgar después. Sus partidarios le llamaban el Justiciero y sus enemigos, el Cruel.

PARA APRENDER VOCABULARIO

Palabras Clave   I

1 **ambas**   las dos cosas, personas, etc.
Visitamos ambas ciudades en Andalucía.

2 **apresuró (apresurarse)**   se dio prisa, no tardó
Rosa se apresuró a identificar al delincuente.

3 **bulto**   figura que se distingue mal, masa indefinible
Notamos un bulto en el rincón que parecía el cuerpo de un hombre.

4 **candil**   lámpara de aceite
Ese candil es muy bonito pero da poca luz.

5 **naranjo**   árbol cuya fruta es la naranja
Este naranjo tiene más de cien años y da naranjas muy dulces.

6 **restaurar**   reparar o reconstruir en su forma original
Los artesanos restauraron el edificio en el estilo morisco.

7 **rezar**   orar de palabra, recitar las oraciones usadas por la Iglesia.
Delante del altar se puso de rodillas para rezarle a Dios.

8 **temporadas** espacios de tiempo que se dedican habitualmente a algo
En la temporada de vacaciones siempre vamos a la playa.

Práctica

Complete con una palabra de la lista.

rezar   candil   temporadas
naranjo   restaurar   ambas
apresuró   bulto

1 Con la luz del _____ Adela pudo ver el camino.
2 Todos los domingos va a la iglesia a _____.
3 Don Pedro hizo _____ el Alcázar de Sevilla para vivir en él.
4 A don Pedro le gustaba pasar largas _____ en el palacio restaurado.
5 No pudo identificar el _____ que vio en la calle.
6 Alguien plantó el _____ en el jardín del palacio hace muchos años.
7 Quería _____ cosas pero tuvo que escoger sólo una.
8 Se _____ a iniciar la reunión porque tenía muchos temas que presentar.

Palabras Clave   II

1 **asunto** tema
Es un asunto de gran importancia para mí.

2 **ejercer** practicar un oficio o facultad
El rey quería ejercer su autoridad de justiciero.

3 **pegado (pegar)** colocado firmemente con clavo, goma, etc.
Han pegado fotos del candidato en todos los árboles del barrio.

4 **prende (prender)** se apodera de un delincuente

Busca al ladrón y préndelo antes de que abandone la ciudad.

Práctica

Complete con una palabra de la lista.

pegado   prende   asunto   ejercer

1 No entendí el _____ que discutían.
2 La víctima, al ver al ladrón, le gritó a su amiga:— ¡_____ a ese miserable!
3 ¿Qué tienes _____ al zapato? ¿Goma de mascar?
4 Es abogada, pero no quiere _____ más su profesión, ya que está vieja y enferma.

Palabras Clave   III

1 **amenazas** declaraciones de malos intentos *(threats)*
No tengo miedo de sus amenazas.

2 **espanto** miedo extremo, terror
El espanto le hizo huir.

3 **prosiguió (proseguir – i)** siguió o continuó después de una interrupción
El Alcalde Mayor entró, y el rey prosiguió con la investigación.

4 **recorría (recorrer)** caminaba, andaba
La policía recorría toda la ciudad en busca del asesino.

5 **temblar (ie)** agitarse con movimiento frecuente y rápido
El culpable va a temblar más al saber su castigo.

Práctica

Complete con una palabra de la lista.

amenazas   prosiguió   recorría
temblar   espanto

1 Yo _____ toda la escuela varias veces al día.

¿De qué se está riendo?

2 Van a _____ del frío si no les permiten entrar.

3 Después de una pausa la doctora _____ con el examen.

4 A pesar de las _____ el rey se portó como un gran líder de su pueblo.

5 Al ver al perro feroz el gato tembló de _____.

La Vieja del Candilejo

Antonio Jiménez-Landi

I

Candilejo lámpara pequeña
sucedido suceso
partidarios followers
Justiciero strictly fair, stern

amplió hizo más grande

retorcido twisted

lóbrega oscura, tenebrosa
angosta estrecha

desfallecida faint

ventanuco ventana pequeña
mortecina dying, pale, wan
membrudo muscular, fuerte
diestra mano derecha

torpeza poca habilidad

pisadas steps
muro pared
choquezuelas, rótulas kneecaps

En Sevilla hay una calle que se llama de la cabeza del Rey don Pedro. Este nombre evoca un sucedido de la época de don Pedro I de Castilla, a quien sus partidarios llamaban el Justiciero y sus enemigos, el Cruel.

Don Pedro gustaba mucho de residir en Sevilla; hizo restaurar su alcázar morisco, lo amplió con magníficos salones y pasaba grandes temporadas en él. Todavía, al cabo de los siglos, se conserva un antiquísimo y retorcido naranjo en sus jardines maravillosos, que, según tradición, fue plantado por el propio don Pedro.

Era una noche lóbrega. No se oía ningún ruido en la angosta callejuela, cuyos vecinos dormían ya, sin duda, salvo la viejecita que habitaba, sola, en una casa muy pobre.

De pronto se oyó el choque de unas espadas, allí mismo, en el esquinazo de la calle y, poco después, una voz agónica, desfallecida, que exclamaba: «¡Dios me valga! ¡Muerto soy!»

La viejecilla, sin pensar en las consecuencias que podría tener aquel acto, cogió el candilejo que la alumbraba y se dirigió a un ventanuco de la habitación. A la mortecina luz del candil pudo ver, entonces, el bulto de un hombre bañado en sangre y caído sobre las piedras de la calle y, a su lado, un caballero membrudo y alto, que permanecía con la espada en la diestra. La luz del candil iluminó el rostro del matador, quien se apresuró a cubrirlo con ambas manos, de manera que la curiosa mujer no pudo conocerle entonces.

Quizá arrepentida por lo que acababa de hacer, la vieja retiróse del ventanuco precipitadamente, pero con tan mala fortuna, quizá torpeza, que el candil se le cayó a la calle.

Su curiosidad no había quedado satisfecha; permaneció detrás de la ventana, para escuchar, y pronto oyó las pisadas del matador, bajo el muro, y el ruido, que ya conocía bien, de sus choquezuelas, o rótulas, al andar.

furtivamente *furtively*

Por ese ruido tan extraño conoció que el matador era el caballero que pasaba todas las noches, a la misma hora, por debajo de su ventana. La viejecita le había visto, furtivamente, más de una vez y sabía quien era.

—¡Sálvanos, Virgen de los Reyes!—exclamó, y se puso a rezar.

alguaciles *bailiffs, constables*
Alcalde Mayor *Lord Mayor*
pesquisas investigaciones

A la mañana siguiente, los alguaciles de la ciudad hallaron el cadáver de la víctima, y el Alcalde Mayor, que era don Martín Fernández Cerón, comenzó rápidamente sus pesquisas para descubrir y encarcelar al asesino.

pobladores habitantes

Se sospechaba de los judíos y de los moriscos, pobladores de aquel barrio. Alguien habló de una hermosa dama que recibía la visita de un personaje principal a altas horas de la noche; pero todos ignoraban quién pudiera ser el galanteador.

galanteador amante

Los vecinos próximos al lugar del criminal suceso no sabían absolutamente nada, ni habían oído nada, ni nada podían declarar.

El hecho levantó muchos comentarios en Sevilla y no pocas censuras contra la negligencia de sus autoridades. Hasta que el rumor público llegó a oídos del propio Rey como una oleada de protestas contra sus justicias, nombre que se daba, genéricamente, a los encargados de ejecutarla.

oleada *big wave*

II

tomar cartas en el asunto *to look into the matter*
premura *urgency, haste*

Don Pedro tuvo que tomar cartas en el asunto y llamó, con premura, al Alcalde Mayor.

—¿Es posible que dentro de Sevilla maten a un hombre y ni tú ni tus alguaciles hayáis averiguado, todavía, quién es el culpable? ¿Ni siquiera habéis encontrado algún indicio que os sirva de rastro para dar con él? ¿Puede ejercerse así la justicia que me ha dado fama?

rastro *track, trail*
dar con *find*

El Alcalde Mayor se excusaba en vano:

—Señor, hemos hecho todas las averiguaciones imaginables; pero he de confesar que, hasta ahora, han resultado inútiles; en el lugar del suceso tan sólo hemos hallado un candil pegado al muro de la casa donde vive una pobre mujer muy viejecilla, a quien, sin duda, pertenece. Pero esto, ¿qué puede probarnos?

—¿Has tomado declaración a esa anciana?

—Sí, Alteza; y ha reconocido el candil como suyo, pero asegura no saber nada más.

—Préndela de nuevo y tráela a mi presencia. Yo te aseguro que delante de mí tendrá que declarar.

El Alcalde Mayor salió del Real Alcázar temeroso y corrido, porque sabía muy bien que si el Rey se interesaba por el asunto y si éste no se esclarecía pronto, su cabeza había de pagar por la del misterioso matador, y le faltaron minutos para dar cumplimiento a la orden recibida.

Algunas horas más tarde don Martín regresó al Alcázar, en uno de cuyos salones moriscos tuvo lugar la escena siguiente:

—Señor, ésta es la vieja—dijo don Martín.

La débil mujer se estremecía de miedo. ¿Cuándo se había visto ella delante del Rey, en un palacio que le pareció de leyenda? Ningún contraste más elocuente que el de aquella vieja arrugada, retorcida como un haz de sarmientos, pequeñita, casi miserable, y del corpulento monarca, de gesto duro, de mirada fría, en lo más florido de su juventud, rodeado de un lujo oriental.

Preguntó el Alcalde Mayor:

—¿Conoces este candil?

—Sí . . . ya he dicho que es mío—balbució la anciana.

—¿Y no has reconocido a la persona que mató al caballero?

—No la vi . . .

—Está bien—continuó el Alcalde—. Quieres que te obliguemos a confesar y vas a hacerlo muy pronto.

Los sayones empuñaron los vergajos, y ya se disponían a descargarlos fieramente sobre la insignificante viejecilla, cuando dijo el monarca:

—Si sabes quién es el matador, te ordeno que declares su nombre. Mi justicia es igual para todos y nada tienes que temer de ella.

Pero la anciana, pálida y temblorosa, no se atrevía a fijar los ojos en don Pedro, que, sin duda, le parecía algún semidiós.

Y solamente pudo balbucear unas palabras ininteligibles.

—Empezad . . . —ordenó don Martín a los sayones.

III

—Todavía no—dijo don Pedro—. Mujer, por última vez te mando que delates al asesino, sea quien fuere, y si no lo haces te mandaré a ti a la horca.

—¡Responde!—gritó, fuera de sí, el Alcalde—. Vamos . . . ¿Quién ha sido?

Pero la vieja callaba. Don Pedro insistió nuevamente, volvió don Martín a sus amenazas, avanzaron los sayones hacia la víctima

acosada *harassed*
aplomo *aplomb, poise*

verdugos *executioners*
selló *sealed*

templada *tempered*

ampara *protects, shelters*
bolsilla *small moneybag*

homicida *murderer*
ajusticiado *executed*

escalofrío *chill, shiver*

se degüelle *be disgorged*

escarmiento *warning,
lesson*

y, tan acosada se vio ésta que, al fin, sacando fuerzas de su debilidad respondió temerosa pero con aplomo:

—El Rey.

El espanto paralizó los brazos de los verdugos y selló la boca de don Martín. ¿Qué iba a suceder, santo Cielo? Mejor era que se abriese la boca.

Pero don Pedro, con voz templada y firme, rompió aquel silencio de muerte para declarar ante el general asombro:

—Has dicho la verdad y la justicia te ampara.

Sacó luego una bolsilla con cien monedas de oro y se la entregó a la mujer, añadiendo:

—Toma; el rey don Pedro sabe premiar a quien le sirve bien.

La viejecilla creyó que estaba soñando, mientras cogía la bolsa . . .

Prosiguió el monarca:

—En cuanto al homicida, será ajusticiado . . . Ya lo oyes, don Martín . . .

El Alcalde empezó a temblar; un escalofrío recorría todo su cuerpo, desde las uñas de los pies hasta las puntas de los cabellos venerables.

Nuevamente la voz de don Pedro, grave, reposada, le sacó de su angustiosa perplejidad. Añadió el soberano:

—Mas como nadie puede dar muerte al rey de Castilla, mando que se degüelle su efigie, que se le corte la cabeza y que ésta se ponga en la misma esquina de la calle donde fue muerto el caballero, para que sirva de escarmiento a todas las gentes.

Y así se hizo. Durante muchos años, una cabeza de don Pedro el Cruel estuvo colgada en aquella esquina de la calle de la cabeza del Rey don Pedro.

PARA APLICAR

Comprensión   I

A Conteste a las siguientes preguntas.

1 ¿En qué ciudad se encuentra la calle de la cabeza del Rey don Pedro?

2 Don Pedro I de Castilla, ¿era don Pedro el Cruel o don Pedro el Justiciero?

3 El antiquísimo naranjo que se conserva todavía, ¿fue plantado por don Pedro o por la viejecita?

4 ¿Quién habitaba sola en la casita pobre de la callejuela?

5 ¿Qué exclamó la voz agónica?

6 ¿Estaba vivo o muerto el hombre bañado en sangre?

7 ¿Por qué no quedó satisfecha la curiosidad de la vieja al iluminar el rostro del asesino?

8 ¿Dónde permaneció para escuchar?

9 ¿Cuándo hallaron el cadáver de la víctima los alguaciles?

10 ¿Qué sabían los vecinos próximos al lugar del suceso criminal?

B ¿Verdadero o falso?

1 Don Pedro I reinó en España hasta 1963.
2 Todos tenían la misma opinión del rey.
3 La acción de esta selección tiene lugar en Sevilla.
4 Don Pedro hizo construir un alcázar morisco.
5 Una noche oscura se oyó el choque de armas blancas en una callejuela.
6 Al abrir la ventana la viejecilla vio a un hombre en el baño.
7 Vio al asesino con la espada en la mano, y él se cubrió la cara con las manos.
8 Al retirarse la vieja dejó caer el candil.
9 Ella reconoció que las pisadas eran las del caballero que andaba por allí todas las noches.
10 La vieja era la única que podía identificar al asesino.

Comprensión   II

A Conteste a las siguientes preguntas.

1 ¿Por qué tuvo que intervenir el propio rey don Pedro?
2 ¿Dónde habían hallado los alguaciles el candil?
3 ¿Por qué salió el Alcalde Mayor muy temeroso a buscar a la vieja?
4 ¿Regresó don Martín con la vieja o solo?
5 ¿Reconoció la vieja el candil?
6 ¿Confesó el Alcalde Mayor que conocía a la persona que mató al caballero?
7 ¿La conocía?

B Escoja la respuesta apropiada.

1 El rey quería
   a. jugar cartas con el Alcalde Mayor.
   b. saber si habían encontrado algún rastro que les ayudara.
   c. matar a los alguaciles.

2 Lo único que habían hallado fue
   a. una viejecilla pegada al lado de la casa donde vivía.
   b. la necesidad de tener todas las averiguaciones posibles.
   c. un candil debajo de una ventana.
3 El rey
   a. asustó al Alcalde Mayor.
   b. fue a prender a la anciana.
   c. reconoció el candil como suyo.
4 Al entrar en el alcázar la anciana
   a. temblaba de miedo.
   b. hizo estremecerse al corpulento monarca.
   c. le dio una mirada fría al joven rey.

Comprensión   III

A Conteste a las siguientes preguntas.

1 ¿Qué castigo prometió don Pedro a la mujer si no declaraba el nombre del asesino?
2 ¿Por qué tenía más miedo la viejecilla de declarar el nombre del asesino que de sufrir castigo por no declararlo?
3 ¿Qué dijo don Pedro ante la terrible acusación?
4 ¿Por qué sabemos si se trata o no se trata de un suceso cierto?
5 ¿Cuántas cabezas de don Pedro el Cruel hubo en Sevilla durante muchos años según se entiende por la leyenda?

B Reenumere las oraciones siguientes en el orden con que ocurrieron en la selección.

1 Los sayones se dispusieron a castigar a la pobre viejecilla.
2 El rey le mandó que dijera quién era el asesino.
3 La señora no se atrevía a mirar al rey.
4 Cuando todos comenzaron a gritarle, amenazándola de muerte, ella encontró fuerzas para nombrar al rey.
5 Por decir la verdad recibió cien monedas de oro como premio.

6 El rey les sorprendió a todos diciendo que el culpable sería castigado.

7 Mandó que se le cortara la cabeza de su efigie para que sirviera de escarmiento a todos.

Más Práctica

A Complete las siguientes oraciones con una palabra de la lista.

temporada, prosiguió, amenazas, ejerce, asunto, me atrevo, restaurar, arrepentida, arrugada, soñando

1 Yo no _____ a acusarle del crimen.
2 Pasaron una _____ en Sevilla.
3 La ladrona se da cuenta de lo serio de sus acciones, y está _____.
4 Yo estoy _____ con conocer Sevilla.
5 Más tarde _____ con la pesquisa.
6 Ellas no se interesan por este _____ personal.
7 El palacio está en malas condiciones, pero lo van a _____.
8 Siempre nos asusta con sus _____.
9 Es ingeniero pero no _____ su profesión.
10 Arrojaron su ropa en la silla y ya está completamente _____.

B Reemplace el verbo *volver* por *regresar*.

1 Vuelven a las ocho.
2 La policía volverá mañana con el criminal.
3 El viejo volvió lleno de terror.

C Reemplace el verbo *ir* por *dirigirse*.

1 La vieja fue hacia el palacio.
2 Van hacia la sierra en busca del asesino.
3 Voy hacia la esquina.

D Reemplace la expresión *ponerse a* por *empezar a*.

1 El señor se pone a llorar.
2 El Alcalde se puso a temblar.
3 Nos pusimos a correr.

Ejercicios Creativos

1 Busque algunos detalles de la vida de don Pedro I de Castilla. Luego, haga uno de los siguientes ejercicios:
   a. Prepare un breve párrafo discutiendo lo que quiere decir el rey don Pedro cuando en el cuento habla de «la justicia que me ha dado fama».
   b. Escriba una composición titulada «El reino tempestuoso de don Pedro el Cruel».
   c. Prepare un informe (oral o escrito) comentando por qué don Pedro I de Castilla merece los dos apodos: el Justiciero y el Cruel.
2 Escriba un diálogo de la última escena, comenzando con el rey ordenando que declare quién es el asesino. Preséntelo a la clase con la ayuda de unos compañeros.
3 ¿En qué consiste el interés del desenlace? ¿Cómo creía Ud. que iba a terminar?

La Camisa de Margarita

Ricardo Palma

PARA PRESENTAR LA LECTURA

Ricardo Palma (1833–1919) es el creador de un género literario llamado «la tradición». Bibliotecario de la Biblioteca Nacional del Perú por unos años, Palma sacó la inspiración de crónicas viejas, documentos legales, dibujos y mapas encontrados allí para desarrollar una especie de anécdota histórica. Al fondo histórico Palma añadió una forma ligera y recogida, narración rápida y humorística, y nos revela no sólo la historia peruana sino la cultura y la gracia de la época colonial.

Como se hace en todas las leyendas, Palma dio rienda suelta a su imaginación para incluir algo de verdad y algo de ficción. A la vez se preocupó mucho del estilo para asegurar una obra de perfección.

La Camisa de Margarita es una de las tradiciones más populares. Los peruanos suelen decir cuando sube el precio de un artículo: — ¡Esto es más caro que la camisa de Margarita Pareja!

PARA APRENDER VOCABULARIO

Palabras Clave   I

1 **al fiado**   dado a crédito, sin pagar en seguida
   Compramos el coche al fiado.

2 **cautivan (cautivar)**   aprisionan, atraen, ganan
   Esos músicos cautivan a su público.

3 **cayó (caer) en gracia**   le gustó
   Al joven no le cayó en gracia que su padre hablara con la profesora.

4 **echó (echar) flores**   dijo cosas bonitas a alguien
   El candidato, buscando votos, le echó flores al grupo.

5 **logro**   lo que uno obtiene como resultado de sus esfuerzos, ganancia
   La señorita Morales trabajó noche y día para el logro de una buena posición.

6   **lucía (lucir)**   brillaba, mostraba física-
mente
   El novio lucía una sonrisa incomparable
   después de la ceremonia.

7   **mimada (mimar)**   tratada con demasiado cariño
   Este niñito ha sido mimado por su tío y
   ya no quiere volver a su propia casa.

Práctica

Complete con una palabra de la lista.

mimados   logro   al fiado
lucía   echarme flores cautivan
cayó en gracia

1   ¡Deja de _____! ¿No ves que tu idea no
    me interesa?
2   Esa carta de su hijo no le _____ al padre.
3   El _____ de una buena educación no es
    fácil.
4   Sus ojos _____ a todos los que los miran.
5   El ganador del premio _____ una ex-
    presión de alegría.
6   Generalmente los nietos son _____ por
    los abuelos.
7   No tengo bastante plata. ¿Me permite
    comprarlo _____?

Palabras Clave   II

1   **botica**   donde se preparan y se venden
medicinas, farmacia
   Se puede comprar aspirina en la botica.

2   **chisme**   murmuración, cuento (gossip)
   El chisme hace enemigos de los que lo
   repiten.

3   **envenenarse**   tomar veneno, tomar algo
que puede matarle o hacerle daño
   Hay peligro de envenenarse tomando
   medicinas no recetadas por el médico.

4   **regalará (regalar)**   dará de regalo
   Prometió regalarle un librito a la niña.

5   **suegro**   padre de uno de los esposos
respecto del otro (father-in-law) (suegros
= in-laws)
   A veces los recién casados tienen que
   vivir en casa de los suegros.

Práctica

Complete con una palabra de la lista.

suegro   regalarles   chisme
botica   envenenarse

1   El señor Torres tenía miedo de _____;
    por eso nunca comía lo que él mismo no
    había preparado.
2   El favorito de todos mis parientes es mi
    _____.
3   Le gustó oír el _____, pero no lo va a
    repetir.
4   El farmacéutico prepara las medicinas en la
    _____.
5   Queremos _____ muebles o plata a los
    novios.

Palabras Clave   III

1   **alfiler**   clavillo de metal con punta por
un extremo y cabeza por el otro
   Al hacer vestidos el alfiler sirve para pegar
   la tela antes de coserla.

2   **arguyó (argüir)**   puso argumentos contra algo
   Yo no quería pelear, pero él arguyó hasta
   la medianoche.

3   **arrodillándose (arrodillarse)**   poniéndose de rodillas
   Arrodillándose en la tierra el campesino
   examinó las nuevas plantitas.

4   **juramento**   lo que uno promete hacer
(oath)
   El juez hizo juramento de obedecer las
   leyes.

Lima: calle comercial

5 **testarudo** que persiste con exceso en su opinión, obstinado

Esta gente es más testaruda que una mula.

Práctica

Complete con una palabra de la lista.

> juramento   arrodillándose   testarudo
> alfiler   arguyó

1 Tienes que ser más razonable; no seas tan
_____ .

2 El hombre testarudo _____ toda la noche.

3 Ella se lastimó el dedo con el _____ dejado en el vestido.

4 El viejo estaba _____ con mucha dificultad delante del altar.

5 Siendo ella misma una persona honrada, la princesa tomó en serio el _____ del caballero.

La Camisa de Margarita

Ricardo Palma

I

Probable es que algunos de mis lectores hayan oído decir a las viejas de Lima, cuando quieren ponderar lo subido de precio de un artículo:—¡Qué! Si esto es más caro que la camisa de Margarita Pareja.

Margarita Pareja era (por los años de 1765) la hija más mimada de don Raimundo Pareja, caballero de Santiago y colector general del Callao.

La muchacha era una de esas limeñitas que, por su belleza, cautivan al mismo diablo y lo hacen persignarse. Lucía un par de ojos negros que eran como dos torpedos cargados de dinamita y que hacían explosión sobre el alma de los galanes limeños.

Llegó por entonces de España un arrogante mancebo llamado don Luis Alcázar. Tenía éste en Lima un tío aragonés, solterón y acaudalado.

Mientras le llegaba la ocasión de heredar al tío, vivía nuestro don Luis tan pelado como una rata. Hasta sus trapicheos eran al fiado y para pagar cuando mejorase de fortuna.

En la procesión de Santa Rosa conoció Alcázar a la linda Margarita. La muchacha le llenó el ojo y le flechó el corazón. Le echó flores, y aunque ella no le contestó ni sí ni no, dio a entender con sonrisitas y demás armas del arsenal femenino que el galán era plato muy de su gusto. La verdad es que se enamoraron hasta la raíz del pelo.

Como los amantes olvidan que existe la aritmética, creyó don Luis que para el logro de sus amores no sería obstáculo su presente pobreza, y fue al padre de Margarita, y le pidió la mano de su hija.

A don Raimundo no le cayó en gracia la petición, y cortésmente despidió al postulante, diciéndole que Margarita era aún muy niña para tomar marido; pues a pesar de sus diez y ocho mayos, todavía jugaba a las muñecas.

---

ponderar lo subido de precio exagerar el valor de algo

caballero de Santiago *knight of the order of St. James, patron saint of Spain*
el Callao puerto de Lima
persignarse hacer la señal de la cruz

mancebo joven
aragonés de Aragón, provincia del norte de España
acaudalado rico
tan pelado como una rata pobre *(poor as a church mouse)*
trapicheos *gambling debts*
le flechó el corazón *drove an arrow through his heart, stole his heart*

postulante el que pide algo

muñecas *dolls*

verdadera madre del ternero razón verdadera	Pero no era ésta la verdadera madre del ternero. La negativa nacía de que don Raimundo no quería ser suegro de un pobretón; y así hubo de decirlo en confianza a sus amigos, uno de los que fue con el chisme a don Honorato, el tío aragonés. Éste, que era más altivo que el Cid, trinó de rabia y dijo:

verdadera madre del ternero razón verdadera

pobretón una persona pobre e insignificante

altivo con cualidad de altivez

el Cid héroe nacional de España, Rodrigo Díaz de Vivar

trinó de rabia gritó enojado

Desairar Insultar

Muchos . . . pecho *Many would be tickled*

emparentar con llegar a ser pariente de

gallardo bien parecido

¿adónde . . . colectorcillo? *what does that petty tax collector think he's doing to me?*

gimoteó lloró

se le sublevaban se excitaban

acontecía sucedía

curanderas personas que hacen de médico sin serlo

encerrarla en el cajón enterrarla

se . . . posta se nos muere

desabrimiento disgusto

varee la plata tenga dinero

borrascoso *stormy*

rogaba *begged*

más . . . parra *the more obstinate the Aragonés became*

desahuciado sin esperanza

terciando en la cuestión interrumpiendo

ochavo moneda de poco valor

Pero no era ésta la verdadera madre del ternero. La negativa nacía de que don Raimundo no quería ser suegro de un pobretón; y así hubo de decirlo en confianza a sus amigos, uno de los que fue con el chisme a don Honorato, el tío aragonés. Éste, que era más altivo que el Cid, trinó de rabia y dijo:

—¡Cómo se entiende! ¡Desairar a mi sobrino! Muchos se darían con un canto en el pecho por emparentar con el muchacho, que no hay más gallardo en todo Lima. Pero, ¿adónde ha de ir conmigo ese colectorcillo?

Margarita gimoteó, y se arrancó el pelo, y si no amenazó con envenenarse, fue porque todavía no se habían inventado los fósforos.

Margarita perdía colores y carnes, se desmejoraba a vista de ojos, hablaba de meterse monja.

—¡O de Luis o de Dios!—gritaba cada vez que los nervios se le sublevaban, lo que acontecía una hora sí y otra también.

Alarmóse el caballero santiagués, llamó físicos y curanderas, y todos declararon que la única medicina salvadora no se vendía en la botica. O casarla con el varón de su gusto, o encerrarla en el cajón. Tal fue el *ultimatum* médico.

Don Raimundo (¡al fin, padre!) se encaminó como loco a casa de don Honorato y le dijo:

—Vengo a que consienta usted en que mañana mismo se case su sobrino con Margarita; porque, si no, la muchacha se nos va por la posta.

—No puede ser—contestó con desabrimiento el tío—. Mi sobrino es un pobretón, y lo que usted debe buscar para su hija es un hombre que varee la plata.

El diálogo fue borrascoso. Mientras más rogaba don Raimundo, más se subía el aragonés a la parra, y ya aquél iba a retirarse desahuciado cuando don Luis, terciando en la cuestión, dijo:

—Pero, tío, no es de cristianos que matemos a quien no tiene la culpa.

—¿Tú te das por satisfecho?

—De todo corazón, tío y señor.

—Pues bien, muchacho, consiento en darte gusto; pero con una condición, y es ésa: don Raimundo me ha de jurar que no regalará un ochavo a su hija ni la dejará un real en la herencia.

III

se entabló comenzó
litigio pelea

de dote *for her dowry*

lo encapillado la ropa que lleva

el ajuar de novia *trousseau*
acomoda acepta

san se acabó eso es todo

perjurare *I perjure myself*

maravedí moneda de poco valor
encajes *lace*
Flandes hoy Holanda y Bélgica
cadeneta de brillantes *small chain of diamonds*
morlacos pesos

a lo más valdría una onza *at the most was worth very little*
Convengamos Pongámonos de acuerdo
merecida *deserved*

Aquí se entabló un nuevo y más agitado litigio.

—Pero, hombre—arguyó don Raimundo—, mi hija tiene veinte mil duros de dote.

—Renunciamos a la dote. La nina vendrá a casa de su marido nada más que con lo encapillado.

—Concédame usted entonces obsequiarla los muebles y el ajuar de novia.

—Ni un alfiler. Si no acomoda, dejarlo y que se muera la chica.

—Sea usted razonable, don Honorato. Mi hija necesita llevar siquiera una camisa para reemplazar la puesta.

—Bien. Para que no me acuse de obstinado, consiento en que le regale la camisa de novia, y san se acabó.

Al día siguiente don Raimundo y don Honorato se dirigieron muy de mañana a San Francisco, arrodillándose para oir misa, y, según lo pactado, en el momento en que el sacerdote elevaba la Hostia divina, dijo el padre de Margarita:—Juro no dar a mi hija más que la camisa de novia. Así Dios me condene si perjurare.

Y don Raimundo Pareja cumplió su juramento; porque ni en vida ni en muerte dio después a su hija cosa que valiera un maravedí.

Los encajes de Flandes que adornaban la camisa de la novia costaron dos mil setecientos duros. El cordoncillo que ajustaba al cuello era una cadeneta de brillantes, valorizada en treinta mil morlacos.

Los recién casados hicieron creer al tío aragonés que la camisa a lo más valdría una onza, porque don Honorato era tan testarudo que, a saber lo cierto, habría forzado al sobrino a divorciarse.

Convengamos en que fue muy merecida la fama que alcanzó la camisa nupcial de Margarita Pareja.

PARA APLICAR

Comprensión   I

A   Conteste a las siguientes preguntas.

1   ¿Qué suelen decir las viejas de Lima al hablar de algo de mucho valor?

2   ¿Cuándo vivía Margarita?

3   ¿Cómo se sabe que el padre la quería mucho?

4   ¿Cómo eran los ojos de Margarita?

5   ¿Por qué vivía don Luis con su tío?

6 ¿Pagaba sus deudas a tiempo?

7 ¿Cuándo conoció a Margarita?

8 ¿Cómo le impresionó Margarita?

9 ¿Cómo respondió Margarita a las flores que él le echó a ella?

10 ¿Qué quiere decir Ricardo Palma con «los amantes olvidan que existe la aritmética»?

11 ¿Qué dijo don Raimundo cuando don Luis le pidió la mano de su hija?

B Escoja la respuesta apropiada.

1 ¿Qué quiere decir «Esto es más caro que la camisa de Margarita Pareja»?
  a. Las viejas de Lima son muy altas.
  b. Un artículo tiene un valor muy exagerado.
  c. Los precios en Lima son altos.

2 ¿Quién era Margarita Pareja?
  a. la hija más mimada del colector general
  b. el diablo en forma humana
  c. una limeña que se persignaba al ver al diablo

3 Describa a don Luis Alcázar.
  a. Era un galán limeño que hacía explosiones de dinamita.
  b. Era solterón y acaudalado.
  c. Era un español joven y altivo.

4 ¿Por qué vivía con su tío?
  a. Esperaba heredar la fortuna de ese pariente.
  b. Era sumamente pobre.
  c. Podía pagar la renta al fiado.

5 ¿Qué sucedió cuando se conocieron?
  a. El Alcázar se rindió.
  b. Se llenó el arsenal de armas.
  c. El galán le cayó en gracia a la limeña.

6 Después de darse cuenta de que estaban enamorados, ¿qué hizo don Luis?
  a. Creyó que Margarita era demasiado grande para jugar a las muñecas.
  b. Estudió la aritmética para lograr sus amores.
  c. Le dijo a don Raimundo Pareja que quería a su hija en matrimonio.

Comprensión   II

A Conteste a las siguientes preguntas.

1 ¿Cuál era la verdadera razón por la cual el padre no permitió que don Luis se casara con su hija?

2 ¿Qué indiscreción cometió don Raimundo?

3 ¿Cómo era el tío de don Luis?

4 ¿Cómo se puso el tío cuando supo el chisme pronunciado al amigo en confianza?

5 ¿Cómo se portó Margarita al tratar de persuadir a su padre?

6 Viendo a Margarita enferma y débil, ¿qué hizo el padre?

7 ¿Cuál fue el diagnóstico de los médicos?

8 Olvidándose de su orgullo y portándose como padre, ¿qué hizo don Raimundo?

9 ¿Qué razón le dio don Honorato para no consentir en la boda?

10 ¿Cómo fue resuelta la pelea entre los dos caballeros?

11 Al ceder a la petición, ¿qué condición impuso el tío?

B ¿Verdadero o falso?

1 Don Raimundo no quería ser pariente del joven sin dinero.

2 Pronunció esta confidencia a una persona poco discreta.

3 El tío era más arrogante que el Cid.

4 Al enterarse del chisme, el tío se echó a reir.

5 Margarita fue al gimnasio.

6 La pobre enamorada se desesperó e hizo cosas para dañarse.

7 Habló con una monja metida en su casa.

8 Constantemente tenía ataques de nervios.

9 Los doctores hicieron el diagnóstico de la enfermedad de la pobrecilla.

10 El padre le rogó al tío que permitiera que su sobrino se casara con su hija.

11 El tío consintió en seguida porque su sobrino era un pobretón.

12 Después de una discusión larga y desagradable el padre se declaró vencido.

Lima: patio colonial

13 Don Luis intervino en el diálogo.
14 El tío consintió que la boda tuviera lugar con una condición muy difícil.

Comprensión   III

A Conteste a las siguientes preguntas.

1 ¿Cuánto valía la dote de la hija?
2 Cite los regalos a los que el tío renunció.
3 ¿En qué consintió para que no lo acusaran de obstinado?
4 ¿Cuándo y dónde prometió don Raimundo que nunca daría nada a su hija?
5 ¿Cumplió con su palabra?
6 ¿Cómo era la camisa regalada a Margarita por su padre?
7 ¿Qué secreto tuvieron que ocultarle al tío?
8 ¿Qué habría hecho don Honorato si hubiera sabido el valor de la camisa?
9 ¿En qué podemos convenir?

B Complete las oraciones según la selección.

1 Se entabló otro litigio más _____.
2 Margarita tenía dote de _____.
3 La niña vendría a casa de su marido con _____.

4 El padre quería obsequiarle los ———— y el ————.

5 El padre insistía que Margarita necesitaba llevar por lo menos ————.

6 En la iglesia de San Francisco, arrodillado delante del altar, el padre dijo:—Así Dios ————.

7 Los ———— de Flandes que adornaban la camisa costaron ————.

8 El ———— era una cadeneta ————.

9 ———— hicieron creer al tío que la camisa valía poco.

10 Don Honorato era tan ———— que, al saber la verdad, habría forzado al ————.

Más Práctica

A Dé un sinónimo de las siguientes expresiones.

1	farmacia	6	joven
2	suceder	7	ponerse de rodillas
3	obsequiar	8	obstinado
4	estar de acuerdo	9	insultar
5	gustar	10	palabra de honor

B Reemplace las palabras en letra bastardilla con una de las palabras o expresiones de la lista.

al fiado, se desmejoraba, solterón, se envenenó, echó flores, un pobretón, mi suegro, el logro de, cautivó, chismes

1 El mancebo le *dijo cosas bonitas.*

2 Margarita *se empeoraba* más cada día.

3 Mi marido no ha llegado, pero *su padre* está.

4 El cazador *aprisionó* al pájaro en una jaula.

5 No te preocupes. Llévatelo *pagando más tarde.*

6 *Se mató* con un ácido fuerte.

7 No quieren oir *murmuraciones* de sus amigos.

8 Por tener la responsabilidad de cuidar a sus padres, él se quedó *sin casarse.*

9 Para *conseguir* su educación, estudió y trabajó.

10 Él es *tan pelado como una rata.*

Ejercicios Creativos

1 ¿Cuáles acciones de los personajes de la selección nos parecen hoy anticuadas y extrañas?

2 Imagínese que el tío sospechó que el padre de Margarita les estuviera regalando dinero, ropa etc. Escriba una escena entre los dos personajes en la cual el padre se defiende, y convence al tío de que no tiene razón. Estas palabras le pueden ayudar en su dramatización. Puede usar los verbos en cualquiera de sus formas conjugadas.

juramento	enfrentarse con
divorciarse	acaudalado
perjurarse	pobretón
camisa de novia	equivocado

El Futuro y el Condicional

Para formar el futuro y el condicional de los verbos regulares, se agregan las apropiadas terminaciones al infinitivo. Las terminaciones del futuro son *é, ás, á, emos, éis, án.* Las terminaciones del condicional son *ía, ías, ía, íamos, íais, ían.*

El Futuro

mirar	comer	vivir
miraré	comeré	viviré
mirarás	comerás	vivirás
mirará	comerá	vivirá
miraremos	comeremos	viviremos
miraréis	comeréis	viviréis
mirarán	comerán	vivirán

El Condicional

mirar	comer	vivir
miraría	comería	viviría
mirarías	comerías	vivirías
miraría	comería	viviría
miraríamos	comeríamos	viviríamos
miraríais	comeríais	viviríais
mirarían	comerían	vivirían

Los siguientes verbos tienen una raíz irregular en el futuro y en el condicional.

infinitivo	raíz	futuro	condicional
caber	cabr-	cabré	cabría
decir	dir-	diré	diría
haber	habr-	habré	habría
hacer	har-	haré	haría
poder	podr-	podré	podría
poner	pondr-	pondré	pondría
querer	querr-	querré	querría
saber	sabr-	sabré	sabría
salir	saldr-	saldré	saldría
tener	tendr-	tendré	tendría
valer	valdr-	valdré	valdría
venir	vendr-	vendré	vendría

Se emplea el futuro para expresar una acción que tendrá lugar en el futuro.

Comerán aquí mañana.
Veremos a los López la semana que viene.

Se emplea el condicional para expresar una condición basada en algo expresado o entendido.

Yo iría contigo pero no tengo el tiempo.
Yo le hablaría para aclarar el asunto.

A Sustituyan según el modelo.

El curaca les contará lo que pasó.
la mensajera/
La mensajera les contará lo que pasó

1 El curaca les contará lo que pasó.
las enfermeras/nosotros/yo/un sacerdote/tú/

2 Todos leerán la leyenda de la urna sagrada.
la clase/yo/la forastera/tú/el jefe y yo/

3 Ima arrojará la urna al lago.
tú y tus amigos/yo/la guerrera/sólo tú/ nosotros/

B Sigan el modelo.

> *Voy a abrir la puerta.*
> *Abriré la puerta.*

1 Voy a cruzar la selva.
2 Voy a evitar el problema.
3 Voy a tener que irme.
4 Vas a ver el fenómeno del lago.
5 Vas a estar inquieta.
6 Vas a hacer una fortuna.
7 Ud. va a salir muy pronto.
8 Él va a disimular su inquietud.
9 Ella va a arrojar la urna al lago.
10 Vamos a perder tiempo buscándolo.
11 Vamos a recibir las primeras noticias.
12 Vamos a guiar a los forasteros.
13 Van a tardar en llegar.
14 Van a valer más en el futuro.
15 Van a querer ir.

C Reemplacen el verbo con la forma apropiada del futuro de los infinitivos indicados.

1 Será muy poco.
   saber/tener/decir/
2 El enemigo comunicará su susto al cura.
   contar/decir/escribir/leer/
3 Yo buscaré el traje recién comprado.
   ponerse/devolver/quitarse/recibir/
4 Los invasores no estarán aquí.
   caber/venir/salir de/ocultarse/
5 La policía no mandará castigarlo.
   poder/querer/permitir/prometer/
6 Tú regresarás muy pronto.
   salir/volver/venir/rendirse/
7 Nosotros llegaremos temprano.
   estar/ir/venir/huir/

D Contesten a las siguientes preguntas según el modelo.

> *¿Qué verás allí?*
> *Veré una carta emocionante.*

1 ¿Qué leerás allí?
2 ¿Qué buscarás allí?
3 ¿Qué recibirás allí?
4 ¿Qué dejarás allí?
5 ¿Qué escribirás allí?
6 ¿Qué llevarás allí?
7 ¿Qué pondrás allí?

E Contesten a las siguientes preguntas según la indicación.

> *¿Cuándo vendrán Uds.?* mañana
> *Vendremos mañana.*

1 ¿Cuándo sabrán Uds. quién lo hizo?
   durante la gran fiesta
2 ¿Cuándo podrán Uds. volar a la Argentina? *muy pronto*
3 ¿Cuándo tendrán Uds. que devolverle el regalo? *la semana que viene*
4 ¿Cuánto le dirán Uds. al juez? *muy poco*
5 ¿Qué harán Uds. con la guitarra? *la tocaremos*
6 ¿Cuándo saldrán Uds. para la selva?
   mañana si no llueve

F Sustituyan según el modelo.

> *No irían sin la carta.*
> *yo/*
> *No iría sin la carta.*

1 No iría sin la carta.
   los vecinos/tú/la abogada/Martín y yo/
   el cura/
2 María no haría eso sin razón.
   yo/el rey/tú/los hombres asustados/
   nosotras/

3 ¿Qué diría el pobre en tal caso?
tú/el cartero/yo/el guerrero atrevido/
nosotros/

4 La viejecilla sabría quién lo mató.
tú/tú y yo/las vecinas/yo/el rey/

G Sigan el modelo.

> *Dice que buscará a la asesina.*
> *Dijo que buscaría a la asesina.*

1 Promete que la castigará.
2 Escribe que vendrán durante la gran fiesta.
3 Cree que le devolverá la urna.
4 La directora dice que tendrás que ayudarle.
5 Las dos lamentan que no serán ricas.
6 El anciano cree que morirá.
7 El jefe dice que los pájaros traerán mala suerte.

8 Yo digo que todos no cabremos en ese cochecito.
9 Yo juro que no pondremos la urna en manos de otros.
10 Tú prometes que dirás la verdad.

H Sigan el modelo.

> *Iba a buscar al asesino.*
> *Buscaría al asesino.*

1 Iba a pagarle al aragonés.
2 Iba a meter sus ideas en la conversación.
3 Ibas a abrir la puerta de la casa.
4 Íbamos a ver a la tía arrogante.
5 Íbamos a regalarle una muñeca al niño.
6 Iban a rezar en la iglesia.
7 Iban a salir después de oir misa.

El Futuro y el Condicional de Probabilidad

Se puede expresar una probabilidad o una conjetura relacionada con el presente por medio del futuro.

> Ahora estarán en casa. → Probablemente están en casa.
> ¿Quién será ella? → ¿Quién puede ser ella?

Si la probabilidad o la conjetura está relacionada con el pasado, se usa el condicional.

> Ayer estarían en casa. → Ayer probablemente estuvieron en casa.
> ¿Quién sería ella? → Me pregunto quién era ella.

I Sigan el modelo.

> *Probablemente están con la reina.*
> *Estarán con la reina.*

1 Probablemente es una embajadora extranjera.
2 Probablemente leen las leyendas pintorescas.
3 Probablemente lucen vestidos elegantes.
4 Probablemente se divierten en sus fiestas.
5 Probablemente los criados juegan en el campo.

J Sigan el modelo.

> *Probablemente estaban en casa.*
> *Estarían en casa.*

1 Probablemente era tarde cuando la descubrieron.
2 Probablemente tenías ganas de confesar la verdad.
3 Probablemente hacían daño a la cosecha.
4 Probablemente pelearon debajo de la ventana.
5 Probablemente hicieron todo lo necesario.
6 Probablemente se convertía en joven serio y honrado.
7 Probablemente encendieron las luces en la sala.

K Sigan el modelo.

> *Me pregunto si es testaruda.*
> *¿Será testaruda?*

1 Me pregunto si la policía sabe quién mató a la joven.
2 Me pregunto si rezan todavía en esa iglesia.
3 Me pregunto si muere víctima de su justicia cruel.
4 Me pregunto si regala otras riquezas a su hija.
5 Me pregunto si puede ver claramente en la oscuridad.
6 Me pregunto si logran decepcionar al tío arrogante.
7 Me pregunto si consiente en que se casen.

L Sigan el modelo.

> *Me pregunto si me dijo la verdad.*
> *¿Me diría la verdad?*

1 Me pregunto si fue posible regalarle el vestido.
2 Me pregunto si le dijo cuánto valía la camisa.
3 Me pregunto si engañó al tío con su regalo tan costoso.
4 Me pregunto si anunciaban los pájaros una calamidad.
5 Me pregunto si se conocieron en la procesión.
6 Me pregunto si tenía miedo de declarar el nombre del culpable.
7 Me pregunto si salieron en busca de médicos y curanderas.

A Personal

Cuando una persona específica sirve de complemento directo del verbo, se usa una *a* entre el verbo y el complemento. Esta *a* se llama la *a personal*.

M Sustituyan según el modelo.

> *¿Vio tu madre el palacio?*
> *Carlos/*
> *¿Vio tu madre a Carlos?*

1 ¿Vio tu madre a Carlos?
el naranjo/el peruano/la mujer atrevida/el candil/los galanes/

2 ¿Conoce Rodolfo a Mari?
esta calle/nuestro primo/el nuevo proyecto/los recién casados/el tío aragonés/

3 ¿Pagó Juana al sastre?
la cuenta/los campesinos/Lorenzo/la nota/las autoridades/

N Sigan los modelos.

> *¿Elena? No la conozco.*
> *No conozco a Elena.*
>
> *¿La calle Colón?*
> *No conozco la calle Colón.*

1 ¿El tío aragonés? No lo conozco.
2 ¿El Diccionario Super? No lo conozco.
3 ¿La ley de impuestos? No la respetamos.
4 ¿El asesino? No lo respetamos.
5 ¿Los músicos populares? Siempre los escuchamos.
6 ¿Los chistes? Siempre los escuchamos.
7 ¿La camisa de la novia? Casi no la veo.
8 ¿La novia joven? Casi no la veo.
9 ¿Margarita de Pareja? Él la quiere mucho.
10 ¿La camisa nueva? Él la usa mucho.

Sentimientos y Pasiones

Adonde el corazón se inclina, el pie camina.

PARA PREPARAR LA ESCENA

Sea el tema principal o no, el sentimiento se expresa en cada trozo literario. No se encuentra la pasión, que es una emoción más profunda, con tanta frecuencia. Sin embargo, muchas obras incluyen el sentimiento y la pasión, y tales obras producen un efecto emocionante y, a veces, inolvidable en el lector.

Los españoles, o sus descendientes, muestran sus emociones fácilmente y sin vergüenza. Por lo general, no dejan de mostrar cómo les afectan sentimientos tales como el amor familial, la alegría o tristeza, o el temor. O pasiones tales como el amor romántico, el odio, el deseo de vengarse, la ira, los celos o el valor.

Para comprender mejor el carácter español, es preciso ver cómo éstos y otros sentimientos y pasiones afectan a la gente hispana—la raza que ha producido guerreros valientes, poetas tiernos y artistas vibrantes.

El Abanico

Vicente Riva Palacio

PARA PRESENTAR LA LECTURA

Vicente Riva Palacio, mexicano (1832–1896), fue periodista, político, general, novelista y, sobre todo, historiador. Pasó mucho tiempo en los archivos estudiando la historia y por eso, conocía muy bien la época colonial. Entrelazados en sus tradiciones y leyendas de aquel entonces hay una ironía ligera y cierto sentido de humor característicos de sus obras.

El abanico es parte integrante de la dama tradicional española. Lo usaba no sólo para abanicarse y como adorno, sino para puntuar su conversación y para coquetear. Sencillamente, la española hablaba con su abanico. Había un verdadero lenguaje del abanico.

Entre las costumbres traídas al Nuevo Mundo por los colonizadores españoles, el uso del abanico es una costumbre que todavía existe. En el cuento que sigue, Riva Palacio nos habla del papel importante que desempeñó un abanico en la selección de una esposa.

PARA APRENDER VOCABULARIO

Palabras Clave   I

1 **abanico**   instrumento manual para mover el aire
   La niña usaba el abanico para refrescarse en el verano.

2 **aborrecer**   odiar, detestar
   Llegará a aborrecer el invierno aquí porque hace mucho frío.

3 **capaz**   que puede hacer una cosa, que tiene un talento, instrucción o fuerza de hacer algo
   Mario no es capaz de hablar delante del público.

4 **daba (dar) con**   encontraba
   Cuando iba de compras, el señor Morales daba con los mismos compañeros.

Dama con abanico (Velázquez)

5 **relámpago**   rayo de luz producido por la electricidad durante una tempestad

Mucha gente tiene miedo de los relámpagos.

6 **suponer**   creer, anticipar *(to suppose)*

Suponer algo no es la misma cosa que saberlo.

7 **tienes (tener) ganas**   tienes deseos

El viejo enfermo no tiene ganas de comer.

Práctica

Complete con una palabra de la lista.

suponer	tengo ganas	daba con
capaz	aborrecer	con
abanicos		relámpago

1 La noticia de las bodas corrió por la ciudad como un _____.

2 ¿Qué haría ella si llegara a _____ que todo iba a cambiar?

3 Es fácil _____ a una persona egoísta.

4 Claudia es _____ de dirigir el departamento de inglés.

5 No voy al baile. No _____ de salir esta noche.

6 En aquella época los salones estaban llenos de damas con _____.

7 El niño buscaba y buscaba pero nunca _____ un gatito tan encantador como aquél.

Palabras Clave   II

1 **embajada**   casa en que reside el embajador

Los terroristas pusieron una bomba en la embajada.

EL ABANICO   141

2 **exige (exigir)** obliga
El profesor exige que estudiemos mucho.

3 **mundanal** mundano, relativo o per-
teneciente al mundo
Él se retiró del ruido mundanal.

4 **soberbia** arrogante, excesivamente orgullosa
Me enojó con su actitud soberbia.

5 **vacilaría (vacilar)** dudaría, estaría indeciso
De tanto vacilar se quedó sin hacer nada.

Práctica

Complete con una palabra de la lista.

exige   soberbio   embajada
mundanal   vacilaría

1 La _____ de los Estados Unidos está en
aquella avenida.
2 De acuerdo. Juan es guapo, pero es frío y
_____.
3 El patrón _____ que yo llegue a tiempo.
4 María nunca _____; por eso la escogieron
para tomar la decisión.
5 A causa de su experiencia _____, mi
amiga siempre podía acompañar sus dis-
cursos con anécdotas.

Palabras Clave   III

1 **apuestos** guapos, bien parecidos
Varios apuestos caballeros asistían a la
tertulia del Alcalde Mayor.

2 **bandeja** platillo que sirve para diversos
usos
La bandeja llena de refrescos está sobre
la mesa.

3 **desplegó (desplegar – ie)** desdobló lo
que estaba doblado, abrió
El niño desplegó el abanico y sin saberlo,
lo rompió.

4 **estorbando (estorbar)** poniendo obstáculo
Estorbando el paso hacia la casa había
muchos automóviles.

5 **rasgó (rasgar)** desgarró, rompió una
cosa de tela o papel
El chico rasgó sus pantalones.

6 **sudando (sudar)** arrojando líquido por
los poros de la piel, a causa del calor, el
miedo o la excitación
El ladrón estaba sudando de terror.

7 **tropezó (tropezar – ie)** chocó con, por
poco cayó *(tripped, stumbled)*
Bajando la escalera, el niño tropezó.

Práctica

Complete con una palabra de la lista.

bandeja   estorbando   tropezó
rasgó   sudando   desplegó
apuestos

1 No vamos a estacionar el auto aquí _____
el paso a los demás.
2 La señora _____ el abanico cuando
cerraron las ventanas.
3 Durante estos días calurosos todos estamos
_____ constantemente.
4 El anciano _____ en la nieve; por suerte
no le pasó nada serio.
5 La niña _____ los papeles porque estaba
enojada.
6 El criado servía los platos de una _____.
7 El salón estaba lleno de _____ caballeros
y damas.

El Abanico

Vicente Riva Palacio

I

El Marqués estaba resuelto a casarse, y había comunicado aquella noticia a sus amigos. La noticia corrió con la velocidad del relámpago por toda la alta sociedad como toque de alarma a todas las madres que tenían hijas **casaderas**, y a todas las chicas que estaban en condiciones y con deseos de contraer matrimonio, que no eran pocas.

Porque, eso sí, el Marqués era **un gran partido**, como se decía entre la gente de mundo. Tenía treinta y nueve años, un gran título, mucho dinero, era muy guapo y estaba cansado de correr el mundo, **haciendo siempre el primer papel** entre los hombres de su edad dentro y fuera del país.

Pero se había cansado de aquella vida de disipación. Algunos hilos de plata comenzaban a aparecer en su negra barba y entre su **sedosa cabellera**; y como era hombre de buena inteligencia y no de escasa lectura, determinó **sentar sus reales** definitivamente, buscando una mujer como él la soñaba para darle su nombre y **partir** con ella las penas o las alegrías del hogar en los muchos años que estaba determinado a vivir todavía sobre la tierra.

Con la noticia de aquella resolución no le faltaron seducciones ni de maternal cariño ni de románticas o alegres bellezas; pero él no daba todavía con su ideal, y pasaban los días, y las semanas y los meses, sin haber hecho la elección.

—Pero, hombre—le decían sus amigos—, ¿hasta cuándo no vas a decidirte?

—Es que no encuentro todavía la mujer que busco.

—Será porque tienes pocas ganas de casarte que muchachas sobran. ¿No es muy guapa la Condesita de Mina de Oro?

—Se ocupa demasiado de sus joyas y de sus trajes; cuidará más de un collar de perlas que de su marido, y será capaz de olvidar a su hijo por un traje de la casa de Worth.

casaderas *eligible for marriage*

un gran partido *a good "catch"*

haciendo siempre el primer papel *always playing the leading role*

sedosa cabellera *silky hair*
sentar sus reales *to settle down*

partir *to share*

—¿Y la Baronesa del Iris?

—Muy guapa y muy buena; es una figura escultórica, pero lo sabe demasiado; el matrimonio sería para ella el peligro de perder su belleza, y llegaría a aborrecer a su marido si llegaba a suponer que su nuevo estado marchitaba su hermosura.

marchitaba *was wilting*

II

—¿Y la Duquesa de Luz Clara?

—Soberbia belleza; pero sólo piensa en divertirse; me dejaría moribundo en la casa por no perder una función del Real, y no vacilaría en abandonar a su hijo enfermo toda una noche por asistir al baile de una embajada.

por no perder una función del Real *in order not to miss a performance at the Opera House*

—¿Y la Marquesa de Cumbre-Nevada, no es guapísima y un modelo de virtud?

—Ciertamente; pero es más religiosa de lo que un marido necesita: ningún cuidado, ninguna pena, ninguna enfermedad de la familia le impediría pasarse toda la mañana en la iglesia, y no vacilaría entre un sermón de cuaresma y la alcobita de su hijo.

sermón de cuaresma *Lenten sermon*

—Vamos; tú quieres una mujer imposible.

—No, nada de imposible; ya veréis cómo la encuentro, aunque no sea una completa belleza; porque la hermosura para el matrimonio no es más que el aperitivo para el almuerzo; la busca sólo el que no lleva apetito, que quien tiene hambre no necesita aperitivos, y el que quiere casarse no exige el atractivo de la completa hermosura.

*   *   *

Tenía el Marqués como un axioma, fruto de sus lecturas y de su mundanal experiencia, que a los hombres, y quien dice a los hombres también dice a las mujeres, no debe medírseles para formar juicio acerca de ellos por las grandes acciones, sino por las acciones insignificantes y familiares; porque los grandes hechos, como tienen siempre muchos testigos presentes o de referencia, son resultado más del cálculo que de las propias inspiraciones, y no traducen con fidelidad las dotes del corazón o del cerebro; al paso que las acciones insignificantes hijas son del espontáneo movimiento de la inteligencia y de los sentimientos, y forman ese botón que, como dice el refrán antiguo, basta para servir de muestra.

medírseles *measure them*

no traducen . . . del cerebro *don't faithfully convey what is in the heart or mind*
al paso que *mientras que*
hijas son *are the result*
ese botón . . . de muestra *that small bit of proof that . . . suffices as an example*

*   *   *

III

Una noche se daba un gran baile en la Embajada de Inglaterra. Los salones estaban literalmente cuajados de hermosas damas y apuestos caballeros, todos flor y nata de las clases más aristocráticas de la sociedad. El Marqués estaba en el comedor, adonde había llevado a la joven Condesita de Valle de Oro, una muchacha de veinte años, inteligente, simpática y distinguida, pero que no llamaba, ni con mucho, la atención por su belleza, ni era una de esas hermosuras cuyo nombre viene a la memoria cada vez que se emprende conversación acerca de mujeres encantadoras.

La joven Condesa era huérfana de madre, y vivía sola con su padre, noble caballero, estimado por todos cuantos le conocían.

La Condesita, después de tomar una taza de té, conversaba con algunas amigas antes de volver a los salones.

—Pero, ¿cómo no estuviste anoche en el Real? Cantaron admirablemente el *Tannhauser*—le decía una de ellas.

—Pues mira: me quedé vestida, porque tenía deseos, muchos deseos, de oir el *Tannhauser*; es una ópera que me encanta.

—¿Y qué pasó?

—Pues que ya tenía el abrigo puesto, cuando la doncella me avisó que Leonor estaba muy grave. Entré a verla, y ya no me atreví a separarme de su lado.

—Y esa Leonor—dijo el Marqués terciando en la conversación—, ¿es alguna señora de la familia de Ud.?

—Casi, Marqués; es el aya que tuvo mi mamá; y como nunca se ha separado de nosotros y me ha querido tanto, yo la veo como de mi familia.

—¡Qué abanico tan precioso traes!—dijo a la Condesita una de las jóvenes que hablaba con ella.

—No me digas, que estoy encantada con él y lo cuido como a las niñas de mis ojos; es un regalo que me hizo mi padre el día de mi santo, y son un primor la pintura y las varillas y todo él; me lo compró en París.

—A ver, a ver—dijeron todas, y se agruparon en derredor de la Condesita, que, con una especie de infantil satisfacción, desplegó a sus ojos el abanico, que realmente era una maravilla del arte.

En este momento, uno de los criados que penosamente cruzaba entre las señoras llevando en las manos una enorme bandeja con helados, tropezó, vaciló y, sin poderse valer, vino a chocar contra el abanico, abierto en aquellos momentos, haciéndolo pedazos. Crujieron las varillas, rasgóse en pedazos la tela y

---

poco faltó para que los fragmentos hirieran la mano de la Condesita.

—¡Qué bruto!—dijo una señora mayor.

—¡Qué animal tan grande!—exclamó un caballero.

—¡Parece que no tiene ojos!—dijo una chiquilla.

Y el pobre criado, rojo de vergüenza y sudando de pena, podía apenas balbucir una disculpa inteligible.

—No se apure Ud., no se mortifique—dijo la Condesita con la mayor tranquilidad—; no tiene Ud. la culpa; nosotras, que estamos aquí estorbando el paso.

Y reuniendo con la mano izquierda los restos del abanico, tomó con la derecha el brazo del Marqués, diciéndole con la mayor naturalidad:

—Están tocando un vals, y yo lo tengo comprometido con Ud.; ¿me lleva Ud. al salón de baile?

—Sí, Condesa; pero no bailaré con Ud. este vals.

—¿Por qué?

—Porque en este momento voy a buscar a su padre para decirle que mañana iré a pedirle a Ud. por esposa, y dentro de ocho días, tiempo suficiente para que Uds. se informen, iré a saber la resolución.

—Pero, Marqués—dijo la Condesita trémula—, ¿es esto puñalada de pícaro?

—No, señora; será cuando más, una estocada de caballero.

*   *   *

Tres meses después se celebraban aquellas bodas; y en una rica moldura bajo cristal, se ostentaba en uno de los salones del palacio de los nuevos desposados el abanico roto.

podía apenas balbucir una disculpa *could scarcely stammer out an apology*
No se apure No se preocupe

comprometido *promised*

puñalada de pícaro *a roguish joke*

estocada de caballero *a gentleman's word*
bodas ceremonia del matrimonio
moldura *showcase*
desposados recién casados

PARA APLICAR

Comprensión   I

A   Conteste a las siguientes preguntas.

1   ¿Quién es el personaje principal de este cuento?

2   ¿Qué había resuelto?

3   ¿Cómo recibió esta noticia la alta sociedad?

4   ¿Por qué era el Marqués un gran partido?

5   Describa al Marqués.

6   ¿Por qué no había hecho la elección el Marqués?

7   ¿Quiénes eran las señoritas elegibles?

8   ¿Cómo era la Condesita de Mina de Oro?

9   ¿Cómo era la Baronesa del Iris?

B Termine las oraciones según la selección.

1 El personaje principal es
2 Él estaba resuelto a
3 La noticia corrió
4 Muchas señoritas querían
5 El Marqués era un
6 El Marqués tenía
7 Quería casarse porque estaba cansado de
8 Quería compartir con su esposa
9 Pasaban los días, las semanas y los meses sin
10 No se casó porque no
11 La Condesita de Mina de Oro es guapa pero
12 Para la Baronesa de Iris el matrimonio

Comprensión   II

A Conteste a las siguientes preguntas.

1 ¿Cómo era la Duquesa de Luz Clara?
2 ¿Cómo era la Marquesa de Cumbre-Nevada?
3 ¿Cómo era la mujer ideal que buscaba el Marqués?
4 ¿Qué dijo el Marqués de la hermosura para el matrimonio?
5 Según el axioma del Marqués, ¿cómo se debe medir a la gente?
6 ¿Dónde hubo un gran baile una noche?
7 ¿Cómo estaban los salones?
8 ¿Cómo era la joven Condesita de Valle de Oro?

B ¿Verdadero o falso?

1 La Duquesa de Luz Clara se dedicaría a cuidar de sus hijos.
2 Ella no vacilaría en abandonar sus fiestas y diversiones.
3 La Marquesa de Cumbre-Nevada es virtuosa.
4 El Marqués necesita religión y entra a oir el sermón de cuaresma.
5 Él quiere un aperitivo antes del almuerzo.
6 Cree que la belleza es agradable, pero él exige más que la belleza física.

7 El Marqués mide a todos por las acciones pequeñas.
8 Las acciones grandes no son sinceras y naturales, según el Marqués.
9 En el trato familiar se puede observar más el carácter de una persona.

Comprensión   III

A Conteste a las siguientes preguntas.

1 ¿Quién era Leonor?
2 ¿Qué quiere decir «terciando en la conversación»?
3 ¿Cómo era el abanico que llevaba la Condesita?
4 ¿Quién se lo había regalado?
5 ¿Qué hizo la Condesita para mejor mostrar el abanico?
6 ¿Quién cruzó entre las señoras?
7 ¿Qué pasó?
8 ¿Qué le pasó al abanico?
9 ¿Cómo reaccionaron las personas que presenciaron el accidente?
10 ¿Cómo reaccionó la Condesita?
11 ¿Qué tocaba la orquesta en aquel momento?
12 ¿Por qué no lo bailó el Marqués?
13 ¿Dónde encontramos el abanico al final?

B Escoja la respuesta apropiada.

1 ¿Por qué no había ido la Condesita a la ópera la noche anterior?
   a. Se había quedado sin vestido.
   b. No quería separarse del aya.
   c. No tenía ganas de oir *Tannhauser*.
2 ¿Qué supo el Marqués de la conversación entre la Condesita y sus amigas?
   a. La Condesa de Valle de Oro era fiel y cariñosa.
   b. Terciar en la conversación es grave.
   c. La Condesa de Valle de Oro se parece a la Duquesa de Luz Clara.

3 ¿Cómo se portó la Condesa de Valle de Oro cuando un criado hizo pedazos al abanico?
   a. Le gritó:—¿Por qué no usa los ojos?
   b. Con serenidad dijo:—No se preocupe.
   c. Comenzó a sudar y balbucir.

4 ¿Por qué no bailó el Marqués con ella?
   a. Tenía otro compromiso.
   b. No sabía bailar el vals.
   c. Fue a anunciar a su padre que había encontrado a la mujer que buscaba.

5 ¿Qué creía la Condesita?
   a. Que él se burlaba de ella.
   b. Que él era un caballero.
   c. Que él arreglaría el abanico.

Más Práctica

A Dé un sinónimo de las palabras en letra bastardilla.

1 No lo debes *odiar* tanto.
2 Muchos caballeros *elegantes* asistieron a la fiesta.
3 Los *recién casados* vinieron a visitarnos.
4 Es mejor no *estar indeciso*.
5 Asistimos *al casamiento* del Marqués.
6 Es *una perfección*.
7 Fue una experiencia *mundana*.

B Reemplace el verbo *encontrar* con *dar con*.

1 No pudo encontrar novia.
2 El otro día encontró a un amigo viejo.
3 Algún día encontrará su ideal.

Ejercicios Creativos

1 Prepare una lista de las cualidades que Ud. busca en un esposo o en una esposa. ¿Cómo las puede medir?

2 Busque información para una discusión sobre las costumbres del noviazgo en los Estados Unidos y en los países de habla española. Sugerencias: la dueña, la serenata, pelando la pava.

3 Tradicionalmente había ciertas expresiones y sentimientos que se podían comunicar con el abanico, es decir, la posición del abanico comunicaba ciertas ideas tales como: pienso en ti, quiero hablarte, te quiero mucho, dame un beso, tengo vergüenza, no hay oportunidad, alguien viene, etc. Prepare una lista de expresiones que se pueden comunicar haciendo gestos pero sin hablar.

"Three Musicians" *por Pablo Picasso* (Philadelphia Museum of Art)

"The Gourmet" *por Pablo Picasso*
(National Gallery of Art, Washington, D.C., Chester Dale Collection)

"Apparition of a Face and Fruit Dish on a Beach" *por Salvador Dalí*
(Wordsworth-Atheneum, Hartford, Connecticut)

"Still Life with Siphon" *por Juan Gris* (Wuppertal City Art Museum)

La Risa por Rufino Tamayo (Private Collection)

"The Bullfight" por Francisco de Goya (The Metropolitan Museum of Art, Wolfe Fund, 1922)

"Starfish" *por Roberto Montenegro* (Private Collection)

Paisaje por David Alfaro Siqueiros (Private Collection)

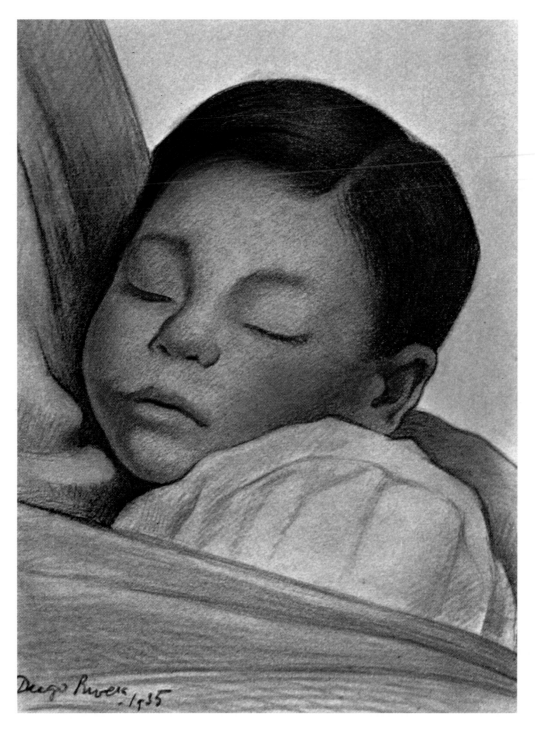

"Sleeping Baby" *por Diego Rivera* (Private Collection)

"A City on a Rock" por Francisco de Goya (The Metropolitan Museum of Art, Bequest of Mrs. H. O. Havemeyer, 1929, The H. O. Havemeyer Collection)

"Cardinal Don Fernando Niño de Guevara" *por El Greco* [*Domenicos Theotocopoulos*] (The Metropolitan Museum of Art, Bequest of Mrs. H. O. Havemeyer, 1929, The H. O. Havemeyer Collection)

"View of Toledo" *por El Greco* [*Domenicos Theotocopoulos*] (The Metropolitan Museum of Art, Bequest of Mrs. H. O. Havemeyer, 1929, The H. O. Havemeyer Collection)

Albarracín por Ignacio Zuloaga (The Hispanic Society of America)

"Sevilla, Opening Salute at a Bullfight" *por Joaquín Sorolla y Bastida*
(The Hispanic Society of America)

"Portrait of a Little Girl" *por Diego Rodríguez de Silva y Velázquez*
(The Hispanic Society of America)

"The Battle with the Moors at Jerez" *por Francisco de Zurbarán*
(The Metropolitan Museum of Art, Kretschmar Fund, 1920)

El Padre

Olegario Lazo Baeza

PARA PRESENTAR LA LECTURA

El lugar: un cuartel de campaña

Los personajes: un padre viejo y su hijo, teniente del ejército; varios soldados del cuartel

La situación: una visita al cuartel por parte del padre quien quiere ver a su hijo

El ambiente: la anticipación

Está preparada la escena para estrenar un drama emocionante. ¡Imagínese los sentimientos de un anciano paisano cuyo corazón está para romperse de amor paternal, de orgullo en los acontecimientos de su hijo, de la alegría de una ocasión especial! Hay pocos sentimientos que puedan compararse con la conmovedora emoción que siente un padre hacia su hijo. Sólo lo iguala el amor de un hijo agradecido hacia el que lo ha criado.

El tema fundamental en las obras de Olegario Lazo Baeza es la vida militar. No toma de ésta el aspecto heroico sino que prefiere entregar al lector los detalles cotidianos de la vida de cuartel y los valores humanos y personales de los soldados allí destacados.

PARA APRENDER VOCABULARIO

Palabras Clave   I

1 **alcance**   distancia a que llega el brazo
El cocinero colocó el plato a su alcance.

2 **gallina**   ave que pone huevos; polla madura
Una gallina bien gorda servirá de cena esta noche.

3 **registrando (registrar)** examinando con detención una cosa

El oficial está registrando el equipaje en la aduana.

4 **repuso (reponer)** volvió a poner, contestó de nuevo

El alumno le repuso al profesor de una manera insolente.

5 **salto** acto de levantarse del suelo con esfuerzo o arrojarse de un lugar a otro

La niña dio un salto largo y llegó al otro lado de la alfombra.

6 **soltó (soltar – ue) la risa** se echó a reir

Cuando oyó el chiste, soltó la risa.

Práctica

Complete con una palabra de la lista.

salto	registrando	gallina
alcance	repuso	soltó

1 Esa señora _____ el coche es la inspectora.
2 Al dar un _____, se cayó en el agua.
3 ¿Cuántos huevos puso la _____ esta semana?
4 No le puedo pasar la sal; no está a mi _____.
5 _____ una risa que despertó a todos.
6 ¿Qué le _____ a su pregunta?

Palabras Clave   II

1 **agregó (agregar)** añadió, dijo más

Creíamos que había terminado de hablar, pero agregó otras ideas suyas.

2 **alzó (alzar)** subió, levantó

No alzó la bandera a causa de la lluvia.

3 **cazuela** sopa de gallina entera con vegetales

Roberto no hace cazuela de gallina hoy porque hace mucho calor.

4 **mareado** enfermo de cabeza y estómago causado por el movimiento, los nervios, las emociones, etc.

El nuevo marinero se sintió mareado en alta mar.

5 **rascándose (rascarse)** rayándose con las uñas

El perro estaba rascándose la cabeza con la pata.

6 **soportar** tolerar

Una persona insegura no puede soportar la crítica.

7 **tosió (toser)** tuvo tos *(coughed)*

Después de fumar, tosió violentamente.

Práctica

Complete con una palabra de la lista.

tosió	cazuela	agregó
rascándose	alzó	mareado
soportar		

1 La estudiante quería contestar y _____ la mano.
2 Para preparar esa _____ se necesita gallina, cebollas, papas, sal y pimienta.
3 A este plato mi cocinera _____ un poco de azúcar.
4 Los malos olores del motor le tienen _____.
5 El pobre niño enfermo _____ toda la noche.
6 Es duro _____ las burlas de sus compañeros.
7 Sara andaba _____ todo el día porque un mosquito le picó.

Palabras Clave   III

1 **arrastrando (arrastrar)** tirando una persona o cosa por el suelo *(dragging)*

Ese niño no camina bien, está arrastrando el pie izquierdo.

Amantes (Picasso)

2 **desengaño**   decepción, descubrimiento de un engaño

Fue difícil mostrarse sereno después del desengaño de su querido hijo.

3 **deslumbrado (deslumbrar)**   ciego temporalmente por una luz muy viva, muy afectado por un sentimiento

Estaba deslumbrado por la luz de la explosión.

4 **desviando (desviar)**   saliendo de su dirección   (detouring, diverting)

Debido a la construcción en la carretera, nosotros nos estamos desviando por este camino.

5 **estiraba (estirar)**   alargaba una cosa extendiéndola   (stretched)

La señora Gómez estiraba las piernas cansadas después de tanto manejar.

6 **secamente**   de manera seria o brusca

El desinteresado contestó a mis preguntas secamente.

Práctica

Complete con una palabra de la lista.

secamente	*estiraban*	*deslumbrado*
desviándonos	*arrastrando*	*desengaño*

1 Se sintió triste con el _____ de su mejor amigo.

2 Para impedir que el público entrara, los dueños _____ un cordón sobre el pasillo.

3 La chiquilla pasó la mañana _____ ese juguete ruidoso sobre el piso.

4 Se quedó en la playa, _____ por el sol brillante.

5 El oficial me respondió _____.

6 _____ aquí, llegaremos antes que ellos.

EL PADRE   151

Un padre acordándose de su hijo

El Padre

Olegario Lazo Baeza

I

enrubiecidos *yellowed*
manta especie de abrigo, poncho
de taco alto *with high heels (like western boots)*
pita *strawlike fiber*

en acecho espiando escondido

Un viejecito de barba blanca y larga, bigotes enrubiecidos por la nicotina, manta roja, zapatos de taco alto, sombrero de pita y un canasto al brazo, se acercaba, se alejaba y volvía tímidamente a la puerta del cuartel. Quiso interrogar al centinela, pero el soldado le cortó la palabra en la boca, con el grito:

—¡Cabo de guardia!

El suboficial apareció de un salto en la puerta, como si hubiera estado en acecho.

Interrogado con la vista y con un movimiento de la cabeza hacia arriba, el desconocido habló:

—¿Estará mi hijo?

El cabo soltó la risa. El centinela permaneció impasible, frío como una estatua de sal.

—El regimiento tiene trescientos hijos; falta saber el nombre del suyo—repuso el suboficial.

—Manuel . . . Manuel Zapata, señor.

El cabo arrugó la frente y repitió, registrando su memoria.

—¿Manuel Zapata? . . . ¿Manuel Zapata . . .?

Y con tono seguro:

—No conozco ningún soldado de este nombre.

irguió levantó
gruesas suelas *thick soles*

El paisano se irguió orgulloso sobre las gruesas suelas de sus zapatos, y sonriendo irónicamente:

—¡Pero si no es soldado! Mi hijo es oficial, oficial de línea . . .

trompeta *bugler*
codeó golpeó con el codo

El trompeta, que desde el cuerpo de guardia oía la conversación, se acercó, codeó al cabo, diciéndole por lo bajo:

—Es el *nuevo*; el recién salido de la Escuela.

palabrea habla

—¡Diablos! El que nos palabrea tanto . . .

El cabo envolvió al hombre en una mirada investigadora, y como lo encontró pobre, no se atrevió a invitarlo al casino de oficiales. Lo hizo pasar al cuerpo de guardia.

El viejecito se sentó sobre un banco de madera y dejó su canasto al lado, al alcance de su mano. Los soldados se acercaron dirigiendo miradas curiosas al campesino e interesadas al canasto. Un canasto chico, cubierto con su pedazo de saco. Por debajo de la tapa de lona empezó a picotear primero, y a asomar la cabeza después, una gallina de cresta roja y pico negro abierto por el calor.

saco *coarse cloth bag*
tapa de lona *canvas top*
picotear *to peck*
asomar *mostrarse*
pico *beak*

II

Al verla, los soldados palmotearon y gritaron como niños: ¡Cazuela! ¡Cazuela!

palmotearon dieron palmadas

El paisano, nervioso por la idea de ver a su hijo, agitado con la vista de tantas armas, reía sin motivo y lanzaba atropelladamente sus pensamientos:

atropelladamente *clumsily*

—¡Ja, ja, ja! . . . Sí. Cazuela . . . , pero para mi niño.

Y con su cara sombreada por una ráfaga de pesar, agregó:

sombreado . . . pesar *shadowed by a sudden feeling of unrest*

—¡Cinco años sin verlo . . . !

Más alegre rascándose detrás de la oreja:

—No quería venirse a este pueblo. Mi patrón lo hizo militar. ¡Ja, ja, ja . . . !

Uno de guardia, pesado y tieso por la bandolera, el cinturón y el sable, fue a llamar al teniente.

pesado y tieso *weighted down and stiff*
sable *saber*
picadero *training stable*

Estaba en el picadero, frente a las tropas en descanso, entre un grupo de oficiales. Era chico, moreno, grueso, de vulgar aspecto.

El soldado se cuadró, levantando tierra con sus pies al juntar los tacos de sus botas, y dijo:

se cuadró *came to attention*
tacos *heels*

—Lo buscan . . . , mi teniente.

No sé por qué fenómeno del pensamiento la encogida figura de su padre relampagueó en su mente . . .

relampagueó *flashed*

Alzó la cabeza y habló fuerte, con tono despectivo, de modo que oyeran sus camaradas:

—En este pueblo . . . no conozco a nadie. . . .

El soldado dio detalles no pedidos:

—Es un hombrecito arrugado, con manta . . . Viene de lejos. Trae un canastito . . .

manta *heavy blanket*

Rojo, mareado por el orgullo, llevó la mano a la visera:

—Está bien . . . ¡Retírese!

orgullo (uso antiguo) vergüenza
visera *visor*

La malicia brilló en la cara de los oficiales. Miraron a Zapata . . .
Y como éste no pudo soportar el peso de tantos ojos interrogativos,

contera *tip*

bajó la cabeza, tosió, encendió un cigarrillo, y empezó a rayar el suelo con la contera de su sable.

muy recluta *newly recruited*
aleteando *flapping*

A los cinco minutos vino otro de guardia. Un conscripto muy sencillo, muy recluta, que parecía caricatura de la posición de firme. A cuatro pasos de distancia le gritó, aleteando con los brazos como un pollo:

—¡Lo buscan, mi teniente! Un hombrecito del campo . . . Dice que es el padre de su mercé . . .

su mercé *(inappropriate address) your grace*

Sin corregir la falta de tratamiento del subalterno, arrojó el cigarro, lo pisó con furia, y repuso:

—¡Váyase! Ya voy.

Y para no entrar en explicaciones, se fue a las pesebreras.

pesebreras *feed troughs*

El oficial de guardia, molesto con la insistencia del viejo, insistencia que el sargento le anunciaba cada cinco minutos, fue a ver a Zapata.

III

tornado *turned*

Mientras tanto, el pobre padre, a quien los años habían tornado el corazón de hombre en el de niño, cada vez más nervioso, quedó con el oído atento. Al menor ruido, miraba hacia afuera y estiraba el cuello, arrugado y rojo como cuello de pavo. Todo paso lo hacía temblar de emoción, creyendo que su hijo venía a abrazarlo, a contarle su nueva vida, a mostrarle sus armas, sus arreos, sus caballos . . .

arreos *trappings*

caballerizas *horse stalls*

El oficial de guardia encontró a Zapata simulando inspeccionar las caballerizas. Le dijo secamente, sin preámbulos:

—Te buscan . . . Dicen que es tu padre.

Zapata, desviando la mirada, no contestó.

—Está en el cuerpo de guardia . . . No quiere moverse.

Zapata golpeó el suelo con el pie, se mordió los labios con furia, y fue allá.

Al entrar, un soldado gritó:

—¡Atenciooón!

resorte *spring*

La tropa se levantó rápida como un resorte. Y la sala se llenó con ruido de sables, movimientos de pies y golpes de taco.

El viejecito, deslumbrado con los honores que le hacían a su hijo, sin acordarse del canasto y de la gallina, con los brazos extendidos, salió a su encuentro. Sonreía con su cara de piel quebrada como corteza de árbol viejo. Temblando de placer gritó:

corteza *bark*

palpitaban *twitched*

soplo *whispered*

pechuga *breast meat*

—¡Mañungo! ¡Mañunguito . . . !

El oficial lo saludó fríamente.

Al campesino se le cayeron los brazos. Le palpitaban los músculos de la cara.

El teniente lo sacó con disimulo del cuartel. En la calle le sopló al oído:

—¡Qué ocurrencia la suya . . . ! ¡Venir a verme . . . ! Tengo servicio . . . No puedo salir.

Y se entró bruscamente.

El campesino volvió a la guardia, desconcertado, tembloroso. Hizo un esfuerzo, sacó la gallina del canasto y se la dio al sargento.

—Tome: para ustedes, para ustedes solos.

Dijo adiós y se fue arrastrando los pies, pesados por el desengaño. Pero desde la puerta se volvió para agregar, con lágrimas en los ojos:

—Al niño le gusta mucho la pechuga. ¡Denle un pedacito . . . !

PARA APLICAR

Comprensión   I

A   Conteste a las siguientes preguntas.

1   Describa al viejecito.
2   ¿Cómo se notaba que era tímido?
3   ¿A quién llamó el centinela?
4   ¿Cómo apareció éste?
5   ¿Qué quería saber el viejecito?
6   ¿Cómo reaccionaron los dos soldados?
7   ¿Qué le contestó el centinela?
8   ¿Qué hizo el padre al oír la palabra «soldado»?
9   ¿Quién aclaró el misterio? ¿Cómo?
10 ¿Qué defecto tiene el hijo?
11 ¿Por qué no le invitó el cabo al padre al casino de oficiales?
12 ¿Dónde se sentó el padre?
13 ¿En qué se interesaron los soldados?
14 Descríbalo y lo que tenía adentro.

B   Termine las oraciones según la selección.

1   El viejecito tenía
2   En vez de entrar en el cuartel
3   Quería preguntarle algo al centinela, pero
4   Cuando llegó el cabo de guardia, el viejo preguntó
5   El cabo
6   En el regimiento hay
7   Al oír el nombre el cabo
8   El paisano muy orgullosamente declaró que
9   El trompeta se acercó al cabo y le
10 Entonces el cabo lo reconoció como el nuevo que
11 Como al cabo el padre le pareció tan pobre, no se atrevió a
12 El viejo dejó su canasto
13 En el canasto había

Comprensión   II

A   Conteste a las siguientes preguntas.

1   ¿En qué pensaron los soldados cuando vieron la gallina?
2   ¿Por qué se puso nervioso el padre?
3   ¿Por qué se puso triste después?
4   ¿Quién le ayudó al hijo a entrar en la milicia?
5   ¿Dónde encontró a Manuel el primero que fue a buscarlo?
6   Describa a Manuel.
7   Al oir que lo buscaban, ¿qué idea apareció en la mente del hijo?
8   ¿Qué le contestó Manuel?
9   ¿Qué dijo el guardia que confirmó la identidad del padre?
10   ¿Cómo se notó su vergüenza?
11   ¿Qué hizo el teniente para evitar los ojos maliciosos de los oficiales?
12   Describa la llegada del conscripto nuevo.
13   Esta vez, ¿cómo mostró su disgusto?
14   ¿Por qué fue el oficial de guardia a llamar al hijo?

B   Escoja la respuesta apropiada.

1   ¿Qué pasó cuando los soldados vieron la gallina?
   a.   El paisano los invitó a comérsela.
   b.   La pusieron en una cazuela.
   c.   El señor se puso nervioso y soltó la risa.
2   ¿Por qué ha venido el padre?
   a.   Hace mucho que no ve a su hijo.
   b.   Su patrón lo hizo venir.
   c.   Quería hacer una cazuela.
3   ¿Quién fue a llamar al teniente?
   a.   Un chico moreno de vulgar aspecto.
   b.   Un grupo de oficiales frente a las tropas en descanso.
   c.   Uno de guardia que llevaba bandolera, cinturón y sable.
4   ¿Qué hizo el hijo al saber que alguien lo buscaba?
   a.   Se cuadró levantando tierra con las botas.

   b.   Dijo que no conocía a nadie por allí.
   c.   Cayó un relámpago.
5   ¿Cómo se sintió al darse cuenta de que era su padre?
   a.   Tenía vergüenza.
   b.   Estaba cansado del peso que llevaba.
   c.   Se sentó en el suelo.
6   ¿Cómo mostró el teniente su enojo?
   a.   Aleteaba con los brazos como un pollo.
   b.   Tiró el cigarro al suelo y lo pisó.
   c.   Corrigió la falta de respeto del conscripto.

Comprensión   III

A   Conteste a las siguientes preguntas.

1   ¿Cómo le habían afectado los años al padre?
2   ¿Cómo creía que su hijo lo recibiría?
3   ¿Por qué había ido el teniente a las caballerizas?
4   Al insistir el oficial que el padre se había negado a irse, ¿cómo manifestó Manuel su descontento?
5   ¿Qué pasó cuando el teniente entró en el cuerpo de guardia?
6   ¿Cómo recibió Manuel a su padre?
7   ¿Cómo reaccionó el padre al saludo?
8   Al llevar al padre fuera del cuartel, ¿qué le dijo el hijo?
9   Describa lo que hizo el padre después.
10   ¿Cómo mostró el padre que todavía quería a su hijo?

B   ¿Verdadero o falso?

1   A pesar de sus años, el padre se portó como un niño.
2   Esperaba muy ansiosamente ver a su querido hijo.
3   Creía que el hijo tendría gusto de abrazarlo y contarle de su vida militar.
4   Por fin, el oficial de guardia montó a caballo.
5   Al ver al teniente inspeccionando las caballerizas, el oficial de guardia dijo al padre que no podía molestarlo.

6 El hijo mostró disgusto porque su padre no se había ido.
7 La llegada del teniente en el cuerpo de guardia causó gran conmoción.
8 El hijo fue corriendo con los brazos extendidos a encontrar al padre.
9 El campesino llevó con dignidad el desaire de su hijo.
10 Se despidió de los soldados, sufriendo una tristeza enorme.
11 Les regaló la gallina entera a los de la guardia con una condición.

Más Práctica

A Dé un sinónimo de las siguientes palabras o expresiones.

1	contestar	6	tolerar
2	echarse a reir	7	seriamente
3	inspeccionar	8	cambiar la ruta
4	rayarse el cuerpo	9	añadir
5	levantar	10	sopa de gallina

B Escoja una palabra de la segunda lista (2) para que corresponda con la definición en la primera lista (1).

1		**2**	
1	enfermo por el movimiento	a.	al alcance
2	hembra del gallo	b.	estirar
3	alargar por extender	c.	desengaño
4	conocimiento de una decepción	d.	arrastrar
5	cerca de	e.	codear
6	tirar por el suelo	f.	gallina
7	levantarse en el aire	g.	grueso
8	sopa	h.	mareado
9	gordo	i.	saltar
10	dar golpes con el codo	j.	cazuela

C Prepárese a demostrar estas acciones en clase.

1	saltar	7	codear
2	soltar la risa	8	erguirse
3	alzar la mano	9	cuadrarse
4	rascarse	10	picotear
5	toser	11	aletear
6	estirar los brazos		

Ejercicios Creativos

1 ¿Por qué se encuentra esta selección en una unidad titulada «Sentimientos y pasiones»? ¿Cuáles son los sentimientos del padre hacia su hijo? ¿Cuáles son los sentimientos del hijo hacia su padre?

2 La vergüenza es un sentimiento penoso que viene del conocimiento de haber hecho algo estúpido, impropio, ridículo, etc. ¿Cuál sería la razón por la que se ve tan avergonzado Manuel Zapata? Desarrolle un párrafo explicándolo.

3 Las siguientes palabras tienen un significado semejante. ¿Puede Ud. distinguir entre ellas dando una definición o un ejemplo?
    a. vergüenza
    b. mortificación
    c. humillación
    d. pesar

4 Un antónimo de «vergüenza» es «orgullo». ¿Cómo hubiera sido la reunión entre padre e hijo si el hijo hubiera sentido el mismo orgullo que sentía su padre? Escriba uno de los siguientes diálogos reflejando tal orgullo:
    a. diálogo entre Manuel Zapata y el guardia que le informó que su padre estaba allí esperando
    b. diálogo entre padre e hijo cuando se ven

5 Prepare una receta para cocinar «cazuela de gallina». Preséntela oralmente a la clase con instrucciones detalladas.

La Pared

Vicente Blasco Ibáñez

PARA PRESENTAR LA LECTURA

El poeta norteamericano Robert Frost en su poema *Mending Wall* dice: «Hay algo que no quiere una pared, que quiere derribarla». Una pared o tapia entre dos casas debe de ser un símbolo de respeto mutuo. Cuando no representa tal respeto llega a ser un testimonio vivo de odio, mezclado con temor, como el infame muro de Berlín. Si un símbolo deja de representar lo decente debe de ser cambiado o destruido.

La Pared nos muestra lo inútil que es vivir consumido por el odio y por deseos de venganza. Sólo cuando los principales fueron impulsados por la compasión humana decidieron salvar una vida en vez de matar. Cuando esto sucedió y fue restaurada la amistad de antaño fue preciso destruir el símbolo de su separación.

PARA APRENDER VOCABULARIO

Palabras Clave   I

1 **agudo**   delgado,   sutil,   penetrante *(pointed, sharp)*
    Sus agudas palabras ofendieron al grupo.

2 **anochecer**   llegar la noche, la oscuridad
    Las gallinas se duermen al anochecer.

3 **descuidos**   faltas de cuidado o atención, omisiones
    Aproveché su descuido para avanzar.

4 **escopetazo**   tiro que sale de la escopeta *(shotgun)*; herida hecha con este tiro
    La mujer murió de un escopetazo.

5 **mocetones**   muchachos jóvenes y robustos
    Su hijo era un mocetón mimado.

6 **odios**   sentimientos que uno siente cuando detesta algo o a alguien

El anciano le guardó un odio profundo a su vecino.

7 **predicaban (predicar)** pronunciaban un sermón, decían en público
El deber del cura es predicar el amor de Dios.

8 **redondo** de figura circular
Colón creía que el mundo era redondo.

9 **rencor** resentimiento, amargura
Por medio de sus feas acciones mostró su rencor.

10 **tendió (tender – ie)** extendió en el suelo
Van a tender a los heridos en la calle.

11 **venganza** revancha *(revenge)*
La venganza causa muchos actos crueles.

Práctica

Complete con una palabra de la lista.

agudo	descuido	predicaban
odio	redondo	anochecer
tendió	rencor	escopetazo
venganza	mocetón	

1 Vamos bien. Llegaremos allí antes del _____ .
2 Los alumnos casi nunca hacían lo que los maestros _____ .
3 Pídale a ese _____ que le ayude a llevar el equipaje.
4 Su acento _____ nos irritó.
5 El _____ no adelanta las buenas relaciones humanas.
6 Hoy día todos saben que el mundo es _____ .
7 Él ayudó al herido y lo _____ en el suelo.
8 Estos instrumentos ya no sirven a causa del _____ .
9 La _____ es siempre mala.
10 El _____ es semejante al odio.
11 El _____ le causó la muerte.

Palabras Clave II

1 **aislarse** separarse de otros
A María le gusta aislarse de los demás cuando tiene que trabajar.

2 **asombro** sorpresa
Su padre no mostró el menor asombro al oir el chisme.

3 **ásperas** de superficie desigual *(rough)*
El mecánico tiene que usar una loción especial para no tener las manos ásperas.

4 **gemía (gemir)** expresaba el dolor con sonidos de sufrimiento
Las víctimas del incendio gemían toda la noche.

5 **leña** trozos de madera que se queman en la chimenea
Antes de hacer el fuego en la chimenea, hay que buscar leña.

6 **roto** quebrado, fracturado, no funcionando
Carmen tiene el brazo roto y no puede escribir.

7 **transcurrió (transcurrir)** pasó el tiempo
Transcurrió un día tras otro sin que llegara la noticia.

Práctica

Complete con una palabra de la lista.

rota	ásperas	transcurrió
leña	asombro	aislarse
gemía		

1 Generalmente cuando un caballo tiene una pierna _____ , lo matan.
2 _____ un año hasta que terminaron la construcción.
3 Por su cara pálida se nota el _____ del ganador.

Berlín

4   Se dice que la madera seca hace muy buena
    ———— .

5   La enfermera tenía las manos ———— de
    haberlas lavado tantas veces.

6   El niño enfermo ———— toda la noche.
    Tenía mucha fiebre y dolor.

7   Es difícil tener amigos si uno insiste en
    ———— todo el tiempo.

La Pared

Vicente Blasco Ibáñez

I

Siempre que los nietos del tío Rabosa se encontraban con los hijos de la viuda de Casporra en las sendas de la huerta o en las calles de Campanar, todo el vecindario comentaba el suceso. ¡Se habían mirado! ¡Se insultaban con el gesto! Aquello acabaría mal, y el día menos pensado el pueblo sufriría un nuevo disgusto.

El alcalde con los vecinos más notables predicaban paz a los mocetones de las dos familias enemigas, y allá iba el cura, un vejete de Dios, de una casa a otra, recomendando el olvido de las ofensas.

Treinta años que los odios de los Rabosas y Casporras traían alborotado a Campanar. Casi en las puertas de Valencia, en el risueño pueblecito que desde la orilla del río miraba a la ciudad con los redondos ventanales de su agudo campanario, repetían aquellos bárbaros, con un rencor africano, la historia de luchas y violencias de las grandes familias italianas en la Edad Media. Habían sido grandes amigos en otro tiempo; sus casas, aunque situadas en distinta calle, lindaban por los corrales, separadas únicamente por una tapia baja. Una noche, por cuestiones de riego, un Casporra tendió en la huerta de un escopetazo a un hijo del tío Rabosa, y el hijo menor de éste, para que no se dijera que en la familia no quedaban hombres, consiguió, después de un mes de acecho, colocarle una bala entre las cejas al matador. Desde entonces las dos familias vivieron para exterminarse, pensando más en aprovechar los descuidos del vecino que en el cultivo de las tierras. Escopetazos en medio de la calle; tiros que al anochecer relampagueaban desde el fondo de una acequia o tras los cañares o ribazos cuando el odiado enemigo regresaba del campo; alguna vez un Rabosa o un Casporra camino del cementerio con una onza de plomo dentro del pellejo, y la sed

extremándose *going to even further extremes*

vientre *insides*

esparto *hemp*

infranqueable *insurmountable*

bardas *hedges*

vara *yard*
desprecio *odio, falta de estimación*
argamasa *cemento*

tejados *clay-tile roofs*
estremecíanse *temblaban*

amasado *cemented*
agredirse *attacking one another*

de venganza sin extinguirse, antes bien, extremándose con las nuevas generaciones, pues parecía que en las dos casas los chiquitines salían ya del vientre de sus madres tendiendo las manos a la escopeta para matar a los vecinos.

Después de treinta años de lucha, en casa de los Casporras sólo quedaban una viuda con tres hijos mocetones que parecían torres de músculos. En la otra estaba el tío Rabosa, con sus ochenta años, inmóvil en un sillón de esparto, con las piernas muertas por la parálisis, como un arrugado ídolo de la venganza, ante el cual juraban sus nietos defender el prestigio de la familia.

Pero los tiempos eran otros. Ya no era posible ir a tiros como sus padres en plena plaza a la salida de la misa mayor. La Guardia Civil no les perdía de vista; los vecinos les vigilaban, y bastaba que uno de ellos se detuviera algunos minutos en una senda o en una esquina, para verse al momento rodeado de gente que le aconsejaba la paz. Cansados de esta vigilancia que degeneraba en persecución y se interponía entre ellos como infranqueable obstáculo, Casporras y Rabosas acabaron por no buscarse, y hasta se huían cuando la casualidad les ponía frente a frente.

II

Tal fue su deseo de aislarse y no verse, que les pareció baja la pared que separaba sus corrales. Las gallinas de unos y otros, escalando los montones de leña, fraternizaban en lo alto de las bardas; las mujeres de las dos casas cambiaban desde las ventanas gestos de desprecio. Aquello no podía resistirse: era como vivir en familia; la viuda de Casporra hizo que sus hijos levantaran la pared una vara. Los vecinos se apresuraron a manifestar su desprecio con piedra y argamasa, y añadieron algunos palmos más a la pared. Y así, en esta muda y repetida manifestación de odio la pared fue subiendo y subiendo. Ya no se veían las ventanas; poco después no se veían los tejados; las pobres aves del corral estremecíanse en la lúgubre sombra de aquel paredón que les ocultaba parte del cielo, y sus cacareos sonaban tristes y apagados a través de aquel muro, monumento de odio, que parecía amasado con los huesos y la sangre de las víctimas.

Así transcurrió el tiempo para las dos familias, sin agredirse como en otra época, pero sin aproximarse: inmóviles y cristalizadas en su odio.

Una tarde sonaron a rebato las campanas del pueblo. Ardía la casa del tío Rabosa. Los nietos estaban en la huerta; la mujer de uno de éstos en el lavadero, y por las rendijas de puertas y ventanas salía un humo denso de paja quemada. Dentro, en aquel infierno que rugía buscando expansión, estaba el abuelo, el pobre tío Rabosa, inmóvil en su sillón. La nieta se mesaba los cabellos, acusándose como autora de todo por su descuido; la gente arremolinábase en la calle, asustada por la fuerza del incendio. Algunos, más valientes, abrieron la puerta, pero fue para retroceder ante la bocanada de denso humo cargada de chispas que se esparció por la calle. ¡El pobre agüelo!

—¡El agüelo!—gritaba la de los Rabosas volviendo en vano la mirada en busca de un salvador.

Los asustados vecinos experimentaron el mismo asombro que si hubieran visto el campanario marchando hacia ellos. Tres mocetones entraban corriendo en la casa incendiada. Eran los Casporras. Se habían mirado cambiando un guiño de inteligencia, y sin más palabras se arrojaron como salamandras en el enorme brasero. La multitud les aplaudió al verles reaparecer llevando en alto como a un santo en sus andas al tío Rabosa en su sillón de esparto. Abandonaron al viejo sin mirarle siquiera, y otra vez adentro.

—¡No, no!—gritaba la gente.

Pero ellos sonreían siguiendo adelante. Iban a salvar algo de los intereses de sus enemigos. Si los nietos del tío Rabosa estuvieran allí, ni se habrían movido ellos de casa. Pero sólo se trataba de un pobre viejo, al que debían proteger como hombres de corazón. Y la gente les veía tan pronto en la calle como dentro de la casa, buceando en el humo, sacudiéndose las chispas como inquietos demonios, arrojando muebles y sacos para volver a meterse entre las llamas.

Lanzó un grito la multitud al ver a los dos hermanos mayores sacando al menor en brazos. Un madero, al caer, le había roto una pierna.

—¡Pronto, una silla!

La gente, en su precipitación, arrancó al viejo Rabosa de su sillón de esparto para sentar al herido.

El muchacho, con el pelo chamuscado y la cara ahumada, sonreía, ocultando los agudos dolores que le hacían fruncir los labios. Sintió que unas manos trémulas, ásperas, con las escamas de la vejez, oprimían las suyas.

¡Fill meu! ¡Hijo mío! *(My son!)*

boca desdentada y profunda *deep, toothless mouth*

albañiles *stone masons*

escombros *rubble*
derribar *tear down*
maldita *cursed*

—¡Fill meu! ¡Fill meu!—gemía la voz del tío Rabosa, quien se arrastraba hacia él.

Y antes que el pobre muchacho pudiera evitarlo, el paralítico buscó con su boca desdentada y profunda las manos que tenía y las besó un sinnúmero de veces, bañándolas con lágrimas.

* * *

Ardió toda la casa. Y cuando los albañiles fueron llamados para construir otra, los nietos del tío Rabosa no les dejaron comenzar por la limpia del terreno, cubierto de negros escombros. Antes tenían que hacer un trabajo más urgente: derribar la pared maldita. Y empuñado el pico, ellos dieron los primeros golpes.

PARA APLICAR

Comprensión   I

A Conteste a las siguientes preguntas.

1 ¿Dónde tiene lugar este cuento?
2 ¿Cómo se llaman las dos familias enemigas de Campanar?
3 ¿Qué suceso comentaba el vecindario?
4 ¿Qué temía el pueblo?
5 ¿Quiénes predicaban la paz?
6 ¿Adónde iba el cura?¿Qué hacía para evitar otra desgracia?
7 ¿Por cuántos años traían alborotado a Campanar?
8 ¿Qué repetían?
9 ¿Cuándo habían sido amigos?
10 ¿Estaban las casas en la misma calle?
11 ¿Qué las separaba?
12 ¿Por qué mató un Casporra a un hijo del tío Rabosa?
13 ¿Cuánto tiempo esperó el Casporra antes de tomar acción?
14 ¿Qué hizo éste?
15 Describa al tío Rabosa.
16 ¿Cómo son los tiempos ahora?

B ¿Verdadero o falso?

1 La gente de Campanar contaba chismes.

2 Temía problemas de los jóvenes Rabosa y Casporra.
3 El alcalde quería paz y amistades.
4 El cura quería que se olvidaran del pasado.
5 Había existido un estado de inseguridad durante mucho tiempo.
6 Las noticias de las luchas de Valencia llegaban al risueño pueblo.
7 Había una tapia alrededor de las dos casas juntas.
8 Un Casporra mató a un hijo del tío Rabosa en una disputa relativa al uso del agua.
9 El hijo menor del muerto observó en secreto al asesino por más de un mes.
10 La rivalidad entre las dos familias aumentó y pasó a las nuevas generaciones.

Comprensión   II

A Conteste a las siguientes preguntas.

1 ¿Qué hacían para evitar enfrentarse el uno con el otro?
2 ¿Por qué levantaron más la pared?
3 ¿Qué oyeron una tarde?
4 ¿Qué hacía la gente enfrente de la casa incendiada?
5 ¿Qué hacía la nieta?

6 ¿Cómo fue salvado el tío?
7 ¿Después de llevarlo afuera de la casa, ¿qué hicieron?
8 ¿Qué le pasó a uno de los Casporras?
9 ¿Qué le llamó el tío Rabosa?
10 ¿Qué hicieron los nietos del tío Rabosa antes de reconstruir la casa?

B Ponga las siguientes oraciones en el orden en que se encuentran en la selección.

1 Debido a la tapia baja, las gallinas fraternizaban.
2 Una tarde comenzó a quemarse la casa del tío.
3 Duraron las luchas por treinta años.
4 La viuda mandó hacer más alta la pared.
5 Aunque algunos querían hacerlo, nadie entró a salvar al pobre viejo.
6 Fue imposible cambiar escopetazos en la calle porque todo el mundo les vigilaba.
7 Mientras más aumentó el odio, más subió la tapia.
8 El tío paralizado parecía un arrugado ídolo cuyo buen nombre sus nietos juraban proteger.
9 Las mujeres cambiaban gestos de desprecio sobre la pared.
10 Terminaron por evitar un encuentro.

C Escoja la respuesta apropiada.

1 ¿Qué sorprendió a los asustados vecinos?
   a. El campanario marchaba hacia ellos.
   b. El tío Rabosa volvió en su silla.
   c. Los tres Casporra entraron en la casa.
2 ¿Cómo reaccionó la gente que los observaba?
   a. Se miraron cambiando un guiño de inteligencia.
   b. Les estimuló a volver a entrar.
   c. Aplaudió al verlos salir con el tío.
3 ¿Por qué entraron de nuevo?
   a. Querían salvar sus muebles y otras posesiones.

b. Los nietos del tío estaban allí.
c. Les gustaba bucear en el humo.
4 ¿Por qué gritó la multitud?
   a. Debía proteger a los hombres de buen corazón.
   b. El Casporra más joven sufrió un accidente.
   c. La gente sintió compasión por el herido.
5 ¿Cómo mostraron un cambio de actitud?
   a. Arrancaron al tío de su silla.
   b. El tío gemía diciendo que quería ver a su hijo.
   c. Antes de volver a construir la casa, derribaron el símbolo de odio.

Más Práctica

A Conteste a las siguientes preguntas según la indicación. Primero será necesario arreglar las palabras en letra bastardilla en un orden lógico.

1 ¿Qué haces con la planta? *tierra, de, arranco, la, la*
2 ¿Quién es aquel chico fuerte? *de, aquel, un, mocetón, barrio*
3 ¿Qué van a hacer con los heridos? *suelo, van, los, a, tender, el, en*
4 ¿Quién es aquella señora que anda descalza? *pobre, cerca, una, vive, viuda, que*
5 ¿Por qué luchan tanto? *venganza, su, quieren*
6 ¿De qué murió? *escopetazo, un, fuerte*
7 ¿Quién va a predicar el sermón? *iglesia, de, el, nuevo, cura, la*
8 ¿Cómo son los alfileres? *peligrosos, muy, agudos, y*

B Complete las siguientes oraciones con una palabra apropiada.

1 El señor murió y dejó a la ———— con cuatro niños.
2 Tenemos que ———— la buena noticia por todo el pueblo.

3 Ellos quieren ——— y no hablar con nadie.
4 Es mejor ——— el amor y no el rencor.
5 La máquina no funciona; está ———.
6 La pelota es ———.
7 El ladrón tenía una ———.
8 Aquel ——— lucha con todo el mundo.

C Dé un sinónimo de las siguientes palabras.

1 pronunciar un sermón
2 retirarse
3 revancha
4 resentimiento
5 circular
6 echar abajo
7 quebrado
8 diseminar

Ejercicios Creativos

1 Haga una lista de las varias pasiones evidentes en la historia. Cite ejemplos.
2 Cite ejemplos de otras disputas ficticias o verdaderas que terminaron con la extinción entera o parcial de las familias.
3 Hoy día en nuestra sociedad no aprobamos la idea de vengarnos por ningún motivo, pero en otros tiempos se consideraba un derecho natural conseguir una satisfacción por una cuestión de honor. ¿Por qué dejaron de buscar su venganza los hijos de los ofendidos? ¿Qué hacían cuando se encontraban? Note el simbolismo en este cuento. ¿Qué simboliza la pared? ¿El fuego? ¿El hecho de los Casporra? ¿El derribo de la pared?
4 Prepare una escena para el noticiero de televisión y entreviste a un nieto del tío y a un hijo de la viuda después del incendio.

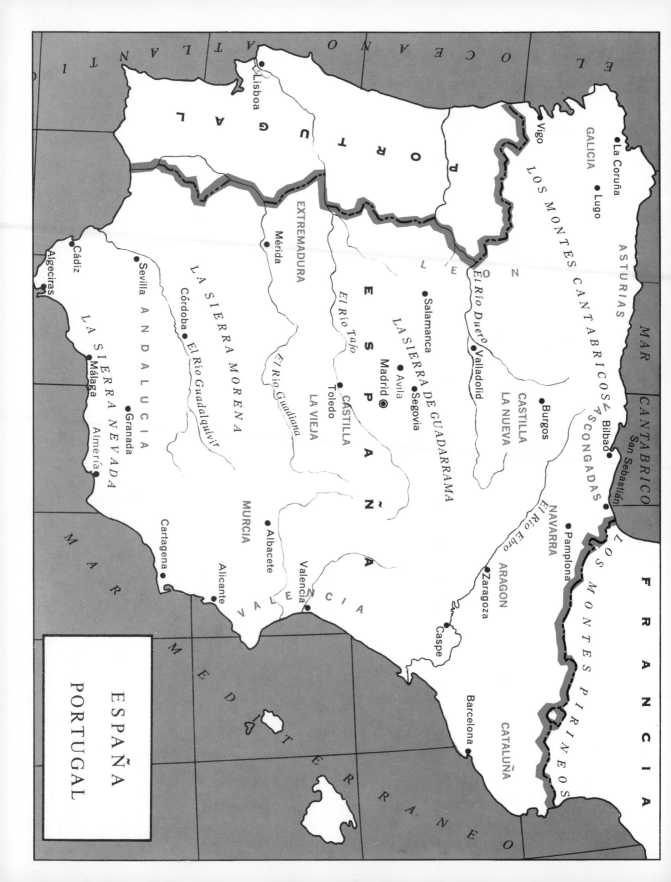

ESTRUCTURA

Mandatos Directos—Formas Formales

Verbos Regulares

Estudien las siguientes formas del mandato formal.

infinitivo	indicativo	mandato singular	mandato plural
tomar	tomo	tome	tomen
vender	vendo	venda	vendan
abrir	abro	abra	abran

Verbos con Raíz Irregular

infinitivo	indicativo	mandato singular	mandato plural
caer	caigo	caiga	caigan
decir	digo	diga	digan
hacer	hago	haga	hagan
huir	huyo	huya	huyan
oir	oigo	oiga	oigan
poner	pongo	ponga	pongan
salir	salgo	salga	salgan
tener	tengo	tenga	tengan
traer	traigo	traiga	traigan
valer	valgo	valga	valgan
vencer	venzo	venza	venzan
venir	vengo	venga	vengan
ver	veo	vea	vean

Verbos de Cambio Ortográfico

infinitivo	indicativo	mandato singular	mandato plural
buscar	busco	busque	busquen
conducir	conduzco	conduzca	conduzcan
escoger	escojo	escoja	escojan
dirigir	dirijo	dirija	dirijan
distinguir	distingo	distinga	distingan
empezar	empiezo	empiece	empiecen
llegar	llego	llegue	lleguen
sacar	saco	saque	saquen
seguir	sigo	siga	sigan

Verbos Irregulares

infinitivo	indicativo	mandato singular	mandato plural
dar	doy	dé	den
estar	estoy	esté	estén
ser	soy	sea	sean
ir	voy	vaya	vayan
saber	sé	sepa	sepan

Se notará que el pronombre de complemento directo o indirecto se agrega al mandato afirmativo. Precede al mandato en la forma negativa.

Levántese Ud.
No se levante Ud.

A Sigan el modelo.

Ud. entra en la iglesia.
Entre Ud. en la iglesia.

1 Ud. trabaja los sábados.
2 Ud. estorba el paso.
3 Ud. pasa por aquí.
4 Ud. habla por teléfono.
5 Ud. regresa a las cuatro.
6 Ud. camina para el colegio.
7 Ud. estudia francés e inglés.
8 Ud. enseña a los niños.
9 Ud. ocupa este asiento.
10 Ud. termina su faena muy pronto.

B Sigan el modelo.

El capitán no baja la bandera.
Capitán, no baje la bandera.

1 La señorita no observa cómo trabajan.
2 El mozo no arroja la bandeja en el suelo.
3 El joven no guarda silencio.
4 El señor no pronuncia ninguna palabra.
5 La profesora no termina temprano.
6 El general no ignora los méritos de mi plan.
7 El señor no enfada a su mujer.
8 El Marqués no vacila en dar su opinión.
9 El soldado no registra a ese pobre señor.
10 El profesor no cambia la tarea.

C Sigan el modelo.

Ud. sorprende al ladrón.
Soprenda Ud. al ladrón.

1 Ud. promete regresar más tarde.
2 Ud. reúne a todos los interesados.
3 Ud. vende la escopeta a los cazadores.
4 Ud. come con nosotros.
5 Ud. vive cerca del edificio alto.
6 Ud. rompe algunas reglas.
7 Ud. abre la puerta de enfrente.
8 Ud. esconde el dinero en el libro.

9 Ud. responde a sus interrogaciones.
10 Ud. esparce verdades, no mentiras.

D Sigan el modelo.

El patrón no vende esa tierra.
Patrón, no venda esa tierra.

1 Mi jefe no responde a tal tontería.
2 La Condesita no esconde el abanico.
3 El padre no escribe ninguna carta.
4 El maestro no prende la luz.
5 El capitán no permite interrupciones.
6 El señor no tose sin cubrirse la boca.
7 La señorita no cree lo que dice Ana.
8 El viejo no rompe el silencio.
9 La maestra no lee nuestras composiciones.
10 El soldado no sube en el avión.

E Sigan el modelo.

¿Debo yo volver?
Sí, vuelva Ud.

1 ¿Debo yo confesar?
2 ¿Debo yo recordar?
3 ¿Debo yo jugar ahora?
4 ¿Debo yo volver mañana?
5 ¿Debo yo volar a España?
6 ¿Debo yo pensar más en eso?
7 ¿Debo yo contar?
8 ¿Debo yo dormir?

F Sigan el modelo.

¿Es propio pedir más?
Claro, pidan Uds. más.

1 ¿Es propio repetir la primera parte?
2 ¿Es propio seguir por aquí?
3 ¿Es propio servir más pan?
4 ¿Es propio conseguir otros boletos?
5 ¿Es propio reir de sus bromas?
6 ¿Es propio medir la distancia así?
7 ¿Es propio vivir en ese barrio?

G Sigan el modelo.

> *Quiero levantarme.*
> *Pues, levántese.*

1 Quiero desayunarme.
2 Quiero defenderme.
3 Quiero sentarme.
4 Quiero retirarme.
5 Quiero vestirme.
6 Quiero esconderme.
7 Quiero rascarme la cabeza.
8 Quiero pararme.
9 Quiero aislarme.
10 Quiero despedirme.

H Sigan el modelo.

> *No queremos levantarnos.*
> *No se levanten Uds.*

1 No quiero moverme.
2 No queremos sentarnos.
3 No quiero bañarme ahora.
4 No queremos quedarnos.
5 No queremos acostarnos.

6 No quiero irme.
7 No queremos enfadarnos.
8 No quiero arrodillarme.

I Sigan el modelo.

> *Ud. viene mañana.*
> *Venga Ud. mañana.*

1 Ud. sale ahora.
2 Uds. dicen algo muy interesante.
3 Uds. tienen mucha paciencia.
4 Ud. no hace nada.
5 Uds. traen buenas noticias.
6 Ud. se pone a trabajar.
7 Uds. ven el lago encantado.
8 Uds. oyen los tiros.
9 Ud. no huye del peligro.
10 Ud. no cae sobre las piedras.
11 Uds. saben la historia de la independencia.
12 Uds. no buscan venganza.
13 Ud. da esperanzas a los demás.
14 Ud. está aquí temprano.

Mandatos Directos—Formas Familiares

Verbos Regulares

El mandato familiar de los verbos regulares es igual que la tercera persona singular del indicativo. La forma negativa es la segunda persona del subjuntivo.

infinitivo	mandato	forma negativa
tomar	toma	no tomes
vender	vende	no vendas
abrir	abre	no abras
comenzar	comienza	no comiences
volver	vuelve	no vuelvas
pedir	pide	no pidas

Verbos Irregulares

El mandato familiar de los siguientes verbos es irregular.

infinitivo	mandato	forma negativa
hacer	haz	no hagas
poner	pon	no pongas
salir	sal	no salgas
tener	ten	no tengas
valer	val	no valgas
venir	ven	no vengas
decir	di	no digas
ir	ve	no vayas
ser	sé	no seas

J Sigan el modelo.

> *Isabel es leal a la causa.*
> *Isabel, sé leal a la causa.*

1 Manuel dice que no estamos de acuerdo.
2 Rosa abre la puerta.
3 Raúl hace otro viajecito al centro.
4 Juana va a la capital.
5 Dolores viene mañana a la misma hora.
6 Ramón estira las piernas.
7 María Teresa sale a la esquina.
8 Teresa vuelve del ejército.
9 Juan pide permiso para ir a las bodas.
10 Victoria resuelve el problema.

K Sigan el modelo.

> *Enrique no trae la bandeja.*
> *Enrique, no traigas la bandeja.*

1 Ricardo no usa la leña.
2 José no dice nada.
3 Tomasina no pide mucho.
4 Inés no prepara la cazuela.
5 Pablo no hace tantas preguntas.
6 Susana no tiene cuidado.
7 Roberto no busca el abanico.
8 Marta no mira al cabo de guardia.
9 Eduardo no agrega nada al plato.

Mandatos Indirectos

El mandato indirecto se expresa por medio de otra persona.

> Consuelo quiere entrar.
> Que entre (ella).

Se expresa con la tercera persona del presente del subjuntivo, singular o plural, según el sujeto. Casi siempre se introduce con *que* y sólo se expresa el sujeto para evitar ambigüedad o para dar énfasis.

L   Sigan el modelo.

> *Elena quiere trabajar.*
> *Que trabaje.*

1   Estela quiere entrar.
2   Roberto quiere comer.
3   Isabel quiere abrir.
4   Las chicas quieren jugar.
5   Juan y Carlos quieren escribir.
6   Mimí quiere leer.
7   Salvador quiere terminar.
8   Luisa quiere insistir.
9   Mis hermanas quieren correr.
10   Eduardo quiere llamar.

M   Sigan el modelo.

> *Creo que Pablo va a bailar.*
> *No, que no baile.*

1   Creo que Celia va a esperar.
2   Creo que Hernán va a llorar.
3   Creo que Rosa va a responder.
4   Creo que los soldados van a sufrir.
5   Creo que la vieja va a toser.
6   Creo que esos niños van a bajar.
7   Creo que Pilar va a decidir.
8   Creo que Pepe y Nacho van a caminar.
9   Creo que van a tocar un vals.
10   Creo que Estela y sus amigos van a subir.

N   Sigan el modelo.

> *Parece que María se levanta.*
> *Está bien. Que se levante.*

1   Parece que el gato se duerme.
2   Parece que los padres se quejan.
3   Parece que Susana se aburre.
4   Parece que Enrique se esconde.
5   Parece que Paco se arregla.
6   Parece que las madres se preocupan.
7   Parece que los jóvenes se van.

O   Sigan el modelo.

> *Ellas cierran la puerta.*
> *Que cierren la puerta.*

1   Ellos se acuestan temprano.
2   Ellas devuelven el libro.
3   Ellos piden más dinero.
4   Ellas se divierten.
5   Ellos duermen mucho.
6   Ellas se visten de uniforme.
7   Ellos recuerdan esta noche.
8   Ellos sirven en el patio.
9   Ellas se ríen de la gallina.
10   Ellos se mueren del frío.

P Sigan el modelo.

Él no dice nada.
Que no diga nada.

1   Él hace otros planes.
2   Ella se pone el sombrero.
3   Ellos salen ahora.
4   Él viene a ayudarnos.
5   Ella ve lo que han hecho.
6   Ellos no van a la oficina de correos.
7   Él sabe esa lección.
8   Ella da el permiso necesario.
9   Ellos traen bastante comida.
10 Ellas no se caen del balcón.
11 Él está impaciente.
12 Ella oye esto.

Q Sigan el modelo.

¿Quién lo saca?
Yo no. Que lo saque otro.

1   ¿Quién lo empieza?
2   ¿Quién lo dirige?
3   ¿Quién lo busca?
4   ¿Quién lo toca?
5   ¿Quién lo paga?
6   ¿Quién lo conduce?
7   ¿Quién lo concluye?
8   ¿Quién lo mide?
9   ¿Quién lo destruye?
10 ¿Quién lo escoge?

La Revolución

Nuevos reyes, nuevas leyes.

PARA PREPARAR LA ESCENA

La historia de la «revolución» en las naciones hispanas encierra muchas lecciones en sus sangrientas páginas. Ella nos enseña que un pueblo oprimido no vacila en cambiar el bienestar por todas las calamidades de la «guerra», con tal de ser dueño de su destino.

Tanto en España como en la América Latina, el espíritu de revolución contra las fuerzas opresoras ha sido el factor que ha ayudado a los pueblos a ascender. El claro ejemplo de los revolucionarios ha infundido incontrastable ánimo en el pueblo hispano.

Algunas veces la lucha y sus ideales originales se extravían por culpa de líderes corrompidos que pierden de vista el bien del pueblo entero. Entonces sigue un período de oscuridad, cuando los revolucionarios sinceros tienen que analizar sus objetivos originales, recobrar la calma y poner manos a la obra nueva. Los cuentos que siguen muestran cuántos sacrificios ha hecho la gente en busca de su ideal.

Una Esperanza

Amado Nervo

PARA PRESENTAR LA LECTURA

Este cuento trata de un joven que está en la cárcel esperando la muerte por haber participado en actos contra el gobierno de México durante la revolución. La familia por su reputación consigue la ayuda de los hombres encargados de la ejecución. Prometen ayudarle a salvar su vida. Hasta un sacerdote hace cosas que no debiera para salvar al joven.

Mientras está esperando su muerte piensa en lo que significa morir por la Patria . . . cambiar su vida real y concreta por una noción abstracta de Patria y de partido. Es una cuestión filosófica sumamente interesante.

Amado Nervo es conocido en el mundo literario principalmente por su poesía, y un tema corriente en sus versos es la cuestión de la existencia de Dios y el significado de la muerte. Este cuento muestra claramente lo que quería decir el autor cuando escribió en una de sus poesías: «Oh, muerte, tú eres madre de la filosofía».

La ironía es un elemento fuerte en este cuento. Trate de notar cómo usa el autor esta técnica estilística para aumentar el conflicto trágico.

PARA APRENDER VOCABULARIO

Palabras Clave   I

1 **abrumado (abrumar)**   muy molesto
Ese sonido agudo le tiene abrumado y no le permite concentrarse.

2 **afiliarse**   asociarse
Los pobres querían afiliarse a la revolución.

3 **desvanecerse**   evaporarse, desaparecer
Cuando el jefe oiga esto, van a desvanecerse sus sueños de victoria.

4 **ensueños**   sueños, ilusiones
Con el vestido blanco lucía como un ensueño.

Zapata (Diego Rivera)

5 **sollozaba (sollozar)**   lloraba con con-
tracciones espasmódicas
Cuando pensaba que iba a morir su padre,
Miguel sollozaba tristemente.

6 **sublevaba (sublevar)**   alzaba en rebelión
Logró sublevar al pueblo contra el
gobierno.

7 **turbación**   confusión, desorden
Cada revolución es una turbación para
todos.

Práctica

Complete con una palabra de la lista.

abrumado	*turbación*	*desvanecerse*
sollozaba	*afiliarse*	*ensueño*
sublevaba		

1 El _____ de su vida era casarse.
2 La vida moderna es una _____ continua.
3 Él quiere _____ a un buen club, pero en
este pueblo es muy difícil encontrar uno.

4   _____ sin parar pensando en su triste destino.

5   El líder revolucionario _____ al pueblo contra el gobierno.

6   Los recuerdos de su juventud tuvieron que _____ para darle una paz completa.

7   Ese hombre parece _____ por el perro.

Palabras Clave   II

1   **aguardar**   esperar
Teresa tiene que aguardar otro día para realizar sus planes.

2   **alba**   luz del día antes de salir el sol, aurora
Lo van a fusilar a las primeras luces del alba.

3   **apenas**   casi no, luego que   (scarcely, as soon as)
Apenas llegó, se fue otra vez.

4   **cuchicheo**   murmullo, acción de hablar en voz baja   (whisper, whispering)
El cuchicheo no es cortés porque no lo pueden entender todos.

5   **sobornar**   corromper con regalos   (to bribe)
Es fácil sobornar a alguien deshonesto.

Práctica

Complete con una palabra de la lista.

apenas   sobornar   cuchicheo
alba   aguardar

1   _____ llegó el cura el joven empezó a sollozar.

2   El _____ del público durante el concierto molestó a los artistas.

3   Tendrá que _____ pacientemente otra oportunidad.

4   Siempre hay alguien que trata de _____ a los que tienen el poder.

5   Cuando llegó el _____, los amantes ya se habían ido.

Palabras Clave   III

1   **ajusticiados**   criminales a quienes se ha aplicado la pena de muerte
El ajusticiado sufre miles de muertes antes de morir.

2   **desigual**   no igual
Es difícil caminar mucho tiempo en un terreno desigual.

3   **endulzar**   hacer dulce, hacer soportable
La presencia de su amigo sirvió para endulzar su sufrimiento.

4   **erguida (erguir –i)**   levantada, puesta derecha
La mujer orgullosa anda con la cabeza erguida.

5   **friolenta**   muy sensible al frío, que da frío
Esta niña es muy friolenta; por eso juega todo el día cerca de la chimenea.

6   **infamias**   deshonras
Robarles a los pobres es una infamia.

7   **leve**   ligero, escaso   (light, faint)
Una leve ilusión entró en el pensamiento de Juana y empezaba a darle esperanzas.

8   **sien**   parte lateral de la frente   (temple)
La sien está cerca de la oreja.

9   **yacía (yacer)**   estaba echado o tendido   (was lying down, laid in the grave)
Aquí yace el grupo de soldados muertos por la patria.

Práctica

Complete con una palabra de la lista.

erguida   infamia   friolenta
leve   yace   endulzar
desigual   sien   ajusticiado

1   A veces ni aun el amor puede _____ los sufrimientos.

Los fusilamientos del 3 de mayo (Goya)

Prado—Art Reference Bureau

2 Jorge siempre tiene frío. Es una persona
_____ .

3 La _____ esperanza había crecido a una
verdad: ¡Iba a vivir!

4 El muchacho se cuadró delante del pelotón
con la cabeza _____ .

5 La descarga de los rifles era _____ ; se
oyó cada tiro.

6 El _____ no estaba muerto a pesar del
balazo recibido en la cabeza.

7 La víctima recibió un golpe fuerte en la
_____ .

8 Fue una _____ lo que hizo, y todos lo
van a reconocer.

9 En este sitio _____ el soldado desconocido.

Una Esperanza

Amado Nervo

I

En un ángulo de la pieza, Luis, el joven militar, abrumado por todo el peso de su mala fortuna, pensaba.

Pensaba en los viejos días de su niñez, en la amplia y tranquila casa de sus padres, uno de esos caserones de provincia, sólidos, vastos, con jardín y huerta, con ventanas que se abrían sobre la solitaria calle de una ciudad de segundo orden (no lejos por cierto de aquella donde iba a morir).

Recordaba su adolescencia, sus primeros ensueños, vagos como luz de estrellas, sus amores con la muchacha de falda corta.

Luego desarrollábase ante sus ojos el claro paisaje de su juventud. Recordaba sus camaradas alegres y sus relaciones, ya serias, con la rubia, vuelta mujer y que ahora, porque él volviese con bien, rezaba ¡ay! en vano, en vano . . .

Y, por último, llegaba a la época más reciente de su vida. Llegaba al período de entusiasmo patriótico que le hizo afiliarse al partido liberal. Se encuentra amenazado de muerte por la reacción a la cual ayudaba en esta vez a un poder extranjero.

Tornaba a ver el momento en que un maldito azar de la guerra le había llevado a aquel espantoso trance.

Cogido con las armas en la mano fue hecho prisionero y ofrecido con otros compañeros a trueque de las vidas de algunos oficiales reaccionarios. Había visto desvanecerse su última esperanza, porque la proposición llegó tarde, cuando los liberales habían fusilado ya a los prisioneros conservadores.

Iba, pues, a morir. Esta idea que había salido por un instante de la zona de su pensamiento, gracias a la excursión amable por los sonrientes recuerdos de su niñez y de la juventud, volvía de pronto, con todo su horror, estremeciéndole de pies a cabeza.

se imponía *asserted itself*
en rededor *alrededor*

rejilla *lattice*

Iba a morir . . . ¡a morir! No podía creerlo, y, sin embargo la verdad tremenda se imponía. Bastaba mirar en rededor. Aquel altar improvisado, aquel Cristo viejo sobre cuyo cuerpo caía la luz amarillenta de las velas, y ahí cerca, visibles a través de la rejilla de la puerta, los centinelas . . . Iba a morir, así, fuerte, joven, rico, amado . . . ¿Y todo por qué? Por una abstracta noción de Patria y de partido . . . ¿Y qué cosa era la Patria? Algo muy impreciso, muy vago para él en aquellos momentos de turbación. En cambio la vida, la vida que iba a perder era algo real, realísimo, concreto, definido . . . ¡era su vida!

¡La Patria! ¡morir por la Patria! . . . pensaba. Pero es que ésta, en su augusta y divina inconciencia, no sabrá siquiera que he muerto por ella . . .

¡Y qué importa si tú lo sabes! . . . le replicaba allá dentro una voz misteriosa. La Patria lo sabrá por tu propio conocimiento, por tu pensamiento propio, que es un pedazo de su pensamiento y de su conciencia colectiva. Eso basta . . .

No, no bastaba eso . . . y, sobre todo, no quería morir. Su vida era muy suya y no se resignaba a que se la quitaran. Un formidable instinto de conservación se sublevaba en todo su ser y ascendía incontenible, torturador y lleno de protestas.

A veces, la fatiga de las prolongadas vigilias anteriores, la intensidad de aquella fermentación de pensamiento, el exceso mismo de la pena, le abrumaban y dormitaba un poco. El despertar brusco y la inmediata y clarísima noción de su fin eran un tormento horrible. El soldado, con las manos sobre el rostro, sollozaba con un sollozo que llegando al oído de los centinelas, hacíales asomar por la rejilla sus caras, en las que se leía la indiferencia del indio.

dormitaba *dozed, napped*

hacíales asomar *made them show (their faces)*

II

Se oyó en la puerta un breve cuchicheo y en seguida ésta se abrió dulcemente para dar entrada a un hombre. Era un sacerdote.

El joven militar, apenas lo vio, se puso en pie y extendió hacia él los brazos como para detenerlo, exclamando:

—¡Es inútil, no quiero confesarme!— Y sin aguardar a que la sombra aquella respondiera, continuó:

no tienen derecho de arrebatármela *they have no right to snatch it away from me*

sucia plazuela *small, dirty square*

pólvora y taco *powder and wadding*

piadosas *kind*

se aleje *se vaya*

—No, no me confieso; es inútil que venga Ud. a molestarse. ¿Sabe Ud. lo que quiero? Quiero la vida, que no me quiten la vida: es mía, muy mía y no tienen derecho de arrebatármela . . .

—Si son cristianos, ¿por qué me matan? En vez de enviarle a Ud. a que me abra las puertas de la vida eterna, que empiecen por no cerrarme las de ésta . . . No quiero morir, ¿entiende Ud.? Me rebelo a morir. Soy joven, estoy sano, soy rico, tengo padres y una novia que me adora. La vida es bella, muy bella para mí . . . Morir en el campo de batalla, en medio del combate, al lado de los compañeros que luchan . . . ¡bueno, bueno! pero morir, oscura y tristemente en el rincón de una sucia plazuela, a las primeras luces del alba, sin que nadie sepa siquiera que ha muerto uno como los hombres . . . padre, padre, ¡eso es horrible! Y el infeliz se echó en el suelo, sollozando.

—Hijo mío—dijo el sacerdote cuando comprendió que podía ser oído—: Yo no vengo a traerle a Ud. los consuelos de la religión. En esta vez soy emisario de los hombres y no de Dios. Si Ud. me hubiese oído con calma desde el principio, hubiera Ud. evitado esa pena que le hace sollozar de tal manera. Yo vengo a traerle justamente la vida, ¿entiende Ud.? esa vida que Ud. pedía hace un instante con tales extremos de angustia . . . ¡la vida que es para Ud. tan preciosa! Oígame con atención, procurando dominar sus nervios y sus emociones, porque no tenemos tiempo que perder. He entrado con el pretexto de confesar a Ud. y es preciso que todos crean que Ud. se confiesa. Arrodíllese, pues y escúcheme. Tiene Ud. amigos poderosos que se interesan por su suerte. Su familia ha hecho hasta lo imposible por salvarlo. No pudiendo obtenerse del jefe de las armas la gracia a Ud., se ha logrado con graves dificultades y riesgos sobornar al jefe del pelotón encargado de fusilarle. Los fusiles estarán cargados sólo con pólvora y taco, al oir el disparo Ud. caerá como los otros y permanecerá inmóvil. La oscuridad de la hora le ayudará a representar esta comedia. Manos piadosas, las de los Hermanos de la Misericordia, ya de acuerdo, lo recogerán a Ud. del sitio en cuanto el pelotón se aleje. Lo ocultarán hasta llegada la noche, durante la cual sus amigos facilitarán su huida. Las tropas liberales avanzan sobre la ciudad, a la que pondrán sin duda cerco dentro de breves horas. Se unirá Ud. a ellas si gusta. Ya lo sabe Ud. todo. Ahora rece en voz alta, mientras pronuncio la fórmula de la absolución. Procure dominar su júbilo durante el tiempo que falta para la ejecución, a fin de que nadie sospeche la verdad.

III

—Padre—murmuró el oficial, a quien la invasión de una alegría loca permitía apenas el uso de la palabra—¡que Dios lo bendiga!

Y luego, una duda terrible: —Pero . . . ¿todo es verdad?—añadió temblando—. ¿No se trata de un engaño piadoso, destinado a endulzar mis últimas horas? ¡Oh, eso sería horrible, padre!

—Hijo mío: un engaño de tal naturaleza constituiría la mayor de las infamias, y yo soy incapaz de cometerla . . .

—Es cierto, padre; perdóneme, no sé lo que digo, ¡estoy loco de contento!

—Calma, hijo, mucha calma y hasta mañana; yo estaré con Ud. en el momento solemne.

Apuntaba Empezaba

Apuntaba apenas el alba, una alba friolenta de febrero, cuando los presos . . . cinco por todos . . . que debían ser ejecutados, fueron sacados de la prisión. Fueron conducidos, en compañía del sacerdote, que rezaba con ellos, a una plazuela donde era costumbre llevar a cabo las ejecuciones.

Nuestro Luis marchaba entre todos con paso firme, con erguida frente. Pero llevaba llena el alma de una emoción desconocida y de un deseo infinito de que acabase pronto aquella horrible farsa.

escoltaba acompañaba

Al llegar a la plazuela, los cinco hombres fueron colocados en fila a cierta distancia. La tropa que los escoltaba se dividió en cinco grupos de a siete hombres según previa distribución hecha en el cuartel.

que vendara a los reos that he blindfold those who were going to be executed

teñir dar color a

El coronel, que asistía a la ejecución, indicó al sacerdote que vendara a los reos y se alejase a cierta distancia. Así lo hizo el padre, y el jefe del pelotón dio las primeras órdenes con voz seca.

La leve sangre de la aurora empezaba a teñir las nubecillas del Oriente y estremecían el silencio de la madrugada los primeros toques de una campanita cercana que llamaba a misa.

De pronto, una espada en el aire y una detonación formidable y desigual llenó de ecos la plazuela, y los cinco cayeron trágicamente.

El jefe del pelotón hizo en seguida desfilar a sus hombres con la cara vuelta hacia los ajusticiados. Con breves órdenes organizó el regreso al cuartel, mientras que los Hermanos de la Misericordia comenzaban a recoger los cadáveres.

granuja vagabundo

En aquel momento, un granuja de los muchos que asistían a la ejecución, gritó, señalando a Luis, que yacía al pie del muro: —¡Ése está vivo! ¡ése está vivo! Ha movido una pierna . . .

desnudando *stripping, baring*
ceñida *girded, tied to the waist*

El jefe del pelotón se detuvo, vaciló un instante, quiso decir algo al granuja, pero sus ojos se encontraron con la mirada interrogativa y fría del coronel, y desnudando la gran pistola de Colt que llevaba ceñida, avanzó hacia Luis que preso del terror más espantoso, casi no respiraba, apoyó el cañón en su sien izquierda e hizo fuego.

PARA APLICAR

Comprensión I

A Conteste a las siguientes preguntas.

1 ¿Dónde estaba Luis al principio del cuento?
2 ¿Por qué se encontraba allí?
3 ¿Iba Luis a morir por su Patria?
4 ¿Qué clase de patriota era Luis?
5 ¿Quería Luis morir por su Patria?

B Termine las oraciones según la selección.

1 Luis estaba pensando en
2 Pasaba su niñez en un caserón
3 De su adolescencia recordaba
4 El paisaje de su juventud se desarrollaba, y él recordaba
5 El entusiasmo patriótico le hizo
6 Va a morir como traidor porque
7 Fue capturado con
8 Fue ofrecido con otros compañeros a cambio de
9 Su última esperanza se desvaneció porque
10 No quería morir porque era
11 Para él la Patria era
12 En cambio la vida era
13 Algo en su conciencia le dijo que la Patria
14 Debido a su tormento el joven lloraba y
15 Al asomarse los centinelas por la rejilla él veía

Comprensión II

A Conteste a las siguientes preguntas.

1 ¿Quién era el personaje que visitó a Luis en la cárcel?

2 ¿De quién era emisario?
3 ¿Qué mensaje le trajo a Luis?
4 ¿Quiénes van a recoger los cuerpos después de la ejecución?
5 ¿Dónde va a tener lugar la ejecución?

B ¿Verdadero o falso?

1 Oyó cucarachas en el suelo.
2 Un sacerdote entró en su celda.
3 El joven lo detuvo para confesarse.
4 Él no quería entrar en la vida eterna todavía.
5 Morir en un campo de batalla no era ninguna deshonra.
6 El sacerdote le trajo consuelos de religión.
7 Luis debía dominarse y escuchar.
8 Sus padres habían sobornado al jefe del pelotón.
9 Mañana temprano van a servir tacos.
10 No habrá balas en los fusiles.
11 Luis es gracioso y va a estar en una comedia.
12 Cuando se oiga el disparo, el joven tendrá que caer como los otros ajusticiados.
13 Las Hermanas de la Misericordia lo ocultarán hasta la llegada de los liberales.
14 Luis gritó porque no podía callarse por su alivio y alegría.
15 Nadie sospechaba que el cura le hubiera dado la absolución.

Comprensión III

A Conteste a las siguientes preguntas.

1 Cuando se oyó la detonación, ¿por qué no murió Luis?

2 ¿Qué dijo el granuja?

3 ¿Cómo lo sabía él?

4 Describa el papel del coronel en la ejecución.

5 ¿Por qué murió Luis al fin?

B Escoja la expresión de la segunda lista (2) que completa la idea empezada en la primera lista (1).

1

1 Luis

2 Temía que

3 El cura

4 Los presos fueron sacados de la prisión

5 En su alma guardaba un deseo infinito de que

6 El coronel indicó al cura que

7 A las primeras luces del alba

8 Se oyó una detonación formidable y desigual

9 Un granuja, señalando a Luis,

10 Puesto que el coronel lo miraba,

2

a. terminara pronto ese horror.

b. y cayeron tristemente los cinco jóvenes.

c. bendijo al sacerdote.

d. cuando apenas amanecía.

e. el jefe del pelotón tuvo que matar a Luis.

f. vendara los ojos de los ajusticiados.

g. fuera un engaño piadoso.

h. las campanas anunciaban la primera misa.

i. era incapaz de tal infamia.

j. gritó que uno vivía.

Más Práctica

A Complete las siguientes oraciones con una palabra apropiada.

1 El pobre ajusticiado tuvo que _____ el momento de la muerte en la cárcel.

2 Era un _____ del joven ver libre a su país.

3 Le tiraron en la _____.

4 Era una mañana _____ que merecía un abrigo.

5 ¡Qué _____ matar a un joven inocente!

6 La revolución causa mucha _____ en la vida diaria de los ciudadanos.

7 El joven orgulloso siempre iba con la cabeza _____.

8 No se puede _____ la amargura del joven condenado.

9 Es un hombre trabajador y serio; no es ningún _____.

10 Allí _____ el cadáver del asesinado.

B Dé un sinónimo de las palabras en letra bastardilla.

1 Es un *vagabundo*.

2 Van a *alzarse en rebelión* contra el régimen.

3 Esto le *molesta* mucho.

4 Pudimos oir el *murmullo* de los espectadores.

5 No se puede *hacer más dulce* tal situación.

6 Sería difícil *corromper* a la jefa.

7 Quería *asociarse* con los revolucionarios.

8 Apareció ante el juez con la cabeza *levantada*.

9 Tendrán que *esperar* a que venga el capitán.

C Conteste a las siguientes preguntas según la indicación.

1 ¿Con quiénes se afilió la joven? *liberales*

2 ¿Por qué no hizo nada de valor? *granuja*

3 ¿Por qué lo visitó el cura? *endulzar su pena*

4   ¿Por qué hay tanta turbación?   *sublevar los revolucionarios*
5   ¿Qué trataron de hacerle al oficial?   *sobornar*
6   ¿Llegó sano y salvo?   *apenas*
7   ¿Qué escucha el guardián?   *cuchicheo del ajusticiado*
8   ¿Qué fue el acto que cometió?   *infamia*

Ejercicios Creativos

1   ¿Cuáles son los aspectos trágicos de la muerte de Luis?
2   Imagine que a Ud., como a Luis, le espera la muerte. ¿En qué pensaría?
3   ¿Cómo emplea el autor la ironía para aumentar el conflicto trágico?

España: 1936

Mejor que perros

José Mancisidor

PARA PRESENTAR LA LECTURA

Cuando tenía más o menos veinte años, José Mancisidor se juntó con las fuerzas revolucionarias de México luchando contra el dictador Victoriano Huerta. Éste se había apoderado de las riendas del gobierno y había ordenado la supresión de los revolucionarios. Había numerosos encuentros entre las tropas federales (huertistas) y los rebeldes. Quizás una experiencia sufrida mientras servía en el ejército de los rebeldes haya dado origen a este cuento.

Mancisidor es un autor que se interesa por los cambios sociales y las razones políticas y económicas que los influyen. Tiene gran simpatía por la clase social de la cual es producto. Es un escritor sensible, interesado, preocupado sobre todo con la confraternidad. En este cuento describe la compasión, el interés común que sienten dos adversarios.

PARA APRENDER VOCABULARIO

Palabras Clave   I

1 **ahogaba (ahogarse)** se sofocaba en agua, humo, pensamiento *(drowned, submerged)*
Se ahogaba el joven en sus pensamientos profundos.

2 **a través de** por, entre
Caminamos muchas horas a través de los campos.

3 **aullido** voz triste y prolongada del lobo y del perro
Se oyó en la noche el aullido de un lobo solitario.

4 **barranco** precipicio causado por las corrientes de las aguas
El caballo se cayó por el barranco y no pudimos salvarlo.

5 **encima de**   sobre   (on top of, above)
El helicóptero pasó justo encima de nuestras cabezas; casi nos mató.

6 **honda**   profunda
Cuando Marta quería expresar su honda sinceridad, le miraba a los ojos a la persona con quien hablaba.

7 **hundir**   meter en lo hondo   (to sink)
Para esconder su dinero, la abuelita lo tenía que hundir en la maleta.

8 **resbalar**   moverse sin fricción sobre algo (to slide)
Hay peligro de resbalar sobre las piedras mojadas.

9 **roncaba (roncar)**   hacía ruido al respirar mientras dormía
Susana roncaba al dormir, pero no lo quería creer.

10 **sacudió (sacudir)**   movió violentamente
La explosión sacudió el edificio y rompió muchas ventanas.

11 **serranía**   terreno compuesto de montañas y sierras
Los caballos eran indispensables en la enorme serranía.

Práctica

Complete con una palabra de la lista.

sacudió	a través de	serranía
encima de	barranco	roncaba
honda	ahogaba	resbalar
aullido	hundir	

1 En el fondo del _____ se veían piedras caídas.
2 Cruzamos _____ las montañas para llegar al campamento.
3 El triste _____ de los perros no me dejó dormir.
4 La mirada que me echó me hizo una _____ impresión.

5 Salimos con precaución para no _____ en la nieve.
6 Su hermano _____ tan fuerte que nadie en la casa podía dormir.
7 Un movimiento rápido de viento helado _____ mi cuerpo.
8 Todos vinieron a salvar a la niñita que se _____ en el río.
9 El avión pasaba _____ la serranía.
10 Se separó de los otros y trató de _____ sus pensamientos en el sueño.
11 El soldado decidió pasar la noche en el pico más alto de la _____.

Palabras Clave   II

1 **apreté (apretar – ie)**   oprimí   (squeezed)
Apreté la mano del joven rebelde.

2 **burlamos (burlarse)**   despreciamos (scoffed, made fun of)
Nos burlamos de su manera de pensar.

3 **párpados**   piel que cubre los ojos para dormir y para protegerlos
Ángela cerró los párpados para meditar y se quedó dormida.

4 **tripas**   intestinos   (guts)
Recibió una bala en las tripas.

Práctica

Complete con una palabra de la lista.

apreté	tripas
burlamos	párpados

1 Cuando yo entré, vi a todos los alumnos con los _____ cerrados, meditando en silencio.
2 El automóvil pasó por encima del animal y lo dejó con las _____ afuera.
3 Nos _____ del granuja que vimos en la calle.
4 Para no caerme, _____ la mano del amigo que me acompañaba.

Mejor que perros

José Mancisidor

I

La noche se nos había venido encima de golpe. El Coronel ordenó hacer alto y pernoctar sobre el elevado picacho de la intrincada serranía. Por valles y colinas y en el fondo del cercano barranco, disparos aislados acosaban a los dispersos. A mi lado, los prisioneros arrebujados en sus tilmas, dejaban al descubierto los ojos negros y expresivos que se extraviaban en insondables lejanías.

Una racha de viento helado sacudió mi cuerpo y un lúgubre aullido hizo crujir entre mis dientes la hoja del cigarro.

El Coronel, mirándome con fijeza, me preguntó:

—¿Cuántos muchachos le faltan?

Llamé al oficial subalterno, le di órdenes de pasar lista y quedé nuevamente de pie, sobre la cúspide pronunciada de la sierra, como un punto luminoso en la impenetrable oscuridad de la noche.

El Coronel volvió a llamarme. Me hizo tomar un trago de alcohol y me ordenó:

—Mañana, a primera hora, fusile a los prisioneros . . .

Luego, sordo al cansancio de la jornada, me recomendó:

—Examínelos primero. Vea qué descubre sobre los planes del enemigo.

Al poco rato, el Coronel roncaba de cara al cielo, en el que la luna pálida trataba de descubrirnos.

* * *

Los prisioneros seguían allí, sin cerrar los ojos, sumidos en un hermetismo profundo que se ahogaba en el dramático silencio de la noche.

---

hacer alto parar
pernoctar pasar la noche
picacho pico
acosaban harassed
arrebujados bundled
tilmas cloaks
se extraviaban wandered
insondables unfathomable
racha gust
crujir creak

subalterno inferior
cúspide summit

sordo oblivious
jornada journey

sumidos en un hermetismo
encerrados en sí mismos

Encima de nuestras cabezas pasaba el cantar del viento y tenue, muy tenue, el susurrar de los montes que murmuraban algo que yo no podía comprender.

Se avivaron los rescoldos de la lumbre y los ojos de los prisioneros brillaron en un relámpago fugaz. Me senté junto a ellos y brindándoles hoja y tabaco, les hablé, con el tono fingido de un amigo, de cosas intrascendentes.

Mi voz, a través del murmullo de los montes, era un murmullo también. Brotaba suave, trémula por la fatiga y parecía dotada de honda sinceridad.

Los prisioneros me miraban sin verme. Fijaban su vista hacia donde yo estaba para resbalarla sobre mi cabeza y hundirla allá en las moles espesas de la abrupta serranía. De sus ojos, como aristas aceradas, brotaba una luz viva y penetrante.

—¿Por qué pelean?—aventuré sin obtener respuesta.

El silencio se hizo más grave aun, casi enojoso.

Me enderecé de un salto, llegué hasta el Coronel y apoderándome de la botella que antes me brindara, la pasé a los prisioneros, invitándoles a beber. Dos de ellos se negaron a hacerlo, pero el otro, temblándole el brazo, se apresuró a aceptar. Después se limpió la boca con el dorso de la mano y me dirigió un gesto amargo que quiso ser una sonrisa.

*   *   *

II

Volví a sentarme junto a los hombres como esfinges, y obedeciendo a un impulso inexplicable, les hablé de mí. De mi niñez, de mi juventud que se deslizaba en la lucha armada y de un sueño que en mis años infantiles había sido como mi compañero inseparable. A veces tenía la impresión de locura, de hablar conmigo mismo y de estar frente a mi propia sombra, descompuesto en múltiples sombras bajo la vaga luz de la luna que huía entre montañas de nubes. Y olvidado de mis oyentes continuaba hablando, más para mí que para ellos, de aquello que de niño tanto había amado.

De repente una voz melodiosa vibró a mi lado y callé sorprendido de escuchar otra que no fuera la mía.

El más joven de los prisioneros, aquel que había aceptado la botella con mano temblorosa, ocultando los ojos tras los párpados cerrados, meditaba:

—Es curiosa la vida . . . Como tú, yo también tuve sueños de niño. Y como tú . . . ¡qué coincidencia! . . . soñé en las mismas cosas de que has hablado. ¿Por qué será así la vida?

Tornó a soplar una racha helada que se hizo más lastimera y más impresionante.

El joven prisionero quedó pensativo para después continuar:

Acosado Perseguido
mendrugos *crusts of bread*

—Me sentí como tú, peor que perro . . . Acosado por todas partes. Comiendo mendrugos y bebiendo el agua negra de los caminos.

gemido *moan*

Calló y luego, quebrándose su voz en un gemido:

—Ahora seré algo peor—dijo—. Seré un perro muerto con las tripas al sol y a las aguas, devorado por los coyotes.

tiritar *to shiver*
filo *edge*

—¡Calla!—ordené con voz cuyo eco parecía tiritar sobre el filo de la noche.

Guardé silencio y me tendí junto a los prisioneros que pensaban tal vez en la oscuridad de otra noche más larga, eterna, de la que nunca habrían de volver.

*   *   *

Poco a poco me fui aproximando a ellos y al oído del que había hablado repetí:

—¿Por qué peleas tú?

—No te lo podría explicar . . . Pero es algo que sube a mi corazón y me ahoga a toda hora. Un intenso deseo de vivir entre hombres cuya vida no sea peor que la vida de los perros.

cobija manta

Saqué mi mano de la cobija que la envolvía y buscando la suya la apreté con emoción profunda. Y luego, acercando mi boca hasta rozar su oreja, le dije velando la voz:

rozar *to touch slightly*

—¿Quieres que busquemos nuestro sueño juntos?

adivinaron *guessed*

Los otros prisioneros adivinaron nuestro diálogo. Nos miraron con interrogaciones en la mirada, y enterados de nuestros planes, se apresuraron a seguirnos.

Nos arrastramos trabajosamente. Cerca, el centinela parecía cristalizado por el frío de la hora, sobre la oscura montaña. Burlamos su vigilancia y nos hundimos en el misterio de la noche. La luna se había ocultado ya y mis nuevos compañeros y yo, dando

dando traspiés *stumbling*

traspiés, corríamos por montes y valles en busca de un mundo en que los hombres, como en nuestros sueños de niños, vivieran una vida mejor que la vida de los perros . . .

PARA APLICAR

Comprensión   I

A   Conteste a las siguientes preguntas.

1   ¿Qué ordenó el Coronel?
2   ¿Qué molestaba a los dispersos?
3   ¿Qué sacudió el cuerpo del joven protagonista?
4   ¿Qué le preguntó el Coronel?
5   ¿Quién tuvo que pasar lista?
6   ¿Quién le dio un trago?
7   ¿Qué ordenó el Coronel?
8   ¿Por qué debía José examinar a los prisioneros?
9   Al poco rato, ¿qué hizo el Coronel?
10 ¿Dónde se sentó José y qué les ofreció a los prisioneros?
11 ¿Qué fingió ser?
12 ¿Qué pregunta les hizo José?
13 ¿Qué contestaron los prisioneros?
14 ¿De qué se apoderó José?
15 ¿A quiénes se la ofreció?
16 ¿Aceptaron ellos?

B   ¿Verdadero o falso?

1   Llegó la noche muy rápidamente.
2   Los prisioneros se envolvían en sus mantas, sin cubrirse los ojos.
3   Hacía calor en la serranía.
4   El Coronel dejó órdenes que lo fusilaran mañana a primera hora.
5   El jefe quería que José interrogara a los prisioneros sobre los planes del enemigo.
6   Los prisioneros estaban sumidos en el silencio de la noche.
7   José les habló sincera y amistosamente a los prisioneros.
8   Los prisioneros le miraban intensamente.
9   Los prisioneros querían saber por qué él peleaba.
10 Cuando José les ofreció la botella todos se apresuraron a aceptar.

Comprensión   II

A   Conteste a las siguientes preguntas.

1   ¿De qué les habló José a los prisioneros?
2   ¿De quién era la voz que oyó José?
3   ¿Por qué le sorprendió a José?
4   ¿Qué tenía también el joven?
5   ¿Cómo había sido el joven?
6   ¿Cómo será?
7   ¿Qué ordenó José?
8   ¿A quién repitió su pregunta?
9   ¿Qué contestó el joven?
10 ¿Qué le sugirió José al joven?
11 ¿Quiénes escaparon?
12 ¿Qué buscaban?

B   Escoja la respuesta apropiada.

1   Después de sentarse de nuevo, ¿de qué habló José?
   a.   de los hombres esfinges
   b.   de un sueño de su compañero inseparable
   c.   de lo que le gustaba cuando era niño
2   ¿Qué le dijo el joven prisionero?
   a.   que él había tenido los mismos sueños también
   b.   que le dolían los ojos aun tras los párpados cerrados
   c.   que su perro fue acosado por todas partes
3   ¿En qué pensarían los prisioneros?
   a.   en el pan que comerían mañana
   b.   en su muerte
   c.   en por qué José se tendió junto a ellos
4   ¿Qué razón le dio a José para pelear?
   a.   Quería una vida mejor que la de los perros.
   b.   Tenía que cuidar su corazón.
   c.   Temía ahogarse a toda hora.
5   ¿De qué se dieron cuenta?
   a.   El centinela había muerto debido al frío.
   b.   Compartían la misma ilusión.
   c.   Habían adivinado los pensamientos de sus nuevos compañeros.

España: nacionalistas vascos

Más Práctica

A Complete las siguientes oraciones con una palabra apropiada.

1 Los _____ protegen los ojos.
2 Pudimos oir el _____ triste del perro salvaje.
3 _____ sobre la nieve y se rompió la pierna.
4 El viento fuerte _____ las casuchas.
5 Corrieron _____ los campos en busca de los revolucionarios.
6 Se durmió y empezó a _____.
7 Era difícil cruzar la _____.

B Conteste a las siguientes preguntas.

1 ¿Qué hacía mientras dormía?
2 ¿Cómo se cayó sobre la nieve?
3 Ya que no le dije nada, ¿cómo lo sabía él?
4 ¿Qué causó la corriente feroz del agua?
5 ¿Qué sacudió los edificios?

Ejercicios Creativos

1 Los protagonistas de este cuento «tenían un sueño». ¿Cuál era? Nombre algunos personajes (de la historia o de la literatura, del pasado o contemporáneos) que buscaban un ideal parecido.
2 Analice el título del cuento. ¿Por qué ha escogido el autor este título? Haga una lista de otros títulos posibles.
3 Un mundo de filosofía existe en la pregunta: «¿Por qué será así la vida?» Prepare algún comentario.

En el Ford azul

Lizandro Otero

PARA PRESENTAR LA LECTURA

En muchas partes del mundo la gente vive bajo dictaduras donde los ciudadanos son vigilados noche y día. Bajo estas condiciones es inevitable que nazcan revoluciones y rebeliones. Siempre habrá gente idealista que trata de cambiar el gobierno y la sociedad. Algunos de éstos creen en la violencia, mientras otros, no menos heroicos, creen que la pluma es más poderosa que la espada. Éstos arriesgan también sus vidas en busca de un ideal.

PARA APRENDER VOCABULARIO

Palabras Clave   I

1 **bujía**   lo que produce la chispa que arranca el motor del automóvil   (*spark plug*)
Si falta aun una bujía el motor no arranca.

2 **loma**   cerro largo y poco elevado
Desde la loma donde está la prisión hay una vista excelente de ese sector de la ciudad.

3 **palpó (palpar)**   tocó con las manos
Elena palpó la manta para ver si todavía estaba mojada.

4 **reposaba (reposar)**   descansaba del trabajo
Hay que dejar reposar un rato esa máquina después de usarla una hora.

5 **ruedas**   objetos circulares de goma que facilitan el movimiento de un vehículo
Los coches corren en cuatro ruedas de goma.

6 **semáforo**   señal iluminada que controla el tráfico, luz de tránsito
Esa esquina es muy peligrosa; realmente necesita un semáforo.

Práctica

Complete con una palabra de la lista.

semáforo	*palpó*	*bujía*
loma	*ruedas*	*reposaba*

1 Después de trabajar diez horas, _____ en casa toda la noche.
2 _____ la fruta para escoger una buena y madura.
3 Es difícil arrancar porque tiene una _____ defectuosa.
4 Es más agradable vivir en la _____ que abajo en la ciudad.
5 Espera hasta que cambie el _____.
6 Se oyó el ruido de _____ en el pavimento.

Palabras Clave   II

1 **acera**   orilla de la calle pavimentada reservada para los que van a pie
   La señora Perales salió de la casa y caminó por la acera.

2 **agarra (agarrar)**   toma bruscamente con las manos   (*grabs*)
   María agarró los paquetes y los llevó al despacho.

3 **calzada**   camino o calle pavimentado
   Siga por esta senda hasta llegar a la calzada.

4 **disfrutaba (disfrutar)**   gozaba, aprovechaba
   Disfrutaba de una libertad sin límites.

Manifestación estudiantil

5 **huelga**   paro colectivo del trabajo para ganar los fines deseados

No llega ninguna mercancía a la ciudad a causa de la huelga de camioneros.

6 **peatones**   los que caminan a pie

Las aceras están reservadas para los peatones.

Práctica

Complete con una palabra de la lista.

huelga	agarra	calzada
acera	peatones	disfrutaba

1 Ramón siempre _____ de su tiempo libre durante las vacaciones.
2 No te pagan si hay _____. ¿Estás segura que vale la pena?
3 Deja que pasen los _____ en la esquina.
4 Los peatones tienen que caminar en la calle porque están reparando la _____.
5 _____ la pistola y escóndela.
6 La lluvia echó a perder toda la _____ y queda puro barro allí. Nadie puede pasar.

Palabras Clave   III

1 **agotado**   fatigado, cansado

Susana está completamente agotada después de hacer tanto trabajo físico.

2 **aguantar**   soportar, sufrir, tolerar

Este profesor no aguanta más las burlas de la clase.

3 **desabotonó (desabotonar)**   desabrochó (*unbuttoned*)

Desabotonó la camisa del ladrón y encontró una pistola.

Práctica

Complete con una palabra de la lista.

aguantar	agotado	desabotonó

1 ¿Por qué llegas a casa tan _____? ¿Caminaste mucho?
2 Vi la cicatriz en el pecho cuando Enrique se _____ la camisa.
3 ¿Quién puede _____ tal insolencia?

En el Ford azul

Lizandro Otero

I

trasladar llevar

Tenían el automóvil, que era lo importante. Para trasladar algo hacen falta cuatro ruedas y lo demás es secundario. El «movimiento» les prestó el Ford azul que, con una bujía defectuosa, podía subir a ochenta en menos de cien metros.

Antonio lo parqueó en el garaje y caminó hasta la casa.

—¿Está bueno?

—Camina bien.

—Pero . . . ¿bueno?

—¿Qué tú quieres? Camina. Hasta corre.

cargar *carry*

—Ayúdame a cargar.

—¿Así, en la calle?

quemada vigilada
chivatos policías, espías

—La casa no está quemada.

—¿No hay chivatos?

—Casi seguro que no.

Entraron en la casa. La sala estaba vacía. En el primer cuarto había un catre de lona y una pistola en el piso. En el segundo

catre de lona *canvas cot*
multilit *copy machine*

cuarto, cubierta con un nailon, reposaba la *multilit*. Junto a ella, cuatro paquetes.

—Lleva tú dos y yo dos—dijo Yoyi.

—Ponlos en el asiento de delante.

—En el maletero es mejor.

maletero *trunk, luggage compartment*

—Es lo primero que registran. En el asiento es más inocente.

baranda *railing*

Al salir, Yoyi descansó sus paquetes en la baranda para cerrar la puerta con doble llave. Subieron al Ford y Antonio salió en marcha atrás. Pasaron del Ensanche a Carlos III. Cruzaron frente a la Quinta de los Molinos.

—Ése es un buen lugar—dijo Yoyi.

FEU Federación Estudiantil Universitaria

—Está muy quemado. La FEU lo quemó muy pronto.

—No fue la FEU.

—Pero es un buen lugar.

—Sí, muy bueno.

—Hasta prácticas de tiro hacían ahí.

—Es muy bueno, qué lástima.

—Hay otros mejores.

—No tan buenos, no con tanto espacio.

—Ahora está muy vigilado.

—Es muy cerca de la Universidad.

Antonio aprovechó la luz roja del semáforo para encender un **regalía** superfino. Palpó los paquetes.

regalía cigarro

—¿Está bueno este número?

—Trae noticias—respondió Yoyi.

—¿De la Sierra?

—De todo.

—Debe estar bueno.

Con la luz verde, continuaron. Antonio cuidaba de no pasar de los cincuenta. El motor ronroneaba seguro. Cruzaron frente al **castillo del Príncipe**. En lo alto de la loma, las **almenas** y las siluetas de los guardias.

castillo del Príncipe
nombre de una prisión
almenas *turrets*

—Tico está ahí—dijo Antonio.

—Si fuera Tico nada más.

—Tico es el último.

—El último nunca existe. Puedo ser yo o tú.

—Tuvo suerte, está vivo.

—¿Sabes cómo lo cogieron, Antonio?

—No, dime.

—Iba en una ruta 28 por la calle 23 y en la esquina de Paseo ve a un señor que lo saluda desde la calle. Tico contestó al saludo. El señor sube a la **guagua** y siguen viaje. A Tico se le parecía un amigo de su padre. En la calle G se baja Tico y el señor también. Tico se le acerca y lo saluda. El señor le dice: «¿Cómo está tu mamá, Tico?» Él contesta que muy bien y por decir algo le pregunta por su esposa. «¿Adónde vas ahora?» Tico le dice que a casa de su primo, al Edificio Chibás, que era donde realmente iba.

guagua autobús

—¿Y qué?

¿Y qué? *So what?*

—A los diez minutos se presentó el tipo de la guagua con tres del buró y se lo llevaron a él y al primo.

—¡Qué idiota!

—A cualquiera le pasa.

—Sí, a cualquiera le pasa **si está suave**.

si está suave *if he's careless*

—En cualquier momento . . .

—No, cuando uno los tiene atrás, camina con cuatro ojos, se cuida hasta de la sombra.

—Pero cuando uno los tiene atrás no se vive. No sabes si vas para el Príncipe o para aquí—dijo Yoyi señalando con un dedo hacia la monumental portada del cementerio de Colón.

II

Habían bajado toda la calzada de Zapata y doblaban frente a Colón para tomar por la calle 12. En ese instante, con un chirriar de gomas, los interceptó la perseguidora.

chirriar de gomas *screeching of tires*

—¡Arrímate ahí! —gritó el cabo bajándose con una ametralladora en la mano. Otro policía se bajó del lado opuesto y el cabo le entregó la ametralladora para que lo cubriera mientras se acercaba al Ford azul.

Arrímate Acércate
ametralladora *machine gun*

Antonio sintió que el estómago se le encogía como si fuese a disolverse.

se le encogía *contracted*

El cabo se acodó en la ventanilla y vio los paquetes.

acodó apoyó el codo sobre

—¿Qué llevan ahí?

—Medicinas —dijo Antonio.

—¿Para los rebeldes? —dijo el cabo sonriendo.

—No juegue con eso, cabo, yo trabajo en un laboratorio.

—¿De quién es este carro?

—Mío.

—Bueno, pues tiene la chapa vencida.

chapa vencida *expired license plate*

—¿Vencida?

—Vencida.

—Pero ¿cómo es posible?

—Ya lo sabes.

—¿Qué puede hacerse?

—Me tengo que llevar el carro.

—Por favor, cabo, déjemelo aunque sea un día más. Hoy mismo le saco la chapa. Es que he tenido mucho trabajo . . .

—De eso nada, me lo tengo que llevar.

El cabo disfrutaba obviamente con el trastorno que le producía al muchacho y Antonio insistió para satisfacer el sadismo del policía en la negación.

—Déjemelo aunque sea un día más, cabo, aunque sea un día.

—No, no, 'ta bueno ya. Vamos para la novena estación. ¿Sabes dónde es?

dale *hit it, get going*

—Sí, ahí en Zapata.

—Bueno, dale. Nosotros te seguimos.

Antonio encendió el motor y esperó que los policías subieran a la perseguidora para poner la primera.

—¿Qué hacemos?—preguntó Yoyi.

apéate *bájate*

—Te tienes que bajar—dijo Antonio—. Agarra los paquetes y apéate en 12 y 23. Hazlo natural, no te apures.

El Ford descendió por la 12, seguido a corta distancia por la perseguidora. Se detuvieron en el semáforo de la calle 23. Yoyi tomó tres paquetes en sus brazos. Apenas podía. El último se lo

tapaba *cubría*

situó Antonio. Casi le tapaba la nariz. Antonio abrió la portezuela y Yoyi descendió haciendo equilibrios con los paquetes.

La perseguidora aceleró en seco para colocarse junto al Ford.

—¿Qué le pasa a ése? —preguntó el cabo.

seguir las diligencias *keep on working*
nos botan *they'll fire us*

—Tiene que seguir las diligencias, cabo. Si no, nos botan.

No contestó. El cabo había almorzado bien y fumaba un buen tabaco. Era feliz.

retrovisor *rearview mirror*

La luz verde. La perseguidora avanzó primero. Antonio la siguió. Al doblar por 23 miró a Yoyi por el retrovisor. En ese instante el cuarto paquete se balanceaba y Yoyi trataba de esta-bilizarlo, pero no pudo y el paquete cayó sobre la acera y se deshizo.

Las hojas volaron, cubrieron la acera y el asfalto de la calle. Dos palabras gruesas, entintadas, podían leerse a distancia: HUELGA y, más abajo, ASESINOS.

Yoyi echó a andar, con los tres paquetes, en dirección de la calle 25. Los peatones que esperaban en la esquina de 12 y 23 vieron los periódicos y leyeron las palabras. Una mujer comenzó a dar un paseíto inquieto y corto. Un hombre caminó hasta la otra esquina para esperar la guagua allí. Nadie dijo nada. Yoyi desapareció doblando por 25.

III

cartera dactilar *I.D. card*
circulación *registration*

En la novena estación de policía, Antonio entregó su cartera dactilar al sargento de guardia y la circulación del Ford.

—La circulación no está a su nombre.

—Ya lo sé—dijo Antonio.

—¿Quién es esta María Ruiz?

—Mi tía.

—Bueno, tiene que ser ella la que recoja el carro cuando tenga la chapa nueva.

El sargento le devolvió los documentos.

—¿Y yo?

—Puede irse.

Antonio iba llegando a la puerta cuando una voz gritó desde el fondo:

—¡Un momento!

El policía de guardia le impidió el paso con su Garand. Antonio se volvió. Era un hombre con un pantalón blanco y una camisa de colores que usaba con los faldones por fuera.

faldones *shirttails*

—Yo te conozco a ti.

Antonio distinguió en la cintura del hombre que se le acercaba el bulto de la 45. Sintió que el estómago se le encogía de nuevo.

—Tú eres Ernesto Suárez, ¿no?

—No, señor.

—¿Cómo que no? ¿Yo soy un mentiroso acaso?

—No, señor, usted no es un mentiroso.

—A ver, Ramón, ¿yo soy un mentiroso?

—No, mi teniente.

—Tú, Candela, ¿me conoces de mentiroso?

—No, señor.

—Tú lo ves, Ernestico. Yo no miento.

—Eso se ve en seguida, teniente.

—¿Cómo sabes que soy teniente?

—Porque lo han llamado aquí.

—¿Tú eres Ernestico Suárez?

Antonio desabotonó el bolsillo superior de la camisa y extrajo la cartera dactilar.

—Mire, teniente, éste soy yo.

El hombre de la camisa de colores examinó atento la identi-ficfición y se volvió hacia el sargento de guardia.

—¿Está limpio?

—Es una chapa vieja—respondió el sargento.

—Bueno, puedes irte, Ernestico . . . porque no eres Ernestico.

manotazo *pat*

Le dio un manotazo a Antonio en el hombro.

—Es una lástima porque tú puedes aguantar unos cuantos

mameyazos *golpes, palos*

mameyazos.

—Lo siento, teniente.

El teniente se rió y caminó, subiéndose el pantalón que se le corría por el peso de la pistola, hacia el bebedero.

Antonio salió contento de la estación porque había pasado bien por todo, pero lo mortificaba haber perdido un carro del «movimiento». Estaba cansado.

chequeado *"bugged"*

Fue a casa de Blanca, que no tenía el teléfono chequeado. Hizo varias llamadas. Supo que Yoyi tomó un taxi, después que bajó del Ford azul, y no paró hasta el Cerro y que los periódicos estaban a salvo.

a salvo *seguro*

Blanca era agradable de ver, joven y todo lo demás. Le ofreció una limonada fría, que Antonio bebió con una aspirina en el portal cruzado por la brisa.

Salió al anochecer. Fue hacia el Mercado Único en una guagua y tomó una sopa china con mucho pan. Cruzó la calle y entró en una casa de dormir para hombres solos y pagó veinticinco centavos por su cama. Se acostó vestido para que no le robaran la ropa. Durmió doce horas seguidas, porque el encuentro con la perseguidora lo había agotado.

PARA APLICAR

Comprensión   I

A Conteste a las siguientes preguntas.

1 ¿Para qué necesitan Antonio y Yoyi un automóvil?
2 Describa el Ford.
3 ¿Por qué está nervioso Antonio?
4 Describa la casa.
5 Según Antonio, ¿cuál es el lugar más seguro para los papeles?
6 ¿Qué hizo Antonio durante la parada en el semáforo?
7 ¿Qué tipo de papeles llevan?
8 Explique «Si fuera Tico nada más».
9 Explique «El último nunca existe. Puedo ser yo o tú».
10 ¿Por qué se lo habían llevado los del buró?
11 ¿Qué significa «Cuando uno tiene los ojos atrás no se vive»?

B Escoja la respuesta que *no* es apropiada para terminar la oración.

1 El Ford
   a. tenía algún defecto.
   b. pertenecía al «movimiento».
   c. no tenía ruedas.
2 En la casa había
   a. una cama.
   b. un cuarto cubierto con un nailon.
   c. un *multilit* recién usado.
3 Los jóvenes pusieron los paquetes de papeles en
   a. el maletero.
   b. el carro.
   c. el asiento delantero.

Ambiente de ira y violencia

4 Tico tuvo suerte de estar en el castillo del
   Príncipe porque
   a. está vivo.
   b. allí puede hacer prácticas de tiro con
       los otros prisioneros.
   c. le gusta estar en lo alto de la loma.
5 La policía lo arrestó a Tico porque
   a. se descuidó.
   b. iba al cementerio en vez del edificio
       Chibás.
   c. saludó a un señor en la guagua.

Comprensión   II

A Conteste a las siguientes preguntas.

1 ¿Qué oyeron cuando doblaban frente a
   Colón?
2 ¿Qué quería el policía que hiciera el chofer
   del Ford azul?
3 ¿Cómo se sintió Antonio?
4 Cite dos mentiras que le contó Antonio al
   cabo.
5 ¿Por qué fueron detenidos?
6 ¿Qué trató de hacer Antonio?

7 ¿Qué consejos le da Antonio a Yoyi?
8 ¿Cuándo bajó Yoyi?
9 ¿Por qué tenía dificultades?
10 ¿Por qué se acercó de nuevo el policía al Ford?
11 ¿Cómo le contestó Antonio?
12 ¿Por qué estaba contento el cabo?
13 ¿Qué le pasó a Yoyi?
14 ¿Qué se podía leer claramente en los papeles?
15 ¿Se interesaron los peatones en los papeles?

B ¿Verdadero o falso?

1 La persiguidora se acercó sin hacer ruido.
2 El cabo le indicó con su ametralladora que se acercara al lado.
3 Antonio trató de esconderse.
4 Antonio llevaba medicinas para los rebeldes.
5 Los detuvo porque el carro no tenía la chapa correcta.
6 El joven quería persuadir al cabo que le concediera un día para corregir el error.
7 Uno de los policías subió al coche con los jóvenes.
8 Antonio le dijo a Yoyi que bajara del coche y que llevara los paquetes.
9 También le dijo que corriera.
10 Los paquetes eran grandes y pesados.
11 Cuando el paquete se cayó, se abrió.
12 Los papeles decían que habría un baile mañana en esa esquina.
13 Todos en la esquina se callaron.
14 Yoyi trató de recogerlos antes de desaparecer.

Comprensión   III

A Conteste a las siguientes preguntas.

1 ¿Qué le entregó Antonio al sargento?
2 ¿A nombre de quién está registrado el Ford?
3 Describa al hombre que le gritó a Antonio.
4 Al ver Antonio que el hombre llevaba un 45, ¿qué le sucedió?

5 ¿En qué consistía la confusión?
6 ¿Cómo fue aclarada?
7 Antonio salió de la estación sintiendo alivio y mortificación. Explique por qué.
8 En la casa de Blanca el joven tuvo dos noticias buenas. ¿Cuáles eran?
9 Al anochecer después de salir de la casa de Blanca, ¿qué hizo?
10 ¿Cómo durmió esa noche?

B Termine las oraciones según la selección.

1 En la novena estación de policía Antonio entrega
2 El coche está registrado a nombre de
3 El sargento le dio permiso de
4 Al llegar Antonio a la puerta
5 El hombre declaró que
6 Otra vez Antonio, asustado, sintió que
7 Hubo confusión acerca de
8 Antonio aclaró el error con su
9 Antonio tuvo suerte porque
10 Se preocupaba Antonio por haber perdido
11 Fue a casa de Blanca porque
12 Supo que Yoyi y los periódicos
13 Al anochecer Antonio comió
14 Antonio durmió doce horas seguidas porque

Más Práctica

A Dé un sinónimo de las palabras en letra bastardilla.

1 *Acércate* al lado de la calle.
2 Antonio *desabrochó* el bolsillo superior de la camisa.
3 *Los que caminan* cruzan en esta esquina.
4 Mañana habrá *paro de trabajo* en el hospital.
5 El joven está *cansadísimo* después de los sustos y emociones del día.
6 Supo que los papeles estaban *seguros*.
7 Ponga estos paquetes en *la parte trasera* del coche.
8 Tuvo que tomar *la guagua*.
9 Durmió en *una camita portátil*.
10 *Gozaba* de las fiestas del fin del año.

B Escoja la palabra o la expresión de la segunda lista (2) que completa la idea empezada en la primera lista (1).

1

1 Cuando cambió la luz del _____ , siguió adelante.
2 Bajó del coche oficial y _____ en la ventanilla para hablarme.
3 Se protegía con su _____ .
4 _____ el bulto del asiento.
5 Pasearon por la _____ .
6 _____ en la próxima esquina.
7 Al llegar a la estación tuvo que presentar su _____ .
8 Por el susto se le _____ el estómago.
9 ¿No ves ese edificio encima de la _____ ?
10 _____ la ametralladora con las dos manos.

2

a. ametralladora
b. agarró
c. cartera dactilar
d. semáforo
e. apéate
f. encogía
g. palpó
h. loma
i. acodó
j. calzada

Ejercicios Creativos

1 Describa el ambiente de la selección. ¿Es un ambiente de horror, de suspenso, de intriga, de alegría, de humorismo? Justifique con ejemplos sus ideas.
2 ¿Cómo se puede clasificar a estos jóvenes rebeldes? ¿Son profesionales? ¿Tienen experiencia en este tipo de actividad?
3 Los jóvenes tuvieron que mentir varias veces para cumplir con su objetivo. Haga una lista de todas las mentiras.
4 ¿Qué va a hacer Antonio ahora? Escriba otro episodio describiendo lo que hace Antonio al día siguiente.

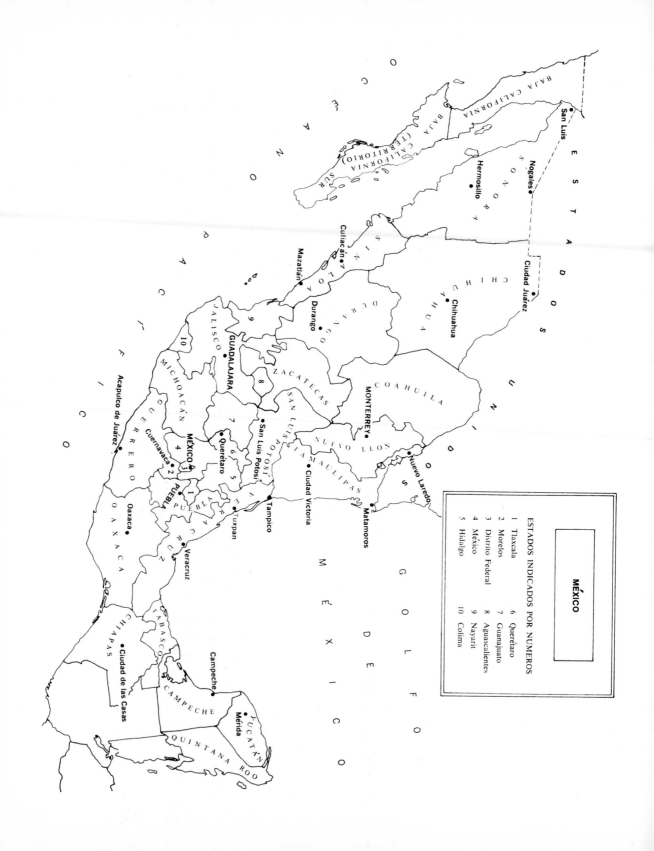

El Gerundio o Participio Presente

Estudien las siguientes formas de los gerundios de los verbos regulares.

infinitivo	gerundio
pasar	pasando
comer	comiendo
recibir	recibiendo

Algunos gerundios terminan en —*yendo*.

infinitivo	gerundio
caer	cayendo
construir	construyendo
creer	creyendo
destruir	destruyendo
huir	huyendo
leer	leyendo
oir	oyendo
traer	trayendo

Los verbos de cambio radical de las segunda y tercera clases exigen un cambio en la raíz del gerundio.

infinitivo	gerundio	infinitivo	gerundio
advertir	advirtiendo	pedir	pidiendo
convertir	convirtiendo	perseguir	persiguiendo
divertir	divirtiendo	reir	riendo
mentir	mintiendo	repetir	repitiendo
preferir	prefiriendo	seguir	siguiendo
sentir	sintiendo	sonreir	sonriendo
venir	viniendo	vestir	vistiendo
decir	diciendo	dormir	durmiendo
despedir	despidiendo	morir	muriendo
medir	midiendo		

Los verbos *ir* y *poder* tienen gerundios irregulares.

infinitivo	gerundio
ir	yendo
poder	pudiendo

El Tiempo Progresivo

La acción progresiva se expresa con un verbo auxiliar más el gerundio para indicar una acción que progresa en el momento indicado.

Ahora estoy leyendo.
En ese momento estábamos comiendo.

El énfasis se concentra en la acción misma y no en las consecuencias. Los verbos auxiliares más comunes son *estar, seguir, continuar, quedar, andar, venir* e *ir.*

Están resistiendo la conquista.
Sigue castigando a los pobres.

Los verbos *ser, estar, tener, haber, ir* y *venir* no se emplean en la forma progresiva.

Voy con él.
Vienen a verme.
Tenemos un examen.

A Sigan el modelo.

Castiga al joven.
Está castigando al joven.

1 Penetro en su casa.
2 Luis solloza desesperadamente.
3 Marta alza la cabeza.
4 Juan escucha al padre sin creerle.
5 Inician un plan para salvarlo.
6 El amor endulza sus pensamientos.
7 Le relata lo que tiene que hacer.
8 Luis reza y confiesa sus pecados.
9 El cura sale con los prisioneros.
10 El joven soldado cae al suelo.

B Sigan el modelo.

> *Notaban el miedo en su cara.*
> *Estaban notando el miedo en su cara.*

1 El joven militar pensaba en su mala fortuna.
2 Carmen recordaba su adolescencia.
3 En ese momento llegaba el sacerdote.
4 El cura trataba de consolarlo.
5 María explicaba lo que hicieron sus padres.
6 Los padres sobornaban al jefe del pelotón.
7 Salían de sus celdas al amanecer.
8 Los presos caminaban en compañía del cura.
9 Los Hermanos de la Misericordia comenzaban a recoger los cadáveres.

C Hagan la sustitución necesaria.

> *Luis está pensando en su vida.*

1 _____ continúa _____.

2 _____ sigue _____.
3 _____ recordando lo bueno de la vida.
4 Los padres _____.
5 _____ están _____.
6 _____ sobornando al jefe.
7 _____ van _____.
8 _____ dudando del plan.
9 Luis _____.

D Hagan la sustitución necesaria.

> *El cura estaba entrando en la sala.*

1 _____ esperando la salvación.
2 Luis _____.
3 _____ sollozando y gimiendo.
4 Los Hermanos de la Misericordia _____.
5 _____ recogiendo los cadáveres.
6 _____ seguían _____.
7 _____ inspeccionando los cadáveres.
8 Un granuja _____.
9 _____ gritando:—¡Éste está vivo!
10 _____ andaba _____.

El Gerundio como Adverbio

Se puede sustituir el gerundio por varias cláusulas adverbiales para indicar duración de tiempo, una condición o circunstancia, una causa o la manera de realizar algo. Corresponde a *-ing* en inglés.

E Sigan el modelo.

> *Cuando viajaba, era feliz.*
> *Viajando, era feliz.*

1 Cuando pensaba en su juventud, recordaba sus camaradas alegres.

2 Cuando recordaba a su novia, lloraba y sollozaba.
3 Mientras esperaba la muerte, se estremecía de pies a cabeza.
4 Mientras escuchaba al sacerdote, temía un engaño.

F Sigan el modelo.

> *Puesto que estaban en la serranía, nadie podía verlos.*
>
> *Estando en la serranía, nadie podía verlos.*

1 Puesto que estaba todo en calma, el coronel quería dormirse.
2 Puesto que tenía mucho sueño, pronto roncaba en su cama.
3 Ya que perdían su desconfianza, me dijeron por qué peleaban.
4 Ya que no queríamos vivir más como perros, volvimos a nuestras casas.

G Sigan el modelo.

> *Si hablas con ellos, comprenderán que quieren una mejor vida.*
>
> *Hablando con ellos, comprenderán que quieren una mejor vida.*

1 Si contestan a sus preguntas, sabrán todo.

2 Si hablo como un amigo, descubriré los planes del enemigo.
3 Si te portas bien, podrás buscar una vida mejor.
4 Si tomo agua, no tengo sed.

H Sigan el modelo.

> *¿Cómo pueden salvarse?* Salen hoy.
> *Saliendo hoy, pueden salvarse.*

1 ¿Cómo se aprende a escribir bien? *Escribe mucho.*
2 ¿Cómo se descubren los planes del enemigo? *Habla con los capturados.*
3 ¿Cómo supo que los otros deseaban irse? *Leyó la carta.*
4 ¿Cómo sabían que era inteligente? *Vio su trabajo.*

Los Pronombres de Complemento

Complementos Directos

El sustantivo que recibe la acción de un verbo es el objeto o el complemento directo. El pronombre que reemplaza el sustantivo complemento es el pronombre de complemento directo.

Los pronombres de complemento directo son:

me	nos
te	os
lo, la	los, las

Sin embargo, cuando en la tercera persona singular el complemento directo es una persona masculina, el pronombre puede ser *le* o *lo*.

> Me obedece.
> No nos mira.
> Toma el café. Lo toma.
> Veo a María. La veo.
> Veo a Carlos. Lo (le) veo.
> Siempre comen las habichuelas. Siempre las comen.

En una oración declarativa o interrogativa, el pronombre precede al verbo conjugado.

A Sustituyan según el modelo.

> *La mujer me vio en el barranco.*
> *nos/*
> *La mujer nos vio en el barranco.*

1 El hombre me vio en el barranco.
te/lo/las/nos/la/me/los/
2 Ella lo observó desde el lomo.
a mí/a nosotros/a ellas/a él/a ti/a ella/a ellos/

B Sigan el modelo.

> *Juana miró al capitán a la luz de la lumbre.*
>
> *Juana lo miró a la luz de la lumbre.*

1 Él ofreció *la botella* a las mujeres frías y asustadas.
2 Oímos *el ruido del viento* durante la noche.
3 No comprendes *el problema*.
4 Ocultó *los ojos* tras los párpados cerrados.

5 Bebió *el agua negra*.
6 Saqué *la mano* del fuego.
7 Busqué *la suya* para apretarla con emoción.
8 Acerqué *la boca* a la taza.
9 Los otros adivinaron *sus pensamientos*.
10 Vi a *Roberto* en el Ford azul.

C Contesten a las siguientes preguntas según el modelo.

> *¿Tienes el libro?*
> *No, no lo tengo.*

1 ¿Tienes las llaves?
2 ¿Tienes la bujía?
3 ¿Tienes el carro?
4 ¿Tienes la planta?
5 ¿Tienes los paquetes?
6 ¿Tienes la ametralladora?
7 ¿Tienes las medicinas?
8 ¿Tienes la chapa vencida?
9 ¿Tienes los billetes?
10 ¿Tienes nuestros pasaportes?

D Contesten a las siguientes preguntas según el modelo.

> ¿Qué prestó el hombre?   el Ford azul
> El hombre prestó el Ford azul.
> El hombre lo prestó.

1 ¿Dónde dejó el carro?   en el garaje
2 ¿Qué vieron en el primer cuarto?   la cama
3 ¿Dónde pusieron los paquetes?   en el asiento
4 ¿Qué hacen allí?   ejercicios de francés
5 ¿Qué señaló con el dedo?   la portada colonial
6 ¿Quién traía la ametralladora?   el cabo
7 ¿Cómo tiene la chapa?   vencida
8 ¿Quién registró la identificación?   el teniente
9 ¿Qué agarra el teniente?   la escopeta
10 ¿Qué tomó con la limonada fría?   la aspirina

Complementos Indirectos

Los pronombres de complemento indirecto son:

me	nos
te	os
le (a Ud., a él, a ella)	les (a Uds., a ellos, a ellas)

En una oración declarativa o interrogativa, el pronombre de complemento indirecto precede al verbo conjugado.

> Rosario me habla.
> Él nos enseña la lección.
> ¿No te explicó nada?
> Le dije la verdad a ella.

E Sigan el modelo.

> Dio agua fría al compañero.
> Le dio agua fría.

1 Dirán lo que sucedió a la policía.
2 Tico prestó un lápiz al señor.
3 Mariana mintió a los señores del buró.
4 Antonio sonrió a los policías.
5 Enseñará los documentos a mí.
6 Adela pasó los periódicos a Marta.
7 El joven entregó su coche a nosotros.
8 El policía impidió el paso a ti.
9 La abogada devolvió los documentos a Ud.
10 El teniente abrió la puerta a nosotros.

Dos Complementos en una Oración

Cuando hay dos pronombres en la misma oración, el pronombre de complemento indirecto precede al pronombre de complemento directo. Se notará que los pronombres *le* y *les* se convierten en *se*.

me		
te	lo	
se	la	
nos	los	da
os	las	
se		

Suele emplearse una preposición para aclarar el pronombre *se*.

> Se lo doy a ella.
> Se la explico a Ud.
> Se lo repito a ellos.

Los dos pronombres preceden al verbo conjugado.

F Sustituyan según los modelos.

> *Él me dio las noticias.*
> *Él me las dio.*
>
> *el regalo/*
> *Él me lo dio.*

1 Él me dio las noticias.
   el regalo/la esperanza/los consejos/la bandera/los periódicos/las velas/las revistas/la carta/los paquetes/
2 Nos mostró el perro.
   el vehículo/el ladrón/las lámparas/la casa/el paraguas/los pedazos/la vista/
3 Carla le devolvió la cartera.
   el coche/la vela/los periódicos/los regalos/las revistas/

G Contesten a las siguientes preguntas según el modelo.

> *¿Quieres traerme el recado?*
> *Te lo traigo en seguida.*

1 ¿Quieres mostrarme la identificación?
2 ¿Quieres explicarme la causa de tu pena?
3 ¿Quieres darme una vela?
4 ¿Quieres describirme la avenida?
5 ¿Quieres ofrecerme el carro?
6 ¿Quieres prenderme la luz?

H Sigan el modelo.

> *Le mandé la noticia ayer.*
> *Se la mandé ayer.*

1 Le dijimos el precio ayer.
2 Le trajeron la chapa ayer.
3 Le quitaron el vehículo ayer.
4 Le dio el regalo ayer.
5 Le explicaron la solución ayer.
6 Le solucionaron el problema ayer.

Colocación de los Pronombres

Como acabamos de ver, en una oración declarativa o interrogativa los pronombres de complemento preceden al verbo conjugado.

> Me lo dijo ayer.

Los pronombres de complemento pueden añadirse al gerundio o al infinitivo o pueden preceder al verbo auxiliar.

> Está diciéndomelo.
> Me lo está diciendo.
>
> Va a dármela.
> Me la va a dar.

Hay que añadir los pronombres de complemento al mandato afirmativo.

> Dígamelo.
> Devuélvenosla.

Los pronombres de complemento preceden al mandato negativo.

> No me lo diga.
> No nos la devuelvas.

I Sigan el modelo.

> *María está reparándome la silla.*
> *María está reparándomela.*

1 Gabriela está mostrándonos la casa.
2 Pedro está arreglándome la habitación.
3 Guillermo está enviándote las rosas y las gardenias.
4 Lupe está trayéndonos la decisión.
5 Manolo está leyéndonos el poema.
6 Juana está diciéndote la verdad.

J Sigan el modelo.

Está prendiéndole la luz.
Está prendiéndosela.

1 Está mostrándole la vista.
2 Está dándole el premio.
3 Está ofreciéndole su cooperación.
4 Está poniéndole la decoración.
5 Está sirviéndole el café.
6 Está escribiéndole la carta.

K Sigan el modelo.

Van a darles tres besos.
Van a dárselos.

1 Van a prestarles el automóvil.
2 Van a concederles la medalla.
3 Van a venderles la casa.
4 Van a lavarles las manos.
5 Van a traerles la taza de café.
6 Van a quitarles el empleo.

L Sigan el modelo.

Dígame su nombre.
Dígamelo.

1 Muéstreme su identificación.
2 Pásele la cartera.
3 Déle estos paquetes.
4 Póngale el abrigo.
5 Apáguenos la luz.
6 Tráiganos la vela.
7 Présteles cinco pesos.
8 Descríbales las casas.

M Sigan el modelo.

Dígamelo.
No me lo diga.

1 Tráigamelo.
2 Muéstremelos.
3 Descríbasela.
4 Déselo.
5 Cuéntenoslo.
6 Préndanosla.
7 Véndaselo.
8 Apáguesela.

N Sigan el modelo.

Consígame el automóvil.
No me lo consiga.

1 Cómpreme el automóvil.
2 Tráigame los papeles.
3 Dígale la respuesta.
4 Quítele esas responsabilidades.
5 Dénos la libertad.
6 Enséñeles el camino.
7 Lléveles este paquete.
8 Cánteles la canción.

O Sigan el modelo.

Consígueme el automóvil.
Pero no me lo consigas ahora.

1 Cómprame el periódico.
2 Tráeme la taza de café.
3 Dile tu nombre.
4 Ponle los zapatos.
5 Hazle la cazuela.
6 Sírvele el pan.
7 Cántales la canción.
8 Llévales el desayuno.

Pronombres con Acciones Imprevistas

A veces uno sufre las consecuencias de un accidente o de una acción hecha sin intención. La acción involuntaria se expresa con el reflexivo y se agrega el complemento indirecto refiriéndose a la persona.

> Se me olvidó la llave.
> Se me olvidaron las flores.

P Sustituyan según el modelo.

> *Se me olvidó la fecha.*
> *las fechas/*
> *Se me olvidaron las fechas.*

1 Se me olvidó la fecha.
   el recado/las reglas/la identificación/los nombres/la carta/
2 Se le acabó el tiempo.
   la paciencia/las armas/el dinero/las fuerzas/la plata/
3 Se nos ocurrió una idea.
   un plan/algo nuevo/otra idea/una inspiración/otras soluciones/

Q Hagan la sustitución necesaria.

> *Se me cayó el plato grande.*

1 _____ pequeño.
2 _____ urna _____.
3 _____ le _____.
4 _____ olvidó _____.
5 _____ preciosa.
6 _____ joyas _____.
7 _____ nos _____.
8 _____ robó _____.
9 _____ me _____.
10 _____ regalos _____.
11 _____ hermosos.
12 _____ quitaron _____.
13 _____ les _____.

Complemento de una Preposición

Se notará que los pronombres que sirven de complemento de una preposición son los mismos que se emplean como sujeto, con la excepción de las primera y segunda personas del singular.

> mí   nosotros
> ti   vosotros
> él, ella, Ud.   ellos, ellas, Uds.
>
> No puedes ir sin mí.
> Quieren viajar con nosotros.
> Es para Uds.

Con la preposición *con*, se forma una sola palabra.

> Él va conmigo.
> ¿Quién hablaba contigo?
> ¿Ud. habla consigo mismo?

R Sustituyan según el modelo.

> *Van a pasar por ella.*
> *él/*
> *Van a pasar por él.*

Van a pasar por él.
nosotros/Uds./ellas/ellos/mí/Ud./ti/

S Contesten a las siguientes preguntas según el modelo.

> *¿Elena no fue?*
> *No, porque salieron sin ella.*

1 ¿Nosotros no fuimos?
2 ¿Ángel no fue?
3 ¿Tú no fuiste?
4 ¿Mis hermanos no fueron?
5 ¿Yo no fui?
6 ¿Uds. no fueron?
7 ¿Las chicas no fueron?

T Sigan el modelo.

> *Bárbara llevó su mapa.*
> *¿Su mapa? Bárbara lo llevó consigo.*

1 Yo llevé mi libro.
2 Marta llevó su paraguas.
3 Llevaste tu abrigo.
4 Ellos llevaron su traje.
5 Llevamos nuestro cuadro.
6 Uds. llevaron su abrigo.

U Contesten a las siguientes preguntas según el modelo.

> *¿Adela está con el sacerdote?*
> *¿No la ves? Adela está enfrente de él.*

1 ¿Adela está con las muchachas?
2 ¿Adela está con nosotros?
3 ¿Adela está con Ud.?
4 ¿Adela está con el maestro?
5 ¿Adela está contigo?
6 ¿Adela está con Uds.?
7 ¿Adela está conmigo?

La Muerte

Quien teme la muerte no goza la vida.

PARA PREPARAR LA ESCENA

La muerte ha sido siempre rodeada de misterio y acompañada de dudas y temores. Sólo pensar en la muerte evoca varias reacciones: la gente primitiva no puede explicarla; los viejos y los enfermos a veces le dan la bienvenida; los niños, si alguna vez piensan en ella, la consideran como un sueño prolongado; los jóvenes creen que es algo que les ocurre a los demás. Algunos la examinan desde el punto de vista de la religión o de la filosofía que tienen del más allá. Muchos la temen; otros se burlan de ella. Pero la muerte es inevitable, y todos nosotros tendremos que prepararnos para el día que llegue.

La Lechuza

Alberto Gerchunoff

PARA PRESENTAR LA LECTURA

Un gato negro que cruza delante de uno, un espejo hecho pedazos, un paraguas abierto dentro de la casa — ¡presagios de desastre! Tales creencias y conceptos han sido populares desde tiempo inmemorial. Nacen de la ignorancia, del miedo y de la incomprensibilidad. Y a pesar de haber pruebas en su contra son nociones muy comunes.

Las supersticiones del mundo se incluyen en muchas formas literarias. En la selección que sigue, una lechuza, frecuentemente nocturna en sus hábitos, es el presagio de la muerte.

El argentino Alberto Gerchunoff emplea las tradiciones hebreas y la vida de la colonia judía de la Argentina como tema de muchos cuentos suyos. A veces trágicos y misteriosos, estos cuentos nos revelan la gran fuerza dramática del autor. Además, Gerchunoff ha captado en prosa la tristeza y la desesperación del pueblo judío que ha sufrido tantas pérdidas y tanta persecución a través de los años.

PARA APRENDER VOCABULARIO

Palabras Clave   I

1 **charcos**   aguas estancadas en un hoyo en el suelo   *(puddles)*
   La rana cantaba en el charco.

2 **jinete**   el que monta a caballo
   Durante la carrera, el jinete se cayó del caballo.

3 **lechuza**   ave nocturna   *(owl)*
   La lechuza duerme con los ojos abiertos.

4 **reflejos**   luces reflejadas, reflexiones de luz
   Los reflejos del sol penetraban por la ventana.

5 **vísperas**   días o noches antes de ciertas fechas   (eves)

La víspera de Pascua comieron poco.

6 **vivaces**   brillantes, vívidos

Ella tenía una sonrisa vivaz.

Práctica

Complete con una palabra de la lista.

reflejo   *charco*   *víspera*
vivaz   *jinete*   *lechuza*

1 El ———— montó a caballo y salió galopando.

2 Fueron al templo la ———— de Pascua.
3 Se dice que la ———— es muy sabia.
4 De repente, el ———— le deslumbró.
5 Brillaba una luz ———— en sus ojos.
6 Por las tardes los pájaros se juntaban cerca del ———— .

Palabras Clave   II

1 **acontecimiento**   suceso, evento

Este acontecimiento fue inesperado.

2 **astro**   estrella, planeta, sol

Aquel astro parece más brillante que la luna.

Un entierro (Urteaga)

3 **comprometió (comprometerse)** se obligó, prometió casarse, dio palabra
   Antonio se comprometió con la novia de su niñez.

4 **espantosa** que causa temor o miedo
   Para mucha gente un viaje en avión es una experiencia espantosa.

5 **maquinalmente** automáticamente
   Raquel apagó maquinalmente su cigarrillo.

6 **piedad** respeto profundo hacia las cosas sagradas; lástima
   El buen sacerdote demostró una piedad sincera.

Práctica

Complete con una palabra de la lista.

acontecimiento	comprometió
piedad	maquinalmente
espantosa	astro

1 Júpiter es un _____ muy brillante del firmamento.
2 Juanita no se _____ con Miguel porque quería más a José.
3 La niña repetía _____ todo lo que oía.
4 Ese _____ sucedió cuando menos lo esperaba.
5 Margarita sentía _____ por los ancianos y los niños.
6 La escena sangrienta era _____ .

Palabras Clave   III

1 **aullaron (aullar)** gritaron con voces lamentosas; se dice de los lobos y los perros *(howled)*
   Los perros aullaron cuando oyeron la sirena.

2 **fantasma** aparición, espíritu visible
   Dicen que en el cementerio hay fantasmas que salen de noche.

3 **oprimida** tensa, dominada, que siente presión *(squeezed)*
   Se sentía oprimida por el terror.

4 **rostro** cara
   Se dice que la tristeza causa cambios permanentes en el rostro.

5 **vago** sutil, indeterminado
   La dueña del restaurante tenía la vaga impresión que sus empleados le robaban.

Práctica

Complete con una palabra de la lista.

oprimido	fantasma	rostro
aullaron	vago	

1 Me cogió un dolor _____ .
2 Roberto gritó cuando vio al _____ .
3 Los perros _____ al oir los ruidos extraños.
4 La hija trató de distraer a su padre _____ por sus temores.
5 Después de la muerte de su perro, Eva anduvo varios días con el _____ bañado de lágrimas.

La Lechuza

Alberto Gerchunoff

I

Jacobo pasó en su caballo ante la casa de Reiner, saludando en español. La vieja contestó en judío, y la muchacha le preguntó si había visto a Moisés, que había partido en la mañana en busca del tordillo.

—¿Moisés?—preguntó el muchacho—. ¿Se fue en el caballo blanco?

—En el blanco.

—¿Salió por el camino de Las Moscas?

—No—respondió Perla—tomó el camino de San Miguel.

—¿De San Miguel? No lo he visto.

La vieja se lamentó, con voz que revelaba su inquietud:

—Ya se hace tarde y mi hijo partió tan sólo con unos mates; no llevó revólver . . .

—No hay cuidado, señora; se pueden recorrer todos los alrededores sin encontrar a nadie.

—Dios te oiga—añadió doña Eva—, dicen que cerca de los campos de Ornstein hay bandidos.

El diálogo terminó con una palabra tranquilizadora de Jacobo; espoleó al caballo, obligándolo a dar un salto, para lucir su habilidad de jinete en presencia de Perla.

El sol declinaba y la tarde de otoño se adormecía bajo el cielo rojo. El tono amarillo de las huertas, el verde pálido del potrero quebrado por el arroyo oscuro daban al paisaje una melancolía dulce, como en los poemas hebraicos en que las pastoras retornan con el rebaño sonámbulo bajo el cielo de Canaán.

Se sumergían en oscuridad las casas de la colonia y en los tejidos de alambre brillaban en reflejos vivaces los últimos rayos del sol.

—Es tarde, hija mía, y Moisés no llega . . .

tordillo *gray horse*

espoleó *spurred*

potrero *pasture*

pastoras . . . sonámbulo
shepherdesses return with their drowsy flock
Se sumergían *Were submerged*
tejidos de alambre *wire fences*

—No hay temor, madre, no es la primera vez. ¿Te acuerdas, el año pasado, en vísperas de Pascua, cuando fue con el carro al bosque de San Gregorio? Vino con la leña al día siguiente.

—Sí, recuerdo; pero llevaba revólver, y además, cerca de San Gregorio hay una colonia . . .

Un silencio penoso siguió a la conversación. En los charcos cantaban las ranas y de los árboles próximos venían ruidos confusos.

Una lechuza voló sobre el corral, graznó lúgubremente y se posó en un poste.

II

—¡Qué feo es aquel pájaro!—dijo la muchacha.

Graznó otra vez la lechuza, y miró a las mujeres, en cuyo espíritu sus ojos hicieron la misma triste impresión.

—Dicen que es de mal agüero.

—Dicen así, pero no creo. ¿Qué saben los campesinos?

—¿No decimos nosotros, los judíos, que el cuervo anuncia la muerte?

—¡Ah, es otra cosa!

La lechuza voló hasta el techo, donde lanzó un graznido y tornó al poste, sin dejar de mirar a las mujeres.

En el extremo del camino lleno de sombra resonaron las pisadas de un caballo. La chica miró, haciendo visera de las manos. Desengañó a la madre.

—No es blanco.

De las casas el viento traía el eco de un canto, uno de esos cantos monótonos y tristes que lamentan la pérdida de Jerusalén y exhortan a las hijas de Sion, «magnífica y única», a llorar en la noche para despertar con sus lágrimas la piedad del Señor. Maquinalmente, Perla repitió en voz baja:

> Llorad y gemid, hijas de Sion . . .

Después, con voz más fuerte, cantó la copla de los judíos de España, que le había enseñado en la escuela el maestro don David Ben-Azán:

> Hemos perdido a Sion,
> hemos perdido a Toledo.
> No queda consolación . . .

Como la madre había continuado inquietándose, la muchacha, para distraerla, continuó la conversación anterior.

graznó lúgubremente y se posó hooted mournfully and lit

pisadas steps (hoofbeats)
visera shield

—¿Tú crees en los sueños? Hace unos días, doña Raquel contó algo que nos dio miedo.

La vieja contó a su vez una historia espantosa.

Una prima suya, hermosa como un astro, se comprometió con un vecino de la aldea. Era **carretero** muy pobre, muy honrado y muy temeroso de Dios. Pero la moza no lo quería, por ser **contrahecho**. En la noche del compromiso, la mujer del **rabino** . . . una santa mujer . . . vio un cuervo.

El novio vendió un caballo y con el dinero compró un misal, que regaló a la novia. Dos días antes del casamiento se anuló el compromiso y la moza se casó al año siguiente con un hombre muy rico del lugar.

El recuerdo del suceso causó honda impresión en el ánimo de doña Eva. Su cara se alargó en la sombra y, en voz baja, contó el milagroso acontecimiento. Se casó la muchacha, y uno a uno fueron muriendo sus hijos. ¿Y el primer novio? El buen hombre había muerto. Entonces el rabino de la ciudad, consultado por la familia, intervino. Examinó los textos sagrados y halló en las viejas tradiciones un caso parecido.

III

Aconsejó a la mujer que devolviera al difunto su lujoso misal. Así **recobraría** la tranquilidad y la dicha.

—Llévalo—le dijo—bajo el brazo derecho, mañana, a la noche, y devuélveselo.

Nada respondió la afligida. Al otro día, al salir la luna, misal bajo el brazo, salió. Una lluvia lenta le golpeaba el rostro, y sus pies, débiles por el miedo, apenas se podían avanzar sobre la dura nieve. En los suburbios ya, muerta de fatiga, **se guareció** junto a una pared; pensaba en los hijos muertos y en el primer novio, cuyo recuerdo había desaparecido de su memoria durante tanto tiempo. Lentamente **hojeaba** el misal, de iniciales **frondosas** y rosas, de estilo arcaico, que le gustaba contemplar en las fiestas de la sinagoga, mientras recitaba en coro las oraciones.

De pronto sus ojos se oscurecieron, y al recobrarse vio en su presencia al carretero, con su cara resignada y su cuerpo deforme . . .

—Es tuyo este misal y te lo devuelvo—le dijo.

El fantasma, que tenía tierra en los ojos, extendió una mano de hueso y recibió el libro.

carretero *wagon driver*

contrahecho *deformed*
rabino *rabbi*

recobraría *would recover*

se guareció *she took refuge*

hojeaba *she leafed through*
frondosas *ornate*

luciérnagas *fireflies*

palenque *stockade*
de imán *magnetic*

jadeante *panting*

alarido *howl*

Entonces la mujer, recordando el consejo del rabino, añadió:

—Que la paz sea contigo, y ruega por mí; yo pediré a Dios por tu salvación.

Perla suspiró. La noche cerraba, tranquila y transparente. A lo lejos, las luciérnagas se agitaban como chispas diminutas y llevaban al espíritu de la anciana y de la chica un vago terror de fantasmas. Y allí sobre el palenque, la lechuza continuaba mirándolas con sus ojos de imán, lucientes y fijos.

Obsesionada por un pensamiento oculto, la niña continuó:

—Pero si el gaucho dice tales cosas del pájaro, bien pudiera ser . . .

Doña Eva miró el palenque y luego hacia el fondo negro del camino y con voz temblorosa, casi imperceptible, murmuró:

—Bien pudiera ser, hija mía . . .

Un frío agudo la estremeció, y Perla, con la garganta oprimida por la misma angustia, se acercó a la viejecita. En esto se oyó el eco de un galope. Las dos se agacharon para oir mejor, tratando de ver en la densa oscuridad. Su respiración era jadeante, y los minutos se deslizaban sobre sus corazones con lentitud opresiva. Aullaron los perros de la vecindad. El galope se oía cada vez más precipitado y claro, y un instante después vieron el caballo blanco que venía en enfurecida carrera. Se pararon madre e hija, llenas de espanto, y de sus bocas salió un grito enorme, como un alarido. El caballo, sudoroso, se detuvo en el portón, sin el jinete, con la silla ensangrentada . . .

PARA APLICAR

Comprensión   I

A Conteste a las siguientes preguntas.

1   ¿Quién pasó por la casa de Reiner?
2   ¿En qué iba?
3   ¿Saludó en español Jacobo?
4   Y la vieja, ¿en qué idioma le contestó?
5   ¿Qué le preguntaron a Jacobo?
6   ¿Dónde andaba Moisés?
7   ¿Qué camino había tomado él?
8   ¿Por qué temían que le pasara algo?

9   ¿Por qué espoleó Jacobo al caballo?
10   Describa el paisaje del potrero.
11   ¿Por qué se preocupaba la vieja?
12   ¿Qué diferencia había entre este viaje de Jacobo y el que hizo al bosque de San Gregorio?
13   Hable del silencio que siguió a la conversación.

B ¿Verdadero o falso?

1   El jinete que pasó les saludó a las mujeres en español.

Lechuza

2 Las mujeres le contestaron en la misma lengua.
3 Moisés había salido a buscar el caballo blanco.
4 La vieja expresó su pena en una voz inquieta.
5 Moisés se había desayunado bien esa mañana.
6 Moisés no llevó consigo ningún arma.
7 Los caminos por allí están muy transitados.
8 Jacobo quería mostrarle a Perla que él era buen jinete.
9 El paisaje era hermoso y melancólico.
10 Moisés tenía la costumbre de regresar en el mismo día.

Comprensión   II

A Conteste a las siguientes preguntas.

1 ¿Qué dijo la muchacha cuando vio la lechuza?

2 ¿Qué hizo la lechuza?
3 Diga algo del diálogo que surgió al llegar la lechuza.
4 ¿Qué se oyó venir del extremo del camino?
5 ¿Era blanco el caballo que venía de la sombra?
6 ¿Qué traía el viento de las casas?
7 ¿Cómo quiso distraer la muchacha a la madre?
8 ¿Quién contó una historia espantosa?
9 Describa la pareja que se comprometió, según la historia.
10 ¿Qué vio la esposa del rabino la noche del compromiso?

B Las cinco oraciones que siguen son falsas. Corríjalas para que correspondan con la selección.

1 Llegó un cuervo que hizo un ruido desagradable.

2 Algunos judíos creían que todos los pájaros traían mala suerte.
3 Doña Eva recitó en voz alta el canto de lamentos por la pérdida de Jerusalén.
4 Perla había aprendido el canto de su madre.
5 Perla trató de calmar a su madre con un cuento espantoso.

Comprensión III

A Conteste a las siguientes preguntas.

1 Relate lo que el rabino aconsejó.
2 ¿Qué papel tiene el misal en esta historia?
3 ¿A quién le dio la afligida mujer el misal?
4 ¿Por qué comenzaron Perla y la anciana a pensar en fantasmas?
5 ¿Cómo se encontraban Perla y la anciana cuando oyeron el eco de un galope?
6 Describa esta última escena.
7 ¿Por qué gritaron la madre y la hija?

B Escoja la respuesta apropiada.

1 ¿Qué hizo el novio contrahecho?
   a. Fue a misa con su novia.
   b. Le obsequió un misal a la novia.
   c. Se casó con un hombre muy rico.
2 ¿Cómo le afectó a doña Eva acordarse del suceso?
   a. Su cara se alarmó.
   b. Su cara se puso triste.
   c. Sucedió un acontecimiento milagroso.
3 ¿Por qué consultaron al rabino?
   a. porque el pobre novio había muerto
   b. para que hallara los textos sagrados
   c. para que les aconsejara
4 ¿Cómo hizo aparecer al novio muerto?
   a. Hizo desaparecer el recuerdo de su memoria.
   b. Hizo iniciales frondosas y rosas en el misal.
   c. Recitaba las oraciones.

5 Al recobrarse, ¿qué vio la mujer?
   a. al fantasma del carretero
   b. al rabino que daba consejos
   c. las fiestas de la sinagoga

Más Práctica

A Dé un antónimo de las palabras en letra bastardilla.

1 Moisés había *vuelto* en la mañana.
2 Es *temprano*, hija mía.
3 Un *ruido* penoso siguió a la conversación.
4 ¡Qué *guapa* es aquella ave!
5 La lechuza voló hacia el *suelo*.
6 Con voz *débil*, cantó la copla.
7 Llevó el misal bajo el brazo *izquierdo*.
8 Al otro día, al *ponerse* la luna, él se fue.
9 De pronto, sus ojos se *esclarecieron*.
10 Se *alejó de* la viejecita.

B Complete las siguientes oraciones con una palabra apropiada.

1 ¡Cuidado! No pongas el pie en el _____ .
2 Tiene un significado _____ ; no es nada claro.
3 Hay muchos _____ en el cielo.
4 Cuando salió tenía el _____ pálido.
5 Los supersticiosos creen en _____ .
6 Algunos perros no hacen nada más que _____ .
7 Su personalidad es muy _____ , llena de vida.
8 La _____ es un ave nocturna.
9 Él lo hizo _____ , sin ningún esfuerzo.
10 Hay un _____ de las estrellas en el agua.

Ejercicios Creativos

1 Describa el ambiente de la selección.
2 En otras culturas, incluyendo la suya, ¿qué animales tienen esta reputación de «mal agüero»?
3 ¿Qué relación tiene el relato de la vieja con los acontecimientos de la selección?

En el fondo del caño hay un negrito

José Luis González

PARA PRESENTAR LA LECTURA

El puertorriqueño José Luis González es un autor moderno que escribe mucho sobre el tema del desempleado. En el cuento que sigue nos habla de un desafortunado que llega del campo a la ciudad en busca de trabajo. Las dificultades materiales de la vida lo hacen establecerse con su familia en el arrabal o barrio construido sobre las márgenes de un caño. Y allí mantiene la lucha contra el ambiente que le rodea.

Un caño es un canal o brazo de mar. Sobre las tierras pantanosas del caño cerca de la ciudad de San Juan, Puerto Rico, creció el arrabal, nido de pobreza, con un amontonamiento de familias, casuchas de aspecto pobre y condiciones insalubres. Entre los arrabales más conocidos son El Fanguito y La Perla.

El ineducado, muchas veces, habla un idioma expresivo, lleno de expresiones familiares. Al leer este cuento, fíjese en el dialecto de los campesinos.

PARA APRENDER VOCABULARIO

Palabras Clave   I

1 **caño**   canal angosto, brazo de mar
   El caño era muy sucio.

2 **chupándose (chuparse)**   produciendo succión con los labios *(sucking)*
   La niña andaba chupándose los dedos.

3 **flojamente**   perezosamente
   Teresa leía flojamente su libro hasta que se durmió.

4 **hacía (hacer) gracia**   causaba diversión
   Le hacía gracia a Mariana que Tony le tuviera miedo.

"Cavalier of Death" (Salvador Dalí), Collection, The Museum of Modern Art, New York

El Caballero de la Muerte (Dalí)

5 **maldad**   malicia, vicio
   Todo lo que hacía el niño era sin maldad.

6 **mudanza**   cambio de domicilio
   El trabajo de la mudanza le cansó.

7 **susto**   impresión de miedo *(scare, sudden terror)*
   Su manera de mirarla le dio un susto.

Práctica

Complete con una palabra de la lista.

caño	flojamente	mudanza
maldad	chupándose	hacía gracia
susto		

1 El ———— pasa cerca de las chozas en el barrio pobre.

2   La ———— le costó más de lo que valían los muebles.

3   Le ———— bailar toda la noche.

4   Cansada, se levantó ————.

5   Por no tener comida, el niño estaba ———— el dedo.

6   El dueño enojado les gritó a sus empleados con ————.

7   Sintió un gran ———— al ver el fantasma.

Palabras Clave   II

1   **arrabal**   barrio, suburbio
    Mucha gente pobre vive en el arrabal cerca del río.

2   **llanto**   efusión de lágrimas con lamentos *(weeping, flood of tears)*
    La pescadora oyó el llanto del niño, lo que le destrozó el alma.

3   **remó (remar)**   hizo adelantar una embarcación con el movimiento de los remos *(rowed a boat, paddled)*
    El pescador remó su bote hasta la otra orilla.

4   **reprimir**   contener, refrenar
    El niño no pudo reprimir el deseo de jugar en el charco.

5   **soga**   cuerda *(rope)*
    El caballo estaba atado al poste con una soga larga.

Práctica

Complete con una palabra de la lista.

arrabal   remó   reprimir
soga   llanto

1   El ———— interminable del viudo me ponía triste.

2   La abogada no pudo ———— una sonrisa cuando oyó la buena noticia.

3   La gente del ———— cerca del río es muy pobre.

4   Tiró la ———— para salvar al hombre en el agua.

5   El pescador ———— una hora sin parar para llegar antes que los otros.

Palabras Clave   III

1   **atardecer**   llegar el fin de la tarde, última parte de la tarde
    El obrero regresó al arrabal al atardecer.

2   **fango**   barro, tierra mezclada con agua
    Cerca del caño hay mucho fango.

3   **muelle**   pared al lado del río o mar para facilitar la carga y descarga de los barcos *(wharf, loading platform)*
    Él encontró trabajo en el muelle cargando mercancías.

4   **súbito**   inmediato, violento, impetuoso
    Susana sintió un deseo súbito de ver a su compañera.

Práctica

Complete con una palabra de la lista.

fango   atardecer
muelle   súbito

1   Los pasajeros desembarcaron en aquel ————.

2   El niño volvió a la casa al ————.

3   Le vino un sentimiento ———— de tristeza y aislamiento.

4   A los niños les gusta jugar con el ————.

En el fondo del caño hay un negrito

José Luis González

I

La primera vez que el negrito Melodía vio al otro negrito en el fondo del caño fue temprano en la mañana del tercer o cuarto día después de la mudanza, cuando llegó gateando hasta la única puerta de la nueva vivienda y se asomó para mirar hacia la quieta superficie del agua allá abajo.

Entonces el padre, que acababa de despertar sobre el montón de sacos vacíos extendidos en el piso junto a la mujer semidesnuda que aún dormía, le gritó:

—Mire . . . , ¡eche p'adentro! ¡Diantre 'e muchacho desinquieto!

Y Melodía, que no había aprendido a entender las palabras, pero sí a obedecer los gritos, gateó otra vez hacia adentro y se quedó silencioso en un rincón, chupándose un dedito porque tenía hambre.

El hombre se incorporó sobre los codos. Miró a la mujer que dormía a su lado y la sacudió flojamente por un brazo. La mujer despertó sobresaltada, mirando al hombre con ojos de susto. El hombre se rió. Todas las mañanas era igual: la mujer despertaba con aquella cara de susto que a él le provocaba una gracia sin maldad. Le hacía gracia verla salir así del sueño todas las mañanas.

El hombre se sentó sobre los sacos vacíos.

—Bueno—se dirigió entonces a ella—. Cuela el café.

La mujer tardó un poco en contestar:

—No queda.

—¿Ah?

—No queda. Se acabó ayer.

Él casi empezó a decir «¿Y por qué no compraste más?» pero se interrumpió cuando vio que la mujer empezaba a poner aquella otra cara, la cara que a él no le hacía gracia y que ella sólo ponía

---

gateando *crawling on all fours, like a cat*

se asomó *peered out*

semidesnuda *half-naked*

¡eche p'adentro! *¡échate para adentro! (get inside!)*

¡Diantre 'e muchacho desinquieto! *Drat that restless kid!*

codos *elbows*

sobresaltada *asustada*

Cuela *Make*

---

cuando él le hacía preguntas como ésa. A él no le gustaba verle aquella cara a la mujer.

—¿Conque se acabó ayer?

—Ajá.

La mujer se puso de pie y empezó a meterse el vestido por la cabeza. El hombre, todavía sentado sobre los sacos vacíos, derrotó su mirada y la fijó un rato en los agujeros de su camiseta.

Melodía, cansado ya de la insipidez del dedo, se decidió a llorar. El hombre lo miró y preguntó a la mujer:

—¿Tampoco hay na' pal nene?

—Sí . . . Conseguí unas hojitah 'e guanábana. Le guá'cer un guarapillo 'horita.

—¿Cuántos díah va que no toma leche?

—¿Leche?—la mujer puso un poco de asombro inconsciente en la voz—. Desde antier.

II

El hombre se puso de pie y se metió los pantalones. Después se acercó a la puerta y miró hacia afuera. Le dijo a la mujer:

—La marea 'ta alta. Hoy hay que dir en bote.

Luego miró hacia arriba, hacia el puente y la carretera. Automóviles, guaguas y camiones pasaban en un desfile interminable. El hombre sonrió viendo como desde casi todos los vehículos alguien miraba con extrañeza hacia la casucha enclavada en medio de aquel brazo de mar: el caño sobre cuyas márgenes pantanosas había ido creciendo hacía años el arrabal. Ese alguien por lo general empezaba a mirar la casucha cuando el automóvil o la guagua o el camión llegaba a la mitad del puente y después seguía mirando, volteando gradualmente la cabeza hasta que el automóvil, la guagua o el camión tomaba la curva allá delante. El hombre sonrió. Y después murmuró: «¡Caramba!»

A poco se metió en el bote y remó hasta la orilla. De la popa del bote a la puerta de la casa había una soga larga que permitía a quien quedara en la casa atraer nuevamente el bote hasta la puerta. De la casa a la orilla había también un puentecito de madera, que se cubría con la marea alta.

Ya en la orilla, el hombre caminó hacia la carretera. Se sintió mejor cuando el ruido de los automóviles ahogó el llanto del negrito en la casucha.

* * *

La segunda vez que el negrito Melodía vio al otro negrito en el fondo del caño fue poco después del mediodía, cuando volvió a gatear hasta la puerta y se asomó y miró hacia abajo. Esta vez el negrito en el fondo del caño le regaló una sonrisa a Melodía. Melodía había sonreído primero y tomó la sonrisa del otro negrito como una respuesta a la suya. Entonces hizo así con la manita, y desde el fondo del caño el otro negrito también hizo así con su manita. Melodía no pudo reprimir la risa, y le pareció que también desde allá abajo llegaba el sonido de otra risa. La madre lo llamó entonces porque el segundo guarapillo de hojas de guanábana ya estaba listo.

III

Dos mujeres, de las afortunadas que vivían en tierra firme, sobre el fango endurecido de las márgenes del caño, comentaban:

—Hay que velo. Si me lo 'bieran contao, 'biera dicho qu'era embuste.

—La necesidá, doña. A mí misma, quién me 'biera dicho que yo diba llegar aquí. Yo que tenía hasta mi tierrita . . .

—Pueh nojotroh fuimoh de los primeroh. Casi no 'bía gente y uno cogía la parte máh sequecita, ¿ve? Pero los que llegan ahora, fújese, tienen que tirarse al agua, como quien dice. Pero, bueno, y . . . esa gente, ¿de onde diantre haberán salío?

—A mí me dijeron que por aí por Isla Verde 'tán orbanizando y han sacao un montón de negroh arrimaoh. A lo mejor son d'esoh.

Hay que velo Hay que verlo
Si me lo 'bieran contao, . . . embuste. Si me lo hubieran contado, hubiera dicho que era embuste (fraud)
quién me 'biera dicho . . . aquí quién me hubiera dicho que yo iba a llegar aquí
Pueh nojotroh fuimoh de los primeroh. Pues nosotros fuimos de los primeros.
Casi no 'bía gente . . . , ¿ve? Casi no había gente y uno cogía la parte más sequecita, ¿ve?
fújese fíjese
como quien dice as one says
¿de onde diantre haberán salío? ¿de dónde diantre habrán salido?
por aí por allí
'tán orbanizando . . . negroh arrimaoh están urbanizando y han sacado un montón de negros arrimados
son d'esoh son de ésos

¿Y usté se ha fijao en el
negrito qué mono? ¿Y Ud.
se ha fijado en el negrito
qué mono? *(Have you
noticed how cute their little
one is?)*
**unas hojitah de algo . . .
quedaban** unas hojitas de
algo para hacerle un
guarapillo, y yo le di unas
poquitas de guanábana que
me quedaban *(a few leaves
of something to make him a
little tea, and I gave her a
few guanabana leaves that I
had left)*
palpando *feeling, handling*
vellón *five-cent piece*
comadrona *midwife*
Se va tirando. *One struggles
along.*
colmado *general store*
habichuelas y unas latitas
beans and a few small cans

—¡Bendito . . . ! ¿Y usté se ha fijao en el negrito qué mono? La mujer vino ayer a ver si yo tenía unas hojitah de algo pa' hacerle un guarapillo, y yo le di unas poquitah de guanábana que me quedaban.

—¡Ay, Virgen, bendito . . . !

Al atardecer, el hombre estaba cansado. Le dolía la espalda. Pero venía palpando las monedas en el fondo del bolsillo, haciéndolas sonar, adivinando con el tacto cuál era un vellón, cuál de diez, cuál una peseta. Bueno . . . hoy había habido suerte. El blanco que pasó por el muelle a recoger su mercancía de Nueva York. Y el obrero que le prestó su carretón toda la tarde porque tuvo que salir corriendo a buscar a la comadrona para su mujer, que estaba echando un pobre más al mundo. Sí, señor. Se va tirando. Mañana será otro día.

Se metió en un colmado y compró café y arroz y habichuelas y unas latitas de leche evaporada. Pensó en Melodía y apresuró el paso. Se había venido a pie desde San Juan para no gastar los cinco centavos de la guagua.

* * *

La tercera vez que el negrito Melodía vio al otro negrito en el fondo del caño fue al atardecer, poco antes de que el padre regresara. Esta vez Melodía venía sonriendo antes de asomarse, y le asombró que el otro también se estuviera sonriendo allá abajo. Volvió a hacer así con la manita y el otro volvió a contestar. Entonces Melodía sintió un súbito entusiasmo y un amor indecible hacia el otro negrito. Y se fue a buscarlo.

PARA APLICAR

Comprensión   I

A Conteste a las siguientes preguntas.

1 ¿Cuándo fue que Melodía vio al otro negrito por primera vez?
2 ¿Dónde lo vio?
3 ¿Cómo llegó hacia la puerta?
4 ¿En qué dormía el padre?
5 ¿Por qué se chupaba el dedo Melodía?
6 ¿Cómo se incorporó el hombre?

7 ¿Cómo despertó a la mujer?
8 Después de despertarla, ¿qué le pidió el hombre a la mujer?
9 ¿Había café o no? ¿Por qué?
10 Cuando comenzó a llorar Melodía, ¿qué le preguntó el hombre a la mujer?
11 ¿Qué había conseguido ella para el nene?

1 ¿Cuándo vio Melodía al otro negrito en el fondo del caño?
   a. cuando llegó el gato
   b. tres o cuatro días después de mudarse allí
   c. cuando salió de la quieta superficie del agua
2 ¿Por qué se alejó del agua?
   a. Se cansó y prefería quedarse en el rincón.
   b. Tenía vergüenza de estar semidesnudo.
   c. Le llamó su padre en tono brusco.
3 ¿Cómo despertó el padre a su mujer?
   a. La sacudió flojamente.
   b. Se incorporó en la cama.
   c. Se chupó un dedo por el susto.
4 ¿Por qué no podían tomar café?
   a. No tenían ganas.
   b. Querían irse.
   c. Se acabó ayer.
5 ¿Por qué lloraba el niño?
   a. Tenía agujeros en su camiseta.
   b. Tenía hambre.
   c. No le gustaba la cara de la mujer.

Comprensión   II

A Conteste a las siguientes preguntas.

1 ¿Qué hizo el hombre antes de acercarse a la puerta?
2 ¿Cómo estaba la marea?
3 ¿Qué indicaba eso?
4 ¿Qué pasaba continuamente por el puente?
5 ¿Qué hacían por lo general los que miraban la casucha desde el puente?
6 Al meterse en el bote, ¿qué hizo?
7 ¿Para qué servía la soga que tenía el bote?
8 ¿Cuándo fue la segunda vez que Melodía vio al negrito?
9 ¿Qué le regaló el negrito a Melodía?
10 ¿Qué seña le hizo Melodía al negrito?
11 Cuando lo llamó su mamá, ¿qué le había preparado?

B ¿Verdadero o falso?

1 El padre durmió con los pantalones puestos.
2 Fue necesario ir en bote porque el agua había subido.
3 Los pasajeros de los vehículos miraban con curiosidad el arrabal.
4 En los últimos años la población del arrabal había disminuido.
5 El hombre se puso triste cuando vio el tráfico.
6 Estaba más contento alejándose de donde se oía el llanto del negrito.
7 Cuando el mar no estaba alto, se podía ir caminando por un puentecito de madera.
8 Al mediodía Melodía volvió a asomarse al caño.
9 El otro negrito le sonrió a Melodía.
10 La mamá oyó la risa que pareció llegar desde allá abajo.

Comprensión   III

A Conteste a las siguientes preguntas.

1 Relate lo que pueda de la conversación de las dos mujeres de la tierra firme.
2 ¿Cómo se sentía el hombre al atardecer?
3 ¿Qué traía en el bolsillo?
4 Relate tres sucesos sobresalientes del día.
5 ¿Qué compró en el colmado?
6 ¿Por qué se fue a pie desde San Juan?
7 ¿Cuándo vio Melodía al negrito por tercera vez?
8 Cuando el negrito le hizo así con la manita, ¿qué sintió Melodía?
9 ¿Qué hizo después?

B Termine las oraciones poniendo en orden las palabras entre paréntesis.

1 Las dos mujeres afortunadas vivían (tierra, firme, en).
2 Comentaban sobre la necesidad de (al, mudarse, arrabal).

3 Los primeros en llegar ocupaban (más, la, sequita, parte).

4 Están urbanizando cerca de Isla Verde y han expulsado de allí (negros, muchos, pobres).

5 Una se ha fijado que (mono, es, niñito, el).

6 El hombre regresaba al arrabal (las, monedas, palpando).

7 Un obrero le había prestado su carretón para (muelle, mercancías, del, recoger).

8 El obrero buscaba a la comadrona porque su mujer (a, otro, dar a luz, iba, niño).

9 El hombre caminaba a su casucha para no gastar (guagua, los, centavos, en, cinco, la).

Más Práctica

A Conteste a las siguientes preguntas según la indicación.

1 ¿Cómo contestó ella? *flojamente*
2 ¿Cuándo salieron al caño? *al atardecer*
3 ¿Lo hizo a propósito? *sí, con maldad*
4 ¿Qué quieres comer esta noche? *habichuelas*
5 ¿Con qué lo van a atar? *soga*
6 ¿Qué le dio el ruido? *susto*
7 ¿Cómo van a cruzar el río? *remando*
8 ¿Dónde viven los pobres? *en aquel arrabal*

B Dé un sinónimo de las palabras en letra bastardilla.

1 Ella recibió la carta con *asombro*.
2 ¿Dónde está la *cuerda*?
3 Siempre lo hace con *malicia*.
4 Esto me *parece divertido*.
5 Ella lo hizo *sin ánimo*.

Ejercicios Creativos

1 Imagine los acontecimientos que siguen a lo que está escrito. ¿Qué hizo Melodía? ¿Qué le pasó? Escriba un párrafo adicional para este cuento.
2 Exprese en un párrafo quién, en su opinión, sufría más. ¿El que murió? ¿La madre? ¿El padre? Justifique su opinión.
3 Describa las condiciones sociales que, como se ve en este cuento, pueden hacer daño a los que residen allí.

La Muerta

Carmen Laforet

PARA PRESENTAR LA LECTURA

Es una experiencia común llegar a apreciar la vida por medio de la
muerte. En el cuento que sigue, el señor Paco se lamentaba de todo
lo que tenía que aguantar en la vida — una mujer siempre enferma,
dos hijas alborotadas y mal habladas como demonios y duro trabajo.
Alguna compensación tenía que ofrecerle el destino. Sin duda,
¡cualquier otro arreglo le sería mejor! Luego, su mujer tuvo «el buen
gusto» de morirse como a veces él lo había especulado, y de repente
se dio cuenta de lo mucho que la enfermiza María había influido en
la vida de toda la familia. Y tras su muerte, casi santificada en la
memoria de sus queridos, María aún estaba por todas partes,
consolando.

Carmen Laforet se consagró como destacada autora con la
publicación de la novela *Nada*, con la cual ganó el Premio Nadal de
literatura cuando sólo tenía veintitrés años. Además, ha escrito
numerosos cuentos y artículos que muestran el genio que tiene para
penetrar en cualquier aspecto de la vida que la rodea.

PARA APRENDER VOCABULARIO

Palabras Clave   I

1 **compadecido (compadecer)**   sentido
compasión por el dolor de otro
> Lo compadezco por la muerte de su padre.

2 **cosido (coser)**   unido con aguja e hilo
(sewn)
> Le había cosido un vestido nuevo a la hija.

3 **emborrachaba (emborracharse)**   perdía
la razón tomando alcohol
> Se emborrachaba para olvidarse de sus
> problemas.

4 **mangas**   partes del vestido que cubren
los brazos

La manga del abrigo se separó y había que coserla otra vez.

5 **olfatear**   oler (sniff)
Al entrar en su casa la señora Chapero olfateaba el aire, notando olores agradables.

Práctica

Complete con una palabra de la lista.

cosido   compadecer   emborrachaba
mangas   olfateaba

1 Tomaba mucho en las fiestas y casi siempre se _____ .
2 El sastre había _____ todo el día y estaba muy cansado.
3 Rosa siempre llevaba blusas de _____ cortas en el verano.
4 Trató de _____ a don Francisco en su tristeza, pero no sabía qué decirle.
5 El perro _____ el aire para ver si había algo que comer.

Palabras Clave   II

1 **padecimientos**   sufrimientos
Miguel nunca se quejaba de sus padecimientos.

2 **no se podían (poder) ver**   no se toleraban uno al otro, no se aguantaban
Las dos hermanas peleaban constantemente; no se podían ver.

3 **torpemente**   sin habilidad (clumsily)
Carmen camina torpemente debido a su enfermedad.

4 **yerno**   marido de la hija de uno (son-in-law)
La hija de la señora Carlota está casada con Manuel; Manuel es el yerno de la señora Carlota.

Práctica

Complete con una palabra de la lista.

no se podían ver   padecimientos
yerno   torpemente

1 Aguantó sus _____ por muchos años.
2 El padre ni siquiera saludó a su _____ cuando llegó con su hija.
3 La enferma se levantó _____ de la cama.
4 Ahora son amigos; pero durante muchos años _____ .

Palabras Clave   III

1 **anudado (anudar)**   juntado con un nudo (knotted)
Había anudado los extremos de la soga.

2 **atravesar (ie)**   cruzar, pasar de un lugar a otro
Al atravesar el pasillo, sintió el calor del sol.

3 **cuello**   parte del cuerpo que une la cabeza con el tronco
Se ató la corbata alrededor del cuello.

4 **empujó (empujar)**   abrió paso usando fuerza (pushed)
Paquita tuvo que empujar la puerta para entrar.

5 **guisos**   platos preparados generalmente con salsa (stews, etc.)
Sus hijos le preparan guisos deliciosos.

6 **mancha**   señal de suciedad o parte con color distinto a lo demás (spot)
El café deja manchas permanentes en la ropa.

7 **sonó (sonarse)**   se limpió las narices (blew his (her) nose)
El enfermo se sonó antes de empezar a hablar.

Anciano parecido al señor Paco

Práctica

Complete con una palabra de la lista.

guisos   sonó   atravesar
cuello   anudado   empujar
mancha

1 Hay que enseñarles a los niños que es necesario _____ la calle con precaución.

2 Aquí sirven unos _____ sin igual.
3 Cuando hace frío hay que protegerse el _____.
4 Se _____ con el pañuelo.
5 Ha _____ la corbata torpemente.
6 Hay que _____ la puerta con fuerza.
7 Se le cayó un poco del guiso, dejándole una _____ en el pantalón.

La Muerta

Carmen Laforet

I

El señor Paco no era un sentimental. Era un buen hombre al que le gustaba beber, en compañía de amigos, algunos traguitos de vino al salir del trabajo y que sólo se emborrachaba en las fiestas grandes, cuando había motivo para ello. Era alegre, con una cara fea y simpática. Debajo de la boina le asomaban unos cabellos blancos, y sobre la bufanda una nariz redonda y colorada.

Al entrar en la casa esta nariz quedó un momento en suspenso, en actitud de olfatear, mientras el señor Paco, que se acababa de quitar la bufanda, abría la boca, con cierto asombro. Luego reaccionó. Se quitó el abrigo viejo, en una de las mangas le habían cosido sus hijas una tira negra de luto, y lo colgó en el perchero que adornaba el pasillo desde hacía treinta años. El señor Paco se frotó las manos, y luego hizo algo totalmente fuera de sus costumbres. Suspiró profundamente.

Había sentido a su muerta. La había sentido, allí, en el callado corredor de la casa, en el rayo de sol que por el ventanuco se colaba hasta los ladrillos rojos que pavimentaban el pasillo. Había notado la presencia de su mujer, como si ella viviese. Como si estuviese esperándolo en la cálida cocina, recién encalada, tal como sucedía en los primeros años de su matrimonio . . . Después las cosas habían cambiado. El señor Paco había sido muy desgraciado y nadie podría reprocharle unos traguitos de vino y algunas aventurillas que costaron, es verdad, sus buenos cuartos . . . Nadie podría reprochárselo con una mujer enferma siempre y dos hijas alborotadas y mal habladas como demonios. Nadie se lo había reprochado jamás. Ni la pobre María, su difunta, ni su propia conciencia. Cuando las lenguas de sus hijas se desataron en alguna ocasión más de lo debido, la misma María había intervenido desde su cama o desde su sillón para callarlas, suavemente, pero con

---

traguitos drinks

boina beret
bufanda scarf

tira . . . luto black band worn for mourning
perchero coat rack
se frotó rubbed

se colaba filtered
ladrillos bricks

encalada whitewashed

alborotadas ruidosas y molestas

firmeza. En la soledad de la alcoba, cuando algunas noches había estado él, malhumorado, inquieto, revolviéndose en la cama, María misma lo había compadecido.

—¡Pobre Paco!

Bien podría compadecerle. Ella bien feliz había sido siempre . . . No le faltó nunca su comida, ni le faltaron sus medicinas, porque Paco trabajó siempre bien, como un burro de carga. Alguna vez, la verdad, había él especulado con la muerte de su mujer. Y esto lo sentía ahora. Pero . . . ¡había estado desahuciada tantas veces! . . . Se avergonzaba de pensarlo, pero no pudo menos de hacer proyectos, en una ocasión, con una viuda de buenas carnes, que vivía en la vecindad, y que le dejaba sin respiración cuando le soltaba una risa para contestar a sus piropos . . . Esto fue en época en que María estaba paralítica . . . «Cosa progresiva—decían los médicos—, llegará el día en que la parálisis ataque al corazón y entonces . . . hay que estar preparados.»

desahuciada *dejada sin esperanza*

piropos *flowery compliments*

II

E l señor Paco estuvo preparado. Ya lo había estado cuando la hidropesía, cuando el tumor en el pecho, cuando . . . La vida de María en los últimos veinte años había sido un ir de una enfermedad mala a otra peor . . . Y ella tan contenta. ¡Con tal de tener sus medicinas! Y hasta sin eso; porque a la hija casada había llegado a darle el dinero de sus medicinas, muchas veces para comprarles cosas a los niños . . . Pero lo que era seguro es que, sufrir, lo que decían los médicos que estaba sufriendo . . . no, María no notaba aquellos padecimientos. Nunca se quejó. Y cuando uno sufre se queja. Esto lo sabe todo el mundo . . . Entre una enfermedad y otra, ayudaba torpemente a las hijas a poner orden en aquella casa descuidada, donde, continuamente, resonaban gritos y discusiones entre las dos hermanas, que no se podían ver . . . Esto sí mortificaba a la pobre, aquellas discusiones que eran el escándalo de la vecindad y nunca, ni en su agonía, pudo gozar de paz.

El señor Paco, durante los tres años de la parálisis de su mujer, había tenido aquellos secretos proyectos respecto a la vecina viuda. Pensaba echar a las hijas como fuera y quedarse con el piso . . . No faltaba más . . . Y luego, a vivir . . . Alguna

hidropesía *exceso de líquidos*

compensación tenía que ofrecerle el destino.

Todos los días acechaba la cara pálida y risueña de María, que hundida en su sillón, en un rincón de la cocina, tenía sobre las rodillas paralíticas al nieto más pequeño, o cosía, con sus manos aún hábiles, sin dar importancia a aquello que al señor Paco le ponía de tan mal humor: que la cocina estuviese sucia, con las paredes negras de no limpiarse en años, y el aire lleno de humo y de olor a aceite malo.

María levantaba hacia él sus ojos suaves, aquella boca pálida donde siempre flotaba la misteriosa e irritante sonrisa, y el señor Paco desviaba los ojos; él notaba que ella le compadecía, como si le adivinara los pensamientos, y desviaba los ojos. Podía compadecerle todo lo que quisiera; pero el caso es que no se moría nunca; aunque por la vida que llevaba como, decía él a sus amigos, cuando el vino le soltaba la lengua, para la vida que llevaba la pobre mujer, mejor estaría ya descansando . . .

Un día el señor Paco sintió derrumbarse todos sus proyectos. Al volver del trabajo, cuando abrió la puerta de la cocina, encontró a la mujer de pie, como si tal cosa, fregando cacharros. La sonrisa con que le recibió fue un poco tímida.

—¿Sabes? . . . Esta mañana vi que me podía lavar sola, que podía andar . . . Me alegré por las chicas . . . ¡Tienen tanto trabajo las pobres! . . .

Parece que también ha salido de ésta.

El señor Paco no dijo nada. No pudo manifestar ninguna clase de alegría ni de asombro. Por otra parte, tampoco hacía falta. Las hijas, el yerno y hasta los nietos, tomaban la curación de la paralítica como la cosa más natural. Discutían lo mismo, cuando la madre estaba en pie y les ayudaba en la medida de sus fuerzas que cuando estaba sentada en un sillón de hule.

Al señor Paco con la imposibilidad de realizar el nuevo matrimonio que soñaba se le pasó el enamoramiento por la viuda frescachona y, en verdad, cuando, al fin, María cayó enferma de muerte, él no tenía ningún deseo del desenlace. Lo que le sucedió fue que hasta el último minuto estuvo sin creerlo. Lo mismo les sucedía a las hijas, que estaban acostumbradas a tener años y años a una madre agonizante. La noche antes de morir, sin poder ya incorporarse en la cama, María hilvanaba torpemente el trajecillo de un nieto . . . Y, como de costumbre, no pudo hacer nada para impedir las discusiones habituales de la familia, en su último día en la tierra.

acechaba observaba

como si tal cosa *as though nothing were wrong*
fregando cacharros *scrubbing pots*

en . . . fuerzas *as her strength allowed*
hule *rubber*

enamoramiento *infatuation*
frescachona muy robusta y sana
desenlace separación *(breakup)*

hilvanaba *was hemming*

III

El señor Paco se portó decentemente en su entierro, con una cara afligida. Pero al volver del cementerio ya la había olvidado. ¡Era tan poca cosa allí aquella mujer menuda y silenciosa!

Habían pasado ya más de tres semanas que estaba bajo la tierra. Y ahora, sin venir a cuento, el señor Paco la sentía. Llevaba varios días sintiéndola al entrar en la casa, y no podía decir por qué. La recordaba como cuando era joven, y él había estado orgulloso de ella, que era limpia y ordenada como ninguna; con aquel cabello negro anudado en un **moño**, siempre brillante, y aquellos dientes blanquísimos. Y aquel olor de limpieza, de buenos guisos que tenía su cocina, que ella misma encalaba cada sábado, y aquella tranquilidad, aquel silencio que ella parecía poner en dondequiera que entraba . . .

Aquel día cayó el señor Paco en la cuenta de que era por eso . . . Aquel silencio . . . Hacía tres semanas que las hijas no discutían.

Ellas también, quizá sentían a la muerta.

—Pero no . . . —el señor Paco se sonó ruidosamente— no . . . eso son cosas de viejo, de lo viejo que está uno ya.

Sin embargo, era indudable que las hijas no discutían. Era indudable que en vez de dejar las cosas por hacer, pretextando cada una que aquel trabajo urgente le pertenecía a la otra, en vez de eso, se repartían las labores, y la casa marchaba mejor. El señor Paco quizá por esto, o quizá porque se iba haciendo viejo, como él pensaba, estaba más en la casa, y hasta se había aficionado algo a uno de los nietos.

Dio unos pasos por el corredor, sintió el calor de la mancha del sol en la nariz y en la **nuca**, al atravesarla, y empujó la puerta de la cocina, quedando unos momentos deslumbrado en el **umbral**.

La cocina estaba blanca y reluciente como en los primeros tiempos de su matrimonio. En la mesa estaban puestos los platos. El yerno estaba comiendo y, cosa nunca vista, lo atendía la hija **soltera**, mientras la hermana se ocupaba de los dos **mocosos** pequeños . . . Aquello era tan raro que le hizo **carraspear**.

—Esto parece otra cosa. ¿Eh, señor Paco?

El yerno estaba satisfecho de aquellas paredes blancas oliendo a cal.

El señor Paco miró a sus hijas. Le parecía que hacía años que no las miraba. Sin saber por qué, dijo que se le estaban pareciendo ahora a la madre.

moño *bun, chignon*

cayó . . . cuenta el señor Paco se dio cuenta

nuca *back of the neck*
umbral *threshold*

soltera *no casada*
mocosos *sniffling*
carraspear *clear his throat*

—Ya quisieran. La señora María era una santa.

Esta idea entró en la cabeza del señor Paco, mientras iba consumiendo su sopa, lenta y silenciosamente. La idea apuntada por el yerno de que la muerta había sido una santa.

—La verdad, padre—dijo de pronto una de la hijas—, que a veces no sabe uno cómo viven algunas personas. La pobre madre no hizo más que sufrir y aguantar todo . . . Yo quisiera saber de qué le sirvió vivir así para morirse sin tener ningún gusto . . .

Después de esto, nada. El señor Paco no tenía ganas de contestar, ni nadie . . . Pero parecía que en la cocina clara hubiese como una respuesta, como una sonrisa, algo . . .

Otra vez suspiró el señor Paco, honda, sentidamente, después de limpiarse los labios con la servilleta.

Mientras se ponía el abrigo para irse a la calle de nuevo, las hijas cuchichearon sobre él, en la cocina.

—¿Te has fijado en el padre? . . . Se está volviendo viejo. ¿Te fijaste cómo se quedó, así, helado, después de comer? Ni se dio cuenta cuando Pepe salió . . .

El señor Paco las estaba oyendo. Sí, él tampoco sabía bien lo que le pasaba. Pero no podía librarse de la evidencia. Estaba sintiendo de nuevo a la muerta, junto a él. No tenía esto nada de terrible. Era algo cálido, infinitamente consolador. Algo inexpresable. Ahora mismo, mientras se enrollaba al cuello la bufanda, era como si las manos de ella se la atasen amorosamente . . . Como en otros tiempos . . . Quizá por eso había vivido y muerto ella, así, doliente y risueña, insignificante y magnífica. Santa . . . para poder volver a todo, y a todos consolarles después de muerta.

apuntada *pointed out*

PARA APLICAR

Comprensión   I

A   Conteste a las siguientes preguntas.

1   ¿Cómo era el señor Paco?
2   ¿Qué hizo al entrar en la casa?
3   ¿Qué llevaba en la manga de su abrigo?
4   ¿Cuánto tiempo hace que vive en esa casa?
5   ¿Qué sentía ese día en el corredor?
6   ¿Cómo eran las hijas?
7   ¿Por qué le compadecía María a su marido?

8   ¿Con qué había especulado una vez?
9   ¿De qué se avergonzaba él?
10   Describa la enfermedad de María.

B   Escoja la respuesta que *no* es apropiada.

1   ¿Cómo era el señor Paco?
    a.   Era alegre, con una cara fea y simpática.
    b.   Solía emborracharse todos los días.
    c.   Se le veían algunos cabellos blancos debajo de la boina.

"The Sob" (David Alfaro Siqueiros). Collection, The Museum of Modern Art, New York

Llanto (Siqueiros)

2 ¿Qué hizo ese día que jamás hacía antes?
   a. Colgó su abrigo en el perchero.
   b. Se frotó las manos.
   c. Suspiró profundamente.
3 ¿Por qué se sentía triste?
   a. Los ladrillos rojos pavimentaban el pasillo.
   b. Su esposa había muerto.
   c. Había sentido la presencia de su mujer como si viviese.
4 ¿Por qué no le había reprochado jamás?
   a. Su mujer estaba enferma por mucho tiempo.
   b. Sus hijas eran mal humoradas y hablaban como demonios.
   c. Su propia conciencia le molestaba bastante.

Comprensión   II

A Conteste a las siguientes preguntas.

1 ¿Durante cuántos años sufrió María?
2 ¿Por qué creían que María no sufría tanto como decían los médicos?
3 ¿Respetaban las hijas a la madre enferma?
4 ¿Qué pensaba hacer el señor Paco durante el período de la parálisis de María?
5 ¿Qué hacía María todos los días?
6 ¿Por qué desviaba los ojos el señor Paco ante la vista de María?
7 ¿Qué decía el señor Paco a sus amigos cuando el vino le soltaba la lengua?
8 ¿Qué le hizo cambiar todos sus planes?
9 ¿Cómo reaccionaron todos a la curación?
10 ¿De qué se dio cuenta el señor Paco?
11 ¿Estaban preparados para la muerte de María?
12 Describa cómo pasó María la última noche de su vida.

B Usando las oraciones que siguen, escriba un párrafo lógico que refleje lo que pasó en la selección.

1 A veces María daba el dinero para las medicinas a su hija.

2 María padecía de varias enfermedades, cada una peor que la otra.
3 A María le mortificaba que las hijas pelearan tanto.
4 Ayudaba a las hijas a arreglar la casa lo mejor que podía.
5 Ella estaba siempre contenta, con o sin sus medicinas.

Comprensión   III

A Conteste a las siguientes preguntas.

1 Describa al señor Paco el día del entierro.
2 ¿Cómo era María de joven?
3 ¿Por qué no habían discutido las hermanas en tres semanas?
4 ¿Qué cambios se notaban en ellas?
5 Al señor Paco, ¿por qué le deslumbraba la cocina?
6 ¿Cómo le parecían sus hijas?
7 Según el yerno, ¿cómo era María?
8 ¿De qué cuchichearon las hijas?
9 ¿Por qué había vivido y muerto María?

B ¿Verdadero o falso?

1 Después del entierro el señor Paco se sintió perdido sin su mujer.
2 Nunca volvió a pensar en ella.
3 Cuando era joven María era una mujer bonita.
4 Cierto día el señor Paco notó que había una tranquilidad completa en la casa.
5 Comenzó a creer que las hijas la sentían también.
6 Creía que la vejez le estaba engañando, haciéndole creer en cambios imposibles.
7 El yerno dijo que las hijas querían ser santas.
8 La madre hizo que otros sufrieran, y ella no tenía ningún gusto.
9 La madre volvió a consolarles.

Más Práctica

A Complete las siguientes oraciones con una palabra de la lista.

atravesó, manga, anudado, empujarla, yerno, hule, coser, se sonó, mancha

1 Llevaba el pelo _____ en la nuca.
2 El marido de su hija es _____.
3 El aceite va a dejar una _____ la blusa.
4 Para llegar a la cocina él _____ el pasillo.
5 La enferma se sentaba en una silla de _____.
6 La puerta está cerrada. Tienes que _____.
7 Le gustaba cocinar y _____.
8 Lleva señal de luto en la _____.
9 Hizo mucho ruido cuando _____.

B Dé un sinónimo de las palabras en letra bastardilla.

1 Al darse cuenta de que sus hijas *no se aguantaban,* el padre se puso triste.
2 *Olía* los aromas deliciosos.
3 Sus *enfermedades* duraron veinte años.
4 Él *tomó demasiado* en la fiesta.

Ejercicios Creativos

1 Los diferentes miembros de la familia no le compadecían a la enferma. ¿Cómo mostró el señor Paco su egoísmo y falta de comprensión? ¿Cómo mostraban sus hijas falta de respeto y cariño?
2 Imagínese en el lugar del señor Paco y las hijas. ¿Podría controlar sus deseos egoístas? ¿Sería difícil ser comprensivo en todo momento? Describa cómo uno debe portarse en tales circunstancias.
3 ¿Por qué Carmen Laforet le llamaría al marido «el señor Paco» y a la esposa «María»? ¿Por qué no les habrá puesto nombres a las hijas?
4 ¿Cuándo ejercía María más influencia sobre su familia? Explique y dé ejemplos.
5 Hemos observado varias muertes — la muerte temida que sí llegó trágicamente, la muerte inesperada e innecesaria y la muerte que tardó en llegar pero dejó sus influencias benéficas. ¿Cuál de las selecciones le gustó más? Justifique su opinión.

El Presente del Subjuntivo

Verbos Regulares

La primera persona singular del presente sirve de raíz para el presente del subjuntivo.

infinitivo	raíz	subjuntivo
mirar	miro	mire, mires, mire, miremos, miréis, miren
comer	como	coma, comas, coma, comamos, comáis, coman
vivir	vivo	viva, vivas, viva, vivamos, viváis, vivan

Verbos con Raíz Irregular

infinitivo	raíz	subjuntivo
caer	caigo	caiga
conducir	conduzco	conduzca
conocer	conozco	conozca
decir	digo	diga
escoger	escojo	escoja
hacer	hago	haga
oir	oigo	oiga
poner	pongo	ponga
salir	salgo	salga
tener	tengo	tenga
traer	traigo	traiga
vencer	venzo	venza
venir	vengo	venga
ver	veo	vea

Verbos Irregulares

Los siguientes verbos son irregulares en el subjuntivo.

infinitivo	subjuntivo
dar	dé
estar	esté
saber	sepa
ser	sea
ir	vaya
haber	haya

Usos del Presente del Subjuntivo

Cláusulas Nominales: Expresiones de Voluntad

El subjuntivo se emplea después de los verbos o expresiones de deseo, voluntad, consejo, preferencia, esperanza, permiso y prohibición.

Quiero que te vayas.
Deseamos que estés bien.
Insisten en que trabajemos.
Mandan que salgamos.
Te aconsejamos que pienses más.
Permiten que nos quedemos.
Les pedimos que nos ayuden.

Nótese que cuando hay un solo sujeto en la oración, se emplea el infinitivo.

Quiero salir.
Insisto en terminar.

A Sustituyan según el modelo.

Quiero que ellos vayan.
mando/
Mando que ellos vayan.

1   Mando que ellos vayan.
deseo/no permito/les aconsejo/prefiero/
espero/ruego/suplico/

2   La profesora manda que escribamos el tema.
permite/insiste en/dice/pide/aconseja/
hace/quiere/exige/

B Sustituyan según el modelo.

Él quiere que entremos en la casa.
los otros hombres/
Él quiere que los otros hombres
entren en la casa.

1 Él quiere que los otros hombres entren en la casa.
tú/su ayudante/yo/los campesinos/nosotros/Ud./

2 El jinete espera que sus amigos lo admiren.
Perla/yo/tú/la vieja/las mujeres/nosotros/

3 El rabino manda que ella devuelva el misal.
tú/la novia/nosotros/alguien/Uds./ellas/

4 Le aconsejan que aprenda a manejar.
me/nos/les/le/te/

5 Preferimos que los obreros aten la soga aquí.
el padre/tú/los niños/Uds./Ud./la mujer/

6 Ella no permite que atravesemos la calle ahora.
los muchachos/yo/Ud./el niño/el público/tú/

7 La joven les pide a todos que no hagan ruido.
a nosotros/a los hombres/a mí/a ti/a Uds./a los otros/

8 Nadie prohibe que volvamos.
los soldados/yo/el pobrecillo/tú/nosotros/los demás/

9 ¡Ojalá que ella se recobre pronto!
el marido/tú/Uds./nosotros/el yerno/ellas/

C Sigan los modelos.

¿Por qué no salen hoy?
Porque quiero que salgan mañana.

1 ¿Por qué no pagan hoy?
2 ¿Por qué no vuelven hoy?
3 ¿Por qué no continúan hoy?

4 ¿Por qué no vienen hoy?
5 ¿Por qué no juegan hoy?
6 ¿Por qué no trabajan hoy?
7 ¿Por qué no siguen hoy?
8 ¿Por qué no se despiden hoy?
9 ¿Por qué no van hoy?
10 ¿Por qué no escriben hoy?

Alicia no quiere ir.
Dígale que vaya.

11 Felipe no quiere contestar.
12 Anita no quiere cruzar la calle.
13 Olga no quiere traer la guitarra.
14 Oscar no quiere atar la soga.
15 Jacinto no quiere guiar al forastero.
16 Eduardo no quiere remar a la otra orilla.
17 Lola no quiere esperar el camión.
18 Eva no quiere venir aquí.
19 Rafael no quiere aprender el verso.
20 Luis no quiere limpiar la casa.

Voy a traer la guitarra.
No quiero que la traigas.

21 Voy a escribir la carta.
22 Voy a cerrar el portón.
23 Voy a dar un examen.
24 Voy a escoger un regalo.
25 Voy a ayudar a la señora.
26 Voy a pagar la cuenta.
27 Voy a devolver el misal.
28 Voy a coser las mangas.
29 Voy a empujar la puerta.
30 Voy a preparar los guisos.

¿Por qué te lavas las manos?
Mi padre insiste en que me las lave.

31 ¿Por qué te quitas la bufanda?
32 ¿Por qué te pones el cinturón?
33 ¿Por qué te cortas el pelo?
34 ¿Por qué te pones la medalla?
35 ¿Por qué te lavas los pies?
36 ¿Por qué te mojas la camisa?
37 ¿Por qué te limpias los dientes?

Expresiones de Emoción

El subjuntivo se emplea con verbos o expresiones de emoción.

> Temen que lo sepamos.
> Nos alegramos de que estés aquí.

D Sustituyan según el modelo.

> Temen que no vengas.
> sienten/
> Sienten que no vengas.

1 Sienten que no vengas.
   les sorprende/tienen miedo de/se alegran de/¡lástima/se preocupan de/les extraña/
2 Tememos que haya perdido la elección.
   sentimos/nos alegramos de/¡qué triste/ tenemos miedo de/¡lástima/nos sorprendemos de/

E Sigan el modelo.

> Juanita sale pronto. ¿Estás alegre?
> Sí, me alegro de que salga pronto.

1 El soldado se va mañana. ¿Lo sientes?
2 La ladrona se ha escapado. ¡Lástima! ¿no?
3 El caballo cae con el jinete. ¿Qué temes?
4 Ella no encuentra al hombre. ¿De qué tienes miedo?
5 El niño se despierta. ¿Te sorprendes de eso?
6 La empleada tiene un buen sueldo. ¿De qué te alegras?

Expresiones de Duda

Se emplea el subjuntivo después de una expresión de duda. Cuando el verbo o expresión indica certidumbre, se emplea el indicativo.

> Creo que llegarán a tiempo.
> No creo que lleguen a tiempo.
>
> Dudo que estén aquí.
> No dudo que están aquí.

F   Sustituyan según el modelo.

> *Dudamos que hayan visto a la niña.*
> *yo no creo/*
> *Yo no creo que hayan visto a la niña.*

1   Yo no creo que hayan visto a la niña.
no creemos/negamos/¿crees/yo dudo/
la joven niega/él no cree/

2   ¿Crees que podamos alcanzarlos?
niegas/¿estás seguro/¿no crees que/yo
dudo/¿creen los jinetes/es cierto/

Expresiones Impersonales

Se emplea el subjuntivo después de las expresiones impersonales que
indican duda, necesidad, probabilidad, posibilidad, voluntad o
cualquier otra opinión.

> Es dudoso que vengan.
> Es preciso que estés aquí.
> Es probable que lo sepan.
> Es posible que volvamos pronto.
> Es mejor que se queden.

G   Sustituyan según el modelo.

> *Es posible que se sienta oprimida*
> *por el terror.*
>
> *es verdad/*
>
> *Es verdad que se siente oprimida*
> *por el terror.*

1   Es verdad que se siente oprimida por
el terror.
es necesario/es probable/es cierto/es
preciso/es lástima/es claro/es dudoso/
es evidente/no es cierto/

2   Es probable que trabaje en el muelle.
es imposible/es verdad/es curioso/es
obvio/es ridículo/es cierto/es claro/es
improbable/no es cierto/

H   Sigan el modelo.

> *Se aburre de la ciudad. ¿Es posible?*
> *Sí, es posible que se aburra de la*
> *ciudad.*

1   Le pagan bien. ¿Es dudoso?
2   Le van a dar una guitarra. ¿Es verdad?
3   La invitan a fiestas elegantes. ¿No es
cierto?
4   Se va antes de Pascua. ¿Será mejor?
5   Se acerca al caño. ¿Es necesario?
6   Se sumergen en el agua. ¿Es posible?
7   Se recobra de la enfermedad. ¿Es
probable?
8   Le pide cincuenta pesos más. ¿Es
necesario?
9   Le han dado un susto tremendo. ¿Es
cierto?
10 Le han robado el dinero. ¿Es lástima?

I Construyan oraciones según los números indicados, escogiendo sucesivamente de cada lista.

Modelo: 1-1-1-1
yo – mandar que – la niña – hacer el trabajo
Yo mando que la niña haga el trabajo.

a. 2-4-6-8   d. 8-2-3-9   g. 5-1-8-4
b. 1-3-5-7   e. 3-8-9-5   h. 9-6-4-3
c. 4-9-7-6   f. 6-5-2-1   i. 7-7-1-2

1	yo	1	mandar que	1	la niña	1	hacer el trabajo
2	Ud.	2	querer que	2	los chicos	2	visitar a un amigo
3	la señora	3	permitir que	3	el viejo	3	ir a la fiesta
4	nosotros	4	dudar que	4	el hombre	4	buscar los detalles
5	Uds.	5	esperar que	5	Marisol	5	comprender todo
6	ella	6	preferir que	6	las mujeres	6	salir pronto
7	Pedro	7	no creer que	7	mi hermana	7	levantarse temprano
8	ellos	8	exigir que	8	Juan	8	venir a la hora fija
9	tú	9	alegrarse de que	9	el sobrino	9	quedarse aquí

Cláusulas Adverbiales

En cláusulas adverbiales introducidas por una expresión temporal, se emplea el subjuntivo si el verbo indica lo que puede suceder. Si el verbo indica lo que ya sucedió, se emplea el indicativo. Las conjunciones temporales son: *luego que, cuando, en cuanto, tan pronto como, hasta que, después de que.*

> Me quedaré aquí hasta que regresen.
> Me quedé aquí hasta que regresaron.
>
> En cuanto llegue, el dueño le servirá la comida.
> En cuanto llegó, el dueño le sirvió la comida.

Con las siguientes conjunciones, se emplea siempre el subjuntivo: *antes de que, a menos que, para que, con tal que, sin que, en caso de que.*

> Nosotros saldremos antes de que ellos vuelvan.
> Lo diré para que tú lo sepas.

Con las siguientes conjunciones se emplea el subjuntivo si el verbo indica incertidumbre, duda o estado indefinido; si el verbo indica una acción realizada se emplea el indicativo: *así que, aunque.*

Aunque llueve, saldremos.	(Está lloviendo)
Aunque llueva, saldremos.	(No sabemos si va a llover).

J Sustituyan según el modelo.

Dormirán hasta que los despertemos.
tú/
Dormirán hasta que tú los despiertes.

1 Dormirán hasta que los despertemos.
tú/yo/la patrona/nosotros/Ud./los padres/

2 Ella estudiará en la biblioteca con tal que Ud. vaya por ella.
su compañero/tú/los interesados/nosotros/yo/Uds./

3 Los jóvenes se quedarán allí a menos que los busque la madre.
sus compañeros/tú/yo/los otros/nosotros/Luis/

4 Preparan mucha comida para que tenga suficiente la familia.
nosotros/los hijos/él y yo/todos los invitados/el ejército/

5 Saldrá para la ciudad cuando le pague el patrón.
yo/la jefa/nosotros/tú/Uds./el teniente/

6 No morirá con tal que le ayude la señora.
nosotros/los doctores/yo/su compañero/tú/la madre/

K Sigan los modelos.

Regresarán si yo los invito.
Regresarán cuando yo los invite.

1 No comerán la cazuela si les traemos otra cosa.
2 Serán felices si alguien les paga el dinero.
3 Se recobrará si va al hospital.
4 Dirá todos los detalles si puede.
5 Recibirá una medalla si encuentra al ladrón.
6 Irán a México si reciben los boletos.
7 Nos llamarán por teléfono si les dicen nuestro número.
8 Saldrán en seguida si los padres les dan permiso.
9 Le daré un regalo si lo veo.
10 Pasaré por tu casa si tengo tiempo.

Al salir Ana, iremos a la playa.
En cuanto salga Ana, iremos a la playa.

11 Al abandonar yo este sitio, Uds. tendrán que venir a verlo.
12 Al sentarse la mujer, empezaremos.
13 Al despertarse los niños, llámame por teléfono.
14 Al ver José la carta, dígale que suba.
15 Al comenzar Marisol el trabajo, consulte conmigo.
16 Al terminar Consuelo la silla, una señora la quiere comprar.

> *Enviarán los paquetes. Yo les pago.*
> *Enviarán los paquetes sin que*
> *yo les pague.*

17 Llevaremos un regalo. Nadie nos ve.
18 Iremos en avión. Mamá nos da permiso.
19 Haremos otros planes. Lo sabe el cabo de guardia.
20 Les da más dinero. Ellos se lo piden.
21 Saldremos súbito. El maestro se da cuenta.
22 Llegarán por la noche. Nadie los oye.
23 Descansaremos. La directora nos observa.
24 Me visitarás a menudo. Nadie se ofende.

> *Entra Lucía. Me voy.*
> *Tan pronto como entre Lucía, me iré.*

25 Los hermanos llegan. Voy a conocerlos.
26 Jacobo pasa en su caballo. Perla estará contenta.
27 Recibe el dinero por el trabajo en el muelle. Regresará a su casa.
28 Comienza a sentirse mejor. Irá a la oficina.
29 Se dan cuenta de la situación. Me llamarán por teléfono.
30 Se mete en el bote. Empezará a remar.

> *Le escribiré una carta. Él está en*
> *España ahora.*

> *Le escribiré una carta en caso de que*
> *esté en España ahora.*

31 Voy a encender el fuego. Ellas regresan más tarde.
32 Él le prepara un poquito de té. Su hijo tiene hambre.
33 Lleva camisa de manga larga. Hace fresco.
34 Decide ir en bote. La marea está alta.
35 Compra medicinas. Su esposa las necesita.
36 Abren todas las ventanas de la cocina. El olor de los guisos es fuerte.

L Reemplacen el verbo con la forma correspondiente del infinitivo indicado.

1 No irá a menos que su mujer _____ también. *ir*
2 En caso de que _____ la esposa, no se quedará solo. *morir*
3 Irá a la doctora luego que _____ a toser. *empezar*
4 Llámame para que _____ las noticias al instante. *saber*
5 Le va a pagar después de que _____ el trabajo. *terminar*
6 Yo haré mis quehaceres con tal que no me _____. *interrumpir*
7 Seguirá así hasta que alguien _____ con ayuda. *venir*
8 Tan pronto como _____ el astro, anunciará su deseo. *ver*
9 Comenzará a construir la casa en cuanto _____ el dinero necesario. *tener*
10 No se cortará el pelo antes de que su padre lo _____. *pedir*
11 Yo saldré cuando _____ los otros. *llegar*
12 No llevaremos impermeables aunque _____. *llover*

Cláusulas Relativas

Si la cláusula relativa modifica un sustantivo o pronombre que sea indefinido o negativo, el verbo de la cláusula se expresa en el subjuntivo. Si el antecedente es definido, se emplea el indicativo.

> Busco un secretario que sepa español.
> Conozco a un secretario que sabe español.
>
> Aquí hay alguien que puede hacer el trabajo.
> Aquí no hay nadie que pueda hacer el trabajo.

M Sustituyan según el modelo.

> *Compraré algo que te guste.*
> *leeré/*
> *Leeré algo que te guste.*

1 Leeré algo que te guste.
demostraré/regalaré/prepararé/
utilizaré/tendré/conseguiré/

2 Busca algún empleado que le pueda ayudar.
algún sacerdote/alguna persona/alguna medicina/algún plan/algunos amigos/algún obrero/

3 ¿Hay aquí una novela que Raquel no haya leído?
Ud./tú/yo/Uds./nosotros/ellas/

N Sigan el modelo.

> *Quiere comprar el coche que no cuesta mucho.*
>
> *Quiere comprar un coche que no cueste mucho.*

1 Busca el camino que pasa por su casa.
2 Necesita la cartera que contiene dinero.

3 Quiere comprar la casa que tiene vista hacia el mar.
4 Quiere leer la novela que trata de la muerte de Manolete.
5 Use Ud. la receta que explica bien la preparación.
6 Evite Ud. la biblioteca que tiene los libros en desorden.

O Sigan el modelo.

> *Hay un cerro que no podemos subir.*
> *No hay cerro que no podamos subir.*

1 Hay un guía que conoce bien esa comarca.
2 Hay un coleccionista que tiene valiosos platos de Sèvres.
3 Hay un amigo que le ayudará a hacer la faena.
4 Hay una enfermera que merece una medalla de honor.
5 Hay un lugar donde se puede descansar.
6 Hay alguien que sabe todos los detalles del acontecimiento.

Caprichos del Destino

Fortuna y aceituna, a veces mucha, y a veces ninguna.

PARA PREPARAR LA ESCENA

El cuento, como casi toda ficción narrativa, habla de la naturaleza humana y su experiencia. En pocas palabras, da un comentario, una interpretación, una visión de la vida. Nos interesamos en los personajes, en el desarrollo de la acción, pero es el fin del cuento lo que nos cautiva. ¿Qué fin tiene para nosotros el autor? ¿Se destaca un noble sentimiento? ¿Se subraya una acción admirable? ¿Se satiriza una costumbre? ¿O hay un desenlace opuesto al anticipado? El destino de cada individuo está frecuentemente en manos de la diosa Fortuna, y nunca se sabe qué viento soplará, qué camino se desviará, qué capricho producirá un trastorno irónico en la vida.

A la deriva

Horacio Quiroga

PARA PRESENTAR LA LECTURA

La selva malsana está llena de riesgos y peligros para todos. Nunca se sabe lo que a uno le espera. Aun la muerte puede ser consecuencia de un momento de descuido.

En este cuento, el uruguayo Horacio Quiroga (1878–1937), el Kipling de la América del Sur, relata el resultado del encuentro entre un hombre y una culebra venenosa.

La selección comienza con la acción ya avanzada. En rápida sucesión el autor nos hace sentir y vivir lo que el protagonista siente y vive. Embárquese con Paulino en su canoa, y ¡ponga *su* vida «a la deriva»!

PARA APRENDER VOCABULARIO

Palabras Clave   I

1 **adelgazada (adelgazar)**   delgada, de menos peso *(thin)*
    En ese vestido largo Rosa parecía adelgazada.

2 **garganta**   parte anterior adentro del cuello
    Con un resfrío, uno tiene la garganta inflamada.

3 **hinchazón**   engrandecimiento *(swelling)*
    A causa de la hinchazón del pie no podía ponerse el zapato.

4 **ojeada**   mirada rápida, vistazo
    Una ojeada le convenció que habría problemas.

5 **reseca**   muy seca, desecada
    Margarita tenía la garganta reseca y pidió agua.

Selva tropical

6 **ronco** áspero, que tiene ronquera
(*hoarse*)
Juan tiene la garganta reseca y está ronco.

7 **tragó (tragar)** hizo pasar comida o
líquido por el esófago
El muchacho tragó mucha agua para
satisfacer la sed.

Práctica

Complete con una palabra de la lista.

adelgazada	ojeada	tragó
garganta	reseca	ronco
hinchazón		

1 Saltó para atrás y dio una _____ a su
alrededor.
2 Tiene fiebre y dolor de _____ .
3 El golpe le causó una _____ grandísima.

4 De una vez _____ todo el líquido.
5 Dio un grito _____ que la mujer apenas
oyó.
6 Después de esa dieta parecía _____ .
7 Tenía mucha sed y la boca estaba _____ .

Palabras Clave II

1 **aliento** respiración, soplo
La doctora sintió el aliento cálido del
paciente y supo que tenía fiebre.

2 **desbordaba (desbordar)** salía de los
bordes (*overflowed*)
En la primavera con las lluvias torrenciales
siempre se desbordaba el río.

3 **ligadura** cinta, atadura de una vena o
arteria (*tourniquet*)
Se aplicó una ligadura para detener la
sangre de la herida.

4 **pala**   remo para canoa, parte plana del remo

   Tomó la pala y se fue en la canoa.

5 **sequedad**   estado de seco

   Sentía una sequedad insaciable en la garganta.

6 **vientre**   panza, parte del cuerpo donde están los intestinos

   Sentía dolores del estómago y del vientre.

Práctica

Complete con una palabra de la lista.

aliento	ligadura	sequedad
desbordaba	pala	vientre

1 Debido a la fiebre su _____ estaba recálido.
2 El _____ le dolía mucho al enfermo.
3 Cada momento le aumentaba más la _____ de la garganta.
4 Puso una _____ sobre la herida.
5 Sin una _____ no podía remar.
6 En las inundaciones anuales se _____ el río.

Palabras Clave   III

1 **enderezó (enderezar)**   puso derecho (straightened)

   Se enderezó en la canoa para poder remar.

2 **escalofrío**   temblor, estremecimiento del cuerpo (shiver, shudder, chill)

   La fiebre le causó un escalofrío tremendo.

3 **girando (girar)**   moviéndose circularmente

   La canoa estaba girando en el remolino del agua.

4 **helado (helar – ie)**   solidificado por medio del frío (frozen)

   El cuerpo estaba helado e inmóvil.

5 **miel**   substancia dulce, espesa y viscosa producida por las abejas

   Puso la miel en el té para endulzarlo.

6 **pesadamente**   de un modo pesado, torpemente

   Levantó la cabeza pesadamente.

7 **remolino**   movimiento circular de agua (whirl, whirlpool, water spout)

   En medio del río había un remolino.

8 **rocío**   gotitas de líquido condensado sobre las plantas por la mañana y por la noche

   El rocío le mojó los pies.

Práctica

Complete con una palabra de la lista.

enderezó	helado	rocío
escalofrío	miel	remolino
girando	pesadamente	

1 El mundo está _____ alrededor del sol.
2 Caminó _____ con el pie hinchado.
3 El enfermo tembló con un fuerte _____.
4 No sintió nada en el cuerpo _____.
5 Las abejas producen la _____.
6 Por un momento se _____, y luego volvió a caerse.
7 Esa mañana había poco _____ en la hierba.
8 Él no pudo controlar la canoa en el _____ del río.

A la deriva

Horacio Quiroga

I

El hombre pisó algo blanduzco, y en seguida sintió la mordedura en el pie. Saltó adelante, y al volverse, con un juramento vio un yararacusú que, arrollada sobre sí misma, esperaba otro ataque.

El hombre echó una veloz ojeada a su pie, donde dos gotitas de sangre engrosaban dificultosamente, y sacó el machete de la cintura. La víbora vio la amenaza y hundió la cabeza en el centro mismo de su espiral; pero el machete cayó en el lomo, dislocándole las vértebras.

El hombre se bajó hasta la mordedura, quitó las gotitas de sangre y durante un instante contempló. Un dolor agudo nacía de los puntitos violeta y comenzaba a invadir todo el pie. Apresuradamente se ligó el tobillo con su pañuelo y siguió por la picada hacia su rancho.

El dolor en el pie aumentaba, con sensación de tirante abultamiento, y de pronto el hombre sintió dos o tres fulgurantes punzadas que, como relámpagos, habían irradiado desde la herida hasta la mitad de la pantorrilla. Movía la pierna con dificultad; una metálica sequedad de garganta, seguida de sed quemante, le arrancó un nuevo juramento.

Llegó por fin al rancho y se echó de brazos sobre la rueda de un trapiche. Los dos puntitos violeta desaparecían ahora en la monstruosa hinchazón del pie entero. La piel parecía adelgazada y a punto de ceder, de tensa. Quiso llamar a su mujer, y la voz se quebró en un ronco arrastre de garganta reseca. La sed lo devoraba.

—¡Dorotea!—alcanzó a lanzar en su estertor—. ¡Dame caña!

Su mujer corrió con un vaso lleno, que el hombre sorbió en tres tragos. Pero no había sentido gusto alguno.

rugió gritó

—¡Te pedí caña, no agua!—rugió de nuevo—. ¡Dame caña!

—¡Pero es caña, Paulino!—protestó la mujer, espantada.

—¡No, me diste agua! ¡Quiero caña, te digo!

damajuana *jug*

La mujer corrió otra vez, volviendo con la damajuana. El hombre tragó uno tras otro dos vasos, pero no sintió nada en la garganta.

II

—**B**ueno; esto se pone feo . . . —murmuró entonces, mirando su pie, lívido y ya con lustre gangrenoso. Sobre la honda ligadura del pañuelo la carne desbordaba como una monstruosa morcilla.

con lustre gangrenoso *with a shiny gangrenous appearance*
morcilla *sausage*

ingle *groin*
caldear *to scorch*
pretendió trató de
fulminante *violent, exploding*
rueda de palo *cane press*

Los dolores fulgurantes se sucedían en continuos relampagueos y llegaban ahora a la ingle. La atroz sequedad de garganta, que el aliento parecía caldear más, aumentaba a la par. Cuando pretendió incorporarse, un fulminante vómito lo mantuvo medio minuto con la frente apoyada en la rueda de palo.

Pero el hombre no quería morir, y descendiendo hasta la costa subió a su canoa. Sentóse en la popa y comenzó a palear hasta el centro del Paraná. Allí la corriente del río, que en las inmediaciones del Iguazú corre seis millas, lo llevaría antes de cinco horas a Tacurú-Pucú.

Iguazú tributario del Paraná

El hombre, con sombría energía, pudo efectivamente llegar hasta el medio del río; pero allí sus manos dormidas dejaron caer la pala en la canoa, y tras un nuevo vómito . . . de sangre esta vez . . . dirigió una mirada al sol, que ya trasponía el monte.

trasponía *was setting behind*

reventaba *was bursting*

La pierna entera, hasta medio muslo, era ya un bloque deforme y durísimo que reventaba la ropa. El hombre cortó la ligadura y abrió el pantalón con su cuchillo: el bajo vientre desbordó hinchado, con grandes manchas lívidas y terriblemente dolorosas. El hombre pensó que no podría jamás llegar él solo a Tacurú-Pucú y se decidió pedir a su compadre Alves, aunque hacía mucho tiempo que estaban disgustados.

estaban disgustados no se podían ver

atracar acercarse a la orilla
cuesta arriba *uphill*

La corriente del río se precipitaba ahora hasta la costa brasileña, y el hombre pudo fácilmente atracar. Se arrastró por la picada en cuesta arriba; pero a los veinte metros, exhausto, quedó tendido de pecho.

—¡Alves!—gritó con cuanta fuerza pudo; y prestó oído en vano.

—¡Compadre Alves! ¡No me niegues este favor!—clamó de nuevo, alzando la cabeza del suelo. En el silencio de la selva no se oyó rumor. El hombre tuvo aún valor para llegar hasta su canoa, y la corriente, cogiéndola de nuevo, la llevó velozmente a la deriva.

III

El Paraná corre allí en el fondo de una inmensa hoya, cuyas paredes, altas de cien metros, encajonan fúnebremente el río. Desde las orillas, bordeadas de negros bloques de basalto, asciende el bosque, negro también. Adelante, a los costados, atrás, siempre la eterna muralla lúgubre, en cuyo fondo el río arremolinado se precipita en incesantes borbollones de agua fangosa. El paisaje es agresivo y reina en él un silencio de muerte. Al atardecer, sin embargo, su belleza sombría y calma cobra una majestad única.

El sol había caído ya cuando el hombre, semitendido en el fondo de la canoa, tuvo un violento escalofrío. Y de pronto, con asombro, enderezó pesadamente la cabeza: se sentía mejor. La pierna le dolía apenas, la sed disminuía y su pecho, libre ya, se abría en lenta inspiración.

El veneno comenzaba a irse, no había duda. Se hallaba casi bien, y aunque no tenía fuerzas para mover la mano, contaba con la caída del rocío para reponerse del todo. Calculó que antes de tres horas estaría en Tacurú-Pucú.

El bienestar avanzaba, y con él una somnolencia llena de recuerdos. No sentía ya nada ni en la pierna ni en el vientre. ¿Viviría aún su compadre Gaona en Tacurú-Pucú? Acaso vería también a su ex-patrón Míster Dougald y al recibidor del obraje.

¿Llegaría pronto? El cielo, al poniente, se abría ahora en pantalla de oro, y el río se había coloreado también. Desde la costa paraguaya, ya entenebrecida, el monte dejaba caer sobre el río su frescura crepuscular en penetrantes efluvios de azahar y miel silvestre. Una pareja de guacamayos cruzó muy alto y en silencio hacia el Paraguay.

Allá abajo, sobre el río de oro, la canoa derivaba velozmente, girando a ratos sobre sí misma ante el borbollón de un remolino. El hombre que iba en ella se sentía cada vez mejor, y pensaba entretanto en el tiempo justo que había pasado sin ver a su ex-patrón Dougald. ¿Tres años? Tal vez no; no tanto. ¿Dos años y nueve meses? Acaso. ¿Ocho meses y medio? Eso sí, seguramente.

De pronto sintió que estaba helado hasta el pecho. ¿Qué sería? Y la respiración . . .

hoya quebrada
encajonan encierran
basalto *basalt, hard volcanic rock*
costados lados
borbollones agitaciones de agua
cobra *takes on*

recibidor *receiving clerk*
obraje *mill*
al poniente al oeste
pantalla *canopy*
entenebrecida *in darkness*
efluvios . . . silvestre *odors of orange blossoms and wild honey*
guacamayos tipo de pájaro
derivaba flotaba sin dirección fija

Al recibidor de maderas de Míster Dougald, Lorenzo Cubilla, lo había conocido en Puerto Esperanza un Viernes Santo . . . ¿Viernes? Sí, o jueves . . .

El hombre estiró lentamente los dedos de la mano.

—Un jueves . . .

Y cesó de respirar.

PARA APLICAR

Comprensión   I

A Conteste a las siguientes preguntas.

1 ¿Qué pisó el hombre?
2 ¿Qué sintió en seguida?
3 ¿Dónde lo hirió la víbora?
4 ¿Con qué amenazó a la víbora?
5 ¿La mató el hombre?
6 ¿Qué hizo con el pañuelo?
7 ¿Podía mover la pierna fácilmente?
8 ¿Qué sensaciones inmediatas produjo la mordedura?
9 ¿Cómo estaba el pie?
10 ¿Qué hizo al llegar a su rancho?
11 Después de llegar a su rancho, ¿qué le pidió a Dorotea?
12 ¿Qué efecto tuvo la caña en su garganta?

B ¿Verdadero o falso?

1 El hombre pisó algo duro.
2 El hombre se sentó en algo blanduzco.
3 La víbora lo mordió.
4 La víbora estaba arrollada alrededor de un árbol.
5 El hombre sacó el machete de la cintura.
6 La víbora lo atacó otra vez.
7 El hombre se dislocó las vértebras.
8 El hombre quitó las gotitas de sangre del pie.
9 El dolor se esparcía por todo el pie.
10 Se ligó el tobillo antes de caminar hacia su casa.
11 La ligadura le quitó el dolor.

12 Él juró otra vez.
13 Cuando llegó al rancho, el pie se veía aun más hinchado.
14 Gritó ruidosamente a su mujer.
15 La caña le dio una sensación de alegría.

Comprensión   II

A Conteste a las siguientes preguntas.

1 ¿Por qué decidió irse el hombre?
2 ¿Cuál fue su medio de transporte?
3 ¿Adónde iba?
4 ¿Hasta dónde llegó antes de dejar caer la pala?
5 ¿Qué le sucedió en seguida?
6 ¿Cómo estaba la pierna entonces?
7 ¿Por qué cortó el pantalón con el cuchillo?
8 ¿Por qué decidió pedirle ayuda a su compadre Alves?
9 ¿Qué le ayudó a atracar fácilmente?
10 ¿Encontró a su compadre Alves?
11 ¿Pudo el hombre volver a su canoa?

B Ponga estas oraciones en el orden en que aparecen en la selección.

1 Bajó hasta la orilla y se metió en su canoa.
2 La atroz sequedad de garganta aumentaba.
3 Miró el pie, lívido y con lustre gangrenoso.
4 Decidió pedirle ayuda a su compadre.
5 Regresó a la canoa y el agua la llevó a la deriva.
6 Cuando trató de incorporarse, comenzó a vomitar.

Una vista del río Amazonas

7 Los dolores se sucedían en continuos relampagueos.

8 Se arrastró cuesta arriba y gritó con cuanta fuerza pudo.

9 El hombre, cuyas fuerzas le escaseaban, pudo llegar al medio del río.

10 Pudo atracar fácilmente porque la corriente se precipitaba hasta la orilla.

11 Tuvo que cortar la ligadura y abrir el pantalón con el cuchillo.

Comprensión   III

A Conteste a las siguientes preguntas.

1 Describa el paisaje de esta región.

2 ¿Cómo se sentía el hombre al ponerse el sol?

3 Relate las diferentes sensaciones que siguieron al violento escalofrío.

4 ¿Pensaba que se había mejorado?

5 Al perder la sensación de la pierna, ¿de quién se acordó?

6 Describa el paisaje al ponerse el sol.

7 ¿Cuándo comenzó a delirar?

8 ¿Qué le sucedió a la canoa?

9 ¿Cómo concluye el cuento?

B Termine las oraciones según la selección.

1 El río que corre allí es el

2 El paisaje es agresivo y reina en él un silencio de

3 Al atardecer el hombre tuvo un

4 De repente, enderezó la cabeza y

5 Él creía que se mejoraba aunque no se podía

6 Comenzó a recordar a sus amigos mientras avanzaba la sensación de

7 La canoa derivaba velozmente, girando a ratos sobre

8 De pronto sintió que estaba

9 Estiró lentamente los dedos de la mano y cesó de

Más Práctica

A Dé un antónimo de las palabras en letra bastardilla.

1 Sentía la cara *muy mojada*.
2 Habló con voz *agradable y clara*.
3 La señora parecía *gorda*.
4 Tenía el cuerpo *acalorado*.
5 Se levantó *con gracia*.
6 Le *habló dulcemente* a su mujer.

B Dé un sinónimo de las palabras en letra bastardilla.

1 El río pasó por una inmensa *concavidad*.
2 Dio una *mirada* al paisaje.
3 Sintió *un dolor agudo* en la pierna.
4 Tenía el pie *muy grande por la herida*.
5 Pisó algo *rígido*.

C Complete las siguientes oraciones con una palabra apropiada.

1 La herida le hace andar _____.
2 El viento frío le causó un _____ por todo el cuerpo.
3 La mordedura de la víbora causó una _____.

4 La herida le dolió más donde estaba la _____ del pañuelo.

5 No puedo remar más porque la _____ se me cayó de las manos.

6 Por la mañana, el barco pequeño estaba cubierto de _____.

7 La chica dio una _____ al chico que pasaba.

8 La herida le causó unas _____ dolorosas.

Ejercicios Creativos

1 Escriba un resumen de *A La Deriva*. Use las siguientes palabras y expresiones: mordedura, machete, dolor agudo, sequedad, escalofrío, cesó de respirar.

2 Se desarrollan muchos cuentos alrededor del tema del ser humano y sus conflictos. Puede ser un conflicto con otra persona, con la naturaleza, con la sociedad, o con un dios. ¿Cuál sería el antagonista de Paulino? Prepare un párrafo escrito en el cual desarrolla su idea.

3 Identifique el desenlace de este cuento. ¿Es un fin anticipado o inesperado? Si Paulino hubiera vivido en otro lugar, ¿estaría aún vivo?

4 Haga una comparación entre la muerte de Paulino y la de Melodía en *En El Fondo del caño hay un negrito*.

5 El ambiente de otros lugares también puede ser peligroso. Haga una lista de los peligros que pueden existir en uno de los siguientes lugares:
   a. en la selva
   b. en una gran ciudad moderna
   c. en alta mar

La Cita

Raquel Banda Farfán

PARA PRESENTAR LA LECTURA

¡Después de treinta y cinco años de ser solterona, la Chona iba a casarse! Iba a casarse con Anselmo, mocetón fuerte y guapo, de un pueblecito lejano, quien la había conocido durante una visita. Recientemente, por carta, la había invitado a reunirse con él.

El chisme voló por la vecindad, y lo que empezó por ser algo privado, acabó por ser asunto de todos. No obstante, como todos sus vecinos la habían creído una «quedada», no le molestaba a la Chona que supieran esta última noticia.

Pero el Destino, siempre inconstante y caprichoso, estaba en ese mismo momento escribiendo en los anales del tiempo otra página de sorpresa para la Chona provinciana.

PARA APRENDER VOCABULARIO

Palabras Clave   I

1 **abrasaba (abrasar)**   quemaba, calentaba
   Hacía mucho calor, y el sol abrasaba el aire seco.

2 **aglomeró (aglomerarse)**   se juntó mucha gente
   Mucha gente se aglomeró en la estación de ferrocarril.

3 **andén**   acera a lo largo de la vía de trenes y autobuses
   Puede tomar el tren a Mendoza en el andén número seis.

4 **hervir (ie)**   llegar a la ebullición *(to boil)*
   El agua va a hervir a cien grados en la escala métrica.

5 **maleta**   receptáculo que sirve para llevar ropa en un viaje, baúl pequeño
   El mozo nos va a subir la maleta a la habitación.

6 **silbar** producir un ruido agudo soplando por los labios o en un silbido *(to whistle)*

La gente esperó en la estación hasta que se oyó silbar el tren.

7 **taquillas** ventanillas en donde se venden boletos

La señora Santos compró su boleto de ferrocarril en la taquilla.

Práctica

Complete con una palabra de la lista.

abrasaba	hervir	silbar
aglomeró	maleta	taquilla
andén		

1 Ponga el agua a _____ para hacer el café.
2 Pregunte en la _____ cuánto es el boleto a Santiago.
3 Los vendedores corrieron a lo largo del _____ .
4 Un grupo de pasajeros se _____ en frente de la taquilla.
5 Cuando oyó _____ el tren, salió con su maleta.
6 El calor sofocante le _____ el cuerpo entero.
7 La _____ pesaba mucho y Ernesto le pidió ayuda al cargador.

Palabras Clave   II

1 **cabaña** casilla rústica *(cabin)*

El campesino construyó la cabaña con troncos largos.

2 **empapado (empapar)** humedecido, mojado *(soaked, drenched)*

Por estar mucho tiempo en la lluvia, su ropa quedó completamente empapada.

3 **resbaladizo** donde se resbala fácilmente *(slippery)*

Con las lluvias el camino está resbaladizo.

4 **seno** pecho *(breast)*

Guardó todo su dinero escondido en el seno, debajo del abrigo.

Práctica

Complete con una palabra de la lista.

cabaña	empapado
resbaladizo	seno

1 Tenía el vestido _____ de agua y vino.
2 Guardó el pañuelo en el _____ .
3 Caminaba lentamente hacia la _____ donde vivía su novio.
4 No tomó el camino directo porque estaba _____ por el aguacero.

La Cita

Raquel Banda Farfán

I

«Aprisa, aprisa», se decía la Chona, «Luisita no tarda en regar la noticia por todo el rancho».

Caminaba presurosa bajo el sol quemante que abrasaba el aire seco. El polvo se le iba metiendo en los zapatos, pero no podía detenerse; en el rancho comenzaría a hervir el escándalo.

Luista debía estar repitiendo a todo el mundo: « La Chona no sabe las letras y me dio su carta a leer. El hombre ese la mandó llamar . . .»

La Chona se limpió el sudor de la cara; el sol se le había adelantado por el camino y los rayos le daban de frente. La maleta pesaba más a cada paso, pero no podía tirarla en el monte, necesitaba la ropa para lucirla cuando estuviera con Anselmo.

Recordó a su novio tal como había llegado dos meses atrás, para visitar al molinero. Era un mocetón fuerte y guapo. Se habían enamorado, y cuando él partió, tres semanas más tarde, le dijo: «Volveré por ti, Chona, y nos casaremos». No había regresado, pero la carta que mandó valía lo mismo. La Chona recordó la cara que puso Luisita al leer aquellas líneas. «Te estaré esperando en la estación de Mendoza el día 4 en la madrugada».

«Si no me creyeran todos una quedada, tal vez no haría esto», pensó la Chona, «tengo ya treinta y cinco años; pero Anselmo me quiere y yo lo quiero a él; ya se callarán los chismes cuando vengamos casados, a visitar al molinero».

Pardeando la tarde llegó a la estación. Con una punta del rebozo se enjugó la cara y luego entró a la sala de espera. No tardaría en pasar «el tren de abajo». Sentada en una banca, miraba las cosas que ocurrían en torno: pero el balanceo constante de sus pies y el continuo limpiarse la cara con el rebozo

---

regar la noticia esparcir la noticia
presurosa con prisa

sudor *sweat*

molinero *miller*

quedada solterona

Pardeando Poniéndose oscura
rebozo chal
se enjugó se secó
en torno alrededor

a carcajadas *muchísimo*
harapienta *in rags*
dormitaba *dozed*
sarnoso *mangy*

condumio *food*

se alborotó *became busy*

indicaban su nerviosidad. Un hombre gordo y sucio reía a carcajadas y junto a él una viejita harapienta dormitaba. Paseando de un lado a otro de la sala, andaba un perro sarnoso. Se detenía frente a las gentes que comían algo y no reanudaba su marcha hasta perder la esperanza de participar en el condumio. Luego, llegaron unas señoras elegantes y la Chona fijó en ellas su atención. No cesó de observarlas hasta que se oyó silbar el tren de abajo y la sala se alborotó con un ir y venir de cargadores. La gente se aglomeró en las taquillas y los vendedores se precipitaron al andén.

II

La Chona no quería correr el riesgo de quedarse sin lugar; corrió a subirse, y antes de que el pasaje hubiera acabado de bajar, ya ella estaba en un buen asiento.

el pasaje *todos los pasajeros*

Cuando el auditor le pidió el boleto, la Chona sacó del seno un pañuelo donde anudaba el dinero: unos cuantos pesos que había juntado vendiendo los huevos de sus gallinas.

—Voy a la estación de Mendoza—dijo.

Llegó en la madrugada. Una lluvia fina la envolvió en su frialdad al bajarse del tren. No había más que dos hombres en la sala de espera.

güero *rubio*

—¿No han visto a un señor . . . a un muchacho güero por aquí?—les interrogó.

—No hemos visto a nadie—dijo fríamente uno de ellos—; tenemos aquí dos horas y no ha llegado nadie más.

—Bueno, voy a esperar—suspiró ella, y sentóse en la banca de enfrente.

no . . . ojos *had not slept a wink*
cabeceando *nodding*

En toda la noche no había pegado los ojos y comenzaba a darle sueño. Pasó un rato cabeceando, hasta que la sala se llenó con el ruido del día. Entonces perdió la esperanza y salió a preguntar por dónde quedaba el camino a Santa Lucía Tampalatín.

pinar *pine grove*
bamboleándose *tripping*

Seguía lloviendo. La Chona caminaba entre el pinar bamboleándose sobre el suelo resbaladizo y empapado. De vez en cuando deteníase bajo la lluvia, y abrazada de un pino tomaba aliento para seguir adelante.

Habría caminado unas dos horas, cuando la cabaña apareció de pronto en un claro de la sierra.

—¿Vive aquí un señor que se llama Anselmo Hernández?—preguntó al viejo que le abrió la puerta.

se cortó tanto *was so embarrassed*

—Sí, aquí vive. Es mi hijo.

La pobre se cortó tanto, que estuvo a punto de echarse a llorar.

—Dígale que aquí está Chona . . . él me mandó una carta.

El viejo la condujo a la cama de un enfermo. Anselmo estaba grave.

—Recibí una carta—dijo ella.

—Sí, te mandé decir que te esperaba en la estación, estaba bueno y sano, pero me agarró la enfermedá.

acurrucada *curled up*

La Chona pasó la noche acurrucada en la cocina. En la madrugada la despertó el viejo, que deseaba un poco de café.

voy a trai *voy a traer*

—Me voy al pueblo—le dijo—, voy a trai al padrecito.

El padre de Anselmo volvió pronto con el cura.

auxilios *last rites*

Después de haber recibido los auxilios, el enfermo pidió que lo casaran con la Chona, y así, en la soledad de la sierra, en una ceremonia triste y oscura, la solterona se convirtió en esposa. La tarde de ese mismo día quedó viuda.

Mientras avanzaba por el pinar, de vuelta a la estación, la Chona lloraba amargamente.

¿Quién la creería en su rancho, cuando dijera que se había casado?

PARA APLICAR

Comprensión   I

A   Conteste a las siguientes preguntas.

1   ¿Por qué tenía prisa la Chona?
2   ¿Por qué leyó Luisita la carta?
3   ¿Por qué no podía la Chona tirar la maleta en el monte?
4   ¿Quién había escrito la carta? ¿Por qué?
5   ¿Cómo se conocieron?
6   Describa a Anselmo.
7   ¿Qué le prometió Anselmo a la Chona?
8   Y ahora, ¿qué quiere Anselmo que haga la Chona?
9   ¿Qué opinión tenían todos de ella?
10   Cuando regresen casados, ¿qué harán todos?
11   ¿Cómo se notó que estaba nerviosa?

12   ¿Quiénes parecían llamar la atención de la Chona?
13   ¿Por qué se alborotó la sala?
14   ¿Qué hizo la gente?

B   Escoja la respuesta apropiada.

1   ¿Por qué tenía tanta prisa la Chona?
   a.   Tenía que regar el rancho.
   b.   Su amiga les diría la noticia a todos.
   c.   Quería oir noticias del rancho.
2   ¿Cuál fue esa noticia importante?
   a.   Debía detenerse en el rancho porque comenzaría a hervir el café.
   b.   La Chona no sabía leer.
   c.   La Chona iba a casarse.

3 ¿Por qué fue difícil caminar?
   a. La maleta pesaba mucho.
   b. Tuvo que limpiarse el sudor de la cara.
   c. No podía tirar la ropa en que se iba a lucir.
4 ¿Qué le prometió Anselmo a la Chona?
   a. Iba a visitar al molinero.
   b. Regresaría para casarse con ella.
   c. Partiría dentro de tres semanas.
5 ¿Cumplió con su promesa?
   a. No, no había regresado.
   b. No, no se habían casado.
   c. Sí, porque le dijo que fuera a Mendoza.
6 ¿Qué deseaba la Chona mostrar a los de su pueblo?
   a. No debían burlarse de ella.
   b. Ya tenía treinta y cinco años.
   c. No le importaba ser soltera.
7 ¿Cómo se veía que estaba nerviosa?
   a. Llegó tarde a la estación.
   b. Movía mucho los pies.
   c. No quería esperar en la sala.
8 ¿Por qué se paraba el perro delante de los pasajeros?
   a. Le gustaba el señor que reía a carcajadas.
   b. Esperaba que alguien le diera de comer.
   c. Quería fijar su atención en la Chona.
9 Antes de oir el ruido anunciando el tren, ¿qué hizo la Chona?
   a. Se alborotó en la sala.
   b. Salió a silbarles a los cargadores.
   c. No cesó de mirar todas las cosas que pasaban a su alrededor.

Comprensión   II

A Conteste a las siguientes preguntas.

1 Describa la llegada de la Chona a Mendoza.
2 ¿Había ido Anselmo a recibirla?
3 ¿Cuánto tiempo se quedó la Chona esperando?
4 ¿Qué decidió hacer?
5 ¿Fue difícil el viaje a la cabaña? ¿Por qué?

6 Describa la llegada de la Chona a la casa.
7 ¿Por qué no había ido Anselmo a la estación por ella?
8 ¿Cómo pasó esa noche la Chona?
9 ¿Qué pidió el enfermo después de haber recibido los auxilios?
10 ¿Por qué está tan triste la Chona?

B ¿Verdadero o falso?

1 La Chona temía no tener un asiento en el tren.
2 Ella compró su boleto antes de subir al tren.
3 Guardó su dinero en el rebozo.
4 Llovía y hacía frío cuando llegó a Mendoza.
5 Un muchacho güero preguntó por ella.
6 Dos hombres habían esperado allí un par de horas.
7 La Chona tenía sueño y se durmió.
8 Por fin perdió la esperanza y decidió regresar a su pueblo.
9 La Chona encontró a Anselmo muy enfermo.
10 Ella durmió cómodamente esa noche.
11 El padre de Anselmo quería casarse con ella.
12 Anselmo murió poco después de la ceremonia.
13 La Chona se sentía amarga porque Anselmo no quería casarse con ella.

Más Práctica

A Complete las siguientes oraciones con una palabra de la lista.

empapado, taquilla, cabaña, hervido, enjugó, resbaladizo, seno, abrasaba, pasaje

1 ¡Cuidado! El andén está _____.
2 Compré mi boleto en la _____.
3 Dejó de llorar y se _____ las lágrimas.
4 Vio la _____ en un cerro del pueblo.
5 El sol le _____ la cara.
6 El suelo quedó _____ por la lluvia.
7 El _____ se aglomeró en la sala de espera.
8 El café _____ tiene un sabor amargo.
9 Guardó su dinero en el _____.

B Escoja una palabra de la segunda lista (2) que
está relacionada con la palabra en la primera
lista (1).

	1		**2**
1	maleta	a.	cabeceaba
2	mal vestida	b.	secó
3	güero	c.	se amontonó
4	abrasaba	d.	harapienta
5	se aglomeró	e.	chal
6	dormitaba	f.	baúl
7	rebozo	g.	oscurecer
8	madrugada	h.	rubio
9	enjugó	i.	alba
10	pardear	j.	calentaba

Ejercicios Creativos

1 ¿Qué evidencias de «tensión» hay en la
selección? Cite varios ejemplos. ¿Qué
importancia tienen?

2 Describa el ambiente. ¿Es fantástico, romántico o realista? Dé ejemplos.

3 Haga una lista de los detalles que muestran
que la Chona es de clase humilde.

4 ¿En qué consiste la ironía de la selección?
¿Por qué estaba triste la Chona al final?

El Diente roto

Pedro Emilio Coll

PARA PRESENTAR LA LECTURA

El refrán español «Cada uno tiene su alguacil» significa que por grande o elevado que uno esté, siempre hay alguien que puede juzgarle.

Juan había sido un niño difícil hasta que, a los doce años, le pasó algo que le cambió la vida por completo. Se puso callado, serio, parecía casi enfermo. Los padres llamaron a un médico que hizo un diagnóstico sorprendente.

Desde ese momento en adelante, la voz del médico llegó a ser la voz del pueblo, y la voz del pueblo es la voz del cielo. Todos aceptaron la opinión médica, e irónicamente, miraron al joven de diferente manera.

Y a Juan le parecía mejor quedarse callado, gozando de sus éxitos, sin abrir la boca para no meter la pata.

PARA APRENDER VOCABULARIO

Palabras Clave   I

1 **genio**   una persona muy inteligente
   Se dice que Edison era un genio.

2 **hartos**   cansados de   *(fed up with)*
   Los padres estaban hartos de sus quejas.

3 **partió (partir)**   dividió, separó
   La piedra le partió el diente.

4 **tentaba (tentar – ie)**   tocaba, palpaba
   Juan tentaba el diente con la punta de la lengua.

Práctica

Complete con una palabra de la lista.

genio	hartos
partió	tentaba

1 Papá ———— el pan con un cuchillo.
2 Sus padres están ———— de que su hijo les pida dinero todo el tiempo.
3 El ciego ———— el camino con un palo para no caerse.
4 Todos saben que Einstein era un ————.

Palabras Clave II

1 **acogida (acoger)**   recibida, admitida
   La pobre niña fue acogida calurosamente por la familia.

2 **alabar**   elogiar, celebrar con palabras *(to praise, to flatter)*
   Es costumbre alabar a los héroes.

3 **coronado (coronar)**   hecho rey o reina; ponerle una corona en la cabeza de alguien
   La reina fue coronada en la catedral.

4 **juicioso**   con sana razón   *(wise)*
   Todos respetan a la jefa porque es juiciosa.

5 **sometió (someterse)**   se rindió   *(submitted)*
   El maestro se sometió a la opinión de los otros.

Práctica

Complete con una palabra de la lista.

acogida	coronado	sometió
alabar	juicioso	

1 El héroe fue _____ con laureles.
2 No luchó contra el presidente y se _____ a sus ideas.
3 La decisión poco popular por fin fue _____ por el pueblo.
4 Muchos le consideraron al doctor benévolo y _____.
5 Vamos afuera. No quiero oirlos _____ a ese político corrupto.

Isla de Pascua: Un capricho del destino

El Diente roto

Pedro Emilio Coll

I

A los doce años, combatiendo Juan Peña con unos granujas, recibió un guijarro sobre un diente; la sangre corrió lavándole el sucio de la cara, y el diente se partió en forma de sierra. Desde ese día principia la edad de oro de Juan Peña.

guijarro piedra pequeña

Con la punta de la lengua, Juan tentaba sin cesar el diente roto; el cuerpo inmóvil, vaga la mirada—sin pensar. Así de alborotador y pendenciero, tornóse en callado y tranquilo.

alborotador y pendenciero *rowdy and quarrelsome*

Los padres de Juan, hartos de escuchar quejas de los vecinos y transeúntes víctimas de las perversidades del chico, y que habían agotado toda clase de reprimendas y castigos, estaban ahora estupefactos y angustiados con la súbita transformación de Juan.

transeúntes los que pasan
reprimendas *reprimands*

Juan no chistaba y permanecía horas enteras en actitud hierática, como en éxtasis; mientras, allá adentro, en la oscuridad de la boca cerrada, su lengua acariciaba el diente roto—sin pensar.

no chistaba guardaba silencio
hierática afectando gran solemnidad

—El niño no está bien, Pablo—decía la madre al marido—; hay que llamar al médico.

Llegó el doctor grave y panzudo y procedió al diagnóstico: buen pulso, mofletes sanguíneos, excelente apetito, ningún síntoma de enfermedad.

panzudo *pot-bellied*
mofletes sanguíneos *healthy cheeks*

—Señora—terminó por decir el sabio después de un largo examen—, la santidad de mi profesión me impone declarar a usted . . .

—¿Qué, señor doctor de mi alma?—interrumpió la angustiada madre.

—Que su hijo está mejor que una manzana. Lo que sí es indiscutible—continuó con voz misteriosa—, es que estamos en presencia de un caso fenomenal: su hijo de usted, mi estimable señora, sufre de lo que hoy llamamos el mal de pensar; en una palabra, su hijo es un filósofo precoz, un genio tal vez.

mal enfermedad, defecto
precoz *precocious*

En la oscuridad de la boca, Juan acariciaba su diente roto—sin pensar.

II

júbilo alegría

Parientes y amigos se hicieron eco de la opinión del doctor, acogida con júbilo indecible por los padres de Juan. Pronto en el pueblo todo, se citó el caso admirable del «niño prodigio», y su fama se aumentó como una bomba de papel hinchada de humo.

lerda poco inteligente

Hasta el maestro de escuela, que lo había tenido por la más lerda cabeza del orbe, se sometió a la opinión general, por aquello de que voz del pueblo es voz del cielo. Quien más, quien menos,

traía a colación mencionó como prueba
pilluelo desarrapado *ragged scamp*

cada cual traía a colación un ejemplo: Demóstenes comía arena, Shakespeare era un pilluelo desarrapado, Edison, etcétera.

Creció Juan Peña en medio de libros abiertos ante sus ojos, pero que no leía, distraído por la tarea de su lengua ocupada en tocar la pequeña sierra del diente roto—sin pensar.

Y con su cuerpo crecía su reputación de hombre juicioso, sabio y «profundo», y nadie se cansaba de alabar el talento maravilloso de Juan. En plena juventud, las más hermosas mujeres trataban de seducir y conquistar aquel espíritu superior, entregado a hondas meditaciones, para los demás, pero que en la oscuridad de su boca tentaba el diente roto—sin pensar.

académico miembro de una academia

Pasaron meses y años, y Juan Peña fue diputado, académico, ministro, y estaba a punto de ser coronado Presidente de la República, cuando la apoplejía lo sorprendió acariciándose su diente roto con la punta de la lengua.

doblaron *rang*
duelo *mourning*

Y doblaron las campanas, y fue decretado un riguroso duelo nacional; un orador lloró en una fúnebre oración a nombre de la patria, y cayeron rosas y lágrimas sobre la tumba del grande hombre que no había tenido tiempo de pensar.

PARA APLICAR

Comprensión   I

A Conteste a las siguientes preguntas.

1 ¿Cómo se le partió el diente a Juan?
2 Para Juan, ¿qué comenzó ese día? Explique.
3 Desde ese día, ¿qué solía hacer Juan?
4 Describa el cambio en su personalidad.

5 ¿De qué estaban hartos los padres?
6 ¿Por qué no castigaban más a su hijo?
7 ¿Qué pensaba la madre acerca de su hijo?
8 Describa al médico que fue a examinar a Juan.
9 ¿Cómo estaba Juan de salud?
10 ¿De qué mal padecía Juan?

B Escoja la expresión de la segunda lista (2) que completa
la idea empezada en la primera lista (1).

<table>
<tr><td colspan="2" align="center">1</td><td colspan="2" align="center">2</td></tr>
<tr><td>1</td><td>A los doce años</td><td>a.</td><td>el diente roto.</td></tr>
<tr><td>2</td><td>Juan tentaba sin cesar</td><td>b.</td><td>estaban ahora estupefactos.</td></tr>
<tr><td>3</td><td>Se convirtió Juan</td><td>c.</td><td>en un muchacho dócil y callado.</td></tr>
<tr><td>4</td><td>Los padres de Juan</td><td>d.</td><td>que Juan estaba muy sano.</td></tr>
<tr><td>5</td><td>Juan hablaba poco y pasaba horas</td><td>e.</td><td>una piedra le rompió un diente a Juan.</td></tr>
<tr><td>6</td><td>La madre temía</td><td>f.</td><td>que Juan era un genio.</td></tr>
<tr><td>7</td><td>El médico fue a la casa</td><td>g.</td><td>sin pensar.</td></tr>
<tr><td>8</td><td>En cuanto a la salud la opinión médica fue</td><td>h.</td><td>e hizo un diagnóstico.</td></tr>
<tr><td>9</td><td>El doctor hizo la declaración indiscutible</td><td>i.</td><td>que su hijo estuviera enfermo.</td></tr>
</table>

9 La gente nunca supo que Juan nunca pensaba.

Comprensión   II

A Conteste a las siguientes preguntas.

1 ¿Qué hicieron todos al oir la opinión del doctor?
2 ¿Qué ejemplos citó el maestro para comprobar la opinión?
3 Describa cómo creció Juan.
4 ¿Qué honores recibió Juan?
5 ¿Por qué no lo hicieron Presidente de la República?
6 Describa el funeral.
7 ¿De qué nunca se enteró el pueblo?

B ¿Verdadero o falso?

1 Todo el mundo aceptó la opinión del médico sin más investigaciones.
2 La fama de Juan creció inmediatamente.
3 El maestro no quería aceptar la opinión de los otros.
4 Algunos creen que si todos repiten una opinión, tiene que ser correcta.
5 Juan estudiaba mucho de los libros mientras crecía.
6 Nunca se distraía.
7 En su juventud comenzó a entregarse a hondas meditaciones.
8 Juan recibió muchos altos honores.

Más Práctica

A Dé un sinónimo de las palabras en letra bastardilla.

1 Estamos *cansados* de comer siempre lo mismo.
2 El señor *tocaba* los bolsillos buscando una pluma.
3 En esa parte de la ceremonia van a *elogiar* al alcalde.
4 Es un político *inteligente* que ha hecho unas contribuciones necesarias.
5 Naturalmente, el padre se *rindió* a las ideas del doctor.
6 Se considera que el niño es *muy inteligente*.
7 Alguien *dividió* el pastel en trozos desiguales.
8 La noticia fue *recibida* felizmente por el abuelo.
9 Él será *declarado* rey en la catedral.

B Conteste a las siguientes preguntas según la indicación.

1 ¿Por qué fue tan famoso el niño? *lo consideraban un genio*

En la oscuridad de la boca, ¿tenta la niñita un diente roto?

2 ¿Por qué no están hablando con los vecinos? *hartos de sus quejas*

3 ¿Por qué está roto el diente? *una piedra lo partió*

4 ¿Cómo pasaba el niño el tiempo? *tentar el diente con la lengua*

5 ¿Por qué se calló el maestro? *someterse a la opinión del pueblo*

6 ¿Cómo fue considerado el doctor? *juicioso*

7 ¿Fue declarado Rey? *morir antes de ser coronado*

8 ¿Quiénes lo querían elogiar? *todos lo alababan*

Ejercicios Creativos

1 En un párrafo identifique el tema de la selección.

2 ¿Cómo ha sufrido una sociedad o una nación por aceptar ciegamente informes y decisiones políticos? ¿Cómo se aplica aquí el refrán «Cada uno tiene su alguacil»?

3 ¿Por qué repite el autor tantas veces «Tentaba el diente—sin pensar»?

4 La sátira y la ironía tienen relación, pero son distintas. Cite un ejemplo de ironía en la selección. Cite otro de sátira.

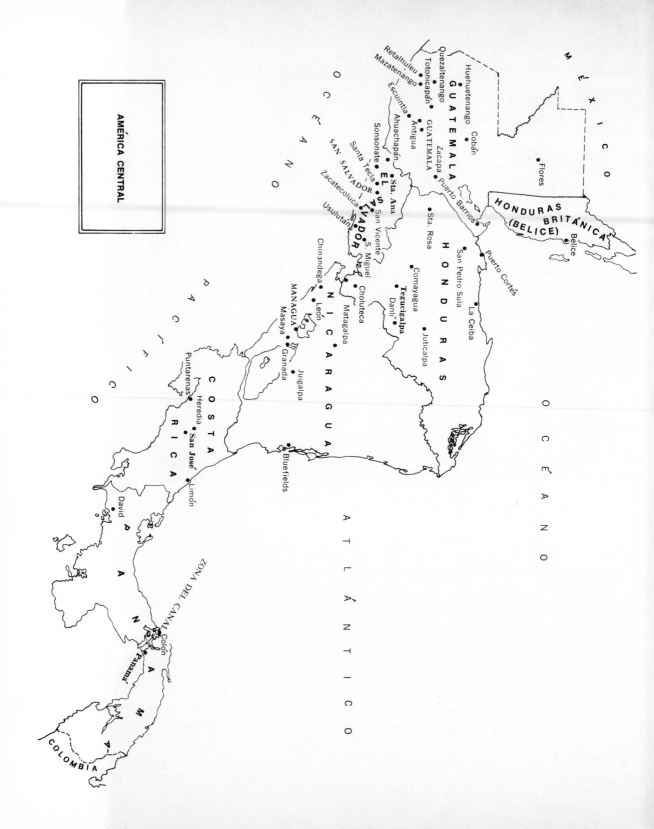

AMÉRICA CENTRAL

M É X I C O

O C É A N O

Retalhuleu
Mazatenango
Quezaltenango
Totonicapán
Huehuetenango
Cobán
Flores
Escuintla
Ahuachapán
Antigua
GUATEMALA
Zacapa
GUATEMALA
Sonsonate
Santa Tecla
Santa Ana
EL
S.
SAN SALVADOR
Zacatecoluca
Usulután
San Vicente
S. Miguel
Sta. Rosa
Puerto Barrios
HONDURAS
BRITÁNICA
(BELICE)
Belice
Puerto Cortés
San Pedro Sula
La Ceiba
Comayagua
Tegucigalpa
Danlí
Juticalpa
H O N D U R A S
Chinandega
León
MANAGUA
Masaya
Granada
Juigalpa
N I C A R A G U A
Matagalpa
Choluteca
Bluefields
O C É A N O
A T L Á N T I C O
P A C Í F I C O
Puntarenas
Heredia
San José
Limón
C O S T A
R I C A
David
P A N A M Á
ZONA DEL CANAL
Colón
Panamá
COLOMBIA

Dixie Belyea

A. 1. El coronel intentó persuadir a miquel

2. Tomo un puñado de monedas de oro.

3.

4.

del testamento

2. La forma en que lo dejó.

3. Sabe usar la tiza con más soltura que
   cualquiero

4. Pídele permiso de hacer la primera
   interpretación,

5. El sobrino no recibe nada.

6. Subsidio dura

El Imperfecto del Subjuntivo

El imperfecto del subjuntivo tiene su raíz en la tercera persona plural del pretérito, del cual se omite –*ron*. A la raíz se agregan las terminaciones apropiadas. Hay dos formas distintas del imperfecto del subjuntivo. Generalmente pueden intercambiarse.

imperfecto del subjuntivo: leer

leyera	leyese
leyeras	leyeses
leyera	leyese
leyéramos	leyésemos
leyerais	leyeseis
leyeran	leyesen

Verbos Regulares

infinitivo	raíz	subjuntivo
amar	amaron	amara, amaras, amara, amáramos, amaran
comer	comieron	comiera, comieras, comiera, comiéramos, comieran
recibir	recibieron	recibiera, recibieras, recibiera, recibiéramos, recibieran

Verbos Irregulares

infinitivo	raíz	subjuntivo
andar	anduvieron	anduviera, anduvieras, anduviera, anduviéramos, anduvieran
caber	cupieron	cupiera, cupieras, cupiera, cupiéramos, cupieran
caer	cayeron	cayera, cayeras, cayera, cayéramos, cayeran

infinitivo	raíz	subjuntivo
dar	dieron	diera, dieras, diera, diéramos, dieran
decir	dijeron	dijera, dijeras, dijera, dijéramos, dijeran
estar	estuvieron	estuviera, estuvieras, estuviera, estuviéramos, estuvieran
haber	hubieron	hubiera, hubieras, hubiera, hubiéramos, hubieran
hacer	hicieron	hiciera, hicieras, hiciera, hiciéramos, hicieran
huir	huyeron	huyera, huyeras, huyera, huyéramos, huyeran
ir	fueron	fuera, fueras, fuera, fuéramos, fueran
leer	leyeron	leyera, leyeras, leyera, leyéramos, leyeran
oir	oyeron	oyera, oyeras, oyera, oyéramos, oyeran
poder	pudieron	pudiera, pudieras, pudiera, pudiéramos, pudieran
poner	pusieron	pusiera, pusieras, pusiera, pusiéramos, pusieran
producir	produjeron	produjera, produjeras, produjera, produjéramos, produjeran
salir	salieron	saliera, salieras, saliera, saliéramos, salieran
ser	fueron	fuera, fueras, fuera, fuéramos, fueran
tener	tuvieron	tuviera, tuvieras, tuviera, tuviéramos, tuvieran
traer	trajeron	trajera, trajeras, trajera, trajéramos, trajeran
venir	vinieron	viniera, vinieras, viniera, viniéramos, vinieran

Verbos de Cambio Radical

infinitivo	raíz	subjuntivo
sentir	sintieron	sintiera, sintieras, sintiera, sintiéramos, sintieran
dormir	durmieron	durmiera, durmieras, durmiera, durmiéramos, durmieran
pedir	pidieron	pidiera, pidieras, pidiera, pidiéramos, pidieran

Usos del Imperfecto del Subjuntivo

Cláusulas Nominales

El imperfecto del subjuntivo se usa en las cláusulas nominales bajo las mismas condiciones que gobiernan el uso del presente del subjuntivo. Si el verbo de la cláusula principal se expresa en el pretérito, el imperfecto o el condicional, el imperfecto del subjuntivo se emplea en la cláusula subordinada.

Fue necesario
Era necesario
Quería   } que salieran.
Preferiría

A Sustituyan según el modelo.

La mujer quería que le llevaras agua.
ellos/
La mujer quería que ellos le llevaran agua.

1 El hombre quería que su novia viniera por él.
nosotros/tú/yo/su amigo/sus compañeros/

2 El herido pidió que todos le ayudaran.
tú/el compadre/yo/nosotros/Uds./

3 Fue importante que Paulino le hiciera una pregunta.
su esposa/sus compadres/tú/tú y yo/yo/

4 Se alegraban de que pudiéramos ofrecerle alivio.
yo/las jóvenes/tú/la patrona/tú y yo/

B Sustituyan según el modelo.

> *Temía que fuéramos a su casa.*
> *dudaba/*
> *Dudaba que fuéramos a su casa.*

1 Temía que fuéramos a su casa.
no esperaba/no quería/tenía miedo de/
fue necesario/prohibió/

2 Mandaron que estuvieses en la estación
del tren.
prefieron/te aconsejaron/rogaron/insis-
tieron en/te dijeron/

3 Fue lástima que la pobre muriera.
era inevitable/me sorprendió/sentimos/
no creían/era probable/

C Sigan los modelos.

> *¿Por qué volvieron?*
> *La patrona les dijo que volvieran.*

1 ¿Por qué se arrollaron la manga?
2 ¿Por qué respondieron?
3 ¿Por qué compusieron la máquina?
4 ¿Por qué no se enojaron?
5 ¿Por qué le extendieron la mano?
6 ¿Por qué se sentaron a su lado?
7 ¿Por qué se asomaron a la puerta?
8 ¿Por qué anduvieron hacia el corral?

> *¿Y nunca regresaste?*
> *Ella no quería que yo regresara.*

9 ¿Y nunca saliste?
10 ¿Y nunca lo supiste?

11 ¿Y nunca te despediste?
12 ¿Y nunca te lo pusiste?
13 ¿Y nunca dormiste?
14 ¿Y nunca oíste de su muerte?
15 ¿Y nunca lo trajiste?
16 ¿Y nunca te divertiste?

D Sigan el modelo.

> *El soltero se alegra de que ella lo*
> *escoja.* se alegró
>
> *El soltero se alegró de que ella lo*
> *escogiera.*

1 Todos le recomiendan que se case.
recomendaron

2 Me sorprende que esté cansado de ser
soltero. *sorprendió*

3 Es lástima que no lo haya encontrado.
fue lástima

4 Siente que Anselmo no la encuentre en
la estación. *sintió*

5 No le agrada que otros se burlen de
ella. *agradaba*

6 Es interesante que ella se forme tal
opinión. *fue interesante*

7 Dígale que venga a verme. *le dije*

8 El padre desea que reciba los auxilios
de la iglesia. *deseaba*

9 Ella lamenta que nadie vaya a creerla.
lamentaba

10 El enfermo pide que el cura los case.
pidió

Cláusulas Adverbiales

En oraciones en que la cláusula adverbial se subordina a un verbo en
el pretérito, el imperfecto o el condicional, el verbo de la cláusula
adverbial se expresa en el imperfecto del subjuntivo.

Sofía se durmió ⎫
Sofía se dormía ⎬ antes de que todos se callaran.
Sofía se dormiría ⎭

Noten que ya hemos aprendido en la lección anterior que las cláusulas adverbiales de tiempo exigen el indicativo cuando la acción está en el pasado.

> Ella me lo dijo cuando lo vi.
> Ellos me saludaron en cuanto llegué.
> Esperé hasta que todos volvieron.

La única excepción es la conjunción *antes de que* que siempre exige el subjuntivo.

> Saldré antes de que vuelvan.
> Salí antes de que volvieran.

E Sustituyan según el modelo.

> *Quería subir antes de que bajaran los pasajeros.*
>
> *con tal que/*
>
> *Quería subir con tal que bajaran los pasajeros.*

1 Quería hablar con tal que le pagaran.
en caso de que/a pesar de que/sin que/ con tal que/para que/

2 No iría a menos que le pidiera la mano.
antes de que/a pesar de que/sin que/ de manera que/hasta que/

3 Anselmo se enfermó antes de que llegara el doctor.
tú/la novia/nosotros/Uds./yo/

4 La Chona se sentó cerca para que lo viera bien.
el padre/tú/nosotros/los angustiados/ yo/

5 Ella lloró sin que su novio se diera cuenta.
yo/los pasajeros/nosotros/el molinero/ tú/

Un Solo Sujeto en la Oración

Cuando hay un solo sujeto en la oración, se emplea el infinitivo en vez de una cláusula.

> Abrí la puerta para entrar.
> *Pero* Abrí la puerta para que entraran.

F Sigan el modelo.

> *Escribieron para saber la hora de la llegada.*
>
> *para que nosotros*
>
> *Escribieron para que nosotros supiéramos la hora de la llegada.*

1 Abrí la puerta para entrar en la casa.
   para que ellos

2 Se sentaron sin hablar.
   sin que nadie

3 Ofrecieron ayudarme a arreglar la boda.
   con tal que yo

4 Dormí bien hasta despertarme.
   hasta que tú

5 Trató de explicarlo sin entenderlo bien.
   sin que yo

6 Vinieron para ver al molinero.
   para que nosotros

7 Yo quería la ropa para lucirla en la boda.
   para que ella

8 Corrió a pesar de tener sueño.
   a pesar de que tú

9 Se quedó con el enfermo hasta dormirse.
   hasta que él

10 Regresó a su pueblo para hablar de su matrimonio.
   para que los otros

Con Adjetivos

Se emplea el subjuntivo con la construcción *por* + adjetivo o adverbio + *que*. Tiene el significado de *however*.

> Por friolenta que sea, no llevará abrigo.

G Sigan los modelos.

> *Aunque saliera muy bueno el rojo, preferiría el verde.*
>
> *Por bueno que saliera el rojo, preferiría el verde.*

1 Aunque supiera mucho, no querría hablar.
2 Aunque fuera muy malo, no castigarían al niño.
3 Aunque supiera poco, todos lo considerarían un genio.
4 Aunque lloviera mucho, tendríamos que salir.

5 Aunque estuviera cansada, seguiría caminando.
6 Aunque hiciera mucho frío, saldrían a jugar.

> *Por bueno que sea, no lo compraré.*
> *Por bueno que fuera, no lo compraría.*

7 Por difícil que sea, lo haré.
8 Por interesante que sea, decidirán no comprarlo.
9 Por caro que resulte, te lo conseguiré.
10 Por barato que salga, te gustará.
11 Por bonito que esté, no te quedará bien.
12 Por tarde que lleguen, estaremos esperando.

13 Por guapo que sea, no saldré con él.
14 Por mucho que viaje, no me cansaré.

15 Por rápido que corra, no lo alcanzará.
16 Por mucho que gane, nunca tendré suficiente.

Cláusulas Relativas

Si la cláusula relativa se subordina a un verbo en el pretérito, el imperfecto o el condicional, el verbo de la cláusula se expresa en el imperfecto del subjuntivo.

> Busqué un rebozo
> Buscaba un rebozo } que fuera bonito.
> Buscaría un rebozo

H Sigan los modelos.

> *¿Qué buscabas?*
> *Busca un libro que estuviera bien escrito.*

1 ¿Qué preferías?
2 ¿Qué deseabas?
3 ¿Qué pedías?
4 ¿Qué buscabas?
5 ¿Qué necesitabas?
6 ¿Qué no tenías?
7 ¿Qué querías?
8 ¿Qué te hacía falta?

> *Ninguna bebida podía quitarle la sed.*

> *No había bebida que pudiera quitarle la sed.*

9 Ninguna persona era perfecta.
10 Ninguna camisa le gustó tanto.
11 Ningún libro le llamó la atención.
12 Ningún otro lo sabía como él.
13 Ninguna acogida le valía tanto.
14 Ninguna mujer negaba eso.

15 Ningún regalo podía complacerle.
16 Ninguna niña quería perder esa oportunidad.

I Sigan el modelo.

> *Buscaba un pueblo. Tenía que ser como Mendoza.*

> *Buscaba un pueblo que fuera como Mendoza.*

1 Buscaba alguien. Tenía que negar lo dicho.
2 Quería oir música. Tenía que llegar al corazón.
3 Deseaba un remedio. Tenía que aliviarlo.
4 Buscaba un libro. Tenía que dar las respuestas.
5 Necesitaba hallar un camino. Tenía que llegar a la cabaña.
6 Quería un marido. Tenía que ser honrado.
7 Buscaba una esposa. Tenía que cuidarlo y protegerlo.

J Sigan el modelo.

> *Aceptaré cualquier libro si tú me lo das.*
>
> *Dije que aceptaría cualquier libro que me dieras.*

1 Iré a cualquier parte si tú me lo dices.
2 Me pondré cualquier rebozo si Uds. me lo compran.

3 Se asustará de cualquier persona si viene por ese camino.
4 Tomaré cualquier tren si va hacia Mendoza.
5 Invitaremos a cualquier muchacho si lo conoces.
6 Se fijarán en cualquier vestido si tú lo llevas.
7 Leerá cualquier carta si cae en sus manos.

Cláusulas con *Si*

Una oración condicional frecuentemente se compone de dos cláusulas. Una expresa una condición contraria a la realidad. Esta cláusula se introduce con *si*. Cuando el verbo de la cláusula independiente está en futuro, se emplea el presente del indicativo después de *si*. Cuando el verbo de la cláusula independiente está en condicional, se emplea el imperfecto del subjuntivo después de *si*.

> Si tengo dinero, iré a España.
> Si tuviera dinero, iría a España.

K Sustituyan según el modelo.

> *Si tuviera el dinero, iría a España.*
> *si tuviera el tiempo/*
> *Si tuviera el tiempo, iría a España.*

1 Si tuviera el dinero, iría a España.
   si me diera un mes libre/si yo pudiera dejar el negocio/si consiguiera un boleto/si me acompañaras/si pudieras ir conmigo/
2 Se casaría con él, si no fuera tan presumido.
   si no se preocupara tanto de su ropa/ si no tuviera miedo de mudarse a otro pueblo/si no pensara tanto en qué dirían los otros/si no estuviera tan enfermo/

L Sigan el modelo.

> *Si me ayudas, acabaremos pronto.*
> *Si me ayudaras, acabaríamos pronto.*

1 Si buscan a la Chona, la hallarán.
2 Si lo escuchamos con atención, entenderemos.
3 Si pido ayuda, me la darán.
4 Si nos invitan a la boda, tendremos que ir.
5 Si te despiertas temprano, tomaremos el tren.
6 Si se fijan en el precio, no escogerán esos boletos.
7 Si compro los zapatos, me los pondré para el viaje.

8   Si nos avisan, esperaremos el tren.
9   Si miran el reloj, se darán cuenta de la hora.
10 Si llega temprano, nadie estará en la estación.

Con *Como Si*

Se emplea el imperfecto del subjuntivo después de la expresión *como si.*

Habla como si fuera rico.

M   Sigan los modelos.

> *Son de España.*
> *Hablaban como si fueran de España.*

1   Tienen bastante dinero.
2   Saben el idioma.
3   Pueden pagar la cuenta.
4   Conocen al viudo.
5   Asisten a la boda.
6   Vienen en seguida.
7   Se dan cuenta del problema.
8   Están solos.
9   Ven todo por la primera vez.
10 Están cansados.

> *Juan habla español. Parece que es mexicano.*
>
> *Juan habla español como si fuera mexicano.*

11 Comes mucho. Parece que tienes hambre.
12 La niña corre. Parece que quiere escapar.
13 La Chona se calla. Parece que quiere llorar.
14 El joven se cae. Parece que está muerto.
15 El cielo está nublado. Parece que va a llover.

Raíces

Dime con quien andas, y te diré quien eres.

PARA PREPARAR LA ESCENA

Las migraciones entre los Estados Unidos y los países de origen hispánico han sido una calle de doble sentido. Los norteamericanos han inundado los países hispánicos a través de empresas comerciales y afiliaciones políticas, como turistas y aventureros. Recientemente se ha visto una gran inmigración de gente de muchos lugares hispano- hablantes. Algunos vienen para conocer otro país, o para escaparse de gobiernos no populares; otros, para buscar empleo o para mejorar su suerte y echar nuevas raíces. Hay que notar que muchos hispanos no llegaron de otros lugares. Muchos ciudadanos de ascendencia mexicana no inmigraron sino que siguen viviendo en tierras que antes eran parte de México. Muchos de éstos guardan la memoria de sus raíces mexicanas.

Para todos en este país el tirón de las viejas raíces es fuerte. Es difícil establecerse en otro lugar. Nunca se pierden por completo las costumbres familiares, el recuerdo de los antepasados, la raza, la patria.

Narración personal de Elías Garza

Elías Garza

PARA PRESENTAR LA LECTURA

Esta narración fue recopilada por Manuel Gamio, distinguido antropólogo de México, que hizo en 1930 un estudio detallado de la inmigración mexicana a los Estados Unidos.

Algunos de estos inmigrantes mexicanos regresaron a su país de origen; muchos se han quedado en el extranjero. Muchos se han adaptado fácilmente al nuevo ambiente; algunos se han dedicado a la protesta social, enfrentando las realidades de prejuicio, discriminación y desigualdades.

Elías Garza, al recordar sus propias experiencias en su tierra natal, así como en los Estados Unidos, nos da un vistazo de sus viajes, empleos, dificultades y penas. Aunque no sea una narración reciente, esta obra nos presenta un tema universal.

PARA APRENDER VOCABULARIO

Palabras Clave   I

1 **exprimen (exprimir)**   extraen el líquido de una cosa (*squeeze*)
   Hay que exprimir la ropa antes de tenderla a secar.

2 **misericordia**   compasión, merced
   Los dueños lo abusaron sin misericordia.

3 **muelen (moler – ue)**   reducen una sustancia a partes pequeñas (*grinds*)
   En el molino se muele la caña de azúcar.

4 **rieles**   barras de metal en que corren los ferrocarriles, etc.
   Los tranvías de San Francisco corren en rieles.

5 **torpes**   que carecen de habilidad o de movimientos libres; pesados
   Los niños parecen torpes, pero la verdad es que están cansados.

Práctica

Complete con una palabra de la lista.

exprimen	rieles	torpes
misericordia	muelen	

1 Quitaron los _____ porque el tren ya no pasa por aquí.
2 Nadie tenía _____ y los obreros tenían que seguir trabajando así.
3 Los dientes traseros _____ bien la comida.
4 Les falta educación. No son _____.
5 Los niños _____ el limón para hacer la limonada que van a vender.

Palabras Clave II

1 **algodón** tela liviana natural, la planta de que se hace esa tela *(cotton)*
    Las camisas de algodón son las más cómodas.

2 **pasaje** precio de viaje en tren, barco, etc.
    Pagué el pasaje y subí al autobús.

3 **reses** ganado vacuno *(cattle)*
    El ranchero cuidaba las reses en el corral.

4 **vías** caminos, canales, medios de transporte
    Trabajaba en las vías de ferrocarril.

Práctica

Complete con una palabra de la lista.

algodón	pasaje	reses	vías

1 Por esa selva no pasan _____ de comunicación.
2 ¿Cuánto es el _____ a Cuernavaca?
3 Los rancheros temían que no hubiera suficiente agua para las _____.
4 Nicanor le compró a su hermano una camisa de _____.

Labradores migratorios

Narración personal de Elías Garza

Elías Garza

I

(Elías Garza es nativo de Cuernavaca, Morelos.)

—Mi vida es una historia interesante, especialmente lo que he pasado aquí en los Estados Unidos, en donde lo vuelven a uno loco con tanto trabajo. Lo exprimen a uno aquí hasta que queda inútil y entonces tiene uno que regresar a México para ser una carga para sus paisanos. Pero lo malo es que eso no solamente sucede aquí, sino también allá. Es un favor que le debemos a don Porfirio: el habernos quedado tan ignorantes y tan torpes que solamente servimos para el trabajo más rudo. Yo comencé a trabajar cuando tenía 12 años de edad. Mi madre era sirvienta y yo trabajaba en uno de esos viejos ingenios que muelen caña de azúcar. Me encargaba de dirigir a los bueyes. Me llamaban El Cochero. Esto fue en el pueblo de La Piedad, en Michoacán. Creo que me pagaban 25 centavos al día y yo tenía que darle vueltas al molino de sol a sol. Mi madre, lo mismo que yo, tenía que trabajar, pues mi padre murió cuando yo era muy pequeño. Seguí en ese trabajo hasta que tenía como 15 o 16 años y entonces me dediqué a plantar maíz a medias. Los dueños nos daban la semilla, la tierra y los animales, pero resultaba que cuando se levantaba la cosecha no quedaba nada para nosotros, aunque hubiéramos trabajado muy duro. Era terrible. Esos terratenientes eran ladrones. En esa época me enteré de que había buenos trabajos aquí en los Estados Unidos y que podía ganarse bastante dinero. Nos juntamos varios amigos y fuimos primero a la ciudad de México y de ahí a Cuidad Juárez. Después pasamos a El Paso y ahí aceptamos un *renganche* para Kansas. Trabajamos en las vías, poniendo y quitando rieles, quitando los durmientes viejos y poniendo nuevos y toda clase de trabajos rudos. Nos pagaban

don Porfirio Porfirio Díaz (1830–1915), dictador mexicano

ingenios *sugar refineries*
bueyes *oxen*

a medias *sharecropping*

renganche *road gang*
durmientes *railroad ties*

comisario *commissary (store) manager*

solamente 1.50 dólares y nos explotaban sin misericordia en el campo del comisario, pues nos vendían todo muy caro. No obstante, como en esa época las cosas eran generalmente baratas, logré reunir algún dinero con el que me fui a La Piedad, para ver a mi madre. Ella murió poco después y esto me dejó muy triste. Decidí regresar a los Estados Unidos y vine a Los Ángeles, California. Aquí me casé con una muchacha mexicana

cantera *quarry*

y entré a trabajar en una cantera. Yo colocaba la dinamita y hacía los trabajos que requerían cuidado. Me pagaban 1.95 dólares por día, pero trabajaba 10 horas. Posteriormente trabajé en una estación ferrocarrilera. Trabaja como remachador y manejaba una

remachador *riveter*

máquina de presión para remachar. Por ese trabajo ganaba 1.50 dólares al día por nueve horas, pero era muy duro. En esa época murió mi esposa. Después conseguí trabajo en una empacadora.

empacadora *packing plant*

Comencé ganando 1.25 dólares al día por nueve horas de trabajo y llegué a ganar 4 dólares al día por ocho horas de trabajo.

II

despellejarlas *to skin them*

—Aprendí a matar las reses y a despellejarlas. El trabajo era muy duro. Posteriormente me casé con una mujer de San Antonio, Texas. Era joven, hermosa y blanca, y tenía dos niños que

entenados *stepchildren*

fueron mis entenados. Juntos nos fuimos a México. Tomamos un barco en San Pedro que nos llevó a Mazatlán y de ahí nos fuimos a Michoacán. Vimos que las cosas andaban mal allá, pues era en 1912 y ya habían comenzado los desórdenes de la revolución, por eso regresamos a los Estados Unidos, por la ruta de Laredo, Texas. En San Antonio nos contratamos para la pizca

pizca *harvest*

de algodón en un campo del Valle del Río Grande. Fuimos a pizcar un grupo de paisanos, mi esposa y yo. Cuando llegamos al campo, el dueño nos dió un viejo jacalón que había sido

jacalón *shack*
a la intemperie *casi afuera cuando hacía mal tiempo*

gallinero para que viviéramos a la intemperie. Yo no quise vivir ahí y le dije que si no nos daba una casita que fuera un poco mejor, nos iríamos. Nos dijo que nos fuéramos y ya nos íbamos mi esposa y yo con mis hijos, cuando nos cayó el comisario. Me llevó a la cárcel y ahí el dueño de la plantación declaró que yo quería irme sin pagarle mi pasaje. Me cobró el doble de lo que costaba el transporte, y aunque al principio traté de no pagarle y después de pagarle solamente el precio justo, no pude lograr nada. Las autoridades solamente le hacían caso a él, y como

confabuladas *in cahoots*

estaban confabuladas con él, me dijeron que si no pagaba se

llevarían a mi esposa y a mis hijitos a trabajar. Entonces les pagué. De ahí nos fuimos a Dallas, Texas, donde trabajamos en las vías hasta El Paso. Seguí en el mismo trabajo hasta Tucson, Arizona, y después hasta Los Ángeles. Desde entonces he trabajado aquí en las plantas empacadoras, en el cemento y en otros trabajos, hasta como jornalero en el campo. A pesar de tanto trabajo solamente he podido ahorrar un poco de dinero para este automóvil y algunas ropas. Ahora he decidido ir a trabajar en la colonia en México y no regresar a este país en el que he dejado lo mejor de mi juventud. He aprendido un poco de inglés de tanto oírlo.

Puedo leerlo y escribirlo, pero no quiero tratos con esos *bolillos*, pues lo cierto es que no quieren a los mexicanos.

recopilada por Manuel Gamio

Trabajando en los campos de repollo

PARA APLICAR

Comprensión   I

A   Conteste a las siguientes preguntas.

1   ¿De dónde es Elías Garza?
2   ¿Qué le deben los mexicanos a don Porfirio Díaz?
3   Describa el trabajo en el ingenio.
4   ¿Tuvo éxito plantando maíz a medias? ¿Qué le pasó?
5   ¿Por qué decidió venirse a los Estados Unidos? ¿Cómo vino?
6   Describa el trabajo en Kansas.
7   ¿Qué injusticias tuvo que aguantar?
8   ¿Por qué no gozó de su regreso a La Piedad?
9   Cite los otros trabajos que tuvo Elías Garza.

B   Escoja la expresión de la segunda lista (2) que completa la idea empezada en la primera lista (1).

1

1   Elías Garza relata
2   Elías opina que en los Estados Unidos
3   A don Porfirio se le debe el favor de
4   En el ingenio se encargaba
5   No ganó nada cuando se dedicó a plantar maíz
6   Al saber que había trabajo en los Estados Unidos salió
7   El trabajo aquí fue duro
8   En los comisarios abusaron con precios altos
9   El trabajo en la cantera
10   Siempre tenía que trabajar duro y

2

a.   y recibió poco sueldo.
b.   era peligroso porque trabajaba con dinamita.
c.   cuando en esa época los precios generalmente eran bajos.
d.   los sueldos nunca subían para darle suficiente para vivir bien.
e.   experiencias personales de su pasado.
f.   porque los dueños se quedaron con toda la cosecha.
g.   uno se vuelve loco con tanto trabajo.
h.   de los bueyes que movían la rueda.
i.   que muchos mexicanos no recibieron buena educación.
j.   de México con esperanzas de mejorar su fortuna.

Comprensión   II

A   Conteste a las siguientes preguntas.

1   ¿Qué hizo Elías en el matadero (*slaughterhouse*)?
2   Describa a su esposa.
3   ¿Cómo eran las condiciones en México en 1912? ¿Por qué?
4   ¿Qué contrato hicieron Elías y su mujer en San Antonio?
5   ¿Por qué dejaron ese trabajo?
6   ¿Qué les sucedió cuando se iban?
7   Describa cómo los trataron después.
8   ¿Qué hizo entonces?
9   ¿Qué ha aprendido Elías aquí?
10   ¿De qué está muy seguro?

B ¿Verdadero o falso?

1 El despellejo de las reses fue un trabajo duro.
2 Elías tuvo dos niños con la segunda esposa.
3 Las condiciones políticas en México no eran favorables.
4 Al regresar a los Estados Unidos fueron a pescar en el Río Grande.
5 El dueño del campo de algodón quería alojarlos dentro de su casa.
6 Elías fue arrestado y llevado ante las autoridades.
7 Elías ofreció pagarle al dueño el doble del precio del pasaje.
8 Elías ha trabajado por todo el suroeste.
9 Después de tantos años de trabajo ha ahorrado mucho dinero.
10 Elías se da cuenta de que hay discriminación contra el mexicano.

Más Práctica

A Escoja una palabra de la segunda lista (2) para que corresponda con la definición en la primera lista (1).

1	**2**
1 sacar el jugo de una fruta	a. algodón
2 lugar donde se hace azúcar de la caña	b. moler
3 compasión que se siente para otros de menos fortuna	c. reses
4 planta de que se hace una tela liviana	d. torpes
5 precio de un viaje	e. exprimir
6 medios de transporte o comunicación	f. pasaje
7 animales que se crían para la carne	g. ingenio
8 lentos o poco inteligentes	h. vías
9 lo que se hace con los dientes	i. misericordia

B Complete las siguientes oraciones con una palabra de la lista.

rieles, res, muelen, misericordia, exprimir, vías, torpe, pasaje

1 No queda más jugo. Tienes que _____ más naranjas.

2 ¿No te gusta el puerco? Hay carne de _____.

3 Me equivoqué. Hoy estoy _____.

4 ¡No camines en los _____! Puede ser peligroso.

5 ¿Me puedes prestar dinero para el _____ del tren?

6 Le castigó al obrero sin _____.

7 Los mexicanos _____ el maíz para hacer tortillas.

8 Hoy día grandes _____ conectan las ciudades.

Labrador migratorio: California

Ejercicios Creativos

1   Haga una lista de las experiencias desagra-
    dables que tuvo Elías Garza durante su vida.
2   Haga una investigación de las condiciones
    sociales en México durante el período de
    don Porfirio Díaz.
3   Elías Garza dijo que no quería quedarse en
    los Estados Unidos. ¿Eran mejores las con-

diciones en México para los que tenían
poca educación? ¿Dónde tenía él sus raíces?
¿Por qué no echó raíces aquí?
4   Consulte libros, revistas y periódicos para
    averiguar la situación actual. ¿Ha cambiado
    la situación hoy día para los que llegan de
    México para trabajar?

Día 50

Luis Ricardo Alonso

PARA PRESENTAR LA LECTURA

Los niños nacen inocentes, ignorantes de los males, prejuicios y agravios que existen en el mundo. ¿Cómo, entonces, aprenden a odiar? ¿A carecer de la bondad? ¿A ser crueles? ¿Cómo pueden, en plena juventud, entender la frialdad de los compañeros, la idea de ser rechazados por el color de la piel?

Tony es puertorriqueño. De niño, su familia se mudó a los Estados Unidos para radicarse en la tierra de las oportunidades. Su papá le había dicho que niño negro era lo mismo que niño blanco, pero pronto Tony se dio cuenta de que no todos compartían la misma idea.

Día 50 es una página de su diario de vida juvenil. Se nos presentan las alegrías, las desilusiones y las angustias de un inocente.

PARA APRENDER VOCABULARIO

Palabras Clave   I

1 **alquilaba (alquilar)**   pagaba por el uso de una cosa, rentaba
    Papá alquilaba una casita de madera.

2 **barrer**   limpiar pisos con escoba *(to sweep)*
    En su trabajo tuvo que barrer el piso.

3 **destreza**   habilidad, dexteridad *(ability, skill)*
    Luis Tiant es un pítcher cubano de gran destreza.

4 **rizaba (rizar)**   hacía rizos en el pelo *(curled)*
    No me rizaba el pelo porque tenía mucho rizo natural.

5 **sinvergüenza**   persona que no tiene vergüenza *(scoundrel)*
    Ese sinvergüenza le robó algo valioso a su propia madre.

Práctica

Complete con una palabra de la lista.

alquilaba	rizaba	destreza
barrer	sinvergüenza	

1 Este patio está muy sucio. Ahora lo voy a _____.
2 Ese niño mal educado es un _____.
3 Como no tenía casa propia, _____ una.
4 Se dejaba el pelo liso; no se lo _____.
5 El manejo de esa máquina requiere _____ de todo el cuerpo.

Palabras Clave   II

1 **basura**   suciedad, papeles y restos de comida que se recogen *(trash)*
     Después del desfile había mucha basura en la calle.

2 **calefacción**   acción y efecto de calentar
     Sentí frío por la falta de calefacción.

3 **capataz**   el que dirige cierto número de operarios *(boss)*
     El capataz contrató a mi padre para un trabajo en la fábrica.

4 **puntiaguda**   de punta aguda
     Le pegó con una roca puntiaguda.

5 **recostado (recostar – ue)**   reclinado contra, apoyado en
     La joven estaba recostada contra un árbol.

6 **tambaleante**   que no puede mantener el equilibrio *(staggering)*
     Llegó del trabajo tambaleante por el cansancio.

Práctica

Complete con una palabra de la lista.

basura	capataz	recostado
calefacción	puntiaguda	tambaleante

1 El alquiler de este apartamento incluye la electricidad y la _____.
2 Salió _____ del accidente.
3 Le pidió al _____ un aumento de sueldo.
4 Cuidado de no pisar aquella piedra _____.
5 No se movió sino que permaneció _____ contra la pared.
6 Luis recogió toda la _____ durante la huelga de los basureros.

Familia hispana inmigrante

Día 50

Luis Ricardo Alonso

I

Hacía pocos meses habíamos dejado Puerto Rico. Norte-américa se preparaba para la guerra. Papá consiguió empleo contestando un anuncio de una fábrica de New Jersey. El empleo era de barrer el piso; pero pagaban bien. Por una módica suma, la fábrica nos alquilaba una casita de madera, limpia y nueva, que olía a pintura fresca, en las afueras del pueblo. Papá compró, con cuarenta dólares de fondo, un automóvil de uso. Yo estaba encantado. Me di cuenta de que, en Estados Unidos, los obreros que tenían empleo, vivían mejor que la clase media de mi pueblo. En éste tenían automóvil, el médico y el dueño de la tienda mixta. Era un pueblito pobre de todo y rico de sol, en las cercanías de Ponce. Nos llevábamos bien, eso sí, e importaba muy poco si la piel era un poquito más clara o un poco más oscura. La mía era más bien esto último, pues sólo me bañaba en el río que era bastante fangoso. En New Jersey había ducha y bañadera, y hasta inodoro de verdad. Los primeros días soñaba que éramos ricos. Papá se había sacado la lotería de Puerto Rico, que aquí está prohibida, y por eso vivíamos en esta casa tan buena. La calle, cuajada de árboles que se besaban al oscurecer, parecía un barrio de ricos. Dios había escuchado las oraciones de abuelita. Al fin habíamos llegado.

*   *   *

Aquellos meses fui feliz en el pueblito verde y blanco de New Jersey. Era un pueblo en crecimiento, pero todavía limpio. La fábrica era hija de Hitler. Hasta entonces había sido un pueblo de granjas y lecherías. Vinimos cuatro familias puertorriqueñas. Tres se marcharon, en cuanto cobraron el primer mes, a New York. Quedamos solos papá, abuelita y yo. Mi hermana se había quedado en Puerto Rico, en casa de tío Dámaso, hasta ver en qué paraban las cosas. Vivíamos en medio de familias rubias y blancas. Había

de fondo *as a down payment*

tienda mixta *general store*

ducha y bañadera *shower and bathtub*
inodoro *toilet*

cuajada de árboles *lined with trees*

granjas y lecherías *farms and dairies*

como tres docenas de americanos negros en el pueblo, pero vivían bastante lejos de nosotros, en una calle sin árboles de casas envejecidas. Trabajaban en las granjas. Venían del Sur y, al parecer, salían muy baratos. A mí, la primera vez que los vi, me extrañó mucho. Nunca había visto negros que no hablaran español. Ni tan tristes.

En la escuela de nuestro barrio, todos los niños y niñas eran blancos. Mi maestro era un hombre muy alto, de carácter muy variable y nariz muy roja. Ahora comprendo que el pobre, debería beber mucho. Y no siempre de buena calidad porque el salario era poco. Al principio gocé de popularidad entre mis compañeros, aunque mi inglés era muy pobre. Nunca habían visto un *spanish*. Los más cultos sabían que los *spanish* eran unos seres morenitos que se pasaban la vida matando toros, tocando la guitarra y gritando olé. Cuando no quemaban gente en las hogueras, con-

forme me dijo, algo temeroso de mi herencia, el hijo de un pastor protestante. Pero aparte de esto, todos fueron muy amables conmigo. Me invitaban a sus casas y así probé muchos dulces nuevos, entre ellos el *pie* de manzana. A las mamás les llamaba mucho la atención mi pelo y me preguntaban si me lo rizaba. Mi amigo favorito era Joe, alto, delgado y pecoso. Él fue quien me enseñó

a jugar al *base-ball*. Yo le tenía un gran afecto. Y admiraba la destreza de su *pitching*.

En casa, todo marchaba bien. Papá hasta había empezado a ahorrar unos dólares. ¡Nosotros que en Puerto Rico le debíamos a las once mil vírgenes! Papá, que era muy honrado, separaba la mitad para los acreedores que dejamos en el pueblo y la otra mitad para el pasaje de mi hermana Carmita. Las compras de

comida, las hacía él mismo, una vez por semana. Como teníamos refrigerador, todo se facilitaba. La abuela no salía nunca, «porque no sé inglés y me da vergüenza», me decía. A mí me parecía que, después de todo, abuela era muy feliz en casa, siempre haciendo algo. Abuelita tenía una gran mano para la cocina, sobre todo para los dulces y para los pasteles puertorriqueños. Yo estaba ansioso de que mis amigos probaran su cocina y a la vez tenía un temor vago, no me gustaba la desconfianza que vi en la calle de los negros. Y así llegó el día de mi primer cumpleaños en los Estados Unidos. Cumplía siete. Yo había ido al de Joe, al de Alvan, al de Dickie, y a los de otros amigos; ahora me tocaba a mí invitar. Ni papá ni la abuela se mostraron muy entusiasmados. «¿Por qué, papá?» «Los niños aquí son distintos, hijo, no es culpa de ellos». «Son mis amigos, papá, tú no los conoces, ¿por qué no vamos a ser iguales que todo el mundo?», insistí. Yo era un niño muy bien educado—no un sinvergüenza como ahora—, pero cuando me ponía tozudo era difícil dominarme. Tuvimos la fiesta. Abuelita se esmeró. Hasta hizo unos pasteles puertorriqueños envueltos en hojas de plátano. No sé de dónde trajeron las hojas, seguramente fue obra de papá que estuvo en New York dos días antes. Había también plátanos verdes fritos, aplastados a puñetazos y churros. Y rosquillas. Y frituritas de yuca. Y empanadillas de chorizo. Y guayaba. Y un dulce de toronja con queso, crema y azúcar prieta, que sólo abuelita sabía hacer. Y mermelada de mango. Los americanos se iban a quedar pasmados.

Fue Joe el primero que expresó su admiración:

—¡Pero tienen criada y todo!

Yo me reí.

—Ésa es abuelita, tonto.

Se marcharon muy temprano.

II

Al día siguiente noté a Joe y a los demás un poco fríos. Sería culpa del maestro que había amanecido el lunes, como de costumbre, con irritación vesicular. Todos nos sentíamos mal. Yo soy de natural expansivo y entiendo la irritación y el váyase usted al diablo o a donde sea, pero no entiendo la frialdad. La atmósfera me recordaba la de Puerto Rico en el mes de octubre cuando se anuncia que el ciclón está al caer pero no cae. A Joe lo castigó el maestro por no sé qué cosa. A mí me llamó *donkey*, que es la palabra inglesa para burro. Todo porque al preguntarme por Lincoln le dije que era el nombre de un auto grande.

Aquello ocurrió al segundo día. Estábamos en el recreo, jugando al *base-ball*, cuando de pronto, Joe soltó el guante y se puso a gritar: «*Tony is a negro, Tony is a negro.*» Yo estaba al bate, y traté de explicar—muy civilmente—que niño negro era lo mismo que niño blanco, conforme me había enseñado papá en Puerto Rico. Tuve poco éxito. Los demás niños seguían riendo. Solté el bate, avergonzado no sé de qué, y entré en la clase. Me senté en un rincón. No lloraba, pero tenía ganas. A Joe lo esperé a la salida de la escuela. Yo estaba recostado en un álamo, mascando chicle para los nervios. Sentía odio y tristeza al mismo tiempo. Había escogido una piedra lustrosa, puntiaguda y bien

tozudo obstinado
se esmeró hizo gran esfuerzo

churros *crullers*
rosquillas *small cakes*
frituritas de yuca *yucca fritters*
empanadillas de chorizo *sausage turnovers*
guayaba *guava (tropical fruit)*
pasmados impresionados

vesicular *of the gall bladder*
natural carácter

álamo *poplar tree*

occipital *back of the head*

negra. Le abrí un hueco en el occipital del tamaño de un *quarter* . . .

Esa noche, el maestro—algo tambaleante—vino a ver a papá. Papá hablaba el inglés bastante bien, así que pudieron entenderse. Se encerraron en un cuarto. Abuela no quería dejarme, pero yo me las arreglé para pegar el oído a la puerta, que estaba, me acuerdo como si fuera hoy, pintada de verde muy claro. Oí frases sueltas. No quiero repetirlas, pero ese día sentí con toda el alma no ser un hombre mayor. El maestro se fue. Papá se encerró con abuela. Al salir, abuela lloraba. Más tarde, el padre de Joe, capataz de la fábrica, vino también. Escuché las palabras *savage, jungle* y *reformatory*. Papá le dio algún dinero. Los médicos aquí cuestan mucho. A las dos semanas nos marchamos para New York. Fuimos a vivir al Harlem Hispano. Es mejor para ti, hijo. Una colección de edificios leprosos, ventanas sin vidrios, alquileres altos, calefacción ártica, basura por recoger, gatos famélicos que ya no maullan salvo de noche, calles sin piedad, muebles a plazos, . . . deudas que nunca terminan de pagarse. Papá no tenía trabajo. Vino la guerra, gracias a Dios. Lo reclutaron. Había, de nuevo, un sueldo.

leprosos *run-down*
famélicos *starved*
a plazos *bought on time payments*

Cuando recuerdo que papá dejó aquel empleo por mí, me siento culpable. De las semanas en que él comió sopa para que yo comiera carne. «Mamá, el niño está creciendo, lo necesita». «Pero hijo, tú tienes . . . » «No, mamá». De su preocupación, que trataba de ocultarme, cuando regresaba cansado de oir la respuesta. «Venga la semana que viene, a lo mejor tengo algo para usted, *I'm sorry*». De la falsa indiferencia que lo llevaba a pasar horas sentado en la escalera, viendo pasar a los demás. Me siento culpable de que Joe no quisiera *pitchear* para mí. Sí, me siento culpable de cosas de las que no tengo la culpa, de no sé qué, de todo lo que sufre en el mundo, de todo lo que veo y está mal, de todo lo que escucho y es injusto. Ser negro, ¿será una culpa? ¿Qué será entonces ser blanco?

PARA APLICAR

Comprensión   I

A   Conteste a las siguientes preguntas.

1   Describa el trabajo del papá.
2   ¿Cuál fue una de las ventajas de trabajar en la fábrica?

3   ¿De qué se puso contento el niño?
4   ¿Cómo se bañaba en Puerto Rico?
5   Ahora, ¿cómo se baña?

«. . . sentí con toda el alma no ser un hombre mayor.»

6 ¿Qué soñaba pocos días después de mudarse a New Jersey?

7 Describa el pueblito en New Jersey.

8 Describa a los americanos negros que vio el niño en New Jersey.

9 ¿Cómo era su maestro?

10 ¿Qué creían sus compañeros de los *spanish*?

11 Describa sus visitas a las casas de sus amigos.

12 Cite ejemplos de la nueva prosperidad de la familia.

13 ¿Por qué tenía ganas de invitar a sus amigos a su casa?

14 ¿Por qué no querían ni su papá ni su abuela que invitara a sus amigos?

15 ¿Tenían razón? Explique.

B Escoja la respuesta apropiada para terminar la oración según la selección.

1 El trabajo de papá consistía en
   a. contestar anuncios de una fábrica.
   b. barrer el piso.
   c. pintar casas en las afueras de la ciudad.

2 Estaba encantado cuando se dio cuenta de que
   a. su papá había comprado un automóvil por cuarenta dólares.
   b. los trabajadores en los Estados Unidos gozaban de más lujos que la clase media en Puerto Rico.
   c. el médico y el dueño de la tienda mixta tenían automóvil.

3 Los primeros días soñaba que eran ricos porque
   a. vivían con más comodidades.
   b. se bañaba en el río.
   c. Papá se había sacado la lotería de Puerto Rico.

4 Al fin del primer mes
   a. llegó su hermana de Puerto Rico.
   b. tres familias fueron a Nueva York.
   c. cuatro familias puertorriqueñas llegaron para quedarse y trabajar.

5 Se sorprendió de que
   a. vivieran en medio de familias blancas y negras.

b. los negros que vio no hablaran español.

c. los negros trabajaran en las granjas.

6 Al principio gozó de popularidad porque

  a. él era una novedad para sus compañeros.

  b. los *spanish* son alegres con costumbres diferentes.

  c. hablaba muy mal el inglés.

7 Una de sus nuevas experiencias fue

  a. rizarse el pelo.

  b. ser invitado a casas donde probó comidas típicas.

  c. enseñar a Joe a jugar al *base-ball*.

8 Uno de los cambios agradables en la vida de ellos fue

  a. rezarles a las mil vírgenes.

  b. poder pagar sus deudas.

  c. marchar en la casa.

9 Cuando llegó su primer cumpleaños en los Estados Unidos

  a. apoyó la desconfianza de los negros en la calle.

  b. su abuela se quedó en casa porque tenía vergüenza de no hablar inglés.

  c. quería tener fiesta e invitar a sus amigos a probar los dulces puertorriqueños.

10 La fiesta no fue un éxito porque

  a. sus amigos comieron demasiados pasteles.

  b. sus amigos se dieron cuenta de que él era negro.

  c. su papá estuvo en Nueva York por dos días.

Comprensión   II

A Conteste a las siguientes preguntas.

1 ¿Cómo se portaron Joe y los demás el día después de la fiesta?

2 Explique algo acerca del carácter de Tony.

3 ¿Por qué resultó ser un día de disgustos?

4 Fue mejor el día siguiente? ¿Por qué?

5 ¿Qué quiere decir Tony con «No lloraba pero tenía ganas» y «Sentía odio y tristeza al mismo tiempo»?

6 ¿Cómo se vengó de las burlas de Joe?

7 Describa la visita del maestro.

8 ¿Por qué dijo Tony «ese día sentí con todo el alma no ser un hombre mayor»?

9 Cuál fue el resultado de la visita del padre de Joe? ¿Por qué?

10 Describa la nueva casa de Tony.

11 ¿De qué se siente culpable Tony?

Familia: Nueva York

B ¿Verdadero o falso?

1 El día siguiente hacía frío.
2 Nadie se sentía bien.
3 El maestro estaba de mal humor.
4 El día después Joe tiró el guante y se burló de Tony.
5 Tony les explicó a sus amigos lo que su papá le había enseñado—que todos son iguales.
6 Después seguían jugando los otros.
7 Cuando terminaron las clases, Tony le pegó a Joe con una piedra.
8 Esa noche mandaron a Tony al *reformatory*.
9 Cuando botaron a su padre de la fábrica, fueron a vivir en Harlem.
10 Tony dijo que quería ser blanco.

Más Práctica

Escoja una palabra de la segunda lista (2) para que corresponda con la definición en la primera lista (1).

1	**2**
1 jefe, patrón	a. pasmados
2 sorprender	b. recostar
3 limpiar con escoba	c. alquilar
4 hacer algo con cuidado y esfuerzo	d. destreza
5 impresionados	e. capataz
6 pagar por el uso de algo	f. tambaleante
7 habilidad, talento	g. extrañar
8 apoyarse	h. barrer
9 sin equilibrio	i. calefacción
10 acto de calentar	j. esmerarse

Ejercicios Creativos

1 ¿Cómo es el ambiente al principio de la selección? ¿Cómo cambia al final de la primera parte? ¿Cómo es al último?
2 Compare esta selección con *Narración personal de Elías Garza*. Cite los elementos que ayudaron a la familia de Tony. ¿Cuál de los dos tenía más posibilidades de echar raíces en los Estados Unidos? ¿Cuál se siente más amargo al final?
3 ¿Cuál es su primer recuerdo de sentirse rechazado por cualquier motivo? Describa lo que Ud. sintió.

En Nueva York

José Luis González

PARA PRESENTAR LA LECTURA

Del campo a la ciudad; de la ciudad al país. Éste ha sido un patrón en el movimiento migratorio de muchos puertorriqueños. En la selección titulada *En el fondo del caño hay un negrito,* leímos sobre la mudanza de una familia del campo a la ciudad de San Juan, donde tuvo que establecerse en el arrabal por razones económicas — primera etapa en la emigración.

El mismo autor, José Luis González, nos ofrece ahora otra etapa en la vida de un joven prometedor que llega a Nueva York para echar raíces en otra localidad. Llega con entusiasmo, con esperanza, con ganas de superarse. Desgraciadamente, aunque sea diferente el medio, surgen los mismos problemas y de mayor magnitud — la pobreza, el desempleo, la insalubridad, el prejuicio, las desigualdades y, finalmente, la desesperación.

PARA APRENDER VOCABULARIO

Palabras Clave   I

1 **acogedora**   que recibe calurosamente a una persona *(welcoming, inviting)*
La sala era muy acogedora y todos querían entrar.

2 **contratiempo**   accidente o evento imprevisto, complicación
El contratiempo frustró sus planes.

3 **deprimente**   que debilita, que deprime *(depressing)*
La pobreza que se ve en muchos lugares es deprimente.

4 **despeinada**   que no está peinada
Estaba despeinada porque acababa de despertarse.

penumbra   sombra *(dimness, half-light)*
Subió la escalera en penumbra.

6   **tallas**   estaturas, tamaños
Llegaron puertorriqueños de todas tallas y edades.

7   **tartamudeó (tartamudear)**   pronunció con trabajo repitiendo las primeras sílabas.
—Mar . . . Mar . . . Marcelino—tartamudeó la joven.

8   **tiritaba (tiritar)**   temblaba de frío
Como no tenía abrigo, tiritaba de frío.

Práctica

Complete con una palabra de la lista.

acogedora	despeinada	tartamudeó
contratiempos	penumbra	tiritaba
deprimente	tallas	

1   No pudo ver bien porque la calle estaba en _____.
2   Encontró la casa cómoda y _____.
3   Los _____ le seguían; tenía muy mala suerte.
4   Soplaba un viento helado, y el pobre _____ de frío.
5   Arréglate, María. A estas horas, ¿por qué andas _____?
6   Por estar nervioso, _____ su nombre.
7   Aunque son de la misma edad, son de _____ diferentes.
8   El ambiente era triste y _____.

Palabras Clave   II

1   **afanaba (afanarse)**   trabajaba muy duro
Se afanaba tanto que de noche estaba fatigado.

2   **aparadores**   escaparates *(showcases)*
Se exhibían las mercancías en los aparadores.

3   **colchoneta**   colchón delgado *(thin mattress)*
La colchoneta no era muy cómoda.

4   **estibador**   cargador que trabaja en los muelles
El trabajo del estibador es muy duro.

5   **plazos**   pagos mensuales cuando uno está comprando a crédito
Los plazos para el abrigo son de diez dólares al mes.

6   **semanales**   cada semana
Arturo trabaja cuatro días semanales.

Práctica

Complete con una palabra de la lista.

estibador	plazos	aparadores
semanales	afanaba	colchoneta

1   Se paró para admirar las camisas en los _____.
2   Recibió un aumento de sueldo porque se _____ en sus obligaciones.
3   Durmió mal en esa _____.
4   Cuando llegué al muelle no vi ni un solo _____ y pensé que había huelga.
5   ¿Tienes bastante dinero para los _____ del coche?
6   Tienes cinco clases _____ de inglés.

Palabras Clave   III

1   **abordó (abordar)**   se acercó para hablarle o proponerle un asunto
El organizador abordó a Mario, proponiéndole un plan.

2   **desafiante**   que provoca, con desafío
El capataz le habló con actitud desafiante.

3   **locuaz**   que habla mucho
El compañero, que era locuaz, no le dio oportunidad de contestar.

Nuevos amigos: Nueva York

4 **remesa**   dinero enviado
Cada semana mandaba una remesa a su madre.

Práctica

Complete con una palabra de la lista.

abordó   desafiante   remesa   locuaz

1 ¿Te fijaste en el tono _____ de esa carta?
2 Marcelino _____ al capataz para pedirle un aumento.
3 Con la _____ semanal que recibe de su hija, vive mejor.
4 A la joven callada le irritó el compañero _____.

Palabras Clave   IV

1 **almohada**   cojín para la cabeza que se usa en la cama
Luisa siempre usa dos almohadas cuando duerme.

2 **estalló (estallar)**   reventó, explotó
Estalló en la mente de Daniel la visión de su pobre madre esperándolo.

3 **náufrago**   perdido en el mar
Elisa era náufraga en una isla tropical.

4 **pesadilla**   sueño angustioso
Trató de dormirse, pero la misma pesadilla volvió a quitarle la serenidad.

Práctica

Complete con una palabra de la lista.

náufrago   almohadas   estalló   pesadilla

1 Una idea revolucionaria _____ en su mente.
2 Le persiguió esa _____ durante varias noches seguidas.
3 A los niños les gusta tirar _____.
4 Robinson Crusoe era un _____ famoso.

En Nueva York

A Demetrio Aguilera Malta

José Luis González

I

camastro cama pobre y mala

yeso *plaster*
agrietado *cracked*

El hombre, aturdido por la fiebre, se revolvió en el camastro y volvió a quedar de cara a la pared. Otra vez ante sus ojos el yeso sucio y agrietado por el cual, a veces, corría desesperadamente una cucarachita. Serían las ocho de la noche. Afuera había oscurecido a las cinco de la tarde, y desde esa hora Marcelino Pérez había hecho luz en el cuartucho. No era gran cosa, una luz amarilla y deprimente, pero preferible a la oscuridad por la que el enfermo había desarrollado una especie de terror.

La habitación estaba en el quinto piso de un viejo edificio de Harlem del Este, y la calefacción, defectuosa en los primeros pisos, no llegaba allá arriba casi nunca. Esa noche, bien entrado ya diciembre y con una temperatura de veinticinco grados en la calle, el enfermo tiritaba en el camastro. Dos días completos hacía ya que la fiebre no cedía, y ese mismo tiempo llevaba sin comer.

Encogido en el camastro, muerto de frío y sudando copiosamente a un tiempo, Marcelino Pérez empezó a rememorar, con una fruición casi morbosa, todo lo que había vivido desde el momento en que el antiguo transporte militar, convertido en barco regular de pasajeros, depositó a cuatrocientos y tantos puertorriqueños en uno de aquellos enormes y lóbregos muelles neoyorquinos.

fruición goce
morbosa mórbida

lóbregos oscuros

El primo que se había ofrecido por carta tantas veces a recibirlo el día que se decidiera a «saltar el charco», no apareció por ningún lado. Ese primer contratiempo empezó a desmoralizarlo. Y el frío, aquel frío que él nunca había podido imaginarse en la isla bañada de sol, lo puso a temblar desde el momento mismo en que subió a cubierta, antes de desembarcar. Una muchacha

saltar el charco *to cross the ocean*

le había preguntado, al verlo encogido y con las manos en los bolsillos:

—Pero, ¿usté no trae abrigo?

Y él había explicado:

—No, yo creí que . . . Como na' más estamos en noviembre . . .

pulmonías infecciones de los pulmones
a dos por chavo *two for a penny*

—Pues consígase uno en seguida, que aquí las pulmonías están a dos por chavo.

Lo ojeó con más detenimiento, y añadió:

—Aunque sea de segunda mano.

Los funcionarios de migración fueron dando paso a docenas de Rodríguez, González y Martínez de todas las tallas, edades y colores. En cierto momento uno de aquéllos comentó con sorna, dirigiéndose a un compañero:

con sorna sarcásticamente

—Fellow Americans all of 'em, believe it or not.

encarguitos *gifts sent by others*
compotas *fruit preserves*

Ya en la calle, con la maleta y una caja de cartón llena de «encarguitos»—quesos del país, pastas, compotas—se decidió a tomar un taxi. El recorrido hasta la calle 112 entre Madison y Quinta le costó más de tres dólares. Lo de la propina, claro, ni se le ocurrió, y el chofer italoamericano se fue maldiciendo en su chapurreado inglés de Brooklyn.

chapurreado *broken speech*

El apartamiento que buscaba quedaba en el tercer piso de un viejo edificio con fachada de color indefinible. Subió las escaleras sucias y en penumbra, saturadas de olor a orines y restos de comida. Tocó a la puerta con timidez, casi con aprensión. Escuchó unos pasos apagados en el interior y poco después la voz de mujer al otro lado de la puerta:

—Who is it?

Por la inflexión de la voz comprendió que se trataba de una pregunta.

—Éste . . . soy yo, Mar . . . Marcelino—tartamudeó su respuesta.—Éste . . . el primo de Luis.

Abrió la puerta una mujer joven, pero pálida y despeinada, con un vestido negro que mostraba un desgarrón en un costado.

desgarrón en un costado *a rip on one side*

—Buenas—dijo él—. Yo . . . yo soy el primo de Luis. Resulta que . . .

farfullaba tartamudeaba

La mujer lo miró fijamente mientras él farfullaba su explicación, fijamente pero con una absoluta falta de expresión en el rostro, como si en lugar de mirarlo estuviera viendo a través de él. De repente se pasó una mano por la frente y dijo:

—Entre . . . entre.

La tibia temperatura de la salita resultaba acogedora, pero en la cocina freían algo y ese olor peculiar de la manteca usada muchas veces parecía haberse metido en todos los rincones. El apartamiento era pequeño, todo en él producía una incómoda sensación de apretujamiento: las personas, los muebles, hasta los cuadros en las paredes.

apretujamiento
overcrowding

—Siéntese—invitó la mujer.

Marcelino advirtió en ese momento que una de las sillas estaba ocupada por un muchachito semidesnudo que dormía en una posición absurda. Se sentó en el desvencijado sofá-cama junto al radiador de la calefacción, y la mujer, todavía de pie, dijo entonces:

desvencijado *falling apart*

—¿Usté . . . no sabe que Luis murió?

Y empezó a sollozar quedamente, inclinando la cabeza como si el llanto la avergonzara.

quedamente *suavemente*

—¿Aaah?—sin darse cuenta, el recién llegado volvió a ponerse de pie—. Pero . . . ¿Luis?

II

La mujer, dominándose y recayendo en su aflicción a ratos, lo contó todo. Luis era estibador en los muelles. Dos días antes estaba en su trabajo, sacando mercancías de un vagón, cuando sintió que alguien chocaba con fuerza contra su espalda. Volvió la cabeza a tiempo para ver al hombre que seguía corriendo y desaparecía entre unas estibas. En ese instante oyó una detonación y sintió un dolor agudo en un costado. Mientras iba cayendo al suelo, dos hombres corrieron hacia él. Uno era un policía con un revólver en la mano. El otro era un compañero de trabajo. Lo último que Luis oyó antes de morirse fueron las palabras del otro estibador al policía:

estibas *piles of freight*
costado *rib, side*

—Dammit, you've shot the wrong man!

Marcelino se encontró ahora sin palabras que ofrecer a la viuda de su primo. Ambos guardaron silencio durante un rato, hasta que ella, sosegada de pronto, preguntó:

sosegada *tranquila*

—¿Y dónde va a vivir usté?

—Bueno, yo . . . yo venía . . .

Ella no lo dejó seguir:

—Mire, hoy supe yo que ahí alantito en la 115 hay unos cuartos furnidos baratos.

alantito *adelantito*
furnidos *amueblados*

—¿Unos cuartos qué?—preguntó él, ignorante todavía del maltratado español neoyorquino.

—Unos cuartos furnidos . . . Amueblados, como dicen por allá.

—Ah.

—Creo que son a cuatro pesos semanales.

—¿Ajá? Pero es que yo . . .

—Porque fíjese, yo tengo aquí ahora a mi tía con dos nenes. Si no, le decía que se quedara, ¿ve? Usté sabe, como de la familia.

—No, no, si yo . . . yo no pensaba . . . ¿En dónde dijo que quedan esos cuartos?

—Ahí en la 115, entre Madison y Quinta, igual que esta calle. A tres bloques de aquí.

—Ajá, bueno . . . Pues me voy en seguida a ver si todavía encuentro uno. Muchas gracias, ah, y a ver si un día de éstos vengo por acá.

—Cómo no, cuando guste.

Ya en la puerta, se acordó de los quesos y las pastas.

—Aquí le mandó tía Lola.

—Ave María, qué bueno. Un millón de gracias.

Tomó un cuarto y tuvo que pagar una semana por adelantado. Así vino a quedar con diecisiete dólares en los bolsillos, sin trabajo y en una ciudad extraña.

Pero al cabo de unos días vino a darse cuenta de que no era realmente tan extraña. Por lo menos este barrio en que vivía, este Harlem del Este lleno de puertorriqueños, donde el inglés era un idioma extranjero; este Harlem del Este con sus cafetines *El Quenepo, Mi Borinquen, Noche y Día;* este Harlem del Este donde ya había encontrado cuatro conocidos de Puerto Rico, que andaban colocando anuncios de un baile para celebrar la reelección de Vito Marcantonio. Por uno de ellos consiguió su primer empleo.

—¿Qué, todavía no tienes yope?—le había preguntado el otro.

—No . . . Ando buscando por ahí.

—Si me hubieras visto ayer, te hubiera puesto a grabar discos en seguida.

—¿A grabar discos?

—Sí, chico, a lavar platos en una cafetería. Pero ya ese chance lo cogió otro paisa.

—Ah . . .

—Pero, mira, si quieres meterte en una factoría de ropa, te puedo dar la dirección.

—Pues venga.

yope *job (slang)*

ese . . . paisa *another fellow countryman got that chance*

—Y agradece que me encontraste a mí, que una agencia de empleos te hubiera sacao un canto.

El trabajo era el más duro y el peor pagado de la fábrica. Durante ocho horas diarias cargaba fardos, empujaba carretones llenos de rollos de tela, subía mercancía a los aparadores, trajinaba y se afanaba de modo que cuando terminaba la jornada, a las cinco de la tarde, sentía que le dolía el último hueso.

Por lo demás, todo marchó bien durante un mes. Pero nunca llegaba a ahorrar los cinco dólares semanales que se había propuesto. Con lo que enviaba a la madre en Puerto Rico, el alquiler del cuarto, la comida, el transporte, la lavandería, los plazos del abrigo que había comprado a crédito, la mala película del domingo y todos los pequeños gastos imposibles de prever, los miércoles sólo venían a quedarle cuatro dólares y pico de los veintidós que le pagaban cada sábado. Esos siempre los guardaba. Por eso el día que pasó lo que pasó tenía dieciséis billetes metidos en un sobre debajo de la colchoneta.

III

Lo que pasó fue que a uno de los compañeros de trabajo, un judío joven y locuaz que trabajaba en la sección de corte, se le metió en la cabeza «unionar» a los obreros de la fábrica. Fue hablándoles a todos, uno por uno, y cuando abordó a Marcelino le dijo, hablando inglés despacio para hacerse entender bien:

—Es una unión del CIO. ¿Tú sabes lo que es eso?

—Sí, seguro. Allá en Puerto Rico una vez hicieron una huelga en los muelles.

—¿Ah, sí? ¿Y qué pasó?

—Pues . . . me parece que al final sacaron un aumento en los jornales.

—¿Ya ves? La cosa es organizarse. Sólo con una unión podemos conseguir aumentos, porque tenemos el arma de la huelga. ¿Entiendes?

—Sí, claro.

—Entonces, ¿cuento contigo?

—Bueno.

Marcelino pensó en la viejita que había dejado en Puerto Rico y en la posibilidad de añadir uno o dos dólares a sus remesas semanales. Pero a poco otro puertorriqueño se le acercó y le advirtió:

soplón *stool pigeon*
botao botado

dizque *talk*

—Mira, yo creo que las uniones son buenas, y yo no soy ningún soplón, pero eso lo hemos querido hacer ya como cinco veces y lo que ha pasao es que han botao un montón de gente. Un día vino hasta la policía y le entró a palos al que más hablaba. Dijeron que era dizque comunista. Así que si quieres un consejo, deja que pase lo que pase sin que tú te metas.

El asunto de la unión, sin embargo, pareció progresar sin contratiempos. El judío aseguraba tener una mayoría comprometida y Marcelino empezó a acariciar la idea de tomar un apartamiento y traer a la madre a vivir con él. Con esos pensamientos, el trabajo lo cansaba menos.

Pero un viernes, a la hora de pagar, el capataz juntó los sobres del judío, Marcelino y otros tres empleados, y en presencia de todos los demás declaró:

—La empresa no requiere de sus servicios a partir de hoy.

Y dirigiéndose al judío que lo miraba en actitud desafiante:

—Qué no vuelva yo a verlo por estos alrededores, óigame bien.

La cosa era clara: alguien había «soplado», pero nadie pudo imaginarse quién, y si pudo no lo dijo.

Así fue como Marcelino Pérez vino a quedar casi en la misma situación en que había llegado. Debajo de la colchoneta tenía los dieciséis dólares ahorrados y en un bolsillo los veintidós que acababa de cobrar. Con eso, calculó, podría aguantarse tres semanas. Al día siguiente se echó los treinta y ocho dólares al bolsillo y salió a la calle. Compró el *Journal-American* y se metió en un cafetín a leer la página de anuncios clasificados. En eso estaba cuando alguien le colocó una mano sobre el hombro. Alzó la mirada y vio al mismo amigo que le había dado la dirección de la fábrica.

—Eh, ¿qué pasa? Siéntate.

El otro preguntó:

—¿Qué, tienes el día libre?

—¿Libre? ¡Qué va a ser! Lo que pasa es que ayer me botaron.

—Adió . . . ¿y qué pasó?

Marcelino se lo dijo y el otro comentó, en tono enterado:

no come cuento *doesn't fool around*

—Ajá. Eso me pasó a mí también dos o tres veces, hasta que en una la ganamos y ahora tenemos una unión que no come cuento. Pero bueno, ¿y qué? ¿Qué piensas hacer ahora?

—Pues . . . estoy buscando aquí en este periódico a ver si encuentro algo. ¿Qué es esto de ty . . . typ . . .

—No, no, brother, eso es para mecanógrafas. Trabajo de oficina, tú sabes.

—Ah . . .

—Bueno, mira, yo sí tengo el día *off*. Te invito a una cervecita y después te voy a explicar lo que hay que hacer para apuntarte en el relief.

—Ah, el relief. Oye, ¿qué es lo que hay que hacer?

—Después te digo, hay tiempo. Vamos a la cervecita ahora.

A las cinco de la tarde seguían en la misma mesa, perdida la cuenta de las botellas que se habían bebido. A Marcelino lo **arrebataba** ya esa felicidad estúpida que invade a algunos borrachos.

*　*　*

(Siguieron tomando hasta muy tarde. Marcelino gastó todo su dinero, y llegó a casa borracho, enfermo y sin el abrigo.)

IV

Lo que no pudo recordar fue cómo había llegado hasta su cuarto. Quiso incorporarse y la habitación entera pareció dar vueltas ante sus ojos. Tuvo que sujetarse la cabeza y echarse otra vez. «Bueno—se dijo—, aquí me quedo hasta que esto se me pase».

Pero no se le pasó. Por la tarde los escalofríos lo tenían sudando y tiritando a un tiempo. El dolor en la espalda y la cabeza se había hecho más intenso. Antes de caer en una especie de **sopor**, alcanzó a pensar: «Si esta noche duermo bien, mañana estaré mejor».

Pero la noche fue una pesadilla continua, un angustioso revolverse en el camastro, un sudar copioso que empapó sábanas y almohada. Y al amanecer del segundo día, no intentó siquiera levantarse.

Y así se encontraba ahora, en la noche del segundo día, echado en el camastro, de cara a la pared de sucio yeso **carcomido**. Por el silencio que reinaba en todo el edificio, calculó que sería medianoche. Se le estaba haciendo dificultosa la respiración, y una angustia sorda, estimulada por la mente enfebrecida, revolvía y confundía sus recuerdos de las últimas horas.

Súbitamente lo asaltó un pensamiento: «¿Por qué quedarme encerrado aquí?» Su cerebro aún tuvo fuerzas para rechazar la idea de salir del cuarto. Al cabo de unos minutos, sin embargo,

arrebataba quitaba con violencia

sopor *stupor*

carcomido *decaying, crumbling*

forcejeo resistencia

el pensamiento recurrió: «¿Qué demonios voy a hacer metido aquí?» Y ya sólo hubo un débil forcejeo interior. «¿Qué demonios voy a hacer aquí?» «Afuera puede que haya algo». «Algo . . . ¿qué?» «Cualquier cosa, qué importa, cualquier cosa . . . ¡Afuera tiene que haber *algo*!»

Casi saltó del camastro. La habitación volvió a dar vueltas, pero ahora no le importó porque él mismo, todo él, también giraba. En otro sentido, de otro modo, pero él también giraba. Y con él giraba todo. Y en ese girar todo, había un orden: el orden del absurdo en que vivía ahora el pobre hombre alucinado. Sudando, tembloroso, se puso la camisa y los pantalones. Sin sentarse, metió los pies en los zapatos y dejó sueltos los cordones. Se abotonó el gabán y bajó como un autómata las escaleras oscuras.

gabán abrigo

No sintió el frío de la calle porque era más intenso el que llevaba por dentro. Caminó una cuadra sin ver a nadie y sin escuchar más sonidos que los de sus propias pisadas. Un súbito golpe de viento lo obligó, ahora sí, a levantarse el cuello del gabán. Caminó otra cuadra. Y otra. Y otra. Hasta que perdió la cuenta. Se detuvo en una esquina y apoyó la espalda en un poste del alumbrado cuya luz exigua sólo alcanzaba a iluminar un pedazo de la calle.

exigua débil

Su confusión persistía, pero se le ocurrió preguntarse qué era lo que esperaba ahora. No supo responderse. Seguía temblando, a sacudidas periódicas. De pronto algo lo alertó: un ruido insignificante, que sólo el profundo silencio nocturno dejaba llegar hasta su oído. Puso atención. Eran pasos de alguien que caminaba hacia él, taconeando a breves intervalos sobre la acera. Una mujer, sin duda. Sí, una mujer sola. Una mujer sola con su cartera. Y la cartera, seguro, con dinero. Con mucho dinero, quizá. Recordó la idea que lo había empujado a la calle: «¡Afuera tiene que haber algo!» Eso era. Eso. Dinero era lo único que necesitaba. Dinero para irse a Puerto Rico. Irse a Puerto Rico, donde hasta en enero el sol es una caricia ardiente. «¡Afuera tiene que haber algo!» ¡Ah!

Se escurrió *He slipped by*
zaguán *vestíbulo*
Aguzó el oído *He listened closely*

Se escurrió dos o tres casas hacia la oscuridad y se metió en un zaguán. Aguzó el oído, los pasos sonaban cada vez más cerca. Asomó ligeramente la cabeza. Como a veinte metros pudo verla. Era una mujer de talla menuda y venía, efectivamente, sola. Miraba hacia atrás cada dos o tres pasos, como temiendo algo. Marcelino volvió a ocultar su cabeza. Transcurrieron unos segundos. El apresurado taconeo resonaba ahora en sus oídos: toc, toc, toc. Ya estaría a unos cinco pasos. Marcelino adelantó un pie hacia la acera, contraídos instintivamente todos los músculos de su cuerpo. Toc, toc, toc. ¡Ahora! Pero el impulso fue demasiado grande y el encontronazo los derribó a los dos. La mano del hombre se extendió hasta la de la mujer y los dedos aferraron la cartera. Un tirón bastó para arrebatársela. Pero en ese instante, mientras él se incorporaba casi de un salto, la víctima, atenazada aún por el terror, gritó:

—¡Ay Dios mío, bendito!

Y Marcelino, con la cartera en la mano, de pie junto a su víctima, se sintió súbitamente paralizado. El grito, proferido en claro español, le golpeó el oído y le llegó como una tempestad hasta el cerebro. Y allí estalló en una increíble imagen relampagueante: la visión de una anciana a la puerta de un ranchito náufrago en el océano verde del cañaveral—toda la angustia inmemorial venida así de golpe a un solo hombre y en ese solo hombre resumida, en una fracción de instante imposible de medir.

La cartera cayó junto al cuerpo de la mujer. Ésta miró al hombre desde el suelo, con ojos agrandados aún por el espanto. Marcelino retrocedió dos pasos, se llevó las manos a la cara y dejó escapar un alarido como de bestia supliciada. Luego emprendió una carrera desesperada por la calle oscura, tropezando al perder un zapato, chocando con los postes y los tachos de basura, hasta desaparecer en una esquina con aquel grito espeluznante quebrado al fin en un ronco sollozo de animal atormentado.

aferraron agarraron

atenazada sujetada con fuerza

resumida reducida

supliciada en agonía

tachos cans *(slang)*

espeluznante que causa terror

PARA APLICAR

Comprensión I

A Conteste a las siguientes preguntas.

1 ¿Qué hizo el hombre aturdido por la fiebre?
2 ¿Cuánto tiempo hacía desde que Marcelino prendió la luz?
3 ¿Por qué no quería el enfermo quedarse en la oscuridad?
4 Describa la temperatura adentro y afuera.
5 ¿Qué comenzó el joven a rememorar?
6 ¿Cuál fue su primer contratiempo en Nueva York?
7 ¿Cómo le afectó el frío cuando desembarcó?
8 ¿Por qué fue importante tener abrigo?
9 ¿Hablaron los funcionarios respetuosamente de los que llegaron en el barco?
10 Dé detalles de la llegada al apartamiento de su primo.
11 ¿Cómo se nota su agitación al llegar a la puerta del apartamiento?
12 ¿Parecía la mujer interesada en ayudarle a Marcelino?
13 Describa la sala.
14 ¿Por qué empezó la mujer a sollozar?

Momento triste

B Escoja la expresión de la segunda lista (2) que completa
la idea empezada en la primera lista (1).

1

1 El hombre aturdido por la fiebre
2 Se sentía el frío en el cuarto sucio
3 Hacía dos días que tenía fiebre
4 Encogido en el camastro empezó a
5 Se sintió desmoralizado
6 Comenzó a tiritar de frío y
7 Tomó un taxi que le costó caro y
8 Contestó tartamudeando su nombre
9 La tibieza de la sala era acogedora
10 Marcelino apenas se había acomodado en
    un sofá

2

a. y no había comido nada.
b. una muchacha le aconsejó que se comprara
    un abrigo.
c. sentía terror de la oscuridad.
d. porque su primo no estuvo allí para
    recibirlo.
e. pensar en su vida desde la llegada a Nueva
    York.
f. porque la calefacción no llegaba hasta el
    quinto piso.
g. y una mujer desarreglada y mal vestida le
    abrió la puerta.
h. cuando la mujer sollozando le comunicó
    una noticia sorprendente.
i. el chofer se enojó por no recibir una
    propina.
j. pero unos olores de aceite viejo penetraron
    en el apartamiento.

Comprensión   II

A   Conteste a las siguientes preguntas.

1   ¿Dónde trabajaba Luis?
2   ¿Qué le sucedió un día en el trabajo?
3   ¿Cómo expresó Marcelino su pesar a la viuda?
4   ¿Por qué no podía quedarse Marcelino con la familia de Luis?
5   ¿Por qué tuvo que gastar algo más ese día de lo que había esperado?
6   ¿Por qué no se sintió extraño por mucho tiempo en el Harlem del Este?
7   ¿Qué le da el amigo?
8   Describa el trabajo que consiguió.
9   ¿En qué gastaba Marcelino su dinero? ¿Cuánto ahorraba?

B   Escoja la respuesta apropiada.

1   ¿Cómo murió Luis?
   a.   Tuvo un choque de vagón.
   b.   Un compañero de trabajo lo mató con un revólver.
   c.   Un policía lo mató por accidente.
2   ¿Dónde intentaba vivir Marcelino?
   a.   En la casa de su primo.
   b.   En unos cuartos amueblados no muy lejos de allí.
   c.   Con un español neoyorquino.
3   ¿Por qué no se sintió extraño por mucho tiempo?
   a.   Porque tenía diecisiete dólares en los bolsillos.
   b.   Vivían muchos puertorriqueños en Harlem del Este donde el inglés es una lengua extranjera.
   c.   Consiguió un trabajo colocando anuncios para un baile.
4   ¿Cómo le ayudó el amigo que había conocido en Puerto Rico?
   a.   Le mandó a una agencia de empleos.
   b.   Le dio la dirección de una fábrica de ropa.

c.   Le recomendó una cafetería donde podría lavar platos.
5   ¿Por qué no podía ahorrar los cinco dólares semanales que se había propuesto?
   a.   Guardó su dinero debajo de la colchoneta.
   b.   No se esmeró en el trabajo, y le rebajaron el sueldo.
   c.   Los gastos excedían lo que él había anticipado.

Comprensión   III

A   Conteste a las siguientes preguntas.

1   ¿Qué se le ocurrió a un joven locuaz del departamento de corte?
2   ¿Cómo le habló al puertorriqueño?
3   ¿Entendía Marcelino algo de las uniones?
4   ¿Por qué se interesó en meterse en ese asunto?
5   Describa lo que le dijo otro puertorriqueño a Marcelino.
6   Con la ilusión de conseguir cambios agradables, ¿cómo le pareció el trabajo?
7   ¿Qué pasó un viernes?
8   ¿Por cuánto tiempo creía Marcelino que podría sostenerse?
9   ¿Con quién se encontró en una cafetería?
10   ¿Cómo pasaron la tarde?

B   ¿Verdadero o falso?

1   Un joven muy hablador decidió «unionar» la fábrica.
2   Cuando el organizador se lo explicó a Marcelino, éste tuvo dificultad en entenderlo.
3   El joven le convenció fácilmente a Marcelino que se afiliara a la organización.
4   Marcelino quería volver a Puerto Rico para ver a su madre.
5   Otro puertorriqueño le avisó que luchara por lo que deseaba ganar.
6   Los esfuerzos anteriores fueron parados por la policía.

Mercado en un barrio hispano: Nueva York

7 Marcelino era comunista.

8 Marcelino tomó un apartamiento y pensaba traer a su madre.

9 La fábrica botó a todos los obreros.

10 Marcelino creía que podría sostenerse durante varios meses.

11 Guardó todo su dinero en el saco y entró en un pequeño café.

12 Mientras leía la página de anuncios clasificados, llegó un conocido.

13 El amigo relató que también lo habían botado ayer.

14 El amigo le explicó lo que tenía que hacer para ser apuntado en el relief.

15 Después de tomar cerveza toda la tarde, Marcelino se sentía mucho mejor.

Comprensión   IV

Conteste a las siguientes preguntas.

1 ¿Cómo llegó a su cuarto?

2 Cuando trató de incorporarse, ¿cómo le pareció el cuarto?

3 ¿Cómo se sintió esa tarde?

4 ¿De qué se convenció?
5 Describa cómo se sentía durante el segundo día.
6 Cuando saltó de la cama, ¿cómo vio todo?
7 Describa cómo se vistió.
8 ¿Qué hizo entonces?
9 Al oir el taconeo en la acera, ¿qué decidió hacer?
10 Si tuviera dinero, ¿qué podría hacer?
11 Describa a la mujer y cómo venía por la calle.
12 ¿Calculó bien su ataque?
13 ¿Se apoderó él de la cartera de la mujer?
14 ¿Cómo reaccionó Marcelino al oirla gritar?
15 ¿Qué le pasó a Marcelino cuando trató de escaparse?

Más Práctica

A Dé un sinónimo de las siguientes palabras.

1	mortificada	6	pasmado
2	sueño horrible	7	escaparate
3	hablador	8	sosegada
4	explotó	9	trajinaba
5	temblaba	10	cargador

B Conteste a las siguientes preguntas. Escoja una palabra de la lista.

se afanaba, colchoneta, aparadores, acoge-dora, se escurrió, contratiempo, deprimente, tartamudeó, despeinado

1 ¿Cómo es esa sala bonita?
2 ¿Cómo es un día frío y lluvioso?

3 ¿Cómo trabajaba para complacer al capataz?
4 Si no habló claramente, ¿cómo habló?
5 ¿Cómo tenía el pelo?
6 ¿En qué durmió?
7 ¿Cómo fue de casa en casa?
8 ¿Qué le parecía a Marcelino no ver a su primo?
9 ¿Dónde se exhibían las mercancías?

Ejercicios Creativos

1 ¿Qué sintió Ud. al terminar la selección? Escoja una de las siguientes emociones y explique su reacción.

a.	compasión	e.	alegría
b.	enojo	f.	desesperación
c.	desprecio	g.	culpa
d.	desilusión	h.	vergüenza

2 Todos los días en los periódicos se lee sobre incidentes parecidos al de Marcelino. En su opinión, ¿quién tiene la culpa? ¿El individuo? ¿El gobierno? ¿El hogar? ¿La sociedad? Defienda su respuesta.
3 ¿Por qué fue difícil que Marcelino echara raíces aquí?
4 Escriba otro episodio expresando lo que le pasa a Marcelino después.
5 En las tres selecciones de este cuadro, uno observa que la familia ocupa un lugar principal en la vida de los personajes. Cite un ejemplo de cada selección que muestre esa importancia.

Ser y **Estar**

Los verbos *ser* y *estar* se traducen *to be* en inglés, pero no son intercambiables. Cada uno tiene sus aplicaciones propias.

Usos del Verbo *Ser*

Ser expresa lo que es el sujeto. Une las siguientes ideas al sujeto:

Descripción o identificación, por medio de adjetivos o sustantivos predicados que expresan cualidades inherentes, características.

> Ella es alta.
> Nicanor es guapo.

Origen

> El abanico es de París.
> Somos de los Estados Unidos.

Nacionalidad

> Nosotros somos norteamericanos.

Profesión u oficio

> Esa mujer es médica.
> El joven es obrero.

Asociación religiosa o política

> Mis padres son presbiterianos.

Posesión

> El auto es de Estela.

Material de construcción o de confección

> La casa es de piedra.
> El reloj era de oro.

Se usa en expresiones impersonales.

> Es necesario.
> Es verdad.
> Es lástima.

Expresa la hora y la fecha.

> ¿Qué hora es? Son las diez de la noche.
> ¿Qué día es hoy? Hoy es miércoles, doce de diciembre.

La hora en el pasado sólo se expresa en el imperfecto.

> Eran las diez y media.

La voz pasiva se expresa con *ser* más el participio pasado.

> El libro fue escrito en el siglo XVI.
> Los hombres fueron llevados a la directora.

Si se expresa quien hizo la acción (el agente), se introduce con la preposición *por*.

> El poema fue escrito por Gabriela Mistral.

Si el participio pasado expresa una emoción o estado mental en vez de una acción física, se introduce el agente con la preposición *de*.

> Ella es admirada (respetada, querida) de todos.

A Sustituyan según el modelo.

> Gabriela es fuerte.
> muy pequeña/
> Gabriela es muy pequeña.

1 Gabriela es fuerte.
inteligente/de Puerto Rico/puertorriqueña/alumna/luterana/muy querida de su padre/

2 Las fotos son hermosas.
claras/de Inglaterra/tomadas en casa/oscuras/de mi familia/buenas/mías/

3 Los hermanos son malos.
serios/españoles/de Barcelona/idénticos/liberales/metodistas/escritores/

B Hagan la sustitución necesaria.

> María es simpática.

1 Felipe es —————————.
2 ————————————— francés.
3 Las señoras —————————.
4 Sus maridos —————————.
5 ————————————— astutos.
6 La madre —————————.
7 Las alumnas —————————.
8 ————————— de la Argentina.
9 ———————————— argentinas.
10 El abuelo —————————.
11 ———————————— valenciano.
12 Sus nietos —————————.
13 ———————————— conservadores.
14 Su nieta —————————.
15 Este libro —————————.
16 ————— vendido por muchas tiendas.
17 Esta medicina —————————.
18 Las colchonetas —————————.
19 ———————————— de algodón.
20 ———————————— baratas.
21 ————————— de la señora Garza.

C Contesten a las siguientes preguntas según la indicación.

> ¿De dónde es Ud.? de Nueva York
> Soy de Nueva York.

1 ¿De dónde es Ud.? de los Estados Unidos
2 ¿Quién es Ud.? Martín Villarreal
3 ¿Qué es Ud.? alumno
4 ¿De quién es este reloj? mío
5 ¿Cuál es su nacionalidad? norteamericano
6 ¿Cuál es su religión? bautista
7 ¿Cómo es Ud.? moreno
8 ¿Es Ud. del Canadá? no, de los Estados Unidos

D Contesten a las siguientes preguntas según la indicación.

> ¿Quiénes son Uds.? sus vecinos
> Somos sus vecinos.

1 ¿Quiénes son Uds.? los rivales de Uds.
2 ¿De dónde son Uds.? de España
3 ¿Cuál es su nacionalidad? españoles
4 ¿Cuál es su profesión? artistas
5 ¿Son Uds. violentos? no, muy pacíficos
6 ¿Cuál es su religión? católicos
7 ¿Cómo son Uds.? altos y rubios
8 ¿Son Uds. amigos? sí

E Contesten a las siguientes preguntas según el modelo.

> ¿Qué es ella, chilena o peruana?
> Es chilena.

1 ¿Qué es ella, mexicana o española?
2 ¿Quién es él, tu padre o tu tío?
3 ¿Qué son ellos, judíos o cristianos?
4 ¿De qué son los rieles, de metal o de madera?

5 ¿Qué hora es, las dos y veinte o las dos y media?

6 ¿De quién es el gato, de Antonio o de Ricardo?

7 ¿Son ellos demócratas o republicanos?

8 ¿Qué día es hoy, martes o miércoles?

9 ¿Cuál es su profesión, profesora o ingeniera?

10 ¿En qué cargo trabaja Ud., jornalero o capataz?

11 ¿Dónde fue dejado primero, en el patio o en el campo?

12 Mira este cuadro. ¿Fue pintado por Picasso o por Dalí?

13 ¿Es estimado de todos o de muy pocos?

Usos del Verbo *Estar*

El verbo *estar* se emplea para expresar un estado o una condición.

Colocación (permanente o no)

> Buenos Aires está en la Argentina.
> La niña estaba en el árbol.

Condición o estado temporal

> El hijo está enfermo.
> Los cuartos estaban limpios.

Se usa *estar* para formar el tiempo progresivo con el gerundio.

> Está jugando con el gato.
> El hombre estaba barriendo el piso.

F Sustituyan según el modelo.

> Marcelino está sorprendido.
> triste/
> Marcelino está triste.

1 Marcelino está triste.
alegre/de buen humor/bien/confuso/listo/malo/

2 La casa está en el campo.
en Valparaíso/muy cerca/bastante lejos/entre unos árboles/delante del parque/

3 El niño está entusiasmado.
agradecido/equivocado/interesado en los animales/parado en el portón/preocupado por el gatito/ocupado con la tarea/

G Sigan los modelos.

Cierra el portón.
Está cerrando el portón.

1 Mira al jinete sobre el caballo.
2 Vuelve adonde está su papá.
3 Juega a la intemperie.
4 Grita con alegría.
5 Pide otra oportunidad.
6 Repite lo que le dice su mamá.
7 Divierte a su amiga.
8 Dice que va a arreglarlo.
9 Elías trabaja como jornalero.
10 Se despide de la abuelita.

Barrían los pisos.
Estaban barriendo los pisos.

11 Exprimían la ropa para quitarle el agua.
12 Trabajaban en las vías, poniendo y quitando rieles.
13 Preparaban churros y pasteles.
14 Se rizaban el pelo.
15 Hacían las compras para la comida.
16 Comían sopa para que el hijo comiera carne.
17 Tiritaban de frío.
18 Subían las escaleras sucias y en penumbra.
19 Lo miraban fijamente mientras él tartamudeaba.
20 Buscaban trabajo en la fábrica.

H Contesten a las siguientes preguntas según la indicación.

¿Dónde está Santiago? en Chile
Santiago está en Chile.

1 ¿Cómo estás hoy? *muy bien*
2 ¿Qué estás leyendo? *una historia interesante*
3 ¿Por qué no miras la televisión? *rota*
4 ¿Por qué estás leyendo? *interesado en la historia*
5 ¿Están ansiosas las hijas de continuar la lucha? *no*
6 ¿A qué están decididos? *a no matar a nadie*
7 ¿Qué está ardiendo? *la casa de la tía Cecilia*
8 ¿Quién está dentro de la casa? *la empleada*
9 ¿Quién está lastimado? *un hijo del viudo*
10 ¿Qué están pintando? *la pared*

Contrastes

Muchas veces el significado de una oración puede cambiar según el uso de *ser* o *estar*. Estudien los siguientes ejemplos:

> María está triste. (condición causada por una desgracia)
> El abuelo es triste. (característica de personalidad)
>
> Marcelino estaba malo. (condición física)
> El capataz era malo. (característica o cualidad moral)
>
> Están listos para salir. (condición de estar preparados)
> Esa niña es lista. (característica)
>
> Está palido. (condición física)
> Es pálido. (descripción o identificación)
>
> María está viva. (condición o estado temporal)
> El gato es muy vivo. (característica de ser animado)
>
> Está alegre. (estado temporal)
> Es feliz. (característica)

I Sustituyan según el modelo.

> *Ms. Brown es de los Estados Unidos y ahora está en España.*
>
> *los Garza/*
>
> *Los Garza son de los Estados Unidos y ahora están en España.*

1 Los Garza son de los Estados Unidos y ahora están en España.
mis primas/nosotros/tú/yo/Marisol/

2 Los nietos son fuertes, pero en este momento están débiles.
el guapo/nosotros/tú/las hermanas/yo/

3 Sara es nueva aquí y está en la clase avanzada.
yo/mis vecinos/tú/nosotros/Uds./

4 El cura es aficionado a la música. Está escuchando el concierto.
la duquesa/Manolo y yo/mis padres/tú/esas alumnas/

J Completen las siguientes oraciones con la forma apropiada del presente de *ser* o *estar*.

1 El hombre está en una fábrica de New Jersey.
2 _____ el padre de Tony.
3 _____ barriendo los pisos.
4 _____ muy trabajador.
5 _____ cansado.
6 Tony _____.
7 _____ en la casa alquilada.
8 _____ contento.
9 _____ en la calle.
10 Los amigos _____.
11 _____ jugando con él.
12 _____ blancos y negros.
13 _____ de carácter variable.
14 _____ amables con Tony.
15 Joe _____.
16 _____ alto, delgado y pecoso.

17 _____ un sinvergüenza.	15 _____ en la página 306.
18 _____ un niño bien educado.	16 _____ corto y emocionante.
19 _____ jugador de béisbol.	17 _____ una buena lección.
20 _____ enseñándole a Tony.	18 _____ un episodio de un
21 _____ aburrido.	diario.

K Completen las siguientes oraciones con la forma apropiada del imperfecto de *ser* o *estar*.

1 La abuelita era muy honrada.
2 _____ como las otras abuelas.
3 _____ trabajando en casa día y noche.
4 _____ buena cocinera.
5 _____ preparando churros y pasteles.
6 _____ muy entusiasmada.
7 _____ de piel oscura.
8 _____ esmerándose en los preparativos.
9 _____ en la cocina.
10 _____ una mujer simpática.
11 _____ admirada de todos.
12 Ese cuento _____.
13 _____ bueno e interesante.
14 _____ de Luis Ricardo Alonso.

L Según los modelos, hagan una oración relacionada, usando *ser* o *estar*.

Ella abre la puerta.
La puerta está abierta.

Ven a los muchachos morenos.
Los muchachos son morenos.

1 Ella cierra la ventana.
2 ¿Conoces al señor simpático?
3 Sirva los pasteles puertorriqueños.
4 Quiero ir en el bote pequeño.
5 Visitan a la abuela en Nueva York.
6 Tengo la foto del capataz.
7 La doctora atiende desde ayer al hombre enfermo.
8 No me gusta el café frío.
9 Sólo esa niña lista sabía resolverlo.
10 Vienen hoy, lunes.
11 Me gusta la cerámica hecha en esa fábrica.
12 ¡Listos por fin! Ya podemos salir.

Por y Para

Se emplea la preposición *para* en los siguientes casos:

Para indicar movimiento hacia un destino que puede ser lugar, persona, evento o tiempo fijo.

Salen para México.
Este regalo es para mi novia.
Estos regalos son para la Navidad.
Llegaremos allí para el dos de mayo.

Para indicar la razón, el propósito de una acción (expresada en el infinitivo), el servicio que ofrece una persona o el uso de una cosa.

Como poco para no engordar.
Estudiamos mucho para obtener buenas notas.
Tienen buenos maestros para enseñarles.
Esto es para escribir.

Para indicar una comparación de desigualdad o una comparación inesperada.

Hace mucho calor para octubre.
Habla muy correctamente para extranjero.

Se emplea la preposición *por* en los siguientes casos:

Para indicar movimiento libre por el espacio.

Él entró por la puerta.   *(through)*
Anduvieron por la orilla del río.   *(along)*
Caminó por el correo.   *(by, in front of)*
Corrieron por la calle.   *(along, down)*

Para indicar el cambio de una cosa por otra.

Pagué veinte pesos por el diccionario.

Para indicar un período de tiempo—la duración de una acción.

Estuvo aquí por dos meses.   *(for, during)*

Para indicar algo hecho en favor de otra persona.

Escribo esta carta por mi hermano.   *(as a favor to)*
Habló elocuentemente por la familia.   *(in behalf of)*
¡Una caridad, por Dios, señor!   *(for the sake of)*

Para indicar lo que uno consigue u obtiene con los verbos *ir, mandar, venir,* etc.

> Voy por el médico.   *(to get)*
> Viene por agua.

Para indicar razón o motivo de una acción.

> Pelean por la honra.
> No fui a la fiesta por falta de ropa.

Para indicar manera o medio.

> Él sacó el diente por la fuerza.
> El paquete llegó por correo.

Para indicar el agente de la voz pasiva.

> El cuento fue escrito por López y Fuentes.
> Los regalos fueron traídos por los Reyes.

Para indicar unidades de medidas o número.

> Los compro por docenas.
> Hay una rebaja de diez por ciento.

Para indicar el bienestar.

> Mis amigas preguntaron por ti, mamá.

Para indicar lo que queda por hacer en el futuro.

> Quedan varias cartas por escribir.

M Contesten a las siguientes preguntas según la indicación.

1 ¿Por dónde pasó Juanito? *las calles céntricas*
2 ¿Para dónde salió el señor? *México*
3 ¿Para cuándo quería regalos? *la Navidad*
4 ¿Por cuánto tiempo se quedó mirando los aparadores? *diez minutos*
5 ¿Por quién fuiste de compras? *mi esposo*
6 ¿Por dónde desfilan los soldados? *las grandes avenidas*
7 ¿Para quién es esta muñeca? *el niño*

N Completen las siguientes oraciones con *por* o *para*.

1 Los indios salieron _____ el cementerio.
2 Fueron allí _____ celebrar su cumpleaños.
3 Caminaron _____ el camino más corto.
4 Caminarán _____ muchas horas.
5 No quieren pasar _____ el centro de Quito.
6 Compraron dulces _____ sus niños.
7 Tienen que estar de vuelta _____ el lunes.
8 Algunos viejos viajaron _____ autobús.
9 Miraron tristemente _____ la ventana.
10 Comienzan sus planes _____ el próximo año.
11 El soldado luchó _____ la patria.
12 Está aquí _____ ganar más dinero.
13 Le pagaron poco _____ su trabajo.
14 _____ principiante trabaja bien.
15 Como su amigo está enfermo, ella hace las compras _____ él.
16 Compró las frutas _____ poco dinero.
17 El artículo fue publicado _____ un periodista.
18 Apretó el botón _____ parar el aparato.
19 Nos queda mucho _____ hacer mañana.
20 Los hijos obedecieron _____ miedo.
21 Fue _____ el cura.
22 Rezaron _____ varias horas.
23 Su pueblo fue destruido _____ el terremoto.

O Reemplacen la expresión en letra bastardilla con *por* o *para*.

1 Vinieron *en busca de* regalos.
2 El avión salió *con destino a* Veracruz.
3 Lo compré *con el propósito de* dárselo a Mariana.
4 *Siendo* brasileño, sabe mucho inglés.
5 No fuimos *a causa de* la lluvia.
6 Le pagó un dólar *a cambio de* un disfraz.
7 Cargué los paquetes *a favor de* la pobre señora.
8 Estuvimos allí *durante* una semana.

Voces de la Juventud

Si la juventud supiera y la vejez pudiera, ¿qué no consiguiera?

PARA PREPARAR LA ESCENA

Así como las costumbres de cada país son distintas y los puntos de vista cambian, la cultura de los jóvenes también varía.

Van cambiando con velocidad los tiempos y, con ellos, las reglas de comportamiento, las actitudes hacia la independencia personal, los modos de vestirse, de portarse, de verse. Es difícil mantenerse al corriente de todos estos cambios. Parece que hoy día los jóvenes están gritando:—¡Escúchennos! Hay que recordar que los jóvenes de hoy son los adultos de mañana, y que la sociedad no puede hacerse la sorda cuando habla la juventud.

En este cuadro suenan voces distintas con el propósito de acortar la distancia entre las generaciones.

Cuando las nubes cambian de nariz

Eduardo Criado

PARA PRESENTAR LA LECTURA

Juan es un hombre dinámico, tan preocupado con sus negocios y quehaceres que ni siquiera tiene un momento para interesarse en los problemas de la familia. Se preocupa sólo de lo suyo, está siempre activo, trabaja como una máquina, y es impaciente con los que lo rodean, aun con su propia familia. Nunca se ha dado tiempo para entenderla. Nunca se ha perdido en un momento de fantasía. Ni siquiera sabe dónde las vacas tienen las orejas o que «las nubes cambian de nariz».

Eduardo Criado ha escrito esta divertida comedia. En la escena que sigue, Jorge, el hijo de Juan, trata de comunicarse con su papá. Jorge quiere que su padre le ayude a resolver un problema. Con el propósito de hablarle a Juan, lo lleva en coche al despacho. Jorge es un muchacho de dieciocho años, nervioso, muy moderno.

PARA APRENDER VOCABULARIO

Palabras Clave

1 **cacharro**   auto u otro vehículo viejo y gastado *(jalopy)*
   ¡No vas a la fiesta en este cacharro!

2 **falla (fallar)**   no funciona *(misfires)*
   El auto tiene gasolina, pero le falla el carburador.

3 **funde (fundirse)**   se une, junta *(fuses, blends)*
   La música se funde con los ruidos de la calle.

4 **hojea (hojear)**   pasa las hojas de un libro, periódico, etc.
   El señor hojea el periódico buscando la sección comercial.

5 **titubea (titubear)**   vacila, no sabe qué hacer
   Una persona que titubea revela su falta de confianza en sí misma.

Práctica

Complete con una palabra de la lista.

cacharro   *hojea*   *funde*
falla   *titubea*

1 Ella _____ una revista en la sala de espera.
2 No arranca porque le _____ el motor.
3 Antes de hablar, _____ y pierde la oportunidad.
4 La plata no se _____ con el oro a esa temperatura.
5 Siempre me voy a acordar de mi primer coche; era un _____ con un carácter muy propio.

«Te doy las llaves del auto.»

Cuando las nubes cambian de nariz

Eduardo Criado

Acto I, Cuadro III: Automóvil en circulación

(Oscuro total. Entra música dinámica que funde con sonido de ambiente callejero. Coches que circulan. La luz va subiendo y vemos un asiento delantero de coche sobre el que están sentados, cara al público, Juan y Jorge. Juan hojea unos papeles y puntea unas notas. Jorge simula llevar el volante del coche imaginario que conduce.)

puntea escribe

Juan: *(viendo que corre demasiado)* ¡Eh, cuidado, chico!

No . . . velocidad *Don't you have the patron saint of speed on the dashboard?*

Jorge: No te preocupes, papá. No llevas en el tablier al Patrón de la velocidad?

Juan: Sí, pero tú ya sabes lo que dicen, ¿no? Que San Cristóbal sólo protege hasta los sesenta por hora.

Jorge: En nuestra época es ridículo, ¿no te parece? Con lo apasionante que es la velocidad. Pero no en coche. No tiene emoción. Lo bueno es que el viento te golpee la cara hasta endurecerte los músculos de frío. Sentir cómo te llena los pulmones el olor a gasolina y que el trepidar de la moto te llegue por los brazos al corazón. Un buen corredor ha de formar cuerpo con la máquina, papá. Entonces sí que hay emoción. Cuando coges una curva bien cerrada, cuando das gas apretando los dientes, cuando pasas dos a la vez, cuando doblas vuelta, créeme esa apasionante sensación es yendo en moto cuando más se nota. Ni en coche, ni siquiera en avioneta.

trepidar *shaking*
moto motocicleta
corredor motociclista

Juan: Pero, ¿tú has volado?

Jorge: En un cacharro que tiene Javier en el Prat. Lo que debe de ser interesante es pilotar un reactor. Quizá tenga ocasión en la «mili».

el Prat aeropuerto de Barcelona
reactor *jet*
«mili» servicio militar obligatorio

Juan: Depende del Arma a que te destinen.

Jorge: Ya he solicitado el ingreso en Milicias Aéreas.

Juan:	¡Ah! Entonces . . .
Jorge:	*(pausa)* Papá . . . , tú, cuando tienes algún problema, ¿cómo lo resuelves?
Juan:	¿Qué?
Jorge:	Que cómo resuelves tus problemas.
Juan:	De frente, hijo, de frente. Cuanto más grave, más rápida ha de ser la solución. No se debe acobardar uno nunca. En la vida, como en los negocios, se han de resolver los problemas con decisión, con rapidez. Y si es preciso, cortando por lo sano. Si el mundo va tan mal es porque hay mucha gente que titubea. Hay mucho Moreno suelto . . .
Jorge:	¿Mucho Moreno suelto?
Juan:	Es una frase que utilizamos Guillermo y yo. Moreno es un cliente nuestro que cuando tiene algún asunto urgente guarda la documentación en una carpeta especial. Al cabo de quince días la abre, y como el asunto ya ha dejado de ser urgente, puede resolverlo con calma. Hay mucho Moreno suelto, hijo. Y hoy, con calma, no se puede resolver nada. De frente y en directa. Si tienes diez problemas, resuelve hoy los diez. Te equivocarás en uno, en dos quizá; pero si quieres resolverlos con calma, cada día dejarás nueve pendientes de solución . . .
Jorge:	Es que yo . . .
Juan:	*(sonriente)* ¿Estás preocupado porque a tu máquina le falla una bujía o por los exámenes trimestrales? ¿No? ¡Je! A tu edad no se tienen problemas. Ya sabrás lo que son cuando seas hombre. *(cambiando el tono)* No te distraigas y cambia de marcha. Aquí ya puedes poner la directa. *(sigue escribiendo en sus papeles)*

acobardar *tener miedo*

cortando por lo sano *with a bold stroke*

carpeta *folder*

cambia de marcha *shift gears*
poner la directa *put on the directional signal*

PARA APLICAR

Comprensión

A Conteste a las siguientes preguntas.

1 ¿Dónde tiene lugar esta escena?
2 ¿Quién maneja?
3 ¿Qué hace el otro?

4 Cuando Juan se queja de la manera en que su hijo maneja, ¿cómo le contesta Jorge?
5 Describa lo que le encanta a Jorge.
6 ¿Cómo prefiere Jorge viajar?
7 ¿En qué Arma quiere hacer el servicio militar?
8 ¿Cómo resuelve Juan sus problemas?

9 ¿Cuál es la anécdota que Juan relata para expresar cómo resuelve los problemas un cliente suyo?

10 ¿Qué hizo el padre para ayudarle a su hijo?

B Complete las siguientes oraciones según la selección.

1 Juan y Jorge pasean en el _____.
2 Jorge está al _____ del coche.
3 En el tablero del coche hay una figurilla de _____.
4 Éste ofrece protección sólo hasta los _____.
5 A Jorge le anima la _____.
6 Es emocionante cuando _____.
7 De todos los medios de transporte su favorito es _____.
8 Cuando ingrese en la «mili» quiere entrar en las _____.
9 Juan dice que resuelve sus problemas _____.
10 Muchos problemas son causados por gente que _____.
11 Juan prefiere resolver problemas con rapidez, no con _____.
12 Jorge quiere hablar, pero su padre _____.
13 Juan se burla de su hijo creyendo que sus únicos problemas son _____ y _____.
14 A Juan le falta comprensión al decir _____.

Más Práctica

A Dé un sinónimo de las siguientes expresiones.

1 pasar páginas rápidamente
2 tener miedo
3 se une
4 acción del inseguro
5 temblar
6 no funciona

B Escriba siete oraciones usando los sinónimos del ejercicio A.

Ejercicios Creativos

1 ¿Por qué quería Jorge acompañar a su padre esa mañana? ¿Fue solamente para tener la ocasión de manejar el coche? ¿Logró Jorge hacer lo que quería?
2 ¿Cuál es la actitud del padre hacia su hijo? ¿Es comprensivo, interesado, amistoso?
3 ¿Cómo se sentiría Ud. si alguien que Ud. respeta le tratara así? Describa cómo deberían ser las relaciones entre padres e hijos.
4 ¿Cree Ud. que si Jorge le hubiera contado a Juan el problema que tenía, éste le hubiera ayudado a buscar una solución satisfactoria?
5 ¿Cómo resuelve Ud. sus problemas íntimos de carácter personal? ¿Tiene con quién hablar? ¿Cómo le ayuda esa persona?

Acabo de alistarme . . .

José Corrales Egea

PARA PRESENTAR LA LECTURA

Enrique está harto de la vida que tiene. Está aburrido. Acaba de tomar una decisión sumamente importante, y la toma a su manera. Ahora tiene que comunicar su decisión a la familia.

La selección es un episodio de *La otra cara* (1962), escrito por José Corrales Egea. El autor nos documenta la vida en España a mediados de este siglo y, con este trozo, subraya la voz de un joven de la época. Es una voz inquieta, impaciente, anhelosa, de un joven en conflicto con la generación de sus padres.

PARA APRENDER VOCABULARIO

Palabras Clave

1 **alistarme (alistarse)** inscribirme en el ejército
 No quiere ser reclutado. Va a alistarse para poder escoger el arma que le gusta.

2 **balbució (balbucir)** se expresó, se articuló con dificultad; tartamudeó
 La víctima del robo balbució una respuesta confusa.

3 **pasmo** asombro *(astonishment)*
 Irene puso cara de pasmo cuando ganó el premio.

4 **sordidez** estado de suciedad, de repugnancia, indecencia, pobreza fea

Tengo que arreglar y limpiar este despacho. No puedo mirar más esta sordidez.

Práctica

Complete con una palabra de la lista.

alistarse balbució pasmo sordidez

1 El nuevo alcalde tolera la _____ de las calles.
2 Al oir la noticia, el pobre _____ algo incoherente.
3 Después de un rato a Raimundo le pasó el _____ y se calmó.
4 En Israel, todas las mujeres tienen que _____ a los dieciocho años.

Acabo de alistarme . . .

José Corrales Egea

—¿Qué hora es ya?—interrogó don Leocadio.

—Las dos.

—¿Dónde se habrá metido Enrique? . . .

Por fin sonó el timbre de la puerta.

—Te estamos esperando.

—Os tengo dicho que cuando tarde no me esperéis; me apartáis la comida. . . . Si he llegado tan tarde es porque he estado haciendo algo importante.

—Algo importante, ¿no lo oís?—repitió con un tono burlón Irene.

Enrique la atravesó con la mirada. Lentamente dejó caer el secreto que llevaba en reserva:

Corea la guerra en Corea

—He ido a enterarme de si admiten voluntarios para Corea. . . .

—¿Qué estás diciendo?—exclamó la madre.

Enrique afectó un aire desdeñoso.

—Lo que acabáis de oir: he ido a enterarme de si admiten voluntarios para Corea.

—No veo lo que a ti te pueda importar esto.

—Ni yo.

—¿No? . . . Entonces es que no me habéis comprendido: he ido a apuntarme.

apuntarme alistarme

Irene puso cara de pasmo.

—Pero . . . ¿tú estás loco?

—¿Loco? Y ¿por qué?

La madre sacó el pañuelo. No podía articular palabra y hacía un esfuerzo para no prorrumpir en sollozos.

prorrumpir en *break into*

—¿Por qué has hecho esto?—balbució. Como si no hubiéramos pasado ya bastante . . .

—No sé por qué os ponéis así . . . Es una oportunidad para ver mundo y ganar dinero.

—Y para recibir un tiro también—añadió Irene.

—Vosotras las mujeres no comprendéis ciertas cosas.

—Claro los hombres sois de una especie superior—respondió, desdeñosa—, sobre todo cuando tenéis veinte años y la cabeza llena de grillos. . . .

—No comprendéis, no comprendéis . . .

Se cogió la cabeza entre las manos. Hablaba con desesperación, con la voz ronca:

—No queréis comprender que no soy un viejo como vosotros, que quiero vivir, vivir, ¿me habéis oído?, disfrutar de la vida. Para que lo sepáis: prefiero disfrutar dos años a vegetar cincuenta como vosotros, como todos vosotros . . . Sí: vegetar, mediocremente, vulgarmente, arrastrándoos por en medio de la pobretería, de la mezquindad, de la estrechez . . . Como gran diversión, una vez al mes al cine, a un cine de barrio naturalmente, de los baratos; como fiesta extraordinaria, medio litro de vino los domingos, para acompañar el cocido; para vestirse, un traje cada tres o cuatro años . . . No, no y no. Estoy harto, harto; quiero vivir, ¿me habéis oído? vivir . . .

Se levantó de la mesa. Le centelleaban las pupilas. Se le había alborotado el cabello y la garganta le escocía de gritar, seca de rabia. Le parecía que la existencia se le escapaba de las manos, para siempre e inútilmente, y que todos los que le rodeaban tenían la culpa.

—Metido aquí no llegaré nunca a nada . . . ¿Qué es lo que me proponéis? . . . Ser un empleado, un chupatintas, un maestro de escuela a lo sumo, como queréis vosotros . . . Yo no sirvo para esto; me horroriza toda esta sordidez, toda esta mezquindad. Antes de verme despreciado y convertido en un desgraciado como vosotros prefiero un tiro, como dice Irene. Mil veces antes . . .

cabeza . . . grillos *bats in the belfry*

mezquindad *pettiness*
estrechez falta de dinero

cocido *stew*

centelleaban brillaban
alborotado despeinado
escocía le dolía

chupatintas *pen pusher*

PARA APLICAR

Comprensión

A Conteste a las siguientes preguntas.

1 ¿A qué hora más o menos llegó Enrique a casa?

2 ¿Qué les había dicho Enrique?

3 ¿Qué ha estado haciendo Enrique?

4 ¿En qué tono le habló Irene?

5 ¿Qué secreto les reveló Enrique?

6 ¿Cómo se portó la madre?

7 ¿Qué edad tiene Enrique?

8 ¿Se quedó calmado Enrique?

9 ¿Qué no comprende su familia?

10 ¿Qué es lo que prefiere Enrique?

11 Describa cómo vive la familia.

12 ¿Cómo se nota que le molesta a Enrique que no lo comprendan?

13 ¿Por qué no quiere quedarse allí?

14 ¿Tiene miedo de un tiro?

B Escoja la expresión de la segunda lista (2) que completa
la idea empezada en la primera lista (1).

<table>
<tr><td colspan="2" align="center">**1**</td><td colspan="2" align="center">**2**</td></tr>
<tr><td>1</td><td>La familia estaba lista para comer cuando</td><td>a.</td><td>les chocó a todos y los dejó pasmados.</td></tr>
<tr><td>2</td><td>Enrique les había dicho</td><td>b.</td><td>en la cual pudiera vivir y escaparse de la mezquindad.</td></tr>
<tr><td>3</td><td>Llegó tarde porque</td><td>c.</td><td>que no lo esperaran; podrían guardarle la comida.</td></tr>
<tr><td>4</td><td>Esa noticia inesperada</td><td>d.</td><td>que le dolía la garganta.</td></tr>
<tr><td>5</td><td>Irene le habló en tono burlón y desdeñoso,</td><td>e.</td><td>Enrique llegó.</td></tr>
<tr><td>6</td><td>Enrique buscaba otra vida</td><td>f.</td><td>acusándolo de estar loco.</td></tr>
<tr><td>7</td><td>Les gritó tanto</td><td>g.</td><td>había acabado de alistarse como voluntario en la guerra de Corea.</td></tr>
</table>

Más Práctica

A Dé un sinónimo de las palabras en letra
bastardilla.

1   No se ha recuperado todavía del *asombro*.

2   *Con dificultad articuló* unas palabras.

3   Las estrellas *brillaban* en el cielo.

4   El hijo fue a *apuntarse* sin la aprobación de
sus padres.

5   Dominándose, trató de no *echarse a llorar*.

6   Quiere escaparse de la *repugnancia* de la
vida en ese lugar.

7   Su tono *irrespetuoso* ofendió a los padres.

B En las dos listas hay expresiones muy parecidas. Escoja
la expresión de la segunda lista (2) que haga juego con otra en
la primera lista (1).

1	**2**
1 ¿Dónde se habrá ido?	a. Puso cara de pasmo.
2 La miró intensamente.	b. Estás loco.
3 Fui a informarme de algo.	c. ¿Dónde se habrá metido?
4 Mostró gran sorpresa.	d. Puedes ser fusilado.
5 Tartamudeaba.	e. Le atravesó con la mirada.
6 Puedes recibir un tiro.	f. Metido aquí no llegaré a nada.
7 Tienes la cabeza llena de grillos.	g. La garganta le escocía de gritar.
8 Tenía el pelo desarreglado.	h. He ido a enterarme de algo.
9 Le dolía la garganta de gritar.	i. Se le había alborotado el cabello.
10 Viviendo aquí no llegaré a nada.	j. Balbucía.

Acaban de alistarse: nuevas astronautas

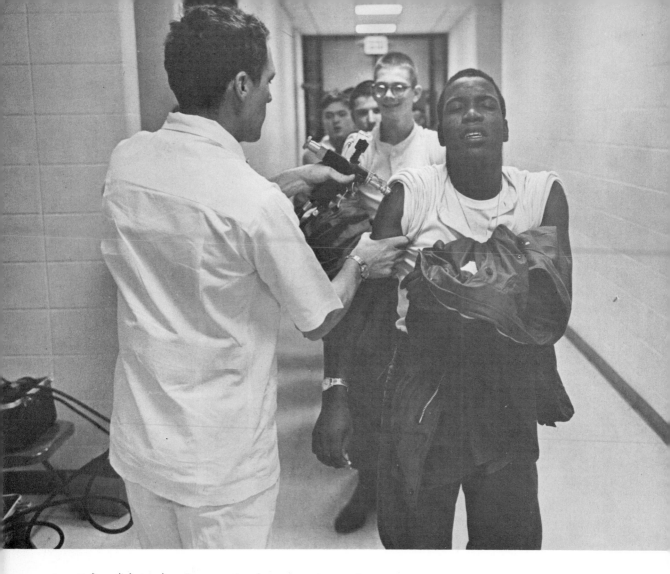

«. . . prefiero disfrutar dos años a vegetar cincuenta como vosotros . . .»

Ejercicios Creativos

1 Describa la actitud de la familia cuando llega Enrique. ¿Cómo lo tratan?

2 Examine las razones que motivaron a Enrique a alistarse. ¿Cree que esta decisión sea válida para siempre?

3 ¿Qué aspectos de la vida de sus padres son intolerables para el hijo? ¿Qué opina Ud. de lo que hizo?

4 Se incluyen aquí tres ideas para otro título. Escoja la que le guste más y explique por qué Ud. cree que es más apropiada.
    a. «Lo hice a mi manera»
    b. «Brecha de generaciones»
    c. «Desafiando a los padres»

5 ¿Reaccionarían los jóvenes de hoy como reaccionaba Enrique en esta selección?

Moda masculina

Francisco Baeza Linares

PARA PRESENTAR LA LECTURA

La selección que sigue fue escrita por Francisco Baeza Linares. Es un trozo de *Al otro lado de la montaña,* primer libro publicado por el autor. El libro es una crónica de una partida de pesca emprendida por cuatro personas de diversas edades.

En este trozo uno de los jóvenes desafía a los mayores. Dice que éstos no respetan a la juventud, que les quitan a los jóvenes las virtudes y les atribuyen los vicios, y que lo hacen sin tratar de comprender la voz de la juventud.

Esta vez estamos ante una voz rebelde que trata de justificar un nuevo estilo de comportamiento, que expresa los ideales de la juventud actual y que pide comprensión.

PARA APRENDER VOCABULARIO

Palabras Clave

1 **ahuyenten (ahuyentar)**   hagan desaparecer o huir una persona o algo
El curandero le dio una bebida para ahuyentar los malos espíritus.

2 **derrota**   destrucción total de un ejército
La batalla de Waterloo fue una derrota para las fuerzas de Napoleón.

3 **mugre**   suciedad, basura
¡Qué desorden hay aquí—mugre en todas partes!

4 **pende (pender)**   cuelga, se suspende
En octubre las manzanas penden de los árboles.

Práctica

Complete con una palabra de la lista.

derrota	mugre
ahuyentar	pende

1   Debes tratar de _____ lo desagradable del presente y del futuro.

2   La bandera de luto _____ de la ventana del palacio presidencial.

3   Después de un año de no vivir nadie aquí hay mucha _____ .

4   Con la llegada de tropas frescas evitaron la _____ que antes parecía inevitable.

Moda masculina

Francisco Baeza Linares

Le niegan Ustedes dicen que no tiene

—Acusan ustedes a la juventud de tantas cosas . . . De todas las cosas. Le niegan la totalidad de las virtudes y no dudan en atribuirle todos los vicios. Se muestran dispuestos no a condenarla sin juzgarla, sino sin siquiera oirla. Yo no pretendo, naturalmente, que se la debe absolver como norma general. Lo que sí quisiera pedir es comprensión: que hicieran un esfuerzo para llegar hasta ella. Que se dieran cuenta de que vivimos en un mundo muy distinto a aquél en que ustedes vivieron su juventud. Que precisamente por esta continua amenaza que pende sobre nuestras cabezas, por esta incertidumbre del vivir actual, la juventud no está dispuesta a frenar sus ansias de vida. Y quiere saborear el día, el minuto, ignorar la preocupación por un mañana incierto al que ni siquiera sabemos si se le va a permitir llegar . . .

ansias deseos vehementes

está . . . encuadrada está incluida

poco hombres falta de masculinidad

No toda la juventud está, por supuesto, encuadrada en esas tendencias de la moda masculina actual en que se apoyan ustedes principalmente para acusar a los jóvenes de hoy de poco hombres. Para ustedes estas tendencias y los que las siguen, representan a la juventud—aunque para mí no la representan en absoluto: son un aspecto, una parte, pero no el todo . . . Debe ser sin duda, que han olvidado ustedes las modas de su tiempo. No pueden compararse con las actuales, ni mucho menos, porque en las de ahora hay una clara tendencia a la comodidad, al trazo simple, a la pura necesidad, junto con un cierto tono de extravagancia en las formas y en los colores. Pero díganme ¿cuándo ha estado la juventud, como hoy lo está, tan totalmente volcada a sus tareas desde la niñez, trabajando en lo que se presente, tan dispuesta a ayudar? ¿Se han visto alguna vez tantos casi-niños como ahora hay con las manos manchadas, vistiendo monos espesos de mugre, con las caras sucias de polvo y de sudor? ¿Ha habido nunca tantas ganas de aprender como ahora

ni mucho menos *not by any means*
trazo líneas, estilo

volcada a sus tareas dedicada a su trabajo

monos *overalls*

se asee se lave
albañil *bricklayer*

les . . . hondo *they are deeply imbued with*

llevarlos *llevar los colores*

son . . . un puro estallido? *do you blow your stack?*

mordiente *gnawing*

hay? Y si es así ¿qué tiene de particular que cuando cesa todo lo que significa tarea, trabajo, esa juventud se asee y se arregle de modo que nadie pueda, a simple vista, distinguir un albañil de un estudiante? Si pueden, y no les preocupa, según yo pienso, un mañana que puede no llegar, ir envueltos en alegres colores que ahuyenten las sombras de su alrededor, esas sombras que tal vez les han calado ya hondo y están dentro de ellos y les duelen, aunque no lo sepamos, ¿por qué los que nos consideramos al margen, los que no podemos, o no nos atrevemos ya, por nuestra edad, a llevarlos, nos resistimos a permitir que esos colores nos contagien su alegría? Es que preferiríamos verles también a ellos ensombrecidos por ese poco de amargura que nosotros llevamos dentro, consecuencia de una derrota que es inútil que no queramos admitir . . .

Todo eso me lleva a preguntarles: ¿Qué tienen ustedes contra la juventud? ¿Qué es lo que hay en el fondo de su ser que les empuja a denigrarla? ¿Por qué son ustedes, cuando de esto se trata, un puro estallido? ¿De dónde les viene ese rencor mordiente con que la atacan? No pretenderán que, como premio, se les muestre amistad, deferencia, cariño. A lo sumo pueden esperar lo que se les da: indiferencia. La juventud no ignora, ni ataca, a quienes no la saben respetar. Se limita en dejarlos donde están.

PARA APLICAR

Comprensión

A Conteste a las siguientes preguntas.

1 ¿Dónde tiene lugar este episodio?
2 Según el que habla, ¿de qué les acusan los adultos a los jóvenes?
3 ¿Qué error cometen los adultos?
4 ¿Qué pide el joven que hagan los más grandes?
5 ¿Por qué no está dispuesta la juventud a frenar sus ansias de vida?
6 ¿Sobre qué basan sus quejas los adultos?
7 ¿Cómo es la moda masculina actual?
8 ¿Cómo son los jóvenes de hoy?
9 ¿Por qué optan por vestirse de colores alegres?

10 Si los adultos no tratan de conocer y comprender a los jóvenes, ¿qué pueden esperar de ellos?

B ¿Verdadero o falso?

1 Los adultos no reconocen lo bueno de los jóvenes.
2 Los adultos quieren ser justos en sus críticas de los jóvenes.
3 Los adultos se dan cuenta de que el mundo ha cambiado mucho desde que ellos mismos eran adolescentes.
4 Hay una amenaza que les quita a los jóvenes la seguridad de tener un futuro.

Moda de los años veinte

5 Básicamente los jóvenes buscan ropa extravagante.
6 La mayoría de los jóvenes están dedicados a trabajar, estudiar y ayudar.
7 Después de asearse y arreglarse se puede distinguir al albañil del estudiante.
8 Los colores que usan hacen la vida más alegre y ahuyentan dudas y sombras.
9 Los adultos se enojan al oir a los jóvenes, pero les muestran comprensión.

Más Práctica

A Escoja la palabra en cada grupo que no se relaciona con las otras.

1 asomarse, ahuyentar, desvanecerse, desaparecerse
2 jabón, limpio, asear, cocido
3 ruido, cañón, talla, estallido
4 incertidumbre, inseguridad, duda, muchedumbre
5 colgar, prender, pender, suspender

B Escoja la palabra entre paréntesis que completa la oración.

1 Había una espada que (pendía, servía) sobre la cabeza de Damocles.
2 Llenos de (intemperie, incertidumbre) vacilan en tomar una decisión.
3 Olvídense de (rencores, monos) y podremos gozar de una buena amistad.
4 Valiente y determinado (huyó, ahuyentó) sus sospechas y dudas.
5 Jamás se ha oído un (estallido, cariño) tan ruidoso.

Ejercicios Creativos

1 ¿Qué opina Ud. sobre las ansias de vida de la juventud? ¿Está Ud. de acuerdo con el autor?
2 ¿Cree que el mundo ha cambiado mucho desde que sus padres eran niños? ¿Cómo?
3 Basándose en su experiencia personal, ¿están los adultos en contra de la juventud? Explique y dé ejemplos.
4 Lea otra vez las últimas tres líneas de la selección. ¿Está Ud. de acuerdo? Si no, ¿cómo las cambiaría?

Revista *Life*, 1926

Los Posesivos

Los adjetivos posesivos son:

mi, mis	nuestro, nuestra, nuestros, nuestras
tu, tus	vuestro, vuestra, vuestros, vuestras
su, sus	su, sus

También pueden emplearse las siguientes formas:

mío, mía, míos, mías	nuestro, nuestra, nuestros, nuestras
tuyo, tuya, tuyos, tuyas	vuestro, vuestra, vuestros, vuestras
suyo, suya, suyos, suyas	suyo, suya, suyos, suyas

Los adjetivos posesivos concuerdan con lo poseído, no con el que lo posee. La forma más larga suele tener un significado especial.

mi amigo	*my friend*
un amigo mío	*a friend of mine*

Para formar el pronombre posesivo se emplea la forma larga del adjetivo más el artículo.

Tengo el mío, no el tuyo.
No sabe lo que ha hecho con las nuestras.

Es corriente omitir el artículo después del verbo *ser*.

Es mío, no tuyo.

A Contesten a las siguientes preguntas según la indicación.

1 ¿Dónde está tu padre? *en el coche*
2 ¿Dónde dejaste tus llaves? *en el bolsillo*
3 ¿Quién tiene tu cartera? *mi madre*
4 ¿De qué hablaste con tu padre? *del cacharro de Javier*
5 ¿Cuándo conversas con tu padre? *cuando lo llevo al trabajo*
6 ¿Cuál es su diversión favorita? *ir rápido en la moto*
7 ¿Por qué consulta él con su padre? *tiene un problema*
8 ¿Cómo resuelve sus problemas? *de frente y en directa*

B Sigan el modelo.

Los problemas de Jorge son insignificantes.

Sus problemas son insignificantes.

1 El coche de Marisol circula por la calle.
2 La diversión favorita del hijo es la velocidad.
3 El cacharro de Javier está en el garaje.
4 Los padres del joven son amables.

5 El cliente del comerciante es bastante excéntrico.
6 No sé dónde está la carpeta del señor Moreno.

C Sigan el modelo.

Es mi decisión.
Esta decisión es mía.

1 Es su motocicleta.
2 Es mi cacharro.
3 Son tus pañuelos.
4 Es mi carpeta.
5 Son sus problemas.
6 Es nuestro dinero.

D Contesten a las siguientes preguntas según el modelo.

¿Tienes tu bolsa?
Sí, tengo la mía.

1 ¿Quiere Ud. el abrigo?
2 ¿Tocas tu guitarra?
3 ¿Prefieren Uds. sus costumbres?
4 ¿Tienes mi libro?
5 ¿Buscan los señores sus billetes?
6 ¿Limpian ellos sus cuartos?

Los Demostrativos

Los adjetivos demostrativos son:

> este, esta, estos, estas
> ese, esa, esos, esas
> aquel, aquella, aquellos, aquellas

Los pronombres demostrativos son los mismos que los adjetivos, pero llevan acento.

> éste, ésta, éstos, éstas
> ése, ésa, ésos, ésas
> aquél, aquélla, aquéllos, aquéllas

Se emplea *este* para indicar lo que está cerca del hablante.

> Este libro que tengo es interesante.

Se emplea *ese* para indicar lo que está cerca de la persona a quien se dirige el hablante.

> Ese libro que tiene Ud. es interesante.

Se emplea *aquel* para indicar lo que está lejos de los dos.

> Aquel libro (allí en la mesa) es interesante.

A Sigan el modelo.

> *El libro que tengo es interesante.*
> *Este libro es interesante.*

1 Las figuritas que Ud. tiene son bonitas.
2 La moto que tengo puede correr muy rápido.
3 La bolsa que Ud. tiene cuesta mucho.
4 Las blusas elegantes que están allí en el escaparate son caras.
5 La camisa que tengo tiene muchos colores.
6 Las rosas que están allí en el jardín son preciosas.
7 La figurilla que tengo representa el patrón de la velocidad.

B Contesten a las siguientes preguntas según el modelo.

> *¿Quieres esta guitarra?*
> *No, no quiero ninguna.*
> *Ni ésta, ni ésa, ni aquélla.*

1 ¿Quieres este plato?
2 ¿Quieres estas maletas?
3 ¿Quieres esta moneda?
4 ¿Quieres estos cuadros?
5 ¿Quieres estos discos?

El de, la de, los de, las de

Suprimiendo el sustantivo, se puede convertir el sustantivo en pronombre. Estudien los siguientes ejemplos.

> El libro de Carmen es interesante.   El de Carmen es interesante.
> Las chicas de Río ganaron.   Las de Río ganaron.

C Contesten a las siguientes preguntas según el modelo.

> *¿Recibiste las tarjetas de Bárbara?*
> *Sí, recibí las de Bárbara.*

1 ¿Te gustan los rebozos de México?
2 ¿Es duro el trabajo de tu madre?
3 ¿Es guapo el chico de la camisa azul?
4 ¿Quieres comprar las camisas de colores vivos?
5 ¿Te impresionó la fiesta del domingo?
6 ¿Son más pequeñas las motos de ellas?
7 ¿Son los mejores los jóvenes de hoy?
8 ¿Es más importante el examen de mañana?

Pronombres Relativos

masculino	femenino	neutro
que	que	lo que
quien, quienes	quien, quienes	
el que, los que	la que, las que	
el cual, los cuales	la cual, las cuales	lo cual
cuyo, cuyos	cuya, cuyas	

El Pronombre *Que*

Un pronombre relativo une dos palabras o dos grupos de palabras que tienen algo en común. Pertenece al segundo y se refiere al primero, que se llama el antecedente. El relativo más común es *que*. Se refiere tanto a personas como a cosas. Se emplea como sujeto o complemento de la cláusula subordinada.

> La mujer que acaba de entrar me trajo la llave que yo quería.

Si una preposición precede el relativo, *que* puede referirse sólo a cosas.

Las ciencias a que me dedico son muy importantes.

A Sustituyan según el modelo.

> *El tráfico que oí a la una me despertó.*
> *el ruido/*
> *El ruido que oí a la una me despertó.*

1 El ruido que oí a la una me despertó.
la moto/el grito/la música/el avión/el cacharro/

2 Vimos una película que nos emocionó.
un programa de televisión/una escena trágica/un drama clásico/una reunión/

B Sigan el modelo.

> *La conversación es frustrante. Tiene lugar en el coche.*
>
> *La conversación que tiene lugar en el coche es frustrante.*

1 La señora es dinámica. Tiene éxito en sus negocios.
2 El padre siempre está de viaje. Presta poca atención a su hijo.
3 La hija quiere consultar con su padre. Tiene un problema serio.
4 La moto no quiere andar. No tiene gasolina.
5 La moto está descompuesta ahora. Antes iba a más de sesenta.
6 La cliente guarda la documentación en una carpeta. No quiere enfrentarse con el problema.

El Pronombre *Quien*

Quien se refiere sólo a personas y concuerda con su antecedente en número. Por lo general una preposición va delante: *a, de, con, por, para, sin, tras.*

Moreno es el cliente de quien me habló.

Cuando se usa impersonalmente, quiere decir *he* or *she who, the one who, those who, whoever.*

Quien estudia aprende.

C Sustituyan según el modelo.

> *La niña de quien hablé acaba de irse.*
> *a quien saludaste/*
> *La niña a quien saludaste acaba de irse.*

1 La niña a quien saludaste acaba de irse.
para quien aparté la comida/con quien fuiste al cine/tras quien andábamos/por quien preguntaron los otros/en quien confiaste/

D Sigan el modelo.

> *La señora salió de su despacho. La conociste ayer.*
>
> *La señora a quien conociste ayer salió de su despacho.*

1 El hijo se enojó. Estás de acuerdo con él.
2 Enrique ha estado haciendo algo importante. Saqué varias fotos de él.

3 Tu amiga afectó un aire desdeñoso. Su madre le gritaba ayer.
4 La mujer acaba de alistarse. Estudié con ella.
5 Los padres pobres ya se sienten mejor. Hicimos los arreglos para ellos.
6 La empleada llegó hace cinco minutos. Te fuiste sin ella.

E Sigan el modelo.

> *El que come bien, sano es.*
> *Quien come bien, sano es.*

1 El que estudia, aprende.
2 El que no sabe eso, es ignorante.
3 El que mucho juega, poco trabaja.
4 El que busca, encuentra.
5 Los que creen eso van a ser felices.

Los Pronombres *El Que, El Cual*

Se usan los relativos *el que, los que, la que, las que* o *el cual, los cuales, la cual, las cuales* con las siguientes preposiciones:

Después de preposiciones de dos sílabas o más: *acerca de, contra, detrás de, delante de* etc. (Con las preposiciones *a* o *de* forman las contracciones *al que, al cual, del que, del cual*.)

> Las motos, detrás de las cuales corren los niños, son nuevas.

Después de las preposiciones *por* y *para*.

> El edificio, por el cual anduvimos, es el Edificio Chapa.

F Sigan el modelo.

> *El coche iba despacio por la calle. Adentro estaban madre e hija.*
>
> *El coche, adentro del cual estaban madre e hija, iba despacio por la calle.*

1 Fui a la esquina. Desde allí vi la circulación del tráfico.
2 La ciudad es bonita. Hay murallas alrededor de la ciudad.
3 El edificio queda en una avenida grande. Cerca del edificio hay un parque.

El Pronombre *Cuyo*

El pronombre *cuyo* significa "whose." Concuerda con lo poseído, no con el que lo posee.

> El hombre de negocios, cuyo chofer lo acompaña, trabaja mucho.

G Sigan el modelo.

> *Enrique está harto de la miseria. Su sorpresa fue inesperada.*
>
> *Enrique, cuya sorpresa fue inesperada, está harto de la miseria.*

1 Enrique llegó tarde. Su madre le guardaba la comida.
2 Los jóvenes son más valientes que nunca. Sus virtudes son grandes.
3 El albañil se lavó después del trabajo. Sus uñas estaban llenas de mugre.
4 Los mayores se enojan al ver la nueva moda. Sus ideas son anticuadas.
5 Rita esperaba unos buenos consejos. Su padre no le hacía caso.
6 La madre comienza a llorar. Su hijo se va a la guerra.

Los Pronombres *Lo Que, Lo Cual*

Lo que y *lo cual* son formas neutras que no se refieren a ninguna persona u objeto, sino a una idea o concepto.

> Se dedicó a sus estudios, lo que (lo cual) nos agradó mucho.

Puede referirse también a una acción, actitud o situación.

> Hace días que mis alumnos no vienen a clase, lo cual me tiene muy deprimido.
> Paula no le quiere hablar a nadie, lo que me parece muy mal.
> La economía de este país empeora día a día, lo cual debe preocupar a todos.

H Sigan el modelo.

> *No dijo nada. Me sorprendió.*
> *No dijo nada, lo que me sorprendió.*
> *No dijo nada, lo cual me sorprendió.*

1 Enrique llegó tarde. Nos enojó.
2 Se fue sin despedirse. Me pareció una falta de cortesía.
3 La llevó a ver el escaparate. Le agradó mucho.
4 Les saludó cordialmente. Era correcto.
5 Los jóvenes llevaban camisas de muchos colores. Produjo una risa burlona del viejo.
6 El albañil trabajaba bien. Le gustó al capataz.

I Completen las siguientes oraciones con el pronombre relativo apropiado.

1 El cielo era oscuro, _____ hizo lucir más los letreros iluminados.
2 Tuve que pagar las entradas al cine, _____ eran baratas.
3 El autor de _____ hablo se llama Baeza Linares.
4 Las tradiciones de los españoles, _____ se vuelven locos en sus fiestas, son interesantes.
5 _____ vea a los jóvenes se quedará contento.
6 Alquilé un cuarto en _____ pasé mucho tiempo.
7 Me acerqué a una señorita _____ cara parecía conocida.
8 Las fábricas, algunas de _____ emplean a cientos de trabajadores, estaban cerradas.
9 Yo quiero ver de nuevo la placita cerca de _____ me esperabas.
10 El tren _____ llegó tarde debe estar en el taller de reparaciones.
11 Los jóvenes, _____ ropa de trabajo tenía manchas, se cambiaron y se arreglaron.
12 La madre, _____ es muy generosa, ofreció su ayuda.
13 Yo sé _____ piensas.
14 _____ haya visto esa comedia te dirá lo mismo.

Los Tiempos Compuestos

Indicativo

Los tiempos compuestos se forman con el tiempo apropiado del auxiliar *haber* y el participio pasado. El participio pasado de los verbos de la primera conjugación termina en *–ado*; el de los verbos de las segunda y tercera conjugaciones termina en *–ido*.

infinitivo	participio pasado	infinitivo	participio pasado
hablar	hablado	vender	vendido
mirar	mirado	vivir	vivido
comer	comido	salir	salido

Los siguientes verbos tienen participio pasado irregular:

infinitivo	participio pasado	infinitivo	participio pasado
abrir	abierto	morir	muerto
cubrir	cubierto	poner	puesto
decir	dicho	romper	roto
escribir	escrito	resolver	resuelto
freir	frito	ver	visto
hacer	hecho	volver	vuelto

El presente perfecto se forma con el presente del verbo *haber* y el participio pasado. Se emplea para expresar una acción terminada en el pasado reciente.

hablar

he hablado	hemos hablado
has hablado	habéis hablado
ha hablado	han hablado

Lo he discutido con él esta mañana.
No sé si se han ido.

El pluscuamperfecto se forma con el imperfecto del verbo *haber* y el participio pasado. Se emplea para expresar una acción pasada terminada anteriormente a otra acción pasada.

comer

había comido	habíamos comido
habías comido	habíais comido
había comido	habían comido

Ella había comido (a las doce) antes de que llegáramos
(a la una).
Ellos habían terminado (el martes) cuando yo los vi
(el miércoles).

El futuro perfecto se forma con el futuro del verbo *haber* y el participio pasado. Se emplea para expresar una acción futura terminada anteriormente a otra acción futura.

salir

habré salido	habremos salido
habrás salido	habréis salido
habrá salido	habrán salido

Ellos habrán salido antes de que lleguemos.
Yo habré empezado cuando tú vengas.

El condicional perfecto se forma con el condicional del verbo *haber* y el participio pasado. Se emplea para expresar lo que habría ocurrido si no fuera por otra cosa que lo interrumpió o prohibió.

escribir

habría escrito	habríamos escrito
habrías escrito	habríais escrito
habría escrito	habrían escrito

Él habría hecho el viaje pero no pudo porque no tenía suficiente dinero.

A Sustituyan según el modelo.

Nosotros hemos salido muy tarde.
comido/
Nosotros hemos comido muy tarde.

1 Nosotros hemos salido muy tarde.
llegado/terminado/ido/concluido/
empezado/
2 Ellos han empezado las ceremonias.
él/los indios/tú/nosotros/yo/

B Contesten a las siguientes preguntas según el modelo.

> *¿Lo vio Ud.?*
> *No, todavía no he visto nada.*

1 ¿Lo hizo la jefa?
2 ¿Lo terminó Felipe?
3 ¿Lo explicó la profesora?
4 ¿Lo leyeron Uds.?
5 ¿Lo reclamó la monja?
6 ¿Lo amarró el niño?
7 ¿Lo intentó el borracho?
8 ¿Lo desarmó el policía?
9 ¿Lo volteó la obrera?

C Sustituyan según el modelo.

> *La chica había manejado el coche.*
> *vendido/*
> *La chica había vendido el coche.*

1 La chica había manejado el coche.
   arreglado/usado/visto/comprado/
   adelantado/
2 El niño no había podido abrir los ojos.
   la pobre vieja/Jorge y Nicolás/yo/Uds./
   tú/

D Contesten a las siguientes preguntas según el modelo.

> *¿Qué dijo Ana?* verlo ayer
> *Ana dijo que lo había visto ayer.*

1 ¿En que insistió María? *llover ayer*
2 ¿Por qué pareció distinto el chico?
   cortarse el pelo
3 ¿Por qué no aprobó el examen la
   estudiante? *no estudiar bastante*
4 ¿Por qué estaba cansado hoy? *no
   dormir bien anoche*
5 ¿Por qué castigó el padre a la niña?
   ser mala

E Sustituyan según el modelo.

> *Para mañana lo habré terminado.*
> *hecho/*
> *Para mañana lo habré. hecho.*

1 Para mañana lo habré terminado.
   conseguido/pedido/contestado/
   acabado/examinado/
2 Ellos ya habrán salido.
   Isabel/yo/Uds./mis padres/tú/nosotros/

F Contesten a las siguientes preguntas según el modelo.

> *¿Terminarás la lección antes del
>   lunes?*
> *Sí, ya habré terminado la lección.*

1 ¿Anunciarán el resultado de la elección
   antes de las ocho?
2 ¿Irás a Bogotá el año que viene?
3 ¿Vendrás a visitarme antes de la semana
   que viene?
4 ¿Comprarán un coche antes de
   septiembre?
5 ¿Me llamarás por teléfono antes del
   lunes?

G Sustituyan según el modelo.

> *Yo no lo habría pagado.*
> *dicho/*
> *Yo no lo habría dicho.*

1 Yo no lo habría pagado.
   hecho/conseguido/llevado/comido/
   querido/puesto/ocultado/
2 Ellas no habrían podido asistir.
   los actores/tú/nosotros/yo/Uds./ella/

H Contesten a las siguientes preguntas según el modelo.

> *¿Asistió Ud. a la escuela el sábado?*
> *No, nunca habría asistido a la escuela el sábado.*

1 ¿Te permitió tu madre ir al baile?

2 ¿Fue María al cine con Jorge?
3 ¿Empezaron las ceremonias a las ocho?
4 ¿Hablaron Uds. por teléfono por tanto tiempo?
5 ¿Terminaste tu trabajo para hoy?
6 ¿Escribiste el ensayo sobre ese tema?

Subjuntivo

El presente perfecto del subjuntivo se forma con el presente del subjuntivo del verbo *haber* y el participio pasado. Se emplea en una cláusula que requiere el subjuntivo cuando la acción de la cláusula está en el pasado.

descubrir	
haya descubierto	hayamos descubierto
hayas descubierto	hayáis descubierto
haya descubierto	hayan descubierto

Dudo que ellos hayan llegado.
Es posible que él lo haya hecho.

El pluscuamperfecto del subjuntivo se forma con el imperfecto del subjuntivo del verbo *haber* y el participio pasado. Se emplea en una cláusula que requiere el subjuntivo cuando el verbo de la cláusula principal está en el pasado o condicional y la acción de la cláusula se ha realizado antes de la de la cláusula principal.

volver	
hubiera vuelto	hubiéramos vuelto
hubieras vuelto	hubiérais vuelto
hubiera vuelto	hubieran vuelto

Dudó que nosotros lo hubiéramos sabido.
Tuve miedo de que tú lo hubieras hecho.

I Sustituyan según el modelo.

> Es lástima que la niña haya sufrido.
> muerto/
> Es lástima que la niña haya muerto.

1 Es lástima que la niña haya sufrido.
desfallecido/roto la pierna/llorado/gritado/caído/

2 ¿Es posible que los padres lo hayan comprobado?
las feministas/tú/el gerente/nosotros/Uds./yo/

J Contesten a las siguientes preguntas según la indicación.

1 ¿Han comprendido bien ellos? *no, no creo*

2 ¿Ha usado ella el puñal? *no, no es posible*

3 ¿Se ha adelantado él en su carrera? *dudo*

4 ¿No se han destacado ellas en los estudios? *es lástima*

5 ¿Ha engañado ella a su padre? *es imposible*

K Sustituyan según el modelo.

> Temíamos que Ana hubiera muerto.
> llorado/
> Temíamos que Ana hubiera llorado.

1 Temíamos que Ana hubiera muerto.
sufrido/vuelto/pecado/recordado/salido/

2 El padre se sintió como si se hubiera enriquecido de repente.
nosotros/la madre/yo/Margot y Arturo/tú/

L Sigan el modelo.

> Ocurrió algo extraordinario.
> Ojalá que hubiera ocurrido algo extraordinario.

1 El predicador habló con firmeza.
2 La hija siguió una carrera bien interesante.
3 Tiene libros de español en su casa.
4 Ocultaron el dinero en un lugar secreto.
5 Cobró mucha fama escribiendo tal libro.

Cláusulas con *Si*

Las cláusulas que empiezan con *si* se emplean para expresar una acción que sea contraria a la realidad. Estas cláusulas exigen una concordancia especial de tiempos.

cláusula principal	cláusula con *si*
futuro	presente del indicativo
condicional	imperfecto del subjuntivo
condicional perfecto	pluscuamperfecto del subjuntivo

> Si puedo, lo haré.
> Si pudiera, lo haría.
> Si hubiera podido, lo habría hecho.

M Sustituyan según el modelo.

> *Si quieres, la confesaré.*
> *mandas/*
> *Si mandas, la confesaré.*

1 Si quieres, la confesaré.
deseas/escuchas/dejas de hablar/me haces caso/

2 Si prometo, lo haré.
lo cumpliré/no lo negaré/te ayudaré/lo buscaré/

3 Si supiera la respuesta, te lo diría.
quisiera ir/supiera la verdad/estuviera lloviendo/pudiera ir/quisiera confesarme/

4 Si no llegaran las enfermeras, no habría manera de resolver el problema.
nosotros/los exigentes/el jefe/yo/la doctora/

5 Si no hubiéramos considerado la fecha, la empresa habría fracasado.
pensado en/recordado/establecido/insistido en/prescindido/

N Sigan el modelo.

> *Prometo hacerlo. Lo hago.*
> *Si hubiera prometido hacerlo, lo*
> *habría hecho.*

1 Le oigo hablar. Me sorprende menos.
2 Él no establece su mandamiento. Los resultados son diferentes.

3 El niño no muere. El padre se siente completamente feliz.
4 No quiero hablar delante del sacerdote. Le suplico que salga por un momento.

O Contesten a las siguientes preguntas según la indicación.

1 ¿Vas a la fiesta? *si Uds. me invitan*
2 ¿Deja solo la niña a su padre? *si la niña muriera*
3 ¿Lo dicen Uds.? *si hubiéramos sabido algo de ella*
4 ¿Pasamos un buen rato? *si tuviéramos algo de beber*
5 ¿Visitan aquel barrio? *si tienen tiempo*

P Sigan el modelo.

> *Si yo voy, él irá.*
> *Si yo fuera, él iría.*
> *Si yo hubiera ido, él habría ido.*

1 Si hablan un lenguaje extraño, nadie los comprenderá.
2 Si agregan una mezcla de frutas, nos gustará más.
3 Si lanzas la flecha, podrás hacer daño a alguien.
4 Si estudias esa carrera, tendrás éxito.
5 Si nos despedimos ahora, llegaremos a casa antes de las cinco.

VERBOS

REGULAR VERBS

Infinitive	**hablar**	**comer**	**vivir**
	to speak	*to eat*	*to live*
Present Participle	hablando	comiendo	viviendo
Past Participle	hablado	comido	vivido

SIMPLE TENSES

Indicative

Present	hablo	como	vivo
	hablas	comes	vives
	habla	come	vive
	hablamos	comemos	vivimos
	habláis	coméis	vivís
	hablan	comen	viven
Imperfect	hablaba	comía	vivía
	hablabas	comías	vivías
	hablaba	comía	vivía
	hablábamos	comíamos	vivíamos
	hablabais	comíais	vivíais
	hablaban	comían	vivían
Preterite	hablé	comí	viví
	hablaste	comiste	viviste
	habló	comió	vivió
	hablamos	comimos	vivimos
	hablasteis	comisteis	vivisteis
	hablaron	comieron	vivieron

Future	hablaré	comeré	viviré
	hablarás	comerás	vivirás
	hablará	comerá	vivirá
	hablaremos	comeremos	viviremos
	hablaréis	comeréis	viviréis
	hablarán	comerán	vivirán
Conditional	hablaría	comería	viviría
	hablarías	comerías	vivirías
	hablaría	comería	viviría
	hablaríamos	comeríamos	viviríamos
	hablaríais	comeríais	viviríais
	hablarían	comerían	vivirían

Subjunctive

Present	hable	coma	viva
	hables	comas	vivas
	hable	coma	viva
	hablemos	comamos	vivamos
	habléis	comáis	viváis
	hablen	coman	vivan
Imperfect	hablara	comiera	viviera
	hablaras	comieras	vivieras
	hablara	comiera	viviera
	habláramos	comiéramos	viviéramos
	hablarais	comierais	vivierais
	hablaran	comieran	vivieran

COMPOUND TENSES

Indicative

Present	he			
	has			
	ha	hablado	comido	vivido
	hemos			
	habéis			
	han			
Pluperfect	había			
	habías			
	había	hablado	comido	vivido
	habíamos			
	habíais			
	habían			

Future	habré			
	habrás			
	habrá			
	habremos	hablado	comido	vivido
	habréis			
	habrán			
Conditional	habría			
	habrías			
	habría			
	habríamos	hablado	comido	vivido
	habríais			
	habrían			

Subjunctive

Present	haya			
	hayas			
	haya			
	hayamos	hablado	comido	vivido
	hayáis			
	hayan			
Pluperfect	hubiera			
	hubieras			
	hubiera			
	hubiéramos	hablado	comido	vivido
	hubierais			
	hubieran			

DIRECT COMMANDS

Informal
(*tú* and *vosotros* forms)

Affirmative	habla (tú)	come (tú)	vive (tú)
	hablad	comed	vivid
Negative	no hables	no comas	no vivas
	no habléis	no comáis	no viváis

Formal

hable Ud.	coma Ud.	viva Ud.
hablen Uds.	coman Uds.	vivan Uds.

STEM-CHANGING VERBS

FIRST CLASS

	—ar verbs		—er verbs	
	$e \rightarrow ie$	$o \rightarrow ue$	$e \rightarrow ie$	$o \rightarrow ue$
Infinitive	**sentar**[1]	**contar**[2]	**perder**[3]	**soler**[4]
	to seat	to tell	to lose	to be accustomed
Present Participle	sentando	contando	perdiendo	soliendo
Past Participle	sentado	contado	perdido	solido

Indicative

Present	siento	cuento	pierdo	suelo
	sientas	cuentas	pierdes	sueles
	sienta	cuenta	pierde	suele
	sentamos	contamos	perdemos	solemos
	sentáis	contáis	perdéis	soléis
	sientan	cuentan	pierden	suelen

Subjunctive

Present	siente	cuente	pierda	suela
	sientes	cuentes	pierdas	suelas
	siente	cuente	pierda	suela
	sentemos	contemos	perdamos	solamos
	sentéis	contéis	perdáis	soláis
	sienten	cuenten	pierdan	suelan

[1] *Cerrar, comenzar, despertar, empezar,* and *pensar* are similar.
[2] *Acordar, acostar, almorzar, apostar, colgar, costar, encontrar, jugar, mostrar, probar, recordar, rogar,* and *volar* are similar.
[3] *Defender* and *entender* are similar.
[4] *Disolver, doler, envolver, llover,* and *volver* are similar.

SECOND AND THIRD CLASSES

	second class		third class
	$e \rightarrow ie, i$	$o \rightarrow ue, u$	$e \rightarrow i, i$
Infinitive	**sentir**[5]	**morir**[6]	**pedir**[7]
	to regret	*to die*	*to ask for, to request*
Present Participle	sintiendo	muriendo	pidiendo
Past Participle	sentido	muerto	pedido

Indicative

Present	siento	muero	pido
	sientes	mueres	pides
	siente	muere	pide
	sentimos	morimos	pedimos
	sentís	morís	pedís
	sienten	mueren	piden
Preterite	sentí	morí	pedí
	sentiste	moriste	pediste
	sintió	murió	pidió
	sentimos	morimos	pedimos
	sentisteis	moristeis	pedisteis
	sintieron	murieron	pidieron

Subjunctive

Present	sienta	muera	pida
	sientas	mueras	pidas
	sienta	muera	pida
	sintamos	muramos	pidamos
	sintáis	muráis	pidáis
	sientan	mueran	pidan
Imperfect	sintiera	muriera	pidiera
	sintieras	murieras	pidieras
	sintiera	muriera	pidiera
	sintiéramos	muriéramos	pidiéramos
	sintierais	murierais	pidierais
	sintieran	murieran	pidieran

[5] *Mentir, preferir,* and *sugerir* are similar.
[6] *Dormir* is similar; however, the past participle is regular—*dormido.*
[7] *Conseguir, despedir, elegir, medir, perseguir, reir, repetir, seguir,* and *servir* are similar.

IRREGULAR VERBS

andar   *to walk, to go*

Preterite   anduve, anduviste, anduvo, anduvimos, anduvisteis, anduvieron

caber   *to fit*

Present Indicative   quepo, cabes, cabe, cabemos, cabéis, caben

Preterite   cupe, cupiste, cupo, cupimos, cupisteis, cupieron

Future   cabré, cabrás, cabrá, cabremos, cabréis, cabrán

Conditional   cabría, cabrías, cabría, cabríamos, cabríais, cabrían

caer[8]   *to fall*

Present Indicative   caigo, caes, cae, caemos, caéis, caen

conocer   *to know, to be acquainted with*

Present Indicative   conozco, conoces, conoce, conocemos, conocéis, conocen

dar   *to give*

Present Indicative   doy, das, da, damos, dais, dan

Present Subjunctive   dé, des, dé, demos, deis, den

Preterite   di, diste, dio, dimos, disteis, dieron

[8] Spelling changes are found in the present participle—*cayendo;* past participle—*caído;* and preterite—*caíste, cayó, caímos, caísteis, cayeron.*

decir   *to say, to tell*

Present Participle	diciendo
Past Participle	dicho
Present Indicative	digo, dices, dice, decimos, decís, dicen
Preterite	dije, dijiste, dijo, dijimos, dijisteis, dijeron
Future	diré, dirás, dirá, diremos, diréis, dirán
Conditional	diría, dirías, diría, diríamos, diríais, dirían
Direct Command	di (tú)

estar   *to be*

Present Indicative	estoy, estás, está, estamos, estáis, están
Present Subjunctive	esté, estés, esté, estemos, estéis, estén
Preterite	estuve, estuviste, estuvo, estuvimos, estuvisteis, estuvieron

haber   *to have*

Present Indicative	he, has, ha, hemos, habéis, han
Present Subjunctive	haya, hayas, haya, hayamos, hayáis, hayan
Preterite	hube, hubiste, hubo, hubimos, hubisteis, hubieron
Future	habré, habrás, habrá, habremos, habréis, habrán
Conditional	habría, habrías, habría, habríamos, habríais, habrían

hacer   *to do, to make*

Past Participle	hecho
Present Indicative	hago, haces, hace, hacemos, hacéis, hacen
Preterite	hice, hiciste, hizo, hicimos, hicisteis, hicieron
Future	haré, harás, hará, haremos, haréis, harán
Conditional	haría, harías, haría, haríamos, haríais, harían
Direct Command	haz (tú)

incluir[9]   *to include*

Present Indicative	incluyo, incluyes, incluye, incluimos, incluís, incluyen

[9] Spelling changes are found in the present participle—*incluyendo*; and preterite—*incluyó, incluyeron*. Similar are *atribuir, constituir, contribuir, distribuir, fluir, huir, influir,* and *sustituir.*

ir[10]   *to go*

Present Indicative	voy, vas, va, vamos, vais, van
Present Subjunctive	vaya, vayas, vaya, vayamos, vayáis, vayan
Imperfect Indicative	iba, ibas, iba, íbamos, ibais, iban
Preterite	fui, fuiste, fue, fuimos, fuisteis, fueron
Direct Command	vé (tú)

oir[11]   *to hear*

Present Indicative	oigo, oyes, oye, oímos, oís, oyen

poder   *to be able*

Present Participle	pudiendo
Preterite	pude, pudiste, pudo, pudimos, pudisteis, pudieron
Future	podré, podrás, podrá, podremos, podréis, podrán
Conditional	podría, podrías, podría, podríamos, podríais, podrían

poner   *to put, to place*

Past Participle	puesto
Present Indicative	pongo, pones, pone, ponemos, ponéis, ponen
Preterite	puse, pusiste, puso, pusimos, pusisteis, pusieron
Future	pondré, pondrás, pondrá, pondremos, pondréis, pondrán
Conditional	pondría, pondrías, pondría, pondríamos, pondríais, pondrían
Direct Command	pon (tú)

producir   *to produce*

Present Indicative	produzco, produces, produce, producimos, producís, producen
Preterite	produje, produjiste, produjo, produjimos, produjisteis, produjeron

[10] A spelling change is found in the present participle—*yendo.*
[11] Spelling changes are found in the present participle—*oyendo;* past participle—*oído;* and preterite—*oíste, oyó, oímos, oísteis, oyeron.*

querer *to wish, to want*

Preterite   quise, quisiste, quiso, quisimos, quisisteis, quisieron

Future   querré, querrás, querrá, querremos, querréis, querrán

Conditional   querría, querrías, querría, querríamos, querríais, querrían

saber *to know*

Present Indicative   sé, sabes, sabe, sabemos, sabéis, saben

Present Subjunctive   sepa, sepas, sepa, sepamos, sepáis, sepan

Preterite   supe, supiste, supo, supimos, supisteis, supieron

Future   sabré, sabrás, sabrá, sabremos, sabréis, sabrán

Conditional   sabría, sabrías, sabría, sabríamos, sabríais, sabrían

salir *to leave, to go out*

Present Indicative   salgo, sales, sale, salimos, salis, salen

Future   saldré, saldrás, saldrá, saldremos, saldréis, saldrán

Conditional   saldría, saldrías, saldría, saldríamos, saldríais, saldrían

Direct Command   sal (tú)

ser *to be*

Present Indicative   soy, eres, es, somos, sois, son

Present Subjunctive   sea, seas, sea, seamos, seáis, sean

Imperfect Indicative   era, eras, era, éramos, erais, eran

Preterite   fui, fuiste, fue, fuimos, fuisteis, fueron

Direct Command   sé (tú)

tener *to have*

Present Indicative   tengo, tienes, tiene, tenemos, tenéis, tienen

Preterite   tuve, tuviste, tuvo, tuvimos, tuvisteis, tuvieron

Future   tendré, tendrás, tendrá, tendremos, tendréis, tendrán

Conditional   tendría, tendrías, tendría, tendríamos, tendríais, tendrían

Direct Command   ten (tú)

traer[12]   *to bring*

Present Indicative	traigo, traes, trae, traemos, traéis, traen
Preterite	traje, trajiste, trajo, trajimos, trajisteis, trajeron

valer   *to be worth*

Present Indicative	valgo, vales, vale, valemos, valéis, valen
Future	valdré, valdrás, valdrá, valdremos, valdréis, valdrán
Conditional	valdría, valdrías, valdría, valdríamos, valdríais, valdrían

venir   *to come*

Present Participle	viniendo
Present Indicative	vengo, vienes, viene, venimos, venís, vienen
Preterite	vine, viniste, vino, vinimos, vinisteis, vinieron
Future	vendré, vendrás, vendrá, vendremos, vendréis, vendrán
Conditional	vendría, vendrías, vendría, vendríamos, vendríais, vendrían
Direct Command	ven (tú)

ver[13]   *to see*

Past Participle	visto
Present Indicative	veo, ves, ve, vemos, veis, ven
Imperfect Indicative	veía, veías, veía, veíamos, veíais, veían

[12] Spelling changes are found in the present participle—*trayendo;* and past participle—*traído.*

[13] Spelling changes are found in the preterite—*vi, vio.*

VOCABULARIO

A

a   to, at, by
abajo   under, below
abanico m   fan
abarcar   to encompass, to include all in one look; to clasp
abatir   to knock down; to overthrow; to sweep over; to discourage
abeja f   bee
abertura f   opening
abogado(a) m or f   lawyer
abordar   to approach
aborrecer   to hate
abrasar   to burn; to be burning up
abrazar   to embrace, to hug
abrigo m   overcoat
abrumar   to annoy; to oppress
aburrir   to bore
acabar   to finish, to end, to complete
   — con   to exterminate, to destroy
   — de   to have just
acalorar   to hear; to incite; to encourage; to become heated
acariciar   to caress
acaso   perhaps
acechar   to watch; to spy on
acecho m   watching; act of lying in ambush
   de —   on the watch
aceite m   oil
aceituna f   olive
acelerar   to hurry
acequia f   ditch, canal
acera f   steel
acercar(se)   to approach, to draw near
acobardarse   to be frightened
acogedor(a)   welcome; inviting
acoger   to receive; to welcome
acompañar   to accompany
aconsejar   to advise, to counsel
acontecer   to happen, to occur
acontecimiento m   happening; event
acosar   to harass; to pester
acostar(se) (ue)   to go to bed; to lie down
acreedor(a) m or f   creditor
acto m   act; public function
actual   present; at the present time
acuclillar   to squat, to crouch

acudir   to come to the aid of; to hang around
acuerdo m   agreement, resolution
   de —   in agreement
acumular   to accumulate
acurrucar   to huddle up
acusar   to accuse; to acknowledge
adelantar   to go forward, to advance; to get ahead of
adelante   ahead, farther on
   en —   in the future
adelgazar   to thin down, to lose weight
ademán m   gesture
además   besides, furthermore, in addition to
adentro   inside
adivinar   to guess
adolecer   to fall sick
   — de   to suffer from
adorno m   decoration, adornment
adquirir (ie)   to acquire
aduana f   customhouse
advertir (ie, i)   to notice; to notify, to warn
aéreo(a)   air
afán m   eagerness, zeal; hard work
afanar(se)   to busy oneself; to strive
afectar   to affect
aferrar (ie)   to seize; to catch
afiliarse a   to join, to affiliate oneself with
afligido(a)   worried; grieved, sorrowed
afligirse   to grieve; to worry
afortunado(a)   fortunate, happy
afrentar   to affront, to face
afuera   outside
agacharse   to squat, to stoop
agarrar   to seize, to grab
ágil   agile, lively; flexible
agitar   to agitate; to shake, to wave
   —se   to become excited
aglomerarse   to increase in size
agotar   to exhaust; to use up
   —se   to become exhausted
agradable   pleasant, agreeable
agravio m   wrong, offense
agregar   to add; to attach
agrícola   agricultural
aguacero m   heavy shower

aguantar   to bear, to endure
aguardar   to wait, to wait for
agudo(a)   sharp, pointed
agüero m   omen; forecast
aguja f   needle; steeple
agujero m   hole
ahogar(se)   to drown; to suffocate
ahorrar   to save
ahumado(a)   smoke, smoked
ahuyentar   to put to flight; to scare away
aislar   to isolate; to separate
   —se   to live in seclusion
ajeno(a)   another's
   — a   free from
ajustar   to adjust
ajusticiar   to execute, to put to death
alabar   to praise
alarmarse   to become alarmed
alba f   dawn, daybreak
albañil m   mason
alborotar   to arouse; to disturb
alcalde m   mayor
alcance m   reach; extent; overtaking
alcanzar   to reach, to attain
alcázar m   fortress; royal palace
alcoba f   bedroom
aldea f   village, hamlet
alegre   happy
alegría f   joy, happiness
alejarse   to go away; to separate
aleta f   small wing; fin of a fish
alfarero m   potter
alfiler m   pin
algodón m   cotton
alguacil m   bailiff
aliento m   breath
alimento m   food, nourishment; pl foodstuffs
alistarse   to enlist
aliviar   to alleviate, to relieve
alma f   soul; ghost
alojar   to lodge
alquilar   to rent
alrededor   around
   — de   around, about, approximately
   —es   environs, outskirts
altivez f   arrogance; haughtiness; pride
alumbrar   to light, to illuminate

alzar   to raise, to lift
allá   there, over there
allende   beyond
   — de   besides; in addition to
ama *f*   housekeeper
   — de casa   homemaker
amanecer *m*   dawn
   al —   at sunrise
amante *m* or *f*   lover
amapola *f*   poppy
amargo(a)   bitter
amarillento(a)   yellowish
amarrar   to tie up; to moor
amasar   to mix; to knead
ambiente *m*   atmosphere, ambiance
ambos(as)   both
amenaza *f*   threat
amenazar   to threaten
ametralladora *f*   machine gun
amistad *f*   friendship
amistosamente   in a friendly way
amolar (ue)   to grind
amor *m*   love
ampliar   to enlarge; to widen
anales *m*   annals, historical records
anciano(a)   old
áncora *f*   anchor
andaluz(a)   Andalusian
andén *m*   railway platform
angosto(a)   narrow
ángulo *m*   corner
angustia *f*   anguish, distress, grief
angustiado(a)   distressed, grieved
anhelo *m*   desire, craving, yearning
anheloso(a)   anxious, eager, desirous
anhelar   to crave, to want badly
ánimo *m*   spirit; courage, valor
anochecer   to grow dark (at night)
   m   nightfall, dusk
ansiar   to long for, to yearn for
ansioso(a)   anxious, uneasy
antaño   of yore, long ago
ante   before, in front of
antepasados *m*   ancestors
anteponer   to place in front; to prefer
anticipio *m*   anticipation; advance
   payment, down payment
anticuado   old-fashioned; obsolete
antigüedad *f*   antique
antiguo(a)   old, ancient
antojo *m*   whim, caprice, fancy
antojarse   to get a whim
anudar   to tie, to fasten, to knot
anverso *m*   obverse, reverse
añadir   to add
apagar   to extinguish, to put out; to
   turn off

aparador *m*   showcase
aparato *m*   apparatus, device
aparecer   to appear
aparentar   to feign, to pretend
apariencia *f*   appearance
apartar   to set apart
apenas   hardly, barely, scarcely
aperitivo *m*   appetizer
aplacar   to appease, to pacify
aplauso *m*   applause; praise
aplicar   to apply
aplomo *m*   poise
apoderar   to authorize
   —se de   to seize; to take possession
   of
apodo *m*   nickname
apostar (ue)   to bet
   —se   to post (in position), to get set
apoyar   to lean; to defend; to aid
apreciar   to appreciate; to esteem
apresurar(se)   to hurry, to hasten
apretar (ie)   to tighten; to squeeze
apretón *m*   pressure; squeeze
   — de manos   handshake
aprisionar   to imprison, to shackle
aprovechar   to take advantage of; to
   make good use of
apuesto(a)   neat; elegant, refined
apuntar   to aid; to point, to point at
apurarse   to hurry
   no te apures   don't worry
apuro *m*   tight spot; urgency; worry
ara *f*   altar
   en —s de   for the sake of
arco *m*   bow
archivo *m*   file; archives
arder   to burn, to blaze
argüir   to argue
arista *f*   edge
armazón   framework
arrabal *m*   suburb, district; slum
arraigar   to establish; to take root
arrancar   to pull out; to start
arrastrar   to drag
arrebatar   to carry away; to move, to
   stir
arreglar   to arrange; to fix; to adjust
arrepentir (ie, i)   to repent, to be
   repentant
   —se de   to repent
arriero *m*   mule driver
arrimarse   to group together
arrodillarse   to kneel
arrojar   to throw, to hurl
arrojo *m*   boldness, fearlessness
arrollar   to roll up, to curl up
arrugar   to wrinkle, to crease

arte *m* or *f*   art; trick
artesanías *f*   native handicrafts
artesano(a) *m* or *f*   artesan
ascender (ie)   to ascend; to be
   promoted
   — a   to amount to
asear   to clean up, to tidy up
asediar   to besiege; to harass
asedio *m*   siege
asegurar   to assure; to fasten, to make
   secure
   —se   to be sure, to assure oneself
asesino(a) *m* or *f*   assassin, killer,
así   thus, so
asiento *m*   seat
asilo *m*   asylum; refuge
asociar   to associate
asomar   to show
   —se   to appear
asombrar   to astonish
asombro *m*   fright, astonishment
aspereza *f*   roughness
áspero(a)   rough; harsh
astro *m*   star
astuto(a)   astute, clever, cunning
asunto *m*   subject, matter; affair
asustar   to frighten
   —se   to be frightened
atadura *f*   fastening, knot; tourniquet
atar   to tie, to fasten
atardecer *m*   late afternoon
atenazado   tortured
atender (ie)   to wait on; to care for
atracar   to moor, to dock
atraer   to attract
atreverse   to dare, to be bold
atrevesar (ie)   to cross; to pass
   through
atrevido(a)   bold, daring
atropelladamente   hastily; brusquely;
   violently
atroz   atrocious, horrible
aturdir   to bewilder; to stun
audacia *f*   daring, boldness
audaz   audacious
auditorio *m*   listener; audience;
   auditorium
aullar   to howl
aullido *m*   howl, howling
aumentar   to increase; to enlarge
aumentativo(a)   augmentative, that
   which makes larger
aún   still, yet
aunque   although, though
auricular *m*   telephone receiver
aurora *f*   dawn
ausencia *f*   absence

auxilio *m* aid, help, assistance
avanzar to advance; to propose (an idea)
aventurar to adventure, to venture
avergonzar to shame, to embarrass
—**se** to be ashamed
averiguar to find out
ávidamente avidly, greedily, eagerly
aviso *m* warning; notice
avivar to revive; to enliven
ayuda *f* help
ayuno *m* fast, period of not eating
azahar *m* orange blossom
azotar to whip, to lash
azote *m* lash with a whip; beating

B

bailador(a) *m or f* dancer
bajar to lower; to go downstairs; to get off
bala *f* bullet
balancear to balance
balazo *m* shot; bullet wound
balbucir to stammer, to stutter
bambolear to sway, to stagger
banco *m* bank; bench
bandeja *f* tray
baraja *f* cards, deck of cards
barba *f* chin; beard
barbaridad *f* barbarism; outrage; piece of folly
¡**Qué —**! What nonsense!
bárbaro(a) barbaric, barbarous
barranco *m* gorge, ravine
barrer to sweep
barril *m* barrel
barrio *m* neighborhood, section
barro *m* mud
bastardilla *f* italics
bastón *m* cane
basura *f* trash, garbage
bata *f* bathrobe
batalla *f* battle
belicoso(a) warlike
belleza *f* beauty
bello(a) beautiful
besar to kiss
beso *m* kiss
bestia *f* beast
bestialidad *f* brutality
bibliotecario(a) *m or f* librarian
bienes *m* wealth, riches, possessions
bienestar *m* well-being, welfare
blanduzco(a) soft
boda *f* wedding
boina *f* beret

bolsa *f* purse; bag, sack
bolsillo *m* pocket
bombero *m* fire fighter
borbollón *m* bubbling
bordar to embroider
borde *m* border, edge; rim
borracho(a) drunk
borrascoso(a) stormy
borrón *m* blot, stain
borroso(a) blurred, smudgy
botar to bounce; to throw out; to fire
botica *f* drugstore
bramar to bellow
bravío(a) ferocious; wild
bravo(a) wild, savage, fierce
brecha *f* opening; break
breve brief, short
brindar to offer; to toast
brío *m* spirit
brisa *f* breeze
broma *f* joke, jest
bronce *m* bronze
brotar to bring forth, to produce
brusco(a) brusque, rough
bucear to dive; to delve
buey *m* ox
bujía *f* spark plug
bulto *m* bulk, volume; package
bullicio *m* uprising, riot
buque *m* boat
burla *f* hoax, trick; joke; ridicule
burlar to make fun of; to deceive
burlón(ona) joking
buró bureau; central office
buscar to look for, to search
buzón *m* mailbox

C

caballeresco(a) chivalrous
caballero *m* gentleman
cabaña *f* cabin
cabo *m* corporal
al — de finally, at the end of
llevar a — to carry out (an order)
cacerola *f* casserole dish
cacique *m* boss; political leader
cacharro *m* jalopy
cada each, every
cadena *f* chain
cadera *f* hip
caer to fall
— en gracia to like
dejar — to drop
cahita *m* language of the Yaqui Indians
caída *f* fall

caja *f* box
cajón *m* large box; drawer
calar to fix bayonets
calefacción *f* heating, heat
calentar (ie) to heat, to warm up
cálido(a) warm
calumniar to slander
calzada *f* highway, broad avenue
calzoncillo *m* underpants
callado(a) silent
callar to silence, to calm
—**se** to keep silent
callejuela *f* side street, alley
cambio *m* change
en — de on the other hand
camino *m* road
camiseta *f* undershirt
campamento *m* camp, encampment
campana *f* bell
campanario *m* bell tower
campaña *f* campaign
campesino(a) *m or f* farmer
campo *m* country; field
candil *m* oil lamp
candilejo *m* small oil lamp
canoa *f* canoe
cansancio *m* fatigue, weariness
cansar to tire
—**se** to become tired
cantante *m or f* singer
cantina *f* bar
caña *f* cane; rum; reed
— de azúcar sugar cane
cañaveral *m* sugar cane plantation
caño *m* channel, canal
cañón *m* canyon; cannon
capa *f* cape
capataz *m* supervisor, boss
capaz capable, able
capilla *f* chapel
capricho *m* caprice, whim, fancy
caprichoso(a) whimsical, fickle
carabina *f* carbine
¡**caramba**! confound it! darn it!
carcajada *f* outburst of laughter
cárcel *f* jail
carecer to lack
cargador *m* porter
caridad *f* charity
cariño *m* love, affection
carrera *f* profession; race
carretón *m* cart
carroza *f* coach, carriage
cartera *f* wallet, billfold
cartero(a) *m or f* mail carrier
cartucho *m* cartridge
casamiento *m* marriage

casar to marry
—**se con** to get married
casero(a) pertaining to the home
casino *m* social club
casta *f* caste, kind; breed, race
castigar to punish
castigo *m* punishment
castizo(a) pure, correct; pure-blooded
casualidad *f* accident, chance; event
por — by chance
casucha *f* hut
catalogar to catalogue; to classify
causa *f* cause
a — de because of, due to
cautivar to attract; to win over; to take possession
caza *f* hunt; game
ir de — to go hunting
cazador(a) *m or f* hunter
cazar to hunt
cazuela *f* casserole; baking dish
ceja *f* eyebrow
célebre celebrated; famous
celos *m* jealousy
celosía *f* jealousy
ceniza *f* ash
centellear to flash; to twinkle
centenar *m* hundred
a —es by the hundreds
centinela *m or f* centinel, guard
cerco *m* fence
cerebro *m* brain; mind
cerezo *m* cherry tree
cerilla *f* match
cerrar (ie) to close, to shut
cerro *m* hill
cerrojo *m* lock
certidumbre *f* certainty
cervecita *f* small beer
cesar to stop, to cease
cesta *f* basket
cicatriz *f* scar
cierto certain
ciervo *m* deer
cinta *f* tape; ribbon
cinturón *m* belt
cirio *m* wax candle
ciudadanía *f* citizenship
ciudadano(a) *m or f* citizen
clarear to brighten, to light up
claridad *f* clarity, clearness, brightness
clavo *m* nail
cobija *f* blanket, coverlet
cobrar to recover; to collect; to cash
coco *m* bogyman, spook
cochero *m* driver

codear to nudge with elbow
coger to seize, catch, take hold of
cola *f* tail
colar (ue) to drip (coffee)
colchoneta *f* mattress, pad
coleccionista *m or f* collector
colegio *m* school, academy
colgar (ue) to hang
colmado *m* grocery store
colmena *f* beehive
colmo *m* overflow
eso es el — that's the limit, that's the last straw
colocar to place, to put
colonia *f* colony; neighborhood
colono *m* colonist, settler
collar *m* necklace
comarca *f* district, region
combatiente *m* combatant, soldier
comerciante *m or f* businessperson; merchant
cometer to commit
comodidad *f* comfort, convenience
compadecer to pity, to feel sorry for
compadre *m* friend, buddy
compañero(a) *m or f* companion
compatriota *m or f* compatriot
compilar to compile
comprar to buy, to purchase
comprobar (ue) to prove, to check
comprometer to endanger, to compromise
—**se** to promise; to become engaged
concavidad *f* concavity
conceder to concede, to give in
concluir to conclude, to finish
concurso *m* contest
condecoración *f* decoration
conducir to conduct, to lead; to drive
conejo *m* rabbit
confesar (ie) to confess
confianza *f* confidence; self-confidence, self-assurance; secret deal
de — reliable
confiar to confide
conforme in agreement
— a in agreement with
congregar to bring together, to gather
—**se** to come together
conjunto *m* ensemble; unit, group
conmovedor(a) touching, moving
conocimiento *m* knowledge; sense, awareness, consciousness; understanding

conquistador(a) *m or f* conqueror
consecuencia *f* consecuence
conseguir (i, i) to get, to obtain
consejo *m* advice
consentido(a) spoiled, pampered
consigo with him, with her, with them
consiguiente consequential
por — consequently, therefore
consistir to consist
— en to consist of
consolar (ue) to console
consuelo *m* consolation
consumir to consume
—**se de** to be consumed by or with
contar (ue) to count; to tell, to relate
contener to contain
contenido *m* content, contents
contingente contingent, depending on
continuar to continue, to keep on
contraer to contract; to condense
contrahecho(a) deformed
contratiempo *m* misfortune, disappointment
contribuir to contribute
convenir to agree; to come to an agreement
convertir (ie) to convert, to change
convocar to call together
copar to cut off and capture
coquetear to flirt
coraje *m* spirit, courage, valor; anger
cordoncillo *m* small cord
corona *f* floral wreath; crown
coronado(a) crowned
correctamente correctly
correo *m* mail, post office
corromper to corrupt
corrompido(a) corrupted
cortejo *m* cortege
cortés polite, courteous
cortina *f* curtain
cosecha *f* crop, harvest
costal *m* bag, sack
costar (ue) to cost
costura *f* sewing; dressmaking;
alta — high fashion
cotidiano daily
crecer to grow; to raise
creencia *f* belief
crepuscular twilight
criar to raise; to bring up; to create
criollo(a) *m or f* creole, native born in America of European parents
cruce *m* cross
crucificar to crucify
crujir to creak; to rustle; to crunch

cuadrado(a)   square
cuadro m   picture, square
cuajado(a)   thickened, coagulated
cualquier   any
cuaresma   Lent
cuartel m   barracks
cubierto(a)   covered
cubrir   to cover
cucaracha f   cockroach
cuchichear   to whisper
cuchicheo m   whisper, whispering
cuchillada f   slash
cuello m   neck
cuenta f   bill, check
cuento m   story
cuerda f   string
cuerno m   horn
cuervo m   crow
cuesta arriba   uphill
cuidado m   care, concern, worry
   tener —   to be aware; to be careful
culminante   highest, zenith, peak
   punto —   climax
culpa f   blame
culpable   guilty,
   m or f   guilty person
cumplimiento m   compliment; fulfillment
cuna f   cradle
cura m   priest
curandero(a) m or f   healer
curiosidad f   curiosity
   tienda de —es   curio shop
cursar   to take a course, to study
cuyo(a)   whose, of which, of whom

Ch

chamuscar   to singe
chapa f   license plate
chapurrear   to jabber, to speak indistinctly
charco m   puddle, pool
charla f   talk; informal lecture; conversation
chico(a)   small
chillido m   screech, scream
chimenea f   chimney
chiquitín(ina) m or f   small child
chisme m   gossip
chispa f   spark
chisporrotear   to spark, to sputter
chisporroteo m   sputtering, sparkling
chiste m   joke, funny story
chistoso(a)   funny, humorous
chofer m   driver

choque m   accident, collision; hit, blow
choquezuela f   kneecap
choza f   hut
chuchería f   piece of junk
chuparse   to suck

D

dama f   lady; maid-in-waiting
damajuana f   jug
daño m   damage, hurt
   hacer —   to cause harm, damage, or injury
dar   to give
   —se con   to run into
   —se cuenta de   to realize
   —se el gusto de   to take pleasure in, to have the pleasure of
dardo m   dart
debajo   beneath, underneath
deber   to owe; must, to have to; m   duty, obligation
debido(a)   proper
   — a   due to
debilidad f   weakness
decapitar   to behead
decentemente   decently
decidir   to decide
decir   to say, to tell
declarar   to declare, to explain
   —se   to make a declaration of love
dedal m   thimble
dedicar   to dedicate
defectuoso(a)   defective
degollar (üe)   to behead
deidad f   deity
dejar   to leave; to let, to allow
delante   before, ahead, in front
   — de   in front of
deleite m   joy
delgado(a)   thin, skinny
delicia f   delight
demanda f   demand, complaint, claim
demandar   to demand
demás   other
   lo —   the rest
   los —   others, the others
demonio m   demon
demostrar (ue)   to demonstrate, to show
dentro   inside, within
depender   to depend
deprimente   depressing
derecho m   right; privilege
deriva f   drift
   a la —   adrift

derivar   to drift
derredor m   circumference
   en — de   around
derribar   to tear down
derrotar   to rout, to put to flight
derrumbarse   to collapse
desabotonar   to unbutton, to unfasten
desafiante   challenging, defying, daring
desafiar   to challenge, to defy; to compete with
desagradable   unpleasant
desahuciar   to deprive of hope
   —se   to lose all hope
desairar   to snub, to disregard
desaparecer   to disappear
desarmar   to disarm
desarrollar   to develop; to unfold
desarrollo m   development
desastre m   disaster
desatar   to untie, to unfasten
desbordar   to overflow
descalzo(a)   barefoot
descarga f   discharge (of a gun); unloading
descargar   to unload; to free; to discharge
descepar   to pull up by the roots; to eradicate
desconcertar (ie)   to disturb, to upset; to disconcert, to bewilder
desconfianza f   lack of confidence
desconocido(a)   unknown, strange
descubierto(a)   open; bareheaded
descuido m   carelessness, negligence
desde   from, since
   — luego   of course
desdén m   disdain
desdeñoso(a)   scornful, disdainful
desdeñosamente   disdainfully
desdicha f   misery, unhappiness
desdoblar   to unfold
desear   to desire
desecador(a)   drying
desempeñar   to play a part; to carry out; to fulfill; to redeem; to perform a duty
desengañar   to disillusion; to disappoint
desengaño m   disillusionment; disappointment
desenlace m   conclusion, end; solution
desenvolvimiento m   development, unfolding
desfilar   to parade; to file by
desgraciadamente   unfortunately

desgraciado(a) unfortunate
deshacer(se) to burst, to come undone
desierto *m* desert
desigual unequal
desigualdad *f* inequality
desilusión *f* disappointment
desilusionar to disappoint
deslizar to slide
—**se** to slide, to slip; to sneak away
deslumbrar to dazzle; to bewilder, to confuse
desmontarse to dismount
desnudar to undress
desnudo(a) naked
desolador(a) desolating
despachar to dispatch; to sell
despacho *m* office
despectivo(a) belittling, insulting
despedirse (i, i) to take one's leave, to say good-bye
despeinado(a) unkempt, uncombed
desplegar (ie) to unfold, to spread
desposado(a) *m* or *f* newly married
despreciable contemptible
desprecio *m* scorn, contempt
destacar(se) to stand out; to emphasize; to be different
desterrar (ie) to exile, to banish
destino *m* destiny, fate
destreza *f* skill
destruir to destroy, to ruin
desvanecer(se) to disappear
desviar to turn aside, to detour
detalle *m* detail
detener to stop, to hold
—**se** to stop
determinadamente decidedly
determinar to determine
detrás de behind
deuda *f* debt
deudo(a) *m* or *f* relative
devolver (ue) to return, to give back
devorar to devour
diablo *m* devil
diabluras *f* mischief
diariamente daily
diario(a) daily
m newspaper
dibujar to draw, to sketch
—**se** to be outlined
dibujo *m* sketch, drawing
dicha *f* joy
dicho stated, aforementioned
diestra *f* right hand
dificultad *f* difficulty
difunto(a) deceased, dead

dignidad *f* dignity
digno(a) worthy
diminutivo(a) diminutive; that which makes smaller
director(a) *m* or *f* principal, director
dirigir to direct
—**se** to address, to speak to
discreto(a) discreet, prudent
disculpar to excuse, to pardon
diseminar to spread
disfraz *m* disguise, mask
disfrutar to enjoy; to use
disgustar to displease
disgusto *m* annoyance, quarrel
disimular to feign, to pretend; to hide the truth
dislocar to dislocate
—**se** to be dislocated
disminuir to make smaller
disolver(se) (ue) to dissolve
disparar to shoot
disparo *m* shot
dispuesto(a) ready, prepared
disputa *f* dispute, disagreement
distinto(a) different
distraer to distract; to amuse, to entertain
—**se** to be absentminded
distribuir to distribute
divertir (ie, i) to divert, to amuse
—**se** to amuse oneself, to have a good time
doblar to fold; to turn
doler (ue) to hurt, to ache
—**se** to feel sorry
dolor *m* pain; sorrow, woe
domesticar to tame
dominar to dominate; to subdue
don *m* title for a man; Mr.; ability, talent
donaire *m* charm; cleverness
dondequiera wherever
dorado(a) golden, gilted
dormir (ue, u) to sleep
—**se** to fall asleep
dorso *m* back
dosis *f* dose
dotar to give a dowry; to endow
dote *m* dowry
ducha *f* shower
duchar to shower
—**se** to take a shower
duda *f* doubt
no cabe — there is no doubt
sin — without a doubt
dudosamente doubtfully
duende *m* elf, goblin

dueño(a) *m* or *f* owner
dulce sweet
m candy
dulcísimo(a) very sweet
durmiente sleeping
duro(a) hard; difficult

E

eco *m* echo
echar to throw; to dismiss; to expel, to drive away
—**se** to lie down
—**se a** to begin
— **flores** to flatter
edad *f* age
efectivamente really, as a matter of fact
efecto *m* effect, consequence
en — indeed, really
efigie *m* effigy
egoísmo *m* selfishness
egoísta selfish, self-centered
ejecutar to execute, to carry out
ejercer to practice, to exert
ejército *m* army
elegir (i, i) to elect; to select
elevar to raise
elogiar to praise
ello it
embajada *f* embassy
embarcar to embark, to board a ship
embargo *m* embargo
sin — however, nevertheless
emborracharse to get drunk
emboscada *f* ambush
embuste *m* lie, falsehood
emocionante emotional, stirring
empapar to soak, to drench
emparentar to relate by marriage
empleo *m* job, employment
agencia de — employment agency
emprender to try, to undertake
empresa *f* enterprise, undertaking
empujar to push
empuñar to seize, to grasp
enamorar to inspire love
—**se de** to fall in love with
encaje *m* lace
encajonar to box, to crate, to squeeze in
encaminar to direct, to show the way
encantar to delight; to enchant
encanto *m* charm
encarcelación *f* imprisonment
encarcelar to imprison
encargar to entrust

—se de to take charge of
encender (ie) to light; to turn on
encerrar (ie) to enclose; to lock up
encima de above, on top of
enclavar to nail
encoger to shrink, to shrivel; to shrug
encomendar (ie) to entrust
encontrar (ue) to find, to meet
enderezar to straighten
—se to straighten up
endotar to endow
endulzar to sweeten; to make pleasant
enfadar to anger
—se to get mad
enfado *m* anger, ire
enfebricido(a) feverish
enfermarse to become ill, to get sick
enfermedad *f* sickness, illness
enfocar to focus
engañar to cheat; to deceive
engaño *m* trick, deceit
engrosarse to swell
enigmático(a) puzzling, not easily understood
enjugar to dry; to wipe off
—se to dry up
enojar to anger
—se to get mad
enojo *m* anger
enjuiciar to judge
enrollar to roll up
ensangrentado(a) bloody, covered with blood
ensayo *m* rehearsal
enseñanza *f* teaching, education
ensillado(a) saddled
ensueño *m* dream, fantasy
entendimiento *m* understanding
  malos —s misunderstandings
enterar to inform, to acquaint
  —se de to find out about
enternecer to move to pity
entero(a) entire, complete, whole
entierro *m* funeral, burial
entintado(a) inked, printed
entonces then
entregar to hand over, to hand in; to give
entrelazar to interlace, to interweave
entremezclado(a) intermingled
entretanto meanwhile
  en el — in the meantime
entrevistar to interview
  ser entrevistado(a) to be interviewed

entristecido(a) saddened
entusiasmo *m* enthusiasm, excitement
entusiasta enthusiastic
  m or f enthusiast
envenenar to poison
enviar to send
envolver (ue) to wrap
envuelto(a) wrapped
épico(a) epic
época *f* epoch, period
equilibrio *m* balance
equipaje *m* baggage; equipment
equipo *m* team, equipment
equivocado(a) mistaken
erguir (i, i) to raise
  —se to swell with pride
errar to err, to wrong
esbelto(a) slender
escalar to scale, to climb
escalofrío *m* chill
escándalo *m* scandal; loud noise
escaparate *m* showcase, display case
escaparse to escape
escarmiento *m* lesson; warning
escaso(a) small, limited
escena *f* scene
esclarecer to lighten up, to brighten
esclavo(a) *m or f* slave
escoger to select, to choose
escombro *m* rubble, ruin
esconder to hide
escopeta *f* shotgun
escopetazo *m* gunshot; gunshot wound
escritor(a) *m or f* author, writer
escultórico(a) sculptural
escurrir to drain
esfuerzo *m* effort, endeavor
esmerar to do one's best
espacio *m* space, room
espada *f* sword
espalda *f* back, shoulder
espantar to scare, to frighten
espanto *m* fright, terror
espantoso(a) frightful, terrifying
esparcir to scatter, to spread
esparto *m* hemp
especie *f* species, type, kind
espectador(a) *m or f* spectator
especular to contemplate; to speculate
espejo *m* mirror
esperanza *f* hope
esperar to hope; to wait for, to expect
espía *m or f* spy

espina *f* thorn
espíritu *m* spirit
espolear to spur, to spur on
espuma *f* foam
esqueleto *m* skeleton
estabilizar to stabilize, to make steady
establecimiento *m* establishment; business
establecer to establish
  —se to settle oneself
estallar to explode; to break out
estallido *m* explosion; outbreak
estampilla *f* stamp
estatua *f* statue
estilo *m* style
estimable esteemed, respected
estimación *f* esteem, estimation
estirar to pull, to stretch
estorbar to disturb; to hinder, to obstruct
estrecho(a) narrow
estrella *f* star
estremecer(se) to tremble, to shake
estrenar to use or wear for the first time
estrepitoso(a) noisy, boisterous
estudio *m* study
  — cinematográfico movie studio
estufa *f* stove, heater
estupefacto(a) dumbfounded
eterno(a) eternal, lasting
evitar to avoid
evocar to evoke, to call forth
exceder to exceed
exhibir to exhibit, to show
exhortar to exhort
exigente demanding
exigir to demand
existencia *f* existence
éxito success
  tener — to be successful
explotar to operate; to exploit; to explode
exponer to expose, to explain
  —se to run a risk
exprimir to squeeze
expulsar to expel
éxtasis ecstasy
extender (ie) to extend, to stretch out; to spread
extinguirse to put out, put an end to
extrañar to surprise; to miss
extrañeza *f* wonder, strangeness
extraño(a) foreign; strange
extraviarse to go astray, to get lost
extremo *m* extreme, end

F

fabricación *f* manufacture
facultad *f* knowledge; skill; power
fachada *f* facade, front
faena *f* work, task, job
falta *f* lack; offense
faltar to be lacking; to falter
fallar to fail, to miss; to misfire
fallecer to die, to expire
fallecido(a) *m or f* deceased person
fama *f* fame; reputation
fango *m* mud
fangoso(a) muddy
fantasma *m* ghost
fascinar to fascinate, to bewitch
fatiga *f* fatigue, exhaustion
fe *f* faith
felicidad *f* happiness
fenómeno *m* phenomenon
feriado holiday
ferocidad *f* ferocity, fierceness
ferrocarril *m* railway
fervor *m* earnestness, zeal; devotion
festejado(a) honored, entertained
festivo(a) festive
fiado(a) guaranteed
  al — on credit
ficticio(a) fictitious
fiebre *f* fever
fiel loyal, faithful, trustworthy
fiera *f* wild animal; savage
fiereza *f* ferocity, fierceness
figurilla *f* figurine
fijar to fix, to fasten
  —se to take notice
fijo(a) fixed, firm, solid, secure
filial brotherly, filial
filo *m* blade; edge; ridge
filosofía *f* philosophy
filósofo(a) *m or f* philosopher
fin *m* end
  a — de que so that
  en — finally
fingir to feign, to pretend
firma *f* signature
firmar to sign
firme firm, steady
firmeza *f* firmness
flaco(a) skinny, thin
flecha *f* arrow
flojamente lazily
flojo(a) lazy
flor *f* flower
  — y nata the choice part
florido(a) flowery

foco light bulb
follaje *m* foliage
folletín *m* small bulletin
fondo *m* bottom, depth; basis;
  pl funds
fontana *f* fountain
forastero(a) *m or f* foreigner
forcejeo *m* struggling, striving
formular to formulate
fortaleza *f* fortress, fort
fortificar to fortify, to make strong
fosa *f* grave
fraile *f* friar
franco(a) frank, sincere, truthful
frenar to restrain; to limit; to brake
frente in front of
  f forehead
  m front
fresco(a) fresh
frialdad *f* coldness, coolness
frijol *m* bean, bean plant
friolento(a) chilly, susceptible to cold
frondoso(a) leafy
fruncir to gather, to pucker
frutal fruit
fruto *m* produce
fuego *m* fire
fuerza *f* force, strength, power; main
  body of an army
fuga *f* flight
fugaz fleeting, passing
fulgurante shining; flashing
fumar to smoke
fumador(a) *m or f* smoker
fundir to smelt; to fuse
furor *m* fury, furor
furtivamente furtively; in a deceptive
  manner
fusil *m* gun, rifle
fusilar to shoot

G

galán *m* suitor, lover
galardón *m* reward, recompense
galopar to gallop
galope *m* gallop
  a — at a gallop; in great haste
gallardo(a) graceful, self-assured
gallina *f* hen
gana *f* appetite, desire
  tener —s de to wish to, to be
  anxious to
ganado *m* cattle, livestock
  — vacuno beef cattle
ganador(a) *m or f* winner, earner

garboso(a) graceful, sprightly
garganta *f* throat
gastar to spend; to waste
gatear to crawl
gatillo *m* trigger
gemido *m* moan
gemir (i, i) to moan, to groan
género *m* genre; gender; kind
genio *m* temperament, disposition;
  genius; spirit
gente *f* people
gesto *m* gesture
gimotear to whine
girar to turn, to rotate, to spin
globo *m* balloon
gobernar to govern
gobierno *m* government
golpe *m* blow, hit, strike
golpear to hit
golpecito *m* tap, light blow
gota *f* drop
gozar to enjoy
grabar to record, to carve
gracia *f* witty remark; grace; pardon
  caer en — to like
  hacer — to strike someone as
  funny
grandeza *f* grandeur, greatness
granizar to hail
granizo *m* hail
granja *f* dairy farm
granuja *m* urchin
grato(a) pleasing
graznar to caw, to cackle
graznido *m* caw, croak, cackle
gritar to shout, to cry
grito *m* cry, shout
grueso(a) thick; large, fat
gruta *f* cave
guagua *f* bus (Caribbean)
guante *m* glove
guapetón *m* bully
guapo(a) good-looking, attractive
guardar to guard; to keep
guarecer to take in, to give shelter
  —se to take refuge or shelter
güero(a) blond (Mexico)
guerrero *m* warrior, soldier
guía *m or f* guide
guiño *m* wink; signal
guisa *f* manner, way
  a — de in the manner of
guisar to cook; to stew
guiso *m* dish; a cooked dish or stew
gusto *m* pleasure; taste
  darse el — to please oneself

H

haber   to have (auxiliary verb)
habichuela *f*   bean
habilidad *f*   ability, skill, capability
habitación *f*   room
habitar   to inhabit
hacer   to make, to do
  — caso   to obey, to pay attention
  — daño   to hurt, to harm
  — falta   to need, to be necessary
  — gracia   to amuse
hacienda   estate, ranch
hallar   to find, to discover
hambre *f*   hunger
  pasar —   to be hungry
  tener —   to be hungry
hambriento(a)   hungry
harapiento(a)   ragged
harina *f*   flour
harto(a)   full; fed up; very much
  — de   sick of
hasta   even; until; to; as far as;
  as much as
  — ahora   until now
  — más no poder   to the utmost
haz *m*   bundle
hazaña *f*   feat, exploit, deed
hebreo(a)   Hebrew
hecho *m*   deed, act; fact; event
helado(a)   frozen, cold,
  m   ice cream
helar (ie)   to freeze
hembra *f*   female
heredero(a) *m or f*   heir
herencia *f*   heritage, inheritance
herida *f*   wound
herir (ie, i)   to wound, to injure
hermoso(a)   beautiful
hervir (ie)   to boil
hidropesía *f*   dropsy
hielo *m*   ice
hierro *m*   iron
hilo *m*   thread
  al —   parallel; the length of
hinchado(a)   swollen
hinchar   to swell
hinchazón *f*   swelling, inflammation
hogar *m*   home, hearth
hoguera *f*   bonfire
hoja *f*   leaf; sheet of paper
hojear   to leaf through
hombría   manliness
hombro *m*   shoulder
hondo(a)   deep
honrado(a)   honorable, honest
honrar   to honor

horca *f*   gallows
hornear   to bake
hospedaje *m*   lodging
hospedar   to lodge
hoy   today
  — en día   nowadays
hoya *f*   hole, pit
hueco   hollow; hole, gap
huelga *f*   strike
huérfano(a) *m or f*   orphan
huerta *f*   orchard
hueso *m*   bone
huir   to flee
hule *m*   rubber
humeante   smoking
humedecer   to moisten, to dampen
húmedo(a)   moist, damp
humildemente   humbly, meekly
humo *m*   smoke
humorista *m or f*   humorist
hundir   to sink

I

ida *f*   departure
ídolo *m*   idol
ignorar   to ignore, to be ignorant of
igualar   to equal, to make equal
igualdad *f*   equality
igualmente   equally
imagen *f*   image
imaginar   to imagine
imán *m*   magnet
impacientarse   to get impatient
ímpetu *m*   impetus; force
imponer   to impose; to dominate
importar   to matter; to be important
impreciso(a)   imprecise
imprudencia *f*   imprudence
impulsar   to impel, to drive
impulso *m*   impulse
incaico(a)   pertaining to the Inca
  Indians of Peru
incendio *m*   fire
incertidumbre *f*   uncertainty
incesante   incessant
incluir   to include
incluso(a)   enclosed, included
incómodo(a)   uncomfortable
incontenible   irrepressible
incontrastable   invincible;
  inconvincible; unanswerable
incorporarse   to sit up; to join
increíble   unbelievable, incredible
indefinible   indefinable
indicar   to indicate; to point out
indígena   native

indomable   indomitable,
  unconquerable
indudable   unquestionable
inesperado(a)   unexpected
infame   infamous
infamia *f*   infamy; disgrace
infelicidad *f*   unhappiness
infierno *m*   hell
informe *m*   report, information
infundir   to infuse, to instill
ingenio *m*   sugar refinery
iniciar   to initiate, to start
ininteligible   unintelligible
injusticia *f*   injustice
inmensurable   immeasurable
inmortalizar   to immortalize
inmóvil   immobile
innegable   undeniable
inodoro *m*   toilet
involvidable   unforgettable
inquietar   to stir up, to excite
  —se   to worry
inquieto(a)   restless
inquietud *f*   restlessness, unrest
insalubre   unhealthy
insipidez *f*   insipidness
insólito(a)   unusual
insondable   inscrutable; fathomless
inspirativo(a)   inspiring, inspirational
insurgente   insurgent, rebel
íntegro(a)   integral, whole; honest
intemperie *f*   bad weather
  a la —   unsheltered, in the open
intentar   to try; to intend
interceptar   to intercept
interés *m*   interest
  —es   property
interesado(a) *m or f*   interested party,
  prospect
interesar   to interest
  —se   to be interested in
interponer   to appoint as mediator
  —se   to intervene
intérprete *m or f*   interpreter
interrogar   to question, to ask
  questions
interrumpir   to interrupt
intervalo *m*   interval
intervenir   to intervene
intraducible   untranslatable
intrépido(a)   brave, courageous
intriga *f*   intrigue
inundar   to inundate, to flood
inútil   useless
invadir   to invade
invasor(a) *m or f*   invader
invitado(a) *m or f*   guest**

inyección *f* injection, shot
ira *f* ire, anger
ironía *f* irony
irónico(a) ironic, ironical
irritar to irritate
izar to hoist, to raise, to haul up
izquierdo(a) left

L

labio *m* lip
labrador(a) *m or f* farmer; peasant
labrar to work; to plow
lado *m* side
ladrillo *m* brick
ladrón(ona) *m or f* thief, robber
lágrima *f* tear
lamentación *f* sorrow
lamentar to lament, to mourn
lamento *m* sorrow, grief
lámpara *f* lamp
lana *f* wool
langosta *f* locust
lanzar to throw, to fling; to cast out;
  to utter sharply
  —se to throw oneself
largo long
  a lo — along, lengthwise
lástima *f* pity, shame, sorrow
lastimar to hurt, to injure
lastimero(a) pitiful, sad
lastimoso(a) pitiful
látigo *m* whip
latita *f* small can
lavadero *m* washroom
lavandería *f* laundry
lavar to wash
leal loyal
lección *f* lesson
lector(a) *m or f* reader
lecho *m* bed
lechuza *f* barn owl
legítimo(a) legitimate, real, genuine
lejanía *f* distance, remoteness
lejano(a) distant, remote
lejos far
  — de far from
lema *m* motto, slogan, theme
lenguaje *m* language
lentamente slowly
lente *m* lense
  —s eyeglasses
lento(a) slow
leña *f* log, firewood
letra *f* letter
levantar to raise, to lift
  —se to get up

leve light; trivial
ley *f* law
leyenda *f* legend
liberar to liberate, to free
libertad *f* liberty, freedom
licencia *f* license; permission
licenciado(a) *m or f* lawyer,
  professional
líder *m* leader
lienzo *m* canvas
ligadura *f* binding, tourniquet
ligar to tie, to bind
limeño(a) from Lima
limosna *f* alms, charity
limpiar to clean
limpio(a) clean
linaje *m* lineage
lindar to border, to be contiguous
línea *f* line
linterna *f* lantern
liso(a) even, smooth; straight (hair)
listo(a) ready; smart, intelligent
litigio *m* litigation, lawsuit; dispute
liviano(a) fickle, inconsistent
lo him; it, the
  — que that which
  — que sea whether it may be
lóbrego(a) dark, gloomy
locuaz loquacious, talkative
locura *f* madness, insanity
lograr to achieve
logro *m* attainment, success, profit
loma *f* low hill
lomo *m* hill; back
lona *f* canvas
lucero *m* bright star; evening star
luciérnaga *m* firefly
lucir to shine
  —se to dress up; to show off
lucha *f* fight, struggle
luchar to struggle, to fight
luego then
  desde — of course
lugar *m* place
  tener — to take place
lúgubremente dismally, gloomily
lujo *m* luxury
lujoso(a) luxurious
lumbre *f* fire
luna *f* moon
  — de miel honeymoon
luto *m* mourning
luz *f* light

LI

llama *f* flame, blaze

llamada *f* call
llanta *f* tire
llanto *m* weeping
llegada *f* arrival
llenar to fill
lleno(a) full; plenty
llevar to take, to carry; to wear
  — a cabo to carry through, to
  accomplish
llorar to cry
llorona *f* weeping person; crybaby
llover (ue) to rain
lluvia *f* rain

M

machetazo *m* blow with a machete
machete *m* long-bladed knife
machismo *m* the quality of being a
  male; male chauvinism
macho male, strong; bully
madera *f* wood
madrugada *f* dawn
madrugar to get up early
madurez *f* maturity
maduro(a) ripe, mature
maestro(a) *m or f* teacher
mágico(a) magic
magnitud *f* magnitude, size
maíz *m* maize, corn
majestad *f* majesty
maldad *f* wickedness
maldecir to curse
maldito(a) cursed, damned
malhumorado(a) ill-humored
malicia *f* malice, evil
malignidad *f* evilness, wickedness
malo(a) bad, evil; mischievous
malsano(a) unhealthy, sickly
maltratar to mistreat, to abuse
manantial *m* spring
mancebo *m* young man
mancha *f* spot, stain
manchar to spot, to stain
mandamiento *m* order, command;
  commandment
mandar to command, to order; to
  send
  — hacer to have made
mandato *m* order, command
mando *m* command
manejar to drive; to manage
manera *f* way, manner
manga *f* sleeve
manifestar (ie) to demonstrate, to
  exhibit
manifiesto *m* manifest, declaration

maniobra *f* procedure; trick; maneuver
manta *f* woolen blanket; coarse cloth
manteca *f* lard, fat
mantener to support, to maintain
manto *m* cloak
manzano *m* apple tree
mañana *f* tomorrow; morning
  de la — in the morning
  por la — in the morning
máquina *f* machine
  — de coser sewing machine
mar *m* (*rarely feminine*) sea
maravilla *f* wonder, marvel
maravillarse to wonder, to marvel
marchar to march
  —se to leave, to go away
marea *f* tide
mareado dizzy; nauseated
marido *m* husband
marina *f* navy; marine
martillo *m* hammer
mártir *m* martyr
mas but
más more
  es — moreover
masa *f* mass; dough;
  pl masses of people
matador(a) *m or f* killer, assassin
matar to kill
mate dull, flat
  m Paraguayan or Uruguayan tea
matrimonio *m* marriage; married couple
maullar to meow
maya Maya Indians of Mexico and Central America
mayor older; greater, larger
mayoría *f* majority
mecanógrafo(a) *m or f* typist
medalla *f* medal
mediados half over; half full
  a —s de about the middle of
medianoche *f* midnight
medida *f* measurement; measure
  a — de in proportion to; according to
medio middle; half
  en — de in the middle of
  por — de by means of
mediodía *m* noon
medios *m* ways, means
medir (i, i) to measure
meditar to meditate; to think
medroso(a) fainthearted; fearful; frightened
mejorar to improve

melancolía *f* melancholy, sadness
melón *m* canteloupe
membrudo(a) muscular, strong
memoria *f* memory
mendigo(a) *m or f* beggar
mendrugo *m* crumb
menor smaller; younger; slight; least
menos less
  al — at least
  por lo — at least
mensaje *m* message
mensajero(a) *m or f* messenger
mente *f* mind
mentir (ie, i) to lie
mentira *f* lie
mentiroso(a) *m or f* liar
menudo(a) small
  a — often
mercancía *f* merchandise
merced *f* favor, grace; mercy
merecer to merit, to deserve
mesar to tear; to pull out
mesero *m* waiter
meta *f* goal, objective
meter to put in, to insert
mezcla *f* mixture; cement
mezclar to mix
miedo *m* fear
miedoso(a) frightened, afraid
miel *f* honey
mientras while
  — tanto meanwhile
mil thousand
milagro *m* miracle
milagroso(a) marvelous, wonderful
militar *m* soldier, person in military service
milla *f* mile
mimar to coax; to pet; to indulge
mimbre *m* wicker
minuciosamente meticulously, with great care or detail
mirada *f* look, glance
misa *f* mass
  — de gallo midnight mass on Christmas Eve
misal *m* prayer book
miseria *f* poverty; misery
misericordia *f* compassion, pity
mitad *f* half; middle
mito *m* myth
mocetón(ona) *m or f* strapping youth
moda *f* style; manner, way
modestamente modestly
modo *m* way
moflete *m* fat cheek, jowl

mohán *m* wizard; priest of an ancient tribe of Indians from Colombia
mojar to wet, to dampen
  —se to get wet
moler (ue) to grind; to mill
molestar to disturb, to bother
molinero *m* miller
molino *m* mill
momento *m* moment
  al — right away
moneda *f* coin, money
mono(a) cute
monja *f* nun
montado(a) mounted on horseback
montar to mount, to ride; to cock a gun
monte *m* mountain, mount
montón *m* heap, pile, stack
moño *m* chignon, bun
moraleja *f* moral, lesson
mordedura *f* bite
morder (ue) to bite
moreno(a) brown, dark, brunette
moribundo(a) dying
  m or f dying person
morisco(a) Moorish
morlaco *m* silver peso
mortificar to worry, to mortify
  —se to be embarrassed
mostrar (ue) to show
motivo *m* motive, reason
mover (ue) to move
movimiento *m* movement
mozo(a) *m or f* youth; waiter
muchedumbre *f* crowd, mob
mudanza *f* change; move (to another house)
mudar to move; to change residence
  —se to be silent
mudo(a) mute; silent
mueble *m* piece of furniture; *pl* furniture
muela *f* tooth
muelle *m* dock
mula *f* mule
mundanal worldly
mundano(a) worldly, common, ordinary
mundial worldwide
mundo *m* world
  todo el — everybody
munición *f* ammunition
muñeca *f* doll; wrist
muralla *f* wall, fence
murmullo *m* murmur, whisper
murmurar to murmur; to whisper; to gossip

muro *m*   wall
musa *f*   muse
músculo *m*   muscle
muslo *m*   thigh
mutuo(a)   mutual

N

nacer   to be born; to start
nacimiento *m*   birth; Nativity scene
nadie   no one
nailon *m*   nylon cloth or fiber
naranjo *m*   orange tree
narración *f*   story
nata *f*   cream
natal   native; pertaining to place of birth
natural *m*   native
naturaleza *f*   nature
naúfrago   sunken
   m   shipwreck
nave *f*   ship
Navidad *f*   Christmas
navideño   pertaining to Christmas
necedad *f*   foolishness
necesitar   to need
necio(a)   foolish
m or f   fool
negar (ie)   to deny; to decline
negocio *m*   business, transaction
nevado(a)   snowcapped
ni   neither, nor
   — siquiera   not even
nieta *f*   granddaughter
nieto *m*   grandson; *pl* grand-children
ningún   apocopated form of **ninguno**, used only before *m sing* nouns
ninguno   none, not any; neither
niña *f*   child, girl
niñez *f*   childhood
niño *m*   child, boy
nivel *m*   level
nocturno(a)   nocturnal, nighttime
nombre *m*   name
noreste *m*   northeast
nostalgia *f*   homesickness
nota *f*   grade; note
notar   to note, to observe, to notice
noticia *f*   news, news item
noticiero *m*   news bulletin; late news
novela *f*   novel
novena   ninth
novia *f*   fiancée, bride, girlfriend
noviazgo *m*   courtship; engagement
novio *m*   fiancé, groom, boyfriend
nube *f*   cloud

nublarse   to become cloudy
nudo *m*   knot

O

obedecer   to obey
obispo *m*   bishop
objeto *m*   object
obra *f*   work
obrero(a) *m or f*   worker, laborer
obsequiar   to present, to give
observar   to observe, to notice
obstante   standing in the way
   no —   nevertheless
obstinadamente   obstinately, stubbornly
obtener   to obtain, to get
ocultar   to hide
oculto(a)   hidden, concealed
ocupar   to occupy
   —se   to busy oneself, to pay attention, to take care of
odiar   to hate
odio *m*   hatred
ofender   to offend, to insult
oficio *m*   occupation, craft, trade
ofrecer   to offer
ofrenda *f*   offering
oído *m*   ear
oir   to hear
ojalá   would that, hopefully
ojeada *f*   glance, glimpse
ojo *m*   eye;
   ¡Ojo!   Watch out!
oleada *f*   large wave
oler (hue)   to smell; to smell fragrant
olfatear   to sniff, to smell
olor *m*   odor
olvidar   to forget
   —se de   to forget
olla *f*   pot, kettle; stew
omitir   to omit
onza *f*   ounce
opaca   opaque, cloudy
operar   to operate
opinar   to think; to have an opinion
opresor(a) *m or f*   oppressor
oprimido(a)   oppressed, squeezed
opuesto(a)   opposite
oración *f*   sentence; prayer
   — revuelta   scrambled sentence
orador(a) *m or f*   speaker, orator
orar   to pray
orden *m*   order (of things)
   f   order (as command)
ordenar   to order, to command
oreja *f*   ear

organizar   to organize
orgullo *m*   pride
   tener —   to be proud
orgulloso(a)   proud
orilla *f*   edge, shore, bank
orín *m*   urine
oscurecer   to grow dark
oscuridad *f*   darkness
oscuro(a)   dark
ostentar   to show, to make a show of
oveja *f*   sheep

P

paciencia *f*   patience
pactar   to agree upon
padecer   to suffer
padecimiento *m*   suffering
pagar   to pay
   ¡Dios se lo pague!   May God reward you!
pago *m*   pay, payment
paisaje *m*   landscape
paisano(a) *m or f*   compatriot
   de —   civilian
paja *f*   straw
pala *f*   shovel; stick; blade of an oar
palabra *f*   word
palacio *m*   palace
paladear   to taste, to relish
palenque *m*   stockade
pálido(a)   pale
palmada *f*   clap
palmo *m*   span, palm
palmotear   to clap
paloma *f*   dove
palomita *f*   popcorn
palpar   to touch, to feel
palpitar   to twitch, to throb
pámpano *m*   leaf; branch of grapevine
pantanoso(a)   marshy, swampy
panza *f*   paunch
panzudo(a)   paunchy
paño *m*   cloth
pañuelo *m*   handkerchief
papanduja   too soft, overripe fruit
parada *f*   stop; parade
paraguas *m*   umbrella
paraje *m*   place, spot
parapeto *m*   parapet
parar   to stop
parco   frugal; moderate
pardear   to become dusky
parecer   to seem; to look like
   al —   apparently
   —se   to resemble

parecido(a) resembling
  bien — good-looking
pared *f* wall
paredón *m* huge wall, thick wall
pareja *f* pair, couple
pariente *m* relative
párpado *m* eyelid
parquear to park
párrafo *m* paragraph
parrandista *m or f* one who "paints the town red"
partidario(a) *m or f* partisan, follower
partido *m* (sports) match, game; political party; group
partir to leave, to depart
  a — de beginning with
parra *f* grapevine
parroquia *f* parish church
pasaje *m* passage, fare; journey; passengers
pasar to pass; to happen; to spend time
paso *m* step, footstep
  de — in passing; at the same time
Pascua *f* Easter
pasillo *m* corridor, hall
pasmado(a) dumbfounded, astounded
pasmo *m* astonishment
patria *f* country, native land
patrón(ona) *m or f* boss
pausadamente slowly
pava *f* turkey
  pelar la — to court; to carry on a flirtation
pavimentar to pave
pavo *m* turkey
paz *f* peace
peatón *m* pedestrian
pecar to sin
pecho *m* chest; breast
pedazo *m* piece
pagajoso(a) sticky
pegar to hit, to stick
pelea *f* fight, struggle
pelear to fight, to struggle
peligro *m* danger
peligroso(a) dangerous
pelotón *m* platoon, squad; firing squad
pena *f* pain; grief, woe, sorrow
pendenciero(a) quarrelsome
pender to hang, to dangle; to be pending
péndulo *m* pendulum
penetrar to penetrate, to enter
penosamente arduously; with difficulty

penoso(a) painful; laborious
pensamiento *m* thought; mind
penumbra *f* half-light
pequeño(a) little, small
pera *f* pear
peral *m* pear tree
percibir to perceive, to observe
perchero *m* clothes rack
pérdida *f* loss
perdonar to forgive, to pardon
perecer to perish
perezoso(a) lazy
perforar to perforate, to puncture
periodista *m or f* journalist
perjurarse to perjure oneself
permanecer to remain
pernoctar to spend the night
perplejo puzzled, perplexed
perseguir (i, i) to pursue; to persecute
persistir to persist; to remain
personaje *m* character (in a play, etc.); important person
personalidad *f* personality
persuadir to persuade
pertenecer to belong
pertrechos *m* supplies, provisions
perversidad *f* perversity, quality of being persistent in what is wrong
pesadamente awkwardly; heavily
pesadilla *f* nightmare
pesar to weigh
  a — de in spite of
pescador(a) *m or f* person who fishes
pescar to fish; to catch
peseta *f* Spanish unit of money
peso *m* weight; unit of money in some Latin American countries
pesquisa *f* investigation
pez *m* fish
picacho *m* peak
picada *f* trail
pico *m* peak
pícaro *m* rogue, scoundrel
piedad *f* pity, mercy
piel *f* skin, hide
pieza *f* piece; room
pintura *f* painting; paint
piñata *f* game of breaking clay jug filled with candy
piropo *m* flattery, compliment
pisada *f* footstep, footprint; hoofbeat
pisar to step on
piscina *f* swimming pool
piso *m* floor; apartment
pista *f* track, trail
pizarra *f* blackboard

placer *m* pleasure
planear to plan
plantar to plant
plata *f* silver; money
plática *f* talk; conversation
plato *m* plate; dish
plazuela *f* small square
pleito *m* dispute, fight; lawsuit
pliegue *m* fold; wrinkle
plomo *m* lead
poblador(a) *m or f* founder, inhabitant, settler
poder (ue) to be able to
  a más no — to the utmost
  no — menos de to not be able to keep from
  m power
poderoso(a) powerful
polvo *m* dirt, dust; powder
pólvora *f* powder; gunpowder
polvorearse to cover oneself with dust or powder
poner to put, to place; to set the table
poniente *m* west
por by, through, by means of, over, during, in, per, along
  — completo completely
  — lo tanto for that reason
  — lo visto apparently
  ¿ — qué? why?
  — su cuenta on one's own
pordiosero(a) *m or f* beggar
pormenor *m* detail
portada *f* book cover; gate
portar to carry
  —se to behave oneself
portátil portable
portezuela *f* little door
porvenir *m* future
posada *f* lodging; Christmas procession
poseer to possess, to own
postal postal
  f post card
poste *m* post
potrero *m* farm for raising horses
preámbulo *m* preamble, preface
precipitar to rush
  —se to throw headlong
precioso(a) precious, dear; beautiful
preciso(a) necessary, precise, exact
precursor *m* forerunner
predicador(a) *m or f* preacher; spokesperson
predicar to preach; to foretell
prejuicio *m* prejudice

premio *m* prize, award

premura *f* urgency, haste

prenda *f* article of clothing

prender to seize, to grasp; to pin; to imprison

preocupar to worry
  —se to become worried, to be worried

preparatorio *m* preparatory school; preparatory

presagio *m* omen

prescindir to leave aside; to do without; to let pass

presenciar to witness

preso(a) *m or f* prisoner

prestar to lend, to loan; to pay attention
  —se to offer

prestigio *m* prestige

pretender to pretend; to aspire to; to try

pretexto *m* excuse

prevenir to prevent; to avoid

prieto(a) dark; dark-complexioned

primor *m* skill; elegance; beauty

principiar to begin

principio *m* principle; start
  al — in the beginning, at first

prisa *f* haste, rush
  darse — to rush, to hurry

privar to deprive
  —se to deprive oneself

probar (ue) to test, to prove; to try
  —se to try on

proceso *m* process
  — legal trial

procurar to try

prodigio *m* prodigy; marvel

profundo(a) profound, deep

prohibir to forbid, to prohibit

promesa *f* promise

prometer to promise

pronóstico *m* forecast, prediction, omen

pronto fast, quick
  de — suddenly

propiedad *f* property

propietario(a) *m or f* proprietor, owner

propina *f* tip

propio(a) own, one's own; proper, correct, suitable

prorrumpir to break forth, to burst out

prosa *f* prose

proseguir (i, i) to continue, to carry on

prosperidad *f* prosperity

proteger to protect

provenir to come from

proyectil *m* projectile

proyecto *m* project

próximo(a) next

prueba *f* test

puerco *m* pig

puerto *m* port

puertorriqueño(a) Puerto Rican

puesto que since, in as much as

punta *f* tip, point

puntiagudo(a) sharp, pointed

puntuación *f* punctuation

puntuar to punctuate

punzada *f* sharp pain

puñado *m* handful, bunch

puñal *m* dagger

puñetazo *m* punch, blow with fist

puño *m* fist

Q

quebrada *f* narrow opening between two mountains, gorge, ravine

quebrar (ie) to break

quedada *f* spinster

quedamente softly, quietly

quedar to remain, to stay
  —se to stay, to be left
  — en to agree on

queja *f* complaint

quejarse to complain

querer (ie) to want, to wish; to love

querido(a) *m* loved one

quieto(a) quiet, calm
  ¡Quieto(a)! Be still!

quitar to take away, to remove
  —se to take off

quizá (quizás) perhaps, maybe

R

rabillo del ojo *m* corner of the eye

rabo *m* tail

racha *f* gust

ráfaga *f* gust of wind; machine gun burst

raíz *f* root

rama *f* branch, bough

rana *f* frog

rápidamente quickly

rascar to scratch

rasgo *m* trait, characteristic

rastro *m* track, trail

rato *m* short time

a cada — frequently
  buen — long time

ratón *m* mouse

rayar to scratch

rayo *m* ray, bolt of lightning

raza *f* race

real royal; real, true

realidad *f* reality

realista realistic
  m royalist

realizar to fulfill, to carry out, to achieve

reanudar to renew; to resume

rebanada *f* slice

rebato *m* alarm

rebelar to rebel

rebelión *f* rebellion, uprising

recado *m* message

recaer to fall again, to fall back

recámara *f* bedroom

recatarse to be afraid to take a stand

receta *f* recipe, prescription

recetar to prescribe

recibidor(a) *m or f* receiving clerk

recién recent

reclamar to claim; to demand

recobrarse to recover, to come to

recoger to gather, to collect, to harvest; to pick up

recogida *f* collection, withdrawal

recomendar (ie) to recommend; to entrust

recompensa *f* recompense; pay, payment

reconstruir to rebuild, to restore

recordar (ue) to remember

recorrer to go over

recostar (ue) to lean
  —se to lean back

recto(a) straight

recuerdo *m* memory; souvenir

recurrir to resort, to have recourse

recurso *m* recourse, appeal

rechazar to reject; to refuse; to repel

red *f* net

rededor *m* surroundings
  al — around
  en — around

redondillas *f* short poems

redondo(a) round

reducir to reduce

reemplazar to replace

referir (ie, i) to refer; to tell

reflejar to reflect
  —se to be reflected

reflejo *m* reflection

refrenar to curb, to check; to restrain

refrán *m*   refrain, saying
regalar   to give a gift
regar (ie)   to water, to sprinkle; to irrigate
  — la noticia   to spread the news around; to gossip
regatear   to haggle over, to bargain
regazo *m*   lap
regir (i, i)   to rule, to govern; to control
registrar   to search; to register
regla *f*   rule
regocijo *m*   joy, gladness
regresar   to return, to go back
regreso *m*   return
rehusar   to refuse; to turn down
reinar   to reign; to prevail
reino *m*   kingdom; reign
rendirse (i, i)   to conquer; to subdue
  —se   to surrender; to give in
renta *f*   income; profit
reparar   to repair; to notice
  —se   to stop, to refrain
repartir   to distribute
repasar   to review
repente *m*   start, sudden movement
  de —   suddenly
repetir (i, i)   to repeat
replicar   to reply
reponer   to replace; to restore
reposar   to rest
representar   to represent; to act; to carry out
reprimir   to repress
repugnancia *f*   repugnance
repugnar   to be repugnant
res *f*   head of cattle
resbaladizo(a)   slippery
resbalar   to slip, to slide
rescatar   to rescue
rescate *m*   ransom; redemption; exchange
rescoldo *m*   ember
resecar   to dry thoroughly
reseco(a)   dried, dried out
resfriado *m*   cold
residir   to reside, to live
resolver (ue)   to resolve
reja *f*   iron bar, protective grating
rejilla *f*   small iron grating
relámpago *m*   lightning
relampaguear   to flash
relampagueo *m*   flashing light
relatar   to relate, to tell
relieve *m*   relief
reluciente   shining, brillant
remar   to row

remedio *m*   remedy
remesa *f*   remittance
remo *m*   oar
remolino *m*   whirlpool, eddy; disturbance
rencor *m*   rancor, resentment, ill-will, malice
rendija *f*   crack
respetar   to respect
respeto *m*   respect, regard
resplandor *m*   brilliance, radiance
responder   to reply, to answer, to respond
respuesta *f*   answer, reply
restar   to subtract
restaurar   to restore
resto *m*   rest, balance
retirar   to retire, to withdraw
retorcer (ue)   to twist; to wring (hands)
  —se   to twist; to writhe
retrasado(a)   backwards
retrato *m*   portrait, picture
retroceder   to retreat
reunir   to gather, to collect; to assemble, to get together
revancha *f*   revenge
revelar   to reveal
reventar (ie)   to burst, to explode
reverencia *f*   bow, curtsy
revés *m*   reverse
  al —   in the opposite direction; on the other side
revivir   to revive
revolver (ue)   to stir, to scramble; to turn around; to toss and turn
rezar   to pray
rezo *m*   prayer, devotions
ribera *f*   bank, shore
riego *m*   irrigation; watering
riel *m*   rail
rienda *f*   bridle rein
  dar — suelta   to allow another to have his (her) own way
riesgo *m*   risk
rígido(a)   rigid, firm
rima *f*   rhyme
rimar   to rhyme
rincón *m*   corner
riña *f*   quarrel
riqueza *f*   wealth; riches, excellence
risa *f*   laugh
risueño(a)   smiling; pleasant
ritmo *m*   rhythm
rito *m*   rite, ceremony
rivalidad *f*   rivalry
rizar   to curl

rocío *m*   dew; drizzle
rodear   to surround
rogar (ue)   to request; to beg; to pray
romper   to break; to tear
ron *m*   rum
roncar   to snore
ronco(a)   hoarse
ronda *f*   rounds (by a guard)
ronronear   to purr
ropa *f*   clothes
rosca *f*   cake served on the Day of the Kings, January 6
rostro *m*   face
roto(a)   broken; torn
rótula *f*   kneecap
rozar   to rub; to touch lightly
rudo(a)   coarse, rough; crude; severe
rueda *f*   wheel
rugir   to roar
ruido *m*   noise
ruidosamente   loudly, noisily
rumbo *m*   course, route, direction
rumor *m*   rumor, murmur

S

sabio(a)   wise; learned
  m or *f*   wise person
sacar   to take out, to remove
sacerdote *m*   priest
saco *m*   coat, jacket; sack
sacudir   to shake; to shake off
salario *m*   salary, wages, pay
salida *f*   exit; departure
salón *m*   large parlor, living room
saltar   to jump, to leap
salto *m*   jump
salud *f*   health
saludar   to greet
saludo *m*   greeting; salute
salvador(a) *m* or *f*   savior; rescuer
salvaje *m* or *f*   savage
salvajismo *m*   savagery
salvar   to save
salvo   excepting
sangre *f*   blood
sangriento(a)   bloody
sano(a)   healthy; of sound mind
santo(a) *m* or *f*   saint
  día del —   saint's day
sargento *m*   sargent
sarmiento *m*   branch of a grapevine
sastre *m*   tailor
sazón *f*   season
  a la —   then, at that time
secamente   dryly
secar   to dry

seco(a) dry
  en — suddenly
secundario(a) secondary
seda *f* silk
sediento(a) thirsty
seguida *f* continuation
  en — immediately, at once
seguir (i, i) to follow; to continue, to keep on
según according to
seguridad *f* security; safety
seleccionar to select
selva *f* jungle
sellar to seal
sello *m* stamp; seal
semáforo *m* traffic light
semanal weekly
  —mente weekly
sembrar (ie) to plant, to sow, to seed
semejante similar; such
semiabierto(a) half-opened
semidesnudo(a) half-dressed
semilla *f* seed
sencillamente simply, plainly; candidly
sencillez *f* simplicity, plainness; candor
sencillo(a) simple, plain
senda *f* path, trail
seno *m* breast; bosom
sensual sensuous
sentar (ie) to seat
  —se to be seated, to sit down
sentenciar to sentence; to pronounce judgment
sentimiento *m* sentiment, emotion, feeling
sentir (ie, i) to be sorry, to regret
  —se to feel
señal *f* sign, marker
señalar to indicate, to point
separar to separate
sepulterero *m* gravedigger
sequedad *f* dryness, drought
ser *m* human being, being
seriedad *f* seriousness
serranía *f* range of mountains; mountainous country
sexo *m* sex
sido been
siembra *f* seeding; sown field
sien *f* temple
sierra *f* mountain range
siglo *m* century
significado *m* meaning
siguiente following, next

silbar to whistle
sillón *m* armchair
simpatizar to be congenial; to get on well together
sin without
  — embargo nevertheless
sinnúmero countless
sino but
síntoma *m* symptom
sinvergüenza shameless
  m or *f* scoundrel, rascal
siquiera even, at least; although, even though
  ni — not even
sirvienta *f* servant, maid
sitio *m* site, place
soberbio(a) proud, haughty; superb
sobornar to bribe
sobrar to exceed, to surpass; to have too much
sobre over; on; above
  m envelope
sobresaliente outstanding; more important
sobresaltar to startle; to frighten
sobrevivir to survive
sociedad *f* society
socio(a) *m* or *f* member; partner
socorro *m* aid, help
soga *f* rope
solemnemente solemnly
solemnidad *f* solemnity
soler (ue) to be accustomed to
solicitud *f* request
solitario(a) solitary, lonely
solo(a) alone
sólo only
soltar la risa (ue) to burst out laughing
soltero(a) *m* or *f* single, unmarried; bachelor
solterona *f* old maid
sollozar to sob
sombra *f* shade; shadow
sombreado(a) shadowed
sombrío shady; somber; gloomy
someter to submit
  —se to yield; to surrender
sonámbulo(a) *m* or *f* sleepwalker
sonar (ue) to sound; to ring
  —se to blow one's nose
sonido *m* sound
sonreir (i, i) to smile
sonrisa *f* smile
soñar (ue) to dream
  — con to dream of
soplar to blow; to whisper

soportar to support; to bear; to endure
sorber to sip
sordidez *f* deafness
sordo(a) deaf
sorpresa *f* surprise
sorteo *m* drawing; raffle
sosegado(a) calm, quiet, peaceful
sospechar to suspect
sospechoso(a) suspicious
sostener to hold; to hold up
suave soft
suavidad *f* softness
subalterno(a) subordinate, of lesser rank
súbito(a) sudden, unexpected; impetuous
sublevar to incite to rebellion
  —se to rise up
subrayar to underline
suceder to happen, to occur
suceso *m* event, happening
sudar to sweat, to perspire
sudoroso(a) sweaty
suegra *f* mother-in-law
suegro *m* father-in-law *pl* in-laws
suela *f* sole of shoe
sueldo *m* salary
suelo *m* floor
suelto(a) loose
sueño *m* dream
  tener — to be sleepy
suerte *f* luck; fate
sufijo *m* suffix
sugerir (ie, i) to suggest
sujetar to subject; to subdue; to hold
sujeto *m* subject
sumergir to submerge
  —se to submerge; to dive
sumido(a) sunk
superficie *f* surface; area
superior upper; superior
superviviente *m* survivor
suplicar to beg, to implore
suponer to suppose
supuestamente supposedly
surgir to appear; to arise; to come forth
suspender to suspend
suspirar to sigh
sustituir to substitute
susto *m* fright, scare
susurrar to whisper
sútil subtle
suyo (a, os, as) of his, of hers, of yours, of theirs

salirse con la suya to have one's own way

T

taberna _f_ tavern
taciturno(a) melancholy; moody; talks little
tal such, so, as
talla _f_ height, stature
tamaño _m_ size
tambaleante staggering
tanto so much, as many, so, so many
  por lo — for that reason
tapar to cover; to hide
tapia _f_ wall
taquilla _f_ box office; ticket window
tardar to delay; to be late
tarea _f_ task; homework
tartamudear to stutter, to stammer
tecla _f_ key (of a piano)
techador _f_ roofer
techo _m_ roof
teja _f_ roof tile
tejado _m_ tile roof
tejido _m_ weaving; textile, cloth
tela _f_ cloth, fabric
tema _m_ theme; subject
temblar (ie) to tremble, to shake, to shiver
tembloroso(a) trembling, shaking
temer to fear
temor fear, dread
tempestad _f_ storm
templado(a) temperate, moderate
templo _m_ temple
temporada _f_ season, period
temprano early
tenacidad _f_ persistence
tender (ie) to stretch, to stretch out
tener to have
  — ganas de to be anxious to
  — la culpa to be guilty
  — lugar to take place
  — razón to be right
  —se en pie to remain standing
teniente _m_ lieutenant
tentación _f_ temptation
tentar (ie) to touch; to feel
tenue soft, subdued
tercio _m_ third part of an entity
terco(a) stubborn
terminar to finish, to end
ternura _f_ tenderness; love
terrateniente _m_ landholder
terremoto _m_ earthquake

terruño _m_ piece of ground, native soil
tertulia _f_ social gathering
tesoro _m_ treasure
testamento _m_ last will, testament
testarudo(a) stubborn; hardheaded
testigo _m_ witness
tibio tepid, warm
tiempo _m_ time; weather
tierno(a) tender
tilma _f_ a cloak fastened at shoulder by a knot
timidez _f_ timidity
  con — timidly
tinta _f_ ink
tirador _m_ shooter; shot
tirar to throw
tiritar to shiver
tiro _m_ shot
  práticas de — target practice
tiroteo _(m)_ shooting at random
titubear to stammer, to stutter
título _m_ title
tobillo _m_ ankle
tocar to touch; to play an instrument
  —le a uno to be one's turn
todavía still, yet
tono _m_ tone
tontería _f_ foolishness
tonto(a) foolish
  _m or f_ fool
toque _m_ ring, ringing of a bell
tordillo(a) grayish
tormenta _f_ storm
tornar to return
  — a + _inf._ to do (inf.) again
torpe slow; clumsy; dull
torpemente clumsily; slowly
torpeza _f_ clumsiness, awkwardness; slowness
torre _f_ tower
toser to cough
tostar (ue) to toast; to tan; to burn
tragar to swallow; to gulp down
traidor(a) _m or f_ traitor
trajecillo _m_ little suit
trajinar to carry; to bustle about
trama _m_ plot, scheme
trance _m_ crisis; peril
tranquilo(a) calm
transcurrir to pass, to elapse
transcurso _m_ course of time
transeúnte _m_ passerby
transformarse to transform
tránsito _m_ traffic
trapiche _m_ sugar press
tras after, behind

trasgo _m_ goblin, hobgoblin
trasladar to transfer; to move
trastorno _m_ upset; disturbance
tratar to treat
  — de to try; to deal with
través _m_ inclination
  a — de through, across
travesura _f_ prank; mischief
tremendo(a) tremendous, huge; terrible
trementina _f_ turpentine
trepar to climb
trepidar to vibrate, to shake; to hesitate
tribu _f_ tribe
tribunal court of justice
tripa _f_ gut, intestine
triste sad
tristeza _f_ sadness, sorrow, grief, woe
tronco _m_ trunk (of a tree or elephant)
tropa _f_ troop
tropezar (ie) to stumble, to slip
  — con to run into; to trip over
trotar to trot
trozo _m_ piece
tumba _f_ tomb
tumbar to knock down
tuna _f_ prickly pear, Indian fig
turbación _f_ confusion; disorder
turbar to disturb, to trouble; to be confused
turno _m_ turn
tutear to address familiarly, to speak with **tú** and **te**

U

ubicarse to be situated, to be located
último(a) last
uncir to yoke, to hitch
único(a) only, unique
  lo — the only thing
unidad _f_ unit; unity
unir to unite
uña _f_ fingernail or toenail
urna _f_ urn, jug
usado(a) used; accustomed; worn out
usar to use, to wear
útil useful
utilizar to use
uva _f_ grape

V

vaciar to empty, to drain
vacilar to hesitate, to waver
vacío(a) empty; unloaded

vacuna *f* vaccine, vaccination
vago(a) vague
valentia *f* valor, courage
valer to be worth; to cost
valentón(ona) *m* or *f* braggart,
  boaster
valeroso(a) brave
valiente brave, valiant
valioso(a) valuable
valor *m* value, worth
vals *m* waltz
valla *f* fence, stockade
valle *f* valley
vano(a) vain, conceited
vaquero(a) *m* or *f* cowboy, cowgirl
variado(a) varying, diverse
variedad *f* variety
varón *m* young man
vasallo *m* vassal, subject
vasto(a) vast, huge, extensive
vecindad *f* neighborhood
vecindario *m* neighborhood
vecino(a) *m* or *f* neighbor
vedado(a) forbidden; closed
vegetar to vegetate
vejez *f* old age
vela *f* candle
velar to watch over; to guard
velocidad *f* speed
veloz swift, speedy
venado *m* deer
vencer to vanquish, to conquer; to
  overcome
vencido(a) out-of-date, expired
vendar to blindfold; to bandage
vendedor(a) *m* or *f* seller, salesperson
vender to sell
veneno *m* poison
venganza *f* vengeance, revenge
vengarse to get revenge
venir to come; to arrive

ventaja *f* advantage
ventana *f* window
ventanal *m* large window
ventanilla *f* small window
ventanuco *m* window
vera *f* edge
  de —s in truth
  ¿de —s? really?
verano *m* summer
verdadero(a) true, real
verdugo *m* executioner
vereda *f* path, narrow trail
vergüenza *f* shame; embarrassment
  sin— *m* rascal, scoundrel
  tener — to be ashamed
verificar to take place; to check, to
  confirm
verso *m* line of poetry
vestido *m* dress
vestir (i, i) to dress
  —se to get dressed
vez *f* time, occasion
  a la — at the same time
  a veces sometimes
  de — en cuando from time to time
  tal — perhaps
vía *f* road, route
víbora *f* snake
vibrante vibrant, exciting
vicio *m* vice
víctima *f* victim
victoria *f* victory
vientre *m* belly, abdomen
vigilia *f* vigil, watch
vil vile, base, mean
vilmente contemptibly; abjectly
villancico *m* Christmas carol
vindicar to avenge
viril virile, manly
virrey *m* viceroy
virtud *f* virtue

viruelas *f* measles
visita *f* visit; visitor
visitar to visit
víspera *f* eve, night before
vista *f* view
vistazo *m* look, glance
viuda *f* widow
viudo *m* widower
vivaz vivacious, lively
víveres *m* food, provisions
vivienda *f* house, dwelling
vivo(a) alive, living; bright
vocal *f* vowel
volar (ue) to fly
voltear to upset, to turn over
voluntad *f* will, determination; good
  will
volver (ue) to return, to come back,
  to go back
  — a + *inf.* to (inf.) again
voz *f* voice
vuelta *f* turn, change
  dar la — to turn around

Y

ya already; now
yacer to lie
yararacusú *m* poisonous snake
yegua *f* mare
yerba (hierba) *f* grass
yerno *m* son-in-law
yerto(a) stiff, rigid
yugo *m* yoke

Z

zanja *f* ditch; irrigation canal
zapatilla *f* slipper
zapato *m* shoe

SOBRE LOS ARTISTAS

Estas breves notas biográficas representan los acontecimientos importantes de la vida de los artistas representados en color en el texto.

SALVADOR DALÍ (1904–   )

Dalí, nacido en Cataluña, es representante del suprarrealismo en el arte español. En sus cuadros hay todos los elementos más extravagantes de esta escuela pictórica. Es el pintor más discutido de hoy.

FRANCISCO DE GOYA (1746–1828)

El rey Carlos III le invitó a Goya a ornamentar el nuevo palacio de Madrid. Todos los palacios requerían tapices para adornar sus salas frías. Entre 1776 y 1791 Goya pintó unos cuarenta y cinco cuadros al óleo. La Real Fábrica de Tapices de Madrid copió estas escenas que hoy se pueden ver en El Prado. El año 1786 Goya fue nombrado Pintor del Rey y más tarde Pintor de Cámara durante el reinado de Carlos IV.

La obra que le dio al pintor mayor fama en el extranjero fue los «Caprichos». Estos son aguafuertes que demuestran unos asuntos caprichosos de la vida como la vio el artista.

EL GRECO (DOMENICOS THEOTOCOPOULOS) (1540–1614)

Nacido en Creta, este gran artista se encontró en Venecia, Italia, a los veinte años. Allá estudió entre las glorias de Ticiano, Tintoretto, Veronés y Miguel Angel. Pero es Toledo que le llevó a la madurez de su arte.

Muy notable en su obra es el alargamiento de las figuras. Algunos han dicho que es a causa de un defecto en la vista del pintor. Pocos son los que toman en serio esta explicación.

El cuadro titulado «El Cardenal» es una de sus más célebres retratos. Representa al cardenal inquisidor Guevara. Esta obra se encuentra hoy en el Metropolitan Museum of Art de Nueva York.

Para todo forastero o extranjero que por primera vez llega a la ciudad imperial es de rigor estacionarse, antes de cruzar el Tajo, en la colina de donde se ve la ciudad tal como la vio El Greco cuando la immortalizó en su «Vista de Toledo».

JUAN GRIS (1887–1927)

La muerte prematura de este pintor español en el pleno apogeo de su arte ha sido una gran pérdida para el mundo de las artes. Otro de los españoles de la escuela de París, era uno de los mayores exponentes del cubismo.

ROBERTO MONTENEGRO (1885–   )

Nació en Guadalajara, Jalisco. Estudió en la Academia de San Carlos, México, D. F. Viajó por Europa y también estudió allí. Organizó el Museo de Artes Populares en México, D. F., en 1934.

Además de ser pintor fue también fresquista, ilustrador, escenógrafo, grabador y editor.

PABLO RUIZ PICASSO (1881–1973)

El pintor español más renombrado de los tiempos modernos es Pablo Picasso, nacido en Málaga. Sus arlequines, sus músicos melancólicos y sus mujeres masivas preocupan a todo el mundo.

En 1900 su padre, profesor de arte de una academia barcelonesa, le envió a París para continuar sus estudios. En 1903 se estableció en Francia definitivamente.

Su obra abarca desde lo realista y común de sus primeros cuadros atravéz del cubismo hasta el simbolismo de «Guernica».

Fue considerado por la mayoría de los críticos como la primera figura del arte contemporáneo.

DIEGO MARÍA RIVERA   (1886–1957)

Nació en Guanajuato, México. Rivera estudió en la Academia de San Carlos. En 1907 viajó a España para continuar con sus estudios.

"Agrarian Leader Zapata" es una variación del fresco que está en el Palacio de Cortés en Cuernavaca, México.

Durante toda su vida tuvo mucho interés no sólo en los asuntos políticos de México sino también en los del mundo.

DIEGO RODRÍGUEZ DE SILVA Y VELÁZQUEZ (1599–1660)

Hijo de padre portugués y madre andaluza, estudió y trabajó en el estudio del pintor Pacheco. Años después se casó con la hija de su maestro. En 1623 fue a la corte y al servicio del rey Felipe IV.

Son numerosas las obras maestras de Velázquez. Entre éstas figuran «Las Meninas», «La Rendición de Breda» y «Los Borrachos». Todo le interesó a Velázquez como tema. Desde los enanos y borrachos hasta las infantas, todos se encontraron fielmente representados en los lienzos del maestro.

DAVID ALFARO SIQUEIROS   (1898–1974)

El pintor nació en Chihuahua, México. Siqueiros igual que Rivera estudió en la Academia de San Carlos. De joven se alistó al ejército de Carranza. Después de viajar por Europa, volvió a México donde se interesó en los asuntos políticos del país.

JOAQUÍN SOROLLA Y BASTIDA   (1863–1923)

Nació en Valencia en 1863. Era uno de los más notables representantes del arte español contemporáneo. Sus cuadros más famosos son los que retratan las diferentes regiones de España.

RUFINO TAMAYO   (1899–   )

El fino pintor mexicano al principio fue muralista como sus compatriotas Rivera, Orozco y Siqueiros. También como ellos metía en su obra el tema revolucionario. Más tarde siguió un camino independiente en que divorció la estética de lo social. Se considera hoy en la tradición de Picasso.

IGNACIO ZULOAGA   (1870–1945)

Ignacio de Zuloaga, pintor del siglo XX, nos presenta retratos sobre fondos de paisaje español. Se distingue por su gran realismo.

En la provincia de Teruel de la región de Aragón se encuentra la antigua ciudad árabe de Albarracín que era capital de un pequeño reino desaparecido. Fue construida a orillas del río Guadalaviar. Las casas se amontonan sobre una rocosa colina. Muy notable es la muralla gótica que sube desde el pueblo a un castillo que hoy está en ruinas.

FRANCISCO DE ZURBARÁN   (1589–1664?)

Hoy día se reconoce el gran valor de este pintor que se encontraba en el olvido el siglo pasado. Forma con Velázquez la pareja de gigantes del arte español del siglo XVII.

Grande es el contraste entre la obra de los dos genios. Velázquez, pintor de la corte, es todo color y vida mientras que Zurbarán sigue el camino de los temas religiosos, de la meditación.

Nació Zurbarán en un pueblecito de Extremadura. A los dieciséis años se marchó a Sevilla donde se estableció. Antes de cumplir los treinta años ya se le consideraba maestro.

De los últimos años de Zurbarán se sabe muy poco. Desapareció después de 1664 y no se sabe cómo, cuándo, ni dónde murió.

ÍNDICE GRAMATICAL